FOR MY LOVE

ISBN 978-0-6151-5441-1

DEEP WINTER

One

Saturday Morning,
January Fourteenth

We were asleep when it hit, and didn't really have any warning.
It was around two a.m. when my wife and I both found ourselves
tossed out of the bed, she to the west, and rapidly covered in books
and clutter from a large bookshelf; me to the east, on top of the dogs'
beds. The dogs were howling and trying I suppose, to get out.

The first shock seemed to raise us up out of the bed and shift the
bed under us. I know I bounced off of the bed, my wife Karen found
herself in mid-dream and in mid-air, and then hit the carpeted floor,
grazing the nightstand with her head on the way. The first thing I
clearly remember is a noise, then the sound of the large double-hung
double-glazed windows in our room exploding from the first wave of
the quake. The crack and splitting of our hundred-year-old wood
frame house, then the dust and large parts of plaster from the lath-
plaster walls then smacked into me as I lay on the floor. Yelling.

They later told us that it lasted under twenty seconds. It seemed
like hours. As the choking dust from the ceilings and walls settled
down on us, I could hear Karen and my daughter Kelly yelling for
help. To say I was disoriented would be to put it mildly. My glasses,
usually on my nightstand, were nowhere to be found. Neither was the
nightstand, the radio, lamp, or my flashlight. All the power was off
of course, and the bitter cold wind now rushed in through the broken
windows and reminded us of what winter really is all about. I
remembered that the weathercast was for lows in the teens, with
wind chills below zero, and snow throughout the night, and
tomorrow. A good Spokane winter storm.

After a few moments that seemed much longer, I was able to
find my glasses (bent, not destroyed) and the big four D-cell

flashlight. Within a minute or so, my wife had freed herself from under her paper mountain, with a few scratches and a couple of good bruises. The dust was rapidly being blown out the master bedroom, toward west side of the house, which we hoped was still there. Kelly's room was on that side. It was cold.

We picked our way through the collapsed ceiling, barefoot of course, through nails, broken glassware and mountains of books. The floor was uneven, although we didn't really notice it that much at the time. We heard Kelly yelling for help, but her door was shut and jammed in the frame. The solid-core five-panel door was split, but still more-or-less intact. I looked around for something to smash the door in, and found a brick, from the collapse of the chimney. The brick chimney was part of the wall in the hallway, and ran from the basement to a height of about forty feet above ground. Now, I could look up and see the snowy sky, and snow blew in through the hole and over the twisted stainless steel chimney liner. Smoke from the still-burning woodstove was pouring through the split seams. I hoped it was only the woodstove. Hundred-year-old wood burns really fast, and really hot.

I pushed in two panels of the door, and managed to shove out one of the rails. I climbed through the hole into the newly devastated bedroom, and dug my daughter out of the lath and plaster that had landed on her old steel frame bed, which likely saved her life. She wasn't even crying, I thought. Kelly had a couple of cuts on her arm where the lath had hit her, and her bed frame was rammed into the floor, the four posts now resting six inches lower than they did a few minutes before. The wind was howling through her large double-hung window, now void of curtains, trim, and glass. Through the snow I could see fires burning in the neighborhood, but had to get us all out of the house. I thought I heard someone outside, and then I heard my son yell out again. 'Good.' I thought. 'Carl's alive.'

I yelled back to him, asking if he was trapped. "No. I'm OK. I'm in the front yard!"

"Is the house on fire?"

"No, but there's lots of fires down the street!"

The cold was really hitting us now, and my hands and feet were going numb. I grabbed clothing as I could for my daughter, and backed us out of the room. The bathroom off to our left was fairly intact--it had been remodeled with sheetrock instead of lath and plaster. The window, of course, was gone. Karen told me to look at the stairs...they were almost all gone. Just a pile of the ceiling plaster, the window at the top of the stairs was gone as was the gable that held it, now open to the sky. I noticed that the dogs were not with us. They were able to traverse the debris and get down to the main floor, I guessed. I yelled to Carl, and asked if he had the dogs. He told me they made it out, but didn't know from where. There was, however, no way that we'd make it down through that pile. We picked our way through the hall, back into our bedroom, with the goal of getting our chain escape-ladder out of the closet and get out through the window.

We then got our first good look at our room. The entire ceiling was down, and some of the lath and nails, poking up at us. I'd stepped on one in my dash to get to Kelly, but it didn't break the skin. The dressers, desk, TV, and nightstands were lying about, although the big bookshelves I'd built for my wife were still screwed to the wall. The closets were racked at crazy angles, and the louvers from the doors littered the place. The cold was getting worse.

By the beam of the flashlight, we retrieved pants, socks and boots from the closets, which still had ceilings—they were sheet rocked. I pulled on some socks, and tossed an armload of clothes and spare blankets out to my son in the front yard. He was standing out there in his pajamas—a t-shirt and lounging pants. 'Barefoot in ten inches of snow,' I thought. Karen and Kelly put on what clothes they could, and I dug out the ladder from the wreckage of the closet. It was colder still. Kelly began to shiver violently.

I pulled the ladder out of the box, and rapidly hooked it over the windowsill. Carl was pulling on clothes in the dark and blowing snow. It seemed much darker than it usually is at this time of night. 'Of course, no power, nothing bouncing off the clouds.' Karen was first out on the metal ladder, and I cautioned her about the glass from the window. The rungs were slippery, and her hands very cold, but she made it to the bottom with Carl holding the chain-ladder for her. Next out, Kelly, who took much longer. I had Carl get the SUV unlocked with the keyless entry, and told him to get the blankets out of the back and everyone warmed up. I realized that there wasn't a spare key in the Ford. Before I left the room, I took the time to get my thermal Carhartt's on, changed socks again (my first pair was now soaked with snow), and put on warm clothes as I could find. I dug through the heavy layers of plaster and found all of my keys,

3

wallet, small AA flashlight, my old Leatherman, a couple of powerbars, and my belt. From one of the attic spaces next to where my dresser was supposed to be, I grabbed as many of the spare sleeping bags as I could, and threw them out the window. Finally, I grabbed the base station CB radio and the hand-held scanner, put them in a pillowcase, and held onto that with my teeth as I made my way out the window.

The wreckage of the house across the street was now completely in flames. I knew that there was one very unpleasant woman that lived there alone, but by the time we got out of the house, it was apparent that if she hadn't made it out by then, she never would. It was a pyre. We had neighbors on all sides, but I knew that at least three families were out of town, and one single man worked nights. We heard sirens in the distance, but nothing near by. Looking around outside, I could see some people in their yards, waving flashlights about, trying to figure out what hit them. Everyone was hit. We had it good—we were all alive. I was sure that there were a whole lot of people who weren't so lucky.

Once I was down, I moved the sleeping bags and other stuff over to the driveway, tossed it in the back of the Ford, and started it up. Karen had already checked out the kids for injuries. Other than some small scratches and bruises, they seemed OK. The first aid kit in the back of the big Ford was rapidly put to use, then we stopped to take stock and to say a prayer. Both dogs showed up at that point, and I got out, put them in the back, and warmed up for a while. Everyone was glad to be alive. Carl dug through the stuff that I'd tossed out of our room and put on some of my clothes and my old boots, which were too small for him. Teenagers, growing like weeds. We were all wondering about the rest of the family across town, and how they'd fared. Karen's eighty-five-year-old mother lived alone, but not far from my brother-in-law.

The garage was still intact, "more or less I suppose," I thought. I decided I better check on the house, especially shutting off the gas and checking to see if there was something I could do about putting out the fire in the woodstove. Karen tried to talk me out of it, but I won out in the end. I did make the concession that Carl could go with me, and hold the flashlight if I needed it.

We made our way first to the garage, which I rightly expected to be a shambles inside. The freezer was upright and apparently had not spilled it's contents, but every other unsecured shelf was now empty, and leaning up against one of the four cars in the garage. My Galaxie convertible was now showered with small cans, stacks of sandpaper, and the trunk was now a resident to one of the wall cabinets, torn off of the wall by the shockwave. The Mustang that my kids and I were restoring had fallen off the jack stands, and landed on the tires stashed under it, crushing one of my toolboxes. I shut off the sub-panel that fed the garage and barn from the house, retrieved a crescent wrench and fire extinguisher and quickly closed the door. It was still warmer in there than outside, and we might be living there, if the barn wasn't intact. The barn was partly remodeled and a couple rooms insulated, with a wood cook stove, stored water and a sizeable portion of our 'just in case' spare supplies. The 'normal' canned goods and all of our home-canned pints and quarts were in the basement of the house, now probably lost forever.

The house, as we could see in the lights from the Ford and the beam of the flashlight, was probably a total loss. Parts of the stone foundation—those we could see—had cracked and were separated, soon turning into individual boulders. The fact that it was two feet thick probably helped, but wouldn't help enough. The house must have shifted I was sure, due to the lift that we felt, and probably didn't come down right where it had been built. The wood lap siding and wood shingles on the upper floor were torn open in several places some bowed and bent. "Damn." I thought. I'd just finished the repaint work last summer. That was the last thing to do on the place, other than maintenance.

I shut off the gas meter on the south side, and then took a good look at it. The pipe was sheared off at the meter on the inlet side, so shutting it off wouldn't do any good anyway...even if there was pressure. I made my way to the back porch, which had separated from the original construction of the house. I tried to open the door, and found it open, hanging over the collapsed oak floor, which was now resting in the crawl space, still fastened to the insulated joists. I climbed in, retrieved several armloads of boots, winter coats, hats and gloves, and told Carl to take them to the car or the garage. I found the second of the big flashlights and the four Family Radio Service (FRS) radios, near the now smashed bread maker, sitting askew on cabinets that had taken me a month to build. 'Damn.' I thought, again.

The house hadn't collapsed into the basement, which was a very lucky thing, I thought. I carefully hopped up into what was the kitchen, which also was in complete disarray. The fridge was still upright but minus some of its contents, and it looked like all of the contents of at least the upper cabinets were tossed out in a like manner. The stove was in the middle of the room, partly blocking the door to the basement. A pile of oak and bricks that had been a corner spice cabinet, formerly on the wall with the chimney, blocked the door to the dining room. Somewhere in that, is the microwave, too." No getting through there.

I lugged a second fire extinguisher out of the wrecked porch, and made my way to the west window of the dining room. The glass was still intact here, but I couldn't get to the window to check on the woodstove, because part of the basement wall below the dining room was gone. 'So much for the bar and all that single malt and tequila.' I thought.

Carl rejoined me, and we made our way into the living room through a hole where the side window used to be. The front door was blocked by the porch ceiling, which was intact but draped like some wooden curtain across the entire front wall. Inside again, collapsed ceiling, furniture covered with plaster and lath. My grandparents silk couch (these days covered with a slip-cover to help preserve it from wear) was looking very out of place, the only furniture in the house that didn't have grey plaster all over it. The woodstove sat on it's shattered hearth, no longer hooked up to the now-collapsed chimney. A slow but steady plume of smoke came out of the outlet. I could only imagine what the basement—and the storeroom with a lot of our canned goods and my computer room—looked like with that chimney down. A blast with the fire extinguisher, and I was reasonably sure that the thing wouldn't catch the house afire. We grabbed some more clothes from Carl's room and made our way back out through the wall. Back to the Ford to warm up. The temperature was thirteen degrees, according to the dashboard.

Karen had picked up the Emergency Broadcast System signals about the quake, and lots of local news and emergency information. Seven point one was the preliminary estimate. We were speechless at first. "Seven point one? Here?" Hundreds were likely dead, with structure fires burning in most neighborhoods, building collapses, and at least one dam failure. We had a powerbar, stashed in the Fords' emergency bag, and considered our next actions. The Ford had a full tank, as did the other cars and our spare gas cans. So we at least had enough gas to get around, keep warm, and make it through the short term. Most of the bulk storage, and a good portion of canned goods and necessities were in the barn. By the look of it through the dark and the blowing snow, it seemed to be OK.

6

The next step would be to check out the barn and get it secured if possible, and to check out the tent trailer, stashed in a metal carport in the back field. I had the feeling that the propane stove it housed would come in really handy very soon.

Forty-seven minutes had passed since the quake.

2

Two-Fifty a.m., Saturday Morning
January Fourteenth

I changed from my 'normal' hiking boots into my newly rescued Sorels, and put on dry socks again while I was at it. I retrieved my hotfingers gloves from the console storage bin, pulled on my Gonzaga Bulldogs cap and my 'work' parka, an old beat up Eddie Bauer down-filled number that I usually wore only to plow snow, and grabbed a flashlight. Carl, Kelly and Karen stayed in the Expedition for now, but Karen had crawled into the back to tend to puncture wounds on Carl's leg, and was cleaning out a cut on one of the retriever's paws. The dog was not cooperative. I'd go see what damage we had to deal with in the barn, the north side of the house, the storage shed that held our spare gas, tillers and summer furniture.

Before making the trek too far, I made another trip into the garage and grabbed a couple of bottles of Gatorade that was left over from our church youth groups' Battleball game. Wasn't that just Tuesday? Seemed like forever ago. I gave my wife the bottles, and told her to let me know on the radio if there was anything she thought I needed to hear.

"Right. Where do I draw the line there?" We both laughed, which we all needed.

"Well, we've got a blizzard, we've had an earthquake, so I guess pestilence and famine are next." Neither of us laughed, then. I noticed then that the tractor was sitting sideways in the driveway. Hmmm.

First, the house. I only did one face-plant on the way around the house, to check out the damage on the north side, twisting my wrist.

Great. The snow was blowing right out of the east, and seemed to be mixed with freezing rain, but I couldn't really tell at that point. The flashlight revealed the collapsed gable that had once covered the stairwell, part of the chimney, and most of the siding on the north side of the house, all in a heap, burying the door that led directly to the basement from that side of the house. It looked like the power line weather head was ripped out of the roof and north wall, when the wires were pulled by something. I couldn't tell what, but the whole weather head, meter, and a big chunk of siding were down, with the wires. The power pole was lying across my neighbors' driveway, and over part of the road. No worse than I expected, since I expected the worst. I could see some light coming from the house, probably from a couple of the power-failure lights that I'd put in. Funny, I didn't remember seeing them when I was inside.

The little metal wood shed looked fine. Filled with firewood for the house, I'm sure it weighed enough to stay put, and with the plywood lining, it probably didn't rack too much in the quake. OK, so two cords of wood available. 'That'll keep Carl busy, splitting,' I thought.

Next, the equipment shed, as we called it. It held our riding mower, the two Troy Bilt tillers, a chipper, and other stuff we used in the summer. More importantly, it held our stash of five-gallon gas cans, stabilized. The shed was tilted, obviously off of its foundation blocks. It'd been converted from a chicken shed, and moved twice in its life, once by me. I pried open the door, and all seemed intact. The gas cans were still in their cubbies, and hadn't spilled. Good for us.

Finally, on to the barn. I made my way through the stock gate, left over from the previous owner twenty years ago, who raised horses. The only current resident was a lone pet rabbit, the sole survivor of several years of Dutch rabbit raising, none of it intended. Rabbits are funny that way. The east end of the twenty-four by sixty barn once held our Rhode Island Reds, which we'd given up on a few years ago. Still had some feed in there and all the equipment I remembered, along with most of the old windows from the house, a lot of two-by stock that I hadn't gotten around to using yet, and a stack plywood. I made it to the east end through the garden, past the little PVC frame and plastic shell of the greenhouse to the end wall of the barn. The barn seemed to have very little damage, and seemed to be sitting on it's foundation as it should, which I found surprising, since the wood sills weren't tied to the concrete.

I opened up the 'tool room', with it's sophisticated hook and eye latch, and played the light around. The garden tools were everywhere, off the walls, in piles, and mostly in my way. The old garbage cans that held my (many) garden tools were tossed over, and all the hoses stored for winter were on the floor. The heavy plastic garbage cans that held the garden fertilizer were still in their corner, behind the tomato cages. The first door, to the woodshop, was closed, and the tempered glass was intact. My keys, rescued from the wreckage of the house, opened the dead bolted door, and I was in. Most of the wall-hung tools were now on the floor and the bench, and my router table was on the wrong end of the shop. All of the vinyl sliding windows were intact, but two of the three had broken latches. I closed the partially opened windows, and kept going on my inspection tour. Most of the sheetrock had cracked, especially the panels that wrapped the ceiling beam. Still, it seemed weather tight, far better than the house. The wood cook stove, an old enameled monster from the Depression was partly off of its base and crooked, but the pipe was still intact through the roof. I'd have to go up there on the roof to make sure, pull the cap off and see if things were really OK, but I was encouraged. Now, on to the storeroom.

Things were a little worse in there. I'd only finished the room the previous summer, and most of the floor-mounted cabinets weren't secured to the walls. I just never got around to it. The walls and ceiling had the same damage to the sheetrock, and the ceiling-mounted 8' fluorescent lights had either shattered in place or dropped their tubes. Either way, glass all over. A wall-mounted mirror in the craft area had cracked and partly shattered, and some of the cabinet doors had popped their magnetic latches and spilled their contents. Nothing breakable though, although a couple of my multi-meters were now on the floor. And all of the packages of small batteries.

The bulk stuff, wheat, rice, sugar, oats, soybeans, and water, all were still upright in their barrels and buckets. Five five-gallon cans of kerosene and a kerosene heater were also all fine, but one of the kerosene cans was dented, and had pooched out some kerosene from the fill cap. The kerosene shouldn't have been stored in the barn anyway, but I'd run out of room in my fuel storage area in the equipment shed. Three small kerosene camp lanterns were one the floor, next to the shelf where they were stored. Their globes were unbroken, fortunately. I wondered how my Model Twelve Aladdin lanterns were, in the house? Three spare chimneys in their 'Lox-On' boxes were still on the shelf in front of me, with a couple spare mantles. Our much newer Coleman dual-fuel lanterns were also there, and below them, both two- and three-burner Coleman stoves. I knew that I had probably ten one-gallon cans of fuel for the Coleman's in the shed and garage, if they'd made it through the shaking without something landing on them. One of the racks of shelves held my collection of old Mac computers, and my old Power Mac was right on the floor, where I left it. The monitor, however, was now in pieces.

The shelves on the north side of the room were designed for a couple of things, including canned good and bulk storage, and if need be, bunks. The shelves had a face-bar that held most of the stuff in place, so only a few small things escaped. Nearly everything that was in the house as far as store-bought goods, was duplicated and then some out here. I did have a couple empty cases of quart and pint Ball canning jars and all of the spare lids and rings, but the great majority of them were filled, and stored in the house. Now, under the house, probably in a smelly pile of tomato soup, peaches, pears, canned meat, and jam. More than a hundred of them, easy. Next to probably seventy-five bottles of wine. All now, probably heading for the drain.

The five kilowatt generator, winterized and stored inside, was in the corner next to the roll of wire that fed the barn through it's dedicated panel. The barn only had twenty amps of power feeding it from the garage, and if I wanted or needed more power, I'd either have to put in a new service, or feed it off of a portable source. The generator had come in handy for the woodshop. I also picked up a PTO-run generator for the Ford 8n at a farm auction, but had never had the chance to make sure it worked properly. It was residing in the only unfinished part of the barn, next to yet another project, my Packard 110, untouched for about five years.

I radioed to Karen to drive the Ford out to the barn and park it tail-first near the outside storeroom door. I found some matches and fired up one of the Coleman gas lanterns for the storeroom. We'd have to clean up the broken florescent lamps, and then off-load the sleeping bags, clothes, dogs and kids into the barn and figure out what was next from there. Once Karen and the kids arrived and the place cleaned up a little, we unloaded the stuff from the car. In the storeroom, I unrolled an old (really old) mattress that I had intended to haul off to the dump, and told the kids to get into their sleeping bags and to listen to the portable radio for news. Karen was picking out batteries for the little twelve-volt TV / radio that resided in the barn, and I was getting ready to take a look at the chimney. We'd need heat, and soon. It was only thirty-five degrees in the barn.

Back outside, I slogged through the field to the metal carport. The glow in the clouds from distant house fires to the north, west, and south of us provided me an uncomfortable light to make the trip. The carport held our tent trailer and that of a friend of ours for the winter, surrounded by stacks of tarped-over scrap two-by mill ends that I used in the shop for heat. The trailers were fine, although the shed was twisted, and had dumped its roof-load of snow. I grabbed one of the ladders that was stored in the shed, and headed back over to the barn. The barn roof is only sloped at four in twelve, so fortunately I didn't have too much trouble getting up on the roof. I pulled off the cap and screen, and shone the flashlight down the chimney pipe. All seemed OK, and I gave my wife the go-ahead on lighting the stove. On went the cap, and back down the ladder I went. We'd have heat shortly.

When I made it back inside, both kids and both dogs were on the mattress, and my wife had set up an old Sixties' era camp cot. Carl, ever hungry, was now munching on one of the oatmeal bars from the Ford, and washing it down with one of the vanilla Cokes from my shop fridge.

"You two should get some sleep. Tomorrow's going to be a very, long day." I looked at my watch, now scratched and dirty. It was only three forty a.m. "No, I was wrong. TODAY'S going to be a very long day," I said as I took the Coleman from the storeroom to the shop, leaving them in the semi-dark.

"What's next?" Karen asked.

"A hug I think," I said.

"What happened?" she asked. "We aren't in earthquake country."

"We are now, apparently. I think I'll go out and see if anybody up the road needs help. That OK with you?"

"Yeah, I think so. Take one of those little radios."

"Let's make sure they're all on the same frequency. I know that two of them were set differently."

I showed her how to unlock the frequency selector, adjust the frequency and 'security key', and re-locked the handset.

"I'll take one of the flashlights. I'll call you if I need anything."

"Don't be gone long."

"I don't intend to. But if there's somebody trapped, or needing help...."

"I know. Go ahead. I'll keep the dogs inside."

"How's his paw?" I said, referring to our male Golden Retriever.

"It'll be OK. A little cut that's all."

"All right. I'll radio in in a few minutes."

"You be careful," she said as I closed the door, going back through the tool room.

I walked across the snowy field, the bitter cold stinging me by the time I hit the front gate. The house across the street was still burning, now collapsed into the foundation hole. There had been some car traffic on the road, as I could see from the tracks in the snow. Looking up the street, I could see fires beyond what looked like some sort of blockage in the road. To the east, smoke rolled toward me from some distant fire.

No one was outside; there were no pleas for help, no cars or trucks, no lights. Nothing but the distant sounds of a siren. I decided to go back inside the barn and wait for daybreak.

There didn't seem much point in looking around, alone.

Four a.m., Saturday Morning
January Fourteenth

Back inside and warm, Karen and I in the woodshop and the kids in the storeroom, where the kids listened to the reports on the radio, turned down low. There wasn't much chance that they'd fall asleep after nearly getting killed in the quake, but at least a little quiet time, and warmth, wouldn't do them any harm. I'd retrieved two of the battery-powered emergency lights, which provided a little light for them. I took the other Coleman lanterns into the other room, along with the three kerosene camp lanterns and some fuel. 'Might as well get to work.' We added some split wood and old untreated cedar shakes to the woodstove, and put some of the stored water on to make some tea.

All of the TV stations were off the air, thousand-foot towers probably in heaps upon Mt. Spokane and Brown's Mountain. The scanner batteries were dead, but we replaced them with fresh NiCad's. The scanner frequencies were still in memory, so we were able to plug right in to the gibberish on ten of the emergency frequencies. We locked on to the local fire department rescue channel, and listened for a few minutes. Nothing good there was happening. The closest operation seemed to be at our own fire station ten blocks away, where the engines were trapped in the partially collapsed masonry firehouse. The paramedics had gotten their truck out, but the pumper and ladder truck were trapped. No water pressure was available for fire fighting due to lack of power and damaged pipes. A big grocery store, part of the strip mall across from the firehouse, was down and burning. The State Patrol frequency told us that several of the overpasses on Interstate Ninety, not far from us, had collapsed as well, blocking the freeway from Idaho into downtown. From the City we heard that the Maple Street bridge had collapsed into the Spokane River, and had crushed several homes in the Peaceful Valley neighborhood as it fell. The dam at Post Falls, holding Lake Coeur d'Alene in check, had partially failed, and the river was now expected to flood with the unexpected flows. I wondered about Upriver Dam downstream of Post Falls, the two dams at Riverfront Park, and the ones from Nine Mile to the Columbia. Could they all be damaged? What about Grand Coulee? Could the damage have gone that far?

Next, I hooked up the CB. The hand-held CB in the barn was fed off of mains power, which was now gone of course, but it had a cigarette lighter plug in available for 12 volt power. I'd never loaded it up with batteries, because I'd never needed to. Karen used to use the CB to call me back to the house when she needed me for something, in more 'normal' times. I had a spare car battery that was stored for the winter in the shop, and hooked up the CB to the terminals with a couple of alligator clips, only remembering after I'd done all that work that there was a battery-powered hand-held in the Ford's emergency kit. More news, all bad, and we didn't know what was real and what was rumor. The first thing we heard was of the train derailment about a mile and a half north and west of us, which was leaking toxic gasses and spreading them downwind, towards Downtown. Away from us, for now. We had one of the busiest rail lines in the northwest, with a great deal of train traffic from the Pacific and mid-west passing through town. Not anymore. Next we heard that High Bridge, crossing the Spokane River and Hangman Creek, was partially down. I hoped no train was on it when it fell. It was once three hundred feet tall.

I pulled the cell phone from my hip pocket, and put it over on the table saw. The battery was fully charged, but without power to the antennas around town, no service was available. No surprise there.

Karen poured us some tea in a couple of old mugs that I'd stashed along with a lot of our non-matching plates, glasses, and old silverware. With a couple of sugar cubes, we listened as things unwound.

Only one of the AM stations was still up full time, and two others were on emergency power. The 'night' staff at the radio stations were trying to do their best to get news out, but their sources weren't much better than what we were hearing on the scanner and CB, and they were obviously not used to dealing with a situation like this. They were after all, caretakers for the station, as the late night national programming always filled this time-slot. The EBS signals continued to come on every fifteen minutes or so, repeating the basics of what had happened. At four-thirty, we found out more.

"......*The magnitude of the earthquake, originally estimated at seven point-one, cannot be verified at this time. Local seismologists monitoring the two thousand four installation of seismographs to cover the local swarm of quakes that began in two thousand two, have not been able to confirm the size or epicenter with the University of Washington Department of Earth and Space Sciences, nor have they been able to contact the other elements of the Pacific Northwest Seismograph Network based at UW. KLXY has been trying to contact Seattle and Portland area media outlets, as well as the UW, but telephone lines are not working at this time. As soon as more news is available regarding the magnitude and epicenter, KLXY will bring it to you. Now, moving on to evacuation centers set up by the Department of Emergency Management...*"

"They can't contact Seattle?" Karen asked with a puzzled look.

"Not yet, they say the lines are down." I was uneasy about this. This wasn't right.

"Don't they have a satellite phone or link or something?" I could tell the wheels were spinning. She didn't like this either.

"Well, they should, assuming the ground station or antenna or whatever is still working."

"That can't be right. They have to be able to contact them some way."

"Yeah. That's what I think, too."

We looked at each other in silence and sipped our tea. I fed the fire, and dug out some of my books. We'd be needing these.

"I wonder if Pauliano's still have laying hens?" I asked Karen.

"Yes, they do," she said, knowing the question that I didn't ask.

"We better talk to them at daylight. We're going to need to get into the house too, and see what we can salvage. We can probably store most of it in the garage, if we can get the big doors open. We'll also need to see how the neighbors made it through. James's are out of town, Brad's in Seattle, and Woolsley's are over in Monroe at the car show. Art works nights at the casino. We'll need to see how Dan and his wife are doing behind us, and those new folks who bought Mrs. Anders place. Dan's house didn't look right. I think part of it's down. We already know that Mrs. Long didn't make it."

"Is there any way to get hold of Mom or Alan?"

"We might be able to use the CB or a relay through CB folks, but it's going to be tough. There's a lot against it now, not the least of which is that they're twelve miles away on the other side of town. The river bridges are probably damaged, so traffic is going to be slow, once the roads ARE cleared. I don't have a Ham radio, and neither does Alan. We'll see what we can do though."

"I'm really worried about Mom."

"I know. Hopefully Alan has been able to get down to her house and check on her by now. Both of there places should've done OK, they're both sitting on solid rock."

"Is that why our house is a mess? Because it's not on rock?"

"Partly. Part of it is due to the way it's built. The foundation is stone, and not reinforced. That's why I had to mortar up the holes after we bought it. It's sand and cement that holds the stone together and seals them up. Then, the wood framing and posts are just sitting on top of the stone foundation. New houses are connected to the concrete foundations with bolts, so the house can't easily lift off the foundation. By the looks of it, ours' went flying."

I started making a list of things that I thought I might be able to salvage from the house, based on what I'd seen earlier. It soon filled three pages.

4

Five a.m., Saturday Morning
January Fourteenth

As the list of possible 'salvage' items grew longer, I wondered what my office downtown must look like right now. The company specialized in planning, wetland restoration, and restoration of contaminated industrial sites...which really meant that we were Swiss-Army knives of our field...'Paying client? Yeah, we can do that.'

Located in an eighteen-nineties vintage non-reinforced masonry building, our company was likely at the bottom of a large heap of red brick and timbers. The quake had probably killed the company, along with the untold thousands. I did have however, DVD backups of the files on the server, the financial information, and the entire contents of my office computer on my iPod, in the Ford. Bringing the company back to life would be interesting.

We were listening to the 'big' radio in the woodshop, a Radio Shack multi-band model that I'd bought at a pawnshop for ten bucks. It'd been brought back to life with a pack of D cells from the craft room, but we still were able to only pull in the lone AM station locally. We did hear snips from KOA and KSL, but their broadcasts faded before we heard much in the way of 'new' material.

I poked my head into the other room to see how the kids were doing. The dogs were fast asleep, sandwiched between Carl and Kelly. Kelly had her eyes closed, and seemed to be asleep, huddled deep in her sleeping bag. I couldn't tell if Carl was asleep or not.

"Two dog night," I said to myself.

I told Karen that I'd take this chance to run up to the garage and bring back one of the bags of dog food, bowls, and some other stuff.

I trudged through the tool-room again, and took a few minutes to clear a path for the return trip.

I was able to get into the garage through the side door, and took a few minutes to look around, with just the beam of the double-A flashlight. I knew that up in the garage attic we'd stashed a bunch of out-grown kids clothes, one small backpacking tent that'd belonged to me before I met Karen and a big family tent that her parents had given to us after they grew too old to camp out I was glad that at present, we weren't sleeping in one of those right now. I also remembered that I had two spare propane tanks on the other side of the garage, probably over by the door by the bikes. We'd probably end up using those on the tent trailer stove.

After two trips between the barn and the garage in the blowing snow, I'd moved dog food, bowls, some car-wash towels, and a bag of old blankets to the barn. The blankets were usually used to cover up our tomato plants in the fall as the weather grew cold, and we stored them in the garage to keep them from being turned into mice nests. One of Kelly's jobs on the last warm day in October had been to string them up on the clothesline and blast them off with water. They dried relatively clean, and then they were bagged up in a big garbage bag.

I left the blankets in the tool room, and hauled the dog food into the woodshop, just as the five a.m. EBS report was coming on. The warning tones ended abruptly, then nothing but static. Karen moved the dial up and down, looking for a signal, but nothing local was up.

"Must've lost their generator. Tune it back to the station, and we'll keep the volume down. If they get back up and going, we'll know pretty quick."

"We're going to need some breakfast stuff from the house. Do you think you can get in?" Karen asked.

"Yeah, shouldn't be too much trouble, although I can state for a fact that if anyone's thinking 'cold cereal', they'll be having it served with bricks. The cabinet under the microwave (where the cereal resided) is now about two-inches tall, including the microwave."

"Great. Just see what you can dig up....no pun intended." At that point, I lost it. I had to leave laughing with tears in my eyes, just to avoid waking up the kids.

We owned two big wheelbarrows and a couple of other garden carts used for a multitude of tasks around the place. I grabbed my grandfather's old contractor wheelbarrow, and dragged it behind me in the snow, across the garden, to the back porch. The wheelbarrow was now my shopping cart.

I was able again to get into the kitchen through the destroyed back porch, and it was apparent that this wasn't going to be easy, to make multiple trips up the stairs, into the hole that the porch had become, and then up four feet to the kitchen floor level. At least for a couple of trips, I'd just have to cowboy up and deal with it. As I hopped up to the kitchen level, I remembered that Karen had had to pick up some new triple-A batteries for my hiking headlamp, and that the last time I saw the headlamp, it was on the counter across from the fridge. The counter was empty, so that meant the floor. Great. I might get lucky and find it, but probably not right this minute. The flashlight would have to do.

The cold in the house served as a big refrigerator, so all of the contents that had spilled had at least stayed plenty cold for the last three hours. I was able to collect much more than I thought, but anything in glass was gone. Two loaves of wheat bread hiding over by the dishwasher. Two gallons of milk. OJ in a Tupperware container. Lots of leftovers. Pork loin steak. Eggs (not broken! Still in the door!) Pepper bacon. Cheese. A bunch of unknown things in frozen packages from the top freezer. Ice. ("Like we need THAT right now!" I thought). Under it all, I found the big lasagna dish, intact, covered with plastic wrap, unbroken and unspoiled, ready to bake. " YES!" I said to myself, then I stopped cold. "Four hours ago you were sound asleep, and your biggest worry was the crappy performance of your retirement fund and how to pay for college. Now you're thrilled to find a lasagna."

I managed to find the kitchen garbage bags (a whole box! Clean!) and filled some of them up with stuff from the fridge. I then collected the canisters of coffee, tea, sugar, and flour, and hopped into the hole where the porch had been. Assembly-line style, passed each of the bags up to the back steps, and then filled my new 'shopping cart'.

I made two more trips that way, until the wheelbarrow was full. I noticed for the first time that anything in cupboards that faced north or south seemed to remain in place—sort of—but anything in east-west facing cabinets or drawers was tossed completely off the shelves. This meant the epicenter was east- or more likely, west of us. Maybe when the radio station got back up and running that we'd hear more.

My next two trips back to the house resulted in retrieval of cooking utensils, pans pots and silverware, although the latter more of a game of pick-up-sticks, since the silverware drawer faced east. Under the gravy ladle, I found my LED headlight, undamaged. 'All right. Now I have both hands free.'

Once I'd returned to the barn, Karen set about making some breakfast. It looked like we'd actually eat pretty well, once we had some clean cookware. For now, we'd plan on something simple.

It was still snowing lightly, but the winds had picked up, and drifts began to build. We could smell the distinctive odor of burning roofing, from somewhere northeast of us. The clouds grew a bit lighter as we moved toward sunrise.

We elected to let the smell of breakfast wake the kids and dogs....and we didn't have to wait long. Breakfast fare included toast cooked over the woodstove on a 'camp toaster', homemade raspberry jam, juice, milk, and coffee. Until we could boil some water in one of the big pots and wash down everything, this was all we could manage. Karen said we'd have a bigger brunch later, after things were sorted out.

The two golden retrievers were very happy to get a big cup of dog chow apiece, and the male managed to nearly drain the water dish, leaving his big sister to look at us with those big brown eyes. Carl pulled on a clean pair of flannel lined Carhartt jeans that used to fit me, and took the dogs out for their morning business.

"Don't let them out of the field, Carl. I don't want them up by the house until we've had a chance to really check it out. And check out the perimeter fence in the field. We need to make sure that they can't get out or other dogs get in. The quake might've dropped some of the fence, and we'll have to get that fixed pretty quick. Grab one of the blue radios too—the channel is already locked in. Don't hesitate to use it. Mom's got her hands-free unit on, so she'll hear you right away."

"'K, Dad."

"And Carl? Be really careful. If you see someone where they're not supposed to be, call on the radio and get back here pronto and we'll figure out what to do."

"K."

I hadn't really thought about looters at this point, but now the potential of some of the residents of the shallow end of the gene pool taking advantage of the situation became a real concern. We'd have to look at that soon. As in, right-darn-now soon. Which meant another trip to the house to find a shotgun, unless it was buried, too. Hadn't thought to look for it last night.

Carl closed the door, and we looked at the dogs as they tore off across the field and drifts. Carl rounded them up after a few minutes and started a loop of the fences in the back field.

With the lessening snow and decreasing gloom of night, we should be able to get a good look at the house, salvage or at least protect some of our belongings, and see how the rest of our neighbors were faring.

And what's up with the radio?

5

Seven a.m., Saturday Morning
January Fourteenth

While Carl and the dogs were out for a walk, Karen and Kelly cleaned up after 'breakfast' and pondered doing 'dishes'. First up, though was sanitation.

"Hon, we don't have a toilet out here. We need to do something about that ...now."

"Nope no toilet, and the house isn't an option either. Is the porta-potty out here, or in the trailer?"

"I think it's in the trailer."

"That wasn't the answer I was hoping for."

"I know it wasn't. Look in the garage first. Quickly, please."

"Gotcha." A little sense of urgency on the ladies part. Not used to going in the woods.....
I put on the big parka again, and slipped into the Sorels. I'd decided to look in the garage first, I thought we might have put the box in question in the garage after our summer camp out, which last year happened to be in the back yard rather than at a campground.
The dogs were most happy to see me, and came tearing up through the field with Carl trailing behind.

"Wow, the house is really trashed."

"Yeah, doesn't look good. Fences OK?"

"Yep. Except for the west side in the middle. The posts are leaning in."

"That's OK, they were doing that before. I was supposed to get those wood posts replaced with the steel ones last fall. We'll have to do something today to make sure we get it straightened up. The houses back there look OK?"

"Not really. The north side of Dan's house looks like it fell in, and the walls are all cracked." Dan had a Fifties era house, built of concrete block. "The empty one behind us is kinda banged up too, not bad though."

"You see anyone?"

"The guy that bought Mrs. Anders' place. His name's Eric, and his wife is Amy. They've got two little girls. He said they're packing up and heading out later today."

"To where? Did he say?"

"I didn't ask."

"That's OK. Maybe we'll see him later this morning." I said as I entered the garage. There it was, on the floor by the Christmas tree box. The porta-potty. "Here—Run this out to your Mom. She's gotta go."

"Hadn't thought about that. Where are we going to put it?"

"Not in the shop or the storeroom. Better plan on being cold for sit downs...."

Carl laughed as he took the box, followed by the Goldens, back out to the barn. I'd let Karen and Kelly figure out where to temporarily install the porta-potty, then we'd have to figure out a better solution.

"Hustle back—without the dogs. We've got stuff to do up here."

24

"K."

In the garage, I decided to get some of the driveway cleared of snow, so we could move Karen's car out and store some of the house salvage there. I found the stack of tarps that were normally stored in the barn, and pulled the big silver one out. We'd use this one first. One of my to-do list things that never got done, moving 'stuff' from 'here' to 'there.'

I caught Carl before he got too far from the barn. "Carl! Grab a milk-crate full of those old sash-weights. And that pack of rope on the wall of the woodshop."

"K."

I had some of the driveway cleared by the time Carl got back with half a milk crate of the cast iron sash weights that I'd removed from the house when I replaced the windows. "I'll have to go back for the others. Weighed too much."

'C'mon, you're almost fifteen! You should be able to handle that!' I kidded him.

"Yeah. Right." He panted as he headed back for a second load.

"You probably have enough here. You're good."

It was 'full' morning now, about eight or so. The fine snow finally stopped, and gave way to a high overcast. The winds finally stopped too. I could hear the sounds of the neighborhood better now, especially the sounds of chainsaws, snowblowers, and the occasional car trying to make it's way up the road.

By the time Carl got back, I had a place cleared for the car, plus a little room to maneuver around, assuming we'd be able to get some furniture out of the house. I noticed several dogs running up the street. None of them looked either familiar, or all that friendly. I was glad Carl put our two away. I didn't need to deal with a dog fight, and I wasn't armed. Yet.

"Let's get this door open." I went inside and disconnected the garage door opener with the emergency rope. The door was heavy, but still on it's track. Once we got some more light inside the garage, we could see that it fared very well in the quake. No apparent structural damage, at least.

"Here," I tossed Carl the keys to the car. "Back it out."

"Really?"

"Yeah, just do it straight. We have enough bodywork to do on the Galaxie and the Mustang without one more banged up Ford. Nice and slow. It's the big key, with the plastic end."

He was overly cautious, but managed to get the sedan out without hitting anything. Big smile on his face, though. He'd be starting Drivers' Ed this spring, if things returned to 'normal' and his grades stayed up.

"Nicely done. I think that the Mustang will be put off for awhile though. Looks like we'll be busy with other things."

"Yeah. What's next?"

"Well, see that hole in the roof of the house? That's part one."

"What, with the bucket truck?" my son said, referring to the big old (cheap) F500 bucket truck that I'd bought to repaint the high parts of the house.

"Nope. Batteries probably down, tires are bald, and there's way too much snow to get it up to the house from the field. We're doing the this the old fashioned way."

"And that would be......"

"You'll see. Did you get that rope?"

"Yep."

"Come on. Time's a-wastin' The snow was back.

We unfolded the tarp and stretched it along the south side of the house. Using a circle of half-inch thick rebar from the garage tied to the first piece of nylon rope, I tossed the metal ring with its' rope tail over the gable, being careful not to drop the weight into the hole over the stairs. Two tries, and it worked. I had Carl go over to the north side, tie on a sash weight, and retrieve the ring. We repeated the process, so we now had two lengths of rope over the house, tied down on the north end. The loose ends of the rope were tied to the corners of the silver tarp, and with no small effort, we pulled the tarp up and over the main gable of the house. Before the trailing edge of the tarp left the ground though, I tied six sash-weights on that edge, and tied two other short pieces of rope from the garage to the corners. Two more sash weights were added to these ropes, then we moved back to the north side, and pulled the now-much-heavier tarp and weight combination up and over the house. The hole was covered, the trailing weights were resting in the gutter as planned, so all I needed to do now was some ladder work up on the north side with more sash weights. Another hour or so on an extension ladder, and I'd have the big hole pretty well covered. At least when the rains came, we could reduce the damage to our belongings by keeping them dry. We'd have to dig out one of the rolls of greenhouse plastic and the staple guns, and tack over the broken windows too.

Once the roof cover was done, Carl and I headed back to the barn to warm up and grab a cup of coffee. The snow flurries were starting again.

We heard them before we saw them—helicopters. Help from the outside was here. The big twin rotor transports, as well as the Blackhawk-style medevacs were coming up from the southeast. We usually only had a Medevac or one of the little police helicopters or the old Huey from Fairchild's Survival School buzzing around. These were quite different.

"Dad, are those Air Force?" Carl asked. "Are they from the Survival School?"

"Nope. I'm thinking the whole area is a survival school now. Those are Army. Looks like a Medevac version of the Blackhawk. Look what's following behind—That's a Marine chopper. A Super Stallion, I think."

"Geez."

"A man of many words, aren't you, son?"

"C'mon. I'm cold."

"Ditto. At least it's not snowing so hard. The weather yesterday said it'd snow till mid morning. We'll see if they were right."

After slogging back to the barn, Karen and Kelly helped us out of our wet coats and boots. In the time we'd been working outside, they'd tidied up my 'man-room' workshop and the storeroom, and were making both livable. Four old cabinets from the kitchen remodel, which were installed but not filled, now contained most of the salvaged items from the kitchen. Two of my new workbenches, which were stacked up with lumber for new glass doors for the upstairs bookcases (now trashed), were now set up for food prep. The base cabinets, left over from an office remodel, held towels, soap and cleaning supplies. To the right, my two grain-grinders were set up, and a bag of wheat awaiting some human-power to convert it to flour.

I almost didn't recognize the place. The scanner was still working, and we could hear the endless chatter on many frequencies. Rescues. Fires. Body recoveries. Too many of those. Reports of looting. Too many of those, too.

"Rick, what are we going to do for a sink? This old pot isn't going to cut it."

"Remember during the remodel when I ripped out the old sink, and bought that plastic laundry tub? It's stashed in with the Packard. I'm sure it's filthy, but it's all there, including all of the drain line, the faucet, and the hoses."

"How are you going to get water running to it?"

"Oh, I'll put my engineering mind to work. Don't be surprised if it looks like something from MacGyver."

Karen laughed. "Hon, today, not much more could surprise me."

"Let's hope that comes true."

"What's 'MacGyver?" Kelly asked.

"An old TV show. The guy saved the world every week with duct tape, a pencil, and a battery. Or, whatever was laying around."

"Oh, Dad, don't exaggerate."

"Obviously, Kel, you have been deprived from one of the great creative geniuses of TV."

Karen interrupted, just in time. "What about a drain?"

"That'll be more interesting. I didn't plumb any drain lines into the barn when I remodeled, and even if we did have water through the built in piping, I don't have a floor drain.......No, wait a minute. There's one under the floor board right there." I pointed to a concrete slab, near the outside entry, where in a past life, cows were milked. "There's a drain pipe in that slab, from the drain trench, to the outside. I don't know where it goes or if it's plugged up though."

"Well, it's not like you have anything to do today. Just make sure it gets on the list soon."

"Yes, Master Chief Sir!"

"Cut it out. You're a bad influence on Carl."

As we sipped our coffee (Carl's with too much sugar, I'm sure), Kelly tried the radio again. "Dad, what channel should I try? Nothing seems to be working."

"Try nine-twenty first. Then fifteen-ten. Those were the big stations. It's almost the top of the hour. Should be something on."

"Karen, are the clothes in here? I'm needing another sweater or sweatshirt. The parka's too heavy, and I need another layer with my shell. Are those in here somewhere? Or in the car?"

"Yep. Yours are in that stack, behind the cot. And your socks.."

"DAD—I've got someone. I think it's the President!"

"Quick. Turn it up." We all gathered around the radio. We'd missed the first part of the broadcast, but we heard plenty.

....we share your suffering and are mobilizing all available resources to respond to this disaster. National Guard as well as FEMA and regular units of the military are responding at this time in rescue efforts and clearing access roads and stabilizing bridges into the Northwest. Emergency shelters are being set up throughout the region, with evacuations planned in heavily affected areas. Michael Brown, Undersecretary for Homeland Security, will now comment on our current situation...."

"Dad, is this more than just Spokane?" Carl asked.

"Sounds like it. Kel, turn it up some more. Batteries are probably going."

"No, it's not a local station, Dad. I think it's KBOI. Is that Boise?

"Yep. Now hush."

The broadcast continued *'.....strongly felt from mid California well into Canada, with extensive damage reports from the entire Pacific Northwest and into western Montana. The full extent of the lahar flow that initiated at Mt. Rainier in the initial event is not known at this time, nor is the extent of ash fall in the Seattle region. As we stated earlier, the current low-pressure system is causing strong winds moving from the southeast to the northwest, which has had the effect of directing the majority of the eruption toward the urban areas of King County....*"

My brother lived in Seattle. I wondered what a 'lahar flow' was. The broadcast faded into static just as we started to hear some real information.

Damn.

6

January Fourteenth

We were all sitting around in shock I suppose. We had thought that the earthquake was just a local event, finally releasing whatever pent-up energy was stored under Eastern Washington. We'd been rattled a few times with quakes literally, under our feet, with the epicenter less than a mile from my office, ten or fifteen miles from home. Until we heard the President and the acting head of FEMA, that is.

"Dad, what about Uncle Alex and Aunt Amber?" Kelly asked.

"I don't know, babe. They're pretty far from Rainier, and on the Puget Sound side of Magnolia. I don't know what a 'lahar' is though, so it's anyone's guess."

"Oh."

My brother and his wife, as well as their two small kids had lived for years in one of the pricier neighborhoods in Seattle. They'd bought before the prices skyrocketed, and would eventually reap the benefits of the real estate bubble. Well, that was the plan anyway. Now what?

"I'm going to see if I can find out what a 'lahar' is. I think there's a dictionary in one of the boxes of books we moved over here after Mom died. Carl, take this one. It should be on top, if memory serves. Kel, here's one for you."

After the fourth box, we found it.

"**la·har**   (lä här)

n.

1. A landslide or mudflow of volcanic fragments on the flanks of a volcano.
2. The deposit produced by such a landslide."

"Mudflow. They didn't say how far it went, did they?"

"No, I don't think so." Karen responded.

"Man, this is bad." Carl said.

"Serious understatement, bud."

"Yeah. I know."

"Honey, will this be like St. Helens here?" Karen asked.

"Maybe. They said the ash was headed north with the winds. When the wind changes, we'll probably see some, especially if Rainier is still in full eruption. St. Helens ash that we saw here was only from the initial explosion. The later stuff never made it past Yakima. We better get ready, either way. Not that there's much we can do about it."

'Never thought about Rainier going,' I thought to myself. 'Never seemed like a threat.'

"Karen, Kelly, how 'bout you clean up in here, then head up to the garage. We're going to see what more we can get out of the house before the weather changes for the worse. I'm sure there's more stuff in there that we can get without getting ourselves killed. And get those leather mittens on over your gloves. There's glass up there."

"Rick, what about the neighbors' places. Have you checked on them yet?"

"No, that'll be next. Once we check out the house and get it secured, I'll take a walk around. Before I do that though, I was hoping I'd find my 870 Express or Dad's 1911."

"Oh," Karen said with a bit of a question in her voice. "Hadn't thought about that. Are you sure you'll need it?"

"No, but I'd rather have it and not need it than need it and not have it."

"True."

"Meet me up at the house."

Back into the boots, wool sweater, shell and hotfingers. One of the hand-knitted ski caps that my late Mom made me for Christmas, nineteen seventy-eight. Back outside.

The snow was just blowing around now, and the overcast was showing. With the wind-chill, it felt like we were working in zero-degree Fahrenheit temperatures.

Now that it was real daylight, and I had a chance to really look over the old house, the damage didn't seem so insurmountable. The house seemed to be on the foundation all the way around, although the back porch foundation had failed completely, tearing the porch off with it. The west wall had failed around the window over the bar, and the entire sill board that I'd spent so much time on, stripping off nearly a hundred years of paint, re-nailing, caulking, and painting, was almost all 'off' of the house frame. As we saw earlier, the north upper gable roof and part of the upper wall at the stairs had collapsed, some of roof framing shifted, buckling the roofing and part of wall. Shingles from the upper gables littered the ground, partly covered with snow. The ceiling on the front porch, pieces of bead board almost an inch thick, had detached from second floor framing in one piece, draped over east wall and covered the front door. Looking in the hole in the foundation wall above the bar, I could see the basement in disarray, but it looked like the entire chimney below the first floor was still where it should be.

"Where do we start?"

"That may be the hardest question I'll have to answer all day. I have no idea. Let's get in the living room and decide from there. Carl, grab the pry bar from the garage. It's next to the red tool box. Or, it was."

"K."

"Dad, can we get up to my room?" Kelly asked.

"Well, eventually I think. I don't think we have a staircase left, and that means using one of the extension ladders. I think the game plan is to get everything that matters off of the first floor, then look at the basement and second floor, probably in that order. I don't think your stuff is going to go anywhere."

"OK, I just wanted some more of my clothes."

"I know. We'll see what we can do. We should be able to get in there today or tomorrow."

"OK. What can I do now?"

"Let's get you and your Mom into the garage and see if there's stuff we need in the barn first. Then we'll have you get this stuff put away as we get it hauled out. All right?"

"K."

Carl was back. "All right. You stay on the front lawn. I'm going to see if I can drop the rest of the porch ceiling."

"Oh no you don't. There's got to be a better way," my better half piped up.

"OK. Carl, grab the tow rope from the garage. I've got an idea."

"How many more things do you want me to retrieve?" Heavy sarcasm. Not one of my son's finer talents, although he was quite skilled at it...

"I expect you to do as you are told, do what is needed, not complain, and excel at what you are asked to do and what you know you must do whether you are told or not. Clear?" My grandfather's legendary battalion commander volume was suddenly apparent.

"Yes sir," he responded with proper respect.

After he returned with the tow-rope, I hooked the heavy nylon through the hole where our porch ceiling light had been, and we all played tug-of-war with the ceiling panel. After about five minutes of yanking on it, the center section tore loose and landed in a heap. We could now see the front door...or what was left of it.

Once I moved the ceiling out of the way (future firewood), and carefully pulled the quarter-inch plate glass out of the way (glass so carefully beveled, etched, and now broken), I was able to get the deadbolt unlocked and pushed the door open. It landed in a heap in the living room.

"I really should have a funny remark here. That was almost a Marx Brothers moment," Carl said.

"It would be funny, if it didn't hurt so much," I said.

"Yeah."

In the next two hours, we managed to retrieve some of the furniture from the living room (including the antique couch, my grandparents first 'nice' piece of furniture, dating from the First War), two equally old side chairs, end tables, an Xbox and stack of controllers, CD's, some of the dining room furniture, and one of my Depression-era Aladdin Model 12's, now missing it's chimney and shade. A second matching model was upstairs, and we'd have to do further excavation to see what else made it.   We'd only seen three people out this morning, walking around. All were from the neighborhood, and we knew them on sight. A couple were looking for lost pets, or heading down the street to the convenience store for cigarettes.

Of course, on hearing this, I immediately thought of Paul Milne, the Y2K doomster that was always predicting on an internet newsgroup, "If you live within five miles of a 7-11, you're toast." Go figure.

The last of the 'stuff' we pulled out of the front of the house included Carl's mattresses (he had a bunk, with a full-size bed on the bottom and twin on top), four bags of his clothes (not that he ever wore anything other than baggy jeans, a sweatshirt over a couple of t-shirts, and shoes that were bigger than my first boat). I didn't know he owned that much clothing. His G4 Macintosh was still intact, including the 17" Apple monitor that for the life of me, reminded me of a giant, one-eyed three-legged spider.

"COOL! My computer made it!"

"Not that we have power to run it."

"You can come up with something. I'd love to hear some music right now."

"Yeah, like I want to hear one more heavy metal artist."

"Naw, that stuff sucks. Bluegrass Rodeo. That's what I want to hear. Or Alison Krauss and Union Station."

"What? You've got to be kidding. I didn't know that you knew that the genre existed."

"Yeah. Annie Womack. She's hot. And she can really fiddle."

You could've knocked me over with a feather. My son likes fiddle music. Karen would never believe it.

"Rick! Carl! Let's go warm up and get some lunch!"

"This oughta be good," I said to Carl. "Wonder what she's come up with?"

"I'm betting on mac and cheese."

"Good luck with that. I'm thinking soup. Head for the barn. I need to cover over the front door."

"K."

I managed to get one of the little five by seven tarps out of the garage and tacked it up above the door. Covered, not secure. Should be OK for a half hour though, without anyone messing with it. They would have to get over the wire fence or through the stock gate if they were bent on getting to the house. Neither was easy to the untrained.

I'd have to get the windows boarded up before dark, check on the neighbor's homes, and think about keeping watch tonight. I'd also need to figure out when I was going to get some sleep.

7

Lunch was indeed a surprise. As Carl and I were pulling stuff out of the house, Karen and Kelly had done some digging of their own in the garage. Karen found five cans of fuel for the Coleman stoves, my gazillion-watt battery-operated spotlight, and unlocked the upright freezer in the garage, which held some of our garden veggies, chicken, fish, and meat. With the power out and the cold, we wouldn't be losing the food anytime soon. The chest freezer was in the basement. I had no idea if it was OK or not.

She also found some more of our lawn furniture, including the big folding 'Costco Couch' and some other fabric folding chairs and both hammocks. All of this stuff was out to the barn by the time we heard her call, and Kelly had lunch going. Spicy chicken fingers, home-made salsa, fried Yukon Gold potatoes and onions, and some of our Early Sunglow corn. And a cold beer. Lunch never looked so good. With the heat from both the woodstove and one of the camp stoves, the rooms were hovering around 70°. Almost too warm with all of our work catching up to us.

During lunch, we talked about what we'd need for the night that we'd salvaged from the house. It would be good to have a real mattress or two (I hate sleeping on the ground), and the garage held stuff that'd let us get by. We had a couple of big air mattresses, bedding, sleeping bags, and pillows from the house. Sleeping arrangements would be tight, only due to floor space. We'd also have to figure out how to keep watch over our house over-night, as well as some of the neighbors' places.

Precious little new information from Seattle came over the radio. Both KDA and KLXY were back up and running, with non-stop reports from all over the city, county, and state. Not much new from the West side of the state though. Both Stevens and Snoqualmie passes were closed. Chinook Pass was of course closed for the winter. State Department of Transportation engineers were reviewing the conditions of all major bridges, after the Highway Three Ninety-

Five bridge through the Tri-Cities landed in the Columbia, a little after seven a.m. apparently with no warning. An undetermined number of cars, busses and semi trucks went with it, with only a handful of survivors making it out of the freezing Columbia. I bet I was on that bridge a hundred times. Unimaginable. I wondered how the WPPSS plant was. That was our state's only operating reactor. If the bridge went down, I wondered how the reactor fared?

After lunch, we decided it was time for a visit to the neighbor's houses, especially those that were empty for the weekend. Against my better judgment, I decided that I'd forego a weapon. My gun safe was still in the house untouched, and at this point unreachable without considerable effort. I knew that we only had maybe four hours of daylight left, and if weather was coming back in, probably less of real working time. And I had a lot of stuff that needed to be done in that time, let alone being caretaker. Still, I was obliged to take a look around the neighborhood.

"Carl, grab the radios. We need to take a walk around and check out the neighbors. Hon, listen in on us. We'll try to give you a report on what we see."

"You be careful and get back here if something doesn't look right," Karen said with concern.

"We will. I'll take Ada. She's pretty good at stuff that doesn't look right. Buck's got too much gung-ho in him yet. Kel, grab the leash for her, OK?"

Buck, our two-year-old golden, obviously expected to go out with his big sister (they weren't actually related), and was eagerly looking at the door. Ada was very calm, a good protector, and had a great demeanor. I needed to spend more time with Buck, and work on his training. Both of his parents were champion hunters, and it was a shame that I didn't use him in that role. He was a natural, but a little squirrelly for what I needed to do today, and more than a little indignant at not getting the invite to come along. Karen reprimanded him strongly, and he settled down, with plainly apparent hurt feelings.

Once we got our gear back on, and plugged the FRS ear buds in, and set mine up for VOX. Carl had his radio in his chest pocket on push-to-talk. I kept mine in my hand. The wind had stopped, and I could tell that the weather was going to change. We'd probably see the winds flip from the cold northeast off of the Rockies, to a southwest flow, much warmer, but now with the possibility of ash heading our way.

We first decided to head to the southwest to Mrs. Anders' old place. The folks that bought it after she'd passed on last fall had met Carl this morning, and I decided to introduce myself over the stock fence.

"Hello the house! Anyone there?"

"Hello!" A pair of voices came from what used to be the garage. A young man and woman appeared.

"Hi-I'm your neighbor Rick Drummond. I believe you met my son Carl this morning."

"Hi—I'm Eric Moore, this is my wife Amy. We already know your dogs—they're always out here to meet us."

"Always looking for a friend. This is Ada, the male is Buck, he's in the barn for a while. Did you guys make it through the quake OK?

"Yeah, but the damage is pretty bad. We've decided to close it up as best we can and head to my parents place. They're down in Valleyford on a farm."

"Do you need any help or supplies?"

They looked at each other for a second, and said quietly, "Yeah. We weren't ready for this."

"I don't know anyone that was." I thought for a second about that look they shared. "Have you had anything to eat today?"

"Not much. And the girls are not dealing with it well."

"That's right. Carl said you had kids. Tell you what, why don't Amy and the girls come for a visit and something warm to eat. I'll have my wife make you a sandwich and some coffee, and you and I can take a look at your place. We'll get you fixed up best we can. Karen?" I said to the radio, "Did you get all of that?"

She responded in my ear, "Yep. Way ahead of you. Send Amy and the girls over, and Carl and Ada. I'll have a sandwich and a thermos ready by the time he gets here. How old are the girls? Do they have enough clothes?"

I relayed to Eric and Amy the questions. "Mary's four, Ruth's two. They've got some clothes, but see what you've got in Kelly's old stuff."

"Gotcha. Coffee's in the thermos, a couple of sandwiches are in a Ziploc. Send 'em in."

"Thanks babe. Right away. Carl, run over to the trailer shed, and get that grey stepladder. We'll put it over the fence so the girls can climb over easier."

"Got it. C'mon Ada! Let's go." Carl tore off through the snow, with Ada trying her best to catch his cuffs.

"Nice radios. I never even saw them.......I can't thank you enough for this," Eric said quietly. Amy was rounding up the little ones.

"Just take care of your family. That's thanks enough. First house?" I said, trying to make Eric feel more at ease.

"Yeah, we got really tired of apartment life. This place was perfect."

"Will be again. Don't let this change your mind. It's a good neighborhood, good schools, and we tend to watch out for each other a bit."

"I've noticed. Are the other neighbors OK? We haven't seen too many today."

"Most around us are out of town for whatever reason. Some are in Seattle, so that's not good."

"Why? What happened there?" Eric said with piercing eyes.

"Rainier went off. That's what started this I guess. Seattle's getting ash fall, or was this morning. And mudflows too. Haven't heard too much other than that. Didn't you have the radio on for news?"

"No batteries, and the radio in the Bronco died. Didn't have money to replace it after we bought the house."

"Well, none of the news is good. No idea how many dead here in Spokane, let alone in the rest of the state."

"God help us."

"He will, I'm sure. Your folks farm in Valleyford?"

"Yeah, mostly wheat, but some peas and lentils. They've also a few head of cattle, goats, sheep and chickens."

"Sounds like a good way of life. Good for them."

"Lot of work though. My Dad won't slow down, and my Mom doesn't know how to."

"I find I'm like that myself. Working to change, though."

Carl showed up with the sandwiches and coffee, and Buck in full bounce-mode. "Here you go!" he said as Buck tried to get the bag.

"Let's go see what we can do about that house," I said as I climbed the ladder over the fence. Amy and the girls met me on the other side. "All right girls, this is my son Carl. I'm Rick. Carl will take you to meet my wife and daughter, and get some hot food in you. Sound good?"

"Yes sir!" they yelled out. They were bundled up in sleepers, boots, coats and mittens. Both of course had runny noses. Off they went. Eric tore into his sandwiches (Two ham, cheese and sweet-hot mustard on wheat), and washed them down with the French Roast.

"OK. Let's go have a look. New homeowner, so I'm betting you don't have anything laying around to cover up the broken windows, right?"

"Yep. And Home Depot is a long walk from here."

"Got that right. I've got a stack of corrugated metal that I tore off the roof of the barn when I rebuilt it. That'll be more than enough. Let's see what else we'll need."

The house had a couple of big foundation cracks, most of the windows were gone, and the chimney was all over the roof and through the carport. Amy's car, a little Nissan Sentra, would need a new windshield, sunroof, and back light, all taken out by bricks that went through the fiberglass carport roof. Eric's late Eighties Bronco was in the driveway, undamaged.

"Looks better than our place. We're going to be living in the barn for a while. Maybe a long while."

"That bad?" Eric asked.

"Yeah, there's a lot gone wrong over there. I don't know if it's salvageable or not. Let's go get some metal and tools and get you going. Are you trying to get out of town today?"

"Yeah I'd like to. The Bronco's packed up and full of gas. We were trying to come up with some way to cover the windows when you called. We were about to cannibalize the garage for wood."

"Well, this will be a little faster. C'mon."

For the next half hour, we bucked the two by eight foot sheets of corrugated steel over the fence and nailed them in place with leftover roofing nails. When we were fairly well done, Karen, Amy and the kids came back over to the fence. Karen had made the Moore's a meal for the trip to Valleyford, which in normal times was a twenty-minute drive. Today, it was anyone's guess how long it would take, or even if it was possible. Karen also had two big plastic bags of what I guessed were extra winter clothes for the girls. We had plenty

43

of stuff that our two had outgrown that we'd never gotten around to donating.

"Got any spray paint?" I asked Eric. "Something dark if you got it."

"Yeah, why?"

"You'll see."

Eric fetched a can from the broken garage. I shook the can and painted on the front of the house: "ALL OK. NO VALUABLES INSIDE."

"Not that it will slow someone who's determined down, but at least the authorities will know that you made it out OK in case they're trying to find you."

"Makes sense. Amy, we better get going."

"OK. C'mon girls, time to say goodbye! We're going to see Grandpa and Grandma!" Amy was putting on her best face for her girls. Good for her.

"Yea!!" they squealed out.

"Rick, thanks again. Here's that thermos."

"You bet. Buy me a beer sometime, we'll call it even."

"You got it."

"Watch yourself. No telling how the roads are with the snow, the quake, and the idiots out there."

"I hear that." Eric grinned as he got behind the wheel. "Say goodbye, girls!"

"Bye!! Thanks for lunch!" more little girl squeals.

Eric backed the fully loaded Bronco out of the drive, and slowly wound his way down the road, over tree branches and around utility poles. It would be quite a while before we saw him again, I was sure.

"One neighbor taken care of, seven or eight to go. Got any more of that coffee?"

"Yep. Fresh pot." We were walking back to the barn hand-in-hand as the kids and dogs ran ahead of us. "That was a nice thing you did, hon."

"Aw, shucks, twarn't nothin', ma'am."

"Quit now, goofball. I mean it."

"I know. They didn't have ANYTHING. They weren't ready for ANYTHING!"

"Amy said all they had in the house were some juice boxes, cold cereal, and leftovers from take out dinner last night. They were going to go shopping this morning after going out to breakfast."

"Going out to breakfast. It would be nice to know that they were the only ones who live paycheck to paycheck, but I'm sure that's not the case. Probably a lot of hungry people in town today. And cold. Nice guy, but I know this is a big wake-up call for him and he's starting to see the errors in his ways. Things are too fragile to live without some sort of safety net. His 'net' is his parents. Hope they make it home OK."

"Me too. C'mon. Let's go warm up," Karen said as she squeezed my hand.

"Yeah. I'm all over that."

8

Kelly had some hot tea ready for us when we got back inside, and a tin of fudge and cookies that I'd found in the wreckage of the back porch.

"Perfect! A nice big mug to warm my hands up, and walnut fudge to keep me going."

"I had to hide it, or Carl would've eaten it all," Kelly told us.

"I would not! I know there's chocolate logs...."

"Did you get your clothes hung up by the fire to dry out?" I asked them both.

"Yep. They're hanging from the workbench, the vise and the table saw."

"We'll need to rig up a better system than that. Carl, why don't you find some of that thin rope we used on the tent trailer last summer, and rig up a clothesline."

"OK. Where do I look for it?"

"Turn around. Look up. Right in front of you." The rope was hanging on a pegboard with some of the tools that were restored to their former spots on the woodshop wall. "If it'd been a snake, it'da bit ya."

"Thanks," he responded sarcastically.

As I took off my ski bibs and changed gloves (again!), and hung up the damp things to dry near the woodstove, I asked Karen what else she'd been able to give to the Moore's, and filled another hot cup of tea.

"Oh, we had those boxes of Kelly's and Carl's old clothes and stuff. I managed a couple off pairs of boots, three sizes of snow-suits, two coats and a couple of sweatshirts. Amy said they'd be all right with what they had on, but if they get stuck, they'd freeze to death. Oh, and a bunch of mittens."

"I packed them a couple of those cans of soup with the pull-tab tops, one of the old thermoses with tea, some juice and some cheese and crackers. You don't think they're going to have an easy time of it, do you?"

"No. Just looking up and down our street, and knowing what the houses look like, I can imagine what the bridges, overpasses, rail crossings and steep hillsides must look like. All kinds of blockages, stuff in the road, landslides. Not to mention about a foot and a half of snow, deeper drifts in other spots, compact snow and ice, and probably rain or freezing rain coming. Still, they've only got to get to Highway Twenty-Seven and down the road a piece. They're going to have more trouble getting south to Thirty-second and Pines than they will the next ten miles. Assuming the two rail overpasses are still in place....."

"Yeah. Hadn't thought about that. It could be a real mess."

"After I finish my tea, I think I'll get the tractor going and do a little plowing. I'd rather get it moved before it either turns to slush or ice, and I don't want to slog all over the place with that much snow, especially if we need to haul some stuff around to cover windows."

"You're not planning on driving anywhere though, are you?" Karen asked skeptically.

"No, no need. There's plenty to do here, and I figure the only people on the road are either headed to a hospital, sightseers, looters, or people that don't have what they need. We're none of those," 'right now', I said to myself.

"Good. I don't want you to go until we know more."

"And then, when we find the world's ended, it's OK for me to go?" I said with a grin.

"Yep. You're well-insured."

"Good to know! I better get going. Carl, gear up! Kelly, you too. I want you to wear those two dogs out so we don't have to fuss with them in the night.....which is coming in about three hours. Make sure that boot on Buck's foot stays in place and dry if you can."

"OK. It's on with....duct tape."

"You'll need to keep an eye on them while I'm out plowing—as in, either you're with them both outside, or you're both inside with them, all right?"

"Sure. What do you want us to do when we come back inside?"

"We'll figure out something. There's a long list of stuff we haven't thought of yet." Which sparked a thought of my own.

"Okay, all. Here's the deal. These two blue drums have all the stored water that we can get to right now. It's also the only drinking water we have stored. So, don't waste it. We'll come up with a plan for washing dishes and such."

"K." Carl responded with his typical long-winded response.

"Dad?" My daughter Kelly asked, "What about washing? You know, showers and stuff?"

"Well my dear, welcome to rural poverty and primitiveness of the Great Depression. See that big galvanized tub?"

"You mean the one we wash the DOGS in?" The tone of her voice said it all.

"Yep. That's our new tub. If we're lucky, I'll be able to cobble up hot water to go with it from the woodstove."

"Swell."

"Hon, you need to remember something here. It's not all about you. Got it? There are dead people because of this, lots of them. At least one on this street, probably more. Think about all the friends of yours from church, middle school, and camp. Chances are, some of them haven't made it through this. Remember what we've been teaching you at church? That you don't know when the end comes, so you need to be ready for it regardless?"

"Yes. I remember. Dad, I'm sorry......it's just so much....."

"Yes it is. For your Mom and I too. Remember, we don't know how the rest of the family's doing in all of this, especially your Grandma."

"I know. I'm sorry."

"That's OK. C'mon. We've lots to do. Sorry I kinda bit your head off there."

"But Grandma's with Uncle Alan's family. She was going to spend the weekend with them and go to Holy Cross with them on Sunday."

"You're right. I'd forgotten."

"Me too—Thanks honey. I've been worried sick about your Grandma all day." Karen said, very relieved. "She's probably OK." She whispered to herself.

"What do you want Carl and I to do?" Kelly asked.

"Here's a clipboard and some paper. I need you to make a list of all of the supplies we've got here in the barn. We need to know how we're going to make do. The list on the clipboard is already an inventory, but I know it's not up to date—by three months. There's probably stuff on there that we need and don't have. We need to know what that is, and figure out how to work around it. Questions?"

"Nope. We'll get on it right now," Carl responded.

"No, you'll get on it when you get back in from playing with the dogs."

"OK. Sorry, I forgot."

"Excellent. And remember, stay out of the s'mores box. That's for later." The s'mores box, Hershey chocolate, graham crackers, marshmallows, sticks, matches and napkins, was found in the garage...and one of the things that they both wanted to get into right away.

"K."

Kelly, Carl and I put our warm, damp coats and outer wear back on, as Karen went back to picking up the shop, sweeping up some of the hundreds of screws, nails and other fasteners up and generally piling them up where we could sort them out someday. In the quake, my metal rack holding several large and many small boxes off fasteners tipped over, hitting the table saw on the way down. The stuff was everywhere.

"Big game of pick-up sticks I have ahead of me, huh babe?"

"Yes you do. Not as big as the house, I'm sure..."

"Got that right. I'll be back in a while. I'm going to go plow and take a quick look around at the neighbors. I'll put the radio on VOX when I'm not plowing."

"Thanks. The drone of the tractor would drive me to distraction I'm sure."

"Be back in awhile." I gave her a quick kiss and headed out the door into the field.

"DAD!!" Kelly called out. "The water tower is gone!"

I quickly looked to the north where the big tower used to be, next to the interstate. "Whoa. I hadn't noticed. That'd help explain why we'd lost water pressure. That tower's been there all of my life. Horizon doesn't look quite the same."

"Are they all gone? Are all the water towers gone?"

"Probably not, babe. Some of the old ones, or ones that weren't being kept up maybe. That tank had probably been there since the early Fifties. I think that held a half-million gallons of water. Probably on I-Ninety right now."

"Wow." The kids looked at each other.

"Yeah." One more thing to think about, right-damn-now. Great.

"OK, get going with those dogs. Make double-sure the fence behind the barn is good, and run 'em hard, but watch Buck's paw. They've been pent-up most of the day and they need a workout. Then make sure that they get fed and get some sleep. I'm going up to the garage and do some plowing."

"OK. I've got my radio if you need help," Carl said.

"Thanks bud. Now get going. That Buck of yours is as wild as a March hare."

"Yeah, but with him around, no hares to worry about."

"So true...."

I slogged off to the garage again, dug out the key to the old Ford, and pulled the canvas Army tarp off of the old beast. I'd bought it three years before more because I wanted it than needed it, and found lots of excuses to use it. I'd finished repainting it last summer, and added new brakes and tires. Other than that and little stuff, it was all original, and seemed to be envied by other folks in the neighborhood, especially when it was snowing........
On the third try, and with a liberal amount of choke, the little four-banger fired up. I didn't bother with tire chains this winter,

51

because of the new lugged rear tires. I hoped I wouldn't need them today—the chains were a real pain to put on.

The weather had 'warmed up' to the high twenties, and the high overcast of late morning had given way to darker grey skies, and lowering. We'd either have rain, or freezing rain before night. Swell.

After a few minutes of maneuvering, I had the Ford ready to go, and quickly cleared our driveway off. I then opened the big metal gate, cleared the approach, then closed the gate behind me. I planned on making a quick few passes up and down the street as far as I could go without running into downed lines, poles or trees. I managed to get most of the way 'down' the street toward the arterial, then turned around at the next cross street, when I heard a loud 'whump'. I looked behind me at one of the newer houses that were built in the late 90's, when prices started to zoom. The big 'custom' house had collapsed in on itself, and the dust cloud settled on the wreckage. Fortunately, it was vacant—the former owner having worked for Hewlett-Packard at the Liberty Lake plant before it closed. They ended up losing it in foreclosure, and we heard later, ended up divorced and living out of his car. 'The bank would have a hard time making money on that property,' I thought. 'Wonder if the tractor noise set it off? Hmmm.'

After a half hour of using the back-blade, I managed to clear most of the street to the south. The north was hopelessly blocked by two large Black Walnut trees that had snapped and crashed into the road two houses north of us. The little shack of a house on that property had also burned to the ground. The car was missing, so I assumed that they'd made it out before the fire got them—probably starting in the ancient oil furnace. A couple of the neighbors that I knew by face if not by name, came out and waved to me, and I then proceeded to drag the snow out of their driveways as well. One of them, an elderly gentleman who lived on the other side of the James' house, introduced himself over the drone of the tractor, and asked me if I had any spare kerosene.

"You bet. Need it for a heater?"

"Yes sir. We're down to about a half-gallon, and it's our only source of heat until my son gets the woodstove hooked back up. He's working on it now, but the place is getting cold."

"I've got lots. I'll get some over to the house in a few minutes. Five gallons enough?"

"That'd be fine, young man."

"Are you keeping enough air in the house? That carbon monoxide is nasty…."

"We have a battery-operated CO2 detector. Hasn't gone off yet, and I just replaced the batteries."

"Sounds good. I'll have my son bring over the kero."

"Oh, are you Carl's Dad?"

"Yes, you've met?"

"When he and Drew play football, the ball sometimes comes in the yard. Good kid, that one."

"Thanks. I'll let him know. Need anything else?"

"Nope, we're doing OK for the moment."

"Sounds good. Look for Carl in a few minutes."

"Thanks again!"

After I drove on to the next house (Brad, our next door neighbor, who was visiting his sister in Bothell, north of Seattle), I asked Karen over the FRS, "Get all of that?"

"I think so, which neighbor is that?"

"The old guy on the other side of James', north side of the street. He says he knows Carl."

"OK. Carl wants to know how he's supposed to get the kerosene over there?"

"Blue wheelbarrow--the one with two front tires. Tell him I'll be right there to plow him a path from the barn to the street. Rest of it's clear."

"OK."

I quickly made a couple of swipes of the driveway at Brad's, and did a quick once-over of his house and shop. The garage was leaning over, hopefully he didn't have much inside of value. It looked like the plastic storm windows were intact, but the glass 'inners' were gone. His chimney was down, and I quickly hopped off of the Ford to re-install two of the little plastic bubbles over the basement windows, which were shattered. 'That'll at least keep a little snow out.'

I put the Ford in third gear and quickly drove off of Brad's property, down the road and back through the gate, where Karen met me. "Figured you'd get tired of gate duty," she told me as I drove through.

"Got that right!" I said as we passed. "Leave it open, I'm not done yet."

"OK!"

Carl was waiting outside the barn with the can of kerosene in the wheelbarrow. 'Good for him. Lifted that in there by himself. Those are heavy,' I thought to myself as I spun the tractor around.

"Follow me out. Hey, did you get the siphon filler too?"

"Yeah. Mom remembered it."

"Good for her." I said as I plowed a path from the barn to the gate. Carl followed slowly, careful not to upset the wheelbarrow and it's cargo.

"I'll be back in about twenty minutes. I've got a few more driveways to do, and I want to check out some of the other houses for damage."

"Be careful. I've still got my radio."

"Will do."

Next up was the James' place. The house was a real mess. It was a Seventies-era split level, and the only part that didn't have obvious structural damage was the garage. A real mess. I hoped they were OK. Tim was a single dad with four boys. They'd gone out of town to the Tri Cities to visit his brother-in-law's family for the weekend. The front deck was tilting, the back one now a heap of firewood.

Joe Pauliano and his wife Joan lived down the road to the south. They were next on the list. Joe, a first-generation Italian, was the toughest old bird I'd ever known. Still working as a part-time contractor in his late seventies, he'd built the house they lived in back in fifty-eight. As I pulled into the driveway, Joan met me with steaming coffee, with her customary hospitality.

"How'd you both do? Everyone OK?"

"We'll be okay. Joe got banged up a little, he slipped on the ice yesterday. He's in lying down on my orders. The quake didn't hurt the house much, two broken windows is all, and the chimney's cracked. He heard that little tractor and had to see who was coming. I told him to stay inside."

I laughed at that. Just like Joe. 'The benefits of living in a house that you designed and built yourself, no doubt.' I knew that the house had been built with quality that today's builders would not recognize.

"Is your family all right? Anyone hurt?" Joan was like a second grandmother to the kids.

"A few cuts and scratches and bruises. Buck and Ada are fine. The house is a different story. We're living in the barn for now."

"Do you need to come down here? We've lots of room."

"Thank you no, we're OK for now. I'll want to talk with Joe when the weather warms up though, about the house. And Karen and I were wondering if you could spare a few laying hens."

"SPARE ANY! I'll say. Joe's been meaning to cull them out since they molted in November and hasn't gotten around to it. We're swimming in eggs. I've had to close up the chicken shed though, with the cold. And their production will fall off without the electric lights."

"True enough. How many can you spare?"

"Oh, golly. Two dozen if there's one. And a rooster or five."

That got me laughing again. "I'll see what I can do to help you out. I'll be back tomorrow with the kids and Karen. You name your price."

"Just keep the road clear for us, and we'll call it even, Rick. I don't know what that man was thinking when he let that flock get so big."

"Consider it done. Better get back inside," I said, handing my cup back to her, "Think we've got rain coming."

"Yes. My hip's been bothering me all day. You be careful."

"I will. Thanks for the coffee—and the bourbon in it too."

Joan blushed. "You looked like you needed it."

"Probably so," I yelled back as I drove off.

The last house I wanted to check was the neighbor to our immediate south, the Woolsleys. He was a serious car nut, while I'm only a nut-in-training. His car mania focused on Model T's, T speedsters, a first-year Model A, and a Ford Lightning pickup. He's one of those guys that had a nicer shop than house. Should be, cost more I'm sure. Nate had wanted to attend a car parts swap in Monroe, north of Seattle over a long weekend. Ginny had gone along to see the grandkids.

I turned the tractor into the drive and bladed off the asphalt, then lifted the blade a bit as I moved onto the gravel path back to the shop. The shop windows were broken out, and the pole building had racked with the movement from west to east. Most of the metal siding had torn loose from the wood framing below it, fasteners ripping through the metal. The roof appeared to be intact, but buckled in many places. I put the tractor in idle, hopped off, and reached through one of the broken windows and unlocked the man-door and let myself in. I'd have to get this secured before looters showed up. Nate had tens of thousands of dollars in tools, let alone the cars.

Using the mini-flashlight in my pocket and what little light came in through the translucent panels (now torn) on the upper walls, I saw that the Model A was OK, as was the Lightning, but the little yellow Speedster was upside-down, smashed into the floor. It had apparently been on the two-post center lift, and flipped off in the quake. Nate would be devastated—he'd spent ten years getting all the right parts for that car. No reproductions, only all original or new-old-stock parts would do.

I checked for spilled flammables, found none, and shut off the breaker panel in the shop on the way out. Outside, I found a few pieces of sheet metal left over from the shop construction, and nailed a few of them up over the windows, with Nate's tools and nails. That'd have to do for now. I locked up and closed the door. It actually stayed closed in the bent doorframe.

"Hon, everything OK? I hear the tractor on idle," Karen buzzed in my ear.

"Yeah, I'm over at Nate's. Just nailed up some metal on the shop. House looks OK, typical damage. Probably nothing we need to mess with today. Saw Joe and Joan. Had a Pauliano Coffee, too. They're both OK, and we'll get some poultry from them tomorrow. I'll give you the full skinny when I get back home."   Pauliano Coffee was different things to different people. To Karen, it meant coffee and brandy. For me, bourbon. To the kids, three sugars and heavy cream.

"OK. See you in a few. Gate's open."

"OK."

I headed back out to the street and turned left as I felt the rain start, and drove past the still-smoldering ruin of the late Mrs. Long's house. 'Hope she went quick,' I thought.

I knew it wasn't going to be warm enough to be straight rain for long.

"One more trial," I said to no one as I drove back to the barn. It was starting to get dark, and there was a lot I wanted to get done before night.

9

By the time I got the tractor back to the barn and shut the engine off, the rain was coming down hard. The little round thermometer on the barn said it was twenty-five degrees. Ice was already building on the old stump of the Siberian Elm that we'd lost in the ice storm of Ninety-Six. We'd thought that a once-in-a-lifetime event at the time. I shut off the fuel valve for the Ford, covered it with a blue tarp and four sash-weights, when I heard the horn.

Turning to look in the driveway, two squarish headlights were peering at me. The horn sounded again. 'Wonder who this is?' I thought, mind racing. 'Who in the heck would be out for a drive after all of this?'

The gate swung open as I crossed from the field into the yard. 'Must be someone I know, not too many strangers can figure out that gate.' I was still blinded by the headlights. They started to look familiar.

"Rick! Is everyone OK?" I knew the voice instantly. My old friend Libby and her husband Ron, driving their Jeep YJ.

"Libby! What brings you out here? Everyone's fine. You're a long way from Five Mile!" I called back out as I finally reached the plowed driveway.

"Tell Ron to drive all the way in. Head for the barn. That's now Chateau Drummond."

"OK!" She closed the fabric door as I closed the gate.

"Hey, wait up. I'll hitch a ride on the running board."

"Hop on!" Ron yelled through the door.

In a minute we were back at the barn. Ron, Libby and their kids John, a senior in high school, and daughter Marie, an eighth-grader, climbed out of the back seat. They all looked awful. They plainly had not traveled out here to see us. 'Well, duh,' I thought to myself. I'd known Lib since college, long before I met Karen. Lib introduced us at her sister Marie's wedding. Funny how things work. Libby's daughter was named for her.

"Come on in. Let's get you warmed up and you can tell us your story."

"It's a beaut," Ron said as Lib and Marie went towards the barn.

"John, grab that tarp. We'll cover up the Jeep before we go inside. No sense on chipping off more ice than we have to."

"Hon, we have dinner guests!" I called inside as Lib and the family entered.

"LIBBY! RON! What are you doing here?"

"My sentiments exactly!" I chimed in.

"We haven't made it home yet. Marie had a youth basketball party until two a.m. at Sports World. We were picking her up when it hit." Sports World was six miles away. Fourteen hours to get here? No, they probably left at daylight. Which meant, nine hours to get this far.

"Come on in by the stove and warm up. I've got spiced cider heating on the stove. Have you eaten?" Karen asked.

"Not since dinner last night." Ron said.

"Whoa. We'll fix that up right quick." I said.

"Kids, get in here and warm up. Here's some cider. Carl, please get out the Cougar Gold and crackers for everyone. Kelly, set up a buffet over there on the workbench. We'll get you taken care of, now take a load off." Karen was taking charge. Atta girl.

"Actually, I think we'd all rather stand. Fourteen hours crammed in a Jeep hasn't been fun. It's been a heckuva day," Libby said.

"Yeah. I bet. Heard the news on the radio?"

"No. The Jeep's radio went missing last fall. We picked up a little from some other folks that were trying to get home, but not much. Something about a volcano and the earthquake. They didn't hear which one," Ron said.

I thought for a second. Lib had family in Seattle, including her sister Marie. "It was Rainier. It's bad."

"Oh God," Lib sobbed, as the questions poured out.

"Slow down, we'll fill you in as much as we know, which isn't much. Every hour it's about the same news, most of it local stuff. We haven't heard much from the West Side since this morning," Karen said as she cracked eggs into a bowl for omelets. Pepper bacon was already in one of my grandmothers' cast iron skillets. "Kelly, if you're done in there come on in and cut up some Cougar Gold and a tomato for these omelets." Cougar Gold was one of my favorite cheeses, produced by college students at Washington State University. Karen's omelets were famous for it, but only on rare occasions did we build them like this.

We filled them in on what we knew about Seattle as 'breakfast' was cooking, and told them of what we knew locally. Ron and Libby had just moved to a newer house four blocks from Grace, Karen's mom, and less than half a mile from Karen's brother Alan's place.

"OK, Martins. Breakfast is ready!" Karen told our hungry guests.

"Dad—It's almost five. Should I try the radio again?" Carl asked.

"Yeah. Turn on both of them. They're on different stations."

We received static from KLXY's frequency until 4:59. KDA had nothing but static.

"Good evening, it is 5:00 pm. A reminder to all within the Spokane Region, that dusk to dawn curfew is now in effect. If you are found on the streets after 5:00 pm, you will be arrested. There are reports of looting from the City and Spokane Valley, and both the Chief of Police and the Sheriff's office have stated that looting will not be tolerated and that homeowners may defend themselves if they deem themselves in imminent danger. Three home-invasion robberies in South Spokane today have resulted in the deaths of two homeowners, one six year old girl, and two invaders."

"Damn vultures," I said quietly.

"Washington State National Guard units have been mobilized to assist in rescue, recovery, and security matters."

'Maybe I better go find those guns,' I thought to myself.

"KLXY News through our regional affiliates and government sources, has confirmed through helicopter over flights of the region that the lahar mudflows from Mt. Rainier's eruption have reached Puget Sound in multiple locations. "

We looked at each other anxiously.   I remembered thinking to myself, 'Holy crap,' as the broadcast went on.

"While the majority of the Seattle region is still unobserved by air or ground forces, it is confirmed that the mudflows have destroyed the Port of Tacoma through the Carbon and Puyallup river drainages, and that the Nisqually river basin is completely covered with the concrete-like mudflow. Radio communications in the region have been seriously compromised by the nature of the ash fall, which has damaged or destroyed most broadcast stations."

"Sketchy reports of similar lahars reaching into the Renton basin and Lake Washington have also come in, and it is believed that the eruption and mudflows have affected the White River, the Green River, the Cedar River, and Renton industrial area. Reports through military sources have indicated that substantial portions of the Boeing plants in these regions have been either buried or swept away in the mudflows."

"Seismologists believe the event at Mt. Rainier, called a 'sector collapse' was similar in nature to the 1980 eruption at Mt. St. Helens, but was far more devastating than that eruption. Preliminary estimates of dead and wounded at this time are approaching a quarter million citizens throughout the region, and are projected to climb as more information becomes available, and rescue crews reach the affected areas.   The Seattle-Bellevue-Redmond area continues to be blanketed by ash fall, which is estimated to reach sixteen inches in the first eighteen hours of the eruption. "

"Mom," Marie asked, "what about Aunt Marie?!" Marie and her family lived in a trendy part of Redmond.

"I don't know, honey. Let's pray for them."

"Meteorologists expect the southeast winds directing the ash fall toward Seattle to gradually change to a southwest wind, which has the potential of bringing ash to Eastern Washington and North Idaho over the next twenty-four to thirty-six hours. The ash cloud is currently topping out above sixty-thousand feet, which could place a significant percentage of the ash in the upper atmosphere, resulting in a potential that the ash cloud could circle the globe. "

"Repeating, a dawn to dusk curfew is now in place..." The first portion of the newscast repeated word for word.

No one had anything to say as we listened again to the curfew notice as the cook stove cracked and popped. Soft kerosene light lit both rooms as the next portion of the report came on. John and Ron had cleaned up their first omelets, and Karen was cooking two more, these two with homemade salsa. I could smell biscuits baking in the oven.

"Besides the obvious and horrible loss of life and property, this is a virtual death blow to the economic engine of Washington state, with the potential loss of major aerospace design and fabrication facilities at Boeing's numerous plants in the damage path, massive disruption of the software headquarters of Microsoft, and similar firms like Adobe Systems and others. "
"USGS observers aboard Air Force planes on the south side of Rainier indicate that smaller mudflows are affecting areas south and

east of the mountain, but to a much smaller degree than the massive outflows to the north. The airborne observers stated that large amounts of steam, rocks, and lava bombs were continuing to shoot from the new crater, and minor earthquakes continue to rock the area."

"Areas outside of the eruption zone have been heavily damaged from the initial series of earthquakes, including the major damage seen in Spokane and Kootenai counties. A preliminary list of affects of the quake includes the following: the closure of Snoqualmie and Stevens passes due to landslides and losses of bridges, the loss of the Vantage Bridge and Highway 395 bridges over the Columbia, and damage to Grand Coulee Dam. The dam continues to generate power and is being inspected at this time by the Army Corps of Engineers. Other dams on the Columbia and Spokane rivers are being inspected by Corps Engineers and local experts to determine the extent of any damage or danger. No report has been made available regarding the status of the Columbia Generating Station, our states' sole operational nuclear plant at Hanford. The loss of Holy Family Hospital in North Spokane has forced relocation of hundreds of patients to the intact portions of Northtown Shopping Center, with new patients being directed to Sacred Heart, Deaconess or Valley Hospital. All local hospitals are currently operating under extremely adverse conditions, with minimal power and damage from the quake."

"Emergency operations at both Fairchild Air Force Base and Spokane International will commence as soon as runway repairs can be completed. The condition of Fairchild's runway is unknown, but the main and auxiliary runways at Spokane International were damaged and buckled in the initial quake. The 'A' concourse collapse did not result in any injuries or deaths, due to the late hour of the quake. Repair operations are being hampered by the cold weather, but are expected to begin within the next twenty-four hours."

"An expanded list of emergency shelters in the Spokane County/Kootenai County will be provided at fifteen and forty-five past the hour. Limited low-power television broadcasts from this and the three other local stations is projected to be re-established within twenty-four hours."

"We at KLXY are holding all of you in our prayers and thoughts, and are asking for the Almighty to see us through this crisis."

"Updating a list of emergency shelters operating at this time....."

"Well. There it is then." I said to no one in particular.

"....Sacred Heart Hospital, Deaconess Hospital and Valley Hospital are all asking for volunteers with medical experience, blood donors, and technicians........"

It would be crowded in the barn tonight.

1 0

After the Martin's had finished 'breakfast', Karen started working on 'dinner' for the rest of us, as well as the Martins. Using the woodstove and one of the Coleman stoves, she and I worked on beef stew in a big cast-iron Dutch oven, cornbread (this was a real experiment for me, I'd never baked in a wood-fired oven before), and for dessert, ice cream from the kitchen freezer.

"Ron, now that 'breakfast' has taken the edge off, how 'bout you tell us about your day."

"I can do that. Well, we showed up at Sports World at about one-thirty to pick up Marie. There were about twenty of her friends from her school team out there, part of a night of basketball shoot-around for the league teams. We met her at the door, and were walking back to the Jeep with all of her stuff when we went flying. The ground just whipped us up in the air, like a carpet ripple."

"All of the cars went flying, several of them hit each other. One guy was crushed between a Suburban and an H2 Hummer as he got out of his car. Never had a chance. His whole family saw it happen, and there was nothing they could do. The buildings didn't fare too well either. In the first wave, the power went out and there were a couple of transformers that 'popped' with sparks and a little fire. One of the poles snapped off about twenty feet up and landed right on the entry vestibule. There were a bunch of people under it. They didn't make it either. Two of Maries' teammates and their families were there too. They're still there. There wasn't anything we could do, and all that steel was too heavy to lift."

"Oh, man," was all I could say.

"Quite a few people made it out, maybe two hundred-fifty. There was a lot going on as usual, you know, ice skating, basketball, weights, the poker tournament in the club. Most people decided to get to their cars and stay in them until they could figure out what to do. I don't think anyone stayed in the buildings, they were afraid they'd come down."

Libby added to the recount. "After we saw what happened to Marie's friends and their families, we tried to pull up the steel, but we knew...... It was snowing, there wasn't any light except from a couple of the building's emergency lights, but....you could tell....." Her voice trailed off as she glanced at her children, then to the floor. "It was too quiet. They were gone. We went back to the car. A lot of people left then, headed for home."

"After about twenty minutes of trying to figure out what to do," Ron continued, we decided to wait for daylight. By then it was maybe two-forty or so, and I could tell by the headlights that we'd have a tough time around all the stuff that was down. During the night, the kids got a little sleep."

"Not much." John said.

"Yeah, John took most of the back seat." Marie replied.

"We weren't exactly planning on camping in the car, you two," Lib quieted them down.

Marie and Kelly moved off into the other room, no doubt to talk about their adventures of the day. And to talk about boys. John and Carl stayed in the shop with us, camped out in one of the big, grey collapsible couches.

"Before you go on, Carl why don't you get John and the girls a soda from the fridge."

"K. Thanks."

"Yeah, thanks Rick."

"That's Mr. Drummond to you, John Martin," Lib said.

"Lib, it's OK." I grinned. She was so **Irish** sometimes.

Ron went on. "Anyway, during the night, a few more of the cars left. Some were running out of gas, so they decided to go while they still could, hoping they'd make it home before they ran out. The Jeep was full, so we were OK at that point."

"We left Sports World at about six-thirty, it was just starting to get light. Without having any traffic, the roads were awful, of course no snowplows, and then all the snow down on all the trees, power lines, poles and stuff. We made it out of the parking lot, no problem. After that, things got hairy."

Karen handed Ron another cup of cider, this time with a little rum.

"We went through—or over—the freeway fence to get on the freeway, because one of the high-tension towers had come down on the frontage road. Anyway, after getting almost a half-mile, the overpass at Barker was down. So I backed up, nearly getting hit by some SOB running without lights. I went up the off-ramp, over the overpass, and saw that there was a huge pile-up on the on-ramp, and with all that snow, there was no way to get around it. Back on the frontage road on the other side. We dodged a bunch of stuff on the frontage road—sometimes going through front yards—until we made it to Flora. The Flora overpass was down, and I knew that we'd have to get to a bridge over the river to head north. That meant Sullivan, Trent, or Argonne. I thought Barker was too far away when I started. Probably should've tried it."

"About ten, we made Sullivan. The south half of the overpass was down, and the hill was covered with snow and ice anyway, and it's steep up hill. The river bridge off to our right was down—the east half."

"Yeah, that'd figure. That was the old part." I said.

"And the west half didn't look much better. So we either had to continue west, or head south. South wasn't an option because of the hill and that snow, so we tried to head west on Indiana."

"Past the Mall."

"Yeah. Mistake. The looting was full-on by then. All the electronics stores, the sporting goods stores, Krispy Kreme, you name it. Krispy Kreme! Why the Hell would you loot a donut shop!?! We saw a couple of cops, but they weren't doing anything but watching it all. One had a video camera, filming the cars as they were coming out. One guy took a shot at 'em. Missed though. There really wasn't anything they could do, there were just too many looters. The store guys at the sporting goods stores though, weren't letting anyone walk off with guns or ammo. Four or five dead guys in the parking lot proved that."

"What'd you guys do?" Karen asked. We were all spellbound by the Martin's story.

"The cops said that we should head back to the freeway up to the exit we'd already passed. The closest overpass was damaged. They also told us that the bridge had been sanded, so we should be able to make it up in four-wheel drive."

"Did you have any trouble with the looters?" Carl asked.

"Not once we drove through the parking lot and back to the freeway approach. We looked back at the overpass and there were two cars and a bus crushed under it, and a tanker had plowed into it after it fell. Burned the whole shebang."

"Once we made Evergreen, we were able to wind our way through the streets over here. If it weren't so cold, we could've walked faster. What is it, six miles?"

"Yeah, something like that. Lots of damage like our street?"

"Yeah. And worse. Those big high-tension lines on Twenty-Seven are laying completely across the road. Those poles must be eighty feet high. The Conoco station was still burning, and the propane tank at the Cenex had blown too."

"How was Valley General?" Karen asked. Valley General was our local hospital, where Carl and Kelly were born.

"Crowded. Lots of tents set up in the parking lot. The new part looked good, still had some glass in the ICU wing and the emergency wing looked fine. The maternity and pediatric wing was pretty broken up. How old was that thing anyway?"

"I think it opened in the mid-Sixties. Probably never saw a seismic upgrade."

"Well, about half of it is unusable. That, from my professional heavy-equipment mechanic point of view on a drive-by in a snowstorm."

I chuckled at that. "Your opinion is at least as good as mine…"

"Which road did you finally use to get here? Ours looks blocked down the road, and the trees north of Brad's have it shut down too," Karen wondered.

"Drove past your church—which doesn't look too good either. The old sanctuary on the east is OK, the wing in the middle is gone, and the new sanctuary on the west looked OK. Couldn't see the gym."

"Thanks. I was wondering if we could go to church tomorrow," Karen responded.

"That's a good idea, babe," I said. "How's that stew coming?"

"Should be ready in an hour or so. Too bad we don't have any of that burgundy. That was one of your Dad's key ingredients."

"Actually, THE key ingredient. Well, that and top sirloin cut up into cubes." My mouth was already watering.

"Ron, how about you and I take a walk up to the house. There's a few things that I think we're gonna need."

"Sure. Got any spare boots?" Ron was wearing short hikers, useless in this weather.

"Yeah, we've got some Sorels over there, and heavy socks are in the bin to the left of the door," Karen said. "Got mittens or gloves?"

"John, give me those snow mobile gloves you had."

"They're over by the stove."

"Thanks."

"Here's a hat," I handed Ron my WSU football knit cap.

"Great. Couldn't be the Huskies, could it?"

"Nope, not in this house. That's a dirty word here!"

"Fine. Better warm than proud."

"Truer words were never spoken," I said as we left the barn through the tool room.

Once we left the barn and slogged through the frozen vegetable garden, Ron told me, "You guys are doing OK in this."

"We're all alive and not hurt, and we've got a place to sleep, and we're warm, and we've got food. I have to agree."

"I can't thank you enough for taking us in."

"Taking you in? Ron, you and Lib and the kids are family. Danged sure closer family than that no-count brother of mine over on Ninth Avenue. Haven't even seen the worthless drunk for two years. There are very few people that I'd want to ride this out with other than you guys. You should know that."

"Thanks. I know that Lib and I feel the same way about you guys too. Once we figured that getting home wasn't an option, this was the only place to go."

"Well, if it were 'summer', we'd be having a barbeque right 'bout now, just like each Independence Day. I guess we'll celebrate 'survival' instead this year."

"No doubt. What do we need to get outta the house?" Ron said.

"I haven't found the gun safe yet. Thought that might be prudent. I didn't plan on having to defend myself with a club or a pitchfork. There aren't too many of the neighbors home right now, and if someone comes callin' who isn't welcome, I'd like to have a 'not welcome' ready for them."

"I hear ya. What do you have?"

"My Dad's Garand, a lever action .45 camp carbine, a couple of 10/22's, a couple of 1911's, a Remington 870 Express 12 gauge. I've got others, but those are the ones I'd like to get now."

"Jeez. What else is there?"

"My grandfathers 1903 Springfield, and two other 1903's that I bought for fun. I don't shoot my grandfather's gun much, trying to preserve it. The others are shooters. The last one is the big family secret. My Dad brought it home after Japan. A Browning Automatic Rifle."

"Holy CRAP! Those things are worth a fortune!"

"Family heirlooms are priceless, actually. And that particular gun can be credited with my existence. Dad took out a Jap sniper after the end of the war with it. Sniper picked off two of my Dad's command as they were building Haneda. Bastard was trying to get to my Dad on his road grader." Haneda was later renamed Tokyo International Airport. "Dad cut the guy in half with it. Lengthwise."

"Is it legal?"

"Strictly speaking? No chance in Hell. It'll still go full auto, and it's never been papered. Well, not since the war anyway."

"Peace through superior firepower."

"Something like that. I just hope to God we don't have to use it. I can't imagine things getting that bad."

"Me either. I'm a bigger fan of 'reach out and touch someone' from a few hundred yards off."

"Yeah. I just can't imagine someone who'd be a looter being anything close to a good shot."

"Yeah. Let's hope we don't have to find out."

"Let's get going. This ice's murder," I said without thinking. "No, this ice is...."

"I get it." Ron said as we put the ladder up to the window.

In we went.

January Fourteenth

After Ron and I had recovered my gun safe and relieved it of it's contents, we wrapped the items up in a bedspread and packed them out of the house. I covered the bedspread with plastic, placed it in a wheelbarrow, and went back in for a few other items that'd caught my eye.

Due to the quake, the safe was in an exposed location, and had a chance of getting rain or snowmelt on it, so I'd emptied it out completely, including the ammunition. I had more bulk ammo stashed in a couple other places around the property, conveniently hidden in plain sight. While my wife knew that I had some ammo in the safe and in the cabinet next to it, she didn't know about the bulk purchases. Some of them were inaccessible due to weather (buried in capped 6" diameter PVC tubes, weather tight and shrink wrapped in plastic). I'd eventually have to explain that to her. Probably should've done it by now. If I would've died in this little fiasco, she would've needed to know that kind of thing.

Next, I had Ron pass me up a roll of plastic from the garage, and one of the staple guns. I spent a little while covering over the exposed windows with plastic, and stapling them up. I managed to get most of the windows covered without killing myself on the now ice-covered ladder, before deciding that it was a really bad idea to continue.

I made one quick trip into part of the house that I'd not yet seen fully, that being the basement—I wanted to surprise Karen and Libby, but knew that Karen wouldn't approve of it if she knew what I was doing. Ron was keeping an eye on me as I went in....through the hole in the foundation. I passed out enough stuff to more than fill the second wheelbarrow, all wrapped up in big garbage bags to keep them clean and dry. I didn't get too far into the basement though, the stair collapse had seen to that, as the door was blocked with the sheetrock ceiling, just opposite of the staircase up to the first floor. Getting the stuff out was a chore.

I tripped over something on my way back to the window—I'd forgotten this one. It was my late father's old bolt-action magazine loading shotgun, a J.C. Higgins, which was a Sears gun from the Fifties. It had hung over the bar for the past fifteen years, unfired. The long barrel had been bent as one of the foundation stones landed on it. I might be able to cut the bent part off and still use it...not that I had ever fired the beast. It weighed a ton. I passed it up to Ron as I started back out of the basement.

I climbed back out of the hole, over foundation stones, earth, and the smashed basement window. He'd wrapped up the old twelve-gauge in the plastic covering by the time I was ready to go. The last of the late afternoon salvage in hand, we headed back out to the barn. With the addition of our guests, it was time to get a supplementary water source going, and pronto. Those two big drums of water wouldn't last long as our sole source of water. I'd have to take that on tomorrow.

We trudged back out to the barn along the path I'd plowed earlier. The freezing rain had solidified the top half-inch or so of snow into a thick layer of ice, and the rain still continued. Walking was tricky. Moving quickly was out of the question. The fences, gates, trees, and my greenhouse were straining under the weight. I'd have to do something about the greenhouse, or I'd lose the covering, and maybe even the frame from the weight of the ice. It was never designed for that.

"Hey! We're back!" I called into the barn. "Hope you've got something warm for us..."

"Irish coffee. I found that bottle of Irish Whiskey that you had out here. Must've been for medicinal purposes, right?" Karen said cynically.

"Yep. Used it for splinters. This IS a woodshop you know."

"Yeah. Suuuure. Here you go. Why are you so dirty?"

"I...I uh, made a couple of trips into the house."

"Uh huh. Try again. Your radio was on VOX. We heard it all. Basement, huh? I should make you sleep in the Ford tonight!"

"Yeah, sorry. Had to get a few things."

"Like what, for example was worth risking your life?"

"I didn't risk my life. The house isn't going to come down on itself, unless we get a couple more big shakes. The foundation is in better shape than I thought, and the basement doesn't have that much damage, or at least not much I could see with the flashlight."

"It's what you don't see that'll kill you. That's what you're always telling me…"

"Here. Pour yourself a nice glass of chocolate Port," I said as I handed her the bottle. The Port was rescued from the bar. I'd bought it at a little Spokane winery that made great wines, and really great Port.

"You didn't."

"I did. Happy Anniversary, babe." She didn't remember it, but this was the twentieth anniversary of our first date. The look of shock grew in her eyes.

"Richard James Drummond…."

"Don't say anything, just give me a kiss."

She complied with the Martin's and our kids applauding. She was crying. "I'd forgotten."

"That's OK. It's not like we've been in a life-endangering situation or anything. I'll just blame it on old age." She had me by six months, which provided a consistent source of ammunition for the perils of getting older.

"You're not making any points there, sweetie."

"I know. You used all three names. I better quit while I'm behind. Here's a bottle of burgundy for that stew. I couldn't imagine it without."

"Perfect timing. The stew's taking longer than I thought—we have to keep feeding that stove. What else did you get from the house? Something useful, I assume?"

Ron and I looked at each other. "Yeah. A few things--Ron and I will get them in here and secured. Best close that door to the woodshop, no sense in letting all the heat out. We've got two loads of stuff to get in, so the store room door will be open a while."

"OK. Just let us know when you're done. Carl, how about you get that other lantern fired up for the store room?"

"OK. Can you show me how?"

Karen showed Carl how to get the old-fashioned kerosene lantern fired up. This was one of the old-fashioned railroad style lanterns, fully enclosed.

Carl helped us get the wheelbarrows moved into the doorway as Karen, Libby and the girls worked on dinner in the woodshop. John was put to work duct-taping cracks in the sheetrock of the storeroom, where cold air was seeping in. The wood shop had a few cracks, but with thicker insulation, the problem wasn't as bad.

Ron and I unloaded the firearms, made sure they were clean and unloaded, and placed them in one of the empty wall cabinets. The Browning was wrapped up in a blanket from the house, and put in the same cabinet after I took a quick look at it. Ammunition, the cleaning kits, and four cans of Hoppe's all ended up in the cabinets and a shelf, and I quickly recognized that all of the guns had at least some ammunition here in the barn. The 10/22's were well stocked with several hundred rounds each; the lever-action .45 and the 1911's had 600 rounds of FMJ that I'd bought locally and from Cabela's; 400 rounds of 30.06 for the Garand, the 1903's, and the BAR. The lone semi-auto shotgun, my 870 Express, had bird shot, deer loads and rifled slugs available.

"Jesus—You planning on a war?" John said.

"No, not right away," I said, seriously.

"Nice one, Dad." Carl smiled.

"Was that a BAR?" John pressed on. "Grandpa Martin ran one of those in Europe. I have a picture of him with one."

"Yep. That one belonged to my Dad. He put it to use in North Africa, the Philippines, and Japan."

"Wow. That's serious hardware."

"War isn't for sissies."

"Yeah. Need any help with the rest of that? I'm out of duct tape."

"No such thing. There's four more rolls in that drawer over there, second drawer down on the left. And more in the garage."

"Well, I've got this room done, I think."

"We'll put you to work. Here, you and Carl grab a couple of these boxes—carefully—and put them on the bench over there. Then the big plastic sacks, OK?"

"Sure."

John was destined to play high school football. A junior, already six-two and about two hundred-thirty pounds, there wasn't an ounce of fat on the kid. Pretty good hunter too, from what Ron had told me.

Once we were done unloading, I closed the outside door and locked it. The remaining boxes and bags were unpacked carefully, and then I told Karen that we'd finished unloading. The shop door opened and the warm air rushed into the chilly room.

"OK, so show us your haul!" Karen and Libby responded together.

"Certainly. Have a seat." Karen and Lib leaned against the workbench on the wall opposite of our 'haul', which we'd covered with a light sheet. Kelly and Marie were in one of the folding couches, John and Carl on the mattress with the dogs. Buck was alternately gnawing on his wrapped foot and Carl's gloved hands. (The dogs know that when family members have work gloves on, it's play time. They know better than to try this with strangers.)

"All right. Here we go. First off..." I pulled a bag from under the sheet, "One wedding dress."

"Oh, you found it! Lib, that was mine, and my mothers' too." It appeared that I was no longer in as much hot water as I was a few minutes before.

"Next, four boxes of photo albums and pictures from the house." Applause greeted Ron and I this time.

"Baptismal gowns, banners and dedication Bibles."

"Good for you!" Libby smiled.

"One 1901 German Bible, one 1860's Bible in Celtic." More applause.

"Your grandmother's and my parents' silver services," I said as I pulled two small cases out.

"One really bent-up shotgun," as I pulled out the old Higgins.

"What about the rest of the guns? Did you get to the safe?" Karen asked.

"Yep. They're all ready in the wall cabinet, with some ammunition."

"Unloaded?"

"Yes, for the moment. We'll have to decide what we need to do regarding security tonight. With any luck, the looting won't come this far in the next day or so. By then, the sheriff and the Guard should have things under control."

"They keep repeating that curfew notice. I heard on one of the CB's that there were home invasions going on on the South Hill and at Liberty Lake," Kelly said. She was getting to be pretty good at snooping out the news.

"Yeah. Not surprised. After dinner, Ron and I and the boys will go out to the other houses we're watching over and we'll do a little spray painting like we did over at Eric and Amy Moore's place. Not that it'll stop them, but it'll make it clear that if someone's breaking in, that they are doing it for less than humanitarian reasons."

"Daddy, did you bring anything else out?" Kelly asked.

"Well I haven't made it back up to your room yet, if that's what you're asking. I did get the window covered so the rain and ice won't get in anymore."

"No, that's not what I meant. I just wondered what else was under the sheet and in those boxes."

"Well, let's have a look. Karen, you have the honors."

"All right. Is this some sort of surprise?"

"Not particularly," I said.

Karen opened the first box. It was filled with quart jars of peaches, pears and apricots that we'd not had room for in the storage room last August. They were all unbroken, and sandwiched in between layers of cardboard.

"Whoooo hoooo!" She said excitedly. "I thought they were all toast."

"Me too. They were stacked up in front of the sewing cabinet. They were just fine."

"Then this one is...YES!!...My tomato soup! And the next one has to be the pickled beans, green beans and stewed tomatoes."

"The next two actually. The other one is over by the door."

"Wow. You didn't have room for four cases of home canned stuff in your fruit room? What DO you have in there then?" Libby asked, amazed.

"More of the same, as well as a bunch of dry goods, pastas, soups, you know. Stuff."

"Our storeroom has Christmas ornaments in it. And old clothes. Nothing like this," Ron said.

"Well, you just never know when the fit will hit the shan, do you?"

"Yesterday, I'd have laughed at you for this, Rick." Lib said.

"Yesterday, I'd have laughed myself if someone said that in twenty-four hours I'd be living in a barn."

"Yeah. I suppose so."

"The last box is for the kids. Kelly, you and Marie open it up."

"OK," Kelly said. She and Marie quickly opened the top of the box and were greeted by an entire box of candy bars, M&M's, nuts, and raisins.

"Cool! Can I have a Snickers?"

"Sure, but I call dibs on all of the Milky Way Dark," I smiled.

"Those were bought for the Bible study kids at church for their verse memorization. Nothing like candy to get a kid to learn God's Word," I told Ron and Lib.

"Sanctioned bribery?"

"Well, of a kind, yes. But when you're dealing with Junior High kids, you do what you can."

"Indeed." Lib said. "Hey! Give me one of the 'Special Darks', John. I need it with my coffee."

"Wait til you try one on a s'more," I told her. "Nothing better."

"Quit that. Dinner's coming soon," Karen said. "You'll spoil your appetites."

"Not bloody likely," I told her. "And babe, you've got a hint of your mother in that tone of voice."

"I'm sure I do. If she were here, she'd be after you with a wooden spoon."

"Yes she would," I thought to myself. 'Sure hope she's OK.'

"So what's on the agenda after dinner?" Carl asked Karen and I.

"Why, got a hot date?" I said to him, which is my usual question to him.

"Nooooo, Dad. John and I wanted to go out." John looked at me from across the room, plainly hopeful that I would give an OK, where his mother I was sure, had not.

"Not a great idea, bud. We don't really know what's going on beyond our street, and we're going to have to figure out how to keep an eye on things tonight. I think after dinner, some of us ought to get some sleep, and we'll have to decide who's going to be on watch and when. And what we're going to do if something happens."

"Something' being what?" Inquisitive little cuss, that boy of mine.

"Someone showing up to rob us or one of our neighbors. There are people who are taking advantage of things right now, and more people that were completely unprepared for this. We're pretty sparsely populated right now, and there aren't enough of us to do a good job of keeping an eye on everything all the time all night. We'll have to set up a watch over night, and if something happens, get on the radios and get help out in case we need it. You need to realize that we are waaay better off than a lot of people in town right now, and far better off than a lot of people in the state. Clear enough?"

"Crystal."

"OK, you deep thinkers, grab a bowl. It's time for stew," Karen called to everyone.

"And don't make a mess of my just-cleaned barn. I slaved away all day on the decorating."

Saturday
January Fourteenth

"Kelly, bring the big radio in here so we can listen during dinner, please." Karen asked Kelly. For the life of me, our little arrangement was reminding me of a 1930's soup line, Karen and Libby dishing us up from the big simmering pot, white aprons and all. After we were dished up, we each took a hunk of (well done) cornbread from one of our old dinner plates. A second cornbread was in the oven.

"How are we doing on batteries for that thing?" I asked.

"Seems good, I changed the old ones this morning, they were five years old, but still had some life in them. The new ones were up in your cupboard."

"Good. I bought those at the after-Christmas sale at Ace."

As soon as we were all served and beverages provided (water for Kelly, her drink of choice, pop for the boys and Marie, and iced tea for the adults), we joined in prayer before eating.

"Dear Father God, we thank you for all that you have provided us, and ask your blessing on your children who do your work. We ask your protection for those who are in danger, for those working to save their brothers, for those who are struggling without your guidance. We ask these things in the name of your beloved Son, Amen."

"Amen," echoed from our assemblage.

"That was very nice, Rick," Libby said quietly.

"Thanks. Nothing like speaking from the heart. We have lots to be thankful for. We've made it through this day safe and sound when many others didn't. We've done this because of Him."

Libby and Ron nodded. The kids dug into their big bowls of stew as the six o'clock broadcast started.

"Good evening, this is KLXY Spokane broadcasting on 920 AM. This is the six o'clock news. KLXY will continue to broadcast throughout the night on reduced power, beginning at seven p.m. "

"Reports of the train derailment east of downtown have been confirmed by our reporters, who have radioed back to the station the details of the major derailment. It should be noted that many derailments in the Yardley railroad yards occurred due to the earthquake, but only two have resulted in major incidents."

"The main derailment, just north of Mission Avenue, has resulted in the loss of the joint City County Emergency Operations Center, or 911 Center, the adjacent National Guard Readiness Center, the City of Spokane Fire Training Center, a fire station, and fire department field house and training facility."

"Oh, crap," I said. "That was one of our projects. We master planned that site for the Community College...."

The announcer went on. *".....derailment was a low-speed event, but the train in question was carrying numerous types of cargo, including bulk goods, fertilizer, and several unknown chemicals. Our reporter on the scene, to the east behind police lines, has reported that the chemical plume from the initial crash and explosion was direct to the south and west, into the East Central and Logan neighborhoods. The fumes were apparently a heavier-than-air mixture of lethal chemicals, which resulted in the deaths of hundreds of residents as they evacuated their homes after the two a.m. quake hit the Northwest. We now go to Amy Johnstone via two-way-radio who is on scene. Amy? Are you there?"*

"Yes, Jim. This is just one of several devastating scenes that I've experienced today, and by far the cause of the single-largest loss of

life that I've seen. I'd like to note that the EOC building and the Fire Department buildings are intact, but as I understand from the local Battalion Commander, all personnel in the buildings were apparently asphyxiated due to the toxic fumes from the train derailment. No contact with any of the buildings has been possible without protective gear, but from the initial visits to the structures, it is my understanding that all staff were killed within minutes of the cloud enveloping the structures. At least two staff of the EOC were killed in their vehicles, which apparently stalled when the gasses overtook them."

"Jim, I've recorded the haz-mat codes on the train cars that I could see through my binoculars, and would like to give them to you now. There is still some fire and smoke rising from the wreckage, which partly obscures the scene. I believe that you have the reference manual for the materials list there at the station?"

"Quick, Karen, get me a pencil from up on the shelf," I asked.

"Why?"

"Tell you in a sec."

"Yes, Amy. Go ahead when you're ready," the announcer continued.

"OK. I'll read these off quick. My batteries are going. 1005, 1051, 1053, 3130, 3307, 3306, and 1978. I better sign off. I'll try to recharge the radio and be ready at forty-five past."

"OK, Amy. Thanks for your report. Our in-house staff is currently reviewing the haz-mat codes found on the train cars, to determine exactly what kind of spill or 'incident' as the authorities typically call it, has resulted in so many deaths....."

"How are you going to decode those numbers?" Ron asked.

"Got a list. In that computer over there," I got up and moved to the Power Mac 8500 that now lived in the store room, sitting on the floor. "Need power though. Wait! I've got the Power Book too. I just need to hook it up to the battery from the lawn tractor and I think I can get it to go. The main battery's shot, and it's not worth buying a new one. Really obsolete."

"Aren't you going to finish your stew?," Karen asked.

"Yeah, in a minute. I want to know what that stuff was."

"OK," she shrugged her shoulders as I took the old Power Book out of the case, hooked up the twelve volt cigarette lighter plug in to the power port, and hooked up the alligator clips to the tiny motorcycle battery that ran my Honda lawn tractor in the summertime. I punched the Power key, and the startup chime rang. After a minute, the screen came to life and the desktop appeared.

"What made you want to know about hazardous materials codes of all things?" Libby asked as I found the file I was looking for, launching Microsoft Word.

"We're about a mile south and west of THE major train line between Chicago and Seattle. Do you know how many trains per day pass through Spokane?"

"No, I never thought about it."

"Dozens. If one of them crashes, and spills something, I wanted to know what danger we were in. Sometimes, it's substantial."

"What have you done about it?"

Sheepishly, I said, "Not much. It was on my list of things to research more. I just never got to it. OK, what are those numbers? Read 'em off to me Carl."

"1005, 1051, 105..."

"One at a time. I need to keyword search them. OK, 1005....is anhydrous ammonia. 1051 is Hydrocyanic acid aqueous solutions with more than 20% hydrogen cyanide."

"Cyanide?" Karen asked with shock.

"Yeah. What's next?"

"One Zero Five Three."

"Hydrogen sulfide."

"Three One Three Zero, then Three Three Zero Seven."

"No specific name, but it says 'Substances, which in contact with water emit flammable gases, liquid, poisonous.' Three Three Oh Seven is......' Liquefied gas, poisonous, oxidizing.'

"Three Three Zero Six and One Nine Seven Eight," Carl finished.

"Lots of entries for Thirty-three-oh-six. 'Compressed gas, poisonous, oxidizing, corrosive, Inhalation Hazards, Zones A through D.' What was the last one?"

"One Nine Seven Eight."

"Propane."

"All of that stuff was on one train?" Libby asked.

"Yeah, probably, and probably more. These were probably all tank cars. If there were bulk chemicals on there, they probably spilled too. Those people never had a chance."

The room was quiet again, except for the broadcast.

"From the Sheriff's Department and Joint Operations Center now located in the Spokane Valley, we have heard numerous reports city-wide of looting of businesses and home break ins. These reports began during the hours after the earthquake and are continuing to increase in number and apparently, violence."

"Business owners and homeowners are encouraged to use their judgment when dealing with life-threatening situations, and the Sheriff's office reminds everyone that a dawn-to-dusk curfew is in place at this time, and that........Please wait one moment, we have

been advised that the entire State of Washington has been declared a disaster area by the President and that the Acting Governor, who until yesterday was our Lieutenant Governor, have declared a state of Martial Law in Washington State due to the natural disaster and ensuing social unrest. At this time, the military has been declared in command of recovery, rescue, and security operations within the State. We have been advised that details of the meaning of this declaration will be coming within the next hour."

"At this time we would urge all listeners to be extremely cautious of carbon monoxide poisoning due to the use of kerosene space heaters, charcoal fired hibachis, and other improvised heat sources. We have reports of more than a dozen deaths due to this silent killer, and more reports of illness. If you are experiencing dizziness or headaches, you may be exposed to excessive amounts of carbon dioxide and KLXY and health authorities urge you to seek shelter in a public facility at once. These shelters are open throughout the city, and a list, by neighborhood, is as follows.........."

"What's next?" Karen asked.

"I finish my stew, that's what's next. After that, some dessert. After that, we'll talk security, then, I'm gonna take a nap."

"That's all?"

"You seem surprised."

"Yeah. Martial Law means the government's in control."

"Right. Like they haven't always pretended to be? Government's not in control, and never has been. That's always been in the hands of a Higher power. You know that, honey."

"Yes. Of course, but....."

"There's things I can do things about. There are things that I can't do anything about. Martial Law would be in the latter category. However, if someone comes for our guns or to unlawfully take our property or that of my neighbors and friends, it'll be a different story,

Martial Law or not. Now, how about some more of that stew? And is there honey for that cornbread?"

As I finished eating, Karen, Libby and the girls took on the task of cleaning up and thinking about breakfast the following morning.

Cleaning up involved washing up the days' dishes, which meant using snow melt water on the stove, boiled, as wash water—a very time-consuming process. Dishes were done in the large banged-up aluminum pot we used for wash-water while camping in the summer, before we bought the tent trailer. Rinsing was done in an old enameled steel pan that dated from the Thirties.

I gave Ron my keys to my old camper van, and he took the four radios and the twin chargers. The Martins' and Drummonds had camped for years together, so he knew our stuff about as well as anyone. He got the old six-cylinder started on the third try, and went to the back of the van to plug in the radios to the inverter, which was powered off of the deep-cycle battery in the back. I figured that if we ran the van for fifteen minutes or so, that the battery's charge would probably be enough to charge the hand-held radios for the next couple of hours. I'd just run the van last weekend, warming it up for an oil change. The van was parked next to the barn, beyond the 'Packard' room. Moving it, of course, would be impossible through the snow and ice, but that hadn't been a problem last weekend.

Karen filled Lib in on our current stocks of supplies, which, though extensive, wasn't exactly like working in our kitchen. We were down to the last half-gallon of store-bought milk, for example, which meant that powdered milk would be used with some of the stored water. We had about eighteen store-bought eggs left, but with luck we'd be in fresh eggs as soon as tomorrow or Monday, depending on how Joe's hens were laying.

Karen had already laid down the law on using the stored water only for cooking and drinking, and that wash water was to be from snow melt, rainfall, or filtered water when we had it available—which wasn't yet. By her records, we'd used perhaps ten gallons of the sixty available in the blue barrels, and four gallons or so of snow melt.

Karen and Libby had also figured out a plan for arranging the store room and woodshop for sleeping, assuming that if someone was out on 'patrol', or whatever we wanted to call it, someone would be up with them, in the shop, listening or talking to them on the radio, keeping them awake. For tonight at least, we had one full-size regular mattress, one twin, and two full-sized air mattresses available for the store room, as well as the ancient mattress that was stored out in the barn. The woodshop would have the World War Two era wood and canvas cot. Bedding for tonight at least would be sleeping bags, which had all been moved to the shop from the house and garage after my initial salvage.

Our 'facilities', meaning our toilet, was located in the unheated, uninsulated part of the barn that held my Packard. The porta-potty had been placed on a piece of plywood atop a wood palette, and offered no privacy whatsoever if the door to the store room was opened. The TP was unceremoniously hung on a sixteen-penny nail, driven into a stud.

Not exactly indoor plumbing, but it'd have to do for now. I'd have to build an outhouse pretty soon. One more thing to do. I'd have to figure a good place to put it, and figure out how to dig through well-frozen ground. Great.

One thing we all were constantly having a problem with was turning on the light switches every time we went into a room. I wondered how long we'd be dealing with that.

While Ron and I talked about security plans for the night, and a staffing rotation, Lib released the girls from their servitude, so that a proper foursome could be had for the boys' game of Texas Hold 'Em, played by the light of two of the old-fashioned camp lanterns. We all decided that this was not a bad idea…it certainly got them into a better frame of mind, if only for a while. Ada and Buck were occupied with all of the smells in the rooms, and were checking out all of the stored boxes, sleeping bags, and odds-and-ends in the shop. Eventually, they staked out spots near the cook stove, evidently deciding that both the warmth and the chance of food being dropped nearby was a bonus.

I was dead tired, and so was Ron. We'd have to wrap this up and get some sleep soon, the boys too. They'd be joining us on 'patrol'.

We were expecting further news or information about our current state of 'Martial Law', before the radio stations powered down, but that didn't happen. KLXY suddenly just dropped off the air, and was gone. Kelly jumped right up and started scanning the dial for more local news, but didn't find any. She settled on KSL for the big radio, and shut off the little GE radio that had been set on the Boise station. The 'big' radio was a Radio Shack model that picked up shortwave, TV, AM/FM, and NOAA weather radio. I think I paid fifteen bucks for it at a pawn shop. We didn't get anything out of

Seattle or Portland even in good weather, so we didn't even bother scanning them. The shortwave bands had a fair amount of information about the quake, but really nothing much we didn't already know or could logically assume. We did hear that between sixteen and thirty inches of ash fall had hit the Seattle metropolitan region, from Tacoma all the way to Lake Sammamish. Survivors were walking out. The Alaska Way Viaduct had collapsed.

Oddly, I wondered how the Trader Joe's in Issaquah was. I bought a case of Two Buck Chuck there two weeks ago, some Ghirardelli chocolate for Kelly and Carl, and some imported tea and exotic coffee for Karen. And my brother in West Seattle. They had such a nice view of the Sound and the Olympics....before.

"Carl and I will take first watch, from nine to midnight. We'll need one of you awake in here listening in during that shift. At eleven-thirty, the watch officer—that's you—wakes up the relief shift and has coffee or cocoa or something ready for two thermoses. Probably some trail mix or jerky too. Your job will be to listen in on the radio during the watch, and contact the patrol every fifteen minutes. More to keep them awake and alert. If anything odd happens during the patrol, the watch will contact you and you will wake the relief. We might need reinforcements out there. Three hour shifts, and the off-duty watch gets at least some sleep. Questions?"

"Are the radios charging?"

"Yeah. Ron put them in the van on the inverter. Should be done for first watch, I hope. The second set will stay on longer, so second watch will have to get them out of the van before they go up front."

"What's your...patrol area?" Lib asked with some hesitation.

"Not far. We should be able to keep an eye on the street from our property alone, but we ideally will be outside of the fence. If someone comes up the road on foot, we need to be able to move. Even with as little light as we have with the cloud cover, we should still hear them before we see them. We're not going to be moving around much, if at all."

"What about....guns?" Lib asked, already very apprehensive.

"We'll all be armed. The boy's will have .22's, Ron and I will have 30.06's, one of us will have a shotgun too."

"What will make you decide to use them?"

"Well, simple looting won't be enough. If we are threatened directly, that will be enough. The boys are painting signs like we put on the Moore's house on each of the vacant houses around us. If someone breaks in, we know they're not there for good reason. Even so, we'll scare them off if we can. That's what the shotgun will primarily be for—noise. If we can't though, well, that will be a tougher decision."

"I don't like this, Rick." Karen said flatly.

"Me either, Karen. You just can't go and shoot someone." Lib added, equally determined.

"Ladies, if it comes to it, this will not be done lightly. But I will defend my family, and the family of my friends. It is as simple as that. It is a duty that I have as a husband and father."

"Libby, I feel exactly the same." Ron added.

Karen was quiet for a moment, and then told us, "You be darned careful. You'll talk to the boys about this?"

"Yep. As soon as they get in."

"OK. Don't tell the girls."

"All right, we'll let you tell them. They need to know," Ron said. "Tomorrow night, if we're still here, they'll probably be on the radios."

"All right. We will."

1 3

Eight Forty-five p.m. Saturday night
January Fourteenth

The alarm on my beat-up Indiglo watch was intruding on my dream. In my dream, I was welding some new floor pans in the old Mustang. I woke up to the 'beep-beep-beep' of the watch, and realized that the sound of my welder in my dream had been static on the big radio. It was eight forty-five, and felt like midnight. Even with the sheets of cardboard that we'd tacked over the windows, we still got a little light in the room from the two-by-two skylight. It didn't sound like it was raining anymore, and I was thankful for that.

Everyone was asleep, the Drummonds in the wood shop, the Martins in the store room, and both dogs were sleeping next to my mattress, both I'm sure, hoping to occupy it as soon as I moved off. Karen rolled out of her sleeping bag and lit the Aladdin lantern, and adjusted the wick to maintain a low flame. 'An old-fashioned nightlight,' I thought to myself.

I'd changed into clean clothes earlier, and was pretty much ready to go. The woodstove was still burning some of the leftover oak flooring scraps, and the room was still pretty warm, at about sixty degrees. Carl finally roused, after I nudged his ribs with my toe and told him to 'get ready for school. You're late for the bus.'

That never failed to get him going. Of course, after he realized where he was, that was a different story.

"Oh, man?!"

"Gotcha. Let's get moving, kiddo."

Karen put the enameled steel coffee pot on for our hot drinks and put some more oak and cedar into the firebox. The water was already warm, and I didn't really want it boiling. We both chose cocoa, and Lib and Karen had already packed us some snacks to keep us occupied. Carl and I would take the nine to midnight shift, with Karen on the radios. We'd do shift change at eleven forty-five, and we'd be back in the barn a little after midnight. We'd overlap a little so we could talk about our patrol and any new information we'd heard through Karen. Then, Ron and John would take the midnight to three, with Lib on the radio. We elected to stop the patrol at the end of the three-o'clock shift, thinking that even looters would be sleeping by then. Really, I think we all wanted sleep and were looking for some justification to be in bed, rather than hunkered down in the snow somewhere.

After we were fully awake, I gave Carl his 10/22, wrapped up in a waterproof ballistic nylon sleeve. I had six of the sleeves, bought at a sporting goods auction a few years ago. They had little Velcro straps on them, basically serving as an anti-scratch cover for travel, with fleece linings. We decided that the guns would stay holstered unless we determined that we had a threat. With luck, they'd never see the dark of night. I also didn't want the guns getting wet or frozen in the snow. They'd all been cleaned within the last month or two, but even so....

"Ready?" I asked Carl.

"Yeah, I guess. This sucks."

"All over that, bud. We'll be OK. Your Mom will keep us awake. Got those gaiters on over the Sorels?"

"Yeah."

"Good. We'll grab two of those brown six by eight tarps up at the garage on the way out. We'll be able to sit or lay on part of it, and put the other part over us. We've got a little cardboard too, so we can use that for insulation against the cold."

"We're not going to be walking around?"

"No, not if we can help it. When you watch a movie with guards in it, what's the first thing that happens to them?"

"They're shot or stabbed or something."

"Why is that?"

"The bad guys want to."

"Yeah, but mostly because they're really visible targets. I'm not about to be a target, and I'm sure as heck not going to make you one. We're going to be 'one' with the background. Think like a sniper in your Halo game."

He smiled. "Gotcha. We'll be fine as long as we don't have the 'Flood' to deal with.' The 'Flood' was a particularly nasty little creature in the X-box game, that was best taken out with a LOT of shotgun blasts or grenades.

"Shouldn't have to worry about those guys. Think of the guys with the glowing swords. That could be your enemy..only in this game, you could die." I was trying to put the real threat in his mind.

"Yeah. The 'Elite's.' They're tough." In the first version of Halo, the Elite's were all but indestructible. They'd killed our screen characters dozens of times before we figured out how to kill them.

"Yeah. But Carl, this isn't a game."

"I know Dad. Real. 'Private Ryan' real."

"Exactly. Hon, got that hot stuff ready?"

"Yeah. And be quiet. We don't need to rile up the dogs or get Lib and Ron up. They're exhausted."

"Yeah, sorry." I replied. "Where'd you dig those up?" I pointed to our 'lunch boxes.' She had four matching soft-sided insulated coolers (warmers?), about six-pack sized. Two were fully packed with our wide-mouth thermoses, the other two were ready to go, without the thermoses.

"Over on the shelf in the back. You never get rid of anything, do you?"

"Not without your permission, babe. Those are yours or the kids."

"Oh. Well, they should work. Just try to keep them off the ice and dry."

"No problem. Let's go kiddo. Hon, the radios are set on 6-21. I think they're all locked in, but that one on the bench reset itself. You might check it before we get too far out."

"OK. Fifteen minutes, right?"

"Yeah. We'll wait for you to call us, unless there's something going on. You could scan for news, and let us know what's going on, if anything. Just don't read to us, unless you want us asleep. We'll try to keep quiet and not use the radios much to save power. OK?"

"Yep. Better get going, it's almost nine."

"We're gone," I said as I gave her a long kiss.

"You watch out for my boy."

"You know it." I took the cases containing the Garand, and the 870 Express. My parka pockets had ammo for both, but not much. I wasn't planning on fighting a battle.

Carl and I had our snow bibs on, boots, gaiters, parkas, snow gloves and a pair of hobo (fingerless) gloves under them. We both had a couple of knit watch caps on, and I had a balaclava around my neck, ready to go. We each had two mini-flashlights, the two double A flavor, in pockets in our parkas. Karen and I had bought four cheap brown PVC rain slickers a few years back on a camp trip to Ocean Shores, when we'd camped with the Martins in the rain. They'd be used again tonight and for the duration I was sure. We each grabbed our wrapped up guns, lunch boxes, and we were out the door. I promptly tripped over something in the gloom and nearly did a face plant into the ramp out of the barn.

"Graceful, Dad."

"Thanks. Stuff like that happens when you hit forty. Your day is coming."

"Coming? I trip up stairs now!"

"Yeah, it's a family thing. Glad to see you're the recipient."

We crunched our way through the heavy ice and with each footstep, plunged into the powder below. The ice was almost thick enough to hold Carl's weight, and I'm sure that the girls would be able to walk on the shell without dropping through to the soft snow, unless they ran. The ice also presented problems, because if you fell in it, it would scratch you nearly as bad as broken glass. I'd forgotten to look at the thermometer on the wall of the barn on the way out, but I was sure it couldn't have been more than fifteen degrees or so. It was COLD. I could hear a generator running somewhere. Just one, by the sound of it, off to the east.

After getting the two tarps out from the garage, and two big hunks of thick cardboard (in a previous life, the cardboard had been shipping boxes for the new windows in the house. Now broken, of course....). The entire driveway that I'd plowed earlier, was a solid sheet of ice over the concrete. We decided to head back toward the house and go to the gate, rather than skate across the driveway.

After more than a little effort, we got the gate open, by chipping some of the ice off of the slide handle with a rock. The gate had a chunk of welded-wire fence tied on the lower sections, which kept Buck-the-Explorer in the yard. This panel was firmly 'one' with the ice now, and there would be no way to get the gate open all the way without considerable effort. Which wasn't going to happen tonight.

Ron and I had talked earlier about locations for our positions, which needed to be both very inconspicuous but still provide a good field of view up and down the roads. We figured that any serious looters would be in vehicles, and that those on foot could be dissuaded without too much trouble. I told Carl to find a spot behind the black locust and black walnut trunks that had come down in the quake, off to the left of the house. This gave him a good view up the road to the east. The road north was blocked in at least two places further north of us, and impassable. I took a position up across from the James's house behind a downed tree, which gave me a view down the road to the south, all the way to the convenience store, which was perfectly black against a dark grey background.

After a few minutes, we'd both 'settled in' as best we could. We each had to find a spot that was fairly flat, and crunch the ice out of the way. We then scooped the loose snow out and got down to the nearly-bare ground underneath. Then, our cardboard layer, and our tarps overhead. They were pretty noisy if you moved around, we both found out. I could hear Carl move from seventy-five feet away, and cautioned him to keep it quiet.

We'd been careful not to disturb the snow in front of our positions with footprints or paths. No sense in drawing any more attention to us than we needed to. If it all worked out, we'd have a nice little stay in the cold, and get back to bed soon. Things would get back to normal soon, we thought.

"Radio check. It's nine p.m."

"South here," I responded.

"North here," Carl mimicked.

"Stay warm," Karen said, "Out."

And so we settled in.

1 4

Saturday night
January Fourteenth

For most of the next two hours, I made a mental list of things that needed doing in the next couple of days. The water situation. Setting up a collector and filter that would give us relatively clean water for washing, and pre-filtered water before we sent it through the Berkey for drinking. Power. I had a number of options available. I'd need to come up with something that was economical regarding gasoline use and gave us enough, not too much, power capacity. Laundry. Eventually, we'd have to wash and dry our clothes. I didn't have a washboard lying around. The outhouse situation. Getting some communication going with the 'outside' world. Which meant, anyone not living within a quarter mile of the place. Security. We couldn't go on like tonight much longer, before we all were too tired to perform. Dealing with the Martin's eventual departure. The list went on and on.

For most of the first shift, we heard only the lone generator, the sound of a chainsaw down to the south, and only one car or truck, somewhere south. No one was outside, other than the stray dog or cat. We had an overcast and no moon, so things were....bleak.

Twice during our radio checks at the ten- and eleven o'clock intervals, Karen gave us a little snippet of news, fed to us through our ear buds.

"They said the eruption is still continuing, but the wind has shifted to the north. By tomorrow night, it's supposed to be headed to the northeast—toward us." Neither Carl nor I responded, per our agreement. If we didn't have anything to say, we'd key the mikes a single time each, and be silent. And cold.

At ten-thirty, I'd had a handful of trail mix, peanuts, raisins, dates, and chocolate chips. Then a second handful. My cocoa I saved for my eleven o'clock break, just to give myself something to look forward to, and to make sure that I didn't have to relieve myself before my shift was over. More the latter than the former. By eleven-thirty, I was also beginning to think that we were worried about nothing, out on a snipe hunt. I was also thinking that we needed some bottled water out here. Cocoa was fine, but water was better.

I assumed that Karen had roused Libby, John and Ron for their shift. I could just see the front of the barn from my viewpoint, and Carl could see the back side. The soft glow of the skylight was the only light I could see in any of the houses, and it wasn't that bright. I heard some noise down the road, probably four blocks south and east. On the arterial. I called on the radio to Ron and John to hustle up. Something was coming, and I wanted them in place before it got here. If, it turned on our street. Ron and John were crunching their way to us when I called.

Libby asked, "What's going on?"

"A car down south of us. I don't know if it's coming our way or not."

"OK. Out."

Ron whispered out to me "Rick! Where are you?" I rustled the tarp and got up to my knees. "Here. Hurry. John—go down by those trees up north. Carl's behind the second clump. Move quick and quiet. Stay outta the road!" I felt that I was overreacting.

It was eleven forty-five. "Radio check," Libby's voice called to us.

"North, check," Carl responded.

"South check," I called back.

"What about Ron and John?"

"They're here. We'll turn over the radios to them when we get ready to head in. Quiet now, something's coming."

"Out." Lib said quietly.

The noise continued to grow louder. A diesel. No lights. Not on our street yet, but coming down the arterial, slow, then it stopped moving. A flashlight or something shone at the intersection. A shape moved onto our street.

"OK, showtime. Something's coming. No lights. Keep cool and out of sight."

"K," the boys responded.

My blood pressure was up and I was sweating. I thought to myself, 'It's just a truck. Calm down. Yeah, a truck, no lights, in creep mode. This isn't good.'

"Take out your weapons, carefully. Safeties off."

"Safeties off."

"You sure about this?" Ron asked.

"No," I replied. "I'm not sure about this. But I'm not taking chances, either."

The truck crept up the road, right past us. A big late model Dodge quad cab, diesel. It was dark blue or black with a big canopy on back, had FEMA stenciled…no, painted…on the side of it in white letters..they'd painted it right over the windows. If this was FEMA, and there was a dusk to dawn curfew in place (which we were choosing to ignore, with our neighbors blessings), why did it look like this was a thief on the prowl?

"Everything all right?" Libby asked, the concern plain in her voice.

"No. Can't talk now. One truck just passed our position, lights off. Doesn't look friendly. More soon. Out."

None of the houses looked occupied, as all lights were out by this time, still, some of them held my neighbors and friends, and we'd already talked to them about what 'might' happen. The Dodge pulled up to our friends the James' vacant home, backed into the driveway, and four men got out. They immediately moved in cover formation, looking around to see if they were being observed. If they'd've had lights on, they would've seen our footprints leading back to the barn, if not our tarp shelters.

"You sure this is it, Levon?"

"Yeah. I delivered it two weeks ago. It's here. The guy said that that house over there," pointing to the Woolsley's, "had one too. That's next, then that old house next door. Lookit that garage. Gotta be tools there, man."

That meant our house.

Two were obviously armed with long-guns. No. 1 kicked in the front door and turned on a flashlight, playing it around inside, obviously searching the place. That was enough for Ron and I. No. 1 and 2 went inside, found it vacant, they returned with a large TV and something smaller. "We've scored dude! C'mon!!"

"Didn't have to off anyone this time. It's all here, the stereo, the flat panel, all of it." They were talking about Tim's new flat-panel TV. He'd had it about two weeks. Had to be a delivery guy, wanting it back.

"OK," I said over the VOX, "It's obvious these guys are looters, and that they've got a list. It's also obvious they're very well armed. I'm not in favor of letting them get this far. How about you, Ron?"

"Rog. No way in Hell. Take 'em now, that's my vote."

"Agreed. Boys, you hear us?"

"Yes sir." John and Carl were together, hiding behind one of the downed Black Walnuts to my left. I was hunkered down right across the street from the truck, behind the root ball of an uprooted tree. Ron moved off to my right slightly, gaining a clear shot.

"Wait one. Ron and I will take the first two when we get a chance…the two that went in the house first. You two get the guys outside when they've let their guard down. You ready?"

"Dad, will this 10/22 do any good?"

"Yes, Carl, with that scope on it and the light from their lantern, you should be able to hit them."

"OK."

No. 3 and 4 then put their guns in the truck and followed 1 and 2 inside, both carrying flashlights. I had the Garand, Ron the 1903, with John and Carl using the matching 10/22's. When all four of them had exited the house, I quietly said, 'Now.' All four guns spoke at once. Three went down immediately, one to go. No. 4 tried to get to his gun as we fired again, and he fell, his flashlight spinning in the air and then landing next to his head. Carl was getting up, ready to move in. I waved him down and told him via the radio, "They're not going anyplace. If they're hit, they're bleeding. If they're bleeding, they'll die. We've got all night for that to happen. If any of them move, shoot 'em again. Insurance."

We waited the better part of an hour before I sent Carl and John back to the barn to warm up. I'd already radioed back after the shooting, and of course Karen and Libby were very concerned. Once I assured her that we were all fine, she calmed down a little. I did have to tell her that we'd probably killed four looters. The silence on the other end of the radio was deafening.

"My God. Has it come to this?" she whispered.

"I'm afraid it has."

"What will you do when the police find out?"

"Tell them the truth. Armed looters invading a neighborhood under the decoy of emergency workers? I don't think the Sheriff will have too much to say about it."

Ron and I approached the bodies carefully. No. 1 took a shot to the upper jaw, and appeared to have died instantly. No. 4 appeared to have taken two shots, at least one from my late father's Garand. The second could have been from either of the 10/22's. No. 2 had reached a rifle, a nice looking Bushmaster, with the sale tag from one of the sporting goods stores at the Mall still on it. Nice of them to borrow it from the store. I'd enjoy returning it. He took a gut shot, and bled out pretty fast. No. 3 was hit a couple of times, once in the head, once in the groin. He had a drum-fed AK, with a Dragunov-type stock. No tags on that one. We also collected a fair amount of cash, six handguns, and a couple cases of ammunition from the truck. There was also a wide variety of porn magazines, DVD's, and bags of what I assumed were crack cocaine, meth, or some other evil in concentrated plastic-wrapped form. Under all of that, there were two cases each of chili, ravioli, and soups, and...a Remington Model 700, Police Model, a big .308 designed for long-distance shooting. 'Must not have been as intimidating as that little AK,' I thought. After we'd relieved the dead of their weapons, we put the bodies in a snow bank and covered them with a foot or two of snow. Seemed like the best thing to do at the time. We left the Dodge in Tim James' driveway. The Sony TV stayed in the back of the truck, with the looters' fingerprints on it. I put the keys and the cash on Tim's kitchen table, and closed the kicked-in door. I called the boys back to the scene to bring the weapons and ammunition back to the barn, carefully preserving fingerprints, if that was necessary.

"I hope all of our shifts won't be this eventful," I said to Ron.

"No kidding. You OK?"

"Me? Yeah, I guess. I haven't thought about it much. I'm sure it'll catch up to me."

"Yeah. You think the boys are all right?"

"No, but I think they will be. They were both shaking."

"Yeah. I'll talk to them with Karen and Libby."

"I'm probably OK out here by myself, if John wants to stay in."

"I thought that it might be good to have him out here with you. You can probably talk about it. Probably don't need to have you two split up tonight," Not anymore, I thought.

"Yeah, probably right."

"See you at three."

"See you then. Goodnight."

"'Night." I walked back to the barn. Time for a long talk, and hopefully, some sleep. 'We've just killed people,' I thought. 'Why did this have to happen?' I asked myself, knowing all along that there was only one answer.

1 5

Early Sunday
January Fifteenth

By the time I crunched through the snow back to the barn, Karen, Libby and the boys were already deep in a discussion about what we'd done. Surprising us all, both John and Carl wondered if WE were all right, rather than having any second thoughts about what they'd done.

"Yeah, Ron and I are OK. Are you guys?"

"Yeah," both responded. "It's not like we had a whole lot of choice. They told us what they were going to do after raiding Tim's. Hit the Woolsley's. Then our house."

"That's right. But it still doesn't make what we did something to make light of or easy to deal with. John, Ron said he'd be OK out there by himself, if you don't want to go back, " I offered.

"No, I'm good, if Mom's OK with it."

"Libby? You all right with John going back up front?"

"Yeah, I guess. How about you stay with your Dad though, instead of splitting up."

"OK. Is that all right, Rick?" John wondered.

"Yeah. I don't think we'll see anyone else tonight. If we do, Libby will get us up and out there right away. Just call."

"OK, I'll tell Dad."

"He's been listening in, haven't you Ron?" Lib said into the radio.

"He said 'yes,'" Lib passed on, the little black ear bud in her left ear.

"K. I'll get going," John said, and was out the door.

"OK, you two. Get to bed. It's almost one-thirty," Lib ordered.

"Yes, ma'am," I answered.

Libby and Karen had created a little corner of privacy for the 'radio room' in the woodshop, using a couple of old well-worn blankets that we used to use to cover our tomatoes in the fall to protect them from frosts as long as possible. They were strung up on a hunk of leftover clothesline and hung from a couple of nails on the walls, and a nail in the ceiling. 'Mighty resourceful, those gals of ours,' I thought as I hit the mattress. The cook stove fire still crackled softly, our only source of heat. Libby turned down the Aladdin lantern to a very soft glow.

It was a long time in coming, sleep. Each time I closed my eyes, I kept seeing the silhouette of the looter that I'd shot, through the sights of the Garand. I was sure that I'd never forget that image as I fired, temporarily blinded by the muzzle-flash and the kick of the old gun. Number 4, I'd labeled him. I wondered if he had kids, a wife, a family. I wondered who'd mourn him.

Eventually, I slept. I woke briefly when Ron and John came in a little after three. I was going to get up to talk to Ron, and he 'shushed' me, and said that there was nothing new. "Get back to sleep," I think was his direct order. I obliged.

I woke up looking through the skylight. 'Sunday morning,' I thought. It was still before sun-up, which meant before seven a.m. I hadn't moved a muscle since three. Buck was on my left at my feet, Ada at my shoulder. She saw me peek at her and her tail thumped twice, then she was asleep again.

I decided to wait a few minutes before I stirred. I thought about my brothers in other parts of the country. One in Seattle, dealing with his own adventure, if he'd made it through the quake alive; another in Utah, settling in to a new business; a third in the Twin Cities, enjoying new grand-fatherhood, a fourth a couple miles from me, a thoroughly useless person. Then the people I knew through the business: Hundreds, probably thousands in my twenty-plus years in the Northwest. My business partners and employees. My vendors and suppliers. The parking attendant. Some of those people were probably dead today. Then the friends I'd made in cyberspace, on the newsgroups that I'd read and lurked in on Usenet. Ol' John on a mountain in Georgia came to mind. A dozen others in cities across the country. People that I'd never met, but among whom we'd communicated off-and on-list about 'stuff', shared life's little and big tragedies, losses, ideas, hopes, prayers. I knew that even as I lay there, they were wondering how we were doing in the Northwest, and praying for our safety. Thinking about my family. About me.

Eventually, I decided to get up. Karen rose at the same time and we shared a quiet moment (and a kiss good morning), looking over at our kids, sound asleep in the half-light. Buck of course then decided that Carl's ear looked good, and started licking him. That was it, the whole barn was up in a minute.

I already had an agenda put together for the day by the time I'd washed my two-day beard in the cold water. 'I'll have to learn to stop making agendas,' I thought to myself. 'Stuff happens too fast.'

Karen and Libby (wearing some of my lounging pants and a thick fleece nightgown of Karen's) got the water for coffee and I lit the old stove with some cedar. Our wives had decided what breakfast fare would be the night before, so they were pretty well in gear by the time I had the fire up to cooking temperatures. Today, they would try whole-wheat pancakes in the cast iron skillet. I thought to myself, 'Glad I'm not trying that out. I'd burn 'em for sure.'

I removed the cardboard window shades that the girls had fabricated for our new 'house', and discovered a brilliant sunrise.

"We should go outside for a minute. I'm sure it's gorgeous out there."

Libby and Karen peeked out the window, and said they'd pass. John, Ron, Kelly and Marie pulled on some clothes quickly and we took the dogs out through the store room door.

"Wow!" Kelly said, "Look at the sun on the ice!!"

"It's like glitter!" Marie responded. I couldn't argue with that. It was stunning.

Buck and Ada were tearing all over the field, having no problem with running on the ice, without punching through. There seemed to be at least a solid half-inch layer on all of the snowfall, and more than that on all the exposed metal and wood. And, on my SUV. The Jeep was covered with a blue tarp, which with all the ice, now resembled a melted Smurf more than anything else. The little Ford 8n was covered from radiator to seat with another blue tarp. I wished I had a camera. The icicles on the headlights nearly reached the ground. The brilliant blue sky though, and warm rays of the sun, was worth the cold temperature...it was probably only twenty outside. I could hear a few more generators this morning, and a few more chainsaws. No air traffic though, which reminded me of Bruce Springsteen's song about September 11, 'Empty Sky'.

I could see across the garden and the yard to the street to the James' house. The truck was still there, the snowpile that held the looter's bodies undisturbed. I heard a car coming up the street...too quickly for the ice that was everywhere. I saw a flash of it between the garage and the house. It didn't appear on the other side. I knew the car belonged to Mrs. Long's son and his girlfriend. The Long's had lived in the house across the street from us for many years, and for those all of those many years, we never once saw anyone who lived there mow the lawn, work on the house, or raise a finger in manual labor. Window panes had literally fallen from the frames for lack of glazing compound and some glazier's points. They just boarded over the window when that happened. Her son seemed at least as unpleasant as she had been. I'm sure he was going to be very upset to see the remains of the home, with his late mother's remains somewhere inside the burned out pile. I decided to trudge up there and see if there was anything I could do, although I knew damn well it'd be a complete waste of time.

"Carl, watch the dogs. I'm going up to talk to Wayne."

"You sure, Dad? You always told me to keep my distance."

"Yeah, that's true. I'll be all right. Join me, Ron?"

"Okey doke. What's the story with this guy?"

On the walk up to the house and the front yard, I filled Ron in. Years of verbal abuse. Strings of four-letter words shouted from inside their house that we could hear in our house, with the doors closed (ours and theirs). Thrown objects. Probable mental illness. The house smelled like a latrine with all of the animals she kept. She yelled at anyone who offered to help. I once mowed her front lawn with my lawn tractor, and received a shovel full of cat manure thrown at me--from inside the front door--for my trouble. (At least the dandelions in the 'yard' didn't spread as far that year....)

"Good for the property values," Ron said.

"Not hardly," I responded.

"No, I mean the fire."

I chuckled in spite of myself. I had to remind myself that someone died over there. We reached the front fence. Wayne was coming toward the front yard after circling the ashes and charred foundation of the house. The whole thing had burned and collapsed into the basement. The concrete steps of the porches climbed to...nothing.

"Wayne? You all right?"

"No, I'm not f*****g all right....."

He went off on a three-minute spew of expletives, stormed back around house again, and started yelling, I couldn't really tell at whom. From what Ron and I could decipher of his monologue, he thought he'd inherit the house and all of the vast wealth, and he'd be set for life. Now, he had 'nothing.'

"You left me NOTHING............ NOTHING!!"

He got back into the beat-up Celebrity, slammed it into drive, and spun the wheels all the way across the front yard, turned around and headed back from where he came from. I never saw him again.

"Well. That was certainly productive," I offered.

"Yeah," Ron said, looking over at the 'FEMA' truck.

"C'mon. Let's go see how the third batch of pancakes has come out. I'm betting the first two oughta've been thrown to the dogs by now."

Ron chuckled." Glad it's not me trying to cook on that thing. That's a frickin' art!"

"I'll say. Hard to screw up coffee though. I think I'll stick to that."

"Wow. I can't believe that greenhouse is still up. Look at all that ice!"

"Yeah. I don't get it. It's only three-quarter's inch PVC with a center rib of PVC and electrical conduit. The shell's only four-mil poly. It blew to smithereens in the windstorm last year."

"We'll see what it'll look like when the ice melts off and the snow gets good and heavy."

"You never know, it might make it through. If not, I've got another skin for it. It's not like I've got seeds going right now. Still a month early for that."

We got back to the barn and opened the door to the smells of breakfast. And were instantly starving.
Ron and I were mostly right, the first three pancakes were being enjoyed by Buck and Ada, who were very much at home on my sleeping bag. The kids were each working on a plate of pancakes, bacon, and juice. Karen and Libby were each nursing a large cup of coffee, not decaf today.

All of the dirty clothes that had collected over night ended up in an ancient wicker laundry basket for later washing. 'One more thing to think about. I've got a lot of junk around here, but I don't have a washboard,' I thought.

Ron and Libby discussed making the attempt to get home after breakfast. We decided to get them 'provisioned' as best we could, like the Moore's, before they left. I knew that I'd need to get some of the stored gas out for the Jeep, and I was considering loaning Ron the shotgun for the trip.

"Any news yet today?" I asked as I munched on my pancake.

"Forgot to check," Karen said. "Kelly, turn on the radio please."

"K", Kelly responded around mouthful of huckleberry syrup and a little pancake.

The local station seemed to be up to full power this morning, and had little static for a change.   A strangers' voice spoke to us over the radio.

"......arterial road clearing schedule. Major east-west arterials, including Francis, Wellesley, Garland, Mission, Broadway, Trent, and Sprague are scheduled for clearing operations this morning. On Monday, major clearing operations are scheduled to resume in the eastern half of the Spokane Valley, progressing westward to meet clearing operations starting at the west edge of downtown, progressing to the east. Arterials on the South side of I-Ninety in the City of Spokane are continuing to progress at this time. Residents are directed to stay off arterials and clear of work operations."

"Interstate Ninety is being re-routed in several locations around damaged overpasses, and traffic control will be provided by manned four-way stops. Where overpasses are damaged, traffic from major arterials will be directed to on-ramps to cross the freeway, through temporary openings in the center median, and to the opposite off-ramp."

"Well. DOT has been busy for a change," I said, probably unfairly.

"These operations are being completed by the Army Corps of Engineers under federal authority."

"I could've been premature in my observation," I continued. Color commentary on the news was one of my favorite sports. I was hushed by Karen, with, which the accompanying flash in her pretty green eyes, was also typical.

"A reminder to listeners: Terms of the state of Martial Law are repeated at the bottom of each hour. The dusk to dawn curfew is still in effect, and will remain so until full mobilization of military police control in urban areas is complete. Residents who have remained in their homes are directed to seek shelter in major public buildings if they are in need of assistance. If directed by military authorities, residents may be asked to leave their homes if the homes are deemed hazardous."

"It is now eight o'clock a.m. This is KLXY Spokane operating military authority."

Sunday morning
January Fifteenth

For the next half hour, we finished breakfast and tried to get more news out of the local stations. All stations were simulcasting the same announcer, so that wasn't going to be much help. The quality of newsgathering was about ten notches below what we were used to. We were also being fed what someone wanted us to know, with little in the way of news from the West side of the state. For some reason, I thought that this must be what Soviet radio must have been like.

The CB radio was a mass of hysterics at the premise of martial law being imposed. Allegations and rumors of men in black kicking down doors and seizing helpless victims were all over channel nineteen, and gradually filled most of the frequencies. After about ten minutes of trying to find something coherent on the little hand-held, I shut it off and disconnected it from the coax antenna. The radio was a small Cobra SSB model, one of two I'd bought maybe six years ago. With the antenna I'd rigged up, it pulled in and broadcast to a respectable distance. No where near as far as ham radios, but good for a couple of miles. These days, Karen used it to page me when I was out in the barn, if I didn't have on one of the radios.

The shortwave frequencies were weak in the daylight. I was just using the stock antenna on the radio, and it wasn't exactly high-performance. We did hear wavering signals from the BBC, and a few words about the disaster in Seattle before the signal faded out. Or 'Say-addle', as the announcer said.

"Martial Law is now in effect in the States of Washington and Oregon until civil authority can be restored. The reason for declaring Martial Law is to effectively establish and preserve public order. In layman's terms, the following rules now apply until further notice:

Dusk to dawn curfew will be strictly enforced. This means that you must remain on your own property or in your own residence during those hours. If you are residing at a public shelter, you must remain inside the shelter during those hours.

Looters will be severely dealt with immediately by military authorities. If you see looting activity, do not take direct action, as you may be putting yourself in mortal danger. If you can identify the looters, or record license plate numbers, do so and pass this information on to the appropriate authorities during daylight hours.

Unauthorized persons found outside of the boundaries of their properties or designated public shelters will be detained for possible military tribunals if questions arise regarding reasons for violating curfew.

Detention centers for military detainees will be established on public property as required by demand. Military tribunals will be held regarding the disposition of military detainees, again as determined by demand. Rights of military detainees will be per the Constitution of the United States of America as administered by the military authority and represented by military legal representation for all parties.

Additional details and full explanation of the terms of Martial Law in the Pacific Northwest are published and available at all public shelters.

Martial Law will be terminated in the Pacific Northwest, or in local regions, as civilian authority is re-established, including civilian order, criminal courts systems, jails, and full compliments of civilian police forces.

Conditions are expected to return to normal, with regards to civilian authority, access, and provision of goods and services, within two weeks.

This message will be repeated at the bottom of each hour."

I pondered the message for a moment. "So that's what all the hullabaloo's about."

"Yeah. I wonder how they think that 'normal's' ever coming back," Ron said. I agreed.

"Still want to head for home this morning?" I asked the Martin's.

"Yes. We need to get home," Libby responded.

"Can't argue with you. I hate to wait to know stuff, too." I hoped for them that their house was in better shape than ours. Their place was only a little over ten years old, and a much better built place than their old home. They'd only moved in last fall. "Well, no time like the present. Let's get you set up. It might be a long day driving home."

"Yeah. Kids, let's pack up our stuff and get ready," Lib directed.

"We'll get the Jeep ready. Karen, would you mind getting a care package put together for them?"

"Way ahead of you."

"You usually are…." I said as I put on a mid-weight fleece and headed out through the tool room. Ron was pulling his boots on, and would join me in a few minutes. Both dogs had to join me, of course.

Ron took the blue tarp off of the Jeep, shattering the heavy ice on the top and sides. The buildup on wipers was beyond help though, and he left them to melt in the sun. I went up to my garden shed to get some of the stored gas. I was thinking about bringing a wheelbarrow to haul a couple cans of gas, but thought that the ice would be too much of a problem both ways. I ended up lugging each five-gallon can in two trips through the heavy ice and snow, and was really winded by the time I was done. The Jeep was fully gassed now, and I put the leftover in Ron's jerry can on the back with another few gallons.

Karen, Libby and our kids met us as we finished up, arms laden with some blankets, a couple sleeping bags, and a large soft-sided cooler with 'lunch' and an old gallon-size insulated jug with hot tea.

"You sure about this?" I asked Libby and Ron.

"Yeah. We have to at least try," Libby responded.

"If you can't get through, come on back, OK? We'll keep an eye out for you. We'll be up on the second floor for a while this morning, after we make a run over to the church."

"Okay, but I'm sure we'll be fine. Everyone ready?" Libby asked the kids.

"Yeah, let's just not make this an all day thing, all right?" Marie asked.

"No promises," her father replied. "Let's take a drive."

The little Jeep fired right up, and Ron backed up slowly, crunching through the heavy ice. In a few moments he was up to the gate, with the rest of us trailing behind. Carl and I forced open the gate through all of the ice, gradually getting it all the way open. We gave the Martins a wave as they turned down the street. In a few minutes, they were out of sight.

"How bout we make a little drive over to church?" I asked as we walked back to the barn.

"Okay, Dad. We don't have to get dressed up, do we?" Kelly asked.

"No, babe we don't. I'm sure if there's a service this morning, our work clothes will be just fine. Go lock up the dogs though in the woodshop and make sure they've got water, and make sure they've been fed. An extra cup each wouldn't hurt them either. I'll see if I can get some of the ice off of the Expedition."

"You really think they'll have services?"

"It'd be nice. I'm sure a lot of people other than me need it this morning."

"Yeah. You doing all right?"

"Yeah, I guess. I'll be OK. Just like everyone else today. Overwhelmed."

"I'll grab our Bible. You sure you can get through that ice?"

"Eventually. It's a ten-minute walk in good weather, or a two minute drive. We still have a little time before regular services, assuming anyone's there."

"Be right back."

I smacked the ice on the drivers' door lock and handle to get access to the cylinder, then remembered that I had a keyless entry, and unlocked it with the key fob. After some careful pulling, I managed to open the door, covered with a good half-inch of ice. I then shut the door with some force, which broke most of the ice off the door. I repeated that on each door after starting it up, hitting the de-ice button, and making sure the wipers were 'off'. I was afraid that the wiper motor would burn up if they were on, and encased in ice. I backed up, turned it into the sun, and turned the defroster on max.

In about ten minutes, the back hatch had melted enough to have the sheet of ice fall off. The windshield was melting slowly, and I had enough free glass to see through, at least to get over to church. I wouldn't do it in traffic though...

Karen and the kids piled into the SUV, which was quite warm by now. The dogs had been sequestered in the woodshop, away from the stored food. With luck, we'd be back in an hour or so.

I drove up from the field to the house, and out the front gate. Carl hopped out and closed the gate behind us as we pulled into the street. No car traffic visible south to the arterial, or in the neighborhood. We did see a few people in working on their houses as we drove the few blocks to church. A few more, loading up their cars.

The building was a mess. The original sanctuary was built in the Forties or so, and later converted to offices. The new sanctuary was built in the Seventies, a soaring structure that held perhaps five hundred or so worshippers. Between the two, a two story concrete block office and classroom wing had been built. It had collapsed completely, as had part of the gymnasium wing's classrooms. The gym seemed intact. A few of the neighbors came out to meet us as we pulled into our customary parking stall right off of the street.

"Good morning. You wouldn't be one of the staff or pastors, would you?," an older gentleman asked as he came through an opening in the fence across the street.

"No, sir, just one of the worshippers. Have you seen any of the staff?"

"No, I've been keeping an eye on the place, watching out for looters. Haven't had a problem yet, but I've got stuff to do myself, and I can't watch it all the time."

"I understand. Has anyone else shown up this morning?"

"A couple cars drove by slow, and then took off. That's about it."

"I'm Rick Drummond, by the way. I'll take a look around if that's all right."

"You betcha. Dan'l Miller. I attend over at St. Mary's."

"That might be quite a hike today."

"I'll say. I'm not about to try it with this hip of mine. Broke it last winter on the ice. Not about to go there again."

"I hear ya. I'll be right back."

"No problem, I'll head back inside if that's OK."

"Yes sir. If you need me, here's my address. I'm just over a couple blocks," I handed him one of my business cards, with our home address on the back.

"Oh, that's the Janowsky place. I grew up with Jake."

"Oh! We bought it after he passed on."

"You've done a nice job keeping it up. His parents and grandparents would be proud."

"Thank you. Sometimes it feels like a real money pit. Today though, the old place isn't quite as pretty as it was on Friday."

"Hit bad?"

"Bad enough. I might be able to salvage it, but it won't be easy."

"That's too bad. I better get going, or Maggie will be on my backside. Nice to meet you Mr. Drummond."

"Likewise. Watch that hill, now."

"Thanks," Dan'l said.

"You guys' stay in the car. I'll be right back," I told Karen and the kids.

I walked to the east, and looked over the carnage of the classroom wing. 'There was no way to get into the building this way,' I thought. I walked all the way around the church, the interior of the church was completely inaccessible due to collapse of the covered entries, effectively sealing the building off. The two fifteen passenger vans were untouched, sitting in the parking lot, covered with ice. There didn't appear to be any way into the building with out a track-hoe to come in and lift up the fallen roof sections. I got back in the Ford.

"Anything we can do?" Karen asked.

"Not without heavy equipment. No services today, that's for sure, even if the pastors made it here. Place is completely sealed off."

"Now what?" Carl asked.

"Back home. Salvage operation Number Two, and we need to get a water collection system back up and going. It's not just for summer anymore."

I backed out of the parking space, turned the car around, and headed home. It looked like this would be another long day.

"Dad, look at the sun. It's turning blue." Kelly told me.

I slammed on the brakes and got out of the car, looking at the sun on what had been a brilliant blue sky.   Kelly was right. The sun was turning steel blue.

"Ash," I said to myself.

"Ash? From Rainier?" Carl and Kelly were looking at me quizzically.

"Yeah. Just like Nineteen Eighty. Only then, St. Helens blew at eight thirty in the morning, and the sun turned blue around eleven. It was pitch black in Pullman by one p.m. The ash fell all night. Burned our eyes."

"So that's going to happen here?" Kelly asked, getting upset.

"Sure might. Let's get home. We've a lot of work to do and dern little time to do it."

Sunday
January Fifteenth

My mind was racing. Earthquake. Bad winter storm. No power.
No water. Now volcanic ash probably in a couple of hours. This was
shaping up to be some week.

"OK, first things first. Kelly, I need you and Carl to get the
chicken coop cleaned out right now. We've got to get those hens up
to our house from Pauliano's as soon as we can, as in, before ten. If
that ash starts coming down, we're not going to want to be out in it.
Your Mom and I will get up to the second floor of the house and do
some more quick salvage work, probably not more than an hour
because we probably don't have much more time if that ash starts
coming down. Then we're going to get the water system setup so that
when we get some clean rain or snowmelt, we can collect it. Sound
like a plan?"

"Oh–kay," Kelly answered, clearly unimpressed with the
importance of the work to be done. Carl had also sunk himself down
in the seat looking as if he'd been sentenced to breaking large rocks
into small ones.

"Listen, guys. This isn't something to take your time with. Ash
fall is NOT pleasant. It hurts to breathe, stings your eyes, can
damage your lungs and in general, is a really crappy way to spend
your time. We do NOT want to be outside in it. Clear?"

"Yes sir," the back seat responded.

"After you get done with that, we'll have to have you get down the road with your Mom and collect some hens."

"Oh, can't wait," Karen said. She loved the eggs, endured the rest of raising hens.

"It'll be fine. We just have to move like there's no tomorrow."

"'What if there is no tomorrow? There wasn't one today!!'" Carl quoted Bill Murray from *Groundhog Day*, which immediately sent us into hysterics.

"Good one, bud," I said as we pulled back into the driveway. Carl hopped out and got the gate. I pulled in and let him get back in after he'd closed it, then goosed the big V-8 back to the barn. "OK, you've got your marching orders. There's two bales of straw in the coop, just get it cleaned out, clean out the laying boxes, and that should be about it."

Everyone climbed out of the car and took off. I unlocked the storeroom, and let the dogs out. By the time Karen and I were geared up to get back in the house, the kids were well on the way to having the coop cleared out. I had Carl get a roll of the welded wire fence from behind the barn and create a new chicken yard, zip-tied to the old steel tee-posts that were left over from our last foray into being 'farmers.' The sun was growing more dim by the minute. We also seemed to have clouds moving in from the west and northwest. The radio was useless for providing us any weather reports.

I had Karen get the roll of big black garbage bags from the garage as I set the ladder up to Kelly's bedroom window. I had to drop the ladder a couple of times on the driveway to break off some of the ice, but felt confident that I could safely make it up, and down once, if I was just bagging stuff up and dropping it down to Karen.

I unrolled about half the remaining roll of plastic bags and stuffed them in the back pocket of my shell, and headed up the ladder. Karen made a trip into the back porch door, and did some salvage work in the kitchen while I raided the upstairs.

I managed to get all of Kelly's bedding, her tennis shoes, and two drawers from her dresser into the first bag, and zip tied it together. The second bag held the rest of the dresser, and two more bags cleared out her closet. With the loss of the plaster ceiling, cellulose insulation that I'd blown in fifteen years before was starting to sift down through the lath, covering everything in a fine, grey powder. It also irritated the lungs. I worked faster. I put my LED headlight on. It was getting to be twilight outside before afternoon. I figured I had a couple of hours, maybe three, if it came down here.

All of the bags from Kelly's room went out the window after I yelled 'Heads UP!!' Carl and Kelly had finished the coop, and dragged the bags out to the barn. I then moved past the hole in the hallway that once held the chimney, and looked down through the floor framing at Karen, working away.

"Hi, there!" I said in a deep voice, scaring her badly.

"OH! I'll get you for that, mister!"

"Sorry, couldn't resist. You always said you wished you had a laundry chute. Of course, this hole only goes halfway to the laundry."

"Do you think the basement freezer's OK?"

"Might be. It looked like the chimney collapsed into the stairs and first floor, not into the basement. It should be OK. God knows it's still cold enough for things to stay frozen."

"Yeah. The freezer in the garage is still rock solid."

"Good. What do you need from up here?"

"Towels, all of our medicine chest stuff, my personal things."

"You got it."

I got to work and made quick work of the bathroom, collecting all of the first-aid stuff, towels, soaps, razors and blades (Hooray! I can shave!) and my contact-lens stuff. It would be good to be able to see clearly again. I only wear glasses when I can't wear contacts, which is about twenty minutes a day. I hate glasses.

The bathroom window was still intact, and I didn't bother opening it. I checked the water in the toilet, and found the tank freezing, and a layer of ice in the bowl too. I shut the water off, and told Karen that I was going to flush the tank, and that she should look out for any leaking water. It drained fine, with no apparent leaks downstairs. 'Thanks for small favors,' I thought. I then opened the sink and tub faucets, hoping to prevent burst pipes. I didn't hear any water flow, or air suck in. I was probably already too late there.

I was about done here. I made a trip into Kelly's room, dropped the last bag out the window, and made another trip into our bedroom. Same grey dust over everything. I decided to empty out our closets and dressers too. I got all of Karen's sweaters and three drawers done when Karen called up to me.

"Honey, you better hurry. You wanted to get the water system set up, didn't you?"

"Yeah, I know. I'm cleaning out our bedroom. I'll be down as soon as I can. You guys go round up those hens from Joe and Joan and get back as soon as you can. If they need anything, send Carl back down."

"OK. You be careful."

"I'm good. I will be."

I heard the gate as they headed down the street. I bagged up four more bags with the last of our clothes and 'useful' shoes and things, and tossed them out the window. The last bag was filled with our spare summer bedding, and the two sets of winter flannels. The bedding was cut by a large hunk of plaster, which buried itself in our new foam mattress—which must have happened after we got out of the house. The last bag went out the window, and I made one last trip to the bedroom. I grabbed the keys to several strong boxes that I had around the place, and a few other things from my dresser. I stapled a piece of plastic over the broken window after pulling the chain ladder back into the room. 'Best forty bucks I ever spent,' I thought. Time to go.

I closed Kelly's curtains and the pull down blind, and re-stapled the plastic cover, backing down the ladder. The sky was full grey to the west, with the only clear light coming from the far southeast, over Mica Peak. 'This could get bad,' I thought as I hauled three bags to the barn. 'Could get bad. Right. Like it's not a bucket of crap right now....'

I heard a motor. The Jeep was back. 'They didn't get far,' I thought. I piled the bags up next to the door and went to see Libby and Ron. I was surprised to see it wasn't them, but Dan, the neighbor to our northwest. He was driving his Modern Electric Company Cherokee.

"Hey, neighbor, how ya doin'" I called out.

"Well, I've had better days," Dan yelled back. "Everyone OK?"

"Yeah, how about you?"

"We don't know where Molly's at. She was staying with her friend Claire, but no one's at the house. Or, at the wreckage of the house. Her car's gone too. I think she went out with friends and was partying someplace, and didn't tell her Mom about it."

Molly was Dan's (wild and uncontrollable) stepdaughter. She tolerated him, that was about it.

"Hope she turns up OK."

"Me too. Sandy's pretty upset."

"I'll bet. How bad's the system?" I asked, changing the subject.

"Pretty bad. It'll be weeks before we can think about getting potable water up and running anywhere near where we should be, power's at least that bad."

"The tank by the interstate can't be helping that."

"That's the least of the problems. Most of the trans-site mains are cracked. Even if we did have the storage capacity, we'd bleed to death before we got pressure."

"What's Allied saying about gas?" Allied Gas and Power—was our homes' natural gas supplier, as well as the major player in the inland Northwest for power and water. They'd 're-imaged' themselves during the dot-com revolution, ala Enron. Hadn't worked out for Allied real well, either.

"Like they answer us when we call them. Honestly? I think they're completely screwed. They cut their crews too deep for too long after the reorganization and essentially castrated themselves. They can't fix anything right now. The headquarters is pancaked, from what Chet told me." Chet Jamieson was the president of our little water and power company, and a guy who knew his stuff. His daughter Kristi and I were in grade school together, forever ago now.

"Your house took a hit too. Lose part of the bedrooms?" I asked.

"Yeah, all of them. We were repainting at the time, so we weren't sleeping in them. If we hadda been, we'd be dead for sure."

"Are you staying there?"

"Yeah, sorta. We're in the travel trailer, and using propane for heat. Other than water, we're doing OK. Beats the crap outta a shelter. The elementary is packed."

"Yeah, I figured."

"I better run. Take care, and let me know if there's anything I can do."

"You too—take care. We had some looters last night."

"No way. What happened?"

"That snow bank, "I said, pointing over Dan's shoulder. "They're under it."

"Good for you. Damned bastards. Take care."

I waved as Dan went back down the street. Karen and the kids were coming back, and Karen waved a hen at Dan as he passed. Each of them had a hen by it's feet, carrying them upside-down up the street to the house. I wish I had a picture of it.

"Looks like something out of the Depression here," I said.

"Feels like it too. Chicken on the hoof." Karen replied. "Salvage done?"

"Done enough. I could spend a lot of time up there, but we've got what we need to be comfortable."

I walked Karen and the kids back to the barn, hauling two more bags of stuff back with me. I finally got all the bags in the store room, and my three chicken wranglers had made two more trips, so we ended up with seventeen hens and one rooster, all Rhode Island Reds. They soon found their homes up on the roost, and I popped open the old barrel of cracked corn, and I scooped up a bunch with a cut-off milk jug, just like the old days. Karen had water on for tea by the time I was done with 'the girls.'

"Dad, do we have to keep working on stuff?" Kelly asked, with Carl sharing the same pleading look.

"You can take a break for awhile. I can do the next chore myself. You can, though, start going through the bags and collect your stuff. Karen, would you mind keeping them on-task?"

"It's what I live for," she smiled. "What kind of tea?"

"Easy. Earl Grey, same as always."

"You got it. I'll call you in when it's done."

"Thank-you-my-dear." I responded. Time for the water system.

With the loss of access to the house, and potentially all of the water trapped in the house pipes, we needed to find a source of water for washing, drinking, and cooking. While the house was quite old in relative terms of the city, it was settled with the promise of domestic water for drinking and farming without the need for a private water well.

I'd shut off the water to the barn in the late fall, same as always, to prevent the exposed hose bibs from freezing and breaking. I also used compressed air to blow out the pipes. This meant now, that there was no water stored in the barn piping, and the shut off valve to the barn was in the house basement, and not accessible. I already knew that the big 10" trans-site water line next to our property was not under pressure, either due to the loss of power or due to breaks somewhere in the lines or the loss of the half-million gallon water tank about a mile from us.

Our 'summer' water collection system to help out in the garden consisted of gutters on the barn, that drained into two settling barrels. Cleaner water overflowed into a series of other barrels, until they reached the final barrel, which was connected to a bonehead simple drip irrigation system, feeding the five thousand square foot vegetable garden with leaky pipe. This simple set up had saved us more than half of our water bill. Now, it might help keep us in drinking water, wash water, and cooking water. With the prospect of warmer weather coming eventually, we'd see some snowmelt and with luck, a serious amount of rain from a chinook. That'd fill the barrels quickly, but I needed to come up with a better filter. I connected the downspout back to the first barrel. I always disconnected it in the fall after watering in the garden tapered off, then drained the system.

I decided to leave the system in place, and add a sand filter. I used the second barrel to construct the sand filter, because most of the crud seemed to settle in the first barrel. First, using a cordless drill from the woodshop, I popped a hole in the 'front' bottom of the barrel. I cleaned the barrel with a water and bleach solution, and did most of the construction work out in the cold. The ash hadn't started to fall yet, but the sky was continuing to darken.

Karen brought me my tea, she knew I was too busy to come and get it. I rewarded her with a kiss and a wink.

Over the hole, I placed a small sheet of filter fabric that we used for keeping weeds down, and then about four inches of (sort of) clean gravel. Next, I added a layer of activated charcoal from the kids old aquarium setup. (Turned out later from my reading of water-storage and filter Frequently Asked Questions that I should've added more than I had available, but this was all I had to work with). On top of the charcoal, I added clean builders sand from the barn. The sand was bagged up for winter bed-weight for my little Ranchero, which was now awaiting a new engine, under all that snow and ice. Six bags was more than enough.

The setup was intended to work this way: Water from the gutters would flow into the first barrel, and the really cruddy stuff would settle out. From the overflow at the top of the barrel, the water would flow into the sand filter. As the water exited the sand filter, we'd pipe it to a storage barrel. This would at least give us cleaner water than straight run-off for washing, showering, and cooking. With the Berkey filter, we'd then get drinking water too. All of the barrels had their covers in place, and covered with a blue tarp, held down by rocks.

Once the sand filter setup was done, all we could do is wait for rain. Without ash, that is. I disconnected the inlet, and waited for the ash to either come down on us or blow over.

I started back inside when I heard the gate open again. 'OK, who's come a'callin' this time?' I asked. Ron's Jeep appeared from around the house. 'Damn. They sure didn't get far.'

I met them at the gate to the field. "Just couldn't bear to stay away, hum?"

"Yes, it's the hospitality. And the beds are to *die* for." Libby said laughing. "National Guard turned us back. They're telling everyone to stay inside. Ash is coming."

"Yeah. You remember back in Eighty in Pullman, don't you?"

"Yep. But I don't think you'll get the last keg of beer in town like you did last time."

"No, and I don't think I could drink that much Coors, either. And there are nowhere near enough sorority girls around here. Make yourself at home."

"We will—and thanks again."

I was soon joined by the dogs as I retrieved the last of the big tarps from the garage, and headed back to cover over the Expedition. I'd spent hours cleaning ash out of my Falcon back after St. Helens, and had no desire to do so again.

Once that was done, everyone came outside for a few minutes. Karen wanted to get a few things out of the garage, and everyone else came to hear about the Martin's latest adventure. I heard a familiar hum coming up from the south.

"About dang time," I said.

"What, Dad?" Kelly asked.

"You'll see. Just wait a minute....Now, look."

The big red and white truck was creeping up the street. The firemen had managed to free their truck from the masonry tomb of the fire station. I knew several of the firemen, after they responded to my late Mother's home during several medical emergencies. I'd respected their dedication by buying the whole station pizza on more than a few occasions, and the occasional steak, baked potato and fresh corn-on-the-cob dinner in the summer. In the seven years since she'd passed on, I still kept them on my list. They were good guys who took good care of our neighborhood.

Two firemen were doing a slow patrol in the oversized paramedic truck, covered with scratches and sporting a cracked windshield, followed by one of the neighborhood 'reserve deputy,' Crown Vic cruisers. Each street was to be visited by this little parade sooner or later, I assumed.

"Nice to see you guys aren't sitting around eating donuts, wondering how in hell to get your fire trucks out of a brick pile," I said to Nick Johnson, who was one of the lead paramedics. "How you all doing? Is that 'Probey' boy in there?"

Probationary fireman Lewis answered back. "Hoo-rah!"

From the corner of my eye, I noticed the driver of the Crown Vic getting out of the car and start walking toward our conversation. He wasn't familiar to me, and was wearing a FEMA jacket and a ball cap with a perfectly flat bill. Balding, over fifty, fat, looked as if he drove a desk for a living. Five-foot-six, maybe, trying to look more tall than round. Not succeeding. I knew the type.

"We just came up to see if you'd spare us a few steaks," Nick said with a broad grin. "Looks like the old girl's seen better days." He said, looking over the house.

"Yeah, but we were lucky. Nothing major, just cuts and bruises. Nothing we could do for that place though," I said, waving over at the Long's house.

"No survivors?"

"Nope. Probably one victim, Mrs. Long. The place was fully involved by the time we came out of the second floor window."

"Hope she went quick."

Mr. FEMA joined us, I glanced his way and nodded.

"Yeah. Me too."

"How's the rest of the neighborhood. Looks quiet."

"Not too many home. A lot of out of town trips this weekend. Had some bad business last night, though."

"What kind of business is that," Mr. FEMA said with a little too much authority, inserting himself into our conversation.

"And you would be….." I responded.

"FEMA officer in charge Donald Brummer. I'm in charge in this sector."

"Mr. Drummond."

"Your first name would be what then?"

"My friends call me by my first name. You haven't earned that yet," I said. 'Might as well test the waters.'

"Now you listen, mister. I'm in charge here and you will do as you are directed by the military authorities in charge."

"Under which, unless I'm Constitutionally-impaired, which I'm not, FEMA does not fall. FEMA is a civilian authority operating under a military commander under Martial Law. So, unless you have a military rank, and are proven by the military command to be in charge, you are just a desk pilot wearing a too-thin jacket on a cold day."

I had, in fact, no idea if this was true or not, but it sure was fun watching this guy get all red in the face. He decided to take on a different tack, and smiled. Or maybe sneered.

"You apparently have not heard the official FEMA instructions broadcast on your radio. These instructions direct you to report to an emergency shelter for disposition immediately. You WILL comply." He sounded like a used car salesman.

"Kinda like 'Resistance is Futile. You will Be Assimilated,' huh?" The Star Trek 'Borg' reference was completely lost on this guy. My friends in the fire truck were chuckling out loud, however.

"You must comply. You must report to the elementary school for disposition and resettlement to an undamaged area," He glanced down at my sidearm, and added, "And you must surrender your firearms." Both Nick and Lewis were shaking their heads and looking sideways at this alleged FEMA authority.

Time for the gloves to come off. "We're well-disposed of here thanks."

"This is not a request. This is an order. And you will surrender that sidearm," he said, pointing at the sixty-five year old 1911 on my hip, in it's equally-aged leather holster.

"And you can kiss my ass. I'm not about to leave this place or these houses. You want us out of here? Try it. Just a little. I guarantee that the first man who lays a hand on one of us won't live to tell about it. After fighting off the looters last night, no one here is about to give up and leave just because some sawed-off alphabet-soup-coat wearing Napoleon wants us to. "

"You are in violation of Martial Law."

Bingo. I had him and I knew it.

"Bullshit, Mister Brummer. I, unlike you, listened word-for-word to the broadcast defining the terms of Martial Law under the current conditions, and you have lost all credibility with me and everyone listening to this conversation by adding and expanding your demands and hiding under the threat of martial law." I was having a ball. This was almost too easy. I continued on. I hadn't had this much fun in months.

"And by the way? You have at least three deer rifles centered on your chest and head. The people on the other ends of those weapons both know how to use them and know these two firemen, as well. They don't know you. I touch the bill of my cap, it's over. You choose. You didn't hear that the looters came after our homes last night in FEMA coats, and with a truck with FEMA spray-painted on it, did you?"

Mr. FEMA obviously hadn't. "No, sir, I did not." The color drained from his face as he looked nervously for those targeting him. There wasn't anyone there of course, but this guy sure as heck didn't know that.

"Well, then you can collect their bodies on the way out, and see what an Ought-Six can do to the human skull. They're over in that snow bank, behind your car. I strongly suggest you consider your next actions and words carefully. Make a sudden move, and it's game over. See this radio?" I showed him my radio.

"It's been open since you stopped your car. I heard what you said, and so did everyone else on this channel. Now be a good boy, get back in your car very slowly, and get the Hell off of my street. I will make sure that word of what you're trying to do will be all over the CB, the FRS and Ham radio in about ten minutes. Now get lost."

He stammered as I continued, more for my benefit than his. "You wanna take care of someone? Go to the 'blue' part of the state. They'll appreciate you over there. As for us, we're taking care of our own." I was, in the words of Charlie Daniels, laying it on thicker and heavier as I went along.

"You will hear from local authorities immediately."

"Good. I might buy 'em a steak and a baked potato. Hell, maybe a Guinness or a nice Cabernet while I'm at it."

I looked at the firemen. They were smiling broadly and chuckling out loud.

FEMA guy backed all the way back to his car, got in the drivers' seat, and over the paramedics truck radio, I heard him call for assistance immediately against a belligerent armed individual.

"Must be talking about me," I told Nick and Lewis. "This is gonna be good," I said. I glanced over at Karen, Ron and Libby. I knew I would catch hell for this later, but I was confident in my position.

"Jesus, Rick. You got big brass ones. He's been getting away with this all morning."

"Not on my street." I replied. I didn't ask them why THEY had put up with it. I'd thought better of them once….

I didn't have long to wait for things to get busy. I heard multiple sirens coming my way as I stood in the street next to the fire truck. I was certain that this would end well for me, badly for the FEMA guy. Fortunately, I knew more about my situation than he did.

As I hoped, the headlights gave way to the green and white cruiser of Sheriff Mike Amberson. The car crept up the icy road, four studded-snow tires making good headway. Mike was followed by a full-on Humvee, including mounted machine gun.

"What seems to be the problem here, Mr. Brummer? This better be good to put out a call like that." Two more Police Interceptors showed up behind me from the east at a respectful distance. I heard the deputies get out of their cars, probably putting their cars between themselves and me. Probably with weapons drawn. I noticed Mike looking over to the Dodge pickup in Tim James' driveway.

"This man is in violation of Martial Law and…….." Mike cut him off.

"That so, Rick?"

"No sir, Mike. I know what the Martial Law order said, and I know the Constitution. This guy apparently doesn't. And how's your lovely wife? Everyone OK?" I attended Mike and Ashley's wedding four years ago. I remembered the wedding well, Mike, however didn't. He was quite intoxicated at the time. I wondered if Ashley'd forgiven him yet.

"She's great. Number One is due in July. Made it through the shake just fine."

"Congrats. She ever forgive you for that bachelor party?"

"Well, let's just say that each anniversary is an effort to establish peace and harmony."

I looked over Mike's shoulder. FEMA guy was livid. "Sheriff, I demand that you...."

"Listen up, Brummer. I've been getting static from people all over your patrol route this morning complaining about a little, pushy, tin-star pissant who has delusions of grandeur. Now that wouldn't be YOU, would it? Do us a favor and get back in your car before I do something I'd love and that'd be to kick your ass. You are ordered to report to command immediately by Lieutenant General James. You're going home. Today." Mike was also suffering from a lack of sleep. It showed. Brummer stormed back to his car, unable to leave because of the Humvee behind him. The Humvee didn't move.

"Glad you don't take that attitude when you're in with the county Commissioners talking about your budget. They'd can your ass for that." I said to my old friend.

"Actually, no they wouldn't. They're the ones who asked me to get out here pronto and rope this SOB in. Why'd he call in, anyway? Made it sound like you were some deranged mad man."

"I stood up to him. He didn't appreciate it."

"I'll bet, " the Sheriff said, waiving off the two cruisers and the Humvee. The all took off to the south, back toward the fire station. "He's from California. San Francisco, to be precise," he said as Brummer's car followed the others.

"Well, that explains some of it. I've got some news to tell you. About last night."

"What happened? Bad?"

I explained the events of the previous night to him, sparing no detail. He considered all I told him carefully and thoughtfully before he spoke. Ron, Carl, John and our wives had joined us in the street by then, and the girls were in the yard with the dogs.

"Tony Johnson was killed by these guys last night." Tony was best man at Mike's wedding. And a Spokane county deputy. And a father of three.

"Oh my God."

"Yeah. You did me a favor by finding them first. I'd've had to arrest them."

"Then it's Tony's Model 700 we recovered."

"Yeah. They left his sidearm. Shot him in the back. Where are the bodies?"

I took Mike over to the snowpile, and pointed. "Composting."

"I'll get our evidence crew here right away and get them out of here. Do you have their weapons?"

"Yeah. We wore gloves, and stored them so they wouldn't get prints on them. I'll have them brought up."

"No, we'll come get them. No need to muddy them up with more chances of prints. Like it matters. We had reports of these guys last night. Killed eleven people, not including Tony. He was at Kelly's

Sports when they got him. Wounded Jefferies, too, also shot in the back. That's his truck."

"Damn."

A few minutes later, Mike's detectives showed up and we showed them the crime scene, letting them in to Tim's house, where they recovered the truck keys. They left the cash on the table. One of the deputies put plastic gloves on, in addition to a plastic bag on the driver's seat of the Dodge, and surgical-style shoe-covers, and drove the truck off for processing. They'd normally trailer it, but they were too busy to bother with formalities. They collected several rounds each from our weapons, and our spent brass, but let us keep our guns.

We turned over Tony's Model 700 as well as all of the looters weapons. Mike told us to keep the ammunition if we could use it. They had plenty of evidence and the ammo might come in handy. I then wondered if he knew something that he couldn't share.

Mike and I shared a look at the darkening sky as we walked away from the rest.

"This is going to hit us. Hard," he said. "You ready for it?"

"Ready? No more so than I was Friday. I think we'll be OK. Is this all ash, or is it snow, too.

"Both. But NOAA says it's going to be a lot of snow. The ash will come down first, snow tonight and all day tomorrow."

"Great."

"I'm serious, Rick. If you have any doubts about keeping warm or fed, you need to get the Hell out of there now and get to a shelter."

"Mike, I'm probably better equipped than the shelter. I have food for eight for a while. A long while. Water will be an issue if the ash is heavy, though."

"Two inches, conservatively."

"Plus snow. I read once that houses can collapse with four inches of ash and rain. Better watch that."

"Thanks. I hadn't heard that. I'll let my guys know. Thanks again for ending those guys. I had to tell Tony's wife last night."

"I'm sorry. He was a good man."

"Yeah he was. Take care and watch your ass."

"You too," I said as I saw the last of the photographs taken of the looters. The bodies were then unceremoniously dumped in body bags then put in the back of a GMC truck.

Before each officer left, they made it a point to come over and thank us. It was obvious that some of them were holding back tears of rage.

Two p.m. Sunday
January Fifteenth

We all walked back to the barn in the growing darkness. It was now almost two o'clock, with the darkness of a mid-December late afternoon. I thought ash would be falling within an hour, certainly no more than that.

"Let's go have some lunch," Karen offered. "I'll have to get that fire going again. I'm sure it's out by now."

"Can I do it Mom?" Kelly asked.

"Yep. But remember to clean out the ashes from below the firebox first into that coal bucket."

"OK. Then what do I do with the ashes?"

"Put them in the chicken yard. C'mon. I'll show you how to get it started."

"K," Kelly and Marie took off through the garden and back into the shop. The rest of us headed back to the barn the long way, 'round the garden. Before we went inside, I made sure the Expedition was covered as well as Ron's Jeep and the tractor. The ash, if it came down dry, was death on air filters, and killed many, many engines in the St. Helen's eruption. I didn't want to rebuild any more engines than I had to, and the current one on the list was just waiting for me to tear into it. All the parts were up in the garage. I just needed to get the Ranchero up there, pull the engine, disassemble it and send it out for machining. Everything else I could handle.

"Are you going to get an outhouse put together today too?" Karen asked as we went inside. Carl lit one of the Aladdin's, which provided a beautiful soft light, and two of the small camp lanterns. The barn had windows, but it was pretty gloomy in there, regardless. John and Carl were going to play some cards.

"That WAS the plan, but I'm not sure we'll get it done. Depends on if we're going to get ash or mud coming down on us."

"What do you have to build one?" Ron asked.

"I've got a bunch of plywood and OSB, a couple bundles of shingles left over from the shed redo, two by fours, hinges, most everything."

"Got a cordless saw?"

"No, I'll have to either use the generator or the inverter—which won't handle the startup load of the DeWalt, now that I think about it. I think it draws something like fifteen amps, which is about the max load on the inverter." The DeWalt was a worm-drive contractor's saw that I bought at a pawn shop before I re-did the barn. Forty bucks for a two-hundred dollar saw was an unbelievably good deal. Sure dimmed the lights in the barn when I fired it up though.

"OK, so we should be able to whack out most of an outhouse in an hour or so. What else do we need to do?" Ron asked as Libby and Karen started on lunch.

"Power. We're going to need to get something rigged up to recharge batteries, and maybe run a few other appliances. Eventually, we're going to need to run a fridge. It's not going to stay cold forever."

"You still have that Generac?" Ron asked, referring to my five-kilowatt generator.

"Yeah, it's over there in the corner, under that plastic. Just needs gas and oil."

"Seems like overkill, we don't really need that much juice."

"Yeah, and I bought a PTO-driven generator last fall at auction."

"You seem to have a thing about redundancy, Rick." Ron kidded me.

"Might as well be my middle name."

"How big's the 'big' generator?"

"It's a Winco. Older model used by a contractor for on-site power. Fifteen thousand watt rating at five hundred-forty RPM. Single phase."

"Holy smokes, that'd run the whole neighborhood!"

"Well, right now it would. I haven't fired it up yet to see if it works OK. I do know that it's trailer set up and PTO shaft fit the Ford, so it could be as simple as plug-and-play."

"Right. Like anything's that easy."

"Hey, now, let me have my fantasies, all right?"

"Sure."

"You guys want soup or chili for lunch?" Karen asked.

"Soup—do you have some of that home-made tomato soup?" Ron asked.

"Yeah. Rick found me a whole case that didn't break," Karen answered.

"C'mon. Be honest. I found a whole case that you forgot about after canning last year."

"Yep. I was saving them for a special occasion. That'd be 'Today.'"

"That's better. Let's go get washed up and you can tell me of your latest adventure into the wilds of Eastern Spokane."

"What'd the generator run you?" Ron asked.

"A hundred and fifty bucks. About a third of what the Generac cost new. I think the current model of the Winco is about two grand, without the trailer or the PTO shaft."

"Man! Why so cheap?"

"Two flat tires on it's trailer, the PTO shaft wasn't part of the same auction lot, and the generator was dirty and had some concrete splash on the case. My buddy Eric worked for a company that was being parted-out, and he said it ran fine the last time he used it. I bought the PTO shaft with a couple of brush hogs and sold them off in a private sale while I was still out at Reinlands. I only wanted the shaft. Ended up getting it for free. The other guys wanted the hogs and didn't care about the driveshaft."

"Jeez. Smokin' deal."

"It will be, as long as the generator doesn't turn INTO a smokin' piece of junk. Oh yeah, I forgot about the little homebuilt."

"Home built what?"

"Well, a kind of a generator. A little guy," I said, wheels turning in my head. "Charges a twelve-volt battery and can run a good sized inverter....."

Our electrical loads consisted of a small black and white TV which we hadn't tried all day, the 'big' radio, the chargers for the FRS's the hand-held CB, a small battery charger, a small fridge and my old Power Book, and hopefully soon my iMac, if it made it through the quake and I could get it out of the basement. If we salvaged some bigger appliances from the house, that'd probably be 'it.' The iMac was important to me because the most current emergency preparations documents, including a ton of FAQ's, .pdf files of A.T. Hagan's food preservation work, and other innumerable resources were stored on it. All of my business files were on the Mac, too. The old PowerMac that was relegated to the shop had some of the information, but the backup CD's and the most current information were in the basement, next to the iMac. Hopefully, intact and not buried. I already knew that the hardcopy of this information was probably ruined in the basement, and the second hardcopy was probably buried at my office, miles away.

Ever since buying the place, I always seemed to have need of power where I didn't have it. For years, I strung extension cords to my project area, then rolled 'em up when I was done. When we built the garage, I had a twenty-amp circuit run from the garage to the barn. Of course, nowhere near enough capacity for what I ended up needing when I converted the horse and cattle stalls to wood shop and store room. The barn only had one circuit from the garage, but I'd wired in six separate circuits to run off of a transfer-type switch through surface-mount conduits to my power tools. Basically, the lights and three convenience outlets ran off of 'mains' power, everything else needed the generator.

Given our current circumstances, we didn't need much, but still needed 'some.' The ten-horse Generac was only used occasionally in 'normal' times. I wasn't sure how it would do 'full time', but I did know that if I had to use it full time with the stored fuel still available, I'd be able to run it for forty hours. I'd stored motor oil and a couple of spare plugs too, but I hoped not to have to use it much.

The second option was the little battery inverter from the van. It'd give us probably almost enough power for charging stuff and a small appliance, but at the cost of running the six-cylinder.

Before I bought the Generac, I had a little home-made generator/inverter setup that I'd constructed from a plan on the internet web-site The Epicenter.com. This used a (tired) five horse Briggs and Stratton engine with a pulley that drove a GM model alternator, charging battery, and a four thousand watt inverter. I hadn't used it in a couple of years, but this seemed to make the most sense for small loads. I'd put it together with an old Troy-Bilt motor, a fifteen-gallon fuel tank from an Austin Healey Sprite, and an electric start switch from an old Ford. All it should need to run, I thought, was an oil change, a cleaned spark plug, and fresh fuel. With luck, of course. Four thousand watts should be plenty for the

Dewalt, and wouldn't drink gas like the other options. It did burn some oil though, which was the reason I'd replaced the tiller motor in the first place.

The 'final' alternative would be the big PTO driven Winco generator for the tractor that I'd picked up in October. The problem with that, was that I had no idea if it worked or not (I wasn't about to tell my wife that, however......She already kidded me plenty about bringing home junk.) It also didn't make a whole lot of sense to run the 8N with a monster generator for a bunch of little stuff.

So, the little home made option seemed to make the most sense right now.

The question I asked myself now was, 'Where did I put the thing?'

"After lunch, I'm going looking for the little thing. I'll get you and the boys lined out on the outhouse. Once the stuff's gathered up, I should have a generator ready, whether it's the Generac or the one I built is still up in the air.

"Sounds good."

"Now, tell me about your morning...."

.

Sunday
January Fifteenth

Ron enlightened us on their morning adventure. "We left here and headed south. The road was blocked a couple streets over by a power pole, all the way across the street. We made it to the freeway frontage road OK, and then had to zig zag through neighborhood streets and in a couple places, front yards to get through."

The new Starbucks building over there had burned, looked like it had been looted. We had to head north from there, up past a gas station. The Guard had a generator set there, and had hooked up the station's pump power and the station operators' were selling gas. We pulled in, there were only two cars there, and asked how much the gas was: They said that it was the same as Friday. All prices west of the Rockies and north of Ashland, Oregon had been frozen to the highest price of the six month average. All prices. For everything."

"Interesting way to do it, not all that unexpected. One way to guarantee prices aren't going to gouge us."

"Yeah, I suppose. Anyway, from there, we headed up toward the freeway. It was blocked, but the bridges looked OK to us. We headed west again, over by the grocery store. Same story there, National Guard troops in place, letting small groups in to buy items. Didn't seem to be any problems, but people seemed to be limited to one cart per family. Only one family member was allowed in. There was a helluva line getting in, I'll tell you." Ron said quietly.

"How long did it take to get over there?" I asked.

"About an hour."

"For a ten minute drive."

"Yeah. Anyway, we drove west from there. We planned on crossing the river someplace, but never got the chance. We got turned back at the Fairgrounds. All traffic was being directed to the south. Both lanes were going right into the parking lot. They were apparently forcing people out of their cars and into the shelter. I took one look at that, and bailed. I don't think the cops appreciated that. One tried to chase me down, but I took off southeast through the old gravel pit, around that electrical warehouse east of the stadium and the old racetrack, and we were gone."

"Did they say why they were forcing you to the shelters?"

"Not at the Fairgrounds, we didn't give them a chance. We tried the crossing at the railroad yards, and the Guardsmen were telling us to get to a shelter, ash was coming and expected within the hour."

"Yeah. Looks like May Eighteen, Nineteen-Eighty out there," I said flatly.

"You boys ready for lunch?"

"You bet!" Ron answered.

"You got the kids fed already?" I asked Karen.

"Yep. They got the Martin's packed lunch, and some soup."

"Anything on the radio?" I asked.

"Yeah, same old stuff. They said we'd be having more 'news' soon," Kelly responded. I didn't think she was even listening.

"Let's find out," I said, taking a bite of cornbread and a spoonful of Karen's soup.

Kelly reached over and turned the 'big' radio on, and it crackled to life.

".........canic ash is expected in the Spokane region within the next hour to two hours. People in exposed locations should seek shelter immediately. Ash fall can be hazardous to the health of those exposed to the fine dust, and can cause long-term illnesses. If you are forced to be exposed to the ash, be sure that your mouth and nose remain covered by adequate means of filtration, and limit exposure to dust........"

"Well, at least they've replaced Mr. Monotone with a female voice," Ron said sarcastically.

"What, being discriminatory? That's probably the only job ol' Monotone could get."

"Hush! You two," Libby said, "They might actually say something we don't already know."

"Don't hold your breath....Sorry, no pun intended." Ron and I both laughed.

"Aerial relief efforts to the Seattle region commenced at ten o'clock this morning, after runways in Everett were cleared of ash. Boeing Field and Sea Tac remain closed, and are buried under up to two feet of coarse and fine ash. Aerial over flights by military helicopters report that the extent of the mudflows that devastated the south Seattle metropolitan region appear to have traveled down the White, Puyallup and Carbon Rivers through Auburn, Buckley, Orting, South Prairie, Sumner, and Puyallup, and on into Tacoma as well as reaching as far north as the Renton area into the southern end of Lake Washington. A further mudflow to the west devastated Ashford along the Nisqually River, but fell short of reaching the Nisqually Basin. The mudflow is estimated to be in excess of one-hundred feet thick."

"The mudflows appear to have reached a depth of up to fifty feet in many areas, stripping trees, homes, freeways, businesses, dams and rivers away. The initial mudflows are estimated to have begun on Mt. Rainier at a speed of over one-hundred miles per hour, eventually decreasing to approximately forty miles per hour before reaching the Sound and Lake Washington."

"Warning systems set up in communities appear to have been partially operational, and several communities report that they did receive warnings and were able to evacuate before power failed. Boulders the size of mini-vans have reportedly been carried as far as thirty miles downstream."

"Damage in the Seattle Metro area from the 8.4 magnitude earthquake include landslides, bridge collapses, massive damage to unreinforced masonry structures, and major damage to virtually all buildings in the Seattle, Tacoma region. The damage is especially severe in areas built on softer soils, similar to the 1989 San Francisco earthquake. Many of the low valley areas and reclaimed wetlands appear to have been especially hard-hit."

"Casualties in the Seattle Tacoma region cannot be accurately estimated at this time, but officials in the Department of Emergency Management report that it is possible that up to fifty-thousand deaths may have occurred in the areas affected by the earthquakes and mudflows on Western Washington alone."

"Numerous casualties have been reported by authorities due to suffocation in the ash fall, carbon monoxide poisoning, and due to crush injuries...."

"From the National Weather Service, volcanic ash is now reported in Moses Lake, Ellensburg, Yakima, Connell, Othello, Pullman, and in the Tri-Cities...."

'They're reporting this like they're going to close schools because of snow...." I thought.

"...expected within an hour to forty-five minutes in the Cheney-Spokane-Coeur d'Alene area. Tonight the weather service is reporting a significant chance of snow, with accumulations in excess of twelve inches expected. Cold temperatures are expected to continue, with lows in the teens and highs in the twenties throughout the week."

"Repeating our broadcast from the top of the hour......."

"You know, you'd think there would be enough news going on to keep 'new' stuff on the air all the time," Libby said

"Yeah, but how many reporters do they have that can call in on a cell phone? Zero." I responded. "We've got some stuff to do outside before it gets here...if it gets here."

"OK. What's first?" Ron asked. "Do we need the boys?"

"No...on second thought, yes. Carl, grab some of that scrap plastic cover from the greenhouse. It's in those two five-gallon buckets in the corner. I'll need you and John to roll it out outside the garden door and the store room door. Weight it down with some snow or something. If the ash comes down, we'll be able to peel it back with the ash on it, and keep some of the mud out."

"K, anything else?" Carl asked.

"Yeah. Close up the door to the chicken shed. Then, make a few runs over to the shed that the tent trailers are in, and get as much wood as you can. We only have about half a cord in the barn, and most of it's cedar. We'll need some of that tamarack and fir for the woodstove, and I'd rather not trudge over there in the ash and the snow. Here's a flashlight. Don't get yourself hurt."

"All right..." Carl answered, plainly unimpressed with my work orders. I think he'd've rather me tell him, 'Yes, just stay inside nice and warm and play Texas Hold'em."

After I grabbed a few tools and fasteners, we put our boots back on and grabbed our gloves. The dogs followed us outside and took off into the dark. I had Ron open up the big wooden doors that enclosed the Packard, our toilet, and my leftover plywood and two-by stock. Ron pulled out the two sawhorses, plopped a sheet of three-quarter inch sheet of shop plywood down, and a few two-by-fours, and started measuring things up. I went on a hunt for the little generator. Even with adding gas and oil, it would probably be faster than digging the big generator out of the store room—it was pretty well buried right now.

I ended up finding it in the shed that held the tillers and mowers, under a piece of the old convertible top off of our Galaxie. I grabbed a couple of quarts of oil and one of the five gallon cans of gas that only held a gallon or two, and stacked them up on top of the tank. The generator was mounted on four small lawn-mower wheels on a flat hunk of plywood, and I'd cobbled up a handle for the beast from an old hand-truck. After ten minutes of pulling the thing back to the barn, I was ready to really take a look at it. It was dusty, but I was hopeful that with fresh gas and oil, we'd be able to fire it up quickly. I checked my watch, having to use the Indiglo button. It was five minutes to three.

"Where's that Dewalt?" Ron asked. "I've got the two-by's all cut with the handsaw, but I need to cut the seat, the door and the roof panel."

"Don't forget the 'moon' symbol...."

"Real funny."

"Saw's in the wood cabinets to the left of the scroll saw. Underneath the drying dishes, now I'm sure. The saber saw's in there too, probably behind the sawzall."

"Got it."

"Extension cord's in the five-gallon bucket next to the sleeping bags."

"Right."

Now I had to get Ron some power. After gassing up the tank, I added thirty-weight oil to the crankcase, retrieved the small battery from the barn that normally sat under the hood of the Honda tractor, and tried the key. Nothing. Ron and I fiddled with it for a few minutes, and found that the wire from the ignition key to the solenoid had broken off. Once I'd stripped the wire and reconnected it to the ignition circuit with my Leatherman, the little five-horse engine turned over, sputtered, and died. Twice.

Finally, we got it going with a large cloud of smoke, eventually decreasing to a slightly less toxic quantity. We plugged the heavy extension cord into the inverter, and we were ready to go.

Ron cut the plywood panels for the door and roof panels, and shut off the saw. All that work getting the generator going for five minutes of cutting. I shut off the generator and moved it to the west wall of the barn, inside the big barn doors. It was pretty well protected here, any ash wouldn't land directly on it, and not much would get near the air cleaner. I raided the pile of junk that was destined to go to the dump in the spring, and found the old shop vac hose with a metal pipe on the end, and with the help of a pipe wrench from the shop, I unscrewed the can-type muffler and pushed the metal pipe over the top of the muffler outlet. Next I grabbed a screw-type hose clamp, and tightened the vacuum hose over the top of the outlet pipe. I fed the hose out through the dilapidated wood door on the west end of the barn. That 'should' prevent too much carbon monoxide from building up in the barn. It was a temporary thing anyway, I hoped.

I took the extension cord and ran it into the barn. I went into the store room, grabbed the radios and their chargers and an old battery charger, loaded them up and headed back out. After restarting the generator, I plugged all of them into the power strip on the side of the contraption, and went back out to help Ron.

In about twenty minutes, we had the outhouse pretty well put together. I knew I had a seat somewhere in the barn, but that could wait. We still had to dig a hole and move the big box over our hole, and get the final touches made…like some sanding. I could already hear the voice of the women, complaining about slivers. Ron and I tilted our new creation up on to it's base and Ron headed inside. I wanted to check the generator. I wanted it to run for a half hour or so, and then let the chargers run off of the battery. If, we had enough time.

"Dad, is that enough wood?" Carl asked, standing next to a fairly impressive stack of wood, which now surrounded the porta-potty.

"Probably good for now. Now run up to the garage, and get the box of painting stuff that's to the left of the Mustang. We're going to need it."

"Painting?"

"No. Four packs of dust masks and two respirators. I've done volcanic ash before."

"Oh yeah. C'mon, John."

The boys were on their way back as I finished up with moving the running generator under the cover of the overhang and the partially closed doors. I was thinking about how lucky we were to have such good kids when I felt something on my cheek.

"Carl—turn on that flashlight."

"Swell. It's here." I checked my watch. It was eleven minutes after four p.m. The ash was coming down like light snow.

"Hustle up. It's ash. Don't breathe it."

The boys hurried back, Carl carrying the box and trying to shield his mouth and nose in his shoulder, John covering his mouth and nose with his hands.

"Inside. Quick."

We all stepped inside…and everyone took a breath. "It's here." I announced.

"Yeah, we can see. You're grey."

"Thanks, it's my new winter wardrobe. Maybe spring too."

"Dad, should we be scared?" Kelly asked. Marie had the same look on her face.

"You mean, more than normal? No. We'll be OK as long as we don't do anything really stupid."

"But they said…" Marie started.

"Honey, we've been through something like this before, we were all about twenty. That's not too much older than you are now. It was in the spring, and it was dry outside, so the dust was pretty bad until the rains came. Then, it was like shoveling wet chalk. Honest, we'll be fine." I said.

"Yeah, Marie," Ron added, "You'll be able to scoop some up, put it in a jar and tell your kids about it. Not everyday we get ash three hundred miles from a volcano. Now, are you all right? There's really nothing to worry about." Ron said. 'Nothing to worry about.......here', I said to myself.

"Yeah, I guess."

"OK then. Let's find you something to do."

"That shouldn't be hard." Karen said.

"I agree. I was thinking about a nap after I shut down the generator. Anything more on the radio?"

"Yeah. They said the ash is here."

"Blinding flash of the obvious," I said. "What else, did they report that it's 'dark' outside, too?"

"No, I'm sure that they reported that earlier..." Karen responded.

"Let's see if the TV's up and running yet," Libby quieted us as she turned on the tiny black and white set. It hummed as it warmed up, running on it's D-cells, as she looked for a station. Channel two came in finally, very fuzzy at first, eventually getting a little clearer.

I recognized the Smith Tower in the picture, once the tallest building in Seattle, now dwarfed by many taller but less distinctive buildings. The images showed everything covered in heavy ash, the wreckage of the Alaska Way Viaduct smothered under the grey blanket. A ferry on it's side at it's dock.

"Look at Safeco...." Carl said.

The home of the Mariners, with it's enormously expensive retractable roof, lay in ruins. The guide tracks for the roof twisted, and the massive trusses collapsed onto the field and seats. We'd seen Edgar Martinez's last game there, fourteen rows back from the plate.

"And Seahawk stadium." I said. Part of the roof had collapsed, and part of the grandstands. The helicopter panned back towards downtown. It looked like they had blue skies in Seattle, and the sun was brightly reflecting off of the grey ash. Most of the buildings had suffered major damage, with some losing all of their glass skins, including the huge Bank of America tower. The top of the Washington Mutual tower, with it's peaked roof and nice styling, was sheared off, the wreckage landing on a lesser building next door. The camera panned off to the west now, showing the wreckage of the piers. We'd had lunch there with my brother and his wife two months ago.

"Libby, where does your sister live?"

"Redmond/Fall City Road. Just off of it in one of the new subdivisions."

The feed switched to another aerial shot from somewhere between Boeing Field and Sea Tac. Both showed aircraft buried in ash, the Museum of Flight hanger shattered, aircraft still visible inside. A building was on fire near Sea Tac, the announcer thought it might have been related to a fueling facility.

Another camera showed people struggling to free themselves of a mudflow, then being swallowed alive. This feed came from Renton. I knew that the damage path of the mudflows included a large percentage of The Boeing Company's work sites, including the developmental center and Museum of Flight at Boeing Field, their corporate centers, the Renton plant, which had been wiped off of the map, by the views of the television; the Space Center over in Kent; the Auburn plant. What ever hadn't been destroyed in the earthquake or the mudflows, was covered with ash. They didn't say anything about the Everett plant, home of the world's largest building, volume-wise.

Other images and commentary came from Olympia, where the recently renovated Capitol was again in ruins, and over Lake Washington, where both bridge links to Mercer Island were......gone. Part of the Five-Twenty floating bridge was adrift, it looked like the south part with the eastbound lanes. They even had a little flyover of one of the multi-million dollar compounds on the lake. A massive garage was still smoking, apparently a car collection had been destroyed in the fire.

'Normal' homes exhibited far more damage overall than we'd seen here, understandably. Many of the newer homes seemed to have been converted into kindling, before being buried. I saw a brief shot over West Seattle and Magnolia, covered in ash, looking remarkably like a wedding cake. I had a brother and sister-in-law down in that mess, if they were still alive.

"We should count ourselves as lucky," I said.

"Or blessed." Carl said, surprising everyone.

"I wonder how Alex and Amber are doing, and the kids," Karen asked.

"I don't know…." I said as I walked away. Some things are just too much to watch. I had had enough television. Libby had too.

I poured myself a medicinal double shot of Irish Whiskey, and one for Libby, who rarely, rarely drank.

"May the roof above us never fall in, and may we friends gathered below never fall out."

2 0

Sunday
January Fifteenth

Libby and I put our glasses down quietly, on the cast-iron deck of the table saw, which was now doubling as a platform for a cutting board.

"I wish I knew how Marie's doing," she said.

"I know. We're all waiting for the other shoe to drop. It might be weeks before we hear from them, as screwed up as things are."

"I know. That's what bothers me...not knowing."

"Try to keep on the upside. There's no point in getting depressed about something that you simply don't know about. She was raised a good Catholic, right?"

"Yeah, but she's been going to some non-denominational church since the priest we had at our parish was...accused of molesting....."

"Oh. I didn't know that. Does she consider herself 'saved?'"

"Yes."

"Then regardless, she's safe. Look at it that way. I do."

"Is that why you seem so calm about all of this? I'm about to explode."

"Yeah, most of it. Sure I've got 'stuff' to get us through hard times or the occasional natural disaster or whatever. But the most important preparation is your faith. Not just Christianity, but faith. I don't have a problem with those who don't believe in Christ as their Savior…the choice is theirs. But if they have a strong faith that is based in good, even though I may not agree with it or it may not be found in the Bible, then I've seen that people with those convictions are much more likely to make it through stuff like this and be more helpful to those that…don't believe. See my point?"

"Yeah, I guess I've never connected the two, you know, faith in God and dealing with….this."

"It's not just dealing with situations that toss your world upside down. For me, it's dealing with the Dilbert-bosses, the everyday crud that wears you down, AND stuff like this. Of course, it only took me about thirty-five years of living to figure that out. It works for me. I have 'stuff' like we're using this weekend, like our stored food and supplies and redundancies because for me, by being prepared and knowing things, I don't need to be afraid of NOT being prepared and NOT having stuff. There's things that I can do to keep us safe in lots of situations. Not all of them, but a lot of them."

"Yeah, that makes sense."

"And your family and mine are descendants of the Irish potato famine and the shake-up in that entire society. You've read a lot of the same history books as I have. For me, a lot of my motivation is never having to put my kids through what my ancestors went through. A safety net. That, and a healthy distrust of things that the government says are what's 'Best For Me.'"

Libby nodded and stared out the window. I hoped that I helped her deal with our present state of life.

"I better get that generator shut off. Be right back."

"OK," Libby responded as I left the shop. Ron was keeping the kids occupied by overacting in another hand of cards, as the dogs wrestled at their feet.

"Everything OK?" Karen whispered to me as she folded clothes.

"Yeah, she's worried about Marie. I can't blame her. I think she's had just about all the stress she can handle today, that's all. I was trying to give her a little pep talk."

"I'll go talk to her too. She's had that thousand-yard stare going for the last hour."

"I know that look well. Sometimes, I think we Irish invented it."

"What, being moody?"

"No, the brooding, worrying, wringing your hands thing."

"Gotcha," Karen giggled. "She'll be all right. I think we could all use a good cry."

"Yeah, you're probably right. An Irish wake would not be a bad idea, either."

"Heaven knows there are enough….." Karen didn't say it.

"Yeah. Enough dead."

"Yeah."

"I'll be right back. I'm going to shut down the generator and close up the barn," I told her.

"Stay out of the ash and get a mask on."

"Yes, ma'am," I said, grabbing one of the big paint-spray respirators I used when I paint cars. "Better?" I said, which sounded like 'budduh?'"

"Much."

I entered the 'Packard' room through the door in the craft area, moving quickly to keep as much heat as I could inside the room. Using my little three-LED headlight, I was able to both use the 'facilities' in the near- dark and negotiate my way through the woodpile that the boys had brought to the barn, over to the noisy little Briggs and Stratton. The fumes weren't too bad in the barn, but my clothes would definitely smell like I'd been mowing the lawn when I went inside. I killed the motor, and checked the radios. They were all now fully charged, which surprised me. I thought they'd take much longer to charge. I left the little battery charger plugged into the inverter, to top off the rechargeable D-cells.

Looking toward the big barn doors, I could see the ash still coming down like grey snow, and as I strained my eyes, I could not make out anything beyond the outlines of the Ford and the Jeep outside. The brilliance of the sunshine on the ice this morning had given way to a dark grey blanket. I knew the tractor was off to the right, but it was invisible....fifteen feet away. The little LED's from my headlamp just lit up the ash. The ice and snow had been covered, and the silence after shutting down the generator was...startling. I strained to hear any noise outside, and ended up just staring for a few minutes. No sound at all, not even the sound of the ash. Only a little had drifted into the barn so far, and there did not seem to be any breeze.

I decided that it was a good time to get a little sleep, and went back inside. I shook off what little dust was on my shell, and hung it up on a newly-hung coat-rack behind the door. The kids and Ron were now into a new game, and Libby and Karen were talking in the woodshop. I sacked out on the cot, my face to the darkened wall, and slept.

When I awoke, everyone except Ron and the dogs were in the woodshop. Karen and Libby had enlisted their 'help' with dinner, which involved baking frozen pizzas in the wood cook stove. Her real motive of course was to let Ron and I get some sleep. Ron had dozed off in one of the fabric folding chairs, feet out on a footstool, hands folded across his belt. I listened to Karen and Libby as they instructed the kids on the use of the woodstove, the little thermometer hanging from the rack, and the different ways to control heat with the air intakes, the damper, and the types of wood for cooking. She was getting to be an expert, and until yesterday, had never even lit a match in the old Monarch.

I looked over at my watch. It was nearly seven thirty. I'd been out for maybe an hour and a half. Felt like a week. I didn't know I was so tired. I tried to get up out of the wood and canvas cot quietly, so that Ron could at least grab a little more sleep. Ada and Buck both thumped their tails at me, flanking Ron in the chair. I hushed them and they both closed their eyes. I pushed open the door to the shop quietly and padded into the woodshop, closing the door behind me.

"Hey, it's Sleeping Beauty," Libby said. She seemed to be in a much better mood.

"More like Rip Van Winkle," I said. " I was out a while."

"Yeah. You and Ron both looked like you needed it. It'll be an early night tonight I'm sure."

"Yep. I don't think we need to worry about security tonight. Only a complete idiot would go out on a night like this."

"Worlds full of 'em," John said.

"Yeah, but most of them live in….." I was going to say Seattle and thought better of it. "Most of them live elsewhere."

"Any news, radio girl?"

"Something about Asia was on at seven. The 'financial markets'. Is that where they sell money or something?" Kelly asked.

"Well, sort of. What did they say?"

"Something about China not using dollars anymore. Why would they use dollars? Don't they have their own money?"

I was still trying to get the fog out of my head when I grasped what she was saying. The Chinese were either dumping dollars, or had switched their financial policy in a big way. Had to, to be broadcast on our station, in this kind of crisis.

"They have their own money, it's called the Yuan, I think. Did they say anything else?"

"No, but the news will be on again in a few minutes. They said they'd repeat the news at the bottom of the hour. Fifteen-ten is back up too, broadcast is different. The Sony is turned to that one."

The little Sony AM radio had been mine since I turned twelve. First Japanese electronics I ever owned, and even though it cost maybe ten dollars when it was new, it was still my sentimental favorite.

"Thanks, babe."

I turned on the little radio and plugged in the earpiece, while cooking lessons went on. Right at seven-thirty, the 'chime' of the network came on and the broadcast came on.

"In an unexpected move, Chinese central bank governor Zhou Xiaochuan says the Yuan is not overvalued early Monday, prior to Asian markets opening. The Dollar fell dramatically against the Yen on the opening."

"The dollar declined to a six-month low against the Yen after the official statement, suggesting it will continue to let the Yuan strengthen."

"Every time China opens the door on a possible revaluation, that causes a strengthening in the Yen," said Neil Ambrose, a director of foreign-exchange sales at BNP Paribas SA in London. ``There were real surprises coming out of China for everyone who had been hoping for some news on revaluation."

"The dollar also reached a nine-month low against the euro after the Administration proposed a record $2.57 trillion budget that expands spending in some areas. Federal Reserve Chairman Michael last week caused concern record current- account and budget deficits will help the dollar."

"The U.S. currency declined to 84.45 Yen at 11:28 a.m. in Asian market trading, from 84.07 late last week, according to electronic currency-trading system EBS. It reached 84.65 today, close to the January high of 84.74, the strongest since January 10. The U.S. currency declined to $1.5614 per euro, from $1.5367."

"Zhou's comments to news agency Xinhua come two days after a meeting of the Group of Seven industrial nations in London ended

with the statement that China is moving closer to eliminating its decade- old peg to the dollar."

"Washington did not have any comments on the Chinese move."

"In other news..."

My mind started to turn off. What did the change in the status of the Dollar mean? I'd read that the Chinese held a substantial portion of the United States debt in the form of bonds and other debt obligation, but didn't understand what the implications could be. There'd been something brewing in the markets for weeks, it was all over the internet...as if you could believe everything you read. Still, the thousand-point decline in the market since the first of the year as something to take heed of. I had, instead of a contribution to my IRA, purchased ninety-percent silver coins with the funds. It had been delivered last Thursday, in a nondescript container. The UPS guy didn't appreciate the value of the box on his hand truck. I didn't enlighten him on it, either.

The first thing that came to mind was a devaluation of the dollar, decline in it's purchasing power both domestically and abroad...which meant dramatically higher prices.

Nationally, this could be a disaster. Locally, it only added fuel to the fire. Most banks were probably heavily damaged from the earthquake, and most people used ATM's these days for 'yuppie food stamps', also know as twenty-dollar bills. So right now, the ATM's were down, banks were in a shambles, power was off and financial records unobtainable, and the dollar stood a good chance of being worth a fraction of it's value the previous week.

Karen looked at me as the broadcast continued in my ear.

"Rick, are you OK? You're pale," Karen said.

"Yeah, I'm all right."

She wasn't convinced. "What's wrong?"

"More than we can know, babe. More than we can know."

Sunday evening
January Fifteenth

"So what's that supposed to mean? 'More than we can know.'"
Karen pressed.

"Something on the radio. It might mean that the US Dollar is in
trouble."

"And that means what?" Libby asked. "How can the dollar be in
'trouble'?"

"It's value can evaporate. Meaning, hyper-inflation. Ala, the
Weimar Republic, Nineteen Twenties."

"Isn't that when they had to use wheelbarrows full of money to
buy bread? We're studying that in Social Studies." Marie chipped in.

"Yes."

"So you think that will happen here?"

"Might. I don't know."

"Why would it? Isn't our money protected by the....oh, what's it
called, the FDIC?" Libby asked.

"Well, that's what the signs say. In reality, no. The FDIC was
intended to save individual savings institutions from insolvency. The
network of big banks and the Federal Reserve, which is a private
bank and not part of the Federal Government, would step in and take

over the bank, making good on bad debts or investments…but not on a nation-wide scale. Or, in this case, world-wide scale."

Karen got it. I could tell by the look in her eyes. Many times we discussed the fiat currency system, and the simple fact that every fiat currency system ever devised eventually failed. Only tangible assets, like gold and silver and real estate, ever kept their value. These days, with the real estate bubbles going full steam, even real estate could be said to be a hugely risky venture.

I could see that Libby was wrestling with the concept. "Listen. Our money used to be backed by the full faith and credit of the United States of America. Meaning, our Treasury. You used to be able to redeem a paper dollar for actual silver or gold. Our dollars used to be tied to the actual price of gold. I think we got to where we are because it was simply easier to create money out of thin air than actually back it with something. The money supply—and therefore the public and all property—is easier manipulated if you're playing with a stacked deck. Or in this case, cards that can say whatever you want them to say. Get it?"

"I'm beginning to. And I'm not liking it."

"You're not supposed to. When the dollar goes the way of the leviathans, so goes the alleged worth of every fake-silver dime and fake copper penny in your savings bank. And all of that pretty-colored paper, too."

"You mean all of our savings, checking, mutual funds, everything."

"And bonds. Government bonds are one of the primary instruments of debt. China owns a lot of it. If they're dumping it or whatever, the fact that we've been bankrupt for a quarter century or so will finally come to light."

"Depression."

"No, more like an economic holocaust. If the Chinese and Europeans play their cards right, and I have no doubt that they're playing them, America will cease to be the financial king of the planet. We've already lost our manufacturing base. We're dependent on our creditors world wide to finance our debt, both personal and public. When was the last time an auto plant was built? Right now. In China. By GM and Ford and Chrysler. We import stuff we used to make here, and it's better, cheaper and faster. And we don't have all of that nasty pollution here and that inconvenient working class. If this is the trigger, we're hosed. The so-called stock prices will plummet too. Kiss our retirement funds goodbye. College funds too," I said, looking at the kids.

Libby was silent for a minute. The kids were listening too. "Now what?"

"I have no idea. I would expect that if the dollar is going to crash, you're going to see dramatic increases in every single item on the shelves and every single commodity within the next week. Maybe less."

"But what about the price controls they put in place because of the earthquake?"

"I'd forgotten about that. That might hold for a while, but think about it. You're in Idaho. Prices have doubled for stuff. Across the state line, they're still cheap. How long do you think that will last before prices go up here? About no-time at all."

"Dad, what do we need to buy? We've been using a lot of stuff it seems, you know, not conserving….."

"Well, that's right. I expected things to return to 'normal' soon, meaning that the stores would still have shipments coming to them on a regular basis. That will probably still happen, but I don't know, honestly. We have a pretty good inventory of stuff here. We will need to get a list of stuff together that might be in short supply or hard to get. And we'll have to be ready to buy it as soon as we can."

"What about the ash?" Kelly asked. "You can't go out shopping in that stuff."

"Well you could, but it'd be ugly. Done that before." I said.

"Libby, you said that the store was open this morning?"

"Yeah, there was a line to get in, but they were letting one family member in at a time, or at least only letting people buy one shopping cart full of stuff."

"Did you see any semis at the loading dock?"

"Couldn't see it. It's on the other end of the store."

"Right. I forgot."

"Besides, what do we use for money? With the power out, it's not like our credit cards will work. I think Ron and I only have fifty bucks between us."

Karen and I exchanged a look.

"Unless they have a lot of faith in you, that's correct. Probably the same for checks. So real soon, it'll be cash only. We'll use what cash we have."

"That won't buy much."

"Don't worry, we'll be fine. We'll talk about it later. After dinner. What's on our menu this fine evening?" I was trying to lighten things up. I wouldn't succeed of course, but it was worth a try.

"Kids'll have a bunch of frozen pizzas from the kitchen fridge. There wasn't room for them in the garage freezer, and they were starting to thaw."

"And we get a pizza apiece!" Carl said.

"Actually, three for you boys, and one each for the girls. I've seen you boys eat." Libby said.

"What about us big kids?" I asked.

"Remember that lasagna you saved?"

"Awesome. If we only had some of that fresh sourdough from Safeway...."

"Can't have everything. We do have two bottles of red table wine that were in the trunk of my car..."

"Then the evening is saved! How long 'til dinner?"

"Pizzas will take an indeterminate amount of time. Lasagna, an indeterminate amount of time squared."

"Gotta love wood-stove time."

"Yeah. Like 'fifteen Hawaiian minutes.'" Carl said, referring to the statement that our tour guide used when shuttling us off to the U.S.S. Arizona and U.S.S. Missouri memorials, a few years back.

"What do you want us to do now?" Carl asked.

"Continue with your woodstove lesson. It's a higher art form, if you were unaware."

"Art? It's a fire! In a metal box!" Carl and the kids giggled.

"Say that after your pizza burns. This isn't electric stove cooking, buddy. Try cooking a meal, and you'll learn. Right, ladies?"

"Yes. And, I think now's a great time. All right boys, you first. Let's get to it."

"All riiight." John said in a descending tone that said 'busted.' This, at least would be good entertainment value.

"Carl, what did you do with that inventory clipboard I gave you to update?"

"Umh, I....didn't get it done."

"Did you, um, get it started?"

"Yeah, we got the first two shelves done, floor to ceiling."

"Well, that's a start. Let's have a look."

"It's on the wall over there by the faucet."

"Thanks."

We'd have some serious thinking to do, if the Martins were to stay with us for any length of time. For several years I had a solid six months of foodstuffs and other consumables. More than once I'd been accused of being a pack rat, and not in a good way. I reviewed the list that Carl started on, and went over what I knew we had in my head. I'd have to find a way to get the other Mac out of the house tomorrow. I knew that it's inventory was current at least to last month. We'd also have to find a way to get into the fruit room in the basement, to see what we could save. And then there was that ancient chest freezer in the laundry.

"Hey, what's up?" Ron said, running his hands through his (thinning) hair.

"Boys are making their dinners. You might want to pull up a chair and critique. Also, there's a fire extinguisher on the wall off to the right, juuuuuust in case."

Everyone laughed, except the boys.

"Hey, there's no light in there," John said, drawing more laughs.

"No kidding. There was barely electricity in these parts when that stove was being used in the house!" Karen said. "You also will want to keep that oven door closed if you ever want to eat. You're letting all the heat out."

"How do I know when the cheese is bubbling if I don't look."

"Intuition."

"Yeah, and good luck with that…." Ron said. "What's new?"

"Plenty." Karen said.

"Hon, you fill Ron-boy in. I need to go see a man 'bout a horse."

"Right. Potty call."

I excused myself, strapped on my little headlamp and headed out to the 'facilities', mostly to scrounge up the plastic laundry sink that we'd used in lieu of our kitchen sink for several months, during the Remodel-From-Hell. After moving a bunch of salvaged tongue-in-groove vertical-grain fir that I really didn't want to go to the dump after the remodel, I found the tub and it's legs, the drain piping, the old faucet and fittings, back in the corner. Filthy, as predicted.

I grabbed a hunk of burlap bag that was on top of the Packard's permanently rolled-down drivers' window, and wiped out as much dust and dirt as I could, and then turned the whole thing upside down to shake it out. After that, I grabbed the whole thing and hauled it into our new 'home'.

"Now that's attractive," Karen said. Ron and Libby were busy making sure the boys didn't develop oversized heads from their first successful baking adventure.

"Nothing too good for our new kitchen."

"Great. AND our new bathroom."

"Better start calling it a 'washroom.' I don't think 'baths' are going to be in order for some time."

"You know, we have that camp shower out in the trailer....."

"Yeah, that's right. Of course, it's pretty well frozen onto the ground buried under snow in a shed, that's covered in ash. And, did I mention the locusts?"

Karen laughed. "No, that would be newsworthy."

"At least."

"Do you think you can hook that thing up?"

"I hope so. The old drain line from the milking-slab is right under your feet. I think it goes out to a drywell or a sump. I never looked, but it drained OK when I washed the place out, before I framed in the floor."

"What do you need to do to get to it? Isn't this board nailed down?"

As she finished her sentence, I took a metal hook out of a drawer in my tool cabinet, walked over, and inserted it into a very small hole toward the end of the board, and lifted. The two-by-eight and its supports lifted up from the slot in the concrete slab, and the drainpipe, capped off with a chunk of rigid insulation.

"And there we go."

"Nice little hiding place."

"Used to be. That's where I hid your Christmas presents, until now, that is."

"Really? I have much better hiding places than this."

"I know. Remember, there isn't a room in that house that I haven't worked over."

"Oh, you just think you know everything," she said with a glint in her eye.

"Me? Not remotely," I said, giving her a little kiss.

Sunday Evening
January Fifteenth

After the last of the pizzas were done and well on their way to being consumed, I loaded up the firebox with some scrap oak from the kitchen floor installation, and found some apple wood from last years' pruning. We'd need the heat to bake the lasagna, which normally cooked at something like three hundred seventy-five degrees for forty-five minutes or so in our electric oven. I knew that the woodshop would get pretty warm, once the fire got going good and strong. Without power, there wasn't really any effective way to fan some of the heat over into the other room, though.

The kids had finally apparently grown tired of cards, and had pulled out one of the oldest games in my family, an ancient game of Scrabble, and a small dictionary that was obsolete in about Nineteen-Seventy to go along with it. Both dogs were sleeping at or on the kids feet, under the small wood drop-leaf table that we'd put together earlier in the day.

Ron, Libby, Karen and I were in the woodshop, waiting to smell the lasagna as it baked. We were all getting pretty hungry, and it would be a good hour before the dish was done. Ron and I were both nursing a Red Hook ale, which we knew might be one of the last we'd have for a long time. The Red Hook brewery was located in the Redmond/Woodinville area, across the street from two of my favorite wineries, Ste. Michelle and Columbia. All were probably covered with ash right now, and probably damaged from the quake. Libby's sister lived a couple of miles from there.

"Lib filled me in on what you'd said earlier. She said we'd talk 'later' about the money situation," Ron said. "I assumed you wanted to be out of earshot of the kids?"

"Yeah, no need for them to know all the details, but if this thing does spin out of control and prices get stupid, we need to be ready for it. To me, it means getting stuff now that we will have a hard time buying at any price later. People will buy things for immediate consumption, and not long-term use that cost much more and delivers much less. We need to work around that. Buy smart, and early. And often."

"But we don't have that much cash to work with, and the banks sure aren't in any shape to open."

"Probably true. It might be a couple of days before they open here. By then, if this goes the way it might, we'll be hearing about effects from other parts of the country here, before most people here can get to physical paper dollars from their banks. Which means, that things could go sideways in other parts of the country before they do here, price-wise."

"So we're screwed. We can't get to money, we're going to have to wait until the crap hits us." Ron said dejectedly.

"Far from it. We're going to get a head start on it if we can. If the ash stops like it probably will soon, the stores may be open again tomorrow, like they were today. Probably Tuesday at the latest."

"That still leaves the cash problem," Libby said.

"No problem at all. We have almost a thousand dollars in paper money between what's in the barn and in the house. In addition to that, we have significant amounts of ninety-percent silver coins and a few gold pieces as well."

"Collector coins?" Ron said with more than a little skepticism.

"No, real money. Silver and gold retain value once paper loses it. Always been that way."

"So we'll be using coins?" Libby asked.

"Probably not at first. We probably won't even be able to spend all the cash, if we're being limited to one cart per person at the store."

"So we go to multiple stores."

"In more than one car."

"More like, three. I'll take the van, you guys in the Jeep, Karen in the Ford. If we can get there, we should be able to buy at multiple stores to the max allowable in multiple trips. I seriously doubt that the government has come up with a way to determine that I've already been to the store today, and therefore not allowed to come back for a week. Not yet, anyway."

"So what's the silver for? What is it, silver dollars?"

"If the dollar crashes like I think it will...or know it will someday...the paper dollars will be worthless. Transactions will have to be done with something of worth. Silver. Gold. Shotgun shells. Barter. Whatever. And no, mostly dimes and quarters."

"So that's why you have silver?"

"That, and the fact that the dollar has been in decline for decades. You do realize that it's lost maybe thirty-five percent of its buying power since 9-11."

"Well, yeah, things are more expensive."

"No, your dollars are worth less. Carl's favorite meal from McDonalds for years was two cheeseburgers, a medium fry and a Coke. Extra Value Meal Number Two. For years it was two-ninety-nine. Now it's four bucks and change. Did hamburger, buns, potatoes or pickles decrease in availability? No. Your dollar is worth less. At the same time, silver went from 4.37 per ounce to 9.07 last Thursday. The last bunch I bought, ten days ago, was at 7.36. What drove it from 7.36 to 9.07? Fear. Fear that something wicked this way comes."

Libby and Ron were both silent, considering what I'd said.

"They reduced the amount of silver in dollars in sixty-four, and eliminated it in sixty-nine, because they were then able to make more money—literally—for much less cost. Get it?"

"Scam." Ron said, lights on. "They've been scamming us."

"Yep. For decades at least." The baking lasagna was now filing the room with it's aroma, which just made our mouths water more.

"All right. So what do we need?" Libby asked.

"Well, just so happens I have this list here...."

The inventory that Carl had been tasked with was obsolete, but not horribly so. I knew that the most current list existed only on the computer in the basement, and was for now at least, inaccessible. The older inventory was printed up at the end of last month, so I knew we'd be in pretty good shape. We were still coming off of the holidays, and weren't exactly eating extravagantly. In January, for us, simpler is better.

"This is a copy of the master inventory of supplies that we have in the barn, the house, and in some cases, out in the root cellar or the shed. It's not quite up to date, but close. I'll need each of you to look it over, and tell me what else we need to stock up on, then we can each make lists and get a game plan put together. If we can get out tomorrow morning, we'll hit what stores we can and get the list taken care of. Here's the list."

I handed them a list, printed out from a spreadsheet that I used to track what we used and what we needed. It ran for eleven pages.

"I don't see the kitchen sink on this list," Ron said with some shock over the contents.

"Already bought it. It's in the other room," Karen said. "And you two have a project—to get us a real sink put together. And a bath tub would be a good idea too. Those boys are starting to get a little ripe."

"Amen," Libby added.

"As you wish, " I replied.   "How's our drinking water situation?"

"I think, if I'm reading this right, at forty-five gallons."

"Sounds right. How about our wash water?"

"Barrels about three-quarters full, so what's that, forty?"

"Yep. Good. This ash is going to screw us up on water from the roof. I'm not sure how I'm going to get that sand filter to give us clean runoff without clogging up the filter completely with mud. I was counting on snowmelt to get us some water to filter. With the dogs and eight people, that drinking water will go fast. Wash water too."

"Nothing you can do about it tonight."

"True. Babe, when was the last time you were in the root cellar?"

"Monday night. Why?"

"Everything holding up OK in there?"

"Yeah, you know, musty as always."

"That's OK. I just wanted to make sure the potatoes haven't gone on us."

"Too early for that. We kept them last year until summer."

"Yeah, but this is THIS year. Nothing seems to have gone the way we planned, you know? Right now, you and I are supposed to be having dinner at the Davenport, and driving home."

"You made reservations?"

"Yes ma'am. Palm Court, grilled filet mignon, champagne and that dessert you like so much. What was it? That's right. Chocolate truffle with raspberry and white chocolate drizzle."

"Stop. You're making me think this lasagna is a poor second."

"Nonsense. We'll have s'mores for dessert and a nice glass of red wine."

"There you go," Karen said. "As long as I'm with you, I'm good."

"Yes, you are." I said with a leer. "Sometimes, very good."

"Quit you two, or we'll get a hose," Libby said.

"Sorry, didn't mean to embarrass you."

"I don't want you giving Ron any ideas. Davenport Hotel indeed."

I reached over and turned on the little TV, just before nine p.m. The CBS affiliate was showing some aerial views of the Spokane area, shot this morning before the ash cloud came over. Must've been about eleven, by the look of the sun angles on some of the landmarks I knew. I was hoping for a picture of the building my office was in.

I wasn't disappointed for long. The images were cobbled together from a hand-held video camera, certainly not professional grade. One of the biggest buildings in town, the former Metropolitan Mortgage building (the company had gone bankrupt in a financial scandal), had lost half of it's aluminum skin, and most of it's glass from the third floor to the seventeenth. The building that held my first professional job, built as the Old National Bank (now US Bank) was almost unrecognizable. The entire terra-cotta façade had been sheared from the building. The Paulsen Center across the street wasn't in much better shape. The ten-year-old Transit Center's skywalks had collapsed across the streets bordering it. The Seafirst building was also heavily damaged. Eventually, the camera panned across the Spokane River, showing the United States Pavilion from Expo '74, our Worlds Fair. The Burlington-Northern clocktower, left over from our days as a railroad hub, was...gone. My office building was an unreinforced brick building, built more than a hundred years before, not far away from the river, and now just coming into view. The roof and two of the six floors had collapsed on one wing, the wing that held my office seemed to be intact, but the upper floor had collapsed on that wing as well. I might still have an office, but it was buried under hundred-year-old brick and Douglas fir beams and joists. So much for hoping.

"Well now. Looks like I have a company to rebuild. This should be fun." I said with no small amount of sarcasm, looking out the window to the dark.

"It's snowing! The ash has stopped!" Will wonders ne'er cease, I thought to myself.

"Good. I'm sure the dogs'll have to go out soon."

"Yes, but that also means that we get to go shopping tomorrow. Why don't you ladies take a look at that, and Ron and I'll see what we can do about the sink."

"OK. Lasagna's probably going to be another ten minutes," Karen said.

"Is that based on actual knowledge, or an educated guess?"

"Four year degree and twenty years of cooking for you, dear."

"Gotcha. Intuition." Ron and I laughed and went into the other room, where the boys had been defeated by the girls. I suggested a Martin vs. Drummond game, and was soundly booed.

"So, what does a plumber make these days," Ron asked.

"Quarter of a lasagna and two glasses of wine, I think, for this job."

"Sounds good to me."

Using the old sink and most of the drain line, we were able to get the piping to line up with the cast-iron drain in the trench, that headed off to the outside at a slight slope. I literally had to use duct-tape to make a joint, but didn't figure that anyone really cared about the aesthetics of the installation. We were able to finish up just as the dish was coming out of the oven. Good thing, the thermometer in the woodshop read eighty-one degrees. The boys had stripped down to their t-shirts, and all of the kids were now barefoot. I knew that in a couple hours though, the rooms would be back down to the high fifties or low sixties.

Ron knocked on the door to the shop, playing a game with the girls. "S'cuse me? I've come to see a lady 'bout a lasagna?"

"Why do come in if you would. My husband's not at home and I've noticed you working soooo hard...." Libby said in her best Scarlett O'Hara voice.

"Now who needs a cold bucket of water?" Karen said. "Let's eat. I'm starving."

"Save some for us," Carl said. "That pizza was a great appetizer."

"Teenagers." I said, sitting down on a stool, next to my table saw. "I'm sure we won't need to worry about leftovers."

2 3

Sunday night
January Fifteenth

Ron and I took a turn doing dishes, which was much easier now that we actually had a sink and not a couple of washtubs. Karen heated up some of the boiled melt-water for dishes, just to the point of scalding. I was always amazed that the girls never seemed to have a problem with hot water, even to the point of burning us poor guys.

As predicted, there was no leftover lasagna, and we polished off the wine with no problem, either. After we put the dinner dishes away (with directions from the girls, they wanted to find them tomorrow. Imagine that.), we discussed our Monday morning plan. The kids had progressed to a cutthroat game of Chutes and Ladders, which had been relegated to the barn when Kelly had turned ten. It was pretty funny to watch teenage boys play this game...

We had decided when we thought up the shopping trip to set some general parameters for our merchandise runs. First, the items had to be in either short supply in the inventory for our new group size; second, they had to by and large be unobtainable locally; third, they had to be non-refrigerated items or could be home-canned; fourth, items like canned soup, ready-to-eats and things like that were not a good use of our money. Finally, we decided to pass on things if someone else appeared to need it more than we did. There was a substantial chance that we already had more than they did, here at home.

Some of the items that ended up on the list included flats for canning jars, pectin, bulk wax, wicks, female supplies, toilet paper, multi-vitamins, disinfectant, cold and flue medicines, allergy medicines, boots for the kids, shotgun shells, ammunition for the twenty-two and the ought-sixes, soap, bulk tobacco, sugar, bacon, beef, salt, spices....needles, yarn thread....rice...on and on.

We each had identical lists, made by hand, with 'target' amounts to obtain for each trip. We didn't want to appear to hoard any particular item, nor did we want to draw attention to us on our mission. We'd rotate between the three major grocery stores within the area, and possibly one other store, although it was a little out of the way. Libby suggested visiting Costco, which was about six miles away. I knew it was a nightmare on normal shopping days, I couldn't imagine what it would be like now. We decided against it.

If a financial meltdown didn't happen, and if recovery and re-supply and outside help happened as it might in California in an earthquake, we'd have enough stuff to last years and years in normal use. If our fears came to pass about a prolonged recovery effort, bad weather, whatever, in addition to the financial problems, we'd be at least better prepared than we sat right now. I still had nagging doubts that I could be dramatically wrong and over-reacting to the whole situation. One of my faults. One of my...many faults, actually.

Ron and I knew that our first task Monday morning would be to get the Jeep, the Expedition and the van cleaned off and started up. I'd need to plow at least to the street too, the van was a mid-engine rear-wheel drive, with a suspension that was almost sophisticated by Prairie Schooner standards. Dawn was around seven. Karen and Libby would make dinner, and the kids would take care of the dogs and cleanup. We'd be getting to the point soon where 'laundry' would be in order. That would be another thing to think about in my abundant spare time. I set the alarm on my watch for six. I also wanted to check on the Pauliano's tomorrow before I hit the stores, to see how they were doing and if they needed anything. At their age, this couldn't have been easy, no matter how tough the constitution.

At ten-thirty, we decided to get ready for bed. This of course resulted in a loud objection from Kelly and Marie, who were dangerously close to beating the boys for the third time in Chutes and Ladders. I decided to take the dogs outside for their evening business, and gave the kids five more minutes to play. I told Karen I'd be back in a few minutes, and took one of the FRS's along.

Buck and Ada were very eager to get outside as we exited through the tool room. I pushed the ancient wooden door to the garden open with some difficulty. The ash was probably an inch or two deep, 'loose', but now that the snow was coming down, it was compacting down to less than half of that. The dogs didn't care either way, they took off running to the gate up to the house. I followed, much slower.

The only sound I could hear was the sound of the dogs, now far off, and the sound of the snow hitting the brim of my hat and my shoulders. I'd never been in a storm like this here, snowing this hard, and have it be this dark. I could hardly see the house.

I walked all the way up to the main gate, and the front fence. I couldn't see any lights in any houses, nor lights or cars on the streets. The whole neighborhood looked deserted.

I called the dogs back to me, and we headed to the south of the garage. I wanted to look over our fruit trees, to see how much damage the heavy ice had caused. The apples on the east end of the rows had some breakage at the tops, and the pears looked fine. One of the four plum trees had split right down to the ground, which didn't really bother me all that much. That particular tree had never fruited like those around it, and wasn't a variety that kept. The cherries on the west end looked fine, other than the big Royal Ann on the end, that had lost about fifteen feet out of the top. We'd have to do some pruning as soon as the thaw hit, both our 'normal' thinning and pruning and some regular surgery.

Funny how a natural disaster never seemed to make the average, every day jobs go away. Just added to them.

Back at the barn, I pointed the flashlight at the dogs, and wiped them off with an old towel. Their golden coats were grey from mid-leg down, from the muddy ash. I then spent the next ten minutes washing them off before letting them in the barn.

They were not amused.

Finally, I got back into the barn and corralled the dogs in a corner with some old blankets. They wouldn't be sleeping with us tonight!

As I finished up and peeled off my snowy coat, Libby asked me if she could speak with me in private. Ron was already in his sleeping bag, and Karen was washing her face.

"I've been thinking about last night all day today. It shouldn't have happened. It's wrong to kill people."

"It is. But Ron and I are entrusted with the safety of our families. You need to understand Libby, that we heard them talk about what they were going to do next, and that they'd already killed people. What did you want us to do, let them kill us and rape you, Karen,

Marie, and Kelly to death? Would you then feel better about what we did?"

"No," she responded quietly, eyes downcast.

"You need to understand that I hated to do that. I ended someone. We ended four someones. They may have been destined to be compost, but we still hated doing it. We will all have nightmares about it for a long time. Maybe for life. I can live with that. My family and yours are still alive. They're not."

"The government should protect us from people like that."

"No, you're wrong. The government's job is not to protect us. The government's job is to defend and maintain our rights and enforce laws. It is our job to defend ourselves. The government has forgotten that, and did so a long time ago. With as many abused kids as you have in your seventh grade classroom, you should know that damn well. The cops don't show up BEFORE something happens. They only show up AFTER. When does Child Protective Services show up? AFTER. The law's been broken, and they're only for clean up. That is all. If they happen to be there when the law is broken, they'll do something about it. Other than that, they don't and can't do anything. It is up to US to protect us. Do you understand?"

"Yes, but…"

"If you were there, with a gun in your hand, and had heard what we heard, you'd have beaten me to the punch. I am not kidding, Lib. You'd have shot them down like dogs."

"What if it happens again?"

"Then we will do the same thing again. Those four we killed were looking for essentially useless stuff. Big screen TV's. DVD players. Cash. Electronics. Porn. The next time we see looters, they'll be better armed, and they'll be looking for food. Bet on it."

"Do you really believe that?"

"If things don't happen perfectly in terms of relief, yes. That is discounting the whole financial thing, which by the sounds of the radio, is unwinding in Europe right now. Inside of a week or two, Bad Things are going to happen here. Again, unless I'm wrong."

"You haven't been wrong lately."

"Yeah. And I hate being right all the time about bad things happening."

"I better get to bed."

"Yeah. Big shopping day tomorrow. Just gear your mind like it's the day after Thanksgiving, and you'll be fine." I said in humor.

"Right," She said as she padded off to bed.

Karen asked, "What was that all about?" in a whisper.

"She's having second thoughts about what we did last night."

"Aren't we all?"

"Yeah, but she seems to have more problems with it than I do, or Ron."

"She'll be all right. Doesn't she know what's at stake?" Karen whispered. "You always say: 'It's not the odds, its the stakes.'"

"Exactly. Let's get some sleep."

"Yeah. I'd like to hit the hay before the wine wears off."

I laughed. "Yeah, I hear you."

We turned out the kerosene lamps and settled down for the night. We could hear the hens on the other side of the wall settling in too. Soon I could hear that Karen was asleep, and I heard snoring from Carl. I was a lot longer in drifting off. I was planning our new washroom layout in my head, as I finally got to sleep.

Monday morning,
January Sixteenth

We awoke to the crow of our un-named rooster, at four a.m. After crowing five or six times, he decided that it wasn't really morning yet, and quieted down. I fell back to sleep by about four-thirty or so, I guessed.

At a few minutes to six, my new alarm rooster let us have it again, right before my watch went off anyway. We let the kids sleep in for awhile, they were growing used to letting us get the fire going and getting the chill off of the rooms before they quit feigning sleep.

It was still full dark outside, but we had work to do. I pulled on clean socks, t-shirt, and flannel-lined jeans, perhaps the greatest invention since mittens. Ron was already up and pulling my old grey parka on over a fleece vest. He was also using my five-year-old Sorels, which in a former life were my 'work' boots. My 'new' Sorels were worn to the office on cruddy, sloppy days, and then I'd change into hikers. No more, so it seemed.

While Karen and Libby were tasked with getting breakfast going and some coffee built, Ron and I had to get the vehicles ready for our shopping excursion. We'd received more than a foot of new snow overnight, sandwiching the ash fall between the ice of a couple days ago, and the light powder. At least it wasn't dusty. Yet.

While Ron pulled the tarps and covers off of the Ford and the Jeep, I attacked the van. The snowfall before the ice made cleaning it off easier, but not exactly 'easy.' With a big push-broom, I managed to get most of the top and windows cleared off, the dark grey muck of the ash mixing with the white powder. I'd run the van a little more than a week before, so I was confident that the big six-cylinder would start. After chipping my way through the ice on the driver's door, I managed to get the button to work and I was in. Sure enough, three tries and the forty-year-old engine kicked to life. I set the heat to 'max' and let the engine run on fast idle while I went about my next task, getting the snow out of the way so we could actually leave the property.

The 8N was similarly encased in ash and snow, which slid off in a heavy clump of grey. With the weight of the layers of snow, ice, ash, and now more snow, we'd have to look at the barn roof and maybe shovel some of that weight off—before we had meltdown or worse, rain, acting like a sponge.

The old tractor spun, coughed and sputtered, finally running smoothly after playing with the choke, same as always. I let the Ford warm up for a while at about three-quarters throttle, while Ron finished up with the other two cars. We decided not to let them idle; there wasn't really a need. We'd warm up with them when we were on the road. Rather, the others would. I'd be driving the van, which I left running to melt off the thick ice from the windows. I shoveled off the snow and ash around our doorway, peeling back the plastic from the original layer of snow. Once that was done, it was time to plow. Turning on the lights, Buck and Ada's eyes reflected back at me from across the field.

While I plowed a path from the barn up to the driveway and to the street, Ron shoveled snow away from the garage doors, in places that the plow could not easily get to. After about a half-hour, I was finally done. Ron had shoveled out a path to the north door of the house that was hidden by the wreckage of the second floor gable. The basement was on our list of places to get to today as well, although less adventuresome than actually leaving the street. After finishing his shoveling, Ron had filled the snowmelt barrels for wash-water and shut down the van. The upper ten inches of the snow were perfectly clean, with a mix of ash and snow in the lower four inches or so. Then, the solid layer of ash. The stratification was striking.

With the last swipe of the back blade, I headed back to the barn, widening out the 'road' that I'd plowed. Ron and I had talked about leaving the place more 'natural', in order to camouflage our location, but really, between the wood smoke and light and the dogs tearing about, there really wasn't any way to 'hide' in plain site. The fact that we had a tall fence around the place had always proved as good a deterrent as any. We'd chance it.

Libby had her first experience at collecting eggs, and managed to only step in one spot of steaming chicken manure. She managed to get six eggs, some of which were used in scratch pancakes, and the last of the bacon from the fridge. Karen said there was more bacon in the freezer, she thought the one in the garage.

It was now nearly seven. Karen cooked up a good sized stack of pancakes for the kids while the rest of us ate. I was scheduled to be first out, because I expected to have more trouble getting around than anyone else. I quickly unbolted the rear-most seat in the van, creating a cavernous space for my shopping trip. Ron rode with me up to the gate, and opened it for me. I drove out and he closed it behind me just as the sun was officially 'up' and the curfew lifted for the day.

Our street was untouched, the fresh snowfall over the ash pushing the light van all over the road. I finally made it to the arterial south of us, noticing that Pauliano's had a light burning in the kitchen, and smoke rising from their chimney. No other lights were burning down the street, and I only noticed one other home that showed any signs of activity since the quake.

I kept heading toward my target store, part of the strip mall across from the fire station, dodging downed trees and power lines along the way. All three fire trucks were outside, covered in tarps. Lights burned brightly in the station, and I heard a generator running. I saw one other vehicle on as I crossed into the mall parking lot, then I noticed the lines. There were about twenty-five cars in the lot, pointed at the store. A State Patrol van was at the door, and a small crowd gathered outside. Four armed MP types, in desert camouflage and helmets, stood at ready positions at both doors, scanning the crowd.

I parked at a respectful distance and got out of the van. I had a sidearm on, but not in a place that was easily accessed. I was hoping not to need it....ever. I walked slowly, as if stiff, and took my place in what seemed to be a line.

"Why aren't they opening?" A whining male voice came from my left. "It's gotta be past seven. C'mon! We're hungry!" Several more voices in the crowd agreed.

"Listen up now. This center will open when we get the word from our operations center, and not before," said the patrolman, not ready to take any crap from anyone.

"Sarge, call just in. We're good to go," said a voice from the state van.

"All right. Single file, starting here. These are the rules. Pay attention to them. This center will remain open until dusk. That does not mean you can shop all day long, however, or keep coming back. To enter, you must show evidence that you have cash money to pay, or a bank statement dated within the last thirty days and a checkbook that shows evidence that you have sufficient funds for your purchase. You are limited to one shopping cart per person, or one-hundred dollars, whichever comes first, excluding prescription drugs obtained with a proper prescription from the pharmacy in this store. This center does not have unlimited resources, and resupply is expected when the roads are clear. All right, five people at a time, you will have store escorts inside with you at all times, so don't think you can five-finger anything. All right, let's go."

The first five, three older men and two older women, not appearing to be related, all went inside the darkened store. The whiney male to my left continued to complain.

"You got a problem here, Mac?" a Marine gunny sergeant asked.

"My name's not Mac, asshole."

"Wow, you must have big brass balls to be speaking to a Marine Gunny that way, pardner," I said. I finally got a good look at the speaker. Too-skinny, long hair, dirty clothes, about twenty-five or so. My mind said, 'Loser.'

"F*ck off. I can talk anyway I like to. This is America."

"No, ass-wipe, this is Spokane, Washington under Martial Law. Martial means 'military,' in case your public-school education has let you down. And you seem to be doing a good job of pissing off the guys in charge. If I were you, I'd be thinking about apologizing."

"For what? Calling it like I see it?"

"No, for being an idiot."

189

Loser took one step toward me just as the Gunny grabbed his chest and lifted him off of the ground in a spin, placing him roughly on the snow and ash-covered ground. "Marine, detain this young man."

"Yes sir!" one of the other Marines responded.

The rest of the crowd gave the respect due, and there were no other problems while I was there. I received a nod from the Gunny. I nodded back.

My turn finally came to go in, escorted by an assistant store manager. Libby and Ron, Karen and I each had identical lists, so we weren't tasked with buying a large quantity of any one thing, which might look odd. We expected a dollar limit, so we were up against an immovable barrier there, however, since no ID record was being made, nor something so simple as a Sharpie permanent-ink mark on our hand or wrist, we theoretically, could go to as many stores as we could to fill out our list.

I grabbed a cart and made my way along the aisles, picking out a variety of things from the list, including sugar, salt, flour, spices, some beef, cold and flu medicines (expensive) and spices (ditto). The store manager ran a running tally on a small hand-held scanner, so he could tell me my balance on the run. Pretty efficient, overall.

"Any idea when more's coming in?" I asked, trying to make conversation.

"Nope." Was the curt reply. It seemed overly abrupt. Maybe the guy was having a bad day. I could understand that.

Within fifteen minutes of arriving inside, I was on my way out. We all made it a point to not be flashy in our dress, or with money, but appear as non-descript as possible. One-hundred and two dollars later, I was out the door.

The huge storage capacity of the van allowed me to stash all of my purchases in the area between the front seats and the middle seat, leaving the back for a second and possibly, third trip to another store. I kept an eye out as I loaded up. No sense in getting robbed now. I covered everything up with a black wool blanket, locked up the back doors, and went over to the Gunny to give him my thanks for his work.

"No problem, sir. Glad to give the young man somewhere to go. Hope it's warm in detention...."

"We haven't heard much about relief. Do you have any news?" I asked, feigning ignorance.

"Trucks supposed to be coming in tomorrow, but we haven't heard for sure yet. You fixed up OK?"

"Yeah, we'll make do. Kids aren't amused, though."

"I hear ya. I have two teenagers back at Camp Pendleton."

"Then this cool weather is a change for you."

He laughed, "Yes sir, Ten days ago I was in Tikrit. They brought the whole unit home on twenty-four hours notice. We knew we'd done a good job, but Hell, we never expected to come home two months early."

"Congrats. Welcome back. We can't thank you enough for what you guys have done over there. I lost one of my classmates over there, year ago Christmas."

"Marine?"

"Army engineer. Reserves. Sent over to build bridges."

"Tough break."

"Yeah. Good man. Take care, Gunny."

"You too, sir."

I headed back for the van, and decided to head up the road a little further. I was taking a chance, heading further 'out' than our plan, but I wanted to check one of the stores that miiiiiiight have no limits, and have a substantial portion of our list. Driving was a chore, with recently-cleared power lines and poles shoved to the side of the road, and barricades directing traffic around obstacles. At the busiest intersection in the Valley, a giant hole took up most of the southern half of the concrete intersection. It didn't take a brain surgeon to know that the sixty-inch sewer main had ruptured.

The car radio, AM only, told me that a stock market slide had begun, if I was correct in my assumptions, as trading curbs were already in place, meaning that at least two-hundred points had already been shed, if not more. This being Monday, only time would tell. There was no news of European or Asian markets. The radio also told me that arterial clearing would continue with snow and debris removal on outgoing roads and highways first, progressing to in-town streets.

I passed 'Rons', which I think was the oldest hamburger joint in the Valley, and still one of my favorite places. I spent a lot of time in the parking lot in high school, eating a Big R burger and a jamocha shake. Good to see it was still there, even though it was missing it's storefront glass.

Bingo. White Elephant was open. White E, as we called it, was originally a surplus store, hence the name. It had evolved into one of the best sporting goods stores in the area. The store was lit up pretty well, a number of Coleman lanterns lit and hanging from overhead wires. There was a pretty good crowd there too, all respectful. Funny how nice people are when you don't know who's armed and who's not. A number of clerks were holding clipboards, and checking them as people bought supplies.

The store didn't have a dollar limit in place, but did limit weapons purchases to two per adult. I didn't have enough money to buy one, even if I did want another gun. I did, however, want more ammunition if possible, if just for barter. I ended up with a shopping cart full of .22 long-rifle, four boxes of .45 ACP, and boxes and boxes of twelve gauge birdshot, deer shot and rifled slugs, topped off by five hundred rounds of 30.06, none of which I ever wanted to use. My old junior high school track coach was checking out the other line, and I waved at him as I left. The last time I saw him, I was getting an MRI on a smashed up elbow. He was getting one for lung cancer. Good to see he was still on this side of the turf. Tough guy, ex-Ranger.

I decided to head home and unload. Among the pleas and statements to seek shelter if your home was damaged or unheated, new reports of home invasion robberies and murders were taking place. Homeless, formerly living in the wooded areas around the city, decided that it was their time. The nearest murder took place twenty-nine blocks from our house, two blocks from our old church. More than fifty deaths had been credited to such invasions.

As I turned on to our street, the radio stated that several price adjustments had been made affecting heating oil prices, gasoline prices, and airline ticket prices, due to unforeseen increases in raw fuel costs. One possible reason was thought to be large advance orders and new contracts for fuel delivery....to China.

Monday morning,
January Sixteenth

I noticed as I turned onto our road that the convenience store had been boarded up with new plywood, although the gas pumps were still accessible. Hmmmm.

As I drove up the street, I stopped off at Pauliano's house. The garage door was open, and the Suburban was in the process of being loaded up. Looked like they were getting out.

"Hello, the house!" I called out as I hopped out of the van.

"Hello there Rick! How's everyone doing?" Joe asked in his thick Italian accent.

"Pretty well, considering. We also have some guests with us, so it's been interesting so far."

"I hear you had some trouble the other night."

"Word gets around."

"Get the bastards?"

"Yes sir. Four of them."

"Four! Good Lord. We'll remember them at Mass in any regard. What were they after?"

"Stuff that doesn't matter right now. TV's, stereos, you know."

"Crap, then. Not worth dyin' over."

"Yes sir. You and Joan getting out?"

"Yes. Joan and I were going up to see you to let you know, and ask a favor. We've decided to go see Don and Lorene in California until this warms up. Joan's having a hard time with the cold, and we're not exactly as mobile as we used to be."

"I understand. Do you want us to look after the place?"

"Please. There's the hens of course, and there's three roosters that need to be culled. We took care of one yesterday."

"Anything else?"

"No not yet. Although, Peretti is supposed to get me a couple-four piglets here, or was, next week. I'm not sure he'll be able to get through. He's out in Otis Orchards."

"I'll see if I can leave him a note, and let him know what's going on, in case I miss him. You sure about this, Joe? You're pretty well fixed up here, it seems."

"Yeah, it's time to go. A couple more days of this and Joan'll end up with pneumonia. She doesn't handle the cold like she used to up in Canada." Joe and Joan had met in Canada, sixty years before. They'd seen interesting things in their lives.

"OK. Anything else I need to know, or can I help load up?"

"No, we've got stuff pretty well loaded. We have lots of food, and the truck's got a full tank and two spares. We should be able to make it to southern Oregon without refueling. If you need it, there's spare gas out by the chicken shed, in the big tank I used to use for the tractor. Gas was fresh in November, and it's got preservative in it."

"Got it. We'll check up on the place a couple times a day, and get the windows boarded up. Looters don't knock."

"Do you have boards?"

"Some, but a lot of corrugated sheet metal and screws. It should work fine, and it's also noisy as hell when you try to pry it off."

"Oh, before you go, you take this box. We don't have room."

"What's in it?"

"Seven dozen eggs. We already packed ten dozen, and Joan boiled a bunch more."

"Wow! You sure?"

"Yes. Just look at this thing—there's no room!"

Joe was right. The full-sized Suburban was loaded—packed—to the ceiling, and the roof rack had a fabric tie-down bag on it.

After a few more minutes of talking with Joe, I said my goodbyes and went back up the road. I sure hoped he made it through OK.

The driveway gate was closed as I pulled in. Carl appeared from a hiding place on the porch, under part of the collapsed porch ceiling. He was carrying his scoped 10/22. John opened the gate—he appeared from the hedge off to the left. 'Good for you two,' I thought. No one told them to keep an eye out. Stupid decision, I thought. John had the other Ruger over his shoulder. I drove through the gate and straight back to the barn. The Ford and Jeep were already there. Ron came out of the barn, followed by Karen, Libby and the girls. The boys stayed up front with the dogs, who were wrestling in the snow under an apple tree.

"You OK? We were getting worried," Karen asked as she gave me a kiss.

'Yeah. No problem, why?"

"Look at the Jeep," she said. Four bullet holes pierced the top, drivers side window, and back window.

"Holy crap!" You all right?" I asked of Ron and Libby.

"Yes, but there is no way we're going out again. That happened on the way TO the store."

"Wow. Honey, did you have any trouble?" I asked Karen.

"Nothing like this, but it wasn't easy, either."

"Let's get this stuff inside. Time to rethink the game plan."

"Amen." Libby said.

I unlocked the side doors and we started unloading. I managed to get about half of my listed items at the grocery, as well as more than what I'd planned to be able to get at the sporting goods store.

"You didn't have any crowds? You got back fast," I asked Karen.

"Not hardly....I was lucky. The crowd was big, but they didn't have any money."

"Wow," Ron said. "You sure as hell didn't get this at the grocery," as he lifted a box of shotgun shells out of the back.

"White Elephant. Busy place too."

"They let you buy ammunition?"

"Yeah, no cops or soldiers there. The terms of Martial Law didn't say anything about getting in the way of commerce, more about law enforcement...but I expect that will change shortly. Besides, it looked like White E was only selling to their customer list.

"They keep a list?"

"Yeah, I guess. I didn't think about it too much. I loaded up what I needed, waved at one of the guys I knew, and paid cash. They didn't even check my ID. They were selling guns too."

"That doesn't sound all that smart."

"Yeah, but now that I think about it, if you're a thief, you're not going to buy a gun, are you?"

"Probably not, unless you're pretty gutsy."

"And if they have a regular list of folks that'd already been through the federal system, and they could prove they'd bought from them before, would you still sell to them?"

"Might. I don't know. No cops though?"

"Not yet anyway. They're usually closed on Sundays, but they probably had the store guarded all day Saturday and Sunday from looters. But honestly, I don't think that it'll be running this afternoon like it was this morning."

"Hmmm."

We finally got the last of the stuff in from the back of the van. Karen's load was already in the barn. It looked like she'd had good luck too.

"OK. Let's hear it. Who's first?" I asked.

"You." Karen and Ron said. "Our story's longer."

"OK." I recapped my visit to the store, including my conversations with the Gunny, the problem-shopper, and what I'd seen inside the store.

"The meat counter was all but empty. I got the last of the beef, a not-very-good looking package of frozen stew beef. Dairy and bread aisles too. About half of the wine was still there, but no beer, almost no pop. No canned soups or prepared foods at all. No candy bars, hard candy, nothing. So I had no problem in getting flour, salt, sugar, brown sugar, molasses, spices, that kinda stuff. The cold medicines were almost gone, and one of the other shoppers was looking at me as I looked over the last few boxes of Contac. I asked her if she needed some and she said yes, so I took two and let her have the other two. Picked up some more Airborne and some of the other stuff you had on the list. Got most of the stuff, before I hit the magic hundred-dollar limit."

"How did you keep track of the cost?"

"One of the managers had a little hand held scanner that gave us a running tally along the way. They only let five in at a time."

"Hmmm. They didn't do it that way at my store," Karen said.

"OK. Your turn. Let's have it."

"I left right after you did, and told Carl and John to keep an eye out. They went and got their twenty-two's, before I could say anything. I thought about it a sec and decided that since they both knew their guns, they'd be OK. John asked to borrow one of the big rifles, but since he'd never shot it before, I thought he should stick to a gun he knew."

"Good thinking." 'Damn straight,' I said to myself. 'How could we just leave and not tell them to keep a weather eye out?'

"Anyway, while you went to Safeway, I headed to Albertsons. The roads weren't cleared, and they're really rough. I put it in four-wheel-drive to make sure I didn't have any problems. I had to dodge a bunch of trees and couple of signs, but finally made it over to Argonne. The lines at the gas stations were stretched up the block. The store wasn't even open yet."

"The Shell station?"

"Yeah. Anyway, I got into the parking lot and parked away from the rest of the cars, where no one could hide. There were maybe two hundred people there, in two groups. Some Air Force reservists had their guns out and were guarding the place. If you had cash, you could get in line on the left. If you didn't, you went to the right. I guess a lot of people tried to pay with checks. The store wasn't ready for that."

"Ours was, or they said they were. I didn't see anyone pay with checks, though, and our crowd was much smaller."

"Anyway, once we were in--they let us in ten at a time--I started going down the list. Same thing you saw too. No cereal, beer, bread, chips, meat, or anything prepared. One guy was demanding that the deli open so he could have chicken for lunch. I honestly don't think the guy knew how to cook. He was standing there in a business suit!"

"I'm afraid there are a lot of people like that out there."

"Yeah. Anyway, again, no dairy, no bottled water, no TV dinners, no soups or stuff. I got a lot of the sewing stuff and some yarn, good amount of baking goods and cleaned up in the medicines, bleach, vitamins and 'ladies' items.'"

"Thank you for that. I hate buying that stuff."

"All guys do..." Ron said.

"Did you hit your limit?" I asked.

"Yeah, and then some. I had cash, and the checker said that if I really needed the stuff, it was OK with her. I slipped her a five dollar tip and she let me go with a smile. I spent one-fifty total, including the tip."

"Wow. I expect that filled your cart."

"Yeah, and the bottom rack too."

"What'd the Air Force guys say when you went back outside?"

"One of them escorted me to my car. Nice kid. Scared though. I don't think they're anywhere enough of them to keep that crowd under control. It was getting loud when I left. Someone threw something at the Expedition as I left. I heard it hit the side. The hotel across the street had busses in the parking lot—they were loading up people when I left."

"One thing though, this lady starts yelling at me. 'You should SHARE! Those that have should SHARE!!' She was obviously in the wrong line to get into the store. And wearing a skirt!"

"I'm glad it's over. OK, Ron, your turn."

"Well, ours was shorter. We didn't get to the grocery store. We did hit Ace down there on Montgomery and picked up some rope and some of the hardware items. Wax. Wicks, dishwashing soap, no kerosene though, or batteries, or flashlights, not that they were on the list. Anyway, we were crossing Montgomery, going over to that Super One across the street. There were about a hundred people in the parking lot, all lined up. Some sonofabitch jumped out from behind a bush and opened up on us with a handgun."

"Thank God that you weren't hit."

"No kidding. I heard the bullets come through the door right by my head."

"What happened to him?"

"I don't know. We took off to the east. The crowd started scattering and running. A couple of cops started after the guy, and opened up on him with shotguns, at least that's what Libby saw. I was busy trying not to get killed. We high-tailed it back here and said 'screw it.'"

"How did the grocery store look?"

"Empty. They were damn near cleaned out of everything—they had lights on inside and the shelves were pretty bare. Must've had a generator for the store."

"Well we're still in one piece at least. I have some other news."

"What's that?" Karen asked.

"Joe and Joan are leaving. They've asked us to look after the place."

"Really? Where are they going?"

"They're packed up and going down to Don and Lorene's. Aren't they in the Bay Area?"

"Yeah, I can't remember where though. Some small town inland. What about the chickens? And doesn't Joe raise pigs and turkeys too?"

"Just chickens for now. One of his Italian buddies was going to get him some piglets next week. Too early for turkeys, I think. I'll have to leave him a note."

"Is their place OK to leave? I mean, is it boarded up?"

"No, I told Joe I'd take care of it for him."

"OK. After all they've done for us, it'd be the least we can do."

"Agreed. Now, how 'bout something warm to drink? Anyone make coffee or tea?"

"Tea. On the stove," Kelly responded. She and Marie had been unpacking the new items, and were trying to find a place to store them.

"So, now what?" Karen asked.

"Welcome to the new 'normal'. Did you listen to the radio at all?" I asked.

"No, I didn't want the distraction."

"Can't blame you."

"Gas prices are going up in other parts of the country. The stock market trading curbs are in, which means that it's sliding downward, quickly."

"What's a 'trading curb?'" Marie asked.

"It's a limit on the amount of stock that can be traded by computer-program, or automated 'sell' calls. There are also 'circuit breakers' that shut down all trading for an hour if the Dow drops more than ten percent. If it drops twenty percent, it shuts down for two hours. If it drops thirty percent…"

"They stop for three hours." Marie chimed in.

"No. They stop for the day."

"What if it goes up by thirty percent in a day?"

"Then the brokers would be very happy."

"So they don't let you sell, but you can buy all you want?"

"Correct."

"That sucks. What if you really need to sell?"

"Tough," I said. "You'll have to wait."

"That's not fair!"

"That's correct. It's not. It is not supposed to be."

"It's cheating."

"Yes, it is. Libby, your daughter has a good grasp of the pitfalls of the stock market."

"She has a good grasp of what's right and wrong, too."

"Same thing."

Ron questioned, "So, worst case scenario, the entire market implodes. It's at ten-thousand something right now. At thirty percent per-day, it takes three days to reach bottom."

"No, your math is too simple. You're dividing the Dow by three, and taking away an equal part each day. It's more complicated. The first day, you're at 10000. Take away 30%. Then you're at 7000. Take away 30% again. You're at 4900. Take away 30%. You're at 3430. See my point?"

"Yes. It takes longer to get to the bottom."

"But the bottom hits, sooner or later. Worst case, full-speed stock market meltdown to where it 'should' be, might take seven trading days to get to a little more than 10% of the value of the peak. Maybe longer. Maybe a month. There's always somebody who'll want to buy, buying on the 'dips.' Calling the bottom isn't for sissies though."

"So where is the bottom? How do you tell?"

"They used to say that the bottom was thirty-five percent of the peak, but in a day's trading, that could be gone. With all the manipulations of the market over the past five years, it's impossible to say what the bottom is."

"You mean all the propping it up that's going on?"

"To put it kindly, yes. To be blunt, out-and-out arm-twisting on the part of the Government to maintain the economy."

"Consumer confidence."

"Yes. Not 'citizen confidence.' 'Consumer'. As if we were just shoppers and not citizens."

"Cramming it down our throats…"

"And us taking it willingly, keeping up with the neighbors."

"Damn."

"Oh, jeez. Almost forgot."

"What?" Karen asked.

"Present from Joe and Joan. In the front seat of the van. Big box, be careful."

"What is it?" She asked.

"That'd spoil the surprise. Just don't drop it."

In a minute, Karen came back in with the precious cargo.

"So do I wait for Christmas?"

"No, now's fine. Hope you like them." She opened the box.

"Oh my. How many?"

"Seven dozen."

"Looks like omelets for lunch."

Nine forty-five a.m.
Monday morning,
January Sixteenth

As Karen and Libby found places to stash the eggs, (They ended up in a big plastic crate with a sealing lid, out in the tool area) I flipped on the radio, more out of looking for something to do that didn't involve a lot of thought, or doing actual work. The schedule we'd been running was getting to me. I was also wishing I had a tall glass of real milk, something I rarely drank in 'normal' times. I had a cup of coffee instead. It wasn't remotely the same.

"....insurers, two of the largest in North America, declared insolvency this morning at eleven a.m., Eastern time. A federal investigation is expected, given the timing of the sudden bankruptcy declaration relative to the earthquake and volcanic eruption in the Pacific Northwest, and the fact that only two weeks ago, both firms reported substantial growth in their quarterly stock reports and filings to the Securities and Exchange Commission."

"What was that?" Karen asked as the broadcast went on.

"Some insurer's went tango-uniform this morning."

"What's 'Tango Uniform?" she asked, which I then explained politely, then she asked, "Why?"

"Probably didn't want to pay out a lot of money."

"Figures."

"Trading circuit breakers slowed trading in the markets this morning, with programmed trading curbs kicking in within the first half-hour of normal trading this morning. Within two hours of opening, automatic circuit breakers kicked in, shutting down trading for two hours. Trading is expected to resume within the next half-hour, with trading curbs remaining in place."

"In local news, major grocery stores in the city opened at seven this morning, and gasoline stations opened at ten a.m. Local officials instituted a buying limit of one-hundred dollars per customer, with cash and local checks being accepted at most locations. Even so, most stores have sold out of many high-demand items as of this time, although more supplies are expected within the day. Most gasoline stations that are open, are operating on portable generator power to provide gasoline to evacuation buses, emergency vehicles, and residents or visitors wishing to leave the region. Major arterials and highways that have been cleared include portions of Interstate ninety, Highway twenty-seven, U.S. two, and Highway one-ninety-five. These routes out of the city are open during daylight hours only for departing traffic, and in-bound supply, relief, and rescue operations only. Residents who may be away from Spokane or the Spokane area are not being allowed to return at this time."

"Federal efforts at relief to the region have seemingly kicked into high gear, with relief aircraft operations landing this morning at Fairchild Air Force Base and Spokane International Airport. Aircraft include military transports with supplies and equipment, personnel arriving in chartered commercial airliners, as well as United Parcel Service and FedEx cargo planes. These operations are expected to continue until further notice, including after dark."

"A reminder, that all sales of gasoline and grocery and retail items will cease at four p.m. this afternoon, and will resume on Tuesday morning. The dusk to dawn curfew is still in force, and will remain so until further notice."

Libby and the girls were putting stuff away, with Kelly occasionally stirring the pot of melt-water to break up clods of snow. It was a slow process, but once it was boiled for a few minutes, we could be reasonably sure that we wouldn't get sick from it. I had a 'thing' about clean water, after losing about fifteen pounds as a result of drinking what was purported to be 'clean' water while on a business trip abroad. Not a great way to lose weight.

The boys were still 'up front', keeping an eye on the street, while Ron was gathering up supplies for our afternoon to-do list. We'd have to get down to Pauliano's place and check the hens, collect any eggs that might be there, and try to get the house secured as much as we could. For that, we'd need the services of our little folding trailer, a four-by-eight platform that in summer, had wood sides for trips to Home Depot or the dump. I'd have to get it out of the spot by the carport across the field, get the sides back on it, and find a way to get it out of the field. The alternative was hauling sheets of ten by two foot corrugated metal several hundred feet, by hand. This would be a job for at least a couple of us, maybe all the men. At least that way, we could get it done quickly.

I set about gathering up my tools for the task: Cordless drill-driver and bits, two boxes of black drywall screws, four pairs of gloves, and a small step-ladder. Pauliano's had a couple big picture windows, and a bunch of smaller three-by-three windows for the bedrooms, baths and kitchen. The basement windows were all solid glass block with a small vent, so we wouldn't have to cover them unless they were broken.

Once I put my outdoor gear back on, I went across the field and assessed the trailer. With it's little wheels, it would probably hydroplane across all the snow and ice, until it got into a cleared area. I had about twenty pieces of two-foot by four-foot scraps of corrugated metal left, in addition to maybe thirty sheets of ten-foot metal, pulled off of the barn when I rebuilt the roof. I was going to recycle it someday, but never got around to it.

Ron came to help muscle the trailer around. It was stored folded up in half, and raised vertically, so that you could store it in your garage when not in use. Since my garage was filled up more often than not, my trailer lived outside. After ten minutes of trying to do it the way that was neat and tidy, we finally just dumped it over in the snow, unfolded it, and bolted on the sides. We'd have to get either the Jeep or the Expedition over to hitch up, and pull it the rest of the way out of it's hole, but with all that snow, it just wasn't going to happen any other way.

Once the sides were on, Ron and I loaded up the three foot pieces, and a half-dozen of the eight and ten-foot pieces of metal. I then tossed in the five-gallon bucket with the driver and screws and stuff, and we were ready to go. Ron told the wives we were heading down the road to take care of Pauliano's, and Karen handed him one of the radios. The boys had two others, and Karen said they hadn't seen anything since we came in.

After hitching up the Ford, and realizing that it's always better to hitch up BEFORE you load the trailer, we took off toward the gate. I asked John over the radio to get the gate for us, and told them to decide which one would stand watch over a lunch break, to 'spell' the other. No sense in getting them worn out, cold and tired of standing there when 'one' will suffice for patrol duties.

In a couple minutes, Ron and I were busy tacking on the metal over the windows. I grabbed a note that Joe had left me, and stuffed it in my coat to read later. I wanted to get this job done quickly and get on about the day. After about an hour, we had the work done. They had four broken windows, and two of the big picture windows had cracked at least one of the three panes of insulated glass. Joe's house had held up very well to the quake. As we finished up, I took a chance to read the note before we went back up to the house.

"Dear Rick and Karen—

We can't thank you enough for watching over the house and the livestock for us. The hens have five hundred pounds of feed, and some oyster shells and some powder for medicine if they need it. The feed is corn, oats, some alfalfa, fishmeal and calcium. Some folks use soybeans but I don't abide it. There's water in the cistern under the barn, and a hand pump. Should be plenty of water, even if the well pump doesn't come on for a while. I think it's five thousand gallons, so you should be good.

The hens are used to light, but without the electric, the egg production's gonna fall off quick. Feel free to cull out those roosters and a few hens if you want, I know that Joan won't miss them. The egg cartons are out there in the room to the left, and there's a candling light there too and matches.

There's gas out in the tank by the barn too. Should be almost three hundred gallons in the tank. The tank's hidden in the east end of the barn, behind a wood wall. The pump handle is just under the window. The hose is under the bench top. You'll see it fine.

If those pigs show up, there's a list on the stall wall for you that tells you what to do and what to feed them. Don't think they will, Peretti's pretty far out and probably has his hands full too.

You take care of those kids.

Signed, Joe"

"Did he get you all lined out?" Ron asked.

"I'll say. I thought I had gas stashed away. He's got a three-hundred gallon tank out there."

"Wow. Wonder why?"

"Used to be a contractor. Probably used it for his work trucks and stuff."

"Glad he kept it filled."

"Yeah, I hope we never need it."

"No doubt."

"Hey you two," Karen buzzed in my ear, "Soup's on."

"Be right there, babe. Lunch is served," I told Ron.

"Good deal. Hope she's got more of that soup."

"I think that's on the menu. After lunch I want to go over to that old guy's house next to the James's, over that way. Haven't seen them to talk to since, what, Saturday? I want to see if they need any more kerosene."

"Why don't we to that now? Won't take a minute, " Ron said.

"Works for me. Karen, you hear that?"

"I'll keep it warm…and I'll keep John and Carl from eating it all."

"Be right back."

We drove the Ford and the little trailer up the street and around the corner, pulling over in front of the house where we'd delivered some kerosene a few days before. I could hear someone in the garage, apparently trying to get the door open. Soon, the man-door opened, and the elderly gentleman appeared.

"Hello! How are you?" I asked. "Need any more kerosene?"

"Fair to middlin'. I'm trying to get the door open so we can get out, but the door's not having any of it. Kerosene's held out fine. Thank you again for that."

"You're welcome. Let's take a look at that door. Where you off to?" I asked as I looked in the garage. Big old Chevy Impala, rear wheel drive. 'Ugly in the snow,' I thought. The big garage door had an electric opener, and the emergency release had been pulled, but the door was frozen to the ground by the ice a few days ago.

"The shelter. We're done here. I can't keep the place warm enough, and the cold's getting to me and the wife. My son left Saturday night for the north side where our grandkids are at. Haven't heard from him since.'

"Do you plan to stay at the shelter?"

"Yeah, that's the plan for now."

"We'll give you a lift. No point in leaving your car down there too. Tell you what, we'll meet you in half an hour, and drive you over. When things warm up, we'll check on you and see if you want to come home. OK?"

"That would be wonderful. By the way, I'm Bob Sorenson."

"Rick Drummond. This is Ron Martin."

"Pleased to meet you both. I'll tell Ellie to get her things together. We'll see you in a bit."

"Be back soon."

"Another Knight In Shining Armor moment?" Karen asked me quietly.

"Yes, fair lady."

"You're a dear."

"Aw, shucks ma'am."

Carl opened the gate for us as we hit the driveway.

"Get some lunch yet?" I asked.

"Nope, I told John to go first."

"I'll save you some," as I grinned.

We drove back out to the barn, Buck trying to catch the trailer and hop on it. Ada was taking a much more casual approach to keep up with us.

We had more of Karen's tomato soup, cold water, and some leftover cornbread. We both ate fairly quickly either due to hunger or enjoyment. The latter for me, the former I suspected, for Ron.

We unhitched the trailer and stored it near the gate from the field to the yard, in case we needed it again. The bucket of tools ended up in the back of the Ford, I suspected I'd be doing more metal work either on our house or one of the other neighbors' places. It seemed our neighborhood was empty.

Ron and I got back in the Ford and Carl again opened the door as John took his place in 'patrol' duties. We picked up the Sorensons, who had a suitcase each, pillows, blankets, and winter coats, and took them over to the elementary school, now a shelter.

As we headed into the parking lot, we were greeted by the sight of sixteen school buses, loading with we assumed, shelter residents. Heading somewhere else.

"What's this about?" said Mr. Sorenson.

"Anyone's guess. Let's find out," I replied, parking next to a Sheriff's Deputy cruiser.

"Ron, grab a couple of those bags. I'll help Mrs. Sorenson on this ice."

"Gotcha."

We headed into the school through the main entry, and into the school office, which was now the registration center for the shelter. The broken glass had been swept up and windows covered with wood or plastic sheet. I was about to ask about the buses when Mike Amberson came around the corner and said, "We don't have room for your kind here, mister."

I immediately started laughing. "Thanks. I love you too, bud."

"Everyone doing OK?" Mike asked.

"Yep, Just helping our neighbors get over here. Their house got cold and they wanted to get somewhere warm."

"Welcome to you both. C'mon into the office, and we'll get you signed in. We're trying to make sure we know where all the residents are, so we can have relatives get in touch with you, and to get a head-count."

"That'd be fine, young man." Mr. And Mrs. Sorenson took a seat at the secretary's desk, where Karen used to volunteer when our kids attended here.

Mike, Ron and I moved out to the hall, and down from the office. "How are things going, really?" I asked quietly.

"Going to Hell in a bucket," Mike replied.

"Really. So Ron's Jeep getting shot up this morning wasn't an isolated incident."

"That was you? Glad you're OK. The guy that did it's warming up a slab downtown. And no, not isolated. Increasingly a problem, becoming widespread."

"What about the buses?"

"They're voluntary evacuees. We can't keep them warm enough here with the building in this kind of shape. We had three hundred in here last night, and we can only handle about fifty the way we should."

"What about supplies?"

"The shelter's OK, but we're sending supplies on the buses with the evacuees. They're headed for warmer weather."

"Where?"

"California. Sacramento area and south."

"Holy smokes."

"You gotta remember, the west side's sucking up all available resources right now. We're gonna have to make do."

"I guess that makes sense."

"You got everything you need?"

"Yeah, we're good. We made a little trip to the stores this morning, got some groceries and medicines and stuff. I made a visit to the White Elephant too."

"I know. I saw the van there. The Guard closed it down at eleven."

"I figured they might." I forgot, the van was kind of a distinctive vehicle. There were only a few left, and only one—mine—painted the way it was.

"They're stretched way too thin to cover everything. Between the grocery stores, the sporting goods places, and all of the other retail targets, there's too much to cover and nowhere near enough manpower. They literally don't have the people in this part of the world to deal with this. And the majority of what they do have is on the other side of the state, dealing with that mess."

"So, worse before better," Ron said.

"Yeah. Afraid so. Much worse. I gotta go. Four more shelters to check before curfew. Get home and stay low. I'll try to send a deputy up your street every once in a while."

"Thanks. We're keeping watch at night, on our property, in case we see someone coming with bad intentions."

"Got a radio?"

"Just FRS's."

"Gimme your frequency. I'll tell the patrol deputy to get a hold of you when they're on the way. We monitor those now too, like citizens-band nine, for emergencies."

"Here's the frequency and code," I said as I gave him a business card with my code and the so-called scrambler code on the back. Contrary to popular belief, anyone on a frequency that you were transmitting on could hear you talk, but couldn't talk back to you or your group, without the CTCSS code.

"Good. Gotta run. Nice to see you."

"You too. Watch your ass."

"Always do," Mike said as he hit the exit door.

"Let's go. We've got stuff to do."

"Yep. And maybe there's some soup left over."

"Good luck with that."

2 7

As we left the shelter, we noticed the long line of people waiting for food at the community center food bank, to the west of the school.

"We're what, three days into this and people are in bread lines?" Ron said.

"Too bad there's no bread," I said as we walked to the car. "Wait a sec. I know that guy. Let's go see him for a minute."

"The guy in the digital camo?"

"Yeah. He's my cousin's boy. I guess that makes him my second cousin."

Matt was about twenty-four, just out of the Navy, I'd heard through my cousins' Christmas card. I'd talked with him last, years before, and had a long talk with him about his finances. I knew from talking with my uncle that he hadn't heard a word of what I had told him.

"Matt! How you doing?"

"Rick! Good to see you," Matt said, plainly uncomfortable to see me.

I knew that he didn't live in the neighborhood, which made me wonder why he was here. He had a box of canned goods and was heading towards a big, new Yukon. There was a young woman inside, and a child in the backseat. I assumed a girlfriend, and either her kid or 'theirs', but I knew he wasn't married, or if he was, my cousin didn't speak of it, but then again, my cousin lived in Denver now.

"Heading out to the lake place. Just topping off the supplies."

'Pretty meager supplies,' I thought to myself. "Made it through things OK?"

"Yeah, we're fine....just decided the lake place is better than the apartment. I better get going. Nice to see you. Tell....tell Karen hello."

"Will do. Stay safe."

"We're fine. Bye," he said as he closed the door.

"What the heck was wrong with him?"

"Acute embarrassment."

"Why?" Ron asked.

"About a conversation I had with him about five years ago. He was just out of basic, making a ton of money, no expenses to speak of, living on base, you know. He was getting his standard pay, overseas pay for TDY—temporary duty—and when the war started, combat pay while they were on missions. I told him that he could easily be a millionaire if he started then, and just did some basic, common sense investing, and wise spending. He was actually making more money that I was, and I had him by twenty years."

"Didn't take the advice, right? Nineteen-year-old's rarely do. I know I didn't," Ron said as we got back in the car and started back home.

"Yeah, me either. I was hoping, though."

"What'd you tell him?"

"Save some money for a house. Buy 'a' vehicle that he'd have until the wheels fell off. Pay for it with cash. Don't buy toys. Invest in appreciating or undervalued items. Buy tools. Learn how to use them. Don't hire done what you can learn to do yourself. Stuff like that."

"And he blew it."

"Yeah, pretty much. New vehicle every year, and not cheap ones. He started off with a Mustang GT. Figured out that that wouldn't haul a new dirt bike. Sold it. Bought a Nissan four-by-four standard cab pickup, then jacked it up with big tires and put a supercharger on it. Wouldn't haul a four-wheeler. Bought an enclosed trailer for that. Got a girlfriend, bought a new Cherokee. Then a ski boat. And a home theater system with the big flat panel. Now, a Yukon."

"That wasn't just a Yukon. That was the Denali version."

"So, OK, what, fifty thousand dollars?"

"In that neighborhood. Still had temporary plates on it."

"And every time he bought one off those cars, he'd buy a new one, then trick it all out with aftermarket stuff. Didn't have any of them more than a year or so."

"Expensive mistakes."

"Yeah. Especially since he probably was upside down in each of the cars, then financed the debt again with the new purchases. I can only imagine what his credit card debt looks like."

"And he said he's in an apartment?"

"Yeah, I thought it was a duplex."

"So he's heading to a lake place? In this weather?"

"That's what he said. That's another story. Place is over on Upper Twin Lakes, his dad's. Denny lives down in Denver full-time now, has for about five years. Used to come up to vacation for a while, then Matt pretty much took over the place—got into a falling out with his dad over that, I don't know if they've reconciled yet. Last time I was out there, it was a really nice setup. The wiring had been updated, had a woodstove, well, really just a summer cabin. I heard Matt had new water put in and capped the well, took out the woodstove and put in electric. Still just a summer cabin, but still….."

"He made it more convenient. Not better. And all-electric? How's he figuring on heating it now? Magic?

"Yep. Well, what's this?" We'd turned back onto the street and were heading back to the house. There were two police cars—one Deputy, one State Patrol—at the next intersection. They appeared to be checking ID's on all cars.

"We'll know in a second."

We were second in line. The car in front of us, a Subaru Outback, was being searched. Ron and I looked at each other for a second. I had my sidearm on, and I knew that Ron had a big ol' skinning knife on his hip. The trooper came toward the Ford and I rolled the window down.

"Step out of the car please, gentlemen, and stand on the curb over there."

"Yes sir, what's up?"

"One moment please. Just step out of the car."

"Yes sir."

Ron and I both got out of the Expedition, and walked to the corner and stood on the curb. The Trooper unlocked the doors, and he was joined by another officer. They did a cursory search of the vehicle, under seats, under the floor panel in the back, glove boxes, under the hood.

The deputy looked at a bag of stuff in the back of the Expedition. "Do you have a receipt for the purchases of those items?"

"That stuff? No, it was salvaged out of the house after the quake and not unloaded."

"Would you please show me the contents? Slowly."

"Yes sir."

I opened the bag up, and slowly took a stack of my daughter's clothes out of the bag. The Trooper had his hand on his nine-millimeter the whole time, and another officer was looking at us, not the bag.

"See, these are all 'used.' From my daughters' room."

"Thank you gentlemen. You may go now."

"What are you looking for?"

"We had a patrol car shot up this morning in an incident at Wal Mart. The officer was wounded, and can't give us a description of the shooter. His service weapons and hand-held radio were stolen, and the suspects came this way."

"Understood. Any idea of what kind of car, or how many?"

"No." Ron and I both raised our eyebrows.

"One more thing to watch out for."

"Yes sir. Thank you for your cooperation," the Trooper said as he went to check the next car.

"Great." I said as I got back in the car.

We arrived home a few minutes later, Carl getting the gate for us. He was taking the afternoon shift, and John would relieve him at two p.m.

We gave Karen and Libby the lowdown on our visit to the shelter, and running into Matt and his 'significant other' at the food bank. And the officers' checkpoint.

"Kids' a dope," Karen said. "Always has been."

"No argument there, he's pretty much followed his father's example." Denny, Matt's father and my cousin, had been 'stuff' oriented all of his life, and was one of those people that demanded constant entertainment. New things, new job(s), new sports, new wife...

"The girls have been busy getting the wash-water refilled. We had a talk with the kids about their clothing. They're used to changing all their clothes every day. That's not practical anymore, both due to the lack of clothes for the Martins, and the lack of laundry facilities. So, if you've got wet clothes, hang 'em up to dry by the stove and rotate them when they're really dirty. Already gave them the lowdown on underwear and socks. Consider yourself warned," Karen said.

"Yes drill sergeant sir!"

"Quit, or I'll smack you."

"Promise?" Ron said.

"What are the girls up to this afternoon?" I asked.

"Not much, we've put away all the stuff from the store, but we really need to re-arrange in here to make it more livable. What do you have in mind?"

"I thought you could show them how to grind some grain into flour. I know we don't need it right now, but it would be a good thing to occupy some idle time."

"Where are the grain mills?" We had two, an old Back to Basics, and a Corona that I used for coarse grinding cornmeal. Both, bought off of eBay.

"Up in the cupboard, above the bench over there."

"You have grain grinders? Why am I not surprised." Libby said.

After remodeling the kitchen, most of the old cupboards and wall units had ended up in the shop. I'd put 'shop' stuff in some of them, but most of them were either empty or had old 'kitchen' stuff in them, mismatched mugs, coffee, or other things I used when working on a project.

"There should also be a box in the woodshop from Mom's place, with a bunch of old baking pans. I know that one of them has a slug of bread loaf pans in it, including those little miniature ones."

"Good. Now what about refrigeration. It's not going to stay cold forever, and food's going to spoil."

"We'll work on it. What's the weather supposed to do for the next couple of days?"

"Warmer tomorrow. They said rain by tomorrow night."

"OK, we'll assume they're right for a change. We'll have to get power for the fridge in here, and maybe we can retrieve the bar fridge from the basement."

"What about the one from the kitchen?"

"That's gonna be tough, with the porch floor down. Also can't get through the dining room because of the chimney brick and plaster. We might be able to bridge over the porch with some lumber, but even so, with all the snow we can't get it out here."

"Oh. I didn't think about that. The small fridges will probably do. Can you get into the tent trailer soon?"

"Maybe. You're thinking the ice-box?" The previous owner of our ancient Coleman was a Survival School instructor at Fairchild. He'd built a portable ice-box for the trailer, and had upgraded it with some other good ideas too. The ice box was just one of them.

"Yep. If it's cold enough outside tonight, we can make some big blocks of ice in plastic bags, and that'll help with the coolers, too."

"Good idea. Hadn't thought about that." We had three or four big camp coolers out in the barn, and we'd only had to use one so far for cooling stuff from the house fridge that'd been salvageable.

"What's new on the radio? I haven't listened much."

"Markets' way down, those circuit breakers you talked about kicked in. Gold's up, silver too. I heard a snip about price increases," Libby said.

"No surprise there. It's almost two. Let's listen in." I switched on KLXY.

"Sounds good," Ron said. "Got any more of that tea?"

"Just making a fresh pot. It's steeping now. Should be ready in a few minutes."

"OK. What's new, Rick?"

"Carbon monoxide deaths. You'd think people would figure it out."

"Yeah, seems like the dumb people are self-eliminating," Ron said.

"Gene pool. Getting cleaned."

"......international discussion of the solvency of the financial system of the United States today. Bankers in Brussels discussed the potential of a wholesale default of the United States on international obligations, and punitive measures that the international banking community would be forced to take should the U.S. renege on debt obligations. "

"In the markets just before the close, trading circuit breakers kicked in this morning, halting trading after a significant decline in the thirty industrials. At the close, the Dow was at seventy-seven-

fifty-one, and the S&P five hundred declined to just over eight hundred, and the NASDAQ tested lows at fifteen-fifty. "

"That's gotta be almost thirty percent...for all of them on one day," I said.

"In precious metals news, gold and silver both increased today on the decline of stocks and bonds, with gold rising in a dramatic one-day price increase of nearly twenty-eight percent, rising to seven hundred thirty-three dollars per ounce. Silver closed at twelve oh-five at the close."

"The President and the Fed Chairman are in meetings at this hour to discuss the looming financial crisis and rampant price increases seen since Saturday. In Chicago, less affluent areas of Los Angeles, Dallas-Fort Worth, Atlanta, and Philadelphia, minor civil unrest has been reported at grocery stores where food stamps have been refused by store operators. No reason has been given for the seemingly coordinated effort on the part of store owners to accept cash only. Fuel price increases, too have resulted in minor problems at gasoline stations."

"From the Pacific Northwest, local reports from our correspondents on the ground report widespread evacuations, many on foot, from the Seattle and Bellevue regions, and widespread devastation in the areas where mudflows raced down Mt. Rainier. Up to fifty-five thousand have been confirmed dead, with many thousands still missing as recovery crews still search the region. It appears that the majority of the Boeing factories in those areas have been completely destroyed, and reports of the collapse of the seawall under the waterfront piers on the Seattle waterfront have been confirmed, further adding to the devastation in that city. Military bases in the area also report significant damage, including Naval Air Station Bremerton, the Bangor Submarine base, home of numerous Ohio-class ballistic missile submarines, McChord Air Force Base, and the Army installations at Fort Lewis and Camp Murray. The U.S.S. Carl Vinson, home at Bremerton for a training operation, has been seen from the air, covered with a coating of ash and apparently is being swept clean by a virtual army of Naval personnel."

"In Richland, Washington, no report has been released on the reactor scram from the Columbia Generating Station in Hanford, north of Richland. The reactor apparently shut down Saturday morning as a result of power failure and the earthquake, but no official report has been made since that time. Observers in the area reported that extensive plumes of steam, far larger than normal, were seen all day Saturday, and that another building on the Hanford Nuclear Reservation, apparently used as an automated building due to high amounts of radioactivity present for its operation, had partially collapsed. This cannot be confirmed by independent sources, and repeated requests made to the US Department of Energy for comment have gone unanswered."

"Now back to our local affiliates on the network for local news. This is ABC News."

"In local news," the local announcers were finally back in place, *"continued unrest has been reported in several parts of the city, with several deaths resulting from looting, robbery, and attempted robbery. Police and military officials report that overall, food purchases and gasoline sales have been peaceful. A reminder to listeners, all local sales of retail items, including food, building materials, and gasoline will end at four p.m. today, and that a strict dusk to dawn curfew will remain in place until further notice."*

"Officials at Sacred Heart, Valley General and Deaconess Hospitals report that over fifteen thousand injuries have been treated since Saturday, and that the death toll has risen to over eleven thousand for Eastern Washington and North Idaho cities reporting in, including those who have been injured or have died as a result of cold, exposure, or accidental death due to carbon monoxide poisoning. A new outbreak of influenza also seems to be affecting the elderly, with several unexpected deaths occurring within the last eight hours."

"FEMA and local emergency management officials have provided numerous shelter residents care, and in many cases, the opportunity to leave the region due to the cold and the inability to deal with so many refugees....."

"Did he say 'refugees?" Libby said.

"Yeah." Ron said.

"......looting in the Spokane Valley, with one State Patrol officer killed. No suspects have been apprehended at this time."

"In a report from North Spokane, soldiers with the Washington National Guard and City of Spokane police officers shot and killed four men who refused to disarm or lower their weapons while refueling at the Conoco station on the Newport Highway. Amateur video of the shootout illustrates a heavily loaded Ford pickup, in camouflage paint, pulling into the gas pumps at the station, which is being guarded by police and military personnel. The four assailants are seen getting out of the vehicle with handguns and rifles drawn, as the driver begins to fuel the vehicle. When confronted by the military to lower their weapons, three of the assailants raised their guns and the military and police opened fire, killing three immediately, with the driver ducking for cover behind the drivers door before being mortally wounded."

"According to an eyewitness on the scene, the driver stated before he died that the four men were afraid that the government was taking over, and that they were just trying to leave the city. The driver passed away before medical treatment could save him. The vehicle was loaded with camping gear, freeze-dried foods, water, and other survival supplies."

"Jesus," I said.

"They just shot them down?" Karen asked.

"Damn straight. You don't point a gun at someone unless you intend to use it. These guys made that one mistake. Well, more than one. They should've been out of town by now, if they were going. They also should've used respect and restraint when dealing with authority. Suicide by cop."

"I bet that'll be all over the news," Libby said

"Yeah. Especially in the Blue States, Evil Government and all," I replied.

"Or the other way, the evil of guns."

"Yeah, that's probably the way they'll spin it. Poor bastards," Ron said.

I reached over and shut off the radio and looked at it for a few seconds. "Better get to work. Stuff to do."

Monday, Three p.m.
January Sixteenth

John was keeping an eye on things on the streets in front of the house, while Carl warmed up and got a snack. Before Ron and I went about our respective tasks before dark, we came up with another item to do today, and that was to get proper observation posts put together for the comfort and concealment of those doing the watching. More concealment, than comfort, for certain.

Far from a military operation, and more akin to a kids' fort, John and Carl had pulled some old plywood from the snow-covered pile of stuff destined for the dump, and grabbed a couple of very weathered wood pallets for side walls and a floor. John was sitting in the 'shelter', on a piece of cardboard, well hidden from the street with a mix of evergreen shrubs and groundcover surrounding the little box. None of it was nailed together, and there was really no way to protect the occupant from hostile fire, without significant effort and a good chance of making it a visible target.

Taking the opposite approach—meaning, stealth and not protection---we decided that two locations for observation—and not patrol—would be preferred. One located near the house but not in it or on the front porch (which had a low wood-siding wall all the way around it), another further south, providing a view to the south that was not possible from the house due to trees and shrubs. With the two locations, we could keep an eye on all road-approaches to the house. This of course, completely ignored the back property line and areas out of sight from either the barn or the observation points. We were hoping that we wouldn't be scouted from that side, and that the fence around the field would protect us. Of course, this was wrong, but we didn't know that at the time. People drove. They didn't come on foot, did they?

Our property was once part of a much larger parcel, sliced up over the years and subdivided as farming became obsolete or cost-prohibitive in a suburban setting. We were left with a parcel that was a little under two acres, twice as deep as wide, and the largest parcel left on the road. Behind us, several homes, one now vacant and for sale, one evacuated, one belonging to our friend Dan, who was now living in his travel trailer due to the damage to the house. Their lots were about a hundred and fifty-feet deep, and at least that wide.

To our north was Brad's house, empty due to his being out of town when the quake hit. To his north, a burned down house. To our northeast, our neighbor Tim's house, which was heavily damaged. Tim was out of town in the Tri-Cities for the weekend. Across the street, the burned out foundation of the Long's. To our southeast, a partially collapsed house that belonged to a single guy, who tended bar at the Coeur d'Alene Casino in Worley. He hadn't made it home after the quake. And finally to the south, the vacant Woolsley's house. They were in Monroe, north of Seattle for a car show. We were almost completely surrounded by empty houses. From our driving up and down the street earlier in the day, it was apparent that few, if any of the twenty or so houses on the street were still occupied.

'Strength in numbers,' I thought. 'And we're weak.'

Ron and I outlined for the boys the overall design, and let them have at it. They scrounged some more lumber and I knew that at least for the post by the house, some of the wreckage from the north gable could be used....just a pile of lumber, no need to pay attention to it....was the thought. We got them set up with some sixteen-penny nails, hammers and odds and ends, and they went at it. Carls' space was next to the house, right north of the porch, amongst some evergreen laurel that I'd planted fifteen years ago. His vantage point looked right down the cross-street, and covered the north as well, which was impassable to vehicles due to downed power poles and several large trees.

From the barn, I had John retrieve a large stack of old black five-gallon paint buckets that we used in the summer for weeding. I had both of the boys fill the buckets with dirt, about half-full, with some of the softly frozen soil from underneath a pile of beauty bark I had in the field...which was also going to be the pit for the outhouse.

Then, I had them load them in the trailer, and we drove several hundred pounds of dirt up toward the front of the house. They off-loaded the buckets, and put them inside their 'rooms' for a very makeshift barrier against a stray shot. Better than nothing, but not by much. It would only protect you if you were plastering yourself to the pallet, and then only from small arms. We'd come up with something better later, depending on how things went. The intention though, was to look and not shoot. I hoped we were right in our planning. Both of the outposts were big enough to sit up in, while seated on the 'floor', but not sit on a chair.

While the boys filled buckets and built their observation posts, Ron got back to work on the outhouse. We'd used a combination of three-quarter inch plywood sheets that I'd salvaged from our office remodel, some oriented-strandboard, and a bunch of odd-sized two-by-fours for the construction. The roof was a piece of OSB, but hadn't been shingled yet, and the sheet had a couple of holes in it. By the time I showed up to help Ron, he'd already tar-papered the roof and was shingling it with some mis-matched asphalt shingles left over from the barn. I reminded him before he got too far, that we could put a vent-pipe in through the seat area, to give the fumes somewhere to go. We used a hunk of downspout for that, a piece that I'd bent up before I had a chance to install it on the barn. We sealed up the hole in the 'seat' that the vent went through with some caulking. Seemed overkill, since the 'seat' hole was so big.

After a lot of digging through stuff in the barn, I found the new toilet seat, cleaned out of my Mom's place after she passed away. It'd lingered in the shop over there for years, after she decided that 'padded' seats were nice. (I hated them. Always felt weird.)

Once the hole was big enough, about three feet square and almost as deep, we grabbed the boys and we slid and lifted the outhouse over the hole. Ron then christened it. I remembered that I'd have to dig out my paperwork on how to best maintain an outhouse. That paperwork was in my iMac, in the basement, which was my next target for salvage. The boys went back about their tasks, and took the pruning shears from the tool room to further camouflage their outposts.

Karen and Libby asked me to start up the generator, so that we could again charge the batteries, and so that Ron could check out the status of the wiring from the generator panel throughout the barn. We'd also check out the panel from the barn to the garage, thinking we might be able to back –feed the garage freezer from the barn. We already knew that the freezer in the basement, assuming it was OK, would have to run off an extension cord—the electric meter, weather-head, and the feeder lines into the panel in the basement were all lying in the yard, on the north side of the house. The gable collapse had taken them out.

Ron checked the continuity of the circuits in the barn with help from Kelly and Marie, who were very thankful to have a break from the grain mills. Ron used a combination of a short-circuit tester I bought for use on our cars, and a multi-meter that I bought from Harbor Freight a few years ago. He was able to make sure that all of the generator circuits checked out OK, but wasn't able to confirm the lighting circuit that fed from the garage. Something was up with that feed.

At least now, we could get a generator hooked up and power us for what we needed, without running extension cords all over the place.

While Ron took care of diagnostics, I went up to the greenhouse to see what I could do about getting some of the snow off of it, and propping it up. It was never designed to handle this much snow, or ice, let alone volcanic ash. After considerable digging, I got the door open, and managed to get some of the snow off of the roof, and propped up the mid-rib in the arch with a couple of eight-foot two by fours. The ice, arriving before the snow and ash, acted like a hard-shell over the thin plastic. I still have no idea why the thing didn't completely collapse. I think I had a hundred-fifty bucks in it, including the pressure-treated base frame, the three-quarter-inch PVC pipe, fittings, and the skin. It extended our growing season for a few crops by two months on both sides of the frost.

Next up, after the greenhouse, was trying to get some of the debris cleared from the side of the house, which had covered the door into the basement. None of the door was visible, buried under roofing, roof framing, siding, and sheathing. Seven feet deep.

I'd armed myself with a large metal pry bar from the garage, and a smaller 'wonder bar' much more suited to nail pulling. After about twenty minutes, I'd managed to get the top of the door exposed, the glass in the storm door shattered from the debris. Carl and John joined me, and eventually Ron. It was nearly dark by the time we had most of the wood, roofing and siding cleared from the door, enough to open the inner door, but not cleared to open the storm to the 'outside'. I smashed what was left of the wood and glass insert panel, and I could then get to the inner door. Fishing through my pocket, I dug out my wad of keys, and unlocked the deadbolt, and shoved the door open with difficulty. Karen had a habit (a bad habit, let me reinforce) of piling stuff up on the landing to the basement. I assumed that's what was blocking the door. I wasn't disappointed.

About the time I was ready to go have a look at the north half of the basement, things got interesting. We heard a honk at the fence, and we looked around to see a little white and rust Mitsubishi pickup with a monster ham antenna, at the fence. None of us were on 'patrol' or 'watch' or whatever, and were surprised if not downright startled. The boys both grabbed their twenty-twos. The driver emerged slowly on the far side of the truck.

"One of you Mr. Drummond?" he asked through the wire fence.

"Yes sir. That'd be me," I responded.

"I've got a message for you over my two-meter from a relative of yours."

"Great. My name's Rick."

"Aaron Watters. I live over on McDonald. I got this message last night before I pulled the plug on the radio. Today, we can't transmit or receive except what the government lets us. We're now using ham for RACES operations....that means emergency communications for the government. Anyway, got this message from one of my buddies up on Five Mile. From a guy named 'Alan.' No last name."

"My brother-in-law."

"Anyway, here's the message: 'G's house down. Staying here. All alive. L&R's house burned, L&R family missing. Reply via ham.' That make sense?"

"Yeah. Perfectly." I looked at Ron. He understood.

"Any reply Mr. Drummond?"

"Will you be able to get through?" I asked.

"Yeah, eventually. Might be a few days though."

"Tell them: 'All OK. L&R here. Living in barn, OK though. Watch looters. X'd 4 here.'"

"Got it. That all?"

"Ron, you have anything?"

"No. We don't have anyone else in town. Can you get a hold of the coast yet?"

"No, not yet. Probably won't for a while, from what I'm hearing."

"No thanks, then."

"OK. You folks going to stay?"

"Yes sir. This is home."

"I know how you feel. Better go. Curfew's on in about ten minutes."

"Thank you, Mr. Watters."

"Glad to help. You watch yourself now, wolves are a'prowlin.'"

"Understood."

Mr. Watters turned around and headed back off to the east. Ron was stoic, just learning that their 'new' home had burned. It had been a long-time coming, and I don't even think all the boxes were unpacked yet.

"C'mon. I'll help you tell Libby."

"What are we going to do?"

"Stay here."

"Yeah. Nothing to go home to."

"It'll be all right," Ron heard me, but wasn't buying it. I doubt I would've either. After twenty years of marriage, and all the accumulated memories one has in that time, to lose one's home.....must be devastating.

"And I'm sure we're not insured for earthquakes."

"Me neither."

"Yeah, but at least your mortgage is paid off. We still owe a hundred and a half on the new place."

I didn't have an answer for him there. I had no idea what he, or tens of thousands of others, would do.

We went back to the barn, walking silently, the only sound the crunching of the ice and snow under foot. Ada and Buck were off on a chase again, out by the back property line. The overcast reflected our moods: Dark grey and lowering.

We finally reached the barn, and went in through the store room. We broke the good news first to Karen, that her Mom, older brother and his family were all OK. Ron then told Libby about their home being destroyed by fire. She spun on her heels and went into the woodshop, crying. Soon Marie and John joined her in a hug as she sobbed.

There really wasn't anything we could do about it, except move on. In my increasingly cynical mind, I thought to myself, 'it's just a house.' Then I remembered what I'd taken from my wrecked home: Karen's wedding dress. Photo albums. Hand me downs from generations past. Our history.

I left the Martins in the woodshop and quietly closed the door most of the way, and turned on the little battery operated TV in the storeroom. Live news continued non-stop, whether it was news or not. They played the video of the shoot-out at the video store, unedited. I could imagine what it looked like in color, all that blood on the snow.

The news reported that the all stores county-wide had been closed at three p.m. due to a shooting at a grocery, where a man walked out without paying, and when confronted drew a gun on the police. More looting happened immediately, and the military units and local police rapidly found themselves outnumbered and withdrew, along with the store personnel.

The store was stripped clean in a half hour.

"Stores are now scheduled to re-open if possible on Tuesday morning, at ten a.m. Stores that will reopen will be listed at each public shelter. National Guard troops will check ID of all shoppers to make certain that no hoarding is taking place, and that shopping limits are enforced."

"In other news, local power and water companies continue to assess the damage caused by the earthquake in the region. Damage done to local dams has been reviewed, and repair plans are in the works at this time. Much larger problems lie in the loss of miles of transmission towers in the Columbia Basin, that transmit power from the hydroelectric dams on the Columbia River throughout the region. Officials have stated that most power generation stations have been damaged to some degree, but that power generation should begin within four days."

"Good! We'll have power!" Carl said.

"No, they said 'power generation' not 'power distribution.' Listen to the words, not what you want to hear, bud."

"Right."

"....systems have been analyzed within parts of the Spokane area, and drinking water has been confirmed to have been contaminated by water seeping in through broken lines. County Health Department workers advise boiling water prior to drinking. No estimates have been provided on restoring full operation of the water system...."

"Weeks. Frickin' weeks," I said.

"Why?" Carl asked.

"Our water comes from the aquifer. Through wells. Powered by electricity, then pumped up to water towers. Distributed through big mainline pipes to meters, then houses. First, no power to run the pumps to the towers. Then, some of the towers have collapsed. Some of the mainline pipes are broken, maybe even the one that runs just north of the barn. That's a ten-inch line. Supplies maybe a couple hundred people with water. Then, you have broken pipes to houses and businesses."

"Weeks."

"Yeah. You gotta get the source up and going. You gotta get storage capacity or booster pumps to put water right into the mains under pressure. You gotta check the mains for breaks and fix them. They're five feet deep, all over the city. You gotta check each customer's pipes for breaks."

"Like starting from scratch."

"Not quite, but close. Power's probably at least as complicated."

"Wow. This is bad."

"Nothing like a healthy dose of reality to kick you in the butt."

"No joke."

The TV was showing the shoot out again.

"I just don't get this. Why didn't they drop their guns?"

"Might've been scared of the military, or the cops, or both. There is a significant group of people that do not trust the government in any way, and believe that they are going to take their rights away."

I went on. "You gotta realize that these guys made several major mistakes that put them in the position in the first place. One, if they intended on getting out of town to avoid the government, they should've done it on Saturday. Or Friday."

"Before the quake? Why would they leave before? How would they know?"

"They wouldn't of course. But the first day of the disaster is actually the second. The first day of the disaster is the day you plan for it. These guys didn't plan, they reacted. If you aren't ahead of the pack, even by a little, the pack is all around you. You lose."

"OK, I guess I get that."

"The second thing they did wrong is on the screen. See anything?"

"No, dead guys, guns, and a truck."

"Right. A truck. Truck needs gas. Gas comes from a station. Everyone buys gas. Everyone goes places. Everyone wants out of town. Everyone runs out of gas eventually, somewhere. Probably in a diameter not too far across. Three, four hundred miles away from their starting point, they start dropping by the side of the road, many of them. Some have no idea where they're going and just hope to hide out until whatever blows over. This is the popular convention. That truck is called a Bug Out Vehicle by a lot of people."

"Lot of good it did them."

"It's easy for me to dissect this—hindsight and all. It's harder to make the decision to do what they did. If they were afraid that the end of civilization was coming, they should've bailed years ago and been ready for it. Living primitively does not come with an instruction manual, and is not easy. People died of simple things not long ago, not far from here. If they weren't ready for living that way," I said nodding at the TV, " then they could just as easily turn into predators."

"And steal stuff."

"Yeah, it's been known to happen. Look at that truck. How much money did that cost, and all the gear in the back?"

"I dunno, forty thousand?"

"Not far off. How much good did it do them?"

"None."

"Right. If someone used the brains God gave them, they would've invested that sum in something that would've worked for them, and be working for them for many years to come. They could've bought property out in the sticks for what that truck cost them, and they'd be sitting there today. This property cost us about ten grand more than that truck, twenty years ago. Since then, we've made conscious decisions to make this house our 'retreat', right in the city. It's not expensive. It's not about guns. It's about making a choice to know how to do things, not waste hard-earned money on stuff that entertains and doesn't have a long-term benefit, but most importantly for us, it's being right with God. Understand?"

"Yeah."

"Unfortunately for these guys, they thought survival was acting like cowboys. Too bad for them, that the real cowboys, the military, thought they looked like outlaws."

"If they wouldn't have pointed their guns…"

"If they hadn't done a lot of things. What that on the screen is, is just the last bad decision they ever made. Too bad. They were somebody's brothers, sons, or fathers."

"Yeah. I hadn't thought about that."

"Don't let the news spin the facts for you. Find them out yourself."

Five p.m.
Monday
January Sixteenth

Ron, Libby, John and Marie finally re-joined us, after about a half hour of privacy to discuss the loss of their home and belongings. They had the clothes on their back and what they'd left home with, their physical assets now consisted of perhaps a checkbook for a bank account that may or may not be worth anything in a week or two; perhaps some information on their IRA's and insurance policies; their soft-top Jeep YJ, the tent trailer that was stored at our house for the winter, and what little cash was in their wallets. Their other cars, a Caravan and a new Chevy Trailblazer, were parked in the garage, and probably burned with the house. Like millions of others worldwide that had money in the stock market, me included, their retirement investments and college funds were shrinking in value before their eyes. Worse for them, their contact information for their insurance policies, credit cards, and investments were probably now lost in the fire, and they probably didn't have copies stored in other locations. They'd have to deal with it from memory.

"Ron, you know that you and Libby are welcome here as long as you want. You don't need to worry about that—ever."

"I know, and we appreciate that. It's just that we assumed that the house was still more-or-less OK, you know? Finding out days later that it's gone is just salt in a wound that we hoped was healing."

"I understand," I lied of course. I didn't know what it was like to lose literally, everything. I could guess though. Marie had gone off to lie down on her bed for a while, and John was turning in early to get some sleep before a late supper and his 'security' shift. Both were silent, and I could tell that all had had a good cry.

"Libby, you OK?" I asked quietly.

"No, but I will be. We'll be fine." 'Resolute, that girl,' I thought.

"Ron, how 'bout you and I go have a look at the basement quick."

"All right."

We donned our coats and boots again, and both grabbed flashlights and headed out through the shop, dogs taking the lead. Carl joined us, I think because he wanted out of the gloomy mood that had overtaken the barn. We slogged through the increasingly sloppy snow and ash back up to the house.

At the house, we went back to getting into the basement for a look-see and a possible salvage operation, although it was too late in the day to do much. Realistically, we should've been having our observation posts manned by now, since it was nearly full-dark, but the full implications of our paradigm-shift hadn't quite struck us yet.

We had the basement door cleared enough to open, and I had already unlocked the door before we got the news about the Martin's house. I pushed the door open, and had to shove hard to get the door open enough to get in.

I had to climb over the lower part of the storm door to get in, while holding the flashlight in one hand and trying not to step on Karen's 'stuff' (groceries, stuff to be mended, etc.) that littered the stair landing. Similar to the main floor and second floor, the stair landing was covered with the fallen plaster, but the lath remained nailed to the house framing. It was more than a little eerie…like watching the wreckage of Titanic on the floor of the North Atlantic.

About the time that I got both feet inside, the room lit up and I heard the 'whoop' of a siren. Carl and Ron had both stuck their heads into the room, and quickly pulled back when the spotlight lit them up.

"POLICE! Step away from the house IMMEDIATELY."

"Oh, crap." I said.

Ron and Carl did as they were ordered, and I stayed in the house until they could talk to the deputy, or trooper, or whatever.

"On your knees with your hands behind your neck. Clasp your fingers. DO NOT MOVE FROM THAT POSITION."

I decided to speak up. "Hey, this is my house!" as I stepped into view.

"Step out of the doorway, slowly."

"Yes sir." The spotlight was blinding, of course by intention, but at least I was able to recognize the new grey and blue Crown Victoria in it's Sheriff's Department livery.

"Sheriff asked me to do a drive by. Can you prove your identity?"

"Yes sir."

"Advance slowly with both hands up and in sight."

"Yes sir." I made my way over to the tall wire fence and stopped. "Can I get my wallet?"

"Slowly, with your left hand." Obviously, hoping I was right-handed.

"You got it." I did as he asked with difficulty, and retrieved my wallet and license. "Here you go," I said as I passed the license through the fence. The officer reviewed it a minute and handed it back.

"Thank you, Mr. Drummond. We've had a lot of calls of looting in the residential areas, and when the Sheriff asked me to do a drive-by, he told me that you were still living here. I didn't expect to see anyone with good intentions trying to get inside at this time of day."

I looked over my shoulder. Ron and Carl had relaxed and were walking over to join us.

"I understand. We've been busy doing things outside today, and this the first chance we had."

"You may not have heard about the new curfew yet. It's dusk to dawn with all people ordered to remain indoors from four p.m. until eight a.m. No exceptions."

"OK, that's all well and good, but you do realize that there is almost no one left living on this street, right? And you expect us to stay all nice and snug in our barn, while the entire street is wide open to looters?"

"I realize the impracticalities of it sir, as does the Sheriff."

"So if, for example, we have two people in concealed locations whose job entails keeping an eye out for looters during say, a four-hour shift, we're breaking the law?"

"No sir. You are breaking a federally-mandated rule."

"Thank you. I think I understand. This is a federal mandate, which is effectively unenforceable, in a long line of federal mandates that the government neither funds, provides manpower for, et cetera."

The deputy was silent for a moment. "That may be a correct interpretation, Mr. Drummond. I am not one to say."

Karen had joined us with three travel mugs of hot chocolate. She was intently listening in on our discussion of the 'hypothetical'.

"So, Deputy, if for example, two residents of a property were keeping an eye on things during the specified curfew, and did see some illegal activity taking place, and did mention on FRS channel four code eighteen that this activity was taking place, what, exactly, would the Federal response be?"

"There would be no federal response, sir. The joint local command of law enforcement assisted by Washington State National Guard troops would respond if at all possible, unless otherwise engaged."

"And if the local law enforcement was otherwise occupied? What then?"

"Where possible, when communications are available, the local residents may be authorized by the local law enforcement officers in charge to use whatever force is necessary to defend the lives of those endangered, but not to use such force if property is endangered."

"You just stated the defense of our actions on Saturday night."

"I fully understand that Mr. Drummond. Sheriff Amberson wanted me to make sure you understand…."

"….the rules of engagement."

"So to speak, yes, sir."

"I understand."

"Deputy, would you like a cup of hot chocolate?" Karen asked, passing him a filled cup.

"Thank you ma'am. I appreciate it."

"Any time, Deputy. Any time. Keep the cup and bring it back for a refill sometime."

"Thank you very much."

"So Deputy, now that we've gone over the purely hypothetical, what's the word on the street?"

"Nothing good, Mr. Drummond."

"Call me Rick. This is my wife Karen and son Carl, and my friend Ron."

"Pleased to meet you. Paul Schmitt."

"Nice to meet you, Paul."

"The word is, that almost all National Guard troops in the state have been called up either to the war or are now on their way over to the coast. We have no problems at all compared to what's going on over there. They did find the Governor's body this morning, and her entourage. They were apparently at a late night Democratic Party function when it blew."

"That's too bad. I didn't vote for her, but nonetheless, we could use a Governor to keep the Federals in line if possible."

"Agreed. Anyway, a substantial chunk of the population here evac'd yesterday and today for warmer weather. Just up and left."

"I can't say I blame them. I know some of those who did. They can't handle the cold, and the uncertainty of when services will be restored."

"Yes sir," Paul sipped on the hot-chocolate. "The lines between here and Grand Coulee, and here and most dams on the Columbia, heck, even from Upriver Dam into the grid, are almost all damaged or down. It's the third week in January. It's the middle of winter."

"Yeah. Our real snow's just begun this year, I'm afraid,"

In one sense--in another 'winter' today was just the first frost of Fall, in the Kondratieff Winter. I knew this and I had talked to Karen and the kids about it. Of all the people that I knew, most didn't understand that economic cycles run in seasons.

"Sheriff had a briefing this morning with our new FEMA administrator. It was closed door, but the sheriff said that relief supplies are going to be slow in coming."

"Going to Seattle?"

"If they make it here at all. FEMA stated that it's about to hit the fan with the economy. Shipping and transportation costs are going to skyrocket, gas is going way up, and the big cities are going to be in trouble. Not 'might be in trouble.' 'GOING to be in trouble.'"

"So as if you don't have enough to deal with, you know it's coming, and can't do anything about it."

"Not much, no sir."

"Well, Paul, you can bet on this. The US Dollar as we know it is done. Any lower income area that has a high proportion of the residents on public assistance will be rioting the day after the checks don't arrive. You can expect the worst there. You can expect the suburbs to be the targets of that aggression, as soon as the first wave is done."

"Can't disagree with any of that. The question becomes, how long will it last?"

"One good thing? This weather. Not too many people want to go out in it or burn their own house down. In that regard, we may be better off than LA, or Chicago, or Atlanta."

"Might be. None of us are betting on it."

"Got family?"

"Yes sir. All of 'em up on Green Bluff." Green Bluff was one of the most productive agricultural areas in the area, just a few miles out of town and now becoming more geared toward 'festivals' where the city-folk could go see what pretend farming looked like—more like tourist-agriculture.

"Good. You don't want to be in East Central." East Central was one of the more crime-ridden areas in Spokane, about five miles from my house. I suddenly had the urge to go load up the 2000 census and pull up the information on my zip code. I wondered what percentage of my neighbors were on food stamps.

"Five-forty-one respond," the cruiser's radio pleaded.

"Five-forty-one," Paul responded.

"Respond code two to Fourth and Dishman-Mica. Multiple gunshots fired. Multiple civilians down."

"Ten-four. Responding code two. Five-forty-one out."

"Five-forty-one."

"Gotta go."

"Watch your six, Paul."

"You got it."

In a few moments, the car was out of site, faster than I'd ever drive in those conditions. I sure hoped that Deputy Schmitt made it home tonight.

"C'mon. Let's have a quick look at the basement and get some dinner."

"You'll have to wait until at least six," Karen said. "Stew's a little slow."

"I'm sure it'll be worth the wait. OK. Third time's a charm. Let's get into the basement and have look."

"You be careful. Thought you might need this," she said as she handed me my LED headlight.

"Thanks. I'll be careful, if I don't break my neck on the stuff you have piled on the stairs and the landing...."

"Sorry."

"I'm getting used to it after all these years of wedded bliss..." I said as I crawled back inside, flipping the switch from the 'green' and 'blue' LED's to the really bright white one. It ate batteries, but man did it light things up.

I made my way over the tumbled groceries from Albertsons that hadn't found their way to the fruit room, to the left of the stairs at the bottom. The basement had been about half-finished when we bought the place, with some of the south half finished, the laundry unfinished, and the fruit room fully framed in, insulated, and furnished with three walls of wood shelving and an 'island' of wood shelves, floor to ceiling. The insulation was left off however, at the rim-joist of the house, with the additional cooling through that uninsulated wall, keeping the room at about fifty-five degrees most of the time. Over the years, I'd developed a taste for cabernets and merlots, and had converted part of the shelving to a simple wine rack, part of which faced north, and part west. Given my experience on the rest of the house, I expected everything in the room on east or west facing walls to be on the floor, and everything on north-south walls to be more-or-less, OK.

The closet at the bottom of the stairs on the far right held our gas furnace, a replacement for the coal-burning monster that was removed in the late sixties. One wall of that closet was the brick chimney and it's base, and the other side of the chimney was exposed in the laundry. I was pleased to see that I wasn't greeted with a pile of shattered red brick at the bottom of the stairs, and could see into the bar area. Other than stuff tossed around, things looked pretty good. My grandfathers' ceremonial cavalry sword and spurs still hung on the wall in the bar area, next to a picture of him atop his mount. He'd joined the Army in the Great War, stayed in the Guard until the second chapter of that fight began, and was in the Pacific as a light-colonel for the duration. Somewhere down here, there was a book with a photograph of him with his unit, standing in his khakis, looking down over a dead Japanese infantryman, his Colt in hand. He'd passed on when I was still in diapers.

I stuck my head into the laundry for a moment, and other than things being all over the floor—which wasn't really anything that was out of the ordinary—all the plumbing appeared to be intact. The waste lines from the toilets on the main floor and second floor hadn't cracked, and there was no evidence of water from the pressurized lines leaking, which meant we still had fifty gallons or so of potable water in the house. There were numerous places in the stone foundation where the mortar had popped out of the joints, littering the room with sand and dust. Only two stones were dislodged, below the boarded-up window where the dryer vent exited the room. One had landed in the laundry tub.

The fruit room door was constructed of two-by-four framing, and sheathed with one-by-six tongue-in-groove pine on a diagonal, and the void filled with sawdust. It was held closed by a simple hook and eye, and I was able to push it open easily on it's big barn-type hinges. As predicted, a fair amount of the wine on the east wall was now wreckage on the floor, landing on the floor drain in the walkway. The west wall of the room to my left had held the empty quarts and pints we'd used since summer. Most were broken on the floor, along with two 'ropes' of canning jar rings that must have fallen from the ceiling joists. The rest of the east wall had boxes and bags of stuff, which was also on the floor, but seemingly still edible. The north wall held more canning jars of peaches, pears, tomato soup, canned tomatoes, meat, sauces, pickled beans and quite a bit of dried food in sealed jars. The island held more of the same, and more store-bought dry goods. Fortunately, those shelves still held most of their contents.

I was just happy to see that we could still get into the room. Having all that food available was reason to celebrate all by itself. I fished out a bottle of Mountain Dome champagne (bottled up in the foothills of Mt. Spokane), and handed it back up the stairs to Ron.

"Here. We'll have this with dinner. Things look OK down here."

"That's great! How's the freezer look?" Karen asked.

"I'll go take a quick look."

I climbed into the overturned laundry baskets and boxes of soap, threading my way over the stack of puzzle boxes and games that once were stored on a metal shelf next to the chimney. The chimney had a large crack running from floor to ceiling on the north side, and I could see all the way up to the first floor through it, catching the reflection of the stainless steel liner for the furnace flue. 'No fixing that,' I thought. I looked up at the big ten-by-ten wood beams and posts, and didn't see any cracks or evidence that they'd even moved. The freezer, an ancient monster from about nineteen sixty-six, was on the side of the room opposite the washer, dryer and water heater. I opened the top with difficulty (the counter-balance springs were shot), and found the freezer still solid, and still in need of being defrosted (it'd been on my to-do list for...months now.) I saw a package on top, and quickly grabbed it and wrapped it up in a pillowcase for dinner.

"Here—Don't peek," I said as I tossed it to Ron. "Freezers' fine. Still needs to be defrosted."

"Good. There's a lot of meat in there, and frozen veggies," Karen said for Ron's benefit.

"I'll be right back. I'm going to snag some books and the iMac," I grabbed another old pillowcase and went into the south half of the basement.   The bookcases were on the south wall, two tall fake-wood particle board units that went almost to the ceiling, and a monster bookcase that we'd moved over from my parents place before we sold it. In them, I had stored my shop manuals for my too-many car projects, novels, and all of my preparedness books. Those were the only things I was interested in getting at the moment. Other stuff would wait.

I quickly grabbed the contents of the entire second shelf and loaded it up in the bag: When There is No Doctor/Dentist; Carla Emery's Old Time Recipe Book/Encyclopedia of Country Living, Back to Basics; Natural Remedies; No Such Thing as Doomsday, Nuclear War Survival Skills, numerous books on food preservation, my year old copy of printed survivalism FAQ's; The bag was almost more than I could lift.

I carried it back over to the bottom of the stairs, and gradually made my way back up." Carl, grab this bag and take it to the barn—don't fall—it's all books and I don't want them wet."

"Books!" he said as he took the heavy load. "Feels like bricks to me."

"I'll give you a hand," Karen said. "Hurry up and get done. You can do this tomorrow."

"I know, I've just a couple more things to get."

"All right."

Back down stairs, quickly unplugged the iMac's power and Ethernet cables and put the keyboard and mouse inside my coat. I grabbed a half-dozen CD's and DVD's that a couple of which I knew contained what I was looking for, but didn't take the time to sort them out. Finally, I took a plastic grocery bag and put the iMac's screen in it. I didn't want to scratch up the flat-panel display. Finally, I headed back upstairs.

"That it? That's what you were looking for?"

"Yeah, that and the books."

"What's on the computer that's so important?"

"Our full inventory of stuff at the house. Insurance information, FAQ's—frequently-asked-questions—of important information on a whole lot of stuff from the internet. Food storage. Water purification. Medical, Dental. Primitive skills. Tactics. You name it. I've literally downloaded whole sites of information onto DVD and CD and flash drives to keep it just in case. That bag that Carl had has some of the most critical information in it. If the fit hits the shan. Grab the door," I told Ron. "Key's in my outer pocket." My hands were full, otherwise I'd have locked it myself."

"Seems kinda silly locking this door," he said as we headed back to the barn.

"Yeah, except when you consider that the value of every single thing in that basement is appreciating at an unheard of pace, in terms of US dollars."

"Yeah. What time are we posting guards?"

Before I could answer, something caught my eye to the south. Light, no, fire. Lots of it up in the hills. "Holy cow," I said. "Look at that fire. No, two fires."

"Houses?"

"Yeah. Big, big houses. Worth a couple million apiece I suppose, which is the high end of our market in town."

"Looters?"

"Has to be. If not, they'd've burned by now, wouldn't they?"

"Probably."

"Let's go." We hurried back to the barn, and inside. "I think night watch starts sooner, rather than later."

3 0

I could smell dinner cooking as we walked back out to the barn, peeling off our coats as we went back inside. A wall of both warmth and onions simmering in beef stew hit us as we opened the door. Ada and Buck were both sniffing around, looking for a bowl of stew of their own. I wondered if they knew that they'd be disappointed, or does hope remain eternal in Golden Retrievers?

The barn was lit for dinner with one of the Aladdin kerosene lanterns, one Coleman white-gas lantern, and two small camp lanterns. During 'normal' evenings, after dinner was done, we'd gotten into a routine of using just one lamp per room. The Aladdin looked distinctly out of place with it's frosted 'Lox-On' chimney and acanthus-leaf shade. I'd never cared much for the style of the shade, and was planning on selling it on EBay in the spring. 'Well, maybe not.' I decided.

"Grab a bowl from the bench over there, and ladies first," Karen said to Kelly and Marie. The boys followed on.

"Hold on just a sec, babe. I've got a surprise."

"Which would be what, exactly?"

"You too—over there. Get a bowl. Now Ron, where's that pillowcase I gave you?"

"Right here," he said, handing over the very cold package.

"Perfect. Bowls please," I said as I unwrapped the package. Last summers home made strawberry ice cream. I worked long and hard on the hand-cranked freezer, and had successfully managed to keep this package tucked away for a special occasion.

"Sometimes having dessert first, is the best thing. Voila—home made strawberry ice cream."

"COOL!" exclaimed the girls.

"And for us adults, we get champagne with that strawberry ice cream…"

" And chocolate sauce," Karen added. "I found a bottle in the kitchen."

"Even better. Stew can simmer a bit more. Kelly, pop that radio on, will you? And Carl, did you feed the dogs?"

"Yep. They snarfed it right down."

"We probably ought to be feeding them a little more—Buck anyway since he's Mr. Hyper. Ada's still got a pretty good layer of fat," I said as I dished Marie up. "All this running around outside is burning a lot of calories."

"Yeah, babe, but I don't see you losing any weight yet," Karen said.

Libby laughed. "Yep. Both you and Ron could stand to lose a few….."

I looked at Ron. "Ron, there is not a good response to that statement, is there?"

"Not if you don't want to sleep in a barn tonight. Oh, wait. We already are," he said.

"Sure there is Dad. 'Pass the ice cream'," Carl said. "Unless Mom and Libby want to think about their own….." Libby and Karen were both giving my son a stern look.

"Son, do NOT go there," I said with a grin. "You're playing with thermo-nuclear stuff there."

"K," he said as he took his bowl to the other room, whispering to me "They can dish it out but…."

"Exactly. Discretion is the better part of valor," I said, dishing up Ron and my bowls as Ron unwrapped the champagne.

With a pop, he uncorked the big bottle, and poured us each a partial coffee mug full.

The radio continued with no good news through our 'dessert' and dinner, of course no surprise that little good news was coming our way.   Among the more notable tidbits were a statement that Federal troops, as opposed to National Guardsmen, would be taking control of all shipping concerns, fuel and food stores in Washington and Oregon, effective at three o'clock this afternoon; confirmation of Deputy Schmitt's statement about the curfew and orders to remain inside; and comments about looting.   There were also some additional advisories about people having serious intestinal problems, probably from contaminated water. Probably.

"After dinner, we better get to our posts. With any luck, we'll have a nice, quiet night."

"Still going to have two people out there, aren't you?" Karen asked.

"Yep, and one on the radio."

"How long a shift?"

"Probably three hours for the outdoor folks, it's up to you on the radio side. This schedule can't go on forever though, it's going to wear us down."

"Yeah. We're all a little sleep deprived."

"I know. And we're just getting started with this little adventure."

"Dad, how long do you think we need to keep up the watch?" Carl asked.

"I have no idea. If we're both lucky and blessed, not long. I'm hoping that the looting will stop after enough bad guys meet their maker and people settle in to a routine, as well as more relief supplies and workers to meet the need."

"How long 'til we're back to normal?" said John.

"I don't know. I'm afraid, a very long time."

"Why? It doesn't ever take Florida that long to get rebuilt after a hurricane."

"Yeah it does. The problem is is that we never see how long it takes. It falls off of the news, and we go about our business. I'd expect that Florida takes years to recover after a big one. We also have other problems. One, the weather. No real rebuilding's going to get going in the middle of the winter. Two, our damage isn't as bad as that on the west side of the Cascades. Three, if the economy is tanking like it seems to be, then recovery may take years. Maybe decades."

"You're kidding, right?" Libby said.

"No."

"How could recovery possibly take years or decades? C'mon."

"All right, let's talk about this place we're sitting in. First, no earthquake insurance. Who's going to pay for fixing my house?"

"The government always helps people in disaster areas."

"Sure, with other people's money, either as a 'grant' or gift, or as a loan."

"Yes, so?"

"The government is bankrupt, and has been for a long time. The news today had the international banking community imposing sanctions on the US for not paying on the debt. If that's true, where do you expect the government to come up with a few trillion to rebuild all the damage in the entire Pacific Northwest?"

"Insurance has to cover some of it."

"I know that mine doesn't. I doubt yours did either. On top of that, the news said that a couple of the big insurers declared bankruptcy this morning, which probably saddles the government with the bill of covering the bankrupt companies' obligations. Adding fuel to the fire."

"Yes, but..."

"But nothing. If the government obligations aren't being met with regards to debt, then they sure as heck aren't going to meet the demands that they've created for servicing Social Security, Medicare, and all of the food stamp charity programs and the military, are they? When word gets out that they can't meet those obligations, riots start. When word goes round that the buying power of the US Dollar is plunging by the minute, the runs on banks and stores and places with 'durable goods' start. And there is nothing the government can do to stop it. Do you see where I'm going?"

"I guess. You're saying that we're going to become yesterday's news."

"Yeah. As soon as the rest of the country starts focusing on gas going up, groceries going up, the stock market going down, their retirement and bank accounts vanishing, we're on our own."

"And no relief comes."

"It can't. The system's not designed with systemic failure in mind. The Red Cross, the National Guard, FEMA, the FDIC, whoever, are designed to deal with isolated incidents that can be addressed through regional response. Not national disasters. Not financial disasters on an epoch scale. When people realize what 'has befallen them', the party is well and truly over."

"And we are well and truly screwed," Ron said.

"Yeah. I'm guessing so."

"How sure are you of all of this?" Karen asked.

"I'm not. I'm making educated guesses."

"So what do you know that is the truth?" Libby continued, a little sarcastically.

"Libby, truth is for philosophers. What I know that is fact is that the US Dollar is no longer the reserve currency of an increasing number of countries, which means that they're not interested in financing us anymore, and that we can't repay what we owe them. That means that even though Congress raises the debt ceiling, if no one wants to finance that debt, we're done. I know that the auto industry has sold too many cars at too low an interest rate to survive on domestic sales alone and that their growth market is China. I know that China is demanding as much oil as we are, and they are five times the size in terms of population, and are the West's major competitor for resources in the world. I know that we haven't the ability to build what we use here. We buy it from…China. I know that civilizations and countries, rise and fall. I know that Russia and Europe are sidling up to Iran, and giving them the OK to build nuclear plants and by extension, nuclear weapons. I also know that the United States as it exists, cannot exist without cheap and abundant gasoline and diesel fuel."

"So how do we….get back to normal?"

"That's what I'm telling you. This may be the 'new' normal."

3 1

Tuesday
January Seventeenth

We had an uneventful Monday night. Carl and I took first watch, and traded off at ten p.m. and again at one a.m. Most of the night had been boring to the point of the extreme, punctuated occasionally be the sound of far-off weapons fire, with single-shot, semi automatic, and occasionally, the sounds of heavy weapons of the military. The latter usually was the last sound heard. Sounded like a mop up operation.

Our little outposts were dry, but far from comfortable. After an hour or so of sitting on a cardboard covered pallet, and then shifting around, and another hour, and then a few minutes kneeling....I knew I'd be feeling it in the morning. The radio checks were helpful in keeping us from dozing off, after the sound of distant gunfire began to be regarded as routine. The temperatures remained in the low twenties until after midnight, when the wind changed from the south and grew dramatically warmer. By the end of my watch at four this morning, the temperature was over thirty, probably thirty-five, and a nice southwest wind was blowing. In the Pacific Northwest, this is known as a 'chinook', which brings dramatically warmer weather and high winds, and sometimes rain. This can result in a dramatic meltdown of ice and snow, and cause flooding in low areas.

By the end of our last shift, there was virtually no gunfire from any direction. I guess even looters need sleep eventually. I had Karen wake Ron briefly to tell him that he could sleep. I'm sure there was some irony in there somewhere, but I was too tired to notice. By ten after four, I was back in the barn and in bed. By twelve after, I'm sure I was sleeping.

Our rooster managed to wake us up at six thirty, and I told Karen that I was sleeping late today. Very late. The rain began not long after, which woke me right up, the sound of the wind driven rain slapping into the metal chimney, and rattling the stove. I roused Ron and John, and let Carl sleep some more. I was worried that more than a foot of wet snow, ice, and ash might be too much for the barn roof. When we'd had heavy snows before, I made it a point to get some of it off of the shallow four-in-twelve barn roof. While we were getting dressed, Karen and Libby got the fire going again, and started coffee.

I felt awful, more walking zombie than man. Buck, however, knew that what I really needed was to play, which is of course his nature. He latched on to my wrist with his mouth, which is his way of saying 'You're mine. Let's go.'

I dug out the snow removal tools, two pretty good sized metal snow shovels, and the pole-puller. This home made tool was a hunk of one by twelve pine, fastened perpendicular to a two inch diameter, twelve-foot long wooden dowel. A couple of metal straps gave it some stability. In heavy snows, I'd used this to pull some snow off of the roof, from the ground. Only in extreme cases did I ever get up on the barn to shovel or push the snow off. I guessed this was an extreme case.

I unhooked one of the short extension ladders that live on the side of the barn, and put it up to the peak of the barn. The barn roof was pretty low on the garden side, only ten feet or so, but fifteen feet on the other end due to the slope of the grade. Ron and John would shovel some of the snow out of the way of the doors and the new chicken yard. They manned the shovels, I would try to shove the upper layer of snow some of the ash and maybe the layer of ice under the ash, off of the roof. Without breaking my neck along the way.

Other than the obvious issues of the weight of saturated snow and an inch or so of saturated volcanic ash, I also wanted to make sure that we got as much of the ash off of the roof so our water collection system would be fairly clear of the heavy muck. The layer of snow and Ice under the ash provided a great separation, if we could make the clearing operation work.

After about ten minutes of trying to clear the entire roof down to the surface, I gave up and decided to be satisfied with getting the upper layer of snow and some of the ash off. I thought I could then pull the ice layer with the ash atop it, off from below, rather than trying to shove it off. After an hour and a half, I had almost all of the roof cleared to the ice-layer, and the rain was washing the ash down the ice to the build up of the upper layer of snow. 'This might actually work.' I thought.

Karen called us in for breakfast around eight-thirty, which was hot cereal, juice, decaf coffee, and scrambled eggs. I reminded her that we'd need to collect eggs at the Pauliano's this morning, and that one of the guys--or two—would need to go with her for protection.

After breakfast, Carl, John and Ron took turns on the shovels, and I finished up as much as I could by pulling the heavy snow off of the roof. After I was done with that, Carl got back up on the peak and managed to push off the entire ice-layer on the north side of the roof, and then moved to the south side. After cleaning out the gutters with melt water and whisk brooms for the muddy ash, the gutters were clean enough to collect all of the remaining snow melt and rainfall. What a miserable job.

I was exhausted and needed to sleep. Ron and John changed their outerwear, which was completely soaked, and Carl changed into drier (not dry) snowmobile pants and my thin shell, over one of my rag wool sweaters. He'd be on 'post' while Karen and Libby and the girls went down street, with Ron and John taking guard duty. I tossed them the keys to the Expedition, and got out of my wet things. The air in the barn was heavy with the humidity and smell of wet clothes. I put on some dry sweatpants, a dry tee-shirt, light socks and a quilted flannel top shirt. I remembered laying down for a nap and hearing the chain rattle on the heavy gate. I didn't wake up until nearly two p.m.

While I slept, Karen showed the Martins and Kelly how to feed and water the Pauliano's hens, collect the eggs, and make sure that no 'varmints' were about or could get in without difficulty. Another two dozen eggs were collected. One thing for sure, our cholesterol sure wouldn't suffer any time soon. Ron showed Karen the location of the cistern for watering the hens, with it's old-fashioned hand-pump. Fortunately, the water in the barn hadn't frozen.

Lunch was fried egg sandwiches, on bread that they baked while I snored ten feet away, behind an old blanket hung from the cracked sheetrock. They also managed to re-arrange the other room to fit the twin mattress from Carl's room, and cleared off two shelves of the storage rack so that John and Carl could sleep on them, submarine-bunk style. I'd designed them to be big enough to do this, but never planned on really having to use them.

Ron had also informed all present that the porta-potty would be used only for 'night water' and that all other bodily functions would be taken care of in the outhouse. I reminded myself to read up on how to best maintain an outhouse, which was a document stored on my recovered iMac.

Libby and Karen had tasked Marie and Kelly with clothes-washing duties, which of course the girls found to be completely disgusting. Libby had dug out a new pair of rubber gloves that I intended to use for chemical-stripping paint off of some old five-panel doors, and gave them to the girls so they would feel a little better about their task, and not have their hands too messed up with the laundry soap. They also discovered that a very little soap will suffice, when doing hand-laundry. Both Kelly and Marie had also had a chance to bathe in the old washtub, and John and Carl would later in the day, so they had a chance to dry their hair before our watch schedule kicked in again full-force. I'd had a chance to wash up yesterday, and needed to again. I'd kill for a hot shower and a decent shave.

Carl and John traded off hourly during the day on watch, and other than three drive-bys by the Deputy on duty, and a wave each time by the person on 'post', no other cars were driving about.

Once I'd finally had enough sleep and snooze time, I rose and dressed in dry clothes (Dry!! DRY!!). I was soon tasked with duties.

"Hon, what's it going to take to get into the root cellar?" Karen asked.

"Shouldn't be anything different than normal, assuming the door's not jammed or frozen."

"We're almost out of potatoes and we could use some onions and carrots too."

"As you wish," I said, mimicking a line from The Princess Bride.

Ron joined me in trekking across the field to the root cellar. He'd seen it, but never really paid much attention to it in all the years we'd been here.

"This come with the house?" he asked as we approached the cellar.

"Well, sort of. There's always been a root cellar, but it's been rebuilt a couple of times, I guess. I've done a little to it, but not much. The roof had a couple of leaks in it that I patched, and I had to do some work on the doors. The roof work was interesting. Had to patch it with hydraulic cement from the inside."

"Hydraulic cement? Never heard of it."

"Cool stuff. You can use it on an active leak—with water flowing through it—and it'll expand and dry, filling the crack and preventing leaks from coming back."

"That's handy. Where did you learn about that?"

"My Dad. We used it on the old house on Alki when I was a kid. Made quite an impression on me…I think I was five."

The cellar was built across the field from the barn, and quite a ways off from the house too. (inconveniently so, most of the time). The cellar was constructed in the early decades of the last century (how odd to say that!) and rebuilt in the late Fifties, I guessed. The 'modern' cellar was almost a hundred fifty square feet, of eight-inch thick concrete walls, and a combination of dirt and wood floors. The walls were lined with shelves about thirty inches deep on the right as you entered, and half that on the opposite wall. There were also a couple of workbenches in the cellar, and an air shaft on the far end, opposite the door, directly through the concrete ceiling.

The ceiling was of later construction than the walls, and was around eight to ten inches thick, arched, and probably reinforced, but I couldn't know that without breaking a hunk out of it. I assumed that the roof had been formed over a plywood and lumber frame, reinforcing placed, concrete poured and cured, and then the wood form removed from below. The stairs entering the cellar entered from the east, along a short wall, with an ancient steel door at the bottom. Six heavy hinges were needed to keep it on it's steel frame. At the top of the stairs, a wooden door hinged to the concrete stair wall kept leaves and snow out. A floor drain, one of two in the cellar, handled what rain made it down the stairs. We usually kept our potatoes and other root crops in the cellar, squash once in awhile, and apples, once. Do not store apples with root crops if you ever want to use them...

Ron and I cleared off the snow and ice with our boots, and I had to kick the door a little to free it up. I really ought to have covered it over with plastic, but never really thought about it that much.

"How much dirt is on top if the roof, anyway?" Ron asked.

"About thirty inches."

"Seems a bit extreme for a root cellar."

"Yeah. But not for fallout," I said, finally getting to the old metal latch.

"You're kidding."

"Hey, I didn't build it. It was here. But it was obviously designed for it. It's almost a duplicate of one that the Feds had in their old brochures—it's even reprinted in one of the books we recovered from the basement—Nuclear War Survival Skills."

I pulled up the door, and dropped it to break loose some more of the ice and snow from the door. The rain was steady, but not as heavy as it had been. Good thing, my gaiters were grey from the muddy ash, and Ron's borrowed Sorels, once black, were now a light grey.

"So what do you keep down here?"

"A bunch of the root crops we grow, potatoes and onions in baskets and burlap bags, carrots layered up in maple leaves in baskets, some other stuff. There's not a ton of stuff in there right now. I cleaned a lot of it out last fall with the intent of re-stocking it eventually. Hadn't gotten to it yet."

We carefully went down the icy steps, and I unlatched the steel door. Removing the rust from both sides of the door had taken me the better part of two days, and I then painted it with a rust-neutralizing primer, and then four coats of polyurethane automotive paint. I had to do it in place, because the door was far too heavy to remove. The hinges were equipped with 'zerk' grease fittings, and I recharged them with graphite grease. I pulled the door open, and we went in.

"Shouldn't the door open in?" Ron asked.

"Yeah, except for a blast wave like you get when a nuke goes off will blow it in. This arrangement would just close it tighter."

"Rick, is there anything you don't know?"

"Me? Plenty. More I don't know every day, is what I'm finding. I know a bunch of stuff about a lot of things, but I'm definitely no expert on most any one of them. There's too much to learn and not enough time to do it in."

Ron had remembered his flashlight, I hadn't. He adjusted the four D-cell beam to it's widest play, and I grabbed a burlap sack from the pile on the shelf, and began filling the bag. Twenty pounds ought to do it, I thought.

"So how does this work as a shelter?"

"I'll show you the book. It's actually not much different than what we're doing now, just underground, more cramped, more humid, and no outside time until the fallout decays."

"How do you tell that?"

"Kearney Fallout Meter, if you don't have proper radiation measuring equipment, which I don't."

"So what is it?"

"It's in the book too. It's a field-expedient way to measure radiation caused by nuclear exchange. Apparently works well, although fortunately for us, field testing is not widely done."

"Good thing. What else is in here?"

"Not much. One barrel of stored water, some canned goods sealed in plastic, some five-gallon buckets of grain, and a five-gallon bucket of stuff for each of us. You know, soap, some clothes, toothbrushes, stuff."

"OK, I gotta ask. How can you afford to do all of this? The stuff in the barn. The books. The supplies. This stuff. All the tools and things? It's gotta cost a fortune."

"Not really. I don't have a boat."

Ron laughed. "Well, neither do I anymore, I suspect."

"I didn't mean you personally. What I meant was, I don't have the need to be entertained or travel to distant places at great expense. I've just used the same resources for acquisition, rather than entertainment. I don't need to go to some distant place to make an impression on my kids. We've gone a few places, but usually on the companies' nickel when I'm already there on a business trip. I can then take time off for 'vacation', and we can go camping around here, work on Carl's baseball skills or Kelly's softball throws, and I can spend all day with them, rather than tow them someplace, strap them on a ride, and then listen to them whine that they're bored or watch them spend thirty bucks on chicken strips, fries, and a Coke."

"But didn't it cost a lot?"

"Not really. I don't hire much of anything done, I learn how to do it myself, so I save. Car repair, house stuff, mowing the lawn. I haven't had a car payment in twelve years. The Expedition's a company car, and we paid cash at a helluva discount, and it was bought used and at wholesale. We grow a lot of our fruits and veggies, and tend to eat pretty simply. I don't buy four-dollar coffees, and rarely eat out at lunch. There aren't many movies Karen and I care to spend twenty dollars on, so we rent them or buy them on DVD when they come out. Think about what a boat costs. First the boat and trailer. Nice little ski boat? Twenty five thousand dollars paid monthly, and realistically, never paid off because everyone always wants a new boat. Then you gotta have something to haul it. So, pickup truck or SUV. Another twenty five or thirty or fifty thousand. Again, probably not paid off, just sold so that Mr. Boat

Guy has a newer ride. Then insurance, accessories, then gas, then time. Pretty soon, you're into that boat for fifty thousand dollars, easy. And, what you buy depreciates quickly, so you might as well just burn a couple years' worth of payments. And that boat never really wears out before it's sold for a newer one. And you only use it four months a year, maybe five."

"I never really thought of it that way."

"Not your fault. You've been marketed and barraged with materialism. You, me and the rest of the world. More is always better. Going places is always better. Experiencing and accepting new and different things is always the right thing to do. Searching for deeper meaning…"

"Is always better."

"Except, when it's not. Too many Americans have bought into the secular world hook, line and sinker. There are so many things around us that are in direct conflict with the Bible that if you think about it, it should literally scare you. The materialism thing has bankrupted our pocketbooks—direct conflict with the Scriptures. The 'new and different things' bit has extended itself to every aspect of our lives. It's now common to see churches surrounded by demonstrators because the Bible speaks against things like homosexuality, immorality, debt, you know, really radical ideas. 'Searching for deeper meaning' now means studying the occult. Most people do not search for deeper meaning in Christ, or God, or the Bible. They'd rather go to Odin, and study Wicca, or Buddhism, or the Great Spirit, or any one of a hundred beliefs except the one that will actually work."

"Funny, I never knew you felt this way."

"Yeah, I'm not exactly a proper evangelist. Not easy to talk to people about stuff like this, especially when like so many, my friends have swallowed the hook."

"There's so many people out there who act just like you described."

"Yep. And not all will be saved, nor will they want to be. They will be consumed either by this world or in the next. C'mon. Let's get back before they send out a search party or figure that we've gone to sleep in here."

We closed the heavy door, and then the wood door at the top of the stairs, and headed back across the field. With luck, I'd catch the news at two thirty.

3 2

Two-thirty p.m.
Tuesday
January Seventeenth

"......*financial meltdown continued today, with trading curbs
and circuit breakers in effect through most of the session. The Dow
Jones thirty industrials closed at fifty-one fifty, and NASDAQ closed
at just under eleven-fifty. The S&P five hundred at the close was
nearly six hundred. CBS Market watch will provide updates as
deemed appropriate on the reactions of the world financial markets
to the continuing slide.*"

"*In other financial news, both gold and silver had dramatic
upturns today, with gold closing at nine-fifty three fifty, and silver at
sixteen forty-one. Silver and gold stocks, however, languished with
the rest of the market. Analysts have expected precious metals
mining firms to profit generously in the current unstable market, but
as of yet those predictions are unrealized.*"

"*Gasoline prices throughout the United States, outside of the
Pacific Northwest where price controls have been imposed as part of
Martial Law, have skyrocketed in the last forty-eight hours, with
regular unleaded now averaging three-fifty a gallon. Diesel is even
more expensive, at four-oh-one per gallon. The dramatic cost
increases are blamed on the announcement that China had secured a
controlling interest in seven major oil fields as well as a fifty-year
contract with Iran to supply China with petroleum products. In
exchange for the petroleum contract, China has pledged support in
the development and enhancement of the Iranian military, with first-
line attack aircraft, surface-to-air missile guidance systems, and new*

anti-satellite weapons on the shopping list. The announcement was condemned by the United States, and Israel pledged that any first strike by Iran on Israel would be met with unlimited release of nuclear weapons in defense of Israel."

"Airline ticket prices have risen accordingly in response to the increase in aviation fuel....."

Ron and I were listening intently to the radio, and Libby and Karen had an ear turned toward it as well.

"Things are coming unwound," Ron said.

"Yeah. Good analogy," I responded. The national broadcast had ended, and the local news was now on.

...borhoods have been evacuated due to lack of available services and repair crews. The affected neighborhoods are almost all at the higher elevations, including Bella Vista, Northwood, and other neighborhoods in the hills above the Spokane area."

"Why don't you guys just tell the looters the addresses while you're at it!" I barked at the radio. "Empty rich-guy houses, free for the taking!"

".......troops are now in place at all major grocery stores, shopping centers, and gas stations and are in control of food distribution, major transportation networks, and physical security. Some of these troops as late as Saturday were performing similar functions in Fallujah and in the northern Kurdish areas of Iraq, and were flown directly from their bases to the United States to help in the relief effort."

"Sucks for them," John said. "First the desert heat, now snow, wet, and cold."

"Yeah," I said. John was getting dressed to go relieve Carl.

"....checks on purchases made at secured facilities are now in place, with identification required for purchases of all items, including gasoline. Rainy weather is expected to continue

269

throughout the afternoon, with clearing after eight p.m. this evening. Tomorrow's weather is expected to be cloudy with a fifty percent chance of rain or snow, continuing through the day. Now back to Pat MacCauley in Olympia, with continuing coverage of recovery efforts in the Puget Sound area......."

I left the others around the little AM radio and moved my bundle of potatoes into the woodshop, finding an old milk crate to put the burlap bag in.

"You OK?" Karen asked.

"Yeah. Just thinking."

"Thought I smelled smoke."

"Funny."

"What's up? Something on the news?"

"Yeah, but more…something that wasn't on the news."

"What's that?"

"It's too clean, neat and simple."

"What? The news?"

"The reporting. Listen. They just told us that inside of three days, the stock market has declined from ten thousand something to five thousand and change, with the Naz and S&P dropping like a rock too."

"Yes, and?"

"And where is the report of panic? People's money—or what they think of as money—is evaporating before their eyes. You can't tell me that watching your investment accounts—which people use for savings accounts these days—going down the drain wouldn't make you act."

"Yeah, that's true. So why aren't we hearing about it?"

"If you—the government—announce that your populace is about to be converted to paupers, you end up with a revolution. Complete with the ruling class getting their heads lopped off or worse."

"So you think that that is really happening, and they're not telling us?"

"I don't see how it could be otherwise! Look at what else they said and make your own judgment: Gas on Friday was what, two-fifteen a gallon? Today it's three-fifty? I would expect that ALONE to be enough to freak people out! Runs on gas stations. Rationing. Theft. We're not hearing any of it."

"Maybe it hasn't sunk in yet."

"How can it not have?" Ron and Libby joined us. "This country depends on gas. And yet we're not hearing about the 'social effect' of a sixty percent increase in the price of gas?"

"Yeah. I see your point." Libby said. "Too...."

"Manufactured." I said for her.

"OK, so now what?"

"Well, I have no idea. There's not much we can do about it anyway, I suppose, even if we could actually make a phone call. There is one thing though...." I said, moving to uncover the 'big' radio with the multiple bands. "We can see if there's any reports on the shortwave that might be a little more reality-based. I don't know how much we'll get during the daylight, I've just never messed around with it too much. I do have a couple of frequencies that have some American stations on them that aren't known for being politically-correct, so maybe we try them first."

"Where are they out of?" Ron asked.

"One's out of Tennessee or Kentucky. The others, I'm not sure. I think I've got some others on the iMac in a pdf file. We'll get Carl to get it set up, and then run the genny for awhile. I want to get one of the printers hooked up to it and print out a bunch of stuff I don't have on hardcopy. That list with the radio stations will be one of them."

"North to barn," the radio called. Carl was still on watch, and John was walking up to relieve him. I went to pick up the hand-held.

"Barn."

"Dad, there's a deputy here to see you."

"I'll be right up." Hmmm. "This is odd." I said. "Join me?" I asked Ron.

"Sure. If I stick around, I'll be stuck peeling spuds."

"Yeah, but you'll be dry."

"Hey—before you go, take this," Karen said, handing us both heavy plastic rain ponchos.

"Cool. Where'd you find them? I thought we'd lost these years ago."

"In the garage, under the kids' life preservers."

"That's logical."

"Yeah. We used them the last time over at Mica Bay, two years ago, remember?"

"That thunderstorm? Yeah, I'll never forget that?" Yeah. I remember that, nearly got me killed when a tree came down next to the outhouse I was…in…at the time.

"I'll take one of the charged radios and leave it on VOX. You'll be able to listen in on what the Deputy wants."

"K. Stay dry."

"Will do."

Ron and I went back out through the garden, and slogged up front to the gate. We'd locked up the gate to prevent someone from easily opening it, although it was more for noise than actual security. The silver Ford was idling in the driveway.

"Good afternoon. What can I do for you?" I asked the Deputy, who was not familiar to me.

"Mr. Drummond?"

"Call me Rick."

"Deputy Jennings—Kurt. The sheriff would like you to meet him at the community center as soon as possible."

"Let's go. Ron? Keep an eye on the place. Kurt, any idea how long it'll take?"

"No sir, but I understand that the meeting is in regards to needing your assistance."

Ron and I looked at each other. "OK, let's get going. I just need a moment with my son, and I'll be right with you."

"That's fine. I'll be in the car."

"Ron, keep an eye on things. If for some reason you don't hear from me within an hour, come and find me. Carl, you and Ron get the little generator fired up and power up the iMac after you get it and one of the printers hooked up. I made a list of files that need to be printed out and left it with the computer. They're all in a file that's called READYSETGO. Use Sherlock to find it. Print them all. It'll take you a while."

"K. Dad, is everything OK?" Carl said quietly over the rain hitting us.

"I don't know, bud. I hope so," I said as I gave him a big hug. "Get inside and get warmed up and some dry clothes on. And get those files printed off. Love you, bud."

"You too. See you soon."

"Yep, I hope so." I said to him as he walked back to the barn. "Hon, you hear all that?"

"Yeah, any idea what's going on?"

"Nary a clue. I love you."

"I love you most."

"See you soon."

"You take care of yourself."

"Always, and you too."

I shook Ron's hand and unchained the gate, and took a seat in the crowded front seat of the cruiser. I was more than a little apprehensive, getting in a police car, even if I did know the sheriff personally. Still, I thought to myself, I wasn't seated in the BACK seat....

We backed out of the driveway and took off down the street, passing the damaged, destroyed and empty homes of many of my neighbors.

"So, Deputy, how is it out there."

"Un-fricken believable. It's like people have lost their minds," he said, rapidly scanning the road and the houses, obviously nervous about the road ahead. "Two patrol cars were ambushed this morning in West Central, and one up in Hillyard."

"Officers OK?"

"No. None of them made it. Head shots from rifles, right through the windshields and side glass."

"Crap."

"Yeah. That about sums it up," he said as we turned toward the community center.

"How's Mike holding up?"

"The sheriff? He's like a regular John Wayne. It's like nothing fazes him."

"Ten years in Rangers will do that for you."

"Yeah, I just had one hitch regular Army," he said as we pulled into the parking lot. There were around twenty cars in the lot, two county buses, and four police vehicles. An Army Humvee—an armored one at that-- complete with it's mounted fifty-caliber on the roof, manned, in the center of the road in front of the community center. The soldiers did not look happy. I wouldn't have been either.

The Deputy and I got out of the Ford and went inside, hung a right, and went down the hall to one of the former administrative offices, now occupied by the sheriff and several military uniforms. 'Hmmmm.' I thought to myself. 'This is damn odd.'

"Mr. Drummond."

"Sheriff. Good to see you."

"You too. This is Lieutenant Chapel, and Gunnery Sergeant Nokes."

"Gentlemen, nice to see the Army and the Marines working together," I said with a grin.

"Thank you sir, good to be here, " the Lieutenant replied. The Gunny just nodded.

"Rick, we have a little problem that you might be able to help us out with."

"Shoot."

"The issue is this: most petroleum shipments to the region come in through a couple of pipelines, both of which are toast right now. What that means is that what we have for fuel is in the tanks over in Yardley, a couple of which were lost in the quake and fire, or in the ground at every gas station in town. We're gonna be fuel-short, and we aren't going to get resupplied in any meaningful quantity before we run out.

"And where do I come in?"

"You have a gas station down the street, and if I recall, a generator for that tractor of yours."

"Yeah that's right. How did you know that?" I was suddenly a little uncomfortable.

"You were bidding against my next door neighbor. I was there that day, and saw you, but didn't get a chance to say hello." There **were** probably five hundred people there that day.

"OK, that's better, I was thinking conspiracy here."

Mike laughed. "No, but you should've seen the look on his face when he found out he'd lost. We had three auctions going on that day, and he was bidding on stuff in two of them," he explained to the Lieutenant and the Gunny. "He did get a nice pickup that day, but he really wanted that gen-set."

"So why my generator?"

"None of the smaller home-owner type generators we've got access to here will do the job."

"And mine will? Hell, I don't even know if it works."

"It should do the job. Can you check it out and let me know?"

"Sure. Tomorrow morning soon enough?"

"Yeah. Meet us at nine at the store. We'll have someone there from Modern Electric to check out the station's electrical system, and make sure we can get the generator hooked up to the panel."

"You got it. Anything else?"

The sheriff looked at the faces across the table and exchanged a glance. "Not at this time," he said. The glance said it all.

"Sounds good. I'll see you tomorrow."

The Deputy escorted me back to the cruiser, and we both got in out of a driving rain.

"That was damn odd," I said aloud. The police frequency radio was a constant chatter of stressed voices, numbers passed, and the occasional request for assistance. I recognized the two main frequencies on the radio as that of the 'Valley' patrol area and that of the State Patrol.'

"Yeah, we're not exactly living in the same place we were a week ago."

"Got that right. I notice that the radio isn't picking up the City frequencies."

Yeah. Too much traffic. They'd drown us out."

I pondered the looks, the unsaid words, and the hidden meanings on the way back home. 'Too much traffic.' That said volumes right there.

"Take it easy, Deputy."

"Thanks. I will," he responded as I got out of the car.

I waved at John in his little cubby hole as I went back through the gate, and chained it closed behind me. I could hear the hum of the Briggs and Stratton on the little generator going, out by the barn.

"I'm back, babe."

"Why thank you kind sir, I haven' been called that in quite some time," Libby responded over the radio.

"Then you're obviously being neglected," I said as I started walking back to the barn.

"Hey now, enough of that," Ron chimed in. "You know, I picked up most of that conversation you had with the deputy, and part of it with the sheriff."

"Really. I never tested the range on these radios." I was very surprised.

"Yeah, pretty good. Got a little fuzzy when you went inside the building."

"Cool. That's good to know."

"I think we can rig up one of these as a base radio with a better antenna, and probably extend the range even more," he said as I got to the barn.

"Sure, assuming we want to go that far afield."

"True."

I entered the tool room, shook off my brown poncho, and hung it up on one of the rakes hanging from the wall. I went back into the shop and sat down to take off my boots. Karen picked up on my mood immediately. I could hear the Epson ink-jet printer working madly.

"What's wrong?"

"I'm not sure. Mike didn't tell me much. It's more what they didn't say, than what they did." I was searching back through the conversation looking for clues, and coming up empty. They were afraid of something. That was plain enough to see, but what did they know that they weren't telling? I'd never seen a Marine Gunny with apprehension in his eyes before, and I'd known a couple in my time.

"What's it going to take to get the generator checked out?" Ron asked, coming in from the other room.

"Darned if I know," I said at first. "No, that's not true. We'll have to get the three-point hitch hooked up, make sure the PTO shaft is the right length and adjust it if it's not, fire up the Ford and make sure everything spins up all right, then check the output with a meter, and then under load."

"Anything else?"

"Yeah. Air up the tires. I'm sure they're flat again."

"Better get to work. It'll be dark soon."

"Yeah. My favorite. Working outside in the rain and slop."

"Me too."

"Karen, what're the girls up to?"

"Kelly's warm. I think she's getting a fever. Marie's a little droopy too. I think they're getting colds."

"No surprise there. Giving them Airborne?" I said, referring to the cold medicine.

"Yep. Second batch."

"Good. That's great stuff. Ron, I'm gonna have a cup of coffee and then we'll get after that gen-set."

"Already up on you there. Whenever you're ready."

"Carl, how's my little project coming?" I said as I stuck my head around the corner.

"Good I guess," he said, pulling the headphones off of his ears. "I think I've printed about fifty pages so far."

"Whatcha listening to?"

"Requiem. Schubert."

"Your concert CD?"

"Yeah. Been a while since I've heard it."

"Share. Dig out some speakers from that bag over there with all the old Mac stuff. I know there's a set inside. It'd be nice to have some music."

"K."

Carl played violin in the high-school orchestra, and one of his recent concerts was recorded on CD. He'd bought a copy, but wouldn't share it with us. It's not like he was a soloist, so I don't know why he had such a problem with it. Teen embarrassment, I'm sure.

"Ready?" Ron asked.

"Yeah, I guess," I said. "Not getting any drier outside."

3 3

Late afternoon
Tuesday
January Seventeenth

For the next two hours, Ron and I went about getting the big generator in running condition. First, we had to deal with all the snow, ice and ash that had covered it since I parked it next to the barn in late fall. Ron then pumped up both tires with a small hand pump, and I retrieved the three-point hitch for the trailer. The trailer had a conventional ball-hitch, and I had a three point implement that let me haul a utility trailer around. I'd need it to hook up the generator trailer. To provide us a little shelter, I pounded a couple of sixteen penny nails into the roof overhang and hung the tarp that we'd used to cover the Jeep in a drape over the trailer. Not wholly inadequate, but nearly so.

Once we got all the right parts together, I adjusted the length of the PTO shaft to match the configuration of the generator to my Ford. The shaft had a number of adjustments to allow shorter- or longer-lengths, made with two nine-sixteenth inch diameter bolts and lock nuts. After that was done, the moment of truth was at hand.

I fired up the Ford, got it to the proper RPM's, and engaged the PTO shaft with the little lever under the metal seat. The generator spun up just fine, tossing a little dust out of the slots in the sides of the case. The plan was to test the output with the little multi-meter. Ron decided to just plug in a trouble light and turned it on. It worked fine on 110V, and we did use the multimeter to test the 220V. That checked out OK too. It looked like we were in business at least on this end of things.

I never really had a reason for buying the generator, it was just something that I thought would be handy to have if I could get it at a decent price. I did get it for what I thought was more than a decent price, like many of the other (well-used) implements for the tractor, and lots of parts that I'd used in its rehabilitation. At auction, I'd bought a Dearborn two-bottom plow that was designed for use on the N Series tractors, a much newer disc, a rake, and a seed drill that I truly had no use for, but it was only ten bucks at a farm auction. It needed new tires, and was a bear to get onto my little trailer, but once I'd de-rusted the outside and cleaned the inside, and repainted it with matching red and grey paint, it looked sharp. Of course, I never intended on using it as it for planting crops, but life has a funny way of taking us in unplanned directions. Most of the implements were stored under plastic to help keep them from rusting more than was their due.

Before we could get the generator trailer down the street, I'd need to plow the road again. The melt-down had exposed most of the ash in the street, and it was extremely slick—more like grease than anything. The trailer also only had about six inches of ground clearance, and I though it best not to 'plow' snow with the generator. Ron and I disconnected the three-point hitch and put the back-blade back on, and I trundled up to the gate again. Carl, now on post, opened the gate for me and I began to clear the street. My .45 was tucked inside my shirt. I'd really need to find a better holster one of these days.

I made four passes, more than enough, up and down the street, getting almost all of the ash and snow off of the pavement. On my final pass to the far end of the road, I cleared off as much of the convenience store parking lot as I could, and then finished up the road. After I'd finished up the road, I made a good effort to get as many driveways cleared, just in case the residents were still there (evidence showed otherwise), and to give the appearance that there were more people there than not. Once our street was cleared, I moved up to the road heading to the east, and cleared it for the better part of a thousand feet, or in other words, as far as we could see from our northern watch-position. I then cleared a half-dozen driveways, again, both as a favor and for appearances sake. I suppose I was thinking that if the places looked lived in, looters might pass them by.

During the entire afternoon, the rain came in waves. Once the majority of the snow was cleared, the rain managed to wash the concrete and asphalt fairly clear, and the thirty-five degree temperatures guaranteed that a more significant melt down would continue at least for a few more hours.

By the time I'd finished, I'd seen sheriff's patrols pass twice down the roads, both times I'd received a wave from the officers, neither whom I recognized. By the time I finished up, it was well past dark, and I drove home with the headlights on. I'd completely forgotten about curfew, and apparently the officers didn't really care that I was out. 'Service of the King', I thought.

John opened the gate for me, and told me that Karen had been trying to get hold of me for dinner for the past hour. My radio batteries were deader than a doornail. I hadn't even thought about it. Lost in the sound of the tractor, trying to do something useful. Three double A's would work longer than the standard battery pack...if I had them, which I didn't.

By the time I reached the barn, the tractor lights showed me that the trailer tire on the left side of the gen-set had gone flat again. No surprise there. I parked the tractor temporarily, took off the back blade, and backed the tractor up to the generator. After I shut down the little four cylinder flathead, I nearly forgot to shut off the gas valve at the bottom of the fuel tank. Did that once—cost me ten gallons of gas. I couldn't afford to do that anymore.

"About darn time, plow-boy," Karen said as I entered the barn. "You and that tractor. Honestly. Trying to get yourself shot?"

"Sorry. Got carried away. The deputies just waved at me."

"What'd you do, plow all the way to Hendrickson's?"

"Now, don't be silly. Not quite that far." Hendrickson's were miles south of us.

"Hurry up. It's bath time."

"Really? Cool. And by the way, you smell very nice."

"You…...don't.'

"I'll blame it on the ten-forty and unburned hydrocarbons."

"HA! I'll blame it on four days without a shower."

"Thanks. I love you too."

"The tub's behind the blanket over there. You can actually have a little privacy. Everyone's in the shop—they're making s'mores at the woodstove."

"Is my razor in here?"

"Yep. On the craft bench."

"Thank you very much!"

I quickly stripped out of my cold, wet things and enjoyed a bath as I'd never had before.

After I'd become somewhat human again, I emptied the tub with a bucket, through the floor drain. Not something that I wanted to repeat many times....

When I rejoined the rest of the family, I ate a late dinner as they enjoyed dessert. Fried chicken, warm mashed potatoes and applesauce has never been so good. I was 'up' for watch duty at ten tonight, so I'd be able to get a little sleep before I had to go sit in the damp for three hours.

We'd arranged a temporary watch schedule, with two on a three-hour watch, usually father and son, with one of our wives on a six-hour radio shift. This allowed at least one of our wives to get a good solid shot at some decent sleep, such as you can when you're sleeping in an earthquake damaged barn, after losing your house, your faith in your money, and in too many cases, losing your faith in the future that you'd been promised.

Marie and Kelly had both caught colds, and although they were getting some rest and taking their medicine, neither was going to contribute a whole lot to either the radio coverage or normal chores for a day or two at least. We'd really have to watch out for our health—a little cold could easily grow into something much worse, and with our medical community having to deal with far more serious injuries, the cold-to-pneumonia chances were probably going to increase dramatically.

Carl had managed to get almost all of the files printed out that I wanted, and Karen had had the girls punch them in the little three-hole punch I kept out in the barn for my equipment manuals, project papers and such. The files were now residing in four three inch binders, and Karen had labeled each section with a bunch of old divider tabs that were in the used binders. (My business associates kidded me about the four cases of binders I'd brought in to the office—I'd literally dumpster dived for them—seeing them peeking out of a large dumpster next to a State office that was relocating. Most of them were nearly new. At eight bucks apiece, it made me mad that someone would throw them away.)

I excused myself from the conversation—which was wandering from plans for 'recovery' to more serious discussion on how far the Market and the Dollar would fall, so I could get a quick nap in. Karen joined me in our blanket-walled bedroom, and Ron, John and Libby started their first shift. I had little trouble falling asleep—freshly bathed, full stomach, warm bed, and Karen snuggled into my back.

At nine-forty five, Libby woke Carl and I for our shift. I'd laid out my dry outerwear already, so getting ready was no big deal. Karen and Libby had each made the 'night shift' fresh cornbread, sliced and honey spread in the middle, and hot tea. Karen gave me a quick kiss and rolled over for another three hours of sleep. The room was lit with one of the Aladdin's, turned way down low, but Libby was good at keeping it from smoking.

"Anything going on out there?" I asked Libby as I grabbed a freshly charged radio and the earpiece. The fire crackled softly in the cook stove.

"Not much. Rain's still coming down, but lighter. Ron's been saying that the wind seems to be changing –from the east again."

"Great. That might mean more snow."

"Any gunfire?" Carl joined me in the shop.

"Nothing close."

"That's a good sign. How about patrols from the sheriff?"

"Haven't had any since eight thirty."

"That might not be unusual."

"These days, no one can tell."

"Too true. Ready, kiddo?" I asked Carl.

"Yeah. But how long does this have to go on?"

"Not forever, I hope."

"It's getting old," Carl said with tired resignation. This from a kid that's used to twelve hours of sleep at a time. I was surprised he was even coherent.

"It is that. Tomorrow we'll get you and John checked out on the ought-sixes, and the girls on the twenty-two's."

"Marie's never shot before," Libby said.

"Ron and I'll teach her. Kelly's a good shot, and she's gone through the safety course."

"Good. I suppose I should learn too."

"You're kidding. You're married to Ron, and have never shot a gun." Amazing.

"Shot? More like 'never touched' a gun."

"That's all right. I wasn't a kid when I learned. It's not that difficult to operate a gun. It is a skill to operate one with skill, like anything."

"Handguns too?"

"Not that different."

"OK. I'll talk to you and Ron about it tomorrow."

"C'mon. Let's go," I said as I turned on the FRS. "Yo, B-Team, the first line's here to relieve you."

"B-Team my ass," Ron said in my ear.

"Carl's coming to John from the west, no lights, round the north side of the house. I'm approaching from the south side of the garage."

"Affirm."

Ron and I reviewed what little had gone on, while the boys did the same. Ron was right, the wind was of the east now, and getting markedly colder. Even through the rain, I could see the glow of fires on the hills surrounding the Spokane Valley. Bella Vista. Northwood. Dishman Hills. Homes that were all but palaces, with kitchen equipment costing more than I'd ever made in a year; with rooms larger than my entire house dedicated to home theaters; monuments to success and wealth and the tool of debt. I'd visited a couple during my career, when the owners (or at least, occupiers) wanted to retain my firm for design services. All had tall metal fences, extensive security systems, cameras, panic buttons. A lot of dang good it did them.

"No local action then?" I asked.

"Nope. Unless you count a dog pack running up the road about an hour ago. A couple of shotgun blasts over to the east."

"Quiet is good."

"Yeah. That's what I thought."

"Go ahead and head back. Hopefully it will stay quiet."

"Good luck."

"Thanks."

Ron and John headed back to the barn. I told Libby to hold off on the quarter-hour radio checks, and just hit us on the half –hour. Every fifteen minutes seemed a little extreme.

The rain on the roof of our little shelters tapped steadily over the next hour and a half without a break. At around eleven thirty, half way through our assigned shift, I heard movement to the east.

"Carl, movement to the east. Over."

"Don't hear anything, can't see squat."

"I think it's coming from behind the Long's house." The house had burned right after the quake.

"Wait, I hear it."

"Do you need help?" Libby asked.

"Not yet. I'll let you know."

"Right."

About five minutes later, I could hear voices, muffled, coming through the yards and staying off of the streets. Had to be looters, I thought. The voices became clearer.

"Libby, get Ron and John up, quietly, and get them up to positions behind the house and the garage. DO NOT use any lights. And keep the dogs inside until I tell you."

"Got it."

This action pretty much woke up the entire barn. Ron and John were in position in less than three minutes. The voices were now almost understandable. At least two adult males, probably not more than that—although I couldn't be sure.

I was sure that they were located about two hundred feet east of me, which put them in the backyards of the homes on the next street. I decided to call in reinforcements and not do something really stupid myself. I'd now see if the sheriff's office really DID monitor the FRS bands.

"Rick Drummond to any law enforcement officer."

"Go, Mr. Drummond." The response was abnormally fast.

"Pretty sure we've got looters, in the back yards of homes one block east. Staying off the roads, moving house-to-house through the yards."

"Any idea on the number?"

"At least two adult males, by the voices I've heard. Unknown if they are armed or of their intentions."

"Understood."

I really had no idea what to expect at this point. I certainly was not expecting a helicopter. Ron and John moved up to the forward positions.

Twenty seconds after my last contact with the Deputy, our road was illuminated by a police searchlight hung from one of the four-place helicopters that the county owned. When the light came on, I could see that they'd rapidly located the looters, and began to follow them over fences, heading to the south. 'Wrong move,' I thought, they were being herded toward the patrols stationed at the convenience store. 'Probably not from the neighborhood, looking for easy pickings.'

Four minutes later, gunfire, sounded like a few handguns, against automatic weapons. It was over very, very quickly. The helo circled once, shut off it's light, and headed southeast. Soon it was out of sight altogether. I noticed that it's anti-collision lights were shut off.

"Holy crap!" Carl said.

"Yeah."

"Radios off VOX everyone," I said. No reason to broadcast what I was about to say.

"Yes sir."

"That wasn't the flying of a Spokane county deputy. Did you see the way he greased that thing along?"

"Nor was it the actions of local police. Those poor bastards were herded to slaughter," Ron said.

"My thoughts exactly. What in the hell is going on?"

"I was about to ask you that," Ron said. "They're letting the rich folks houses up in the hills get robbed and burned, and then they come in and shoot the poor S.O.B.'s down here? Doesn't make sense."

"Not really. Unless the police and military really don't have anywhere enough forces to stop it everywhere, then it makes perfect sense."

"Isn't this backwards to the way they normally do it?"

"You mean the rich people getting better protection and response than us just average folks? Yeah. It's completely backwards. And as a regular Joe, I'd say it's about damn time."

Ron thought about that for a minute. "You know, what they're doing is writing off the indefensible neighborhoods."

"Maybe. I think they're writing off the neighborhoods that can't survive without massive support from the rest of us. They weren't ever designed to be remotely self-sufficient. Water piped up there from below, or pumped from wells five or six hundred feet down. Long, narrow roads that only serve the neighborhoods. No stores, businesses, or schools within walking distance. No ability to grow food on those rocky, dry slopes."

"Cynical mood, this one."

"More so e're I grow older."

"So, now that we're looking at midnight and mid-shift, what do we do?"

"You and John head back to bed. We'll hold down the fort until two. That'll give you an extra hour, and I suspect that we can close up at four a.m."

"You sure?"

"Yeah, I'm OK. Carl might have an issue with it though."

"I'll go tell him," Ron said.

"Thanks for the quick thinking. I never would've thought to call the cops."

"It was worth a try. Still though, it bugs me….."

"You can't say they weren't warned."

"True. But in four days we've come to this."

"Makes you think about the next four."

"No doubt," I thought. "No doubt."

Tuesday, January 17-Wednesday, January 18

After Ron headed back to the barn, I thought about what I'd just seen, and helped cause. No, helped...end?

I heard voices. I knew they were out of place. I was prepared to defend myself. Instead, I called on Big Brother, who ended it with a clinical sterility. Of course, I was assuming that the final burst of gunfire had killed the alleged looters, and not just been a warning. I decided to find out for sure, what I'd heard. If, of course, the other end of the radio would tell me.

"Drummond to law enforcement."

A few moments of quiet, then "Go, Mr. Drummond."

"What the hell was that?"

"The situation is over."

"Custody or a slab at the morgue?"

"Custody. That last burst was from the mounted fifty on the Humvee. Two suspects, one will need to change his pants. They ran right to us, saw the burst from the fifty, and dropped like rocks."

"Good to know. Are they from around here?"

"No sir. Not your neighborhood. They're headed to detention at this time."

"Thanks for the quick response."

"You're quite welcome. The residents of the house where they were caught are appreciative as well. Good night."

"Good night," I said, bewildered. Maybe my faith in humanity wasn't completely gone, after all.

"Did I hear that right?" Libby said.

"Yeah, I guess."

"They just arrested them?"

"Yeah. Maybe they've got their reasons. Like using a mounted machine gun against looters in a residential neighborhood might not be the smartest thing to do. Or all that sporting."

"Ron said he thought they 'greased' them, whatever that means."

"Killed them."

"And the deputy said they didn't."

"Affirmative. We'll talk about this later." Meaning, off the radio.

"Agreed."

For the rest of my shift, I did little but think. 'What weren't they telling us?'

Wednesday morning, like all mornings since the earthquake, came way too dang early. Karen and I had had chickens years before, and I never did get used to hearing that rooster announce to the world that he was ready to start his day. This day was no different, except we had work to do down the road.

Ron's shift had ended at four, with no other incidents or anything, other than the rain finally quitting, to report. We set our alarms for six-thirty, our rooster beat that by a half-hour.

Karen and Libby got the fire going again, while we stood in line for the 'facilities.' We decided to let the boys stay in bed, and the girls too, to give them a chance to rest up from their colds.

Libby was working on getting some pancakes mixed up when I got back inside, and Karen had the fire going nicely. The wall thermometer said the woodshop was a little over fifty degrees, and I knew that the store room was cooler than that. The clouds had thinned out overnight, and the coming from the northwest. Never a good sign, as it usually meant that extremely cold weather—usually single digits or lower—was coming our way.

"So what's on your game plan today, Coach?" Karen asked me.

"I'm not sure how long it'll take me down the road, so I'm kinda up in the air."

"What do you want done around here?" Karen asked as she poured a pancake into the cast iron pan.

"Weather seems to be changing to one of our favorites—arctic blast. Have the boys muck some wood over from the shed, and make sure they get a lot of it. That'll cut down on trips across the field once what's in here runs low."

"OK, I'm sure they'll be thrilled at that chore."

"No doubt."

"What needs doing in here, other than the obvious?"

"You might find out what we've got room to store in here that we've got in the basement that we're short on, although there's no way that we can do it all. Libby, if you can give Karen John's clothes sizes, we can maybe get into the house later and see if there's something he can wear, although pickings are pretty slim in his size, I'm afraid."

"Yeah, he's a big kid."

"No, he's a big man. He's got me by forty pounds, and an inch!" I'm six two, and John had been looking down at me for a year.

"Anything else?"

"Just to check on supplies. We do need to get the inventory updated…"

"Here. Done." Karen said as she handed me the clipboard.

"Cool. Now we can update the spreadsheets on the computer."

"Why? The inventory's done. I don't get it."

"The spreadsheets list quantities of items. I can set up a link to another spreadsheet that can guesstimate the nutritional intake of our food, so that if things get scarce, we can make sure that we're getting enough of each kind of food to eat."

"How on earth are you going to do that?" Libby asked.

"I downloaded a sample from the 'net. It provided guidelines on creating a nutritionally balanced diet based on somewhat non-traditional food combinations. If for example, meat is scarce, you can substitute other types of food to make sure that you're getting the right percentages of proteins, amino acids, starch and sugar. Most of the bulk stored foods fit into that program."

"Wow." Karen said. "What made you want to know this kind of stuff?"

"The writing's been on the wall for me for a while. After that trip to Africa a couple of years ago, it was reinforced. We cannot exist on what we grow here on this land. The Africans can't either on their land, unless they are diligent, and our Western example of 'civilization' doesn't work for them and that is part of the tragedy of that continent. Our example is also starting to not work for us. We need to adapt. With luck and planning, the stored foods will give us time, but we don't have enough to last forever, so we have to find other ways to feed ourselves. All of this of course, is based on the premise that things are not returning to normal. I could be wrong."

"Your track record over the past four days has not lent itself to us betting against you," Ron said.

"Luck runs in streaks. Both good, and bad."

"So this trip this morning. I assume that I should come along?"

"I'd feel better about it. I have no idea what to expect. If it all looks OK, you can just walk back up the street."

"Armed?"

"I will be, I'm taking a 1911—my grandfather's. There's a newer one in the cabinet that you can take. I think long-guns are probably not the wisest thing to come strolling in with, if the Marines, Army and the sheriff's department are there."

"Makes sense. Now, assuming you're on tractor-duty for the day, what do you need me to do around here?"

"I'm thinking another observation post—this time in the field someplace, with a good field of vision—would be a good idea. If looters are coming at us from the west, we'd never know it until they were at the barn and attacking it."

"Yeah. That's true. We can scout out a spot and get something put together."

"Remember that pile of brush on the southeast corner—you can probably build a decent shelter, and then camo it with that."

"Good idea," Ron said, already thinking about where to build a third observation post.

"So what would you do, man all three, or pull someone from the front?" Karen asked as she flipped another pancake onto a plate, and handed it to me.

"Probably pull someone, but that is open to discussion and the situation at hand."

"Good to know this isn't a dictatorship," She said with a wink. "Here, have another."

"We probably better make sure all the rechargeable batteries are topped off, and run the fridge for a while. And don't forget the Pauliano's hens."

"We're going to be buried in eggs shortly," Libby said.

"That's OK. They're a valuable commodity. Anything on the radio yet?"

"Yeah. Dollars way down, the market circuit breakers closed it down again, and the European and Asian markets tanked overnight," Libby said. She had temporarily taken over monitoring the radio while Kelly and Marie rested.

"Might be using eggs for money, soon enough. How far's the market down?"

"They didn't give numbers."

"Imagine that."

We finished breakfast, and I put on my heavy outerwear and my sidearm, under my parka. Ron did likewise. It was cold outside, no more than twenty. I asked Ron to get me one of the five-gallon cans of gas from the shed, and I hooked up the three-point hitch and the PTO generator. Karen had dressed in the meantime, and brought us out a thermos of coffee and a bagged lunch. I then pumped up both tires, both now flat, and set off to the gate after Ron filled up the tank. Ron followed along, getting the gate for me, and then rode along on one of the running boards. We were a little early, it was only eight-forty or so.

We passed the wrecked, burned and abandoned homes along the way to the end of the street, and met a desert-camouflaged Humvee, in pickup-truck configuration, in the parking lot of the convenience store. Two desert-camo'd soldiers manned the top gun, which was definitely not a fifty-caliber gun. I'd never seen anything like it before—a single large tube, with something resembling glass at the end of the 'barrel'. What the hell?

I waved as we turned around into the parking lot, and backed the generator up to where the electrical panel for the store. I shut down the tractor after I'd backed up into position, and Ron and I hopped off.

"Good morning, gentlemen. How's it going this fine day?"

"Good, sir, all things considered."

"If I might ask, what the Hell is that thing?" I asked, pointing at the odd-looking weapon.

"You can ask, I can't tell you," the Spec 4 responded.

"I thought as much. How about I describe it for you? Lethal or non-lethal directed energy weapon."

"Like I said sir, I can't say."

"That's OK. You boys have breakfast yet?"

"No sir, we don't really count MRE's as food."

I laughed. "Yeah, I can understand that." I had brought one of the radio with me resting in my pocket, and had the ear bud in. I switched it to VOX, turned away from the Humvee, and quietly spoke. "Karen, you there?"

A few moments passed. "Yep, whatcha need?"

"I've got a couple of soldiers down here who'd appreciate some real food. Any chance you can fix 'em up?"

"If they like eggs, I can help them out. I've got some cornbread too."

"That'd probably do. How bout you make up a mess of 'em, put them in that small Dutch oven, and then drive the Expedition down when you're done."

"Making friends?"

"In a manner of speaking, yes."

"Attaboy. Give me fifteen minutes."

"Thanks—love you most."

"Love you best."

"How to win friends and influence people, huh?" Ron said with a grin.

"Yeah. I figure it's best to make a good impression on the local constabulatory until things settle down."

"You're assuming they DO settle down."

"True. Give me a break. I'm trying to be a glass-half-full kinda guy."

"Yeah. Sure you are," Ron said with a smirk.

At five minutes to nine, the big Expedition came down the street, with Libby driving. I waved her into the lot, and she backed up next to the tractor.

"Soldiers, breakfast is served," I announced.

"You gotta be kidding," the Spec 4 said.

"Nope. C'mon down. Should be fresh eggs and cornbread." The soldiers didn't wait long.

Libby popped the locks on the Ford and I opened up the tailgate. True to our plan, there was the little –four quart—Dutch oven, and a foil wrapped pan of cornbread, with butter and honey. A big insulated cooler—which we used in the summer for lemonade—now held the rest of the big camp coffee percolator. Four old mugs were in a box, and some plastic utensils.

"No way," said the Spec 4, whose name read 'Alvarez.' He was joined by another soldier, who went by the name of Beck.

"Yes, way. Grab a plate and dig in. There's probably coffee in that cooler."

"Thank you ma'am," both said to Libby.

"My pleasure, boys. Gotta keep you on our good side, don't we?" Libby chuckled.

"This is the way to do it," Spec Alvarez said. "First fresh eggs I've had since God knows when."

"Yeah, the powdered stuff leaves a little to be desired."

"Yes sir," Beck said around a half-mouthful.

"Where you guys from?" Ron asked.

"Lately, somewhere hot and sandy. This is a little of a shock."

"To us all, be assured."

"Saturday night, our time, they packed us up—minus our gear—and put us on an airliner. Not a transport, a frickin' Seven Sixty-Seven!" I slept all the way home...er, well, all the way here. We were in Karbala, and now we're here."

"How many of you made it?"

"Two divisions, from what the scuttlebutt is telling us. One of ours, and a Marine Division."

I whistled. "That's what, thirty-thousand men?"

"Yeah, maybe more."

"And they're all headed here?"

"No, two brigades in Spokane, the other is detached to someplace called Yakima. Marine brigades are headed to the Tri-Cities…is that what it's called?…and the other Division is headed to Seattle. Or what's left of it."

"Wow. That's a lot of men."

"Yeah, and that's just us. I know that Guard units are getting pulled out too, and the Marines. They can't use that many men all in Seattle, so it's anybody's guess."

"Yeah, that it is. Here. Get some more before they get cold. And some more cornbread. That honey was made right down the street."

I moved away from the Expedition and back over to the tractor as the Deputy's car and a one-ton truck from our electric co-operative showed up.

"Sorry guys, I don't know if there's leftovers," Libby said as Deputy Schmitt and the electrician looked over the back of the Ford.

"That's OK, ma'am, I've eaten."

"Hey, there's still some left," said Alvarez. "C'mon. These eggs are killer."

"That'd be the green Tabasco sauce my wife tossed in."

"Awesome," Beck said. "and that coffee's the real deal too."

"French roast, I think. Enjoy. C'mon, Paul, get in there." I said to the Deputy.

For the next few minutes, the Deputy Schmitt and the electrician, a very weathered gentleman who went by the name of Samuel, got acquainted with the remaining eggs and the two soldiers just home from Iraq. This gave Ron and I a chance to talk off to the side.

"You hear that?" I said.

"Yeah. If I gather, they're pulling what, seventy thousand men out of Iraq?"

"Army Divisions are different than Marine Divisions. Figure thirty thousand in the Army division, maybe a little more than half-that for the Marines. Plus reserve units. Yeah, could be seventy thousand. Remember, that's scuttlebutt from a Spec 4. Not worth gold, but worth something."

"So where are they redeploying to?"

"Or, are they redeploying FROM, and why now, and where to?"

"Yeah. Hadn't thought about why they're leaving, just that they were called home."

"Yeah. Tell you what. You and Libby head on back to the house after they've cleaned up breakfast. I'll be fine here. I'll leave the radio on push-to-talk instead of VOX. I'll let you know what's going on every half-hour."

"Sounds good. Man it's cold."

"Yeah. That reminds me. Be sure to check the weather forecast—I think we've got a little present coming down from the Gulf of Alaska."

"Great. One more thing to work through."

"Yep."

In a few more minutes, the eggs and all of the cornbread was finished off, and the coffee as well. I didn't know at the time, but Karen had spiked the coffee with a couple shots of Bourbon, Pauliano-style. No wonder the Army liked it. Ron packed up the Ford and he and Libby headed back home, in a shower of thanks from our neighborhood soldiers.

Alvarez was from West Texas, and Beck was from West Virginia. Neither looked more than about twenty. I hoped they made it out of the Army and back home, after all this was over.

'Samuel'—he never gave a last name, got to work on the electrical panel, pulling the meter out of it's socket, and Paul unlocked the padlocked hasp on the heavy plywood doors that covered the broken storefront—he had a ring of master keys. Samuel unrolled a large diameter cable from his truck and snaked it through a hole in the poorly-fit plywood, and ran it back to the mechanical room which held the breaker panel. He then wired it in directly to the feeder lines that ran back to the meter. Since the meter was pulled, there was no danger that the electricity would flow back out of the building, into the lines on the street, and kill someone by accident.

After that was done, he shut off all the breakers except those to the pumps, hooked a sample load up to the panel, and checked to make sure that the wires weren't pulled out or shorted somewhere. Things checked out OK, so we were at least ready on the building-side.

"Samuel, I've got a question for you. The sheriff told me that the smaller generators they had wouldn't work on this setup. It looks to me like we're only going to use one-ten here, so why does my generator work where the smaller ones won't?"

"Clean power. That generator supplies power in a clean sine-wave. Most of those little generators don't do that. The wave isn't a wave, but more like a 'U' and a lower case 'N'. The computer controlling the pumps would just shut down if you supplied it with that kind of power. Safety precaution. It thinks that it's a power surge, so it resets. So here, dirty power equals no gasoline pumps."

"Got it. Thanks." 'Learn something new every day,' I thought to myself.

About fifteen minutes later, Samuel had cobbled up a plug to connect to my generator. He did wire it for two-twenty, so that he could theoretically supply the whole store with power, should he need to. I wondered if my generator and more importantly, my tractor, were being requisitioned...on a permanent basis?

Nine-thirty a.m.
Wednesday
January Eighteenth

As soon as Samuel had the cable hooked up, he gave me the OK to fire up the tractor and engage the generator. I turned on the gas, hopped up on the Ford, pushed in the clutch with my left foot and held my right foot down on both brake pedals, turned on the key and pushed the starter button, located next to the shift lever. After turning over twice, the old tractor sputtered and fired up. I ran the engine up to speed to get the PTO revolutions at about five hundred-forty RPM, engaged the PTO, and let the clutch out. Keeping my foot on the brake pedals (two, one for each side so you can turn quickly while plowing, by keeping one foot on a brake), I reached under the seat and engaged both parking brake levers, little quarter-inch-thick serrated plates that held the brake pedals down. Simple, but effective. I'm sure there would be no way to legally create such a simple mechanism today.

As I got the brakes set, a red Buick sedan that had seen better days pulled into the lot. I recognized it as belonging to one of the store clerks. A pleasant enough guy, but he seemed like he never quite operated on full power.

I looked up to the east at the sound of a low jet, which I'd seldom heard since last Friday. A FEDEX transport plane, was following a C-17 on approach to the airport. A constant stream of transport aircraft would follow for the rest of the day, and the occasional military helicopter buzzed about too, once in a while one of the big, twin rotors.

When the generator was at it's operating speed, Samuel threw the breakers in the building that operated the pump computer, pump motor, and a couple of convenience light circuits. This at least provided about half of the normal light inside the store, even though some of the fixtures had broken in the quake.

I left the tractor after grabbing a couple of concrete blocks that had fallen off of the dumpster enclosure, and blocked the big back tires of the Ford—one of the little parking brake tabs was broken. The Deputy and the store clerk were already heading in the door as I tagged along.

The clerk, Andy, had been to the store on Saturday, and had stayed until somebody showed up with plywood and a shotgun to secure the store. It had been unmolested since then. They had cleaned up the broken storefront and broken glass in one of the cooler doors, and had picked up the food and other items that had fallen in the quake. The place looked almost presentable—other than the daylight coming through the concrete block walls where they'd split.

The store was almost more of an old-fashioned general store than a 7-11. It had been built in the Twenties or Thirties, when the neighborhood was working-class agricultural, and although it'd been rebuilt, it never really forgot it's roots.

Andy moved behind the counter, hit a 'reset' button on the pump controls, and the LED panels lit up with all 'eights'. In a few moments, more numbers came up, and then finally a green LED came up in the corner of the display. Then it went blank.

"We're ready to pump, unless there's something wrong between the tank and the pump," He said.

"OK, let's find out," Samuel said as he left the building for his truck.

"Hi, I'm Rick Drummond from up the street," I said to the clerk."

"Hi. Thought I recognized you. Andy Welt. My uncle owns the place."

"Nice to meet you. You think things will work as normal?"

"No, but they'll work. Credit card sales won't work. Each card sale is done with a connect to the main company computer to verify the card is good. Without phones, it's cash-only, or an override."

Mike Amberson walked in. I hadn't heard him pull in over the noise of the tractor. "This setup going to work, Mr. Welt?"

"I think so, sheriff."

"Rick, got a minute?"

"Yep," I said, moving outside. Samuel had moved his Modern Electric truck to one of the pumps, and was filling the saddle tanks. Things were apparently working.

"Your tank's full, I see," Mike said as he peeked under the battery and fuel filler door on the Ford. "OK, here's the deal. In exchange for use of your tractor and generator, the cdounty will pay you in fuel at the rate of three times what you're using during a shift, as well as preferential treatment on food and supply distribution. How does that sound?"

I expected much less. "Sounds OK. One thing—well, more than one thing—we'll need is clothing for a couple of our unexpected guests. Can you help out there?"

"Probably. See Andrea at the community center. Give her your name and this card. It's got a Vendor ID number. That should get you set up."

"How long do you need me to stay here today?"

"I'd like to set up a regular schedule, daily, for two hours, maybe three today."

"Sounds OK. Who's gassing up?"

"This station will be serving the central part of this zip code, with priority given to all emergency and military vehicles that are able to fuel here, evacuation buses, ambulances, aid cars, and residents who are evacuating. Not staying, evacuating."

"Don't all military vehicles use gas or diesel?"

"No. A lot use kerosene."

"Really. I never knew that." Kerosene? I wondered why. "So, the fuel that I get paid for using my tractor and generator I can use in my car, without restriction?"

"Yes. So long as it's done during non-curfew periods." Andy joined us from the store.

"How long do you think this gas will last—I mean, how long until resupply? There can't be that much in the tanks."

"Three tanks. One regular unleaded, one premium, one diesel. Ten thousand gallons each, filled last week," Andy said. The store on Argonne is almost three times that—higher traffic, bigger tanks, more of 'em."

"Wow. I had no idea," I said. I'd obviously not given Andy a fair shake. He knew his business. Samuel called Andy over to the pumps for a minute, where Samuel signed for the gas on a legal pad. Buses were showing up and getting in line.

"The stations on Argonne, Andy's and the other two, will be open to the public for evacuation purposes. Cash sales only. The store owner's made a good point in that they don't know if the cards are good without verification from the credit card processing centers, and they don't want to get ripped off," Mike said.

"Can't blame them, but what about people that don't have cash?"

"If they need gas for evac, they can get on a bus. The buses are more efficient at moving people, and we don't need a bunch of gawkers running around—or looters checking out the pickings."

"What if they're just buying gas for generators?"

"That's fine, if they've got cash," Mike said.

"You're going to have a situation on your hands, my friend. Not too many people buy stuff with cash in the kinds of quantities that you're talking about."

"Not my problem. If they need assistance, they can get to a shelter. If they want to leave, they can get on a bus. I gotta get going. Maybe I'll see you tomorrow."

"Sounds good. Give Ashley my best."

"Will do, when I see her. I haven't been home since Monday. I'm headed home for some sleep right now."

"She doing OK?"

"Yeah, she's got her folks there. I called her on a radio this morning. Her folks grew up in Oklahoma during the Thirties and Forties. They know how to **do** things."

"Vanishing knowledge these days."

"Yeah. See ya."

"Hey—before you go, if you have a minute, run up to the house. I'll have Karen run you out some eggs. We've got a ton."

"Thanks. That'd be great. Those things'll be worth their weight in gold before this is over," Mike said as he got in the Crown Vic.

"Maybe so," I said quietly. That statement surprised me. There were obviously things that he knew about what was coming that he couldn't or wouldn't talk about just yet, although that was certainly one big dot in the 'connect the dots' picture.

The drivers window rolled down after he started up the car. "One more thing. There is going to be a CERT team in the neighborhood today. They're doing a census to find how many folks were killed and are still here. Military's escorting them."

"OK. Thanks." CERT was an acronym for Community Emergency Response Team. 'About four days late,' I thought.

"Karen, you there?" A few seconds passed.

"Yep. What's up?"

"Could you box up some eggs for Mike Amberson? He should be in the driveway in a minute."

"Sure. Libby and Ron are down at Pauliano's right now with the Expedition, getting more. Couple dozen work?"

"Sure, I s'pose."

"Done. How's it going?"

"Good. Call me back after Mike leaves."

"Will do. Out."

By the time Mike had pulled out of the parking lot, eleven buses were in line.

"Hey, Andy. Are you open for business?"

"Yeah, for cash customers."

"I'll get out my wallet. Need some eggs?"

"Let's continue this conversation inside," meaning, away from the authorities.

"Hell yes. Those are gonna be worth money. Real money."

"What'll you give me for three dozen?" I thought, doing a little quick math in my head.

He smiled slowly. "I'm sure we can work something out."

Karen was back in my ear. "OK, babe, Mike just left with a big smile on his face. Whatcha need?"

"Excuse me, Andy, my wife's in my ear," I said.

"No problem."

I went back outside and around the corner. "I'm back. You know what we need that we weren't able to buy Monday? We might have a second chance. Get the list and get down here pronto. And bring a lot of cash and six dozen eggs."

"Six dozen?"

"Yeah. We got a little bartering to do."

"K. Out."

I walked back toward the door to the store, thinking about what Andy's store might contain that I might need from our list, that we couldn't buy with Dollars. I wasn't coming up with much, but maybe there was something we could find.

"So, Mr. Drummond, what can I do for you?"

"Well, I may be able to supply a few dozen eggs every couple of days, but I'm not sure what in exchange you have that I need."

"What kind of shape is your house in?" This question came out of left field, I thought.

"Probably a lot like everyone else's. Beat up. Bad."

"I might be able to help you out with that."

"How so?"

"I own a building supply company. More correctly, my late father owned it. He didn't make it through the quake."

"I'm sorry to hear that."

"Don't be. He was a real bastard. Used to beat the crap out of us kids. I'm the only one that stayed. Everyone else left town to get away from the abuse."

"Then I'm doubly sorry that you had to put up with that."

"Now to business. We should be able to work out something that will be mutually beneficial using our resources at hand, agreed?"

"Potentially, yes."

"Potentially? Listen. That generator of yours is making me a fortune. I owe you big time. The government is paying me non-regulated prices for every drop that comes out of every tank I've got, so I'm not hurting for money, for the first time in my life. Everyone who has a clue realizes that the dollar is history, and until something else takes its' place, trading is going to be the way to go. So every paper dollar that I get, I'm getting rid of as soon as I can, buying things that will be worth something later. Diversifying, so to speak."

I was completely wrong about this guy. He was one of the few people I'd met that not only 'got it', but was trying to position himself to be on the upside before anyone realized the seriousness of the situation. I had to regard him with both respect and…caution.

"The problem being, is that not many have a clue."

"Too bad for them, good for me."

"That's one way to look at it."

"Hey. I'm not taking advantage of anyone here. I'm charging regulated prices for my goods and my gas that goes to the public. I hammered out the deal with the Feds on my gas that I get paid a national market rate, every day. If people want to sell me goods in exchange for paper, that's their problem."

"Yes, as long as you're not taking advantage of them." Karen showed up behind me.

"Store open?" she asked.

"Andy, this is my wife Karen."

"Ma'am, nice to meet you," Andy said as he shook Karen's gloved hand. "Yes, the store's open if you've got cash."

"We've got cash."

"Then whatever's in here you can buy, so long as it's within limits," meaning, at a hundred dollars or less. "for each of you, of course."

"You sure?" I asked.

"I'm the one selling. No one's ripping me off, and I'm making money."

"You heard him, hon. Go shopping."

"Will do!" She said with a smile.

"OK, building supplies. What can you help me out with?"

"What do you need?"

"A sh•tload of sheetrock, drywall tape and mud, window glazing, probably some two-by sixes, rolled insulation, four squares of roofing, mortar....and about fifty feet of eight inch double walled chimney stack."

"That's not a bad list."

"That's off the top of my head."

"Tell you what. You get me a list, and we'll talk. I can sell all that for cash, right now."

"Market rate?"   I could see Karen was listening in, while filling a basket.

He smiled. "We'll work something out. Goods like that are hard to come by."

"What I just listed is about two grand in materials."

"Retail, yeah, probably."

"You can get me that material?"

"No problem. If you got the cash. Not a check, cash."

"I'll see what I can do." If I could get to the bank, and if the bank were actually open, I might be able to do something meaningful. If.

"Now, what about those eggs?" Andy asked.

"We have laying hens. They're able to supply us a fair amount per day."

"A little advice. Don't sell them. Stock 'em up and wait as long as you can. They're appreciating by the minute."

"Kind of. It's not the eggs that are worth more, it's the dollar—the medium of exchange—that's worth less."

Andy grinned. "You get it good enough."

"Yeah. Didn't think it'd happen this soon though, or this fast."

"This ain't nothin'. Store prices on your eggs are regulated right now at last weeks price. What's that, under three bucks a dozen? In Coeur d'Alene right now, those are selling for more than six bucks."

"You're kidding."

"No I am not. I heard it on their radio station this morning."

"Well, that puts a different spin on things."

"No kidding. So what's your first priority on your house?"

"Getting the roof fixed, I guess."

"What's it gonna take?"

I thought for a minute, and wrote up what I thought I would need to fill in the hole where the north gable back used to be, as well as the work for the chimney for the woodstove.

"That's probably a good start."

"What's your address?"

I gave it to him.

"The stuff'll be there tomorrow morning."

"I don't have that kind of cash."

"Don't worry about it. My way of saying thanks for that generator. By the time those tanks are dry, I'll be a very wealthy man. If they resupply, even more so. Get the rest of your list together and you pay for that. This stuff's on me. Or, my old man, more correctly."

"I'm not getting it. How are you making money on this?"

"I told you. I negotiated national market rate for my gas. National market rate is an average of unleaded fuels, nation wide. I paid for it already, and I'm being paid for it more, every day, in cash by the Feds. The national price per gallon average today is four-fifty a gallon. I paid a buck ten. Do the math. I've got thirty thousand gallons here, eighty-two thousand at the other stores. What kind of profit am I making here?"

"A serious one. But it's in evaporating money."

"Right. Which is why I'm buying stuff so fast I'm losing sleep."

"And you gotta be making money on the sales of building materials, after all, the whole Northwest is gonna be a big construction zone."

"Yeah, and whatever's left in inventory when the world opens back up for business will go into probate. Tying it up for months."

"Oh. Gotcha. So whatever you get rid of before 'the world' opens back up for business…."

"Is mine."

I could see where Andy was going with this, and although I didn't like the reasoning, I did need the materials to get the house livable again, even if things returned to 'normal'…the chances of which I thought were fading like a dream upon waking.

"All right. Sounds like a deal. How are you getting power to your other stations?" I asked.

"Military helicoptered in generators. We'll open the stores up tomorrow morning. Might even sell latte's."

"So, the governments paying you every day?"

"Yep. Cash. Collect it at the start of curfew. I've been sleeping at the store since then. Paying three guys to watch over my house and the building supply and the store when I'm not there. A couple hours a day, I go…shopping."

His tone meant, buying black-market at whatever the going rate was.

"So what've you bought so far?"

"Stuff that'll be worth it's weight. That's all I'm gonna say, and don't ask again."

"I won't, assuming it wasn't stolen."

"Not stolen. But, not all of it was bought within the rules and regs of Martial Law, either. Enough said."

"Indeed. I'll be right back. Gotta check on the tractor."

I went out front and checked the tractor for fuel. The aftermarket gauge that I'd put in the tank showed a little under half full. Close enough for now. I headed back inside.

"Karen, you done?"

"I think so. I don't know the total cost though."

"I'll add it up," Andy said. He rang up the purchases at the cash register as Karen loaded the bags up. The total came to a little over three hundred dollars.

"That's a little more than two hundred," Andy said, "but I don't see a Fed in here."

"Works for me." I said. "Pay the man, hon. Andy, how about a couple dozen eggs."

"That'd be just fine, Mr. Drummond. Just fine."

Late morning
Wednesday
January Eighteenth

Karen and I loaded the Expedition up with our purchases. From what I was able to see as we loaded the bags, Karen had loaded up on canning flats, pectin, yeast, thread, wax, cold and flu medicine, cheese, honey, spices, coffee beans, sugar, bleach and a bunch of other stuff that she or Andy loaded and I didn't see. I never imagined spending a hundred bucks at a convenience store, let alone more than three.

"Go and head on back home. Did you get what you needed?"

"And then some. But there's probably still some stuff that Libby could use. Should I send her down?"

"Yeah, but make sure she drives the Jeep. I don't want it advertised that we're buying that much stuff. And have her bring a couple of empty five-gallon gas cans."

"Got it."

"We'll talk more later. I should be home for lunch."

"Got a surprise going for lunch. Dinner will be fried egg sandwiches—fresh bread too if the girls kept an eye on it."

"Cool! That and some of that Nine Fingers Mustard, and I'm set."

"You are twisted, Rick Drummond."

"Yes ma'am. That I am. Oh. Almost forgot. Tell John that we're going to the community center this afternoon to see if there's any clothes at the clothing bank that'll fit."

"How did you work that out?"

"Tell you later. Get going."

"K. Love you."

"You too."

The Expedition wound it's way around the last of the buses that was in line. Ambulances, fire trucks and paramedic units had now taken their places, and a big county snowplow, soon followed by a road grader, got in line. At this rate, I wondered how long thirty-thousand gallons of fuel would last?

About fifteen minutes later, the Jeep showed up with Libby. I introduced Libby to Andy, and he quietly opened the door for her to shop. She ended up with around eighty dollars in goods, loaded into the back of the Jeep, next to three empty gas cans. The last of the gas fueled vehicles was at the pump now, leaving only the diesel grader in line. I had Libby drive over to the pump and I filled two gas cans. I'd fill the tractor up with the third. Specialist Alvarez wrote down the pump reading as I finished the cans, and waved to Libby in the Jeep as she drove back to the house.

"You feel free to build us some of those eggs, any time Mr. Drummond."

"That's my wife's recipe. You guys pulling the same duty shifts? No rotation?"

"Yep. We're up the middle. Second crew will be here at eighteen hundred through oh-six-hundred. There's four on late duty. Should be a mobile patrol running with two of them, with the other two manning this post. Problem is they're green as grass."

"Does that mean that we can actually get some sleep tonight?"

"Sheriff said you had a couple of LP/OP's up the road for the past couple of nights." An LP/OP was the military term for 'listening post/observation post. I didn't tell Alvarez that ours were hardly military.....

"Yeah. Had a little business one night too."

"I heard that too. Rocked their world."

"Yeah, bad stuff."

"You should be able to get some sleep. We'll have continuous patrols, between us and the sheriff's office. The core areas are easy to patrol. The foothills are another story."

"Yeah, pretty spread out up there."

"Yep, both houses and patrols. Not worth protecting after a point."

"I figured as much. Why don't you have your second shift CO stop by the house after shift change. I'll see if we can fix them up with a meal or a coffee break."

"I'm sure they'd appreciate that, Mr. Drummond."

"After what you guys have done for us, I think we're all OK with a little pay back."

"Thank you, sir."

"You're more than welcome," I said as the road grader pulled off. "Looks like we're about done here today. I'll be back in the morning."

"Sounds good. We'll see you then," Alvarez said as I carried the can over to the tractor. I told Andy I was shutting down, and he came out with a bag of groceries for Alvarez and Beck.

"Y'all like Twinkies?"

'Staying on their good side,' I thought.

After pumping up the trailer tires (with the stations' air compressor!) and topping off the tank, I towed the generator back up the road.

The weather had never really warmed up much, it was around twenty-five as the first snowflake hit my cheek. By the time I was halfway home, big white flakes had started to obscure the far end of the street.

"Comin' home." I said into the radio, after pushing the button. "Anyone on gate duty?"

"Yeah, Carl and Ron are up there. Can you guys get the gate?"

"Yep." Ron responded.

By the time I'd driven the few hundred yards home, my black ski bibs were white with snow, and the red running boards were covered. I pulled into the yard and drove straight to the barn, backing the generator trailer up to the big barn door in front of my Packard. Ron and Carl had been busy, I could now see the front wall of the house, after they'd pulled down the bead-board porch ceiling that had draped over most of the first floor façade. After I shut off the engine, I hopped off and shut off the fuel feed. I then covered both the generator and trailer with tarps and went inside for lunch. It was a little after noon. Both dogs came running, Buck with the remains of his treasured old shoe in his mouth, trying to tell me of his morning adventure with his characteristic growl and whine. Ada of course just wagged her tail hard enough to swing her entire hindquarters about and pleaded at me with those soft brown eyes.
Ron had chained the gate back up and he and Carl were coming back for lunch.

"How'd it go?" he asked as he got back to the barn. .

"An adventure, like every other day this week."

"Karen said you worked out some creative acquisitions."

I laughed a little. "Yeah, I guess. I'm still trying to figure it out. C'mon. I'm half popsicle," I said as we went inside.

"Just in time," Karen said. "Lunch is just about ready."

"Good thing. I'm starved." I said. "What's on the menu? Smells Chinese."

"Good guess. I didn't have a recipe, so I winged it. Rice, some of that sauce that we like on our Chinese stuff, and I sliced up a couple of pork chops. And some peas. And some fried onions."

"Works for me," Ron said.

"Hope you made a lot, you know the way the boys eat."

"I do indeed. I used the big wok on the woodstove. I pulled off one of the burner covers and it fit right in. It came out great."

"Cool. I never thought of that. I...uh committed us to providing a meal or a coffee break to our Army friends tonight."

"That suspiciously sounds like you committed 'me' to that, Mr. Richard Drummond," Karen said, with that tone in her voice.

"Well, kinda."

"How many, just two again?"

"Um, four. Two guys will be at the station, two on mobile patrol." I received a stern look from both Karen AND Libby.

"Just don't make this a regular thing, OK?"

"I'll try not to. There is an upside. We don't have to pull watch duty. They're on regular patrols through the neighborhoods, with the sheriff's office."

"They guarantee that looters won't get us?"

"No, no one could do that before the quake either. Still, it looks like they're finally getting their....stuff together."

"I'm sure I can come up with something. What time?"

"They're running twelve hour shifts, from six a.m. to six p.m. I told the guys down the road to have the second shift commander to stop by a little after six, and we'd figure something out. It looks to me like all of the guys we're getting here are straight from Iraq. Real food is probably foreign to them."

"That's what I thought when I saw them this morning," Libby said with a smile. "I thought I was feeding John's football team the way they ate!"

"Well, we've got time to figure out something. I'd like to take care of them once in a while, but I don't think we can do it every day."

"Amen to that," Karen said. I knew she shared my feelings, but taking care of the family was first in her mind, mine too of course.

"Let's eat. I'm not getting fed just smelling lunch."

I gave everyone a recap of my morning as we ate, especially the comment that Mike told me about eggs being 'worth their weight in gold,' and my conversation with Andy Welt.

"You're getting all of that stuff, he's gonna deliver it? For free?"

"So he says. He did make a good point. The fuel would remain in the ground if it weren't for me...at least until the military moved another generator over, or decides that it's easier just to take the fuel and not pay him for it. I think he's trying to get his profit while he can. I can't say I blame him, he's very shrewd. Completely backwards of my first impression of the guy. Honestly, I thought he was learning – impaired or something. He never struck me as all that bright. Man, was I wrong. I'm hoping that he's just wanting to repay the favor."

"We'll have to wait and see," Karen said. "I think he's gaining the world at the cost of his soul."

I thought about what Karen said for a moment. "Yeah. You're probably right. So, do I do business with him?"

"If you can do so and not put yourself at risk, sure." Libby said. "Otherwise, walk away running."

"Yeah. Embrace him at arms' length."

"If that close," Ron said.

"So if he comes through, we need to get ready for some building supplies arriving tomorrow, which means clearing a spot in the garage or the driveway. If it arrives while I'm on gas station duty, Ron'll have to figure out how to get it unloaded and secured. All of that's going to change my afternoon around a bit, and so's this snow. Did the boys get the wood moved?"

"Yeah, but they're getting the crud that the girls have got, so they're in for the day. I don't want to risk something serious."

"That's OK. We're either a little ahead of the curve or we're not. I can't think of anything that they need to do out there this afternoon. How much did they move?"

"Half a cord."

"Wow—more than I expected. Good for them. I do need to take John over to the community center to see if there's some clothes that'll fit. Other than that, he should be good to stay inside."

Ron recapped the location and construction of the third observation post, which ended up toward the southwest corner of the property on high ground, with a good view of the Moore's back yard, the remaining yards to the west of us, and a big chunk of the field in front of the Woolsley's big car-barn. From the barn, it looked like a brush pile, just like we'd talked about, now being covered with snow, which further hid the post.

The morning egg trip to the Pauliano's barn and our own hen-house had netted five dozen eggs from the hundred and four hens, which is about what Joe's note told us to expect. He had a number of little side-ventures that brought extra income to his household, probably a tradition borne out of want. If Andy's information was right, then the five dozen eggs were worth well over thirty bucks, since brown eggs always sold for more than 'white' ones. 'Not bad,' I thought. Of course, production would fall off soon enough without artificial light.

The plan for the afternoon included a trip for John and I to the clothing bank, getting the small generator running, and charging up the batteries. Libby and Karen would do some more baking, and of course the endless washing of dishes and keeping the place in operation.

I was particularly enamored of the thought of sleeping a whole night through, something I'd not enjoyed since last Thursday night. I was starting to feel like a new father, functioning on five of eight-cylinders.

"Anyone had the radio on today?"

"Yeah, a little while ago, before you came in. Markets in the tank again, they said trading circuit breakers had ended trading early," Libby responded as she dished us up a second time.

"Hmmm. You remember the numbers?"

"Wrote them down for you, Mr. Crystal Ball," Libby said with a smirk. "Here you go," she said as she handed me a piece of notebook paper.

"How 'bout the weather? Any news? Seems like we've got cold weather from the northwest."

"Haven't heard. I'll check at half-past," Karen said.

I looked at the hand-written note.

Dow	*4277.15*
NASDAQ	*801.22*
S&P 500	*505.70*

Gold	*1007.26*
Silver	*17.86*

"Broke a thousand," I said, half to myself.

"What'd you say?" Ron said.

"Gold. Over a grand an ounce."

"That's what Libby said. And silver way up too."

"Yeah. That retirement fund of mine just bit it though."

"Yours, mine, and everyone's."

'Not everyone's,' I thought to myself. Someone—probably a group of someone's—were cleaning up like nothing seen since Twenty-Nine. Contrary to popular belief, not everyone got creamed in that crash. I was sure that was the case this time, too. Some were probably like Andy Welt. Some were much more ruthless, I was sure.

I looked out the shop window as the snow fell, now in small flakes, indicating the drop in temperature. 'So the markets were finally tanking like I thought,' I thought to myself. 'No, worse than I thought. So when does the generally dumb public realize it? Have they already? Are we being kept in the dark?'

"Whatcha thinking," Karen said as she embraced me from behind, her cheek against my shoulder.

"How bumpy it's going to be on the way down."

"No telling. Have you heard anything about the banks reopening?"

"Not a word. I'll see if I can find something out at the community center this afternoon. They should know something. Oh, also Mike said that census takers were coming around today. They're trying to find out how many casualties there were and how many people are still here."

"What else are they trying to find out? How much stuff we've got?"

I was silent for a minute, pondering what she'd said. "I never thought about that. Quite possible."

"Then we better not advertise."

"Yeah, but it's not gonna be hard for them to figure it out."

"We can always look poor."

"You mean like on the old Jack Benny show when the tax man came?"

"Yep. Not too much of a stretch right now. Look around! We're living in a barn!"

"True enough. How 'bout you, Libby and the girls work on that project. Hide the stuff that makes it look like we prepared in the first place. The kerosene lamps, throw some clothes over the shelves over there, mess the place up, and air it out. It smells like the Mustard Seed in here with that lunch we just enjoyed. We need to look like...."

"Peasants."

"Yeah. Think Dr. Zhivago."

"Where's my balalaika when I really need it?"

"It might work, no guarantees. But there was no point in preparing for something like this if we're going to let the government take it from us."

"What if they figure it out?"

"We'll cross that bridge when we come to it. We have a friend or two in higher places, that might help. The hospitality we've been providing to the military and law enforcement folks can't hurt either, I hope."

"Let's hope you're right," Ron said. "We should go get our outside duties taken care of. It's not getting any nicer out there."

"Yep. Back to the salt mines...."

Ron and I put our outerwear back on, and I grabbed a drier pair of glove liners and my mittens, and one of the charged radios. We headed out through the tool room, and up toward the garage, dogs leading the way, when they weren't tackling each other and biting at each other's hind leg. 'As long as they're fed, they're happy,' I thought.

"How much room do you think we need to make?"

"Well, if he comes through with the list I gave him, we'll have ten or twelve sheets of plywood, thirty two-by-sixes, twenty two-by-fours, a dozen rolls of insulation, a three-by three double glazed window, ten to fifteen sheets of five-eighths sheetrock, tape, mud."

"That's a pretty sizeable order."

"Forgot the chimney stuff too. That's about fifty feet of double-walled stainless chimney pipe, eight inch. I think I can salvage some of what came down, maybe only the stove fitting and the cap."

"Sounds like that'll fill up a good chunk of part of the garage."

"Yeah. And we just filled it up with furniture. I guess we can stack it up and see how it comes out."

"What's the game plan for the house?"

"I've been thinking about that, but we need to do some forensics on the place to see what's damaged behind what we can see. The foundation's damaged, but not terminally, from what I know right now, but that opinion might change. If we were lucky, we can clean the place out of all the contents, get the lath and plaster cleared out, repair the damaged framing, put in new windows (from God knows where), fix the roof and chimney, and get it weather tight again. Then we can do the sheetrock, refinish it, and move back in."

"Nice and tidy description."

"Yeah. The reality however is somewhat different."

"Always is. This will take a serious amount of time."

"Yep, considering it took the better part of twenty years to do the functional and cosmetic work on it to get it to where it was on Friday."

"You really think that the economy's not coming back?"

"No, I think that 'an' economy will come back. Not the one that we've participated in for the past three generations."

Ron thought about that as I opened up the man-door on the side of the garage, and peered into the darkness. "It's going to be a wild ride, and no one knows were it'll end up. We have a good chance of the government nationalizing critical industries, seizing transportation networks and commodities, and essentially ending up in a dictatorship to preserve a system that doesn't work anymore. We have a chance to create an economy that is based on honest work for honest pay, for a currency based on recognized standards of value—meaning gold or silver—and going on from there into a future that understands the danger of creating something from nothing. We have a chance of failing at both."

"Ever the optimist."

"Well, it's gotten me this far...." I laughed. "C'mon. Let's move some stuff and make a hole."

Wednesday Afternoon
January Eighteenth

Ron and I assessed the contents of the garage with an eye toward filling it up with building materials that may, or may not arrive tomorrow. We elected to move the row of boxes that resided in the center of the garage before the quake toward the south wall, and stacked them floor to ceiling in a row, partly occupying the spot where I used to park. We then moved the furniture we'd removed from the house against the boxes, and stacked up what we could. This provided a space about fifteen feet wide, and twenty-four feet deep, where Karen's car normally resided. It was parked in the driveway and covered with a plastic sheet, left over from repainting the house last year.

I also took the time to get out the floor jack, and lifted the old Mustang back up off of the floor. Carl, Kelly and I had been working on it with the goal of getting it restored before Carl started Drivers Ed. I'd been replacing the upper control arms the weekend before, and my back had decided to let me know that it didn't appreciate all the time spent working under the fender, so I'd put it off for the next weekend. The back tires were still on the car, and the quake had shoved the little coupe to the east and off of it's jackstands, one of which was crushed by the weight. My old tool box, home to my favorite tools, was similarly smashed. That'd wait for another day. I found a couple of really old jackstands from my teenage years, and jacked the car back up, and rested it back on the stands. It seemed doubtful if we'd finish the two-day project in two years, at that point.

The cream-yellow Galaxie convertible, under it's padded cover and residing in the back corner of the garage, had received the contents of two wood shelves mounted on the south wall, showering the passenger side of the car. The wall cabinet that used to be on the west wall, had torn off, landed on the workbench below it, and fallen over onto the trunk. The cabinet was almost empty, only holding some air tools and some miscellaneous stuff that I hadn't sorted out after I'd finished the wood shop. I'd spent a couple thousand hours putting that car back together, and I wasn't all that eager to see how much damage was done. Ron and I moved the cabinet off of the trunk, and stacked it between the Galaxie and the Mustang. I ran my hand over the still-covered trunk, and was rewarded with a large dent where there was once smooth metal. Damn.

As we were moving back toward the front of the garage, I heard the chain rattle on the gate. I hadn't heard a car.

Cautiously, Ron and I looked out the man-door, and saw three bundled-up pedestrians, two with clipboards. "Must be the CERT survey team. Keep an eye on them from here. I'll go out."

"Got it," Ron replied.

I gave him the radio. "Tell the girls what's going on."

"Will do."

The CERT team was baffled by the gate. Most people were, and I liked that. They were still staring at the chain and latch as I approached through the snow. One guy, two women. Interesting.

"Howdy," I called out.

"Hello. We're here to do a survey of the neighborhood residents to determine population and casualties from the earthquake."

"I heard you were coming. The sheriff let me know."

"Very good. I'm Zach, this is Sharon and Deborah." The young man had an accent. Midwest.

"Nice to meet you. I'm Rick Drummond."

"Can you tell me how many people you have living here?" Zach was reading from a list. One of the young women was taking notes on waterproof paper on her clipboard.

"Normally four. Since Sunday, eight."

"Are all residents here related?"

"Our guests are friends."

"Has their family been notified that they are here?"

"No. Most of their families are, or were, in the Seattle area."

"Are they from this neighborhood?"

"No. North side, Five Mile."

"I see. Has anyone informed their neighbors that they are here?"

"No. No way to do so."

"Was anyone seriously injured in the quake?"

"No, cuts, scratches, that kind of stuff. We were lucky."

"Do you know the disposition of your neighbors?"

"Yes, some of them." I told them what I knew of our neighbors, who was out of town, who was working late that night, who was dead.

"Do you know that public shelters are available for your use?"

"Yes."

"Are you planning on relocating to a shelter or evacuating the region?"

"No."

"Do you have adequate supplies to remain where you are?"

"Probably. That depends on how long the supply lines are down. What can you tell me?"

"What we know is that most supply lines this side of the Continental Divide in Montana are in tough shape. Same thing coming up from California into Central Oregon. The quake severely damaged most infrastructure within a two-hundred mile radius of Mt. Rainier. Virtually every bridge over I-Five, and all bridges between here and Seattle, and overpasses too, are damaged or down."

"About what we've heard on the radio."

"Do you need any assistance to remain where you are?"

"Probably not."

"I've gotta say, that's the first time I've heard that this week."

"How long you been surveying?"

One of the young ladies answered. "Since Monday afternoon. Our response rate has plummeted since then."

"Not surprised. People are getting out of the cold and going somewhere warm. Where you all from?"

"Oklahoma City."

"Thought so. Accent."

"Yeah, pretty hard to blend in here."

"That's all right. Seems like there's not many people to blend in with right now. What's your population count telling you?"

"Not too many deaths from the quake directly, twenty that we've counted since Monday, but we're not in a heavy damage zone or the chemical contaminant zone to the west. Eighty percent mortality downwind of that. So far in this zip code, we've had maybe forty percent of the residents still at their house as of Monday and Tuesday, probably only thirty percent today. The roads south are pretty busy."

"Yeah. Welcome to winter."

"So I gotta ask you," 'Sharon' asked, "How do you people heat your houses around here? With all these trees around I thought there'd be a ton of wood heaters going. Most people are leaving because of cold."

"Most are either gas or electric. Those that used to have fireplaces that burned wood, or wood-fired furnaces or woodstoves, converted them to gas for convenience, and because the state was leaning on the county's air-quality. Wood stoves aren't always good for your breathing air, the government tells us."

"Doesn't seem to me that air quality matters if you're freezing to death," Deborah responded.

"Yep, and we haven't seen the coldest temperatures yet."

"So you heat with wood?"

"When we can, that is, before the quake hit, we'd have to quit burning wood if the air quality alerts went up. Then we used natural gas. Not anymore, it appears."

"Yeah, probably not for a while, either. Well, we better get going. We're trying to finish up between here and the next arterial before dark."

"Good luck. Watch yourself. We had some trouble with looters the other night."

"Thanks. We'll keep an eye out. We've got a police radio if we need help, and we're never more than a half-mile from a patrol."

'Good to know,' I thought. "All right then, we'll see you around."

"Thanks for your cooperation," Deborah said as they headed off into the snow.

'Hmmm.' I thought. 'They didn't even want to see where we were living. I could've been a looter for all they knew.' I walked back into the garage.

"Didn't invite them in?"

"Nope. Nice enough kids, but they were just going down their list of standard questions it seemed. They must know who lives where though, one of the girls was checking off boxes as I listed who was still in the neighborhood and who was out of town."

"No ulterior motives?"

"Seemingly not. The jury's still out on that though. Did you let Karen and Libby know?"

"Yeah. I think Libby was a little disappointed that the Jack Benny thing wasn't going to play before an audience."

"I'm not. The less they know the better at this point."

"Think we've got enough room?"

"Probably more than enough. I want to get back into the basement before dark. If it gets as cold as it could, the pipes in the house will freeze. That'll add insult to injury."

"What do you plan on doing?"

"Drain at least the second floor, if not the main floor too."

"You plan on collecting the water?"

"Probably wouldn't hurt. Do you know what we've got for containers?"

"Nope. Let's check with the ladies. 'Bout time for a coffee break anyway."

"Yeah. Something warm would be good."

Ron and I walked back out to the barn. I checked the temperature on the little plastic thermometer on the side of the garage, it read twenty-one degrees. It was still snowing hard, but if the 'arctic blast' was coming, the snow would taper off and we'd probably see clear, very cold weather by morning, and wind from the northeast. Since the house wasn't weather tight anymore, I didn't expect the pipes to stay warm enough with no heat source to keep them from freezing and splitting. Draining the place could be a real job.

"Hey, got any coffee on?" I asked as we came into the shop.

"Hush. Weather's on," Libby said quietly.

......tures in the single digits by morning in the majority of Eastern Washington, with temperatures in the teens in the coastal regions. Gusty winds are expected to pick up by ten p.m., with wind chills expected to be minus twenty and colder for twenty-four to forty-eight hours. Extreme cold temperature will lead to frostbite on exposed skin and danger of death due to exposure. If you are in an exposed location or have the slightest doubt that you can remain warm during this arctic outbreak, seek shelter in a public facility immediately."

"Swell." I said as I poured a cup of coffee. 'Somewhere along the line today, I picked up a sore throat. Funny I didn't notice it before,' I thought.

"Hey, John, let's get over to the community center. I want to get back sooner rather than later."

"OK," he groaned. Obviously not feeling good. He always responded in a positive manner to Karen and I, much less so to his parents.

"Hon, we need to drain some of the water out of the house. Do we have any containers for potable water that we can lug out here?"

"Why carry them? Just put them in the Expedition."

"Duh. Glad you thought of that."

"How many gallons do you think?"

"No idea. I just don't want to waste it, even if we've got a decent filter setup going."

"I know we've got that big blue five-gallon jug, and two five gallon collapsibles. That's all that I know of."

"That'll have to do. I don't want to drain the water heater, but we might have to. If it's around freezing in there now, we'll have to. It'll be really cold this time tomorrow."

"How big's the tank?"

"Fifty."

"No way we've got room for that."

"I know. It'll just have to go down the drain."

"What about the other houses? Do we do anything with them?"

"No keys for Nate and Ginny's, although we could probably get in through the broken windows that we covered. Tim's is trashed, Brad's is in the same shape as Woolsley's. Joe drained his before they left. We can't do them all, and I'm not sure that the problems will be that bad if the houses are mostly secure, even though they haven't been heated for the last five days. Mostly, I've got enough to do right here."

"OK. I'll give Ron the water containers and I'll go up with him to the house. Do we drain them into the laundry sink, and fill the containers from there?" Karen asked.

"Yep. Just the same procedure as I had you do when I messed up the shower faucet." I'd tried to replace the washers in the Delta shower faucet, and ended up breaking the pipe, inside the wall. Karen had to run downstairs, shut the house water off, and open up the laundry faucet to drain the pipes so I could fix the shower. Another example of a fifteen-minute job that took me five hours.

"Hopefully not so well-planned."

"Thanks. I love you too. John, you ready?"

"Yep."

"OK, let's roll."

"Remember, babe, if you can see your breath in the laundry, drain the tank. There should be that hunk of hose in there that I use when I flush it out."

"Got it."

"OK. See you in a little while."

"Hurry back. More fun to have here."

"I'm sure."

John and I left through the garden, then wound around to the front of the barn to keep the heat in the store room, where Carl and the girls were reading, sacked out on their beds.

We piled in the Expedition, and after scraping the well-frozen windshield, drove up to the front gate. John hopped out and got it open, and closed it behind me when I pulled through. We had about three inches of fresh snow.

At least one vehicle had been up the road since I came back by the tracks in the snow, probably a police car by the treads. We passed our Army friends at the corner, honked, and headed up to the community center.

The center was more full than it had been during my previous visits, and the shelter at the elementary school seemed to be much more full as well. Three school buses were idling at the curb, and they were being loaded as we got out of the Ford.

Entering the community center, a nice young lady—Andrea, as the sheriff said--asked if I needed assistance, and showed us to the clothing bank on the basement level after I showed her the card that Mike gave me. The food bank was also located there, and I was not surprised to see that it was closed. Through the windows, I could see that it was stripped bare. It looked like a new building—nothing of any kind on any of the shelves.

The clothing bank had been picked over pretty well too, but given John's larger than average size, we were able to get a nice pair of hiking boots, a pair of Sorel knock-offs that my whole boot could fit in (John wore size 14 shoes), a rather ratty snowmobile suit that we could patch up, an Army parka and shell (complete with furry fringe on the olive-drab shell), jeans, socks, underwear, and a couple of sweaters.

"What do I owe you for the clothes?" I asked.

"There's no charge if you can't afford it."

"I've got cash. If it'll help the shelter out, I'd just as soon pay for what we've picked out."

"If you're sure," Andrea said, somewhat surprised that we just didn't take the stuff and go. "Twenty dollars would be fine."

I pulled out my wallet and paid her a nice, new bill that was evaporating in value even as I handed it to her. "There you go. Hope you can get some food for the food bank with that."

"I don't think that'll happen. What was left was taken over to the shelter yesterday afternoon. They're probably shipping in a couple of trucks to the shelter tomorrow. They're running low."

"Are they still evacuating people?"

"Yes. We shipped out twenty buses today from here alone."

"Whoa. What is that, a thousand people?"

"Twelve hundred fifty, actually."

"Not too many left in the old neighborhood."

"No sir. Probably stay that way until spring, I guess."

"You might be right." I said. "Thanks again."

"You're very welcome. Take care of yourself," she said, smiling warmly at young John, who was instantly embarrassed. We headed up the stairs and back to the Ford.

"You go, boy!" I kidded.

"C'mon, don't tell Mom."

"No problem bud. I just thought it was funny that a pretty mid-twenty something was looking over an eighteen year old like that. Makes me feel young again."

"Quit, please."

"No prob." I smiled as we drove home. 'Nice to know some things don't change.'

Late Afternoon
Wednesday
January Eighteenth

I pulled into the gate and John hopped out and got the gate for me—I asked him to lock it up when he closed it. Ron had two of the five-gallon water carriers in the driveway ready to pick up, and as I pulled into the drive, he rounded the corner with the last of the jugs. I unlocked the doors and he piled the containers in the back.

"How'd it go?"

"Good. John cleaned up."

"What'd it cost?" Karen asked, carrying a box and something wrapped in blankets.

"It was supposed to be free. I gave the young lady twenty bucks any way. We ended up on the good end of that deal by a long, long ways."

"That's good. How'd the food bank look?"

"Stone cold and stripped to the walls."

"No."

"Yeah. They shipped the food over to the shelter. The young lady, Andrea, said that food was running low. They've moved out something like twelve hundred people from there so far, headed south."

"Wow. I wonder where they're going?"

"Somewhere where it's not winter, I suspect. What's in the bag?"

"Something for you. Here," she said as she handed me the blankets.

I unwrapped the long package after setting it in the back of the Ford next to the water jugs. It was my grandfather's polished and engraved Cavalry sword and spurs, from the wall by the bar, a bottle of very old cognac, and several framed photos, also from the bar. The first, of my Dad was taken when he'd been stationed in Manila and building airstrips for the Army Air Corps. The second was a shot of him in Greenland, where he built radar directional stations for cross-Atlantic bomber and transport traffic, seated inside a tent, in formal wear, with a full beard. My Mom hated that picture. I thought it illustrated his occasional irreverence quite well. The final shot was of my parents, right after their engagement. Mom with a beaming smile and a new engagement ring, and my Dad in his Lieutenant's uniform, arm-in-arm, walking down Riverside in Downtown Spokane. April, nineteen forty-four. They met while he was on leave, passing through town. Proposed on the second date. She accepted immediately. Married in June of forty-seven. Mom always said he was the last man out of the Pacific Theater.

"Thanks." I said quietly.

"You're welcome. The envelope behind the pictures has the negatives and the CD ROM too."

The CD held the scanned images of not only the three framed pictures, but was filled with scanned images of hundreds of family pictures stretching back to the eighteen-nineties. Even a couple of tintypes that were older than that.

"I figured those ought to be someplace safe."

"Yeah, they were just stacked up on the back bar, weren't they?"

"Yep."

"I see you got fifteen gallons. Did you drain the tank too?"

"Yeah. That's where it all came from. The kitchen lines were already either dry or frozen. There's a puddle on the floor of the laundry, under one of the valves for the bathroom, and all the dirty laundry on the floor is soaked. I think it drained the upstairs."

"Or already froze and split. Dang. Let's get back inside. I want to get John into a warm room." 'Me too,' I didn't say. I was getting a cold or something, sure as the snow.

Everyone piled into the Ford and we drove back out to the field. John made a beeline for the storeroom, and we hauled the water through into the woodshop, setting it down near the big barrel of water that had run through the Berkey filter.

"What is that lovely aroma?" It hit me like a wall.

"Not for you. Not the first one, anyway. Peach cobbler for your friends down the street. The girls' idea."

"And you thought I was buttering them up!"

"No harder to make than anything else. There's a second one ready to go in the oven soon."

Karen re-wrapped the sword, pictures, and cognac, and brought them in, putting them on a workbench that until recently held my Dremel, a decent sized grinder, and an unfinished baseball display case I was building for Carl. Now, it was a sideboard for our food preparation.

Carl was napping on his bed, with Ada curled up next to him. Buck was nearby, his nose covered by a paw. He looked up at us briefly as we came in, and promptly went back to sleep. All the outdoor activity was wearing on the dogs too.

Kelly and Marie were both reading by the light of the Coleman camp lantern, turned down to a comfortable light.

"What are you two reading?" I asked.

"Marie's reading 'Cold Mountain.' I'm reading a book called 'Andersonville.' It's good."

"Yes it is. Both of them are—they're both favorites of mine." 'Funny they're both reading Civil War novels. I hope that isn't a sign of things to come.' I thought to myself. "Have you heard any news on the shortwave or the local channels?"

"Same old warnings about the cold on the local channels, and the stuff about curfew, and gas, and price controls, and spending limits," Kelly answered.

"Shortwave's where it's at," Marie said. "It's wild. We picked up a station, no, a man with a bunch of letters and numbers as his 'call sign', from outside of Denver. He was talking to someone in California. They were talking about all kinds of stuff."

"Well?" I waited for her to continue. "Spill it, girl!" I said with a laugh.

"They said people were trying to get money out of the banks and the banks were only letting them take a little cash. The gas cards and credit cards weren't bein' accepted by stores."

"Really...Hmmm. What else?"

"They said that gas and grocery prices were going crazy."

"Do you remember what they were? I mean, the prices?" Libby asked her daughter.

"No. I wrote them down. I thought you'd want to see them. I tried to listen for as long as I could, but they faded out."

"Shortwave'll do that, especially with an antenna that's not all that great."

"Here's the list."

I scanned it quickly. "You did very well. Both of you. We'll have to promote you from mere working slave, to working slave, first class."

"Gee, thanks a lot."

"Seriously. You both did well. We'll have to set up a system and schedule for you two to listen in and take notes on the frequencies you're picking up, when you're hearing them, and what's important to write down."

"How do we do that? I mean, how do we tell what's important."

"We can give you a list of things that might be worth writing down, or getting one of us to listen in too."

"OK. Sounds fun," she said as she went back to her book. 'Andersonville' in my opinion, was the greatest Civil War novel of its day. 'Cold Mountain', a good second, but more about the love story than the war.

'Might be,' I thought. 'Might be terminally boring.' I looked the list over. If the radio operators were telling the truth, the value of the dollar was plummeting faster than I had imagined it could.

Message from Denver
Coffee   Not available
Milk $6.30/gal.
Mac and Cheese $6.56/5 pack
Steak $10.99/lb.
Butter $7.69 lb.
Bread $3.25/loaf
Gas $4.72 9/gallon

Message from California. Susanville?
Gas $5.65 9/gallon
Canned Veggies $2/can small size
Potatoes $2.49/lb.
Chicken $8.00 each
Eggs $6.73/dozen

"Marie, you sure you wrote these down right?"

"Yes sir. Just like they said them. I didn't understand the gas prices though. They always gave a 'nine' after the dollars."

"You did it right. The prices are listed at four dollars, seventy-two and nine-tenths per gallon."

"That's stupid."

"Can't disagree with you there."

"And why won't the banks let people get their money?" Kelly asked. "It's theirs, they should be able to get it when they want. THEY didn't go through an earthquake, so that's no excuse."

"Yep, that's right. But there is not enough physical paper money to go around. It's mostly on computers."

"So what happens when they run out?"

"We'll likely hear about that from your shortwave, if we don't hear about it on AM," I said, as we moved back into the shop and partially closed the door. John had tossed his large frame down on his mattress, and was nearly asleep already.

"Did I hear you right?" Karen asked. "Four seventy two for gas?"

"Five sixty-five in California. That's not all. Look at the rest of the list. Think about what you paid the last time you bought that stuff."

"A third of these prices," she said as Libby looked over her shoulder.

"My God. What's happening?" Libby said with shock.

"The dollar is rapidly becoming worthless."

"What will we do?"

"Use it up while we can here, that is, the physical paper and coins that we have, as long as price controls exist and there's stuff to buy. Once price controls end, it's Goodnight Irene to the dollar as we know it."

"Then what?" I could see the fear in her eyes. 'I thought we'd discussed this already,' I thought to myself.

"Then we find a new way."

"All of our money is gone. Or will be soon."

"Yep. And there's not a damn thing you or I can do about it."

"We're broke."

"The government is broke. We're, temporarily without funds. Or will be soon."

"Same thing."

"No it's not. The government is broke. They've already—or are about to—renege on their obligations to pay back the interest and principal that they've been living on for a few generations. That means that the lenders will be really pissed, and will retaliate."

"But we're the lenders."

"Some of us are small lenders. The big lenders though, are foreign governments. China. Japan. Europe. A hundred others."

"So what happens then? I mean, what will they do?"

"Wars have started for less. That's an option for them. So is seizing assets of companies that are based in the US, when those assets are located overseas."

"What we did to Al Qaida."

"Yep."

"So we're toast," Ron said.

"The government's gonna get hammered for sure. The military will have too many things to deal with all at once everywhere. Corporations like GM, Ford and others that have built big plants in China for that market did the Chinese a real big favor. They built state of the art auto plants for the Chinese, and now they're going to lose them to the Chinese."

"Checkmate," Ron said.

"Probably not that simple. We--the U.S.--is THE market for Chinese and Asian goods and products. Without us, they don't have a whole lot of people to sell to. Which means, their people don't have much to do, work wise. Which can mean, revolution."

"This just gets better and better, doesn't it?" Karen said as she got things ready for dinner.

"These are only possibilities."

"Look like probabilities to me."

"But remember, the dollar may be gone as we know it, but we're not broke. The dollar is a medium of exchange, that's all. We'll have a new one, sooner or later. Hopefully something that's grounded in reality."

"Like eggs," Libby said.

"Like eggs or those silver coins. Which brings up a point. Those layers are worth something. Someone else—like our 'friend' Andy—are going to figure that out. We need to either post someone down at Paulianos, or move the hens up here."

"You've got to be kidding. Joe's henhouse is sized for a hundred fifty hens. Ours holds twenty-five."

"Chickens can be eaten, as well as kept for layers. Look at those prices again for a dressed bird and tell me I'm smoking something illegal."

"I know, but where are we going to put them?" Karen pleaded.

"I don't know, but we better deal with it soon. Otherwise, they're gonna be gone."

"Married to a farmer," she muttered.

"Yes. A reluctant one." I answered.

"C'mon, Ron. Let's go dig out those books we rescued from the basement. I know there's a poultry book in that stack from the last time we were egg ranchers." Libby and Karen were slicing up four loaves of bread for our camouflaged-clad soldiers, who'd get a couple of fried-egg sandwiches apiece.

It turned out that according to a book that actually came with the house, and the lone rooster that resided here as well, that we actually had room for about fifty chickens in our current coop. One laying box per four hens, roost space was adequate, but we'd have to find a place to either add on for the remaining hens, or risk losing them to two-legged varmints.

Ron and I had already looked over the stash of building materials around the place, so we had a good idea of what we had and didn't have. We probably had enough 'stuff' to recycle or build straight out a new coop attached to the existing barn. We'd have to move the hen yard, which was no big deal, and enlarge that dramatically for the larger flock. Other than those minor hurdles, and of course doing all of this in sub-freezing weather, or even sub-zero weather, it'd be fine. Right.

"How long you figure it'll take us?" Ron asked.

"You banged out that outhouse pretty fast. This is almost as simple, just bigger. We don't have a foundation, can't pour concrete, so we'll use some of that pressure-treated lumber that I'd planned on for the back deck this summer for the bottom sill. The rest is two-by four framing, and either OSB sheathing or some more of that metal from the old barn roof. Roosts can be whatever; the existing ones are two-by-two's. Then we gotta build nesting boxes."

"Isn't there stuff at Joe's that you could use?"

I hadn't thought about that. "Yeah. A lot of it. Thanks for bringing that up. The roosts he built are portable, sort of. They're on wheels so he can move the whole rack out and clean it. The nesting boxes too. They're old gym lockers with the doors removed and shelves built in."

"We can move those easy."

"Yeah. We just need a big box to put them in."

"That's easy enough. I don't look forward to framing a bunch of stuff in this cold though."

"We've got the magic of power tools for that. We'll fire up the generator, and the air compressor, and frame it up with the framing nailer. We've got three walls to build, a space for a door, probably some windows—we might use some of the old house glass for that—some roof framing, sheathing and we're done. The framing nailer is a huge time saver."

"Good. Got anything that can raise the temperatures by forty degrees?" Karen said as she served Ron two fried-egg sandwiches.

"Not hardly."

"Then you're going to have a busy day tomorrow. Gas duty and building a new chicken shed?"

"So it would appear."

"What time are you expecting the Army to arrive?"

"Oh, jeez. Forgot about them. I told Alvarez to have the second shift commander stop by a little after six."

"That'd be about now," Ron said. "I'll keep your sandwiches company."

"I'm sure you will," I said as I put my boots and coat back on, plugging in the FRS and grabbing my hat. "Hon, listen in on the radio. Hopefully I'll be back soon."

"You know you're breaking curfew, right?" She asked with that look in her eye.

"Yeah. I'll be careful."

"You better. I'm no darn good with a hammer."

"Yes, but you are good with….other things."

That resulted in a wet dishrag thrown my way as I left the room.

Evening
Wednesday
January Eighteenth

I made my way through the snow up to the front porch of the house, which provided little shelter from the wind and blowing snow, now coming from the northeast. I cleared off some snow from one of the Adirondack chairs that we used in the warmer months, sat down, and waited for the Army patrol to come this way.

About twenty past six, lights appeared to the south, and a Humvee came into view –a different vehicle than had been stationed at the store earlier in the day. This had a different body configuration, and was set up like a pickup truck. A large dark box was mounted in the bed area. The vehicle stopped in the middle of the street and a spotlight came on and played across the front of the house. I turned the radio on to VOX. "They're here babe. Listen in."

"Will do," said the voice in my ear.

"Good evening," I called out.

"Hello. You Mr. Drummond?"

"Yes sir. And you are?" I asked as I left the porch for the gate.

"Second Lieutenant James Dixon, US Army. This is Specialist Olathe Johnson."

"Sir." A distinctly female voice answered from behind the spotlight.

A woman on patrol duty? Hmmmm. I guess that's not out of the ordinary these days. "Nice to meet you both. Were you here last night too?"

"In Spokane, but not here. We were in a place called East Central."

"Bet that was a big bucket of no fun."

They both looked at each other. "You got that right."

"One of the roughest neighborhoods in town. Hillyard's rough too, and so are some parts west of Downtown."

"Some of the civilians like taking pot shots at us over there."

"Yeah, Mike Amberson—the sheriff—said that too. They lost some city officers there."

"Yep. We got the guys that were doing that. That is, Oletha did."

"Good for you. Let's hope this doesn't go much farther down the old toilet bowl."

"Yes sir," Specialist Johnson replied.

"I had a talk with first shift this morning. Said you boys might appreciate some real food."

"Well, yes sir. MRE's are getting a bit thin on the novelty scale."

"How does a couple of fried-egg sandwiches sound? We'll have some other stuff too, I'm sure. Think of it as a home made MRE."

"That'd be great. We haven't had real food in….a while."

"So the first shift said. How 'bout you come back by in fifteen minutes or so, and we'll be ready. We'll meet you at the gate, and have enough for the boys down at the store too. We'll put the food in an insulated box. You just take the whole box with you and bring it back when you're done. That way you won't have to miss patrol time."

"Thanks. See you in a few."

"You got it." I waved as they continued up the street, and turned at the corner.

"Get all that?"

"Yep. Eggs are in the pan, coffee's in that big pump pot of Mom's, and we're ready for an assembly line of sandwich construction. Kelly had a bright idea too—she took one of those hunks of metal that you had laying around and heated it up on the stove. We'll wrap it up in a towel or something to keep the box warm."

"Atta girl. I'm heading back."

"K."

The insulated box that I planned on using was a homemade wood crate I'd built around a Styrofoam container. There was a great rib place in Tennessee, the Germantown Commissary that my brother's wife knew from her youth there. They'd FEDEX us big orders of ribs and pulled pork, and that great sauce each year, sometimes for our Independence Day party, sometimes for Christmas. The order would arrive on dry ice, in a big insulated cardboard box. I'd taken a few of the foam liners and built wood cases for them, two of which I gave to a Civil War re-enactor friend of mine, with appropriate stencils for his unit, the Twenty-Sixth North Carolina Infantry. They used the camouflaged coolers in their encampments at Fort George Wright, west of downtown Spokane, each summer, when they fought the Battle of Spokane Falls. Their opponents were often the Twentieth Maine, the Seventh Wisconsin, and the Third Michigan. Hardly seemed fair that the Confederates had so many blue uniforms to shoot at with their fifty-four caliber rifles.

Other folks from the Third Michigan liked my crates too, but since I became of the age where I could discern the real reasons for the Civil War, I've favored the Confederacy in the War of Northern Aggression.

At the appointed time, Ron and I lugged the crate by it's rope handles up to the gate, unlocked the chain, and hauled the crate out of the gate just as the Humvee came back from it's loop. Ron kept his word, he just watched my dinner, and didn't eat it.

"Good evening. Got a little something you will appreciate here."

"I'm sure that we will. Our patrol would like to thank you for doing this."

"Like I told the morning crew, after what you all have been through, it's no problem at all. We're proud to do it."

"Thank you."

"Anyway, here you go. There's some sandwiches wrapped up in here, two apiece, fried egg on wheat bread. Bread's fresh this afternoon. There's some condiment packages in there too and some plastic utensils. The pump pot's got hot coffee in it, a darn sight better than mess-hall coffee, I'm sure. On the bottom, is the surprise. Save it for last. It's still hot from the oven. Careful of the bottom hot plate—it's a hunk of half-inch steel that's wrapped up in an old towel."

"Will do, sir. We'll keep the box down at the store and have the day shift get it back to you."

"That'd be fine. You better get going. This stuff's not getting any warmer."

"Yes sir. Goodnight," both Dixon and Johnson answered. "Take care."

"Always do. You too." We waved as they went back down the street.

"That ought to make a favorable impression."

"I'll say," Ron said. "Must be our turn for our cobbler."

"Amen."

I locked up the gate and we headed back to the barn.

Karen and Libby were listening to the shortwave when we got back inside. Aftershocks of around six-point-oh had hit the Seattle region, with an epicenter around Olympia. We hadn't felt a thing. More casualties were expected in collapses of damaged buildings.

"We better expect that here, too," I told everyone.

"Why? The quake wasn't here in the first place."

"Yeah, but that quake shook loose a lot of things. That fault going under downtown might wanna let go again like it did a couple years ago."

"What'll that do?" Carl asked.

"Shake us up some more, no doubt. The ones we had were little, only three-point-five or so. No real damage. Hard to say what'll happen next."

"How do we get ready?" Kelly asked.

"Anything that could tip over has got to be secured. Anything breakable should be stowed when we're not using it."

"What else?" Karen asked.

"You know from your time in California. Get into a doorway."

"OK," the kids answered.

"You guys get some rest. We need to get you all healthy again."

"Yes sir," John answered from his bed.

The adults went into the woodshop, and Karen brought the radio with her.

"Do you think we'll have another quake?"

"Yes, sooner or later. Aftershocks will keep happening until things settle in again. How have the dogs been behaving?"

"Same as always."

"If they start acting weird, that might be a sign. Now let's listen in and see what else we can hear. And I'm about ready for some cobbler, if that's allowed."

"I'll dish you up," Libby answered.

"....south of Seattle registered at six-point-two in the revised readings from Golden, Colorado. Numerous casualties from this strong aftershock have been reported, including several deaths. Aftershocks around Mt. Rainier have been reported at two-point five to four-point three since the eruption early Saturday morning."

"In news from Rainier, the lava flows reported yesterday could not be observed today due to heavy clouds and snowfall. Ash has tapered off to irregular plumes since Tuesday morning."

"The National Weather Service has issued a warning for the Pacific Northwest. An air mass of arctic air is headed for the region, with lows expected in the Spokane and Coeur d'Alene region of minus twenty degrees accompanied by winds in excess of twenty five miles an hour from the east. The severe cold is expected to last until at least Saturday and possibly Sunday before a warming trend is forecast. Residents of the region who have any doubt about keeping warm in these temperatures should take shelter in a public shelter or evacuate the area on public transport. FEMA has organized additional transport which will be available on Thursday morning beginning at nine a.m."

"In national news, price increases in virtually all commodities have been observed in all major markets across the country in the *past three days. Some items have been observed in short supply, and disputes have broken out in several cities."*

"The Federal Reserve has issued a statement assuring America that the dollar is sound and will remain the flagship currency of the world. This statement was made after China, quickly followed by other countries holding large amounts of US debt obligations, effectively dumped the US Dollar as an investment instrument and terminated agreements with United States corporations nation-wide. It is unknown at this time the status of Americans in the country, but it is known from radio broadcasts that two major US manufacturing plants have been occupied by Chinese Army soldiers and the American representatives removed from the premises."

"Holy crap." I said.

"What?" Libby asked.

"Shh. In a minute."

".....governors were reported missing late this afternoon. The Fed is effectively ruled by a small group of private bankers, determining monetary policy in the United States and within the world banking community. It is unknown where the three members of the board of governors had gone, or if this was a planned vacation or if foul play may be suspected. FBI and National Security Agents were seen leaving the Fed offices in New York, San Francisco, and Washington, prior to the announcement that the members were not present for a scheduled conference call with the Fed Chairman. Unconfirmed reports of a private plane that left the United States without a flight plan late Tuesday lend credence to a rumor that at least one of the Fed Governors may have left the country. The plane later was observed landing in Brussels."

"KLXY will shut down in five minutes for maintenance, and will be back on the air at six a.m. Thursday. Repeating the National Weather Service warning, a severe cold air..."

I shut the radio off.

"OK, so what was that?"

"Sounds like first, the Chinese are taking the US factories in lieu of US debt. Second, sounds like the Fed is in full meltdown. Third, and more importantly, we're going to be really cold tonight."

"They took our factories?"

"Sure. Wouldn't you repo something that wasn't getting paid for?"

"Yeah. I suppose," Libby answered, mental wheels spinning.

"The Fed thing is no big deal. What else would they say? 'Go ahead, wipe your butts with that twenty, cause that's all its worth?'"

"Of course not."

"Right. And the fact that three of the board of governors of the Fed, the ruling council if you will, have gone missing, what's that tell you?"

"They're bailing. They're saving their skins," Ron said.

"Rats, leaving a sinking ship."

"Heading for Europe."

"Heading for Brussels." I corrected. "Capital of Europe's banks. Where their masters are."

"Masters?" Libby asked.

"Masters." I affirmed. The room got very quiet. "Things are coming unwound. Don't sweat it much. Pray about it before bedtime, and wake up and go about our new lives. Worrying about it isn't going to collect any eggs."

"It's really happening...." Karen said flatly.

"Never had any doubt it would. The only question, ever since I knew what was coming, was, 'when'. Now, that's been answered. 'Now.'"

Ron was looking out the window, where we hadn't put our improvised blinds down yet. "Snow's letting up."

"Good. Less we'll have to futz with in the morning."

"How big you figure the hen-house outta be?"

Ron and I spent the next hour or so figuring out the game plan for getting the henhouse built with the least amount of trouble-and work—involved. We decided that we could probably build it in panels inside, and then assemble them outside quickly.

Around eight thirty, we decided to get the as-yet unused kerosene heater out and set it up in the storeroom. If it got really cold, we'd need it before morning. Hopefully not, as I hated the smell of the thing. The lamps were bad enough.

By nine, we'd heated up the woodstove with apple wood and oak scraps, and heated the place up as warm as practical, and we all got ready for bed.

One thing I can tell you, using an outhouse in single-digit temperatures makes you really respect your ancestors. By nine-fifteen, everyone was in bed. We did the nightly 'Walton's' goodnight. I think I was probably asleep by nine thirty.

I was walking along a road, in the brilliant sunshine. The cold air though, was wrong. It was summer. My old dog was beside me, walking up a hill, with grass on both sides of the road, and split rail fences and a farmer with a draft-horse, turning the soil. But the air was wrong. It was too crisp in my nose.

I awoke with a start. My dream of summer, interrupted by the reality that the fire had died and the temperature had plummeted inside the barn. Buck and Ada had both climbed up on the mattress, Buck between Karen and I, Ada at Karen's feet. The temperature had to be thirty in the shop, I thought.

"What's wrong?" Karen asked. "Man it's cold."

359

"That's what's wrong. We've gotta get the fire started again." I reached over and turned on one of the big flashlights. I'd cobbled up a little stand for the big flashlight, so that when it was needed to light up the room, it was held in a little wooden stand that directed the beam up to the ceiling, where it splashed off of the white paint.

"It went out?"

"Sure. No one to feed it all night like you've been doing on radio duty."

"Forgot all about it," she said. "That was dumb."

"Didn't think about it. That's all."   The dial thermometer in the woodshop said thirty-eight degrees.   Seeing our breath was no problem.

I gathered up kindling and paper, and relit the fire. It'd be a good hour before we had the room warm again, even with both the woodstove and the kerosene heater.

"Here-keep an eye on the fire and get it going good and hot. I'm going to light the kerosene heater in the storeroom."

"K."

The kerosene heater was used out in the garage before I put an electric ceiling-mounted heater in. It was effective in warming the place up, but at the cost of the smell of the kerosene. The lamps were bad enough, but now we'd have to put up with the heater too. And we had to watch out for carbon monoxide buildup.

The heater had a little 'glow-plug' switch, that when tripped, lit the heater without use of a match.

"What's up?" Ron asked through fogged over eyes.

"Fire's died. Gotta get some more heat in here. Stay in the sack. I'll take care of it."

"OK." He turned over and covered back up. The kids were similarly burrowed down in their sleeping bags and blankets.

'Hope no one catches their death from this,' I thought as I went back to the shop.

"Get back in bed. I'll stay up and keep the fire going, and shut down the kerosene heater when I can."

"You sure?" Karen asked. She wouldn't need much convincing.

"Yeah, I'm fine. I'll see if I can catch up on the outside world. Shortwave's much better after dark, and I might even be able to pull something from Europe."

"OK. The headphones…."

"Are right here. Back to sleep. You still have time for a good dream or two."

"That'd be nice. I keep waiting to awaken from this one."

"Me too. Good night, babe."

"'Night." Karen retreated back into her 'blanket room', and I sat down at the radio desk, in normal times, my router table.

Twelve forty-eight a.m. 'This is going to be a long night,' I thought as I plugged in the headphones and turned on the radio.

4 0

Thursday
January Nineteenth

The night passed very slowly. I'd picked out a stack of things to re-read in my 'spare' time, which was to this point non-existent. The first was a review of the material that Carl had printed off for me, to make sure it had all come out of the printer like I'd hoped. The big binder included a whole series of FAQ's (frequently asked questions) from numerous internet sources on preparedness. I wanted to make sure that Libby, Karen and Ron read them, and had at least as good a working knowledge as I did. Carl and John and the girls should read them too, I realized later.

The first FAQ I skimmed through was on sanitation, including basic construction of an outhouse and it's operation. It was also covered in some other texts that I had. Next up, were water treatment, smoking and curing meat, a food storage text put together by Alan Hagan on the opposite end of the country, and a few others about primitive skills. These would be a good primer for everyone to read up on.

While I was reading and skimming, I was listening in on shortwave radio communications coming from several stations in the US and Canada, and recording the frequencies and times on a pad by the radio, in case we were looking for them later on. It was becoming apparent that the prices of items denominated in dollars was skyrocketing. While the broadcasts were amateur, the information they conveyed was not the same picture that I received during a two a.m. broadcast from ABC radio news. The network broadcast talked of 'mild unrest' in several major cities in response to 'unforeseen price increases in several items', and 'spot shortages of gasoline' in 'limited areas.' A brief one-sentence comment was made regarding the Federal Reserve's three missing members of the Board of

Governors, and then a commercial came back on. The Fed, if I recalled, only had seven members of the board, so losing three—and mentioning it as if they'd simply been misplaced like an errant sock in the laundry—struck me as so obviously underplayed that it in and of itself screamed 'censorship.' To those with a clue and a glimmer of understanding, this story demanded far more attention and emphasis.

By two-twenty a.m., I was able to shut off the kerosene heater, but had to continue stoking the woodstove about every forty-five minutes or so to keep the barn relatively warm. John was snoring peacefully, and I could just make out Carl's head from under the covers through the dim light of the Aladdin in the woodshop.

Our broadcast news was being fed to us as if we were babies, needing to be sheltered from the bad things going on outside our nursery doors. My pessimism only deepened for the future.

In contrast to the broadcast news (the version on CBS at two-thirty was nearly identical, with a few words changed and the order of the stories altered), the half-dozen or so conversations that I heard on the receiver talked of serious shortages in major supermarkets, some armed (private) guards at stores, and in two cases—Philadelphia and Detroit—National Guard troops and police in riot gear at major suburban shopping centers. No discussion of the 'urban' areas in either city. Gasoline lines were long, and common, in all areas of the shortwave broadcasts that I received. Gas in Davenport, Iowa (home of one of the broadcasters), topped six dollars a gallon at the end of business on Wednesday. In Chicago, gas was rumored to be almost eight dollars a gallon, self-serve.

Banking seemed to be having its problems too. I was wishing I had a transmitter so I could ask questions of those I was listening to, but I'd never gotten around to it. In most areas that reports were coming from, physical 'cash' withdrawals were limited to five hundred dollars a day, maximum. Businesses were apparently neither accepting checks nor credit cards in most major cities, and rumors of letters being sent out by major credit card companies, mortgage banks and other major financial institutions regarding the potential negative implications of missing payments on personal debt, house payments, or home equity loans consumed fifteen or twenty minutes of my listening time. The gist of the rumor was that the debtor would be pursued to the ends of the Earth by the creditor for payment. That seemed to make things pretty clear to me that the financial institutions smelled the change in the wind, and didn't like what the wind foretold. 'Good luck trying to collect on that,' I thought. 'Party's over. Tell that to your stockholders, Citibank.'

The news from Europe seemed to be going downhill rapidly too. Europeans were obviously hoping to avoid the crash that was now tearing the US economy apart, and while hoping for the best is always a noble effort, they were realizing that without American spending in goods, services and tourism, they now felt the foreshocks themselves. I wondered how their social spending programs would survive as the Euro plummeted and those millions of recipients of government charity would react. I also wondered how the 'guest workers' would react when their hosts suddenly realized that they were unable to pay, were outnumbered, and were culturally in a minority?

The speculation on a shortwave broadcast from Tennessee turned to Asia. The broadcaster speculated that the Asian markets were now realizing that without the massive consumption of the United States, even though it was paying with worthless paper, they would soon be flooded with inventory with no one to buy it.

The huge production infrastructure that made textiles, shoes, consumer electronics, and a million other useful and useless items, built over decades of off-shoring and outsourcing, would die in a matter of weeks without buyers of their products. There was literally, nothing they could do about it.

I thought to myself, 'What does it take to make a pair of shoes? Or gloves? Or a pair of jeans?'

Having had enough of international doom-speculation, I decided to shut the big radio off, and plugged my headphones into the small scanner we'd salvaged from the house.

".....10-15 Video City, Valley Mall. Officers respond."

"Nine seventy-one, two minutes."

"Five sixty-two heavy, one minute."

"Nine-seventy one."

I wondered what a 10-15 was. I knew that the first numbers were the units responding, but I didn't know what the term 'heavy' meant. The repeated unit numbers were from the dispatcher. Video City was maybe, two miles away.

"Five sixty-two, shots fired."

"Five sixty-two."

"Nine sixty- six!!"

"All officers, sniper at Valley Mall."

"Air six en route."

"Hurry your ass up! My partners hit!"

"Air six inbound hot."

The worst thing about scanners, is that you never really knew what was going on during the interminable silences between the cryptic broadcasts. This particular one was no different. Almost three minutes passed before the radio came back to life.

"Air six, multiple snipers neutralized."

"Five sixty-two, report status." Nothing.

"Five sixty-two, repeat. Report status please."

"Nine seventy-one. Five six two, two down. Repeat two down, life-threatening injuries. Send the bird."

I didn't need a translator for that. Two officers down, send medevac helicopter. Selfishly, I hoped they weren't someone I knew. I then prayed for them, and shut off the scanner. I also prayed that this was not a 'typical' night for law-enforcement.

In the quiet, I read Isaiah, looking for a verse that I'd been wrestling with. I found it finally, the last part of 27:11 *"......For this is a people without understanding; therefore He that made them will not have compassion on them, He that formed them will show them no favor."*

Indeed.

Between repeated trips to feed the woodstove and another cup of spearmint tea, I took the mini-flashlight and shone it out the window at the barn thermometer. Minus eleven. 'A possible warming trend!' I thought as I settled back in. I dozed a little, and managed to develop a pretty good sense of when I should wake up to feed the fire again, and still get in a nap.

Around six thirty, our rooster decided it was time to get up. Three crows, and then he settled back down again. I put the big coffee pot on, and put the teapot to the side, warming up the fire again. I then turned the big radio back on, hoping to pick up some more local news. KLXY was still off the air, but KDA, and its alleged fifty thousand watts, was up and going. They'd repeated the National Weather Service warning about the severe cold, and then began to list the access points through town that were now open. There weren't many. More reports that ID was required for those traveling, and all vehicles were subject to search.

Karen arose without an alarm at quarter 'til seven. Libby and Ron were up a few minutes later, and made a visit to the sub-zero porta-potty. I was third in line. By then, before sun-up, the temperature had reached as far as twenty-six below. Other than a few whispered 'good mornings,' we kept quiet to avoid rousing the kids and the dogs, That lasted about three minutes, and then Buck decided that it was time to play, grabbed a shoe and was announcing that he was ready for them to chase him. Soon, everyone was awake, if not vertical.

"Nice weather for a gas station attendant," Ron said.

"I was thinking that myself. Only problem is, I'm afraid if I fire up that old iron in this weather, I'd risk losing a connecting rod."

"Agreed," Ron said. "Good to know you've got some common sense in that big heart of yours." Ron knew of what he spoke. He was a heavy-equipment mechanic for fifteen years before he landed in management at a big service company in town.

"I'll have to let the sheriff know."

"Fire up the radio. No point in going down the road when you can phone it in."

"Man I'm glad you're here. You are full of good ideas today."

"And I haven't had my first cup of coffee yet."

"It's ready. Go pour yourself one hotshot. I'll go make a call."

"What's up?" Karen asked.

"We think it's too cold to run the tractor for the gas station. I'm afraid we'll break it."

"Even in normal times, you wouldn't use your precious antique in weather this cold. And even when you did, you'd park it in the heated garage the night before."

"Frozen hydraulics are no use to anyone, and I've rebuilt that pump the one time that I care to."

"Gonna call the boys down the road?"

"Yep."

"What about your construction project?"

"I don't know. We'll probably still do it, but most of it inside. Then move it outside, set it up, and be done with it."

"Easier said than done," Libby said as she sipped her coffee.

"Yes, ma'am. That it will be," I said as I picked up the FRS and plugged the ear bud in.

"Drummond to law enforcement." A long pause.

"Go ahead Mr. Drummond." Sounded like Alvarez.

"Is this the morning crew?"

"Yes sir."

"This cold is too much for my tractor. I think I'd break it if I try to fire it up."

"Affirm. Operations suspended in any regard. Too cold for evac on the buses, and not much else is moving. Please check in later this morning if conditions improve."

"Affirm."

"Out."

I looked at the radio as I put it back in its charger. Sure. They were using diesel school buses, and they weren't plugged in last night to keep them warm. Probably frozen solid. But that wasn't all.

"What's wrong?" Libby asked.

"I don't know. I think that was Alvarez. Sounded....odd."

"Maybe something's happened."

"Maybe. Last night was active over at the mall."

"Shooting?"

"Yeah, you could say that." I recapped everyone on what I'd heard. They were all quiet when I was done.

"Think it was someone we knew?"

"Could be. I'll see if we can find out later. Man I hate not knowing."

"Could've been Mike."

"I thought that too, but it's not his call sign. At least, not his car number. His is five-oh-one.'

"Well, you can run down there later with something to eat and maybe pry it out of them." Karen said with a smile.

"So how are you doing on virtually no sleep?" Libby asked.

"Not bad, actually, I'm starting to perfect the art of cat-napping. I know that I'll need some real sleep later though. I know by noon I'll be toast."

"Then we better get a lot done this morning," Ron said as he sipped is coffee from an old mug that read 'World's Greatest Boss.'

"Fitting mug," I said as I pointed out the inscription.

"Yes it is. It's good to be king."

I laughed. "Yes, your majesty. Isn't it your turn to empty the porta-potty?"

"My kingdom is a small domain, but yes, the price of majesty is the occasional tour of duty as serf."

"Good. Just wanted to remind you of that. And not a 'serf'. I think the proper term is 'cottar.'

"Thanks. Libby doesn't do that often enough."

"Apparently," she chimed in.

"And what's a 'cottar?'"

"The lowest of the peasantry. Think, 'swine-herd', or better yet, you're a gong-farmer!"

"Which is what exactly? And how do you know stuff like this?"

"Medieval literature. A gong-farmer is someone who empties the latrine pit."

That brought them all to laughter.

"Perfect," Libby said. "Just perfect."

Karen made us a dish of scrambled eggs blended in with the leftover rice and pork, and some of the previous day's bread. She also made some orange juice in the late afternoon, and left it outside the warmed spaces to chill. It did, into a nearly solid block. Add some tequila, and we'd have tequila-drivers....if it were August, I might've done just that.

Coffee would have to suffice until the OJ thawed out. The kids grabbed their plates and then retreated back to the warmth of their beds. The boys later had a bowl of cold cereal and powdered milk, and Buck and Ada were not entirely satisfied with their dry food and cold water.

Karen made sure that we all were getting normal batches of multi-vitamins and was making sure we were keeping up with a balanced, if occasionally different, diet. I was sure that this would be more of an issue in a month or three, if things didn't return to something approaching 'normal' in that time. We had lots of food to survive on, but it would get pretty boring, pretty fast unless we worked something out with local growers, dairymen, and butchers. I had no illusions that my little piece of property with a garden, some field space that could be converted to row-crops or grain or pasture, and my fruit trees would keep us all alive and thriving. Alive, barely, perhaps. Barely.

The morning TV broadcast, on the little battery-powered set, was distinctly void of any news that was other than 'normal' in tone and content. No 'special reports.' No aerial coverage. No live-on-the-scene stuff. The briefest mention of 'unrest' in 'impoverished neighborhoods.' No mention of riots or killings or robberies or stores being cleaned out, only passing comments on the Fed governors who'd apparently fled the country for Europe. A great deal of talk about price increases and the market declines, but tempered with the news that both were bound to improve soon and rebound.

'Sure they were,' I thought. As the 'financial' portion of the news came to a close, a brief sentence that trading on the New York markets was delayed on opening due to a 'power outage.'

'Power outage. Right. More like a full-on panic,' I said to myself. I wondered when the government would be forced to come clean? Couldn't last long at this pace.

The national weather reported that our cold was not an isolated incident, and that the 'dip' in the jet stream extended well into northern California. Video feeds of evacuees from the Puget Sound and Eastern Washington/Oregon areas streaming into Redding, Stockton, Sacramento, and points south were shown. Lines of buses—both school buses and city mass-transit types—were intermingled with hundreds of vehicles of all kinds. It looked weirdly enough like a twenty-first century version of The Grapes of Wrath. Seeing an F-150 pickup—the Harley Davidson model—loaded with belongings and 'stuff' strapped to the roof, hood, and sides—made me wonder if today's Tom Joad family was any better off, or just drove to their next life in more style. It didn't seem to hold as much as the Joad's—of course, theirs was a working truck. This guy probably never even loaded it up before.

The weather report for the 'Live West Coast Edition' ended with images of light snow falling on the Cal State campus, now flooded with refugees. Even with the fuzzy picture that the station put out on reduced power, you could see the ground was white. I wondered how often it snowed in Sacramento. I'd never heard of it before, but then again, why would I?

Thursday,
January Nineteenth

After breakfast and a nice hot shave (what a luxury!), Ron and I started gathering up our tools and lumber for the henhouse construction project.

Neither of us cared for spending any more time outside than absolutely necessary, but we had to move around quite a bit of stuff to get to my dimensional lumber supply and the remaining few sheets of oriented-strand board and scrap plywood. The cold made our eyes water, and after a few minutes outside, the frost on my balaclava turned the green fabric to white. My radio was still in my pocket, although at least I'd remembered to shut it off.

We'd already cleared out the wood shop of anything the rest of the family would likely need while we were working, because we wanted to keep the warmth in the store room and the sawdust to a minimum. I showed Carl and the kids how to run the kerosene heater, and they lit it up as we shut the door to the adjoining woodshop.

In order to power the shop up, we oiled and fueled up the Generac, and connected the pigtail to the transfer panel to feed the shop and storeroom circuits. After a couple of pulls, the generator fired up, and was soon running all of the power in the barn. Oddly now, you could turn on a light switch and have electric light. A novelty.

I'd told Karen and the kids that once power was up, they should be able to use the computer, but to get the radios and all the rechargeable batteries plugged in. We had the need of power for the small Senco pancake air compressor to feed my framing nailer, and my worm-drive seven and a quarter inch saw, for now. The constant movement of hauling lumber and sheet goods in- and out of the shop rapidly dropped the temperature, even though we were feeding the woodstove.

The overall plan Ron and I came up with was to cut as little wood as possible, which meant eight-foot walls designed around the standard lumber. We decided to frame up sections in four-foot chunks inside, and then take them outside, lay them down and screw a couple of them together with a cordless drill-driver, and then sheet the lower half with OSB. Once two wall sections were done this way, I finished the third standard wall section, and Ron built a narrow door section. Construction was not much different than framing a house, with a pressure-treated bottom plate, two-by-four studs at sixteen inches on center (I've never liked doing stuff at twenty-four, too rickety), and a single top-plate. We'd add another two-by-four top plate when the whole thing was up, before the roof went on.

While we were busy serving as carpenters, Karen and Libby were reading two separate copies—new and old—of Carla Emery's Encyclopedia of Country Living, and Marie was browsing through Back to Basics. Kelly was writing a story on the computer (one of her favorite pastimes, writing), and Carl and John were enlisted to help set up the walls and help out with construction. Grumbling along the way. When we were done in the shop, Karen closed it up and started working on lunch.

John and Carl's first task was to remove the recently installed hen yard fence and posts, due to the addition of the new henhouse. By nine-thirty, work was ready to start on assembly of the new room, and Ron and the boys lifted the panels up, while I screwed them together. Once the east wall was 'up', Ron checked it for level and plumb on the frozen ground, made some adjustments, and I screwed through the stud into the ancient barn wall. A half-dozen more screws, and the east wall was secure. The south-, and west walls went up much faster, and then we realized that we needed to pull the west wall down temporarily to load the portable roosts that Joe had built, and the nesting boxes. We couldn't roof the room until those were in, either.

I asked Libby and Karen and the girls to get ready to go collect eggs from Joe's, and filled them in on what we needed to do. While they were getting the eggs collected, we'd pull the roosts and nesting boxes out, load them on my little trailer, and haul them home. Libby was going to stay at the barn to make our local Army folks some lunch—obviously something was in the oven. Of course, the trailer had been stowed for the winter in its vertical position next to the tent trailer, and was now covered with snow, ice and ash. Great.

By eleven-thirty, we had muscled the trailer around and had it re-assembled. It was a four-by-eight trailer, that folded in half and could be stored vertically when not in use (which was seldom, around here). The side panels were one-by-fours, with half-inch plywood screwed to the framing, and then fastened at the front corners with angle brackets and more screws. We left the drop-in tailgate off for today.

We drove up to the gate and the insulated crate from the night shift was there waiting for us. I had Carl hop out and run it back to the barn. It was pretty light by then. I reminded him to tell Libby to take out the hunk of half-inch steel and warm it up on the stove before she re-loaded it.

Ron and the boys and I drove the Expedition and the trailer down to Pauliano's, getting a wave from Deputy Schmitt along the way. I was glad to see he wasn't one of the victims of last night's ambush.

Karen and the girls were finishing up with the egg collection, which hadn't dropped off as much as I thought it would. They loaded the eggs in the flats that Joe had, and gently stacked them up in the cavernous back of the Ford.

While Ron and the boys loaded up three of the ex-school lockers now nesting boxes, I looked over the roosts, now occupied unhappily by Joe's flock. They were obviously wondering what was going on. The 'extra' roosters were in a separate pen, and we'd have to make sure they stayed separated. 'One more thing I didn't think of.'

"Hey, Dad. Look at this stuff," Carl called to me.

"Whatchya got?"

"Panels of that fiberglass stuff. You know, like at Grandmas. On her patio cover. Can't we use this on the hen house instead of wood? Or those old windows like you were planning?"

"Yes we can. They'll need the light and it'll be faster than putting in glass. How many sheets are there?"

"Let me count......twelve."

"We won't need that many. Let's get eight. That should be more than plenty."

Ron and I hadn't planned on windows for the hen house, and were wondering what we'd do about light. My going-on fifteen-year-old just solved that for us. Smart kid.

We picked up the lightweight sheets of nearly clear fiberglass, and fit them into the trailer next to the nesting boxes. I told Ron and the rest to head home and unload, and get back as soon as they could. I was going to walk the few hundred feet to the store, and visit Specialists' Alvarez and Beck. It had warmed up to the high teens, and by now, getting the tractor going shouldn't be a problem—I hoped.

There were still several loads—not including the hens, which would be an adventure all by itself—to retrieve from Joe and Joan's place. Straw (which we hadn't thought of), feed (which we had), waterers (hadn't), feeding boxes (had), light strings (hadn't) and of course the three spare roosters (hadn't). 'There should be time enough to get the big stuff moved in, the roof on, and the hens moved by dusk. Should be,' as I walked down the road.

"Hello the store," I called out. The store was locked up, and a different Humvee was parked at the intersection. No mounted gun, no one outside. There were two figures inside though. The drivers' door opened.

"Good morning, Mr. Drummond."

"Mr. Alvarez, how are you this fine sunny day?"

"Colder than a witches….."

"Yes, I believe I get the sentiment. What's your first name? I don't see calling you by rank all the time or your last name. Seems uncivilized."

"Jeremy. Beck's name is Matthew."

"Well, Jeremy, I know our wives are working on something to warm you up. Should be ready about any time. Let me check here," I said as I plugged the ear bud in and turned on the radio and punched the call-button. "Yo, Libby, you there?" a long pause.

"Yes. I couldn't put the ear-thing in after it beeped."

"How's lunch for our desert-camo neighbors coming?"

"Karen and Ron will run it down as soon as they get the truck unloaded."

"What'd you and Karen come up with?"

"Marie's idea. Scrambled eggs, some pepper-cheese and breakfast sausage links baked in the oven with a can of cream-of-mushroom soup. Casserole-style. And biscuits. They're just coming out of the oven now. Got some utensils and napkins in there too. And coffee in that pump-pot."

"Superb. Thank you my dear. Out."

"I won't tell you what's for lunch. Suffice it to say, you're going to love it."

"Thanks. We appreciate it. The night guys said you fixed them up too."

"Just some fried egg sandwiches. And a cobbler."

"Wow. Real food!"

"No doubt. With these temperatures, I can get that tractor going and the station fired up. Can you let the sheriff know?"

"I'll tell my CO, and he'll relay it. Hang on a minute."

"No prob."

I walked around the parking lot a little, trying to shake off the cold, as Alvarez called in.

"Says thirteen-thirty hours will work, sir."

"Good. Then I better move and get back here. Gotta get some lunch myself."

"You haven't eaten yet?"

"No, we've been busy getting some stuff done."

"Understood."

"Be back soon."

As I was about halfway home, my big red Ford passed me with Libby behind the wheel. She looked a little intimidated driving the big thing. Ron had unhitched the trailer, and had it mostly unloaded by the time I got back to the barn.

"Can you handle the rest of the construction without me?" I asked Ron as he and John were moving the last of the nesting boxes in.

"Gas station operator this afternoon?"

"Yep."

"Sure. Let's go over the roof trusses before you go though."

"OK. Carl? I'm going to have you finish up the window panels out of that fiberglass while Ron and John get the next couple loads of stuff down the road."

"Got the better end of that deal," John said.

"Not hardly. He gets to build the trusses too."

"I thought that's what Ron was going to do."

"Sort of. But it's nothing you can't handle. I'll sketch up something for Ron, he can get you lined out on getting the parts put together the right way and check it out before you get too far, and you're in business."

"I don't think I can do that."

"Sure you can. Think 'Lego' with an air nailer. Just don't put an eye out or nail your foot to the ground."

"No big deal, Carl. I'll show you how to get started."

"OK...." He said with some trepidation.

"And remember to wear these goggles. Only get one set of eyes."

"K. What're you going to do?"

"Gas station. Warmed up enough to run the Ford, and the powers-that-be think that they can make use of it."

Ron and I spent a few minutes going over the design of the roof trusses, which were all two-by-four dimensional lumber, with plywood panels (scrap) used to reinforce the joints. The joints would be glued, the panels applied to one side, and screwed in place with one-inch screws. I knew the glue wouldn't set up in these temperatures, but eventually it would. Hopefully it would be enough. Ten trusses were needed. It'd take the three of them to get them up on top of the walls, set them vertical, and temporarily secure them. One of them—Ron got to decide who—would then secure them permanently and then roof the structure with the last of the sheet metal I'd torn off of the barn when I rebuilt it. With luck, there'd be two whole pieces left over. With luck.

"Ready for lunch? I hear you're gas-man again." Karen called through the window.

"You bet," I said, expecting the same fare as the soldiers. "Be right in."

Karen handed me a peanut butter sandwich on home made bread, and a big plastic sports bottle of cold water (my preferred beverage). "Wait a sec. I thought...."

"You thought wrong. You'll have to wait for dinner for your turn."

"Dang. My mouth was watering when Lib described it on the radio." I took a bite of the sandwich. At least it was raspberry jam.

"Poor pitiful you!" Karen responded with a smile. "Them's the breaks."

"That's OK. I'll survive."

"I'm sure you will. Now eat up and get moving."

"Yes, ma'am," I said as I took another big bite. "Better run. I'll call in after while. Remember to have someone on the FRS."

"K. Love you."

"You too," I said around the last of my sandwich.

I headed out to the tractor, uncovered it, and went through the start up procedures. Gas on. Brakes off. Choke out. Shift in neutral. PTO off. Depress clutch. Turn on key. Push starter.

Nothing. Push starter again. Nothing.

'Dang. This is one of THOSE days.'

I hopped off the tractor, opened up the little battery cover door, and fiddled around with the ignition wiring, not really having any idea of why the engine didn't turn over. I touched the wire at the ignition switch, and it came apart in my fingers. 'Problem solved.'
In a few minutes with the help of my Leatherman, I'd stripped off a new hunk of the wire, and run it back to the screw terminal on the back of the switch. The tractor started right up, on full choke. After a few minutes running time, I was able to adjust the choke and head up to the gate.

Libby had returned, and Ron took the wheel of the Expedition, and backed up to hook the trailer up again. He'd have a busy afternoon, while I baby-sat the tractor at the gas station.

"Need anything else from me?" I called over the exhaust and clatter.

"No, we're OK. I'll call if I need something."

"K."

I pulled up into the yard and hopped off of the tractor, in time to see a semi-tractor stop in front of the house. 'Welt Building Supplies' was painted on the door. "Holy crap," I said aloud as the driver climbed out.

I pulled the tractor on to the street and shut it off.

"You Drummond?" asked the stocky driver.

"Yes sir."

"Here's your delivery. Please sign here," he said as he handed me a clipboard with the manifest—each item marked with a 'no-charge sale' on the subtotal line. The sheet was signed by Andy Welt at the bottom, with 'THANKS' written in the memo line.

"I'll be damned." I said.

"Mr. Welt thought you'd say something like that," said the driver. "I've worked for the old man for fifteen years and I've never seen him do anything like his kid's doing. Screwy."

"I'm helping him out with the gas station down the street."

"That 'splains it then. He's rakin' it in. Gave me and the missus two grand in cash yesterday, 'belated Christmas bonus.' Where you want the stuff?"

"Let me get my friend up here. It'll go in the garage. Pain to unload it all."

"No sir, there's a forklift back there on the back."

I hadn't noticed. A small lift was plugged into the trailer deck, and raised up off of the ground. The driver just had to start it up, lower the forklift down, and then go about his work.

"Wow. I hadn't seen it. Let me get the garage door, and we'll get it loaded inside."

"Sounds fine. I'll get'er unstrapped."

Ron and the boys joined me. "Is that stuff all for us?" Carl asked.

"No, there's too much on there for the list I gave Andy. About a third of that, maybe. Ron, let's get that door open. Boys, help the driver see what he's doing and keep the dogs outta the way. I gotta get down the street—I'm late."

"K."

I told the driver that Ron would show him where to put the material, and told him that I had to get down to 'Mr. Welt's' station. He shook my hand and I hopped back up on the tractor.

'Don't that beat all.' I said as I looked over my shoulder one last time.

The line at the gas station was all ready to go by the time I got there, and folks were getting impatient, I could tell. I swung the tractor into position, left it running, and set the brake. I then plugged the pigtail into the generator and revved up the engine, and engaged the PTO. The lights on the pumps came to life as one of the soldiers appeared from inside the store. Andy was nowhere in sight, nor was his old car.

"Where's Andy?" I asked Jeremy.

"Haven't seen him. Unlocked it myself and turned on the key."

"You doing records on the pumps?"

"Yep. Great lunch, by the way, and thanks again."

"Our pleasure. I'll pass along the compliments."

The first vehicles in line were five Crown Victoria cruisers, manned by a couple of deputies I knew, and some I didn't. One had a window taped over with plastic, and four round holes in the passenger door. The unit number was five sixty-two. I went over and talked with Deputy Schmitt while five sixty two, in front of his five forty-one, refueled. A non-uniformed officer was at the pump, badge on his service belt, which I noticed, held twin nine-millimeter Rugers.

"Paul, how you doing?"

"OK, how about you guys?"

"Good. You guys are keeping things quiet for us, so we're able to get some sleep. Ever since the Army showed up, we discontinued our night duty. I heard the scanner last night. The Mall."

"Yeah. That was rough. Two wounded."

"They gonna be all right?"

"One for sure, leg wounds. The other was a City cop helping us out. He's iffy. Took a shot in the side at the thin spot of his vest. Went out his back. He's pretty torn up. They evac'd him to Boise last night."

"How many snipers?"

"Six. They were working cover for looters who came into the store from the back. Drove down the Centennial Trail, up the hill, right to the back of the store. Snipers on all four corners plus two in the bushes."

"So what was 'Air Six?' I heard they took care of them."

"Air Cav."

"Really…..." I was very surprised. "I figured it was just a police helo."

"No, it was a little more brutal than that. Apache Longbow, from what I heard from the incident commander. Thirty-millimeter chain-gun. Didn't take long to end them."

"Holy crap."

"You can say that again."

"That's an anti-tank helicopter," I said.

"In normal times. These aren't normal times."

I remembered the gun-camera footage of Desert Storm, with the AH-64's cutting down the Iraqi troops, and using the Hellfire anti-tank missiles against the hapless Russian T-72's. "Where'd they come from? We don't have anything like that around here, or even in the Northwest."

"Fort Rucker, Alabama."

"You're kidding me."

"No sir. They're barracked over at Felts Field. Night duty only. Keep your eyes open. You'll see the little observation helos and maybe a Blackhawk once in awhile during daylight, never one of those babies."

"Afraid of scaring people."

"Imagine," Paul responded.

4 2

Thursday Afternoon
January Nineteenth

After the police cruisers, finished gassing up, the ambulances and aid cars took their place, followed by six Spokane Transit Authority buses at the diesel pump.

"Don't they have their own station out here in the Valley?" I asked Alvarez.

"Empty. That was the primary station for the evac buses," a voice from behind me answered. The Marine Gunny from my lone shopping trip a few days ago. Seemed like weeks. Alvarez looked...very respectful.

"I thought this one was, Gunny. Good to see you again. I met you at the grocery store on Monday. You're just back from Tikrit, right?" I said as I walked back to the Ford to check an uneven idle.

"Yes sir. McGlocklin, Scott McGlocklin. First Marine Division."

"'No better friend, no worse enemy.'"

"Yes sir."

"Pleased to meet you. Rick Drummond," We shook hands. Rather, his massive paw shook my 'normal-sized' hand. I thought to myself, 'This guy could squish me like a bug.'

"These Army pukes keeping things quiet here?"

"These guys? Yeah, they're doing a good job. I think they're a little shell-shocked to be fighting in an urban environment in a desert country one week and fighting at home the next."

"Can't blame 'em there. Screwed up world right now."

"Got quite a line today," I said, looking at the twenty or so vehicles lined up on each side of the pumps.

"This? Naw. This is nothing. I don't think there's more than a half dozen city buses left in town. Probably fewer school buses than that. That's what we're hearin.'"

"I had no idea."

"How would you? News is fer sh*t. They're not telling anybody anything."

"That much I figured out on my own, of course I hoped I was just being paranoid."

"You're not paranoid. The stuff we've seen on TV and heard on the radio ain't what's really going on."

"I know. Just listen to shortwave or a police scanner and you can figure that out. How long you figure they can keep the lid on?"

"Ever seen a pressure-cooker go?"

"Yeah. Twice. Once was enough."

"Well, the heat's up and she's a cookin'. Not long. Gonna hit the fan soon."

"Speaking from the point of view of someone who's already been the recipient of it hitting the fan, what more can come our way?"

"Here? You're not bad off. When the rest of the country goes hot butter, it's gonna get downright interesting."

"Any advice?"

"From a broke down Gunny? Yeah. Keep your head down."

"I heard they're using Apaches on looters."

"'Nother thing you won't see on the news. I better get goin'. Nice talkin' Mr. Drummond."

"You too, Gunny. Watch your ass."

"Always do. Save it for my wife to chew on."

"Attaboy."

The Gunny climbed in an open Humvee—no doors or top—parked around the corner of the building, and headed west. Open cockpit, twenty degrees, and thirty miles per hour. No parka, no gloves.

I moved around the corner and pushed the radio push-to-talk button. "Yo, anyone there?" A brief pause.

"Yep," Karen answered. "What's up?"

"Just gas-man checking in."

"Let me get Ron. He wanted to talk to you when you called in."

"K." A few moments passed.

"Ya there?" Ron asked.

"Yep. What's up?"

"Either that Welt guy screwed your order up or the driver did, and the driver said he didn't."

'Great.' I thought. "What's missing?"

"It's not what's missing, it's that you got a whole lot more than you had on your list."

"How so?"

"You asked for something like a dozen sheets of plywood. You got a whole pallet. And whole pallets of everything else. Looks like the only thing you got verbatim was the pipe for the chimney and the window. No way on God's green Earth it'd fit in the garage."

I was dumbfounded. "Where'd you put it all?"

"Sheetrock, insulation, roofing and plywood inside. Dimensional lumber outside. Nails, tar-paper, drywall tape, and the window and the mud inside."

"OK."

"You all right?"

"Surprised as Hell, I guess. Driver say anything?"

"Said that's what Mr. Welt told him to deliver. Don't mess with half pallets just load the whole thing. He still had two other deliveries to make too—full pallets too by the look of it."

"OK. Sounds like you got that under control. How's the framing coming?"

"All the trusses built and up, but none vertical, plus the cricket to tie it into the barn roof."

"Forgot about that."

"Yeah. It's gonna be a pain in the ass too. Nothing on the barn is square or plumb."

"Never was."

"Carl doing all right with the framing?"

"Yeah, pretty well. Slow to start, did good though. We got the straw in the hen house, all the roosts we could fit, and the nesting boxes. Boys are getting the feed barrels off the trailer and the feed boxes and waterers. Going slow 'cause of the cold."

"Yeah. I hear ya. Gonna get it finished before dark?"

"Good chance. Karen and Libby are emptying some big boxes now to put the hens in for the move."

"That sounds like something I'd like to see."

"Me too. Glad it's them and not me."

"I'll try to be back by three-thirty and help finish up."

"Sounds good. We've got the fiberglass panels up already. Just need to finish getting the trusses up, tie 'em down, and we can get the purlins on, then the metal."

"Home Makeover, Barn Edition."

"You got it."

"See you soon. Out."

"Out."

'What the heck is Welt doing?' I thought to myself. 'Am I on the hook for something I can't pay for?' I pondered those questions, seated on the Ford, as the fueling continued.

I noticed the Modern Electric truck belonging to my neighbor Dan pull into line. I hopped off the Ford and went over to talk as he waited his turn.

"Dan! How you doing?"

"Hey, Rick. Crappy, actually. Getting things put back together—or patched back together—is a helluva deal."

"Things at the house OK?"

"House? Yeah, but we're gonna be in the shelter tonight. Out of propane for the furnace in the trailer, and the house is a mess. No way to heat it without the oil furnace."

"No fireplace?"

"Nope, never had one. We figure we got enough fuel for today, but it'll run out tonight. Can't get any at the stores or stations, either. Cleaned out."

"How much you need?"

"You got some?"

"Yeah."

"We started off on Saturday with a thirty-pound tank. It's about gone."

"I bet. You must've nursed it to get it THIS far. Let me call my buddy Ron at the house. We've got two tent trailers with full tanks, and I have a tank on my barbeque, and a spare for the barbeque. They're all thirty pounders."

"How much you want for them?"

"I want my water back on. To do that, you need to be working. I also want you at your house. You're my back perimeter. We'll work something out sometime. Maybe you catch me some of that Northern Pike next summer and remember me then."

"You sure?"

"Yes. I'm not gonna be the only one left on the whole damn block. Go stop by the house when you're gassed up. Ron'll have a couple of them waiting. One'll come off the barbeque, and it's pretty full, but not all the way. The other one I filled two weeks ago when propane was cheap."

"It sure isn't anymore."

"Nothing is," I said as he pulled forward. "They'll be ready for you."

"Thanks, Rick."

"No prob. Neighbors, bud," I said as I again dug out the radio.

At quarter to four, the last of the vehicles—the last of the Humvees—was gassed up and Specialist Alvarez locked up the store as I unplugged the generator pigtail and wound up the cord. I'd gassed up the tractor with a five-gallon can from the store, and the 'store' owed me another ten gallons. I was wondering where I'd put it if this continued.

"Sir, got a message from the night crew a few minutes ago. They said thanks for dinner last night, and wanted to let you know that they're getting hot food again at the mess. They didn't want to put you out anymore—as in, don't cut yourselves short. We'd second that, Mr. Drummond."

"Understood. I'll still see what we can do once in awhile."

"Thank you again, sir."

"Our duty, soldier. See you on the morrow."

"Have a good evening."

'What a good kid,' I thought. 'Hope his parents know that,' I thought as I hopped back on the Ford and headed home. How did the saying go?

'Good people sleep peaceably in their beds at night only because rough men stand ready to do violence on their behalf.'

I thought that it fit the Gunny more than the young Army soldiers.

Amen, Gunnery Sergeant. Amen.

It was nearly half-past four by the time I ended up getting home. The sun was low in the cold western sky. It's not often, if ever, that I've ever seen a red sunset in January, but there it was, bloody red. I trailed along behind the Expedition and the van headed up the street, where they'd just left Pauliano's. I hoped this was their last trip. Curfew was less than a half-hour away, at little before five p.m., and I had hoped to be home well before then.

The gate was kept open for me as I trailed far behind the little caravan. Carl closed the gate and chained it as I passed, having to dodge two tarped bundles of building supplies. Ron was finishing up the last of the metal roofing on the cricket between the new hen house and the barn, as John was finishing up the installation of the translucent fiberglass on the south side. It looked like they'd had a good afternoon, after all.

Libby, in the Expedition, and Karen, in the van, both backed up as close to the hen house as they could. I pulled the tractor around them and nosed in to the south side of the barn, leaving room for them to move out when they were done. After I'd shut down and turned off the gas, I went over to help them unload.

They'd made a couple trips already, and had emptied a number of large cardboard boxes and loaded them up with hens. Ron had already moved the roosters into a separate enclosed pen.

"You've done well."

"We're looking forward to being done. It's getting cold."

"Yeah, probably another cold one tonight. This the last trip?"

"For tonight, yeah. There's still more stuff to get down there, but we're good for now," Karen said as she pulled the second of three large boxes out of the van. I got the third, which shifted in my hands as the birds inside moved about, very displeased with their treatment.

"You didn't find any gas cans down there, did you?"

"Didn't look. Why?"

"Well, I think all the vehicles here are full or nearly so, and the cans are too. They owe me ten gallons of gas for today, and probably another ten tomorrow."

"Tough problem to have. We'll find something. Might have to look at your neighbors' places,' Ron said as he stowed the ladder.

"What's left?"

"More feed, for one. And a brooder, other stuff for chicks."

"Hadn't thought about that. I guess we should plan on replacing or expanding the flock as we go."

"Yep. I married a chicken rancher."

"Reluctantly, a chicken rancher. We'll have to get the hen yard put together in the next day or so. They probably won't go out in the cold."

"Our old Rhode Islands didn't, I don't think these will either. How'd it go down the street?"

"Good, I suppose. Andy never showed up, but Alvarez and Beck were there, and I ran into Deputy Schmitt and that Marine Gunny that I told you about—from my grocery trip."

"Social butterfly, huh?"

"Dead-tired social butterfly. Catching up on all the gossip that's not fit for broadcast. Literally."

"Let's get done and get inside. Then you can fill us all in," Libby said.

A few minutes later, as the sun finally set to the west, we were done unloading. The boxes were no longer serviceable for storing anything other than hens in, and we broke them down and stuffed them behind the nesting boxes.

Once we were all back inside and warming by the fire, we were able to catch up.

"Did Dan get by to get those propane tanks?"

"Yep, John said. I gave him the one from the barbeque and the spare from the garage, once Carl found it for me."

"Good deal."

"I've never seen a guy so happy to see a propane tank before, let alone two."

"He's about out of fuel. That'll let him stay at home—and not be evac'd—a little longer. Maybe long enough. He's one of the lead plumbers for the water district—so the longer we can keep him here, the sooner we'll have running water again."

"Makes sense," John said.

"Any trouble with construction?" I asked Ron.

"Other than whacking my hand with that big framing hammer, and a couple of cuts for each of us, no."

"Did you guys get those cuts cleaned out?"

"Yeah, we washed them," Carl said as he sipped a cup of coffee.

"Did you have your Mom or Libby look them over?"

"No, it's just a cut."

"No such thing anymore, bud. A little infection in these conditions can kill you one piece at a time. Karen, could you…."

"Way ahead of you." She said as she came back in with the first aid kit, alcohol, and cotton balls. "Let's see," she said to the boys. She then went about cleaning and disinfecting the wounds first with alcohol, then peroxide, which delivered the predictable 'ouch!' from each of them—Ron included.

"Alvarez said that they were OK tonight without a care package. They're getting hot food again at their mess hall."

"You sure?" Karen asked as she examined a cut on the back of John's hand, near the wrist.

"Yeah, they said we should hang on to what we've got. As in, 'we're going to need it.'"

That elicited a look at me over her reading glasses she sometimes wore for close work. "Really."

"Yeah. The Gunny also confirmed that what the news is saying is not what's going on. He thinks the lid's coming off soon. Pretty frank talk."

"Think he's right?" Libby asked.

"More like, 'Afraid' he's right. He said that he didn't think that we had it too bad here, but that in the rest of the country—and I quote—'when the rest of the country goes hot butter, it's gonna get downright interesting.'"

"What's that mean?" Marie asked.

"I think it means that prices are going to skyrocket, which means that people are going to stampede the stores, if they haven't already. Shortages, which could drive riots. Bad stuff."

"Everywhere? Here too?"

"Everywhere—probably not just the States either."

"Why would it spread to other countries?" Kelly asked.

"We're the big dog. We go down, they all go down."

"Oh."

"Don't get that upset about it. We've got a couple things going for us. First, we've already been whacked, which means a lot of stuff is already headed here or here, ready to be distributed or sold. We had a three or five day head start on the rest of the country, and we have price controls in place for the moment. Second, the military's already in control and not afraid to take charge—that'll cut down or eliminate looting and riots. Third, a big chunk of our population isn't here anymore. They're headed south or in warmer areas already. Fewer people, more resources available."

"For us, not them," Kelly said.

"Unfortunately for them, yes."

"So anyone that evacuated might be worse off than we are," asked Carl.

"Almost certainly."

Karen had finished up on John and Carl, and now was cleaning out a deep scratch on Ron's hand, which reflected the corner of the waffle-pattern of my big framing hammer.

"When's dinner ready? I gotta get some sleep," I asked.

"Now. It went in early. Kel and Marie put a schedule together for tonight for keeping the stove going. You're not on it.'

"Yea for me."

"Go get washed up, and I'll dish you up," Libby said.

"K. Thanks."

I took off my boots, and finally felt warm enough to shed my snowmobile bibs. I then padded around in an ancient pair of Fila tennis shoes that I'd retrieved from the porch. I usually wore them in the summer, when I was mowing the field or the lawn.

After I used the 'facilities' and washed up, Karen handed me a big plate of the casserole dish she'd made for the Army guys earlier, and three warm biscuits. I savored each bite, and washed it down with ice-cold water. By five-thirty, I was headed for bed, either for a nice nap or a twelve-hour snooze, either of which was fine by me. Ron and the boys were dragging, too, and as I lay on my bed, I heard Carl turn on the iMac, now running off of the battery-powered inverter, and play some music. 'Better Days', by Annie Womack and her Bluegrass Rodeo. 'What a lovely voice she has,' I thought as I drifted off, hearing the last of the song.

".......I can only live
right here and now.
All my promises and dreams
Still live on.

My kin been tellin' me,
That things will turn around
Once the angels and the Son
Come back about.

Oh, Better Days,
they're coming round,
My sins been paid for
long since now.
I don't deserve Him,
The Gift he gave.
And I'll tell him soon,
In Better Days.

Twelve oh nine a.m.
Friday morning,
January Twentieth

It was still dark out, and the dogs were whining to go outside. Kelly was up, listening to the shortwave and tending the fire. It was a little after midnight when Buck stuck his cold, wet nose against my cheek, waking me up in more than a little of a mood. The thin glimmer of light came from one of the Coleman lanterns, hissing a little as it burned low.

"Sorry, Dad. He just started doing that. Ada's pacing around too," she said from under her blankets, pulling the headphones around her neck.

"Have they been out?"

"Not since nine."

"Did someone watch them do their business?"

"Yep. Carl did."

"What's up?" Karen asked with sleepy eyes.

"Dogs. Something's bothering them."

"Something outside?"

"Dunno. I'm about to find out."

I got up, slipped my boots on, and unlocked the door from the shop to the tool room. The bitter cold went right through my t-shirt and the quilted top shirt I'd worn to bed, as well as my long johns and flannel lounging pants.

The rumble hit as I started to close the door. I was about to say 'aftershock', but by the time I did, it was over. Just a quick 'bump', and as quickly as it had started, it was gone. Nothing like last Saturday morning.

"Aftershock. C'mon, dogs. You got us up, let's get you outside," I told the dogs.

"That was an aftershock?"

"Yep. Most likely. What's the radio say?"

She pulled the headphones back on. In a few moments, she said "Seattle again."

"Be back in a minute."

I closed the door to the woodshop and went out into the tool room, and then into the garden. The dogs went out, had a sniff at the air, and both took off at a tear across the garden and *over* the three-foot wire fence – they'd never done that before, ever. There was something out there they didn't like. Buck went forward, stopped, and let us know that there was something out there, after all. Toward the street. In the dark, I couldn't see a thing and couldn't tell exactly where he was from the barn. On the other hand, whoever was out there, couldn't see us, either, and the wind was from the east, which should help mask the sound of our approach.

I quickly went in, and pulled my coat on. "Get Ron and the boys. NOW." I grabbed the Remington twelve-gauge, the bazillion candlepower spotlight, and thought better of it. I put the shotgun back and took the Garand. "Karen, call for law-enforcement NOW. There's something out there the dogs don't like and we need them to flank it."

"Got it," she said, now fully awake as she made the call on the radio. Ron and the boys came into the light in various states of awareness. "Guns, now. Something's out there. Dogs are out on a tear." I could still hear them barking, even Ada, with her 'defender' bark going. "We'll stay in the yard. I plan on lighting up the world when we're in position. You need to be ready for whatever when that happens."

"Understood." The boys had their 10/22's, and Ron took the twelve gauge and one of the .45's.

"Let's go. I'll take the spotlight and my rifle. Train your guns on whatever the dogs are barking at when I light it up."

"If someone's out there and armed, they could shoot at you with the light," Ron said.

"I'll be next to it on the ground. And if so, you better nail their ass. C'mon."

"Sheriff or whoever's on the way-five minutes," Karen said.

"K. Let's go."

We headed out across the garden, Carl and I heading straight to the front, Ron and John bearing right. They'd go around the front of the house the long way. We hugged close to the side of the house for lack of available cover. Buck was no more than twenty feet ahead of me, barking toward the house. 'Somebody's trying to get in," I thought.

As I moved to the north side of the half-walled porch, I could see a figure crouching on the porch, or a shadow or something—not moving. I motioned Carl to my left and to raise his gun. I saw Ron and John come around the other side of the house as both Buck and Ada moved with us to the front. Someone was at the front door, trying to hide.

With three guns trained on the motionless lump, I moved the Garand's strap around my shoulder, and took out the big, blinding spotlight. I could see a light coming up the street---either a Deputy's cruiser or a military vehicle, couldn't tell which.

"LIGHTS!" I yelled as I turned on the spotlight. The figure flinched, huddled low. A companion spotlight played across the front of the house, and the headlights began to flash and the marker lights lit up.

"GET UP REAL SLOW." I yelled to the blanketed form. It moved, but not much. "I WON'T ASK AGAIN." The blanket fell away. "Oh, crap. You," I said with disgust. My brother. The one I didn't claim. "Move really carefully, Joe."

"You wouldn't shoot me," he said with no small amount of anger.

"Don't lay a bet on it. You wouldn't be the first looter I've shot this week," I kept the light trained on him. He was a real mess. I hadn't seen him in more than six months. It looked like it'd been that long since he'd bathed.

"You HAVE to take me in. I'm family!!"

John went over and opened the gate for the deputies—two of them, full riot gear and M-16's. They headed up to the house as I spoke with my brother, one of four, this one nine years my elder.

"I don't have anywhere to go."

"You sure as Hell don't. This home isn't welcoming you."

"What's going on, Mr. Drummond?" asked Deputy Schmitt.

"MISTER Drummond is it! Well you stupid cop, there are TWO Mr. Drummonds here, and one of us is a Doctor! And it isn't him!" he said, pointing to me.

"This guy related to you?"

"Only by our parents. Certainly by nothing else," I responded.

"Listen up you little sh*t, I'm staying. You can't do a damn thing about it. You HAVE to take me in."

"Wrong. Get off of my porch and off of my property. Now." The dogs were both growling, and baring their teeth.

"I'm staying. I'm all you've got for family here."

"Wrong again. Get out. Now." I said as I set the big flashlight down on the porch half-wall, and shouldered the Garand. "Recognize this gun?"

"That was Grandpa's. I wanted it and you took it when you split up the house."

"It was given to me in the will, which also specifically denied that you get this, or any other gun. Mom was afraid you'd eat one of them. She was probably right."

"You asshole. I'll get you for everything you've done against me...." Joe lunged at me. Paul's companion, clad in all black with no name badge, clocked my brother in the chest with the butt of his rifle. He dropped like a sack of wet mud.

"Load him up, Jimmy. I'll talk to Rick about this matter."

"Yes sir."

'Jimmy' literally dragged my brother by the coat to the driveway, and roughly tossed him in the back of the cruiser.

"New guy?" I asked.

"Out of the academy ten days ago. Used to be a lineman for the Vandals," Paul said. The Vandals were the University of Idaho Vandals. A decent team, but not much competition for my Cougars. "Now, what's up with him? He really your brother?"

"I've seen him twice in the past year. Not by my choice. Thirty-five year alcoholic. Earned his Ph.D. at Colorado back in the seventies. Could have been top of his field. Decided bourbon was more fun. Moved back here in ninety-six, lost his job, moved in with our mother, ran the house down, verbally abused my Mom, threatened me with a shotgun one particular August night. I booted him out. He thinks the rest of us are out to get him."

"I see his type all the time."

"Then you'll find an appropriate place for him."

"Detention's pretty full up. They're putting them on prison buses and sending them out to God knows where."

"Works for me."

"You serious?"

"Deadly. We've done all we can over the years, and we're done. The entire family. The one adjective that is truly fitting is 'evil.' I will not go into the details."

"All right. I'll take your word for it. Anything else going on?"

"Other than I feel like crap, no. Must be getting a bug."

"Flu. Watch out for it. Valley General's overrun with it, and people are dying from it."

"Great. Thanks. One more gem in a crown of them."

"Just telling you like it is."

"More than the TV and radio are doing."

"Yep. Sheriff's gonna want to meet with you in a couple days. Maybe Monday. Can't go into the topic, but it's important."

"Understood. What time?"

"Ten, at the community center. He also said that gas station duty is postponed until at least then. We've got enough fuel in the tanks until then, we're not selling it from that station to the public, and the buses are all out of state. If they come back, we'll need you sooner. Unless you hear from the sheriff though, you've got a couple days off."

"Good. I can sleep in tomorrow. Today was a real bear."

"I'll get your brother situated. He won't bother you again."

"Thanks—have a good night."

"You too," Paul said has he walked back to the gate, where John closed it and locked it behind him.

"Dad, that was really Uncle Joe? I didn't recognize him."

"I almost didn't either, bud. He's going down fast. I just don't want to be around when he hits bottom again."

"Isn't there anything anyone can do for him?"

"Not if he won't accept their help. In his mind, he doesn't have a problem."

"Wow. I could smell the booze on him from here."

"Yep. C'mon y'all. Let's go get some sleep."

As we walked back through the garden gate to the now-lighted barn, we could hear the unmistakable sound of a gun battle to our northwest. Shotguns, probably handguns, and heavy weapons fire.

"What happened?" Karen asked with no small amount of worry. The girls were up too.

"Joe paid us a visit."

"Your brother?"

"One and the same."

"What happened?"

"He's on his way to a detention center somewhere. Deputy Schmitt's taking good care of him."

"We also get the pleasure of having Rick around for the next couple of days. No gas-station duty until further notice," Ron said.

"Is that a good thing, or a bad thing," Kelly asked.

I thought about it for a minute. "I don't know. Paul said all the buses are gone. So either they're done evacuating, and those of us that are left are here to stay, or there's a bunch of folks still at the shelters with nowhere to go. One thing we know for sure, the shooting's not over. Gunfight going on over west of here."

"I heard it on the scanner. One of the grocery stores. Sounded like the supply trucks showed up and got…what's the right word? Oh yeah. Ambushed."

"What about the aftershock? Any news on that?"

"Yeah, over near Ellensburg this time. Six point something. They said the first time it was six point one. The last time I heard it it was up to six point seven."

"OK. That's enough for tonight. Who's up on stove and radio duty?"

"That'd be me," Libby said, already getting settled in the 'radio room', which was nothing more than a corner of the shop.

"Hon, got some Tylenol or something? I feel awful."

"Let's check you out," she said as she put her hand against my forehead. "Lie down. You've got a fever, mister."

"The Deputy said that flu's bad at the hospital. Think that's what it is?"

"Don't know. Might be a cold. Kelly, grab the medicine kit. The digital thermometer is inside. Front compartment."

"K."

My temperature was 102.1. No wonder I felt like crap.

"You're not going anywhere for a while. Get to bed and get covered up. Kelly, get some of that juice for your dad. Take these," Karen said, handing me a couple of pills.

I got back into my nightclothes, and climbed into the bed. Kelly brought me some orange juice, in a plastic water bottle.

"Thanks, babe."

"You're welcome. I'll pray for you. Get some rest."

"I will. You too."

"I will. After Libby's shift, the boys are up. So I get to sleep all night!"

"Good for you. 'Night."

"Night, daddy."

"Hey, and if the dogs act up again, pay attention."

"Will do," Libby said through the curtains.

I took a couple of drinks of the juice, and collapsed into bed. Karen came to bed later, but I had no idea when.

I had a miserable night. That happens when I have a fever, I get loopy. Hallucinations even, before the fever breaks. Karen has gotten used to dealing with me when I get 'out of my head.' Fevers like this usually come with a bad bout of stomach flu or something…this one was different. Just a fever, no intestinal problems, but an aching in my chest I'd never had before. It hurt to breathe. I felt as if I were drowning, and had to sit up most of the early morning hours, while trying to rest.

Some time during the night, I couldn't tell when, Karen had me start drinking something other than juice. It turned out to be a re-hydration solution, made from salt, baking soda, sugar, and water. It tasted awful. She later told me that she was afraid that I was already dehydrated, and that my fever was aggravated by that. She also gave me some elderberry concoction, but I don't remember much of that.

When I woke up again, it was daylight. I'd apparently missed the morning rooster-call, and breakfast too. By the look of things through the walls of my blanketed room, it looked like late morning. I still felt awful, but I could tell that my fever was gone and that my chest didn't hurt as much when I took a breath. I coughed to clear my throat as I sat up on the edge of the bed.

"About time you woke up. We were worried about you," Karen said, peeking in to our room.

"What time is it?"

"A better question is 'what day is it.' It's Saturday. You missed Friday."

"No way."

"Yeah. You slept through almost all of it."

"Wow."

"You hungry?"

"I don't know. I guess I am. I feel like I've slept for a week. Still foggy."

'We were starting to call you Rip Van Winkle."

"Funny. Thanks. I just hope I didn't sleep for the twenty years and two days he did. Got some water?"

"Here," she said, handing me my favorite water bottle as she sat on the bed next to me and held my hand. I felt….thin.

"Thanks." I said after taking a big drink. "What have I missed out on?"

"Enough. Weather's the same, still cold. Clear now though. Two more aftershocks in Seattle, felt the first one, and the dogs warned us first. Second one was too small to feel here. We also got a note from Alan. They're coming out here Monday—and leaving town. The cold's too much for Mom and they're going to see Diana in Fresno." Diana was Karen's sister-in-law.

"They holding up other than that?"

"Yeah. We actually got a letter from them-sort of. Relayed over the radio. Mike Amberson delivered it himself. It was only an hour old. He told us to keep you out of the hospital. It's bad there."

"Hmmmph. What else?"

"Alan wants to know if we have diesel. He's loading up a lot of stuff and needs more fuel. The stations up on the north side are out."

"The station down the road owes me some fuel. I suppose I could take diesel for Alan. All our tanks and cans are full. Did they say what time they'd be here?"

"They were going to leave as soon as curfew was lifted."

"So in other words, no idea."

"Probably. Who knows what shape the roads are in?"

"Somebody must, if he's crossing the river and driving twelve miles to get here, with all his stuff. What other news?"

"Get cleaned up first. I'll make you some lunch and get you caught up."

"K. Where's the rest of the gang?"

"Ron's got them to work in the house. They're cleaning up the main floor and getting the plaster out of there. He said you'd probably do that sooner or later."

"Yeah, he's right. Are they warm enough in there?"

"They're only working an hour or so at a time, then warming up."

"OK, I guess."

"There's also a surprise for you. Ron got into the tent trailer and got the solar shower out. You can actually have a shower if you want."

"Hallelujah. You have water?"

"Five gallons on the stove, steaming."

"Outstanding," I said as I got to my feet, weakly. I could barely stay upright. I wondered how long this would take me to get over.

Two p.m.
Saturday afternoon
January Twenty-first

There is nothing like a hot shower after you've not had one for a while. It seemed like years since I'd had clean hair. It was one week and one day in reality, and while this 'camp shower' was a far cry from the steamy morning shower I'd become accustomed to, on this day, it was perfect. The 'bag' of water over my head, hung from a wood plate that Ron had screwed to the ceiling rafters, had a nozzle that I could turn on and off, while standing in the big galvanized wash tub. Might as well been the Fairmont Hotel in San Francisco for all I cared. It was glorious.

After showering and changing into clean clothes, I felt like a new guy. Weak, sore and probably ten pounds lighter, but new. As soon as I had a sip of juice, I was instantly hungry. I was a little lightheaded while on my feet smelling 'breakfast' cooking. I took my seat in the newly re-assembled Nineteen-Fifties chrome-and-linoleum kitchenette set that I'd cleaned out of my parents place and stored in the barn. Felt like home, right down to the marbled tabletop. Of course, my Mom never dried laundry in the kitchen before, and we had a fresh crop of sheets and underwear all over the room. They'd been busy while I was 'out.' The beds had been re-arranged, and Kelly's antique steel bed frame now housed her mattress. The bed had belonged to Karen's parents, and grandparents before her. (A number of her family, and ours, were conceived in that bed.)

"You all have been busy. Look at this place! And where did you get the idea for keeping me in fluids? I mean, the hydration solution?"

"That big binder of yours. There's a formula in there. It's your book, don't you remember?"

Through the fog, I did. "Yeah, I guess. I'd forgotten it. Too much to memorize."

"Libby found it a few nights ago. She dug it out when your fever went up. Bet you don't remember the ice-down, either."

"I thought that was a dream. More correctly, nightmare. I dreamed I fell through the ice on a river."

"Nope. Broke your fever. You went right to sleep after."

"What's for breakfast?"

"Something easy. Toast and plain eggs."

"Toast? How'd you manage that?"

"That little camp toaster that goes over the propane burners in the camp stove, remember? Works OK on the woodstove too if you know how to do it."

"Cool. So what else did I miss out on?"

"Kelly and Marie started to take radio notes for you. We all ended up writing something. Sort of a newspaper. Here you go. It's not good." Karen said as she handed me a clipboard.

"Busy," I said as I briefly looked at the pages.

"Yep. You need to read it in order. You'll see why."

"That good, huh?"

"That bad. You predict too well."

"Great. So Ron's got everyone working in the house?"

"Yep. Ron figured they needed to get out of here and get some air. They've been cooped up in here for a while."

"Which I slept through."

"If you can call that sleep."

"Yeah," I said as she handed me a plate with a small pile of eggs and two pieces of toast. Karen was careful to give me no more than what I could reasonably eat, although at that point, a side of beef and a gallon of Longhorn Barbeque sauce would've done nicely.

"More if you can do it."

"Thanks," I said as I took the plate. "Ron put the table together?" I said around a fork full of eggs.

"Nope. Carl did. Ron did retrieve Kelly's bed from upstairs though. Had to move a lot of plaster and lath off of the frame. Managed to get it out the window after he pulled the top sash out—intact. Box spring too. Said the posts had punched right through the floor. He roped up the box spring and mattress and lowered it down to the boys."

"Yeah. I remember that from when it happened. I figured that bed saved her life."

"Appropriate, since that's where she was made," she said with a smirk.

"Good thing she doesn't know that."

"Good thing. Need more?"

"The eyes are willing, but I better not."

"You can have some more later. I'm going up to the house to check on the gang. You OK by yourself?" she said as she pulled on her heavy coat and boots.

"Yep. I've got my reading material to keep me occupied."

"And it will. Be right back."

"Before you go, let's talk about Alan and your Mom. Are you sure you want them to up and go to California with all of this stuff going on?"

"No. I'm not sure, and I'm going to let Alan know. I think it's hare-brained and I don't know what he could possibly be thinking."

"Good. Tell me how you really feel," I said with a grin. "First off, I don't think they'll make it. Second, It might be the last time you see your Mom."

"I know. I want them to stay."

"Then we better come up with a contingency plan for them. If they're leaving, they're doing so because they have to. Not because they want to."

"So what can we do?"

"We need more living space if they're going to be here. We're going to have to look around at the houses around us, and assuming that the owners are coming back someday, make an excuse for breaking into one of them and moving a family in."

"I hadn't considered that."

"Things aren't coming at us in ones-and-twos these days babe, they're coming at us in platoons, battalions, and divisions."

"More to deal with and less time to decide."

"Precisely."

"I'll be back in a little bit."

"K. Love you babe."

"You too mister. And you better not scare us like that again or I'll kick your butt."

"Yes'm," I said as she closed the door to the tool room.

The girls had done an excellent job at note taking while I was ill. They managed to log the time of the message, the general content, the source, and the frequency, list-style, on eight hand-written pages. 'They could be reporters if they live that long,' I thought.

'Now where did that pessimistic view come from,' I wondered to myself. I read the reports:

Friday Morning:

5.45 am SWR discussion between California and Idaho regarding default of federal obligations. CA says government will lie about it to the last minute. ID agrees. ID says contacts in LDS church are in 'lockdown mode.' CA says police and troops are isolating poor neighborhoods. Says that food stamps were not shipped this week and complaints are turning to violence. Not on TV or radio. Says that 'poor bastards' in Seattle will never have a chance to recover. FREQ SW2—see chart.

6.00 broadcast. CBS. Banks across country will open at 10 am local time for cash withdrawals limited to $200 per account. Treasury secretary says that US gov't maintains assurance that all deposits in banks and savings accounts will be safe. Commentator sounds funny. Skeptical? Rail traffic to Washington re-opened through Oregon. Statement from head of 'fed' is expected later this morning. Lines in LA, NY, Denver, DFW for gas, at banks, and stores. Report of American held hostage by Venezuela until America pays company debt. Wants payment in gold. FREQ 1510AM

6.15 scanner. Not able to get police, State Patrol or Valley patrol frequencies. Garbled. Worked at 5am. FREQ scanner 1,2, 3, 4. checked frequencies. Still not working. Weather channel comes in OK. FREQ 5.

I scanned the morning notes. More stock market drops.

......Trading halted at ten am PST. DJ 2414.20, NAZ 498.21 S&P 286.20 Gold 1239.55 Silver 21.45. No statement from 'fed.' FREQ 920 AM

'There's all the signs of a Depression.' I wondered where James Wesley, Rawles was right now? I noticed earlier that one of the boys had my copy of 'Patriots' out, laying on one of the beds.

I scanned through the rest of Friday, looking for key information. I found it later on

Friday afternoon. I wondered if the government still thought that if it was broadcast on late Friday afternoons, that it would be forgotten by Monday?

3 pm broadcast. Federal gov't says that they have declared that the Federal Reserve is unable to pay foreign obligations. Say that domestic bonds and domestic accounts are safe and the Fed will be able to address them in due time. End of news. No other stories (!!) 920 AM.

"Well, there it is." I said to the empty rooms. "The sh•t will now officially hit the fan." I continued reading.

4 pm broadcast. Reports from Asia that U.S. factories have been seized in Taiwan, China, Indonesia, Korea, others. Reports that troops occupied factories and escorted Americans out of buildings and transported them off-site. No report on whereabouts. Report that Ford Motor executive and Delphi electronics workers killed. Reports that protests around US military bases appearing within last hour in Europe, Korea and Japan. 1510 AM.

'Perfect timing,' I thought. 'Too perfect.'

The remaining reports from Friday spelled out the ultimate result of outsourcing American businesses to foreign countries. The businesses were almost all nationalized as part of 'debt-seizure.' Thousands of Americans were 'missing.' 'More likely, 'hostages,' I thought.

By the seven p.m. Friday report, international news was non-existent and domestic news was, while not 'rosy', was certainly rose-colored. I could tell by the girls' notes that even they were frustrated with the obvious censorship.

Before I read farther into the Friday night radio logs, I sat and thought about what I'd just read and it's implications. The US owed money, a lot of it, to a lot of countries and companies. They (we) just said that we weren't able—or going to—pay those debts. As a result of corporate greed, we'd gutted ourselves by selling off the most critical manufacturing and R&D processes to our competitors. China. India. Japan. Korea. Europe. We as a country had doomed ourselves. The ultimate problem though, was that we doomed everyone else along with us.

This is how wars start. Was this worth a war? Probably, to someone. Not me.

I read the remaining Friday radio notes. Shortwave was going crazy, and the girls—or Karen or Libby—the notes grew remarkably more legible and 'female' at ten p.m.—were very busy changing frequencies and writing cryptic notes.

10.14P   CO reports riot in downtown Denver. SACramento reports NG troops around Gov mansion. No food stamps distributed, none honored. Bank robberies by mobs in east LA. SFO reports looting in Marina district. Fires seen. ID-Boise reports shooting at grocery and LDS warehouse. WWCR reports wide unrest in urban areas from reports through it's 'network.' Advises all to pray and prepare.' SWR

"Little late for that, guys," I said aloud. 'Unless you're talking spiritually, I suppose. Never too late for that.'

11.00P. No national news broadcast?? 1510, 920AM??? Same 12AM. Both silent, but open....not static.

12AM—Scanner not working. Garbled.

The notes for the remainder of early Saturday morning were hourly. The 'recorders' had either tired of hearing the same thing over and over again, or were trying to save batteries. Either of which, was OK by me.

9AM—WWCR reports riots in DC, Atlanta, Philadelphia, DFW, LA via ham reports. Bank runs becoming widely known. Lines for gasoline, food. SWR LIST.

10AM—President asks 'for calm and for people to stand fast and remain in their homes.' Says that 'adversity has struck us again and we will prevail.' 'Citizens will be protected world-wide and those that are held against their will in foreign lands will come home soon.' 920AM

10.15AM—Fed chairman resigns. Treasury sect resigns. 920AM

I heard Ada bark in that pleading, 'play with me' bark out the window. The whole gang was coming back in to warm up. There were a lot of smiles, all things considered.

"Welcome back to the land of the living," Ron said as he came in through the storeroom door.

"Yeah, I thought you were just getting out of the really fun jobs," smirked Libby, just behind Ron.

"Thanks. Yeah. That's it. Yeah. Shirking my duty."

"How ya doing, Daddy?" Kelly said as she gave me a big hug, soon joined by Carl.

"Much better, now that I've had a hug. What have they been keeping you busy doing?"

"Cleaning up the living room and the dining room."

"Now that sounds like fun. Not."

"Not bad. We have a huge pile of broken plaster in the living room, and the boys have been stacking bricks on the front lawn."

"Really?" I asked Carl.

"Yeah. Now I know what it's like to be a slave."

"Hardly. You're too well-fed and rested and haven't had a taste of the lash."

"Funny, Dad."

"Hey, I'm trying. I'm a little off my game."

"Off, is right."

"Ooohh."

"Take those dirty gloves and put them in a pile. We'll shake out the dirt and get them dry again. John, let's get that knee looked at," Karen said.

"What happened?"

"Nail. He was moving some bricks and one of the ceiling lath boards came up and bit him."

"John, when was the last time you had a tetanus shot?" I asked.

"Last summer. We did the Habitat for Humanity thing on the coast. We had to get one before that."

"OK, then you should be all right. Karen'll get you cleaned up."

"Get caught up on the world?" Karen asked.

"Yeah. Really gonna hit the fan now."

"That's what Ron thought too. Oh. Almost forgot. Tim James just made it home. Said he'd stop by in a few minutes," Karen said.

I was very surprised. They'd been in the Tri-Cities. "They OK? The boys too?"

"They're all OK, but they're not staying. They were in Kennewick at his brother-in-law's. Says things there are weird. No one's talking about the reactor."

"No small wonder, but that's not something that you can keep quiet forever if there's really something wrong with it."

"They said that no one was allowed north of town."

"That'd be the first indicator that something's wrong."

"That's what he said too. They're packing up some stuff and going to his folks place in San Diego. His brother-in-law is heading down there too, with his sister. They're going to be here until Monday, and then go back to the Tri-Cities, meet his brother-in-law, and go, caravan style."

"Dang. Hate to see him leave. He's been a good neighbor. And a great guy."

"Yeah, it's too bad. He said he'd stop by though today and talk."

"K." Tim was a good man and he'd made a difference in our neighborhood. Carl was good friends with all four of his boys. Their mother had decided more than a year before, that she was tired of married life....to Tim anyway, and had up and moved out. I knew that Tim still loved her, but was resigned to the fact that she was gone for good. He was way more understanding than I would've been.

"So what do you think about the President's statement?" Libby said quietly.

"Doesn't matter. It's beyond his control and ours. The economy is not something that the President or the federal government should've had a whole lot to do with, other than maintaining free trade and minimizing onerous regulation, but I'm an idealist. Of course, that hasn't been the case in about a hundred years. Probably a whole lot longer. Out of their control, nothing to do about it except let it do what it's going to do. That won't happen of course. They can't resist fuddling around with it, which usually does nothing but aggravate things, either making them worse or prolonging the bottom."

"Did you see that note about the 'poor bastards in Seattle?' The shortwave one?"

"Yeah I did. Guy's probably right. The country can help an area bounce back after something like that because it's got the resources to do so. It probably won't now. I have no idea what that means, something's going to happen over there. I just don't know what. The state can't do it alone."

"Can the country? Even if the economy wasn't tanking? It'd take years."

"The country could, sure. On credit. Which is entirely the problem," I said before changing the subject. "How much did you get done on the house?" I asked Ron and Libby.

"Got the living room and dining room debris pretty well picked up. All the broken glass is in a metal trashcan. The rest of the furniture is set back up and a little worse for wear. We boxed up a bunch of the nick-nacks and set them off to the side. Started clearing the stairs—that's where the brick came from. John and Carl and I moved the woodstove off the hearth, it's sitting in the middle of the dining room. Libby was downstairs with the girls picking through stuff—in the dark."

"Not entirely dark. We had that laser beam of a flashlight of yours. We picked through the canned goods and jars in the fruit room and got some of that cleaned up. What was salvageable, we put back on the shelves after getting it wiped off. The rest we shoveled into a little garbage can."

"You were busy today."

"Yesterday too, remember."

"Yeah. I keep forgetting."

"You're allowed. You look a lot better."

"For someone that looks like crap, yeah." Ron said.

"Thanks. I appreciate that, ya big jerk."

That drew a round of laughter.

"Glad you are back to your normal repartee," Karen said looking out the window. "Tim's on his way, he's coming with Drew. Carl, get the door please."

Libby had taken out a plate of cookies (cookies? Where did those come from?) and had some pop for the kids. We'd known the James family for about five years, and Carl and Drew were the best of friends.

"Welcome to our humble abode," Karen said as they came inside. The dogs were very happy to see them too, with Drew smacking Buck around like usual.

"Thanks. It's nice to be back, even if our house is a shambles," Tim said. He looked very weary. I suppose we all did.

"Don't get too close to Rick. He's just coming off the flu."

"Drew got it Monday. I empathize. He's still not back to all eight cylinders. Three days in bed." Drew and the boys had already started comparing stories about their respective weeks. The girls were huddled by the fire, warming up some water for tea.

"I hear ya. I've only been out of bed since about one today."

"It's bad. I know it's killed folks in the Tri-Cities. Ritzville too."

"So what's your plan?"

"Can't stay here. My boss in Kennewick—he was in the same shelter that we were in—said that the company's gone. Declared bankruptcy on Tuesday and no hope of restarting it. He heard from his boss's boss. So with no job, no meaningful equity in the house, Margie's up and took off with another guy, to Hell with it. We're goin' home."

"You sure you can get there?"

"Beats freezing to death up here. My parents have a big place. They already said if I wanted out---when Margie left---that they'd put us up. They've got a couple acres."

"Aren't they in San Diego? That's one helluva drive. And it's all suburbia."

"They're actually in Spring Valley. Not far from SD. It is a helluva drive. I figure if the roads are better than the crap we just went through, we'll be OK. Once we get back to the Tri-Cities, we'll hook up with my brother-in-law and we'll caravan down."

"You know you stand a good chance of not making it," I said with some determination.

"We stand a better chance than here," Tim replied, equally resolute.

"There's riots in most of the cities. Food stamps aren't getting accepted or maybe even sent out anymore. Prices are skyrocketing. Gas is going to be short in supply at any price. The Honda gets, what, maybe twenty-five miles per gallon?"

"Bout that."

"And a fifteen-hundred mile drive? That's sixty gallons of gas assuming things go well for you. At what per gallon, eight bucks? Do you have five hundred bucks for gas?"

"Thanks to that pile of cash on the kitchen table of my house, I have twelve hundred. Ron filled me in on the looters and the FEMA guy."

"Tim, I think you're nuts for doing this."

"I know. But I also think you're crazy for staying in a barn in a state that has no chance of recovery."

"Ron, go get Mr. James one of those Red Hook ESB's and one for yourself. I'm gonna try to talk him out of this yet."

"Keep trying, but my hole card is that both my parents are terminally ill. The kids don't know it yet, but they will, soon enough," he said quietly.

That shut me up. "God, Tim. I'm sorry to hear that."

"You couldn't've known."

"Still."

"It's OK. We're going to get through it. I'd planned on selling the place in the spring anyway and going back down home, even before I talked with my Dad last Thursday. Now, I'll just leave the keys for Bank of America and they can go stuff themselves."

I thought about it for a moment. "I guess you're credit won't exactly be ruined, will it?"

The adults all laughed quietly. "I guess not. But I will take you up on that beer."

"Here you go," Ron said as he handed him the last of the Red Hook.

"Karen's also heard from her brother Alan. Alan and his family, and Karen's Mom Grace are heading south on Monday too. Any chance they could caravan along with you, assuming that we can't talk them out of going?"

"You bet. Safety in numbers."

"That's what I was thinking too. Alan will certainly be armed. He's got a fair sized arsenal of his own." Alan was our family hunter. I had no idea how many rifles, shotguns and handguns he had, but it was 'many.'

"Hadn't thought about that, but not a bad idea. When's he coming out?"

"In theory, he's coming out here from Five Mile on Monday morning, after curfew's up. We have no idea when he'll arrive here."

"We can wait for him. It doesn't take that long—or shouldn't take that long—to get back to Kennewick."

"As long as you've got that black card, that is."

"True. Do you guys have more family down there?"

"Alan's wife's sister Diana. Fresno. We've only heard twice from Alan, so we don't know the full reason for leaving, but Karen's Mom is eighty-five, so I'm sure the cold's gotta be getting to her if they've been in a shelter or even at Alan's place."

"But," Karen added, "I'm--that is, WE ARE--- going to try to talk them into staying."

"Can't say I blame you," Tim added.

"Now let's hear about your week," I asked.

Three-thirty p.m.
Saturday
January Twenty-first

Tim took a seat on the folding 'Costco couch' and took a long draw on his beer.

"We were all in bed of course when it hit. My brother-in-law's place is in Kennewick, about two blocks off of Three Ninety-Five, just west of that Fred Meyer. You know the one?"

"Yep. We worked on a couple of projects there. The Utility District maintenance annex. Did the remediation plan for the site."

"That's the one. Anyway, I was in the guest bedroom, the boys were in the basement with Chuck's kids. The quake sounded like—and acted like—a bomb going off. Everything just exploded in the first shock." Tim took another sip and stared off out the window as he continued.

"We spent the first night huddled in the cars. It was cold—maybe thirty—and they were having a rare snowstorm. The next day, Chuck and I boarded up the place with plywood they were giving away at the Fred Meyer, and we went to the elementary school to get warm and to get fed. We spent Sunday there, too. Chuck and Nancy didn't have much food in the place, just a couple days worth. No pantry, nothing. Just what was in the kitchen. The store made it handy I guess to just stop by every couple days."

"Anyway, Sunday afternoon, Chuck gets this call on his mobile. He has some fancy little radio. He's got some hush-hush job up north on the reservation, working on the cleanup of the reactors and all the contamination in the soil. He goes off by himself and talks, then shows up about ten minutes later. That was about three o'clock on Sunday. A blue Suburban shows up, you know, with the blacked-out windows an' the government plates, and he takes off. We didn't see him again until Friday. He wouldn't say a word, but I could tell, something scared him, bad. As soon as he got back, he said 'we're outta here' and started making plans to head south."

"Whoa. Does that mean the reactor went off or something? Or the contamination spread, or what?"

"No idea. He wouldn't say, even when I pressed him on it."

"Swell."

"So while he was gone, we were at the school, and made a few trips back to the house. On Wednesday, somebody got in and picked it over. The gangs are moving in packs, and have carved up the place into their own little Mexicos—that's what they are, all Hispanic gangs. I don't remember that many down there before, but they're sure there now."

"How bad was the physical damage?" I asked, realizing I was more than a little tired.

"Bad enough. The Three Ninety-Five bridge, the big steel one, is still up. The cable suspension bridge is down, the rail bridges are down, and the bridges over the Yakima are damaged and closed. Tough to get around. The first couple days were OK, but after about three or four days, the lines for food and gas got bad, and the cops couldn't do squat about it. You're way more organized up here. More military, checkpoints, all of it. They're way too thin down there. We were seeing ATM machines hauled off in pickup trucks. Thursday, the Army Airborne units showed up. They're kicking ass big time. Doesn't pay to be on the street when a gunship's looking at you."

"We had a little of that up here, after dark the other night."

"Not down there. Full daylight, they're going house to house, and they know what and who they're looking for."

"Wonder how they know that?"

"Yeah. Me too," Tim said.

"What about the trip up here? They let you go? They're sending everyone south from what I heard, and no one's coming back in."

"Only because of Chuck. He gave us a pass," he said as he fished it out of his pocket, "here it is. This got us through everything. Got us gassed up too."

"I got one of those from the sheriff. Mine's blue." Tim's was black, but otherwise identical in shape, weight of the paper, and the type style. His said "12148", where mine said 'Official.' I wondered what the numbers meant.

"Once we got out of the city, such as Kennewick and Pasco are, the roads were pretty good. Some cracks and detours around broken pavement, and some of the overpasses were down. The one at Lind for one. The rest area halfway up to Ritzville was more like a campground. There were at least two dozen RV's there, maybe twenty cars, and some semis. No idea why they weren't being allowed to leave. Lots of buses though getting through. The other weird thing we saw were farm trucks and farm equipment that had closed the access roads off of Three Ninety-Five. Some of them had guys with guns manning them. No idea what that's about."

"Simple. They don't want visitors or looters coming into their towns or their farms. If they close off the roads, then the looters are on foot. Looters are lazy. They'd rather drive."

"Hadn't thought of that. By the time we got to Ritzville, we'd passed two big train derailments on that line off to the west of the highway. One had what looked like coal. The other had boxcars. Some had obviously been looted, even though we were in the middle of nowhere. That was this morning. Took us five hours to get home.

We had lunch at a restaurant in Ritzville too—the black pass got us in."

"I guess it opens all kinds of doors. That's not bad for a two hour drive. How much was gas selling for?"

"You mean if you wanted it? Nine bucks a gallon was the black market price. Two fifty at the posted price, but damn if there wasn't a shortage of two-fifty a gallon gas. Had plenty at nine bucks though, twelve bucks at the rest-stop at Sprague Lake. That was an 'aid station' for people stuck on the road. A semi-driver for Conoco had a good business going there, as long as you had cash."

"No shock there. Free enterprise and all. Any other surprises?"

"Other than the Hispanic gangs...the general Hispanic population is bailing. Either it's too cold, or they figure that the farm and general labor economy will never come back."

"Probably a little of both. Or a lot of both. Was any traffic on Ninety going west from Ritzville to Moses Lake or Ellensburg?"

"Nope. Blocked off."

"Hmmm, wonder why?"

"Overpasses might be down, hard to say."

"Yeah. Hard to say," I said as I thought about what Tim had told us.

"Here, Tim. Have some cornbread. Where are you going to spend the night?"

"The travel trailer. It's behind the house and has full propane tanks. It'll be tight, but we're used to that. We could use some water if you have some to spare."

"We can give you one of the five-gallon containers, would that work?"

"Perfect. We can fill up the on-board tank and use it then."

"Not unless you want it to freeze. Your on-board has a heater inside—that runs off of shore power or your van."

"Right. I forgot about that."

"Good thing I didn't. That tank was a chrome plated b•tch to replace the last time it froze, remember?" Tim had asked for my help a couple years before, when he brought the trailer home and got it ready to go camping, and then found this huge leak. It'd taken all day to pull the tank and replace it. "You aren't going to haul that all the way to San Diego with the Honda, are you? It'll never make the passes."

"Nope, just back down to Kennewick. Chuck's truck will haul it from there. His wife's driving their Bronco."

"Good. You'd toast that transmission if you did."

"We'll be OK on flat ground if we don't go too fast."

"What are you planning on taking with you? You can't take it all, obviously."

"Clothes, food, pictures, some tools. The rest of it is yours if you want it."

"Take the stuff you can sell along the way too. That new flat-panel would be a good idea to sell to someone for something other than paper money, but be damn careful. Ron can probably look over the place and pick out some other things that have transitory value right now. Four men died for that TV set and your home audio system. People will still do stupid things to gain material goods. You might consider that."

"I will. Like I said though, I'm leaving the keys for the place and I'm gone. Not coming back. What's left is yours if you want it."

"We appreciate that, but I'm not sure what we'd do with it," I said.

"Things will get back to something approaching normal, someday, but there's nothing there that we'll need. You probably will, or can, at least use the stuff we leave. The house is pretty hammered, and I know that our insurance company, well the one that we had before they went under on Tuesday, didn't cover earthquakes, and I had so little equity in it after the divorce that the bank can have it back."

"Assuming the bank is still in business," Ron added.

"True. Blood sucking bastards."

"Can't argue with you. I'm sure they're going to be looking for the car payment at the end of the month on the charred wreckage of Libby's new Trailblazer. Wonder what it's worth in trade right now? It only had fourteen-hundred miles," said Ron.

"Why, lots, as long as you don't look too close, or under the hood, assuming it still has a hood," I said.

We all had a good laugh at that. For me, it didn't take much to make me laugh. Sometimes you just have to. There's too much sadness and depression around not to get set off at the least little thing.

We chatted with Tim for a few more minutes before he and Drew went back to the house to get situated for the night and to start sorting out the 'takes' from the 'leaves'. We loaned him one of the kerosene camp lanterns to help them out for the evening.

The conversation left me tired, more so than was due, so I excused myself from the rest of the family and went back to bed for a late nap, which I hoped to get in before they came back in at dusk. It felt during my visit with Tim that my internal batteries were draining, minute-to-minute. Libby stayed in the barn, working on dinner—some frozen chicken from the basement freezer, and she was boiling some potatoes for mashing. Karen, Ron and the boys were headed back up to the house, and the girls would be tasked with helping Libby.

As I lay there, drifting off, I thought about where we could house Alan, his family, and Karen's mom. More complications. And losing

Tim would be a loss to the neighborhood, such as we had these days, and to our family. He was one of the few neighbors we had that we knew, and could really trust, no matter what.

Karen woke me a little before six. "Dinner time. Can you come to the table?"

"Yep. Man that was a nice nap."

"Didn't want you sleeping too much. You might be up all night."

"Thanks. Something smells good."

"Kelly's lemon chicken recipe. The one she has in marinade."

"But not on the grill? This should be good."

"I had a sniglet. It's great."

I washed up for dinner. The kids had already eaten, and were crashed on their beds. John was reading Patriots, and Carl was working his way through the first C.S. Forester book of Horatio Hornblower. "Careful, John. Remember that's just a story."

"Yeah. They call this the 'Crunch' in the book."

"A rose by any other name…"

"Yep."

"Carl, how's Horatio?"

"That'd be 'Midshipman' Hornblower to you, sir," he said with some authority.

"Very good sir," I said with a bad English accent as I bowed and backed out of the room. I liked 'Flying Colours' better than the other novels. I still don't know why, just do.

During dinner, the adults talked about the progress on the house, and a possible schedule for putting it back into habitable shape. All of which depended on the weather, which would be cruddy for at least the next two months, almost guaranteed.

"We can at least get most of the demo taken care of, the stuff that obviously has to go or get pulled out to get to things we know need to be rebuilt. We can also sort out stuff that came down in the quake to figure out if there's anything we can salvage and reuse," I said.

"So now that we've beat that horse to death, where do you see us in six months? I mean, recovery?" Ron asked.

"Now there's a question with endless possible answers," I said.

"Opinion, not prediction," Libby said. "We already know your predictive ability."

"Don't take that too seriously. It's just when a school bus full of kids is parked on a train track, you can figure that sooner or later a train's gonna come. I wasn't the only one seeing it, you know."
"Maybe, but you're the only one WE know that saw it."

I paused for a few moments before answering. "That may be so. OK. Six months. I can't answer that without mapping it out, literally, on paper. Cause and effect style. Or more correctly, Event and potential impact, locally and on a wider scale. The longer you get away from the present, the fuzzier it gets. We're not supposed to know the future you know. There are too many things in play to know where we'll be."

"OK, that sounds reasonable. That said, best guess," Ron said.
"All right, let's postulate. One, the world won't end, although it will be a whole lot different when the dust settles. If the U.S. is still the big economic power, I can't see how that will happen. We've broken the bank of the world, and we're not to be trusted. Two, it is quite possible that our military dominance in all areas of the world is over. We can't afford it, and we're probably no longer welcome.....most everywhere," I said, thinking about those words and their meaning. "Third, if I were some two-bit country (in the

431

view of certain members of the current Administration) wanting to take advantage of the situation, we could easily be at war. If we're attacked and don't have the support of the country in which we're attacked, we lose face, or we have one option that'll wake everyone up and not mess with us again. Nuclear. Fourth, we don't make anything here anymore, and what took us years to lose through bad business decisions and greed and government corruption will take us years and decades to replace…if we can do it even then. I could go on."

"What about here? What do you think will happen here?" Libby asked.

"Assume the worst. No assistance to rebuild. Gasoline and fossil fuels in short supply and expensive. That changes a lot of things. Everything is shipped using fossil fuels and people depend on them to get to their jobs, grow their food, heat their homes. When the gas runs out, people can't get around. Can't get to jobs. Can't get home. Can't grow food like they used to—meaning that agricultural production plummets, and people get hungry and starve to death." I paused again, not wanting to, but scaring some people around the room nonetheless. "That is a very real possibility. Here, though, at least right here, we have something of a fighting chance. We have some ground, trees that can help feed us, people in the area that grow food and livestock, and live near their jobs. We're surrounded by agricultural land on three sides that needs no irrigation water, and one side that does need water. I could do my job, if there ever were a need for my old job again, land planning and infill development, from my house." A light went off in my head. "You two could teach. Ron could work on equipment. Farming stuff will have the highest priority for fuel, to grow food consumed locally."

"You think we can survive all that?" Karen asked. My mind was still bouncing about. Infill…… Local food production……

"I think we have a fighting chance. If those things come to pass, people in urban areas in America might become familiar with the stories of the siege of Stalingrad."

"My God." Libby said. "I just showed my classes the documentary on that."

"I've told you that this wasn't a rosy path that I was leading you down."

"Starvation? In America?"

"Why not? What makes you think we're exempt from the laws of carrying capacity?"

"Well we're not, obviously, it's just so...."

"Profoundly disturbing," I said, finishing her sentence. "Remember our ancestors, my dear. We're both here because of a certain famine in a certain small island country a hundred fifty-odd years ago."

"Yeah." She looked off over my shoulder, imagining the implications.

"Enough doom and gloom. I'm scaring even myself. How about some cribbage?"

"Haven't found the board yet," Karen said.

"Dang. What else do we have to do?"

"Scrabble, for one. The kids have dug out some other board games."

"No, that'll do. One rule. No 'doomer' words."

"Works for me," Ron said.

"Let me get a refill on my water. I work up a sweat when I'm spelling," I said.

"You?" Libby said. "I never knew you had a problem spelling."

"Me? I don't. I spell very well. It's just that I need to use up the Q, Z, and X."

"Funny."

"I live to serve, m'lady."

Eight twenty p.m.
Saturday,
January Twenty-first

The Scrabble game was an unmitigated disaster. Five games, Ron and I lost four. The ladies in their victory, were insufferable. I couldn't blame them, we would've been too.

"That's what we get for marrying teachers," Ron said. Karen taught K-6 before Carl was born, and Libby was a working mom, teaching middle-school kids at one of the tougher schools in the city.

The kids had again headed for bed, with Buck taking a try at snuggling Carl on his bed, and Ada on the floor by the woodstove, the warmest place in the barn. All four were reading, by light of the Aladdin or the Coleman lanterns. Our wives were continuing to gloat, and we let them, as I turned on the radio on the pretense of gathering the latest news, in fact trying to hush the girls.

I tried KLXY first, for the eight-thirty news. I picked up a national talk show, which went right over the bottom of the hour break. That was odd.

"Listen. I'm telling you what I'm seeing, and what I'm seeing is not what I'm hearing about on TV or network news."

"We're hearing that a lot, caller. Where are you?"

"Atlanta."

"How are things there?"

"Ever see Gone With the Wind? Picture that fire going through the poor parts of town, and no one showing up to fight it."

"Any idea what started it?"

"You mean other than the riots? No, I have no frickin' idea. How stupid are you?" The sarcasm stretched far beyond the continent that separated the caller and our little group.

"Calm down, caller. I'm in Tennessee. We're not getting anything from the TV news. You are our reporter there."

"Well then get this through your thick heads, America. If you're rich, you're a target. If you have a business, you're a target. If you have food next week, you're a target. The food stamps and the welfare checks and the Social Security checks didn't show up in the mail on Thursday and Friday, and it hit the fan. Those people are Sherman's army reincarnated. If it hasn't happened in your city, it's gonna, and you better be ready."

"Thank you caller. Keep the ammo dry."

"Yeah. Right. Like that's gonna stop a half-million hungry people," the caller said as the host moved on.

"What's going on? This isn't CBS, is it?" Libby asked.

"It isn't CBS radio. Sounds like one of the shortwave broadcasts got picked up either by the network or by the local station," I said.

"......different in Philly. ATMS are getting hauled out of stores and the owners are getting shot if they do anything. If you're at a store, you're either looting it or trying to. The cops can't do anything to stop it."

"What kind of stores...."

"Electronics. Car dealerships. Food. Clothes....doesn't matter." The phone clicked as if cut off.

"Caller? Philadelphia, are you there?"

436

"....*if you are trying to make a call, please hang up and* ...." The host clicked the next caller on.

"*Hello caller this is WWCR Nashville, where are you please?*"

"*Dallas.*"

"*Can you tell me how things are there?*"

"*Better than 'lanta, I kin tell ya,*" the accented voice said. "*But I gotta tell ya this. It started before the ry-uts there. It's getting' ready to pop here too, when the stores run outta food, it'll hit the fan.*"

"*That seems to be the common thread.*"

"*You gotta understand somethin'. Food ain't getting ship'd ta parts of the country, and some cities in paticulah, and some neighbahoods in paticulah.*"

"*Can I ask you how you know this?*"

"*Simple. They don' have money, they don' get food. We drivers know which'd neighbahoods is po'. Comp'ny know it too. Not goin' where we gonna get jumped.*"

"*How long has this been going on?*"

"*Friday moanin' in the Nowtheas' and Souf. Cahlafohnya since Wednesday. 'Zona, too. No cash, no truck.*"

"*Can I ask you who you work for?*"

"*You kin ask. I ain't tellin'. Lissen. Yo' faith in God all that gonna get you through dis.*"

"*Understood. Thank you caller.*"

"*Night, y'all.*" The phone clicked off. We were all looking at each other as the calls went on.

"On to Portland, Oregon via ham radio. Caller are you there?"

"I'm here."

"Please describe how things are going there for our listeners."

"Seattle without the ash and snow. Everything's wrecked. Lloyd Center collapsed—that's a big shopping mall with an ice rink too. The Eye-Five bridge across to Washington's gone, and it's down right in the middle of the Willamette too. The Four-oh-Five's gone. The Two-oh-Five's gone. The KOIN tower's a wreck. The pyramid on the top is just.....gone. The US Bank building has half it's glass gone and whenever the wind blows, more comes out. Half of Wells Fargo landed on the building next door—that's twenty stories of building gone. The airport got creamed after one of the dams upstream on the Columbia went. The poor neighborhoods are rioting. There's fire all the way out to Gresham."

"Can you get supplies? Are you keeping warm?"

"Last night it was fifteen degrees. The night before, it was zero. I dunno how many people are even left in town, and aid is tough to get. The Army's pretty much written off parts of the city. They aren't even going in there, just blocked off the roads. If I didn't have my RV, I'd have frozen to death. My house is a pile of wood and brick. Can't get out of the neighborhood though. All the streets are wrecked."

"Will you be able to get out if you have to?"

"Sonny, I'm seventy-six years old and all crippled up. I'm here until gravity is all that's needed to hold me down."

"Understood. God bless you, sir."

"And our country."

"And our country. Amen. Next caller is from Helena, Montana. Go ahead caller."

438

"I'm here. It's pretty busy here. Lots of folks from Idaho and Washington bugged out to Montana. No room at the inn is an understatement."

"How is the population reacting to what's going on?"

"What, you mean the money stuff?" Same as ever'where, I guess. But we're not shootin' anybody over it. Pays to be a million miles from D.C."

"What about the Presidents announcement of martial law?" This was news to me.

"He declared Martial Law in the rest of the country?" I asked. Everyone else looked surprised too. We hadn't listened since the afternoon, so we'd missed out, obviously.

"Our governor negated that. Pretty much telling the Federal Government to stuff it."

"We've heard that from several other states as well, including Arkansas, Idaho, Wyoming and the Dakotas, unconfirmed of course."

"When this blows over, it'll be clear on who got all girly and who cowboy'd up. He may be from Texas, but he's all hat and no horse."

The host had a laugh over that. "Haven't heard that in a while. Washington will corrupt even a good man given enough time."

"Yep. Pays to flush the toilet ever' once in a while."

"Thank you caller. This is WWCR Nashville. It is midnight eastern time, nine pm Pacific standard time."

"I thought you turned on KLXY?" Karen said.

"I did. This is it. They dumped the network feed."

"Good. About time. How long are you planning on staying up?"

"Not. I'm thrashed."

"Us too," Libby said.

"Then get to bed. I'm first up on the feed-the-fire watch. I'll listen some more," Karen said.

"OK, who's up after you?"

"Let me check the list…."

"Me," Ron said. "Four on, four off, right?"

"Yep,' Said Karen.

"Me then Libby."

"What about the kids?"

"Let them sleep. No point in grouchy kids who haven't had enough sleep. I'd rather deal with just being tired than put up with that." Libby said.

"All right. I'll make a trip to the outhouse, and then head for bed," I said.

I slipped on my big boots and my coat, and took the long way 'round to the outhouse, with Buck leading the way. The overcast was back, covering the veil of stars that was newly revealed after our electric lights went down. I fished out my little flashlight to give me a little help—it was that dark, even with the snow on the ground. Maybe people would appreciate the impacts of light pollution better after this. Probably not, though.

Fifteen degrees and a plastic toilet seat. I need not say any more. Brrrr.

When I got back to the barn, I noted some other stuff that Ron or Karen had retrieved from the camp trailer when they had it opened up—two extra sleeping bags (with broken zippers) several bundles of rope that we used to make clotheslines of when we were up at the lake, and two gallons of Coleman fuel. We had only used two tanks for the lantern in the week that we'd used it, and one refill per camp lantern. The Aladdin's were even more stingy. I'd never thought about how much fuel I'd need long-term for lighting in the event of a permanent or semi-permanent outage of power, and I certainly didn't plan on it. Still, it was good to know that it seemed that we had plenty of fuel for a while.

The kids and the Martins had already turned in, and Karen was sequestered in her radio cubby.

"Anything new on the radio?" I asked in a whisper.

"More businessmen taken hostage in Central America. Seems that that one guy who's being ransomed for gold was only the first. The governments are being pretty ballsy about it too—no pretense, they've just stated that fifty-five Americans are now being held in 'protective custody' until 'American obligations' have been satisfied. What is that supposed to mean? 'Obligations?' They haven't figured out that we've been giving them foreign aid forever? They want more?"

"Sure. They think they're entitled to it. Addiction is a tough thing to break. Right now, there's a lot of folks worried about coming down off the high of excess spending and dependence on government funds. Which aren't 'government funds' at all of course. They're ours and our future generations. Were, at least. Anything else?"

"CBS finally came back on to KLXY. They're reporting widespread unrest in most major cities. Seems California didn't get their food stamps or aid to dependent checks or checks for the illegal aliens out---that's what they called them—checks for illegals!"

"Whoa. Honesty at CBS. Never thought I'd see the day. I better go," I said as I gave her a kiss goodnight. "Love you."

"You too. Most. See you in four hours."

"Hope so!" I said as I climbed into bed.

I was asleep fairly quickly, even though I had a million things racing around in my head. Tomorrow, I'd do some scenario work and try to figure out the housing situation, with Alan's family and Grace potentially staying out here for the remainder of the winter....at least.

Karen crawled into bed a little after one. "Everything OK?" I asked quietly.

"More shortwave broadcasts, KLXY went off completely. I went to another frequency and heard more reports....'bout the same. The President didn't declare Martial Law nationwide, either. He suggested to the governors that if they feel the need to do so, that the Federal government would support them fully. Most of the states with 'blue' cities took him up on it—that's where the troubles seem to be."

"Certainly not limited to them."

"No."

"Any weather news?"

"Twenties tomorrow. Chance of flurries."

"K," I said as I kissed her goodnight again. "'night."

"G'night."

Sunday morning, I woke up at five to the smell of coffee brewing. Libby was up making coffee, and getting the ingredients ready for pancakes. This was a rare morning, as I was wide awake, and felt...great. Karen rolled over toward the blanketed wall and went back to sleep. It was still black outside.

"Morning." I whispered.

"Hi—feeling better?" Lib whispered back, a novel in her hands. She was always an early riser, I remembered.

"Much. Human again."

"I hope none of the rest of us get that."

"Me either. Not something to strive for. Any news?"

"Not much. Ron didn't have much either. Things got quiet about two, he told me. He just went to bed."

"Anything on the scanner? Local stuff?"

"Nada. That is, nothing he could understand. Why is that? It worked a couple days ago."

"They're scrambling the transmissions, I'm betting. I have a scanner, thieves do too."

"Oh. Hadn't considered that."

"Glad they finally did. Should've days ago. What's on the calendar today? I've kinda slacked off on the keeping tabs end of things."

"Ron was thinking about …doing nothing. It's Sunday, and he and I thought it would be a good thing to just rest."

"Biblically sound idea."

"That too."

"I do want to see if I can help Tim and the boys out though, load up, sort out, whatever."

"That makes sense."

"Is the Powerbook still hooked up to the inverter?"

"No idea. I think Carl plugged the iMac in instead."

"That'll work too. I'll use it."

"What for?"

"A little scenario planning. 'If this then that' stuff. Lists. Things we need to do or think about or prep for."

"Sounds busy."

"It's kinda the way I think."

"I've always wondered…" she smirked.

"Hey now, I was always there for you in Sociology Three-Thirty when you wanted to bail and go watch 'Days of Our Lives.' You seemed to appreciate my notes."

"I did. And thanks again."

I moved over to where the iMac was set up, plugged in the earphones into the speaker jack, and punched up the power. The startup 'chime' sounded in the headphones, rather than the main speaker, which preserved a little more quiet. Buck moved from his bed to my feet, and curled up and went back to sleep. Ada hadn't moved.

I fired up Microsoft Excel, my scenario-outlining tool of choice. I then listed the items that came to mind that demanded immediate attention, and lower-priority items and 'stuff' to think about. As I noodled each one over, I put comments and further ideas to explore in descending cells, working down and to the right as I went. The process let me identify at least SOME of the issues relative to each option or choice made.

First up was our living situation. We'd camped with Ron and Libby for up to a week at a time, and I could tell from the way the kids were starting to behave that the novelty was off. We all simply needed some more privacy and some time to be 'alone.' I also knew that Libby spent more than her share of private moments mourning the loss of their home, and I couldn't blame her for that. With the potential added population of Alan, his wife Mary, and our niece Rachel and Mark, our nephew and Karen's elderly mother, the situation rapidly went from merely difficult to literally impossible.

The house wasn't yet an option. It would take a serious commitment to put it back into shape to live in, which merited its own to-do list in order of deconstruction and reconstruction. Knowing how long things 'should' take versus how long they 'actually' take, and my experience of 'open up a wall and always find something ugly,' I was pessimistic that we could be back in the house by the next winter, even assuming that I could get all the materials to do so. Andy Welt had certainly helped, but I knew that custom-sized insulated glass wasn't something that anyone around here had laying around. My windows were double-insulated double-hung units from Marvin, manufactured in Minnesota. That was a long way from here, these days, and probably getting farther away as time went by.

Next up, we could use the barn, clean up and clean out the garage, and convert that. Primitive at best. I'd have to duplicate the work we'd done in the barn, including heat, temporary plumbing, probably another outhouse or some other means of dealing with human waste. It was also pretty dark in there, with only windows on the north side, and no skylight. Bad option.

We could use the tent trailers in warmer weather…which wouldn't be here for three months at least. Bad option.

Fourth, we could use one of the vacant homes around us, and repair them enough to live in. Tim's place was probably not an option. Just my cursory look at it said the best remedy would be a D-8 Cat. Woolsley's had gas heat, no fireplace, and was a 'rancher'—meaning all spread out and not designed to be heated from a single point-source. Brad's place to the north was a possible option, but small. He had a basement wood stove but from my earlier look, saw that the small brick chimney had gone down in the quake. I held out hope that both he and the Woolsley's would return home from the Coast. Better option, but still not ideal.

Fifth, and most promising, seemed to be the vacant home behind us. Listed for sale just before the New Year, the house was sandwiched between Dan and Sandy's place on the north, and the Moore's vacated house on the south. I hadn't looked it over for damage to any great degree, but the cursory examination that I'd given it made it look promising. I'd have to get over the fence and take a look later in the morning. I then had to figure out if I could get 'permission' to set up housekeeping in the place from the authorities. Somehow, that seemed most daunting. I knew from previous visits to the home, which was sold by a family that relocated to Las Vegas, that it had not only wood heat, but an honest to goodness wood furnace. It was newer than our house by five years. Almost modern. Had a concrete foundation! First on the block!

After considering the housing situation, and mulling that over for a while, the next thing that I needed to think on concerned Tim James' place, and materials that might be salvaged or moved to the 'new' house....assuming that there was anything useable. I made another list.

Libby handed me a cup of coffee as I started the next list. "Thanks," I whispered.

We needed water. We needed power. We'd need them soon. Water we could not depend on until Modern Electric got through examining and repairing the system. Power came from Modern too, and was supplied by Bonneville Power Administration, and I had no idea what their status was. We'd need refrigeration in less than a month, I guessed. Could we freeze enough ice to put off our need? Build an ice-house? I'd have to research that. I knew that somewhere in one of the computers, maybe this one, I had some info on ice-house construction.

Next, I looked forward into the later spring. I always planted the outdoor garden on the first weekend in May, if the snows were off of Mica Peak, which is about fifty-two-hundred feet above sea level. We're about two thousand feet. The greenhouse starts were usually started in the house in February, moved to the greenhouse in March, and some pulled out and planted in the garden in May and June. Some things—tomatoes in particular, and peppers—I forced in the greenhouse and left them there for the summer. We'd have to map out planting schedules and quantities for much greater than normal production.

Even with the stored bulk foods, I had no illusion that they would last forever. We needed to add to them. I'd never grown grain crops before, nor harvested them, nor had modern equipment to do so...other than a small grain drill to tow behind the Ford. No 'combine' meant that for what we planted, we'd have to scythe and collect the grain by hand, bundle it in sheaves, thresh it by hand, collect it by hand. A huge labor investment.

The other issue of course was available land. We had a little under two acres within our fenced boundaries. Seven thousand square feet of that was vegetable garden, which we didn't typically plant all that intensely. That would be different this year. About half of the property was either covered in turf grass, buildings, garden or fruit trees. The remainder—the field, was just native grass, that the neighborhood kids played softball on all summer long. Brad to the north, had a lot about two-thirds the size of ours, with the majority in native grasses—little lawn, and the buildings were up toward the street. Houses to the north, all the way to the cross-street, had 'open' back fields. The homes to the south had chopped up the properties with subdivided lots and more homes. There was acreage available, if we were to attempt to grow food here. Again, at a high labor cost. I had no idea how many people were still in their homes beyond the blockage in the road. We'd not seen any signs of life whatsoever. Twenty plus houses on the street, about that many behind us, two houses occupied. Not a good labor pool to draw from, but then again, not many mouths to feed.

We'd need more than produce, again assuming the worst that the grocers could not supply what they'd once supplied. We'd need meat, and chickens would get pretty tiresome if that's all we had. No beef cattle around here, no one to butcher them in any regard. Half a dozen horses within a mile or so, if things came to horse power. Nobody I knew raised hogs or goats. Pauliano's did---but they'd left town. His contact out east of us hadn't stopped by with the promised piglets. Even if he did, I had no experience in raising them. I did have a book or two, but like so many things, that's not quite the same thing.

It came down to this: If things were really going to be as bad as they seemed they might, we'd be scrambling to generate enough food to keep thirteen people going. No one ever appreciated how easy food was to come by. Until now, that is.

For the next hour, I worked on the computer, working on what-ifs and the many potential evils lurking out there. As usual, I generated more questions than I could answers. The thing that kept surfacing in my mind, and had ever since the night before, was that the suburb as a concept was dying. It lived on fuel, and if fuel was gone, and it seemed that could be the case, whole sections of the country could quickly be unlivable. One of the worst scenarios imaginable: Money is worthless, massive unemployment, very few if any countries friendly to us, a cut-off of foreign-generated oil, and no viable alternative. A work-around put me back to nineteen-twenty or earlier.

'Local goods. Local food. Local jobs,' I thought to myself.

In my former (?) profession, that was something I knew how to do—work with communities to reinvigorate themselves and adapt to change. For me at least, that had meant adapting to sprawling development and creating something from something else. If this country were to have a chance, people would have to adapt to living differently. The government would have to adapt too, from local planning right up the food chain. If money was worthless, governments as we knew them were bankrupt and out of business. If the States kept some semblance of organization about them, the many power grabs by the federal government at the expense of the states......might be wiped clean too. Maybe this is a chance to remake things on a larger scale. Or the 'vortex' could take it all down.

Libby handed me another cup of coffee as I leaned back in my chair.

"Done?"

"No. Just getting started. But I need to ruminate on it for a while."

Sunday Morning,
January Twenty-second

By nine, everyone was up and fed. Carl and John expected to be put to work as soon as they were dressed, when we gave them the news.

"Nope. Day off. It's Sunday and Ron came up with the brilliant idea to just rest."

"Cool. You mean we can do anything?"

"Or nothing."

"Excellent. Can we play the iMac? Or set up the Xbox?"

"I reckon. I'm going to go help Tim get packed up for a while though."

"We need to find a TV that didn't break in the quake," John said. They were off and going. That alone went a long way in relieving a rapidly growing pressure-cooker. The girls were looking at me expectantly. "You too—anything you want."

"Can I use the iMac to write a story?" Kelly asked.

"Yep."

"What can I do?" Marie asked.

"What do you want to do?"

"Go back to bed."

"Go right ahead," her Mom replied.

"K!" Marie was quickly under the covers in her dark corner, with Ada to keep her company.

"Hon, I'm going over to Tim's for a while."

"Take him this."

"Whatcha got?"

"Extra pancakes."

"You will be revered in the halls of the James family for generations to come…"

"Oh, stop. Those boys are probably hungry for some real food."

"No doubt. I've seen them eat. Not pretty."

"Get going. Take a radio. And don't stay too long. You need some more rest, whether you know it or not."

"Yes, dear. What are your plans for the morning?"

"First Corinthians."

"Good idea, although I would've chosen Proverbs 31."

"You would. Now shoo."

"As you wish."

For a change, neither of the dogs followed me out as I headed over to Tim's place. There were a few flakes falling as I went out the gate, and noticed the tire tracks from one of the patrols. A State Patrol cruiser was parked over at the James. That was odd.

When I announced myself to the damaged house, Drew met me where the front porch was supposed to be. "C'mon in. The cop thought we might be looters."

"Sure. This house would be a jewel in a crown of jewels."

Drew smiled. "Maybe the TV and the home theater system."

"Yep."

I climbed up to the front door landing, and up the stairs. A State Trooper, new to me at least, was talking with Tim. Identification issues seemed to have been resolved, and they were talking about the Tri-Cities.

"Morning," I said.

"Howdy—how's it going today?"

"Good. Here—" I said as I handed the package to Tim, "Pancakes that Karen made."

"Fantastic. David! Get up here please." A face appeared from the basement. "Take these out to the trailer and share with your brothers. That means—equally."

"OK. Hi, Rick."

"Hiya, Davey. Have an adventure last night?" Davey was eight.

"Yes sir. Camped outside in the winter!"

"Very good. Stay warm?"

"Yep. I was in the middle!"

"Good for you. Almost as good as a dog. Now get going!"

"K! See ya!"

The three adults stood for a moment. Tim said. "Must be nice to be eight."

"No kidding," I said. "I'm Rick Drummond," to the Trooper. He must've been six-five.

"Tony Daniels. Nice to meet you."

"Likewise. We don't usually see Troopers around here."

"We're getting familiar with the territory. Literally. And I'm also supposed to remind you of a ten a.m. meeting on Monday."

"Thanks, I remembered, even without my Palm Pilot. And welcome. This part of your regular area?"

"Pretty much, although we're usually just supposed to be on the interstate and the state highways. Command is reorganizing areas so that we can assist the Guard and the sheriff's office. That means knowing the roads and who's where."

"Not many around on this street," I commented.

"Nope. You and Mr. James here. All the others are empty."

"And I'm outta here tomorrow," Tim said. "We were just talking about the Tri-Cities. Tony's from down that way."

"Kennewick?"

"West Richland, actually."

"Really. I know it well. Whereabouts?"

"Bombing Range Road. Top of the hill. My folks built it in the seventies."

"Know the spot. Not far from the churches, if I remember."

"Yep. That's the area."

"Love the name of that road. Talk about politically incorrect!"

"Yep. My dad just about stroked when they changed the name of the freeway exit to 'Queensgate."

"I had a good laugh over that too. Trying to be PC and all."

"Yep. Well, I better get back on the road. Just making sure you're supposed to be here."

"If you don't mind, can you tell me how many families are left around us?"

"Sure. Let me check my list." Trooper Daniels pulled out a laser-printed sheet, and found the road behind us. "Two on the road to the west. Six on the north, but you can't get there from here on the roads. Two families, south. No one else that way all the way to the arterials."

"I had no idea there were so few." The population of the streets he described—basically our block—should've been over fifty families.

"Yep. The whole area's pretty well cleared out. Sheriff said that the zip code is less than thirty percent of its normal population.'

"That many evac'd?"

"Pretty close. Said that the census they did a few days ago showed a five percent mortality rate from the quake."

"Two thousand dead in this zip code? What's it like across the rest of the city?"

"Bout the same." That meant around ten thousand.

"How about Seattle? Anybody done an educated guess yet?"

"I don't know about educated, but King county's supposed to have a half-million dead. Thurston county about sixty-thousand.

Over a million in Washington and Oregon, the FEMA guys figure. A bunch more up in Canada, from what I hear."

"Canada? They got hit?"

"Yeah. The quake, not the ash."

I considered the words the Trooper told me. The numbers added up to perhaps fifteen percent of our state's population, plus the deaths in Oregon, plus those in Canada, which I never even considered. "Good God."

"Yes sir. Gentlemen, it's been good to meet you. I better get going."

"Thanks for keeping an eye out for us."

"No problem. You all take care."

"You too."

After the Trooper left, Tim asked, "Meeting? With the cops? They looking into your nefarious past? The midnight Tequila shots on Independence Day?" He was grinning.

"Nothing like that. Besides. I've had a deputy or firemen or five over for that party in years past. I expect they've finally gotten a little better organized and may even want to provide us some information."

"On what? Getting back to normal?"

"That's not going to happen anytime soon, and you know that as well as I do. Hopefully though, they can at least shine some light on things. I know that Dan's been working his ass off trying to get the water system checked out and going. I assume that the power guys and the natural gas guys are too."

"It'll be months."

"Yep. But if they can get ONE of the services back up—power—then the others aren't so tough. Can't pump water without power. Can't keep it warm enough to keep from freezing either."

"True, but with the country falling apart, you really think they're getting things PUT TOGETHER?"

"We can hope. Let's get to work. What do you need help with?"

"Getting the boys to realize that we can't take everything with them."

"I know what you mean. Carl and John are trying to get one of the Xboxes hooked up, and a working TV."

"You got enough power for that?"

"They can run them off an inverter, from a little tiny generator I built."

"Wow. I never knew."

"I got a bigger one, five thousand watts, and a monster that runs off the tractor too. I've been powering up the gas station down the street for that. The evac buses, fire trucks, and the Army have been gassing up there."

"Supply sergeant."

"Of a distinctly civilian kind, perhaps. C'mon. I promised Karen I'd be home in time for a nap. I'm still not back to normal."

"You never were."

"Love ya' man. Love ya."

We spent about two hours with the boys, sorting out stuff to take and stuff to leave, which had to be confined to the space of Tim's travel trailer and the back of the Honda van. The list included all of the food in the house that was still good—including the contents of the small refrigerator freezer—as many clothes as they could take, and personal belongings including the photo albums. The trailer already had the family sleeping bags and the rest of the camping gear, so at least that stuff didn't have to be re-packed. The boys were---typically—thrashing each other in one of the bedrooms. We got more done without the boys 'helping' than with. By eleven or so, Tim had a good start on getting the first load of stuff taken care of. We'd arranged it in order of necessity, so that the late-to-pack items, if they didn't fit, wouldn't be something they couldn't live without.

I also made some mental notes on what Tim was lacking, and ended up calling Karen to write them down for me.

"Karen, you there?" A few moments passed.

"Yep. Whatcha need?"

"Well, I've got a list of stuff that I think Tim oughta have on the trip."

"I hope eggs are on the list."

"As a matter of fact, yes."

"Why don't you guys take a break and bring the boys over. Carl got the Xbox working with the TV from the basement. I'm sure they'd love to play."

"You sure you're ready to be invaded? Clear it with our guests?"

"Did already. And I've got popcorn right off the woodstove."

"You found your popper."

"I did. And it's reeeeeally good. If Tim's got margarine, tell him to bring a lump."

"Will do." I walked back out to the garage, where Tim was looking at a size C pile, and a size A hole to fill in the van. "Looking at it isn't going to make it bigger, or the pile smaller."

"I know. There's just too much stuff."

"We've got a car-top carrier you can have. That'll take care of some of it."

"Thanks." Tim sounded more depressed than I'd heard him since his wife left.

"C'mon. Time for a break. We've got a surprise for you."

"We could use a pleasant one."

"Yep. You could. Go get the boys and a stick of butter if you've got one. I'll close up the van and the garage."

"OK." Tim turned and went back into the house.

He gathered up the boys and we walked through the light snow back to our house. Buck and Ada met us at the fence, demanding the boys to play Right Now. I didn't tell them that Carl had video games to play this afternoon, I thought it best to surprise them. I was to be surprised too, when I opened the barn door.

"Oh my..." I said.

"Welcome to Sunday dinner," Libby said. They'd set up dinner for all of us—scattered around the shop and store room sure—but everyone had a place setting.

"Marie's idea."

"And a good one at that," Tim said.

I made sure that everyone was reintroduced. Everyone had met before at one or another party that we'd had, and the boys naturally went straight to the video game, where John and Carl let the younger boys take over. With some cajoling, Drew joined in too. I knew he wanted to play, but I think he thought it was not the grown up thing to do.

"Something smells wonderful," I said.

"Thanks to Ron, we're now minus two pesky roosters. They're baking right now, along with baked potatoes and we've got some sweet corn from the freezer."

"You've been busy. And you said you just had popcorn."

"We do. Those roosters still have a while to go. We don't have this science down yet," Libby said as she handed a big plastic bowl to the kids.

"This is amazing," Tim said as he chomped on a handful of hot popcorn. "If my folks were in better shape, and I were set up like this, I'd be tempted to stay. How long has this taken you? I mean, getting ready and all?"

"Well, first, it's not really 'getting ready.' It's 'being ready.' See the difference?"

"Not really."

"'Getting ready' implies that you're preparing for a single event or situation or a point in time when something happens. 'Being ready' is being prepared for most things, at most times. Can't be ready for everything though. To answer your question though, I've been 'being ready' for years. It's never really something that I decided to do, it's just the way I was raised."

"Why? I mean....."

"It's OK. I get it. Big family. 'Eat what's in front of you' and all that. Parents that had seen the first Great Depression and what it could do to a family. Grandparents that told stories of their ancestors' having to leave Ireland because of starvation and oppression by the English. For me, its watching my back. Making sure my wife and kids are provided for. Making sure they learn too."

"I'm afraid I've let my kids down on that department."

"Never too late to change."

"Here you two--have some popcorn before the wolves devour it all," Libby said. The younger boys were huddled around the TV, busy helping each other crash their cars in the digital version of San Francisco.

"We figured that a mid-day dinner was a better idea, what with the curfew," Karen said. "And I figured that Tim would want to get a good nights sleep before heading out."

"Probably a good idea.'

"We also have a care package put together for you, based on what Rick told me over the radio. Stuff you might be short on or missing entirely."

"You don't have to do that."

"'Do not neglect to do good and to share what you have, for such sacrifices are pleasing to God,'" Karen said.

"Where's that from," Tim asked.

"Hebrews thirteen, verse sixteen," I responded.

"You know it well."

"I do. That one and many others. My owner's manual for life."

"I wasn't raised that way...."

"Never too late to learn, brother."

"I suppose so."

"I better go sit down for a while. Feeling a little light-headed."

"Couple days. That'll pass."

"I hope so. I've never been one to sit around."

While I took a few minutes to cat-nap amongst the clatter of the kids playing (the girls were giving the boys a run for their money, and had best lap times on the race three turns in a row), Karen showed Tim around the barn and detailed our living arrangements. Finally, she showed him the box of stuff that I'd asked her to assemble. In it, she'd put a gallon of bleach, bar soap, batteries for his flashlights, a small first-aid kit, some rope, a bag that had some baked flatbread, and a foil wrapped cornbread. There was space in the box for several dozen egg cartons too, which would be packed in as soon as dinner was over. He accepted in hushed tones. I dozed for a while longer, and was awakened by Ada, jumping up on the bed next to me, for her afternoon nap.

We enjoyed a great dinner, and a bottle of chardonnay, rescued from the basement. Dessert was a surprise too—brownies, hot from the oven. Things were almost 'normal'.

Around three, Tim gathered up his boys and headed back home. He still had several rooms to finish going through and wanted to get the kids settled down and the trailer warmed up for the night. We sent home some 'dinner' too, in the form of some canned soups and a half-loaf of bread. We made plans to meet up in the morning, as soon as curfew was lifted, to plan out the day. If Alan was dead-set on going to Fresno, we'd have to get Tim and Alan acquainted and have them get set up with their CB's on the way south, as well as logical stopping points along the way…assuming logic still played a role.

After the James' clan left, Ron and I put our coats on for a quick walk to the house behind us, to check it out for damage. If it was trashed, there was no point in talking to the sheriff about using it for the foreseeable future. We took a stepladder to the back fence and straddled the fence with it, and climbed over into the property's back yard. We'd picked up another couple inches of snow over the past couple hours.

We kept to the north property line that bordered Dan's property. His travel trailer was in the driveway, and there were lights on inside. "Hello the trailer!" I called out. Dan's wife Alicia—she hated that name though, and went by 'Sandy'—appeared at the window. She waved and in a moment, stepped outside.

"Hiya, neighbor! Thanks for the propane."

"You bet. You keeping warm enough?"

"Just fine, thanks. Hi, I'm Sandy," she said as she shook hands with Ron.

"Nice to meet you. I'm Ron Martin. Reluctant houseguest of the Drummonds."

"You could do worse."

"We could. Our house burned to the ground, so we've heard."

"I'm very sorry," Sandy said, meaning it.

"Have you heard from your daughter?" I asked Sandy. Her daughter from her first marriage had been missing the last time I remembered to ask Dan about her.

"She showed up on Monday in her boyfriends' truck, and announced they were leaving for good."

"You OK?"

"Honestly? Yes. Dan and I are tired of bailing her out all the time. She's just so irresponsible! She thinks the world owes her......the world!"

"I know the type. Did they say where they're heading?"

"Republic. That's where her boyfriend's from."

"Tough place to get to in bad weather, even before all this."

"Tried to tell her. Might has well been talking to a log. She packed her cosmetic bag and left. That's it, no goodbye, no clothes, nothing. Gone."

"If she's lucky, she's still alive."

"If she has half a brain, she won't come back here," Sandy said. "But I'm afraid she leans toward her father in that department."

"Takes all kinds."

"What brings you over?" she said, changing the subject.

"We thought we'd check out the vacant house here. Karen's brother's family and her Mom are planning on going to California in the morning. We think it's a dumb idea, but we're full up now. If the place is livable, I'm going to ask the sheriff if we can take it over temporarily. But what about your place? Is it salvageable?"

"Dan thinks so—although at first he was also looking at the house on the south, too. He thought it looked better than our place. He's already started some work on our house though. We just paid it off in October and we're not about to let it go to Hell now. We're going to be back inside as of tomorrow we think. The first floor is in good shape, other than one window. The second floor bedroom is toast—the wall came in and brought part of the roof with it--but we can close that off. He's also thinking that water could be back in the main part of the system by the end of the week."

"Really? That's awesome news."

"They've been busting their asses to get it fixed."

"I know. And completely under-appreciated."

"Got that right. We did get a food priority, and Dan said that he's got a line on a used generator that threw a rod. He's going to take the motor out of the lawn mower, and get it going again. His buddy Samuel said it would fit."

"Samuel knows his stuff. I met him the other day."

"Anyway, Dan should be home soon. They're working three eights instead of twelve's."

"No point in wearing them out completely."

"No joke. I better get inside. You too. It's getting cold again."

"We're finally getting the winter they warned us about for all those years."

"Nice timing. Good to meet you, Ron."

"Likewise, Sandy. I'll have the boys send over some eggs tomorrow if you like."

"That'd be great! We sure appreciated those eggs that Carl brought by the other day."

"He did? He didn't tell me."

"Yep. Same day that Dan got the propane."

"Good kid," Ron said.

"Yes, he is. See ya soon Sandy."

"Bye," she said as she went back inside.

"Nice lady." Ron said.

"She is. Deserves better than that daughter of hers. That kid's been a whack job all her life. I don't get it."

"Some things are beyond understanding."

"Amen to that. C'mon. Let's check out the house and kick some tires."

We made it inside just before curfew, through the east wind and now-drifting snow. The house wasn't in too bad of shape, with cracks in several of the recently-installed vinyl windows, and the back deck in a heap. The top of the chimney was also gone--a pile on the back yard. The rest of it though, looked good. We couldn't see much inside, though, through the mostly-closed blinds.

"Not a bad place," Ron said.

"Yeah. If Alan's agreeable, I'll talk to the sheriff about getting him inside and setup. If he's not, we should get you guys in there. Regardless, we should scout out a place for you guys. Barn living is getting old for everyone, I'm afraid."

"It is, but it beats the heck out of a shelter, or a trailer."

"Yeah. Tomorrow at the meeting we'll see if they've established any rules for such things."

"Rules? It's the government. That's all they do is make rules."

"No argument with that. But at least here, I think we have people with brains and common-sense in decision-making positions."

"That'd be unique these days."

"Indeed."

Sunday Evening
January Twenty-second

"So, the house looks to be in pretty good shape," I recapped for Libby and Karen over soup and bread. "If there's some way that I can talk Mike into letting us use it, we might be able to move Alan and your Mom in there. We can probably use a bunch of what Tim couldn't take, and the rest we can use for Libby and Ron's place, which we don't have figured out yet."

"There's still a lot of empty houses though," Karen said. "Can't we use one?"

"It's tough to feel good about up and moving in on someone's house if you don't know they're coming back, or have relatives who are," I said.

"Yes, but it would only be temporarily," Karen countered.

"Still, it'd be weird. I was thinking of asking Mike or whoever's in charge of stuff like this if they're other empty houses that are repairable around us."

"That'd be slim chances you know, as hot as the housing market is."

"That'd be 'was'. I don't think it's too hot anymore, or ever will be again."

"Probably true," Libby said.

"Anyway, it's on my to-do list for tomorrow. I know that patience will wear thin pretty soon. I've already seen it in the kids and the way they're acting around each other."

"Yeah, that started and we shut them down. Made them go pick up a book to get away from each other."

"Smart. Me the slave driver would've just put them to work."

"I know. We need to get you to slow down a little," Karen said.

"I know. Too much to do though. There's just so much to do...or was anyway. We've gotten through the first week. We can now start looking ahead a little and catch our breath."

"Assuming nothing else bad comes our way," Ron added.

"I think we've seen our share of personal life-changing events for a while."

"Right. You think so?" Ron asked.

"I can be an optimist."

"On the rare occasion, lately," Libby smirked.

"Can't live on the Dark Side all the time, sweetie. Now let me get to work."

"More computer time?"

"Some. I need to do some research more than anything else."

"What this time? Libby asked.

"Lots of stuff. First, assuming that things that we're seeing now extrapolate into bad things continuing along for the foreseeable future, how much food do we need to generate to maintain ourselves and get through the winter. That means not only what we grow here, but what's grown in the neighborhood and the Valley in general. What we can grow, what we can't, where we're going to get it if we can't. That extends to Pauliano's hens, we're going to need milk, meat, and list goes on."

"Sounds like a doctoral thesis level of work."

"Everything does at first. I've got a little of a head start, knowing what we grow and our immediate neighbors, and some of what some of the other folks on the block grow…or grew. I also have to figure out how much farmable land area is available around us. That's not that tough to figure out, though, I can figure it out from a satellite photo of the neighborhood that I downloaded from a program we use at work. I do, however, have some things that any one of you could read up on…"

"Like what?" Ron asked.

"Poultry for one. One of the books that Karen and I used to read up on when we were in the egg hobby had statistics on production, lifespan…and in general stuff we don't know."

"K, what else?" Libby said.

"Help with area calculations on the food production end of things would be handy. That's mostly right now at least, reading from Carla Emery's book and gleaning some stuff from there. A couple other sources too. Basically, how much area to generate how many pounds or bushels of food per acre. Then I have to figure out how much our growing group will need to make it and produce a comfortable overage."

"Why? You mean, grow more than we can eat?"

"Yeah."

"Why bother?"

"We're not the only ones who eat? Duh!" I said with grin. "If we want to remain relatively safe…"

"….we have to provide a resource that's big enough to support those who protect us."

467

"Bingo. And, this neighborhood is not going to be empty forever. And we can't grow enough to maintain ourselves if we've got twelve people to work it the hard way."

"There's thirteen though, assuming Mom and Alan's family are in the count."

"They are, but your Mom is well beyond the age where she can work the fields."

"Yeah, but she can still help."

"Yes she can. She can teach us not to make stupid mistakes. She grew up in the Depression. She's seen something of a more simple lifestyle that she knew."

"I'll make you some tea. You still aren't on stove-duty tonight," Karen said.

"Good for me. I'm not going to get much done anyway, I can tell. I'm already fading."

"Go ahead and get to work and get those books out. We'll figure out who gets to be the expert in each area."

"Find a quarter. That'd be good for flipping. God knows that they're not worth much as money anymore."

I worked until long after I should have, with the dull throb building behind my eyes. I managed to get a fair bit of work done, at least a good start. Libby was busy reading up on knowledge from Carla Emery, Karen was re-reading the poultry book, 'Raising Poultry the Modern Way.' Ron was reading the 'old' copy of Carla Emery's Encyclopedia of Country Living, and our copy of 'Back to Basics' was on the table as well. I finally turned in at eight after a snowy trip to the 'facilities' and was joined by Karen for at least four hours. Libby and Ron were 'up' for stove duty tonight, with Karen following them in the four hour shifts. Both Ron and Libby were making hand-written notes on some five-by-seven yellow pads to give me in the morning.

After I'd gone to bed, as is my unfortunate habit, I had a difficult time turning off my brain. I kept going over the lists of food crops we'd need, what we'd grown in the past, average production, questions on where we'd get meat, milk, and fish......finally I drifted off.

I dreamed that night of riding on the tractor, pulling a trailer full of apples. A nice dream.

Monday
January Twenty-third

I woke at six-thirty Monday morning in the same position I fell asleep in. It felt great. I crawled out of our blanket-room, pulled on my insulated Carhartts, some old boots, and an old ragg wool sweater and kissed Karen good-morning. She hushed me and handed me a stack of papers and a cup of sweet coffee. They'd been busy overnight.

After a quiet breakfast of scrambled eggs and toast (what else?), I went outside through the tool room to clean off the tractor and get it ready for plowing again. Ron and Libby were just getting up when I fired up the Ford, unhooked the generator trailer, and put the six-foot back blade back on. At least for now, the tires on the generator trailer weren't flat. Curfew was just lifted when I started to plow a path up to the street. We ended up with deep packed drifts in some places. After about a half-hour, I'd managed to clear the path and the driveway of drifts up to two feet. I opened the gate and found the drift between the driveway gate and the fences on either side to be formidable: Four feet deep. 'Ain't no way the tractor's gonna clear that,' I thought. Shoveling. By hand. Great. I shut down the Ford and walked back to the barn for reinforcements. I'd need a few, the drift was twenty-feet long and I'd need to get at least five feet clear for the tractor, more for one of the vehicles.

After letting everyone in on the news that all hands were needed with shovels, I retrieved two 'push' type snow shovels from the tool room, two 'scoop' shovels, and some assorted flat-bladed shovels that I'd picked up over the years at garage sales and auctions and re-handled as needed. I was a sucker for a garage sale or estate sale or whatever...and my tool room was evidence of that. One memorable weekend netted me more than a dozen forged hay forks, pitch forks and potato hooks, as well as many small hand tools, shovels and spades. None of them had handles, either they'd rotted out or been through a fire. The seller was using them for 'yard art' in the front yard of their fifties ranch-style house. The final find of that day was at an auction they had for the house next door: A Dearborn two-bottom plow, holding up a pot of geraniums. Fifteen bucks, and it was mine. I didn't even need to put new plowshares on it! I'd 'restored' it to its factory colors when I repainted the 8N. I'd only used it a couple of times over the years, as it was more efficient to use the Troy-Bilt tillers in the garden, which was surrounded by fences.

"Do we HAVE to do this?" Kelly asked.

"'fraid so, babe. Unless you fancy being snowbound as well as living in a barn."

"This sucks."

"Yep."

"That's all we do around here is work. We haven't been able to go anywhere since the quake."

"I know, Kel. We weren't sure how safe things were out there. I'll take you along with me today though, if you want. Tell Marie that she can come with Ron and I, OK?"

"OK," she said, not particularly impressed. "Where are we going?"

"Meeting at the community center."

"Big whoop."

"Hon, I'm sorry if this doesn't meet your agenda, but this is the way things are. You can come with us and at least get a look around at things off the property, or you can stay here. You can choose. You have until quarter of ten or when we're done with the snow drift, your choice."

"OK. We'll go."

"Atta girl. Now go get those mittens."

The boys were not in a particularly good mood when the girls started teasing them that they got to go with us this morning, and the boys didn't. I stopped that quickly.

"Kel, I didn't say the boys couldn't go."

"Really?" Carl asked.

"Sure. You can come with us, but I'm not sure if the sheriff will want you there or let you in on the meeting."

"That's OK. At least we're out of the barn and the house for a while," John said.

"Works for me," Carl added.

"All right, let's get shoveling. As soon as you've got five feet or so clear, I can get through it with the Ford. I can widen it out pretty quick then, but you'll still have to help clean up."

"All right," Carl said in a descending tone that said, 'I don't want to do this.'

We worked for the better part of an hour getting a path cleared wide enough for me to work the Ford into the channel. 'If this snow keeps up, I'm going to need the chains,' I thought to myself. With another fifteen minutes of work, I had the driveway cleared all the way to the street. All of this could be for naught, if the road was blocked further down. I didn't see any evidence of a recent police patrol, which was also damned odd.

"I'm gonna run this up the road and see if it's open. You head back to the barn and bring up the Expedition. I'll be back quick, just a couple of passes and then we'll go to the meeting—I don't want to be late. Grab my clipboard too, and the radios."

"K," Ron said. I heard the kids ask, 'Are we done yet?' as I pulled out.

I chugged the little tractor up the road, dragging snow off to the right as I went. No big drifts were evident all the way to the corner. The Army Humvee had been there recently at least, by the tire tracks in the parking lot, but the store was both closed up and unmanned. 'What is up with that?'

I made my way back up to the house, where Ron had the Expedition in the driveway, kids already inside. I pulled the tractor back by the barn, shut it down and closed off the fuel line, and jogged back up to the gate. I closed the gate and hopped in.

"Wives OK with us taking the kids?" I asked Ron as I put the ear bud in.

"Yes we are," the voice in my ear replied. "Just leave the radio on VOX in the meeting. If we have any questions we want answered, we'll talk to you."

"Thanks, babe." I said as Ron turned down the street. The girls were in the third row of seats, John and Carl in the middle row. Ron had already placed the SUV in four-wheel-drive.

"Besides, this gives Libby and I a chance to talk in privacy, which has been sorely lacking of late."

"Know what you mean."

We turned left toward the community center, plowed through some drifts, and in a few minutes pulled into the mostly-empty lot. Two Humvees were there, unmanned. Hmmm. I looked over at Ron, and he glanced over at me too. Hmmm.

It was five minutes to ten when we walked into the assembly room and sat down. The kids sat in the back row (just like they would in church, if we didn't make them sit up front somewhere). Ron and I sat up front, in the first two seats to the left of what was passing for a lectern. There were perhaps fifty people in the assembly hall, with chairs set up for around a hundred. I recognized the uniform coveralls of all the utility providers and several other unfamiliar uniforms. Two military uniforms joined us in the room, trailed by a Deputy I didn't recognize, four firemen that I nodded to, and finally the sheriff.

"Good morning, thank you for joining me. For those of you that don't know me, I'm Sheriff Mike Amberson. To my left is Lieutenant Peter Wolfson, my logistical officer. To my right are Colonel Michaels of the Washington State Army National Guard. The Colonel is in command of the Spokane region's military presence, which crosses the lines between military branches."

"The purpose of today's meeting is to provide you an update on local recovery efforts. This is one of a series of meetings held in the county. My City of Spokane counterpart will be conducting similar neighborhood meetings this week as well. I would like to turn over the initial portion of today's briefing to the Colonel."

"Thank you, Mike," the Colonel responded. "First, I would like to thank you all for assisting us in maintaining a sense of order and civilization over the past week. As many of you know, we as a state have suffered deaths in the hundreds of thousands, probably exceeding the scope of the Indonesian tsunami. Additionally, we've lost most of the major economic resources of the State. The majority of Boeing's Washington state facilities have been destroyed, most of the high-tech firms in the Seattle region have been either destroyed or heavily damaged, the Ports of Tacoma and Seattle have been wiped out and will take generations to restore, if possible. Additionally, major military bases in the state have been significantly damaged or destroyed completely. These include McChord Air Force Base, Fort Lewis, the Naval facilities at Bremerton and in the Sound. The devastation in Seattle, even in normal times, would tax the nations' resources to the breaking point. But as you know, these are not normal times, nor will they be for the foreseeable future. The primary reason that we requested this meeting is to inform you that we expect recovery of the damage to take much longer than anyone could expect."

I interrupted, which I'm prone to do, speaking my mind before I've given the speaker time to finish. "So what you're expecting is no relief from the rest of the country, starting, let me guess, last Friday?"

The Colonel narrowed his look to me as Mike whispered something in his ear. "Essentially correct. Nothing is being stated to that effect in official channels, but that's what we're expecting."

"With all due respect, Colonel, is any of this information coming from the federal authorities, or is the State stepping up?"

"The latter. The federal government, by the military's assessment, is either in, or soon going to be in, full meltdown mode. That is to say, the various departments that have become institutionalized will soon cease to function as recognized entities. The Pacific Northwest was merely on the leading edge of a twin disaster of unparalleled proportions."

The room was dead quiet, for what seemed like an hour.

"Are you saying that you expect the elected governmental officials to….fall?" The question came from behind me. I was thinking the same thing.

"It is the belief of the military that that will be the case."

"OK, so let me get this straight," Ron said. "You are briefing us, without orders from your civilian government leaders, and telling us that the civilian government is about to fall. Is that right?"

"Yes sir."

"So what will the military's role be in this collapse?" a voice from my left.

"We will defend the Constitution of the United States of America, and do what is necessary to meet that obligation, whether that takes place on United States soil or internationally."

Questions were racing through my head. Where to start? What to ask first? Karen's voice sounded in my ear with the proper question.

"What about the President? The Vice-President? The Cabinet? Congress?"

"It is my understanding that the full Cabinet, the Supreme Court, and a large percentage of congressmen are being protected at this time." I could hear Karen's facial expression over the radio. She was more than a little cynical.

"Protection, or custody?" I asked.

"Protection. This is not a coup, and the military authorities will protect the elected government if and as required."

"What about foreign engagements?"

"A full pull-out of American forces is underway in the Middle East. Not just Iraq, but in the entire region. This actually began two days before the quake..." The Colonel was interrupted by a woman in the back.

"BEFORE? Did they know this was coming?" She was irate.

"It appears so, ma'am. I do not have the full report, but from my sources, which are pretty far up the food chain, that appears to be the case. The civilian government was expecting a financial meltdown to begin, and recognized the ramifications that such a meltdown would have on U.S. interests worldwide. Other forces have been designated for relocation to U.S. soil, but have been stopped by foreign governments."

"Stopped? What the Hell does that mean?" a much older man asked from right behind me. I turned and saw the VFW cap and Korean War and Vietnam patches and pins.

"Sir, that means that foreign installations, including all forces in Europe, Korea, Japan, and numerous other nations, have essentially been barred from leaving those countries unless they choose to fight their way out."

"Hostages," the old man said. The room erupted in anger.

"Yes sir," The Colonel responded flatly.

"What are we doing about it?" I asked.

"That is being addressed at a much higher pay grade."

"When will we know that our boys are safe?"

"I would expect soon. I would like to get onto other matters that we need to discuss. The military command in Washington state will not allow this state to devolve into anarchy. As with the federal government, our role is to protect and defend the Constitution. Plans are being put in place to restore as much infrastructure as possible, and hold new elections for the state government. As you have heard, the majority of the state leadership was lost in the earthquake. Only five percent of the former leadership survived."

"OK, this is turning out to be much worse than anyone feared. What other curves are you going to toss our way?" I said as I leaned forward.

"That, sir, is the big money question, isn't it?"

"Depends what you consider to be money," someone behind me said.

Monday Morning
January Twenty-third

I took a glance over my shoulder at the kids. They were still in the back row, and very interested at the discussion going on in front of them. 'History in the making, and they're on the front row,' I remember thinking.

"So, Colonel Michaels, can you explain what chain of command you are operating under?" the Korean War vet asked pointedly.

"Certainly sir. The state Guard command is operating under direct military authority of the Department of Defense, as are all other state Guard units nationwide. The respective Governors of each state are in direct contact with commanders of military units assigned to each state, and each Governor is in direct contact with the Joint Chiefs."

"Complicated," came a voice behind me.

"Yes, but it allows local flexibility and control, with a minimum of federal governmental interference."

"Or input."

"Yes sir. However, our field commanders, while available to each Governor for defensive operations in each state, also have the ability if needed to exercise discretion should orders from the states' leaders go counter to constitutional mandates."

"So you're saying that's supposed to keep local leaders from acting on their own with State military forces to do whatever they please."

"Exactly. California and two northeastern states have already tried to institute some measures upon the civilian population that cannot be supported constitutionally."

"What exactly, were they trying to do?"

"Disarm the population, among other things."

"And the result was?"

"Not good for the state leadership in those states. They are in custody and military commanders have taken control until civilian authority can be restored to responsible parties, which should be within the next ten days."

I spoke up again. "OK, Gotta ask this. What I'm hearing, or seeming to hear, is that the military is not putting up with anything that is literally, not in the Constitution. Is that correct?"

"Essentially, yes. Since the President allowed each state to declare martial law and a number of states have done so, the military authorities in those regions are operating and will continue to operate under military authority, and under this evolving situation, we expect that civilian law will be interpreted by military authority, much more strictly according to the Constitution than the Ninth Circuit Court or the Supreme Court has for the past several decades."

"Good. Then they can start with the Patriot Act."

"It remains to be seen what the process will be of interpreting laws and the legality of laws passed prior to the current crisis," the Colonel replied.

"Well that's one helluva re-set that you're putting in place," I said. "You're potentially removing decades of judicial interpretation."

"That may well be," the Colonel replied. "As I said, it remains to be seen if any different interpretations will remain once full civilian control is restored. I would like to continue this conversation, but I know that there are other issues that need to be brought up, and we do have a schedule to keep in order to meet with other neighborhoods. Sheriff?"

"So what's driven this bass-ackwards chain of command? Doesn't stuff like this have to go through the Pentagon? This doesn't sound normal," the Korean vet said suspiciously.

"Therein lies the problem. There are major ideological differences in the management of this situation. It appears that the President and White House staff are on one side of the table, with the Joint Chiefs; and staff in large portions of other agencies and the upper levels of the Pentagon are on the other. The President has directed this simplified chain of command in order to respond quickly to the situation, rather than letting it fester in the E-Ring of the Pentagon."

My mind was racing. Had I heard that right?

"Thank you Colonel. I would like to assure all of the residents here that it is not the intention of either the military command or the civilian law enforcement to overstep the bounds of the Constitution. There will be no gun seizures. There will be no seizures of private property. There will be due process. The Bill of Rights will be maintained and enforced. I know there are many questions that you have, but I would like to move on right now to the infrastructure issues that we all face. I have Earl Cannavelli and Ken Snow with us to provide an update on water and power systems. Earl, could you provide an update for us?"

A shortish, round man in his mid-fifties took the stand. For the life of me, he reminded me of Gimli, the dwarf in the Lord of the Rings, without the accent. "Thank you sheriff. I want to let you know that we have made substantial progress in restoring water within the systems primary areas of service. Fourteen of our staff, joined by seven workers from out of the region, have been working non-stop on analysis of the existing system and restoration of system operation. We have suffered the loss of one of the three aboveground water tanks in this area as you know, and thirty-five percent of our mainlines have been damaged beyond repair. Water service to the remaining operational mainlines will be brought back on line as soon as electric power can be restored to the well pumps and boosters, and as individual residences can be isolated from the mains."

"Isolated? You mean cut off?"

"Yes sir, temporarily. You see the system can't pressurize if there are a hundred broken lines downstream of your curb stop. And there are at least that many. Starting today, our crews will be shutting off curb stops for every connection in the system, and the system pressurized on generator power. Once that's done, active connections—meaning houses that are being lived in or businesses that are essential—will be turned on and checked for breaks."

"Sewer. What about the sewer?"

"By our analysis, it's probably 75% intact. Without power, the lift stations won't work though. And the breaks that we know about—and those aren't our department, but Spokane county's—are in large transport lines heading to the sewage treatment plant."

"So all that money that we had to spend on abandoning our septic tanks was for nothing. And the county made us fill our tanks in and destroy the lines to the houses."

"I'm afraid so. We will have some paperwork on a do-it-yourself rebuild of the septic-type system, assuming the drain field is still intact."

"That beats the heck out of going in a bucket," a woman said to my left.

"OK. Now what about power?" came another voice.

"Power's tougher. We get the line right from Bonneville Power Administration. BPA got hammered. They lost forty percent off their transmission lines, and thirty percent of their generating capacity, or so we've heard."

"They lost dams?" A female voice asked. Marie, sitting in the back. 'Good for you,' I thought.

"We've heard that Bonneville and John Day were heavily damaged and breached. Don't know how. We also know that a number of the generation stations were shut down due to the ash fall, and have not been cleaned to the point where they can operate again."

"What about Grand Coulee?" I asked.

"Third powerhouse—the one built in the seventies—was damaged. Overall the dam is OK—again, so we've heard. The big problem right now is getting the downed lines back up. They can generate power all day long, but without those lines there's no way to get it onto the grid."

"What about Hanford?" Ron asked. The answer was a long time in coming.

"The Columbia Generating Station is off-line," the power rep said.

"We figured that much already. How bad is it damaged and is there any radioactivity?"

"I'll answer that," Colonel Michaels said. "FEMA clamped down on all information from the Hanford Reservation when the quake hit. They didn't want any information to get out prematurely."

"OK, that's all well and good, but from a guy I know who was there in Richland, they're not letting anyone north of the city and he got so spooked he's bugging out to California," I said.

"The reactor was damaged. It was in full operation when the quake hit, and had just been brought back on line the week before for maintenance. There was no release of radioactivity into the atmosphere. The reactor containment vessel prevented that. The reactor building as I understand it, was heavily damaged both due to the quake and the reactor control system was damaged in the quake and the shutdown. It will never operate again. The federal government is removing the fuel from the reactor at this time. The building will then be secured as much as possible. Permanently."

"So you're saying it didn't melt down," someone to my left asked.

"That's what I'm saying."

"What about the other facilities on the reservation?" I asked.

"What are you referring to?" There was that narrowed, focused gaze at me again. Dang. I hate drawing attention like that….

"The reactor isn't the only radioactive facility down there, Colonel. Back in the early nineties, I toured the reservation by invite. The insides of some of those buildings will never be seen by human eyes because of the radiation. Are they intact?"

"That is my understanding," he said with a steely voice.

"You might want to investigate further to find out for yourself," Ron added. The Colonel did not look happy. I wouldn't have been either if I were in his shoes. There was an uncomfortable silence, broken by the power guy.

"With regards to interim power distribution, we're in the process of getting our local generation capacity tied into the local distribution network. As you can imagine, this is no small job—we have over three hundred people working on it in Spokane, Kootenai, Lincoln, Adams and Stevens Counties. Similar to the water system, we have to find out what's intact and what's not. We're starting with the distribution system and going from there. We have already restored power to parts of downtown, with the hospitals and shelters being the obvious priority."

"What's our timeline? I mean here?" I asked.

"Probably two to four more weeks. Part of the problem for full restoration of services is going to be parts availability—especially transformers and conductor material. Those are made in China." The room groaned.

"Hold on, now. Don't get too worried about that. We think that based on the current population, we can restore electric power to the majority of the occupied area within that time frame by salvaging equipment from outlying and unoccupied areas. You, in this area, are in the heart of the Valley. You have transmission lines on two sides that are relatively undamaged. I suspect you'll have juice back on the front end of that timeline."

"What about that main line over on Twenty-Seven? That thing went down all the way across the street."

"Downed lines've been cleared. Poles will be up tomorrow by dark, and conductors strung by the end of Wednesday."

Someone let out a low descending whistle. "Someone's been busy."

"Yes sir. Sixteen hour days, since the ash quit. They've made good progress."

"OK, so that's power and water. How about gas? I mean, natural gas?"

Again, the power guy. "That's the bad news. The distribution network isn't too badly beat up, but a lot of the natural gas we use in the States comes from Canada. And right now, they're keeping it. The prime company has reneged on distribution agreements at the behest of their French owners. Not just ours, we're small fry compared to the rest of the country. The upper Midwest and Northeast are getting hit hardest. The Californians are going to have it bad too, this summer. Their power stations are heavily dependent on natural gas for operations."

"Sh•t," came from my far right.

"There is no answer there. The issue is economics," the company rep said.

483

"More correctly, economic warfare."

"Yes sir. On multiple fronts," the Colonel responded.

"OK, now about our neighborhood. Mike? What's our game plan. Or are we tasked with coming up with that ourselves?"

"I'm not sure I understand the question, Rick."

"Are we supposed to rebuild our homes, find a way to subsist on what we can produce locally, or can we expect stores to reopen at some point in the future? I've heard about power, water, gas, and the government situation. I haven't heard about distribution of goods and provision services."

"Distribution of goods and provision of services are being restored as soon as we can make them happen," the logistical officer said, eyes shifting around a bit. "Stores will re-open for four hours per day, from ten a.m. until two p.m. if goods are available."

"OK, Understood. But," I said in a warning tone, "Life as we knew it is gone. What's going to take its place?"

"We will have to make do."

A voice from behind me said, "What the Hell does that mean, 'make do?' Answer the question. When are the stores going to reopen?"

Mike looked at his lieutenant, and the Colonel answered for them. "Frankly, I'm not sure. The rest of the country is unraveling at a rate that is unheard of. Domestic shipping is all but breaking down completely. Availability of foreign goods is zero. Availability of foodstuffs produced outside of the U.S. for U.S. consumers is becoming close to zero. The food products that are produced in the U.S. could still be produced if the energy situation and domestic unrest stabilizes. The last food truck we expect to see anytime soon arrived this morning." The room almost erupted at that point. Mike shouted for attention, and finally got it.

"Listen, folks. You know this is bad. We're not going to spin it like the federal government seems to be trying to do. This is the Second Great Depression. Get used to hearing that."

"Mike, are we going to starve, or not," the Korean vet asked.

"It's going to be different, Jimmy. I can tell you that. I don't think we'll starve."

"Then we better get to planning. With no offense intended," I said to my fellow attendees, "I doubt the majority of folks in this room have any idea what it takes to grow enough food to live on, let alone thrive on," I said.

"That's probably true. And with all the restrictions that the county's put on us, we can't grow livestock anymore," an older woman said from my right.

"That's changed. If it's related to food production or transportation, livestock will be allowed in the suburban areas and even in the city, as long as basic hygienic procedures are followed."

"And who's going to do the butchering if we grow....cattle and whatnot?" said a voice a few rows back.

"I don't know," Mike said. "Like I said, this is going to be different. I'd encourage all of you to get introduced after we leave-- and make sure you sign in on the sign in sheet-- and see if you can put your minds together for the good of all of you. You are all still here because you have had the resources to get this far and the spirit to stay where you are and tough it out. I know most of you, some quite well. I know that you have much in common. I'm afraid that we need to move along to our next meeting. Any questions before I go?"

"Will we meet regularly?"

"That can be arranged. I'll have the community center director contact me and we can set up a schedule."

"Mike, I have—potentially—a brother-in-law, his family, and my mother-in-law arriving this morning. I…"

"My condolences," he interrupted. A quiet chuckle went through the room.

"Funny. Thanks. But I have a problem. I don't have the room, and I'm wondering if it is possible to use one of the vacant houses behind us. It was for sale, and empty. Damage doesn't look too bad."

"Yep. I'll see to it. That all?"

"This one's more sticky. As you know, Ron Martin here and his family have been with us in the barn since the quake."

"And things are a little cozy."

"Yes sir, they're getting that way. Are there other empty homes on the block that are useable? I mean…."

"I know what you mean. I'll look into it. This does bring up a topic that we need to cover before we go. There is a common understanding that your neighbors' property is still your neighbors. If they've evac'd or haven't made it home since the quake, law enforcement expects you to treat those properties as if they were still occupied. That means, unless you have specific permission from the owners, you are to leave them alone. No looting. No use of the buildings or other consumables. Is that clear?"

"And when food starts running low, the food in the kitchens and pantries…." A voice asked.

"Is not yours. If it looks like it's coming to that, we will address it well ahead of time. Understood?"

A mumble of agreement went through the room.

"What about security? Do we still need to worry about looters?" I asked.

"Security patrols will continue, but have tapered off in frequency. This is due to the fact that most, if not all looters have been caught or killed. This area is now one of the safer areas within the urban areas of the county."

"What about fuel? I mean, gas?" a female voice asked. "And travel? Can we go places?"

"Fuel is available for critical uses only. There will be no pleasure travel. If you need fuel for a generator, you can see the manager here at the center and get on a list. If you choose to evac, you will be fueled up at one of the local stations. However, if that is the case, you are expected to leave. If you are caught or observed going back home or in other areas, you will be detained."

"What about the banks? Are they going to reopen?"

"I expect to hear something about that later today. I will post a memo at the center, and there should be something on the radio. Folks, I do need to get going. I do know that mail deliveries will be made to this center today for residents still in the area. That was coordinated as part of the CERT census last week. The post office can't field vehicles for widespread delivery, but you should expect to see mail arrive later today. The mail delivery is limited to letters and packages only. Junk mail and catalogs aren't going to leave the mail distribution center."

"Can we send letters?"

"Yes. Same as always. Remember your stamps." That brought laughter.

"Shouldn't we just tape a dollar bill on the envelope?"

Mike smiled. "No, just a stamp, same as always. Thank you folks for coming," Mike said as he left the lectern. "Rick, a moment, please?"

"You bet," I said. Ron and I went to meet the group that had just spoken. After shaking hands, Mike took me aside. "What's up?"

"What do you think of what you just heard?"

"Definitely some surprises in there."

"Stands to reason. Getting your family into that vacant house won't be a problem. There won't be any keys though, just go ahead and find a way in."

"There's a lock box," Ron said. "Key's probably inside."

"Just pop it open and use it, then. I'll see to some paperwork about it. Ron, about another house, I know that you're going to need housing, but at the moment, I'm not sure what's available. I can't put you up in someone else's home, not knowing if they're alive or dead."

"Understood."

"Gentlemen, I will tell you this. If they are not here now, the chances of them getting home are slim, especially if they were on the Coast when the quake hit. Both Stevens and Snoqualmie passes are closed and will be months or years in being cleared. Hell, they can't make it on U.S. Two even if they made the pass, the bridges at Wenatchee are gone, so there's no way to cross the Columbia. Vantage is gone too. The North Cascades highway's closed of course for the winter. The Gorge highway is still open, more or less, but they're having issues with cars being shot up down there by gangs."

"We have two neighbors on either side who were on the Coast last weekend." The kids had joined us, and hovered at our backs.

"If they're still alive, the chances of you seeing them in the foreseeable future are very, very slim."

"That said, how long will those properties be required to be vacant?"

"I don't know. We've never had to deal with anything like this before. If you can secure them though, you know, keep them weather-safe, you'll at least protect them a little from the elements until we can figure it out."

"Did that already to five houses around us, including Pauliano's place."

"Old Joe was smart in getting out when he did, but I hope he had as good a setup as he had here wherever he bugged out to," Mike said.

"His son's place. I think they're in the Bay Area. I'm sure they'd be pretty well set up."

"Good for them. Good folks. We'll miss them. Gotta run guys. Rick, gas station duty tomorrow afternoon OK? Starting at one?"

"Sure."

"Probably run an hour, maybe two."

"That'll work. I'll clear my busy schedule."

"Take care."

"You too."

The room cleared out fairly quickly. Most of the attendees picked up flyers from the county on the way out. I grabbed one of each as I left the assembly hall. 'Not bad,' I thought. The five flyers included information on basic sanitation, warnings and procedures on boiling water, improvised heat and light sources, a map of stores in the area that were slated for operation, and a schedule of communications broadcasts on AM, FM, and shortwave.

"Interesting," Ron said.

"Yeah. I was thinking that too."

"Nothing like the library you've got though."

"Not yet. I'm going over to talk to the center manager for a sec. You wanna get the kids loaded up?"

"Sure. I'm certain they're thrilled with going back home."

"No doubt. Be right back," I said as I went down the hall to the managers' office. When I arrived, I knocked on the doorframe.

"Good morning, may I help you?" It was the young lady from the clothing bank, now serving as secretary apparently to the community center manager.

"Andrea, right?"

"Yes sir. You visited us the other day with that nice young man for some clothes," That's right. She was 'checking him out.'

"Yep. That's my friend's son. John Martin's his name."

"Can I help you?"

"I wondered if I might help the center out, actually. I have a fair amount of information stored on my computer that may be useful to the community right now. I could set it up as a resource base for people to use, if the manager's interested."

"I'm interested. I'm the manager."

"Oh, pardon me. I thought…"

"That's OK. I get that a lot. Mr. Parker left his position on Friday for Nevada. I got a field promotion."

"Congratulations, I guess. I'm Rick Drummond."

"Pleased to meet you. It's a small empire, but it's all mine," she giggled, "such as it is. Tell me about your materials."

"It's quite a list, and fairly comprehensive. Covers a pretty broad spectrum of items. The Readers' Digest Condensed version would fill two three-ring binders, both sides of each sheet. I don't remember how many gigabytes the files consume, but it's a lot."

"Can you get me a disc so I can review it?"

"Yep, I think so. I'll be over at the gas station this afternoon. I'll bring one by then if I can get one burned."

"I'll be here. We're setting up a clinic in the education wing today. Should be up and running by the end of tomorrow."

"Really? Doc's and everything?"

"Safer than going to the hospital for minor stuff with the flu bug and everything else they're dealing with. We're doing a series of clinics that rotate around the Valley each day."

"Makes sense. I'll be back later today, Miss…"

"Britton."

"Thanks again. I'll see you in a while."

"Thank you, Mr. Drummond. I look forward to it."

5 0

Monday
January Twenty-third

"How'd it go?" Ron asked as I got back in the Ford.

"Good. I'm going to get them a CD of some of the prep information that I've got. Interesting meeting, huh kids?"

"Sort of," Kelly said. "Sort of boring."

"Better than sitting in the barn though."

"True."

"Let's go see if your Grandma and Uncle Alan and Aunt Mary and your cousins have arrived yet," I said as Ron pulled out of the parking lot.

"K."

"Don't be so glum."

"Dad, we're tired of this. All of us, OK?"

"I know, we are too. Getting all snippy about it is not going to make it go away. Sorry guys, but this, for now, is the way things are."

"I want to go to the mall…" Marie said in a trailing voice.

"Yeah? Well, I want a Big Mac and a Mocha shake. I don't think either one of us is going to get our wishes though," Ron said.

"Pizza." Carl said.

"Krispy Kreme donuts. Hot. Free." John added.

"So that's the game, huh?" I smiled. "All right. Crab Louis at Scoma's on the pier in San Francisco. With fresh sourdough, a nice Beefeater Gin and Tonic, followed by their chocolate brownie with raspberry drizzle and white chocolate flakes...or maybe that white chocolate soup. Then, one of those great cups of coffee."

"That is so unfair," Kelly laughed. "OK, my turn. Steak. Baked potato. Corn on the cob. Butter. Cold milk." Everyone groaned.

"Me next," Kelly said. "Starbucks double tall mocha and a hot chocolate chip cookie." More groans.

"OK, we're here. And no guests yet. Almost eleven thirty. 'bout time for lunch." I looked up the street toward Tim's. He'd hooked up the trailer, and looked about ready to take off.

"Good. All this talk of food's got me starving," Carl said as he piled out of the back to get the gate.

I thought to myself, 'I hope that is never true, young man.'

I pulled the Expedition in, waited for Carl to close the gate and hop back in, and then we drove back to the barn. We parked behind the Jeep, and went inside for lunch.

"Well that was an interesting little meeting," Libby said as we took our coats off, and I unplugged my FRS from my ear and set it in its charger.

"Yep. I'm sure there's more to come too," I said. "Tomato soup for lunch?"

"Yep. Sorry, no sandwiches. We made Tim and the boys a lunch for the road, and that took a while."

493

"That's OK."

"And while we're at it, 'Crème Brule' and a tawny Port," Karen said. The kids started laughing. "I was listening in."

'At least they can still laugh,' I thought as I washed up. "Nothing from Alan yet?"

"Nope," Karen said with disappointment.

"They'll be OK, Kare," I said.

"I know. But seeing is believing."

"They should be here soon. Besides that, Tim's gotta get going before one if he's going to make it before curfew."

"I know," she said as she dished me up.

I heard the clatter just after the dogs did, their ears perking up and whining insistently at the door, as if poking it with their noses would make it open sooner. "I think they're here!" I said as I loosed the dogs. "Yep. Truck's in the driveway. Got a big trailer too."

"Good." Karen said breathlessly. "Let's go welcome them."

Everyone grabbed their coats and slipped their boots on as Alan's wife Mary opened the gate and he pulled into the driveway. Our kids were running up to meet them, as was Karen. I was moving a little slower. Ron and Libby, who knew Alan's family as well, tagged along with me. Ron had hunted with Alan a time or two, for upland grouse and pheasant, out west of the city and north, up toward Colville and Tiger.

By the time I reached them, hugs were already well under way. Karen's Mom was in the front seat, looking frail but excited. Up until quite recently, she'd been very active, with trips to see friends around the country, and in general, acting like a sixty-year-old, not someone who was just eighty-five. There were a lot of tears flowing. We chatted briefly in the driveway, shaking hands and giving hugs to all of them. I thought Mary would crack one of my ribs.

Alan and Mary looked weathered, which was not something I'd seen on either of them before. Rachel and Mark both looked OK, but bedraggled. Each had paired off with the boys and girls in our little group and were talking. I finally decided to get things moved inside.

"Hey now, let's move this inside. This weather's probably not the best for you, Mom."

"Agreed," she said in her Kansas accent. "I can't get warm these days."

"Alan, got a minute? In private?"

"Sure. That was a heckuva drive," he said.

"You aren't serious about leaving."

"We don't have a helluva lot of choices."

"Sure you do. That house back beyond the back property line is vacant. For sale. I spoke with the sheriff this morning, he said we could use it if we needed. For you and Mom and your family."

"You're kidding."

"No sir."

"Well that beats all."

"Close. Agreed?"

"Let me talk to Mary and Mom for a minute."

"Make it quick. If you're going, I've got a caravan buddy for you. If not, I need to let him go, right now."

Alan went back over to the truck, and spoke with Karen and his Mom and Mary. I could tell by the hug that Karen gave Mary and Alan that they were staying.

"Go tell Tim, honey. They're staying."

"Will do. Alan, go ahead and drive on back to the barn. I need to run over to the neighbor's quick. I'll be right back."

"K." He hopped back in the F350—a diesel crew cab and four-wheel drive—and headed out. The trailer was well loaded too, and tarped over with a big grey tarp. I didn't know where Alan got the trailer, it was a double-axle model, more suited to hauling cars. 'Must've done some horse-trading,' I thought.

I jogged through the snow up to Tim's place, where he had loaded the last of his stuff.

"They coming?" Tim asked.

"Looks like not. We're going to put them up in that house behind us."

"Well, like I said yesterday, anything you want out of this place is yours."

"I'm sure we can use it. Tim, may God watch over you on your trip."

"I'm hoping He will. Take care, Rick. It's been good living up the road from you and Karen. You've been good friends."

"You too. Best get going, it's getting late."

"Thanks. Tell Karen and Libby goodbye again for me."

"I will."

"C'mon, boys. Let's fire this thing up."

The boys jumped out of the front door of the house, where the steps used to be. Drew was the last one out, and closed the door behind him.

"Take care, Drew. Remember to write."

"I will, once we get settled."

"And watch out for your old man. Don't want him getting hooked up with that Cuervo. Wouldn't want to inflict that singing on anyone. Even in California."

"Hey, now. I heard that," Tim said.

"See ya, buddy," I said as I walked back up the street. I had a lump in my throat. The sky was lowering again. 'Probably more snow,' I thought as I went back to the barn.

By the time I got back inside, everyone had taken their heavy coats off and tried to squeeze in and find a place to sit. Twelve people in two rooms wasn't going to work for long.

"Grab some soup, hon, before it's gone. I'm warming up some more."

"K," I said as the chatter grew louder. The room was already quite warm, I was sure it would overheat with all of us in there.

"This is quite the setup you've got, Rick." Alan said.

"It was a nice shop. It's not a great house."

"Better than our place. We were living in the boat for the last two days. The rest of the time we were in the RV garage. There wasn't any way to keep the house warm once the gas was gone."

"I thought as much. House bad hit?"

"Bad enough. Cracked the walls at the dogleg all the way from the ground up. You could see daylight standing in the hall by the garage, all the way through the second floor and roof."

"Natural ventilation. Got some of that ourselves. We have a nice big hole where the chimney and the stair gable used to be."

"That's why you're out here."

"Beats a shelter or the tent trailer. As much as I want to hear your stories, and I'm sure you want to hear ours, we're on a tight timeline. I don't want to break curfew, and I know we've only got about four hours of time to get into that house and see what kinda shape it's in. If it's good, we have stuff to move over there pronto. But it's gonna be work. There is obviously no way we can sleep twelve people in here tonight."

"Work's better'n sitting around."

"How's Mom been holding up?" I asked quietly."

"Better than I thought, but the cold's really getting to her. That was one of the big drivers. We took one look at the shelter and heard all the coughing, and the flu, and the pneumonia, and decided to get out."

"I can understand that. Let's finish up lunch and get to it."

"That'll work. Mom's soup recipe?" he asked as he took another sip.

"Yep. We didn't lose too much of it in the quake."

"Lost all of ours, what, four jars?" He looked mad at himself for getting caught low. I'd be mad too. I knew that they had a pantry, but nothing like ours.

"You guys do OK for food?"

"At first. After five days though, things ran out pretty quick. Ended up with mac and cheese, water, crackers, and dinners were canned soup. At least they were warm. We had the camp stoves and lanterns, the wood stove out in the RV garage until we ran out of wood. After that, we were in the boat." Alan had a big 26' cruiser stored in the shop for the winter. I could only imagine what that must've been like. "The novelty wore off quickly for Rachel. Mark was a little more manageable, but only a little."

"Have much looting up there?"

"Did at first. Not around us, not after our neighbor lit up a car with his AR-15."

"We had a little of that here, too. A little closer to home."

"You guys take care of it?"

"You could say that, Ron and the boys and I took out four of them across the street, over at Tim James' place."

"No sh*t."

"No sh*t. After that though, between the deputies and the Army, we haven't had any real trouble."

"You've got some stories to tell," Alan said in a low voice

"I'm sure we all will, once this is over."

"Depends what you mean by 'over', I think."

"For me it means 'spring.' That's about as optimistic as I can be," I said as I took a gulp of soup and looked outside. It was snowing harder. "But right now, that to me is a long ways off."

After another twenty minutes of 'lunch time', Alan, Ron and I had come up with 'teams' to complete as much work as we could in the afternoon before curfew. The goal, of course, was to get the other house livable. That meant getting in, determining if the wood-fired furnace was operational, securing damage to the shell to make it more air-tight, and get furnishings in for at least the night. For at least the first couple hours, we figured that Mary, Karen, her Mom and the younger kids could stay inside, until we got the house and some furnishings inside, and then we could have the kids come over to help set up. I wanted to make sure that Mom stayed as warm as she could, and had enough to eat and drink. She looked very frail. Much more so than she had ten days before, when we'd seen her last.

I suggested that Ron and Alan get some tools and break open the lock box and get inside the house to assess its condition. We already knew that even if it needed work, it was in better shape than our place, and if the wood furnace couldn't be made to work tonight or tomorrow, the kerosene heater we had could be used in a pinch. While they looked over the house, I'd take the boys and my small trailer over to the James' former home, and start loading up what we could make use of. I knew that we'd need all the beds, which included two queen-size sets and three full/twin bunk sets. Other stuff would come to, but beds were the first priority. If we could at least get the preliminaries taken care of before dark, we could get them fairly well set up by bed time, working with flashlights, lanterns, and candles. Once they were 'in' the house and the preliminary assessment taken care of, we'd use all the guys to move stuff from the James' to Alan's new digs. The plan also included Libby, who'd take a look at the James' kitchen equipment and designate what should be moved. It was almost one-thirty before we got moving. About three hours 'til curfew.

I rounded up a few things from the woodshop for Ron and Alan to use to get into the other house. One of the first things though, were wire cutters to cut through the stock fence surrounding our field. The vacant houses' yard was fenced with six-foot chain link on the sides, and five-foot around the front yard, so it would be easy to keep the dogs in between the two yards. We talked about moving an unused stock gate from the fence between the 'field' of our place and the 'yard', to keep Buck and Ada in sight. The other tools I thought they could use I tossed in a five-gallon bucket. Alan retrieved two big flashlights from his pickup, and they set off across the field.

Carl, John and I took the Expedition with the folding trailer, and made several trips through our property with furnishings. Libby spent about an hour going through the James' house, collecting salvageable kitchen items and household stuff to move. It was quite a chore, sorting through the wrecked and already picked over contents. By three p.m., we had most of the 'essentials' moved and at least in the house.

This was all prefaced of course on Alan and Ron's work. They'd smacked open the lock box, which was cast from pot-metal and crumbled easily. The house keys were inside, and they let themselves in as a Deputy stopped out front. He had Alan sign a document stating that he was accepting responsibility for the condition of the home and that any damage beyond that caused by the quake, would be his responsibility. It seemed pretty silly to me.

The house was built in the Thirties, and updated sometime in the Seventies, we guessed by the cabinetry in the kitchen. The whole house had been gutted and sheetrocked, as well as re-wired. The original double-hung windows were still in place, several of them cracked or broken, or the storm windows shattered. Their survey of the place still showed significant damage, but even so, the place was in better shape than Tim's house or ours. A crack in the foundation ran all the way across the basement floor, but hadn't displaced the concrete. The pipes had been drained when the home was put up for sale, back in December. Part of a ceiling on the second floor, on the south end, had collapsed into a bedroom. Fiberglass insulation draped from the rafters to the oak hardwood floors. Other damage was similar to our barn, with cracks in the sheetrock, broken or cracked windows, and more significant damage to the attached garage. The main concern of course was heat. The wood-burning furnace, by appearance ten to fifteen years old, seemed undamaged. The flue was lined with a stainless steel liner, and the chimney, other than some minor cracks at the brick joints, was in very good shape. The top two feet of brick was gone, in the back yard. The liner though, extended to its original height.   The gas furnace, fed by a black iron pipe, had pulled loose of its mount, and lay on the floor in the basement.

By the time we got the third load of stuff over to the house, Alan had fired up the wood furnace for an operations check with some scrap lumber from our house. Ron had closed up the doors to other rooms, and soon the house was warming up nicely. Even without an electric blower, the place would stay warm. One battle won, at least.

Our final load of furniture, and then two loads of 'stuff' from Tim's house, completed our outside work before curfew. The younger kids had all now relocated to the 'new' house, and they were kept busy by Libby and Mary in cleaning up and putting stuff away. Cracked glass had been taped over inside and out, and missing glass covered up with cardboard and plastic, and then duct-taped.

Alan had moved his truck and trailer into the back yard, and was busy with John, Carl and Mark unloading his stuff into the main floor. It piled up pretty fast. It was well after curfew by the time the truck and trailer were off-loaded. We knocked off about five-thirty, when Karen called on the radio announcing 'first shift' for dinner. That meant the kids. Alan made sure everyone was out of the house, and shut off the Coleman lanterns that he'd brought.   I noticed his reloading equipment and a number of long-gun shaped bundles in the back bedroom. The gun safe was still on the trailer, too heavy to move tonight. I was surprised he brought it, but then remembered that his grandfather had built it.

"That was a good days' work," I said as we walked back to the barn trailing the others.

"At least. I think we're all about ready for bed. Hey, what's in the shed over there?"

"Don't know. I never saw it open before the folks moved. I assumed in was mowers and stuff."

We walked over to the eight-by-ten shed and with some effort, slid the door open. It was full of unsplit wood.

"Don't that beat all," Alan said.

"I don't suppose they thought it was worth moving."

"Ten days ago, it wasn't," he said as he slid the door closed again.

"C'mon. Food then some storytelling, then bed."

"Looking forward to the latter."

"Don't get too fond of the notion. Karen's got my little generator going. I wouldn't be a bit surprised to see a number of kids playing video games after dinner."

"That'd be a change. They've been going through withdrawal."

"Ours too a bit. Hasn't been too bad though…yet."

Buck was nibbling at my hand as we headed inside, trying to get me to play. "C'mon, dog. I'm betting it's dinner time for you too."

"Lasagna," Alan said as he inhaled. "Aaahh."

"Hopefully more than one. We had one leftover from before the quake and it lasted about fifteen minutes." The kids were already washed up and in the chow line. Karen had put out a card table for the girls, and the boys and some of the food was on the old kitchen table. The grown ups were going to have to make do on finding a spot to sit until the kids were done. Grace was in the midst of it all, sitting near the warmth of the woodstove with a cup of tea.

"Sheer pandemonium, huh Mom?" I asked.

"About the same as when I was a girl. Eight of us kids and Mother and Dad for each meal. Got a little busy!"

"I'll say. But you weren't in a barn."

"This barn is nicer than our kitchen was by a long shot. It's warm."

"Feeling OK?"

"I'm much better. Karen's been keeping me in tea, which means that I've had to make not two, but three trips to the outhouse—does that bring back memories!—and we've been catching up. It's been a delight."

"Good. I'm glad. You let me know if there's anything you need…"

"Stop, now. I'm no invalid."

"Never said you were. But we've got stuff scattered from here to yon, and we can find stuff quicker, that's all."

"All right then," she said. "I'll be sure to let you know," she smiled.

"Let's go catch the news if we can," I told Alan and Ron. "And, if I'm not mistaken, I have a case of beer or two in here somewhere."

"I thought you said we had the last one already."

"Last of the Red Hook. Not the last of the beer."

"Holding out on us, huh?"

"No, no. 'Preserving it for worthy occasions,' is more what I had in mind."

"Riiiight," Ron said.

We went into the other room and turned on the smaller battery operated radio. It was already tuned to 920AM, the local CBS affiliate. I rummaged around a bit and found the beer, hidden behind a couple of boxes. In former days, I'd have a few beers in the shop fridge, in case I developed a dreadful case of thirst after completing my work. I never drank of course, before or during the use of the power tools. I had a healthy respect for things that can cause amputation or blindness or worse.

I pulled out three bottles of Kokanee and handed one each to Alan and Ron as the 'chime' at the top of the hour came on.

"This is a CBS News Special Report. Reporting from the White House, we have David Jefferies, where the President is about to address the nation. David?"

"Hush now in there," I said. "The President's coming on," Karen hopped over a chair and turned the other radio on. Both rooms grew silent.

"Thank you Bob. This address was announced only fifteen minutes ago in the press room, and will take place in the Oval Office. It is being broadcast, we understand, on all television channels in the United States and throughout the world including all cable channels. This is a most unprecedented situation, and no one can recall any situation where access has been demanded, and provided, for a Presidential address....we understand the President is about to speak."

"....Ladies and Gentlemen, the President of the United States."

"Good Evening, my fellow Americans. I address you this evening during a period of growing tension, uncertainty and fear. Our

nation's economy is being rocked by numerous forces that we are striving to control. International relationships are being strained to the breaking point. Nations that were formerly partners in efforts such as the War on Terror and coalitions to fight evil have turned on our country, our soldiers and sailors, our citizens and our corporations.

I am here to tell you more, and to issue a warning to these nations and these governments and their leaders.

Beginning at ten a.m. last Thursday morning, United States military bases, Embassies and Consulates throughout the world were surrounded by what were touted to be peaceful protesters, demonstrating against errant US economic policies that are being blamed for the current world-wide economic crisis.

Within one hour of the initiation of these protests, it became known to our government through the resources of our intelligence services that these protests were being coordinated between each nation, at the highest levels, and that further, no Americans or American military forces were to be allowed to leave these countries or bases. In many cases, harassment by foreign forces has taken place, including violation of airspace over American bases, interdiction of US aircraft, and deployment of host-country military forces around each base. Several American servicemen were killed in these actions. US Naval ships have been targeted and defended themselves.

I am here to tell this nation and the leaders of the world and these nations in particular—you know who you are--that you have until midnight, Eastern Standard Time to cease these operations and remove your protesters from around American bases and return all hostage American citizens to our Embassies and Consulates or you will face a military response the likes of which have not been seen in decades. This nation will not tolerate foreign governments holding the American citizen and the American soldier hostage. I will not target civilians. I will target the leadership of each country that we have identified as participating in this nefarious scheme. I know the locations of each leader and his family. I know the places that you intend to go to hide. I know the locations of your assets. I know the capabilities of your military forces, and I can assure you that you are no match for the wrath that will come your way should you continue on your present course.

To the leaders of international business concerns that are participating in this scheme: It is open season on you as well, starting in three hours. Should you continue on this course to assist in the seizure of Americans and American assets beyond midnight tonight, I can assure you that you will be hunted down. Mark those words: Hunted down. Being in a neutral country will NOT keep you safe.

To the American people: We face a crisis of unprecedented proportions. Excesses of the past have come back to bite us. It is time for the books to balance. We will work with every fiber of our being to restore the confidence of the citizen in your government. We will defend our Constitution, we will protect our citizens, we will protect our country, and we will not tolerate international thugs who would threaten our citizens. And I assure you this: We will prevail.

I ask for your prayers this night, but not for me or my family. I ask you to pray for this great land, this country of boundless opportunity. I ask you to pray for her defenders around the world. May He in His infinite Mercy watch over them and guide them to safety.

Good night."

"Oh my Lord," Grace said almost in a whisper.

Monday night
January Twenty-third

"We could be at war in three hours," Ron said.

"No, we're already at war. Have been since last week, by the sounds of it," Alan said.

"Just have to see how far it goes, now," I said. I had a sick feeling in my stomach. "C'mon. Let's get some dinner."

The kids were very quiet as they finished eating. "Dad, is it going to be all right?" Rachel asked Alan.

"I don't know, bumblebee. I just don't know."

"C'mon you men. Get some food in you," Libby said. I could see she was trying not to cry.

Karen was holding her Mom's hand. They were praying silently.

Ron, Alan and I went back to the other room with our plates, and the beers that were open and no longer so appealing. We ate in silence as the commentators continued their 'analysis' of the speech.

"As if we needed one more thing to deal with," I said finally.

"Had to come sooner or later," Alan replied, equally downcast.

"What do you think he's got planned?" Ron said.

"I don't know, but if I were in those countries, I wouldn't want to be in the capitals," Alan said.

"You think he'd nuke them?"

"Right now, I'm not a betting man, either way. Sounds like he's making it more personal, and rightly so. Always thought that wars should be fought by the leaders, not the kids anyway," I said.

"Let's get another plateful and get back to work. We can at least make progress on that front before bed."

"Yeah. Suddenly story telling doesn't matter as much right now."

We each dished up another square of lasagna, and Alan gave us a quick overview of what he'd brought with him. By the time he was done, I was wondering how he got it all in the truck and on the trailer. I hadn't had much time to pay attention to the stuff piled up in the house. Overall, it was a lighter version of the 'preps' that I had, but his was more geared toward his hunting and boating hobby, which managed to furnish most of his gear. He was obviously light on food though.

"Sounds like you're in OK shape then," I said.

"Until the food runs low."

"That's a topic we can tackle tomorrow. We'll be all right for a while. God knows we have eggs."

"How many do you have? I saw the rack through the window in the tool room."

"Last I heard, ten dozen. Probably more now."

"Better start working on setting up some bartering."

"Yep. I plan on doing that very thing tomorrow," I said wondering to myself, 'If there's a tomorrow.' "I could use your salesmanship skills in that department."

"Happy to oblige." Alan could sell sand to Iraqis. In his former job—assuming it wasn't coming back of course—he was a low-pressure, very successful software salesman.

"Let's get back to it. We should get you guys to bed by eight or so. We're finding that the extra sleep is very nice after days like this."

"Can't imagine why," he said as he pulled on a coat.

"Ron, could you keep the kids entertained while we take the women-folk over to the new house?" Ron was a big kid himself, and the kids naturally gravitated toward his outsized-teenager attitude.

"Sure! That means I can beat Kelly finally at hearts," he said with an evil tone, his eyes looking toward the shop.

"Not likely, mister!" she called back from the other room.

"Ladies, your presence is requested. Grace, if you would make sure Ron isn't beaten too badly by the kids, I'd appreciate it."

"That'll be fun. Deal me in once in awhile too, Ronny."

"Yes, ma'am! OK. Who's ready?" All the kids yelled out. John and Carl were enjoying watching Ron over-act. Marie and Kelly were shuffling already. I knew that both Mark and Rachel were ready too.

"Carl, got a sec?" I said as the other adults left the room.

"Yeah?" he said as he came over to me.

"Keep an eye on the fire for me, and please get the dishes rinsed off OK? I thought it'd be nice to get your Mom and Libby out of dish-duty."

"John and I will take care of it," he said.

"Thanks buddy. Tell your Grandma that it's OK with me if you and John split a beer, all right?"

"Really?"

"Unless she says no, sure."

"Thanks. Never had a beer before."

"Do NOT tell your mother. She'd skin me for sure."

"K. Thanks, Dad."

"You worked hard today. We all appreciate it."

"Awww…go on now. This is getting all girly."

"Yep."

I grabbed my ancient grey parka and my watch cap, and headed out the door. The snow had finally stopped, and through patches in the clouds, I could see the Milky Way over head. I'd almost forgotten the colors of the stars.

When I let myself in the back door, Karen, Libby and Mary were making the first bed that was assembled by Ron and Alan. They were now wrestling with a metal bunk bed. The queen sized bed for Grace was much simpler, just a box spring and mattress on a frame. I started un-piling the goods that Alan had unloaded from the trailer, and like a good delivery boy, putting them where Mary wanted.

We knocked off at quarter to eight, with the set up of Alan's camp porta-potty in the surprisingly intact bathroom. The house was a very pleasant sixty-five degrees, and Alan had moved some of the smaller unsplit wood into the basement for the furnace. With any luck at all, he'd be able to feed it once during the night to keep the house relatively warm. With the stair door to the second floor closed, and the den and a dining room converted to bedrooms, the four main rooms on the floor should stay comfortable, even if the furnace blower wasn't working.

Karen, Libby and I said our goodnights to Mary, and Alan went with us back to the house to collect Grace and his kids.

"I can't thank you enough for all the work you guys did for us today."

"That's what families are for," Karen said. "It's good to have you close by, big brother."

"It's good to be here. I was dreading that drive to California."

"Is Mary OK with it? Really OK I mean?"

"More than she will let on. She and her sister get along all right, but only for about three days. Heaven knows that's all I'm good for there."

"Then it's a blessing."

"It is certainly, that."

"How about a night cap?" Alan and I were famous for having a nightcap before turning in on our camp trips.

"You bet. What do you have?"

"Cutty Sark do?"

He looked shocked as he took a half-step backwards and his eyes widened. "Set me up!"

We went inside and gave the kids—and Ron—five minutes warning til the game had to end and Alan's horde headed over to their new house. I'd drive Grace over. I didn't want a broken hip to worry about tonight too.

I went over to my sanding station, where my little bench top belt sander used to reside, and pulled the bottom drawer open. In the very back, a small silver flask in a leather pouch resided, with six nesting cups. I'd bought it years ago, the day I turned twenty-one. I carefully poured out the liquid, and handed a cup to Ron and Alan, and asked Karen, Libby and Grace if they wanted to join us. They smiled and passed, knowing that partaking of the last nightcap, as well as us asking them to join us, was a 'guy thing.' We each sipped, then drank our little shot, and started getting Alan's kids ready to go to their new home.

"Grace, you can ride over with me."

"Not before visiting the facilities."

"That can be arranged."

"Karen, I need you to hold the light."

"Can't do it in the dark?"

"Could, yes. Will, no." We laughed about that.

"I'll take Mom home, honey. You stay inside with Carl and Kelly. I think Carl wants a shot at beating you, too."

"Shouldn't be hard. I'm awful at cards. Little Bee, Sparky, you have a good night, OK?"

"We will, Uncle Rick. Thanks!" Mark said. Rachel gave me a hug as she headed toward the door, her straight blond hair in stark contrast to her red coat.

I looked at my watch. An hour and ten minutes until the Presidents' ultimatum was up. I turned the radio on and sat down at the card table with Carl.

"What's gonna happen, Dad?"

"I'm hoping they fold."

"What if they don't?"

"Then people will die. Maybe, a lot of people. Let's listen and see if anything's changed."

"Grandma had it on earlier, no one's responded. At least that's what the radio says."

"And they always tell the truth on the radio...."

"Right. Sure they do," Carl said.

512

"They did say something about Mexico though. Some weird word....re, recon..."

"Reconquista?"

"Yeah. They said it's 'started.' What does that mean?"

"The Mexicans want to take back the American southwest—re-conquer it. Did they say that the Mexican government is part of it too?"

"No, just that a lot of Mexicans were crossing the border and that there was lots of trouble in the Hispanic neighborhoods in the border states."

"That'll be taken care of shortly, I'd suspect." Holy cow. What next.

"I wonder how things are up here? I mean, with all the migrant workers in the state..." Libby asked.

"Not too many this time of year, but plenty of Mexicans, regardless."

"Gonna be a turkey-shoot, I'm thinking," Ron said.

'That it might,' I thought. 'But on whose side?'

The radio commentators were counting down the minutes as well, a more serious and perverse version of a New Years Eve countdown. We still had an hour until the ultimatum passed.

"......nations that are likely to be on the list, based on information collected by our correspondents around the world. In addition to nations that would be expected to protest the American government, such as North Korea and some of the European Union states, we have seen protests in countries formerly allies to the US in conflicts of the past. Belgium, Germany, civilian protests in England. Mexico, South Korea, Egypt, and China. Word from Saudi Arabia that the US Embassy and military facilities are under a virtual siege.

As the President stated earlier tonight in an unprecedented warning to these nations, this may turn out to be a real Texas showdown."

"Mike, do we have any word from the State Department on a response so far?" I recognized the voice as that of Alex Wittkopf. Alex used to do weather on one of our local TV affiliates.

"None whatsoever, Alex. Hundreds of journalists are here at State, standing in the rain, waiting for a statement of some kind. We have been told that something should be forthcoming after eleven p.m., Eastern time."

"The President referred to deaths of American military personnel that were caused by these so-called 'protests.' Do you have any information on the locations or units involved?"

"Alex, the rumors we've heard are that an aircraft returning to Ramstein Air Force Base with Marines wounded in Iraq crashed after being harassed by an unknown aircraft, with the loss of all aboard."

"Good God," I said. Libby and Ron shared the same look. Marie and Kelly had their books on their laps, but were listening as well.

".....government disavowed any responsibility in the matter, although the aircraft involved was later observed landing at a German military base. We do know that twenty-seven Americans, three Turks, and five Iraqis were aboard that aircraft."

"The President also mentioned that Naval vessels have also been involved. Does your source have any information on that?"

"A reporter from NBC news provided us information on that. The reporter, Dan Ellingston, was kind enough to provide the information to all American news organizations, and we are seeing a widespread sharing of resources to put this information together. What we do know is that a Perry-Class frigate, U.S.S. Reuben James, was targeted by a missile while serving as part of an escort screen with the U.S.S. Abraham Lincoln's Task Force Seven in the western Pacific. We do not know where the ship was located when it was

targeted, who may have fired at them, or what defensive measures or retaliation was taken. It is our understanding that this attack took place this morning, before dawn. It is now mid-day in the western Pacific."

"It seems to me, that the commander of that task force must be exercising extreme restraint in the face of an unprovoked attack."

"Agreed, Alex. That is the consensus here as well."

"I assume that diplomatic hot lines around the world have been red-hot all day."

"Longer than that, Alex. According to a source first identified in the first Gulf War, DoD, State, and NSA departments have all been putting in long hours since Wednesday night last week. That source is...Dominos Pizza. As humorous as that may sound, the 'pizza index' has been a very reliable indicator of pending military operations or reactions to unpublicized crises. The 'pizza indicator' has been running wild since then."

"Thank you, Mike. On to other news for a few minutes. We will return to Alex Wittkopf at the State Department as events warrant. We go now to New York, to Deborah Sexton on Wall Street. Deborah?"

"Thank you, Alex. Wall Street analysts are remaining gun-shy in calling the bottom of the stock market crash. With today's Dow closing at sixteen eighty-one, and gold's corresponding jump to over sixteen hundred dollars an ounce, an old rule-of-thumb may be coming back into play, that is, one ounce of gold being able to buy one Dow Jones average."

"This relationship has fluctuated over the decades, even back to the time before the nineteen twenty-nine Crash, when eighteen ounces of gold were needed to buy one share of the Dow. After the twenty-nine Crash, only two ounces of gold were needed. At the peak of the most recent bull run in the stock market where the Dow peaked at eleven seven twenty-three, gold closed at a little under two-hundred eighty-two dollars an ounce, or forty-one ounces of gold per Dow Jones average share. Right now, it's a one-to-one

515

relationship. The analysts, in my opinion, are afraid to call the bottom, for fear that the swing of the pendulum still has a ways to go."

"Corresponding falls in all stock markets world-wide are ostensibly credited as the cause of the current crisis between the US and other nations, and China shocked the world earlier today by stating that their dumping of the US Dollar is merely the final signal that the Renminbi—or People's Currency, also known as the Yuan—is destined to be the replacement standard for the reserve funds of nations around the world. The E.U. bristled at this remark, as the forum in Brussels firmly believes that it is time that the Euro took its place as the world standard. It appears that the Chinese statement may be little more than wishful thinking, as the initial offering of Chinese government bonds went nowhere fast...."

"Deborah, I'm afraid I have to cut in here, we have a statement coming from the Secretary of State and the Secretary of Defense at the Pentagon."

"Thank you, Alex." Karen came back in as the broadcast continued.

"All right, over to our Washington bureau chief, Elizabeth Reckman. Elizabeth?"

"Thank you Alex. We just received notice that a statement will be made momentarily regarding the Presidential ultimatum to numerous countries around the world who have detained or seized Americans, American military forces, and American businesses in the past several days. The Secretary of State's office has provided us a list of these countries, their leaders, and the locations of each leader and each leaders family, per the Presidents address earlier this evening... I'm sorry, the Secretary is about to speak....Here she is."

"Good evening. As you have been provided a list of countries involved and the governmental leadership directly responsible for the actions against US citizens and forces world wide, I would like to address the current status. Eleven nations on that list have complied with the ultimatum as of twenty-two thirty hours Eastern time. Those nations include England, Germany, Algeria, Afghanistan, India,

Morocco, Turkey, Yemen, and Italy. German Chancellor Dieter Bruck has been removed from office by his government for direct involvement in the downing of the US transport aircraft and is in the custody of the United States Marine Security Guard at US Embassy Berlin. It is my understanding that Americans held as hostages, detained American forces, and American Embassies and Consulates in these countries have been freed and in many cases, are preparing to leave those countries at this time to return to the U.S.

Nations that have not responded include China, Mexico, Belgium, Egypt, France, North Korea, South Korea, Saudi Arabia, Venezuela and the United Arab Emirates. The deadline stands, there will be no extension offered.

With regards to the border incursions in the southwest, US military forces at this time are engaged with organized combatants in the region. Unrest in Hispanic neighborhoods in the border states and within other states with significant Hispanic populations are being addressed in a similar manner. The President will address the nation, shortly after midnight, Eastern time. Thank you."

The room erupted into shouts for responses and questions before the network went back to their reporter. We sat looking at each other in the dimming light of the lantern.

"You kids get ready for bed now," I said. "And do a good job on those teeth."

"Did you hear that list? The ones that haven't responded?"

"Yeah. Most of them weren't surprises. Mexico surprised me a bit, but if they want to re-enact the Alamo, this time's gonna be different. And she didn't list eleven nations that had complied. I think she listed nine," Ron said. I hadn't noticed.

"Wonder who else is on the list?" Libby asked.

"Yeah." I was wondering about my root cellar, and whether or not we'd need it for a fallout shelter. 'There could not be a worse time of year,' I thought.

"So we wait until nine to find out?" Kelly asked as she got her toothbrush ready.

"Maybe. Maybe not that long."

"How come?"

"In card playing terms, they know we're not bluffing. We've seen their hand and we know ours is stronger. Those nations may react before the deadline, one way or the other."

"You mean they'll fold?"

"Or call. In this case, fight."

"Oh," she said as she came over for a hug.

Within a few minutes, all the kids were in their beds, although still listening to the radio along with us. Karen had made some tea for us while we listened and watched the clock.

Assuming World War Three didn't start tonight, I started making yet another list of things to do on Tuesday.

5 2

Two-fifteen a.m.
Tuesday Morning
January Twenty-fourth

I took over from Karen for stove duty at two. I had turned in at ten, along with the others, with the instructions that if or when the President spoke, I be awakened. The address never came, so I—eventually--slept. Karen woke me right at two, gave me the written notes that she'd taken on the radio broadcasts, and crawled into the warm spot I'd left her in bed. She also told me that Alan had FRS's too—with better range than mine--and she gave him our frequency and set his on push-to-talk, so that if any alert about war came, either she or I could let him know. He was to keep the radio next to his bed on 'standby.'

I started again on the seemingly endless lists of stuff to do now that we had more bodies to feed, water, and keep warm, as well as work that needed to be done. After a half hour, I felt like I was trying to reinvent the wheel. How, exactly, does someone list all the efforts needed to keep one alive for.....an indeterminate period of time?

And yet this was what I was trying to do.

Finally, in some fit of frustration, I listed needs, and ideas on how to meet them. More crude, less exact, but quicker and probably as effective. At least it felt like I was making progress. I think in the end, what concerned me is that I was planning things, based on shaky ground. If I KNEW at least a few things, I could create a to-do list with some reasonable sense of accuracy. But right now, what I didn't know about where our country, our state, our city, and our population far outweighed what I could assume to be correct.

We'd have to inventory Alan's belongings....finally, I just gave up and tackled something that I at least, knew that I could accomplish. That was creating a series of CD's with my library of knowledge relative to primitive living, survival, medical treatment, growing stuff, preserving....on and on.

Karen had noted that that all countries with the exceptions of China, Mexico and Venezuela had complied to the Presidential ultimatum. At three fifteen, KLXY reported that China had issued a statement that demanded the United States cease its threats against peaceful nations and individuals protesting the failure of the capitalist system. China was also reported to have seized control of the U.S. Embassy and consulates throughout China. CBS also reported that four U.S. businessmen died in an 'escape attempt' in Venezuela. Why was I not surprised.

I was realizing that the news reports were as paralyzing to me as watching the second airliner slam into the World Trade Center.

The network coverage was unabashedly pessimistic about the fact that the President had not addressed the nation as expected. As for me, I was wondering if he was even still in D.C. or not. Did China have ICBM's? And why had we not heard boo from Russia?

A few minutes before three in the morning, CBS reported on an unconfirmed source stating knowledge of U.S. navy actions in the western Pacific. 'Well, now.' I thought. I put the computer to sleep, and just listened to the radio. I did take a break now and then to feed the fire. Almost forgot, once. I started taking notes for the 'day shift,' similar to the notes they left me.

--Three-fifteen news bulletin confirmed that U.S. naval vessels including submarines and surface craft were attacked by mainland Chinese forces at eleven-thirty five p.m., Eastern Standard time and had retaliated. U.S. reports loss of four aircraft, and crew losses of six airmen.--

--Three-twenty, CBS reports that the Battle of Taiwan had begun with an aerial attack of missiles and aircraft. The attack, so far, had been repulsed, with heavy damage to Taipei, ports, industrial areas and heavy casualties.

By three-thirty, a report had been forwarded that the missile defenses were overwhelmed by the sheer volume of the attack. I debated on whether I should awaken Alan. I debated for all of five minutes, before I pushed the button.

"Yep, I'm here. What's going on?"

"China attacked Taiwan a half-hour before midnight, Eastern-time."

"Pulled a 'Pearl,' huh?"

"Could be. No reports yet on how we're doing, or the Taiwanese. Thought you'd want to know."

"I'll turn it on over here. If things get dicey, I'll be back in touch."

"Agreed. Out."

"Out."

By four a.m., we at least had some news from the Department of Defense. The Sec Def himself, behind a desk, speaking to the camera, so the radio voice told me.

"......attack on Taiwan has been repulsed and the enemy forces suffered major losses to all attacking forces. The initial attack on U.S.S. Rueben James was carried out by a Chinese submarine, prematurely it appears. U.S.S. Rueben James suffered serious damage and casualties in the attack, which triggered a significant response from the United States military forces world-wide.

"The President was informed at eleven-ten p.m. Eastern that the Chinese appeared to be about to launch a major attack on the island of Taiwan. The President ordered all United States military forces world wide to be prepared for this attack and to defend U.S. interests and assist the Taipei government in the defense of their country.

The Chinese attack was multi-faceted, with the initial attack coming in the form of an electro-magnetic pulse carried out in near space to bring down the power and communications grid on the island. This attack failed when the warhead—a nuclear warhead—was destroyed by a laser hit from one of our airborne assets. Simultaneously, a massive series of ground-to-ground and ship-launched missiles bore in toward the island.

The sheer number of missiles overwhelmed both US and Taiwanese defenses, with approximately thirty-five percent of incoming missiles making it through the defensive screen. Most of these missiles were targeted on industrial and civilian government command and control targets. The initial wave of missiles was targeted on key military targets, with civilian and governmental targets in subsequent waves.

The Battle of Taiwan is now concluded. The United States and Taiwan have won the day.

Ships of the U.S. Navy that participated in the defense of Taiwan included the U.S.S. Essex, a light carrier deployed from Sasebo, Japan, which is on fire and listing at this time. Also damaged, Ticonderoga-Class Aegis cruiser, U.S.S. Antietam, which took four missile hits. U.S.S. Harpers Ferry, a Marine amphibious assault ship, was sunk by a Chinese submarine. No United States submarines were lost or damaged in the battle.

Our response to the attack was swift and severe, but appropriate to the level of force needed to defeat the enemy. Upon the news of the attack on U.S.S. Rueben James, the Commander, Pacific Fleet informed all U.S. warships in the theater of operations of the attack, the casualties, and the target package for each ship. As of five a.m. this morning, Eastern time, the Communist Chinese Navy has permanently ceased to exist as a viable fighting force in the world.

Our submarine and surface vessels have sunk more than sixty submarines in port or at sea, including two ballistic-missile submarines, one off of Hawaii, the other off of San Francisco. All surface vessels worldwide belonging to the Communist Chinese, have been sunk or destroyed, with the exception of four vessels which surrendered to U.S.S. Abraham Lincoln's battle group upon threat of sinking. Forty-two merchant vessels were also destroyed, after refusing orders to heave to for boarding, threatening U.S. military or civilian ships with illegally-mounted weapons, or in one case, attempting to ram a U.S. Coast-Guard cutter in San Francisco Bay.

The President, when informed of the initial attack, was relocated to a secure location. I now will transfer this briefing to the Presidents' location."

A few moments of silence.... "Good morning. I am speaking to you from Camp David, to inform you of the defeat of the People's Republic of China in their attack on Taiwan. The losses in Taiwan are high--they have paid a dear price for their freedom.

There is also news from Beijing. The ruling government of Communist China has been removed from within. The U.S. Embassy and consulate staffs have been released. At this hour, massive demonstrations are taking place for peace and democracy in major Chinese cities. It appears that this may be another country about to turn the corner to freedom and democracy, and away from enslavement, from evil, and from an ever-shrinking number of nations that wish to deny basic human rights upon their citizens.

The news—and results--of this pre-meditated attack on the U.S. and Taiwan and the resulting Communist Chinese defeat were leaked to the Chinese people almost as soon as the first missiles flew. It is our understanding that more than a million Chinese citizens stormed the Chinese Premier's home and homes of other government leaders. Almost to a man, the former leadership was immediately taken into custody by the Chinese Army forces in the areas, which refused to defend the indefensible. It is our understanding that some of the military leaders responsible for this course of action either committed suicide or were executed by their own troops before the former government was deposed.

To the Chinese people, I wish to welcome you on the path to freedom and democracy. As part of the terms of surrender, the mainland Chinese have agreed to full reparations to the island democracy of Taiwan, to the United States government, and to all other injured parties.

To the people of the island democracy of Taiwan, I wish to commend you on your bravery, your sacrifice, and your kindness in helping injured U.S. soldiers, sailors, and Marines. These acts,

*which will become known soon, will be long-remembered and held
with honor by many.*

*To the people of the United States, it is a new day. We will make
the most of it and heal the fresh wounds on our country and our
countrymen. While this war with Communist China was brief,
consuming only a little more than a days time, the repercussions will
be with the world forever. With losses in the thousands and tens of
thousands,, but not millions, and none shall be trivialized on either
side. Often, death came without warning, either from the missiles
striking cities and ships, to the torpedoes suddenly sinking the pride
of the Communist Navy throughout the world's oceans. Brave men
fought and died, as did innocent civilians. We will remember the
sacrifices of all, with the goal of never having to fight another war.*

*Please pray for the souls of all the dead, and hold them in your
hearts this day. I will return to you later this day, to discuss events
on our southern border, and the actions taken to defend our land.
Good day."*

The radio commentator seemed as shocked as I was.

"Holy smokes," I said. We fought a war in one night.

"Did I hear that right?" Alan asked on the radio.

"Yes you did, unless you and I are sharing some sort of
delusion."

"We're not."

"What now?"

"That may be the most-asked question of the day."

"Have you heard anything about Mexico?" he asked.

"Nothing all night, other than that little cryptic comment."

"I never thought that a war with China would be quicker to fight
than one with Mexico."

"Me either. Welcome to the brave, new world."

"Funny. I'm going to try to go back to sleep."

"And good luck with that."

"I'll need it."

I got up and fed the fire again, and put some water on for coffee. I knew that Libby would be up soon, and then I could try to sleep. Right. Sleep.

After more analysis and near hysterical interviews on CBS radio, I finally switched frequencies and found some more news, this time on the Mexican frontier.

"....missiles fired from enemy combatants have shot down at least four U.S. aircraft attacking the Mexican invaders, including at least one A-10 Thunderbolt training in the Arizona desert. U.S. ground troops, backed by air support, have turned back the majority of the attack and are progressing into Mexico at this hour. We've heard from volunteer Militiamen who were overwhelmed by the initial invasion, that U.S. forces are literally, shooting anything that moves within twenty miles of the border, and appear to be moving farther south by the hour. We have confirmed that two helicopter gunships were downed by enemy gunfire, and that the crews were alive after the choppers went down. We have also confirmed that the crews were executed after they were taken prisoner."

"The invasion force appears to have been armed with Chinese-style surface to air missiles, shoulder fired weapons, and heavy machine guns of foreign manufacture. Captured equipment is labeled in Chinese figures, English and Spanish. U.S. Army mechanized units were reported to have captured and pacified parts of Tijuana, Nuevo Laredo, Ciudad Juarez, and Mexicali. Intense urban battles rage at this time in Brownsville, El Paso, the San Diego region, and as far north as Tucson. In addition to highways and airports, PEMEX—the Mexican national oil company—resources including oil fields such as the huge Cantarell field, refineries and pipelines, have also been seized by American forces."

525

"In the U.S., urban battles at this hour continue to side with the guerilla force, with most active-duty and reserve police units being killed in an initial series of car bombings and sniper attacks. Given the battles fought in the western Pacific today, and the nature of the surprise attacks and invasions, it only seems a matter of time before the Mexican attackers, as well as innocent Hispanics caught up in the battles, are killed. Urban areas with high percentages of Hispanics and illegals in many U.S. cities also report vicious attacks on whites, police officers, and military forces."

"Within the hour on the East Coast, a vicious car-bomb attack has occurred in suburban Alexandria, Virginia. The bomb has apparently leveled a child-care facility used almost exclusively by Congressional staffers families. Two Mexican illegals seen running from the delivery van were captured after the explosion and beaten to death before police could arrive. They have been identified as in this country illegally through government records listing previous deportation. At this hour, the death toll is rising, with forty-seven children under the age of five killed, thirty more missing, and more than twenty adults missing and presumed killed. Eleven adults and four children were pulled from the wreckage and taken to local hospitals."

A chill ran down my spine. The commentator paused for a moment. *"An editorial comment here, I would add,"* he paused again. *"In my forty years in journalism, I have never seen such brutality inflicted upon such a group of helpless victims. If there ever was a galvanizing event so brutal as to unite the American people against a common enemy, we must look back to the attack on Pearl Harbor for comparison. Within the space of a single day, the United States has been attacked by the Communist Chinese, and our neighbor to the south, Mexico. The defeat of one was rapid and decisive. If you are a Mexican listening to this now, I can assure you that your defeat is coming, and it will be equally decisive and infinitely more painful...for you."* The radio clicked for a moment and a different voice came on.

"This is FOX news." The broadcast went to static.

I heard Libby stirring, and in a minute she came into the 'radio room.' "What's new?" she said in a hushed tone.

"Where do I start?" I whispered back.

"What happened with China? And the other countries?"

"China attacked us and Taiwan. I did tell Alan what was going on, by the way. It's over. They lost." Her eyes were like dinner plates.

"No way."

"Yes. The government was removed. The war's over...on that front it seems. It didn't go nuclear."

"Well that's a good thing."

"Yep."

"How about the others?"

"Mexico invaded. They also are attacking cities from within with folks, I suspect, that aren't legally here."

"Big shock there," she said.

"They also may have bombed a day care in Virginia. That was just on."

"What, do they have a suicide-by-soldier wish or something? A day-care?"

"That's what the radio said. I'm just telling you."

"Think it's on the up-and-up?"

"You mean, is the government lying?"

"Yeah, to be blunt about it."

"Honestly? I doubt it, but it could certainly be the case."

"I guess we'll never know about some things."

"That is correct."

"What do you think will happen next?"

"I predict that you will make tea, and I will make a trip to the facilities, and then back to bed. Sometime after that, I predict that the more important parts of Mexico, including the parts that make oil and have factories, will be solidly inside of U.S. territory. I also predict that a lot of Hispanic folk are going to die today. A lot of them will be innocent."

"You think we're going to....."

"Invade? Conquer? Undoubtedly. And it will be justified with 'they started it.'"

"You're awfully cynical for this early."

"It's not often that the vision of a blown-up day-care is thrust into my mind. Water's on for tea or coffee. I'll go make a pit-stop, then I'm turning in."

"K."

Tuesday Morning,
January Twenty-fourth

It was a little after eight when I finally woke up. Everyone else was being very considerate in keeping quiet until I (the last) was up and going. Ada decided that my recently-vacated warm bed was a nice place to spend the morning, and helped herself as I pulled on some clean socks and my boots.

"So what kind of world did I wake up to this time?" I asked.

"Good question. Mexico's getting their asses handed to them, and Venezuela decided that offing our Ambassador was a good idea," Ron said.

"No one's that stupi...."

"Yes, I'm afraid someone is that stupid."

I sat there for a second, trying to both wake up fully and process the information. "Coffee."

"Yeah. You'll need all of that," Karen said. "Breakfast for second-rounders will be ready shortly."

"Second rounders?"

"That'd be you, John, Carl, the girls, my Mom, and Alan's kids."

"Everyone else's eaten?"

"Yep. We cooked up a mess of stuff and sent a load over to Alan's place."

"Smart."

"One-time offer. I almost dropped the fried eggs on the way."

"You walked?"

"Have you looked outside? Not worth scraping the windows on the Ford to drive two hundred feet."

The sun was streaming into the room from the east. A hard, heavy frost covered everything. It almost hurt my eyes to look at it—it glittered.

"What a beautiful sight."

"The sunrise was nice too—reddish, then pink," Libby said.

"Probably helped out by a lot of ash."

"That's what I figured too."

"The Pres been back on?"

"Nope, not yet. Nothing official since you turned in. That hasn't stopped the talking, though."

"Anything more on the daycare?"

"Seventy-one dead. Most kids," Ron said with disgust. "Gimme a gun and a target-rich environment, and I'll go hunting illegals."

"I'm sure there's plenty of that going on. I just hope that people are using some level of common sense and not going after anyone that looks Hispanic."

"Not going to happen," Ron said.

"That's what I'm afraid of."

530

"Here. Scrambled eggs, cheese and peppers. Biscuits are in the oven."

"You," I said as I kissed my wife, "are an angel."

"So it's been reported. But Libby made breakfast today."

"Better not, Lib. Don't want the wife getting all jealous," I tried to say with a straight face.

"That's OK, we'll just wait 'til they leave," I lost it then.

"Ron, where's that bucket of cold water?"

"Water? I think we've got some 'night water' for them both..."

"Sorry, couldn't resist," I said.

"That's perfectly all right. I think we could all use a laugh."

"Yeah, but my mind is resting on other things, and on families that won't see their loved ones again." I was silent for a moment. "Children. How could they?"

No one answered a question that had no answer.

After a breakfast spent quietly, turning over the events of the previous night and the morning over in our minds, we set about putting the day in order. The President's address was to be broadcast at ten a.m. I wanted to be somewhere near the radio or the TV when it came on.

Once all the kids were up, they were told of the night's events. They were both scared and excited at the news, and saddened as we were by the news about the attack on the day care. I noticed that Carl and Marie spoke to each other quietly, and a bit off to themselves. 'Better keep an eye on that,' I thought. Libby had seen it too, and shared the same look.

I had another cup of French Roast, with a dollop of honey this time.

"John, you and Carl up to a little field trip today?"

"Sure, anything beats moving furniture."

"This is a little lighter. I'll need you to go over to the community center and find the manager. I've got a series of CD's for the community center to use. Also, I'd like you to see if you can get a copy of the list of meeting attendees from yesterday, and ask the manager if it's possible to set up a bartering store there at the center. Can you handle that?"

"I think so, sounds easy enough."

"Should be. You can either take my Ford or the Jeep, if it's all right with your Dad," I'd already cleared it with Ron, so I knew it wouldn't be a problem.

"That OK Dad?"

"Yep. Finish up breakfast, then get cleaned up and get going. We still have some stuff to move, but most of the heavy stuff's taken care of. After that, we'll need you both to help us out with some salvage. You should be done with that by afternoon. Then, you get free time."

"Cool," Carl said.

"Not so fast, young man." Karen said. "You've had a week off of school, all of you. That's going to come to screeching halt pretty soon. Better be ready for it."

"But the school's miles away," Carl said correctly. His school was fifty blocks away.

"So's mine," Kelly said. "Though not as far as Carl's."

"The elementary is still there. We're going to talk with the community center later today, Libby and I. We can't have you out of school forever, and if gas isn't available, then buses aren't going to be either, and I'm betting you aren't the only kids around who're out of school."

"Trying to get rid of us, huh, Mom?" John said.

"There is something to be said for peace and quiet several hours a day," Libby said.

"Man...." Carl said.

"Back to the idea of a one room school, sounds like to me," I said.

"Great. Just great." Marie was not impressed.

"Before you get all whiny, you better remember to thank God that you weren't all vaporized last night, OK? The Navy sank a couple of ballistic missile subs, and you can bet real money that at least a couple of those warheads were scheduled to land twelve miles from here at Fairchild." That certainly shut them up.

"Yes sir," Carl and Kelly said.

"Now go on, get cleaned up and teeth brushed and dressed. It's a new day, so get on it."

"K."

Libby said to me quietly," You sure know how to somber up a room."

"Libby, my heart is breaking for what's going on right now, and I'm not one to cry."

"I know. It'll be OK."

"Yeah. It will. I know it will. Doesn't make it easier though. I haven't been this edgy in years. Maybe decades."

Once you are a parent, you begin to understand true loss, because of the sheer joy of being a parent and the void that appears when your child leaves you, even for just a little while. The unimaginable had happened in Virginia. Children murdered. It had happened in the Pacific too, with sons and daughters killed in war. In the American Southwest. And it was happening Right Now.

While Ron prodded the kids into getting ready, and visiting the 'facilities' himself, Karen and Libby finished up breakfast and started gathering clothing for the laundry. I decided to read. I picked up First Thessalonians. I felt better when I'd finished it. I don't know still, why I read that chapter that day. It has stuck with me though, and I hope it will for a long time.

"Be joyful always; pray continually; give thanks in all circumstances, for this is God's will for you in Christ Jesus."

"Hey guys, I'm sorry I bit your head off. It was a bad night last night."

"That's OK, Dad. We understand," Kelly said. Both she and Carl came over and gave me a big hug.

"I love you both."

"We know. But we love you most," Kelly said. Eventually I let them go.

"OK, boss. What's on our menu today?" Ron said as he came into the room.

"I want to listen to the President's address, that's supposed to be at ten. I've got gas-man duty at one. Other than that, about fifty things."

"Cool. We get to multi-task."

"We're perfecting it, bud. Here's my list. We should get Alan in on it too."

"More the merrier."

"He's on the way," Karen said. "I just called him. Libby is going to get the girls going on laundry here, I'll go over and collect Mary's stuff and wash it here too. After that, we're going over to help them get settled in."

"Anyone staying here?"

"Just to feed the fire, someone can pop back in."

"Sounds OK. Remember to take a radio."

"What have you got planned?"

"First, I thought we'd go back over to Tim's and figure out if there's anything else we want to clean out, even if we're not going to use it."

"To what end? We don't have anywhere to put it here."

"Alan does, and what he doesn't want or need, we can trade."

"Gotcha. What else?"

"I'd like to get back into the house and look it over for damage, and figure out what a game plan might be for putting it back together."

"Start with the laundry. We're tired of washing stuff by hand."

"Actually, that might be easier than you might think. Tim's laundry was right off the garage, and it's still intact. We can probably salvage the equipment over to Alan's place, then use a generator to run a washer. The dryer's gas though, so that's a non-starter."

"If you can swing it, that would be great."

"Anything to keep you happy babe."

"Really? Good. I'll keep that in mind," she said with a smile.

"C'mon. Let's get you out of here before you dig a deeper hole."

"I do seem to be at the bottom…"

"Which means you need to quit shoveling."

"Aye," I responded.

We met Alan in the 'front yard' of the barn. He looked much better than he did last evening.

"And how are things in the Bauer Haus this fine morning?"

"Very good, thank you. I'm a little unsure about the title of the place though."

"It's yours until the sheriff says it isn't. Might as well call it by name."

"Better than 'Camp Bauer,' I suppose."

"Yep. Stay warm enough?"

"Yeah it was great. That furnace does a good job, even without power."

"Good. Everyone doing better today?"

"Yep. The kids are back in bed though, coming down with colds."

"Stay after it. If it goes to flu, it's bad."

"We know. Saw plenty of that at the shelter up north. What's on tap this morning?"

I noticed Alan was wearing one of his revolvers on his hip. "Thought we'd go over to Tim's place and figure out what's there we can either use or barter later. John and Carl are going over to the community center with some stuff I promised the manager, who I think has taken a shine to young John. I wanted to be around the radio when the President comes on, and I wanted to get back into the house to look her over for damage. I want to start thinking about putting it back together. I'll be at the gas station at one to pump gas, too."

"Things always this busy around here?" Alan asked.

"Busier, most days," Ron said.

"You're going to wear us out."

"I'm trying to pace myself a little better. One big thing per day is probably enough, I'm thinking."

"Good. Starting today?" Ron said.

"Yeah, probably. I know I'm going to need to turn in early or nap when I'm done at the station, too. Running on about five cylinders today."

John and Carl were busy getting the Jeep cleaned off, and the windshield scraped. "You two give Andrea my regards," I said as we walked up to the front gate. John looked....uneasy.

Once we were through the gate, I recognized that I should plow sometime today or tomorrow too. With so few people on the street, and infrequent police patrols, the snow was a bit deep, and drifted in again.

While at Tim's, we managed to collect a sizeable amount of stuff that Alan's place could use, we decided. Aside from the washer, which was old but undamaged, we designated a couch, recliner, dining set and dressers to be relocated, as well as all of the remaining utensils, towels and bedding, hand tools from the garage, and mundane things like light bulbs. We also found a twenty-five pound bag of basmati rice that was up on a shelf in a closet. Tim had obviously missed it, or hadn't had room in the van or the eighteen-foot trailer. I was betting on the former.

The second pile of stuff ended up in the living room, which we decided to have the girls look over too. That pile was intended to be 'barter' goods, but until we had all decided on what could 'go', it was just one more pile of stuff.

At nine forty-five, we headed back to the barn for the scheduled address. We'd come back later with Alan's truck and his trailer, and hopefully finish it up in no more than two loads.

As soon as we were clear of the house, I heard Buck and Ada barking at something behind us. We all turned to see four or five dogs coming at us....quickly.

Before I even had a chance to move, Alan had calmly unsheathed his big revolver and taken aim. The roar was enough, I think to have scared the dogs off. One dropped stone dead in its tracks, a second was hit as it turned and ran. The others ran off.

Ron and I just looked at Alan for a moment. "Nice shooting, Tex."

"You just never know when an Anaconda might be useful."

"That's what that is? I've never seen it before."

The gun was seemingly huge. Eight-inch barrel, stainless steel, with bone grips. Must've weighed a ton.

"Bought it for protection on the boat, when we used to fish out in the Sound."

"Afraid of pirates?" Ron asked in jest.

"It has been known to happen, especially when you start getting close to international waters. Got an 870 Marine Magnum too. Drug running is a real thing."

"I had no idea," Ron said.

"Me either. Let's....get rid of these dogs."

"Where?"

"At least out of the street." I recognized the remains of the lead dog, a rottweiler with an absolutely massive skull—now shattered—as a pet of the people that used to live on the other side of our neighbor Brad. When they abandoned their home, they apparently left their dogs. The second was one of theirs too, a tan pit-bull, which was hit in the side. The forty-four probably shattered it's spine on its way through. Ron and I grabbed a leg, and dragged both off to the side of the road. The swaths of red trailed each dog, in stark contrast to the sunlit snow.

"Well, that's one way to get your adrenaline going." I said. "Now if I could get the ringing in my ears to stop..."

"Better start going around with your sidearms or long-guns," Alan said. "How many starving dogs are out there, do you wonder?"

"More dogs than cats, right now, I'd bet."

"That'd be a safe assumption," Alan said as we got to our gate.

"Did you have this problem up on Five Mile?"

"Coyotes more than anything else."

"Wonder what the President will say?" Ron asked.

"'That we're kicking ass and taking names, and we're fresh out of pencils and paper.'"

Ron and I had a good chuckle over that. The Jeep was still gone. I hoped the boys weren't getting into any trouble. I decided to find out, and called Carl on the radio. It beeped twice on his end, before he answered.

"Yep?"

"Things OK? You still at the center?"

"Yep. We'll be on our way soon. There's some other people here, and we had to wait for them to finish. They're...collecting bodies too. They call themselves a 'recovery team'."

"Oh. Well that makes sense. Come straight home when you're done. Don't want you getting into trouble."

"K. See you soon."

"Out."

"Out."

When I got back inside, the tiny black and white TV was on and Libby, Kelly and Marie were taking a break from the laundry and enjoying some tea. Ron and Alan each had a cup of coffee, and Alan handed me a steaming cup as I took my boots off. Alan was filling everyone in on our canine adventure.

"Any more real news?" I asked Libby.

"Yakima, Ellensburg, some of the smaller towns in Oregon, oh, and Wenatchee. All have had some trouble with Hispanics."

"What kind of trouble?"

"Shooting at cops, mostly."

"Not a wise way to grow old," I said.

"Shh. It's starting," Kelly said.

".....news from the White House press room. The President's helicopter landed forty minutes ago, and we understand that the address will come from the East Room. As with all Presidential addresses, there will be no question and answer session, this is strictly a speech to the American people and to the world. The President of the United States..."

"Good afternoon, my fellow Americans.

I am speaking to you about the invasion of the American Southwest by forces harbored, sheltered and sponsored by the enemies of the United States and enemies of the freedoms we enjoy.

In a synchronized attack against U.S. forces in the Far East and at home, terrorists backed and supported by Mexican army troops have staged a series of attacks and invasions on the border cities shared by our countries. This effort, widely called the opening of the Reconquista—or re-conquering—of the Southwest, was joined nation-wide by terrorist cells operating in predominantly Hispanic areas of the country.

These attacks included the bombing of a daycare center not far from here, in Alexandria, Virginia. This attack wounded and killed people that I know personally. Children that I have met. Network television has broadcast all day the results of this bombing, in graphic detail. But that is not all. This type of attack has been used in many of our cities, against police forces, hospitals, and schools. Eleven such attacks have occurred so far today, fourteen have been stopped. At this hour, five hundred and seven have been killed, and over two thousand injured.

Units of the U.S. military have eliminated Mexican Army units at the border, and are working both south into Mexico in pursuit of these attacking units, and north, into cities and neighborhoods where these terrorists have hidden like cowards. The U.S. military, acting on my orders, has seized major economic centers and resources of the Mexican people, and will retain these until a peaceful and unconditional surrender of enemy forces occurs and a stable government is in place. Funds received by the operations of these facilities will be retained for the Mexican people.

Using our national resources and intelligence assets, we have determined without question that the current invasion of American soil was led by none other than the president of Mexico and his leaders, in concert with the Chinese and other nations. This man I called friend, who I have dined with, who I believe shared a vision for the common good of both countries and our common peoples, has betrayed his people, the people of the United States, and the good will of neighboring nations.

Working with the leader of Venezuela, one of the attacks first actions was to seize our diplomatic staffs in both countries. I am sorry to report that both the Mexican and Venezuelan governments have executed all American diplomatic personnel and numerous American citizen contractors in both countries, and did so before we could mount any meaningful response to their seizure.

There will be no safe harbor for people such as these."

I watched as his eyes narrowed.

"When this war is over, I pray that there will be a new world, one which has no room for men like these, for countries like these, for evil such as has been committed this day. I will do all in my power to ensure this is so.

Good afternoon."

The anger was palpable, and not just on the television.

"Bastards...God-damned bastards....." Alan said. What I wanted to say, I could not in front of my daughter. Ron, I'm sure, felt the same.

"Gonna be a lot of hunting today," I finally said.

"Open season. I wouldn't want to be Hispanic today for all the money in the world."

"Yeah. Like Muslims after nine-eleven."

"Not all Hispanics did this."

"Nor did all Muslims. But the net being thrown will not discriminate all that well."

We sat there for a full minute in silence, only interrupted by the continuing coverage of the daycare center, the Battle of Taiwan, and now, Mexico.

"Dad, how are they going to tell them apart? I mean, the good guys and the bad guys?" Kelly asked.

"If it were me, if they point a gun at you, they die. If they don't, and can prove they're a legal citizen, they live, same as you or me."

"So they have to sort them all out? Sounds impossible."

"Yes, it does. Some bad guys will get through, some good guys will be wrongly accused. This is what happens when you allow your borders to be as air-tight as a screen door."

"Oh."

"C'mon and give me a hug. We need to move some more stuff and you need to finish the laundry."

"I hate the laundry."

"I know. This might be the last time though. We're thinking about hooking up a washing machine."

"Yea!" Kelly said. "That would be cool."

"Yep. It'd free you up to do other things."

"Killjoy."

"Not intentionally, but quite often by accident," I responded.

Tuesday
January Twenty-fourth

The boys returned home about ten minutes after the speech ended, and we worked until around noon getting the rest of the 'stuff' moved over to Alan's new home.

Alan had enlisted all of the men to help move the big gun safe into the house, and we then carefully handed him his collection to store. While many of his guns were strictly hunting pieces, he also had twin Bushmasters, three Colt 1911's (National Match models!), and more reloading stuff than I'd ever seen in one location outside of a gunsmith's shop. The reloading bench was moved to the basement (no small feat) and set up far away from the wood furnace.

Grace looked much better today, I thought, as we moved more furniture into the house, and the smaller fry helped put things away. Karen made me a sandwich and a thermos of coffee, while I got the tractor ready to go. The trailer tires had again both gone flat, so that took a few minutes to take care of. As long as they held air for a while, I'd be OK.

I took Alan's advice and strapped on my own 1911, a lowly and well-worn service automatic and two spare seven-round magazines, and headed out the gate. I'd decided to forego salvage work in our house until I got back, and let Karen know that the older boys were free for a couple hours.

It felt odd, driving a fifty-five-year-old tractor, with a sixty-year-old gun strapped to my belt. I didn't see any evidence that any of the houses between our place and the gas station still had anyone living there. 'Weren't there a couple, yesterday or day before?' I thought.

At five 'til one, Deputy Schmitt showed up to open up the store, followed by five State Patrol cars, a number of Patrol Expedition models, and six or seven additional Crown Vic cruisers belonging to the city or the county. No military vehicles or buses this time.

"Afternoon, Paul. How's things going?"

"Nothing earthshaking...no pun intended."

"That's good. Where's Andy Welt? I thought he'd be here to open up," I said as I hooked up the power to the generator and engaged the PTO for the generator.

"You haven't heard...obviously. He was found on Sunday morning. He was murdered. Probably by one of his employees. Robbery, it looked like. Haven't found the guy or guys who did it yet, but we have a pretty good idea who it was."

"Wow. He seemed like he was pretty well ready."

"So he thought. But he was also a little too indiscreet with his money, which in these times, was as good as an invitation to come on in and steal everything he's got. Which was pretty much what they did."

"He told me that he was buying up stuff that would be 'worth it's weight'. What was it?"

"Crystal methamphetamine. Grow lights. Fertilizers. Hydroponics. Seeds."

"All drugs."

"Yep."

"So should I assume that whoever killed him is now a big player in the drug market?"

"You may. And you should also assume that the price of a bag is very high. Which means that robberies and thefts and out-and-out murder are going up. The dopers didn't leave town in the same rates as people who hadn't cooked their brains." The first State Patrol vehicles had fueled up and left, and the next two were now in line.

"Great. On another topic, how are you making out? Doing OK?"

"Yeah, the family place has always been setup for getting by without power. It's been in the family since it was homesteaded."

"Doing OK for food?"

"Yeah, my brother and dad raise beef, hogs and goats, in addition to all the orchard stuff. Apples and peaches, mostly."

"We may have to do a little talking. Be interested in a little bartering?"

"Could be. Whatcha got in mind?" he smiled.

"We've got thirteen people up the street right now, and while our stored food will hold up for awhile, we're eventually going to need meat, milk, that kind of stuff. We've got laying hens that are putting out a very good count per day."

"That'd be worth talking about. By the way, who's got your back up there? I heard someone moved in next to the guy from the power company."

"My brother-in-law's family. Wife, two kids, mother-in-law too."

"Pays to have them close. He armed?"

"Yep."

"Good. Little spooky around these streets without either lights or people living in the houses."

"Yeah, we know."

"Mike wanted me to let you know that your family's on the list for priority food distributions when they get here this afternoon."

"We really don't need anything, Paul."

"That's what he said you'd say. He said to tell you to take it anyway. I'll drop it by later on. I have no idea what they're distributing. Could be some of that nice federal cheese."

"Well you know the saying, what you subsidize, you get more of."

"That's a fact." Just then, Ron's Jeep, with Carl and John behind the wheel, pulled into the lot and parked.

"Howdy, boys. What's new over at the center?" I asked, as if I didn't know....

"Not much. Andrea told us to tell you 'thanks' for the CD's. There's a lot of stuff on them that she was looking for."

"Yeah, it's a little tough to Google-up something these days around here." I noticed an unmarked City car pull into line. It looked like the community center manager, Andrea, behind the wheel.

"What do we do now, go home?"

"Not yet. The Jeep's tanks aren't full, and the county owes me some fuel. Get in line behind the last of the cars, and we'll fill you up. I'm going to get Alan down here next time to fill up his diesel."

"We owe you that much?" Paul said.

"You will as of today. My tanks, other than the Jeep and the tractor, are pretty well full."

"Better not advertise that."

"I won't." At that point, Andrea joined us. "Miss Britton. Nice to see you. This is Paul Schmitt, if you haven't been introduced."

"We've met. Nice to see you Paul."

"Likewise."

"The boys tell me that the CD's might be useful?"

"I'll say. I was looking through the texts that FEMA gave us, but yours is more concise, and searchable on the computers."

"What's on the CD's?" Paul asked.

"A bunch of survival info. Primitive living. Sanitation. Stuff we take—or took—for granted. Thought it'd be a good idea to share."

"Good idea. I might have a look myself."

"That's what it's for. Of course that's only the start of our work," I said.

"What do you mean?" Andrea said, as only a young woman in her early twenties can. 'Was I ever that naïve?' I thought, already knowing the answer.

"Look around. Within the last week or two, we entered the Second Great Depression, and that's what the press is calling it. We've also been thwacked by a major earthquake that's devastated our state...."

"Three, actually," Paul said.

"Three what?" I asked.

"Three quakes. They're calling it the Domino Quake."

"I don't understand."

"The Seattle quake triggered Rainier going off, our quake on the Latah Creek Fault and the Mid Columbia Fault right in between us and Seattle."

"Columbia Fault? Why haven't I heard about this on the news already?"

"Oh, I dunno, war with Mexico, war with China...."

"Yeah. Yesterdays news."

"Affirmative."

"OK, as I was saying. Where was I?"

"Earthquake," Paul reminded me.

"Right. Sorry. Lack of sleep. OK, so we've been hit by earthquakes, our ecology temporarily or permanently whacked by the volcano. Millions dead. Most of the rest of the world is pissed at us because we bankrupted them...and us. Our currency is rapidly approaching that of toilet paper as far as purchasing power goes. Gas is unobtainable from outside countries, or probably will be. The point is, the way of life we've enjoyed for three generations is over. And we damn well better be ready to deal with a whole new way to live, and we better start figuring it out right-damn-now."

"How do we do that?" Clearly I had her attention. She looked scared.

"Adapt. The bananas that you had two weeks ago from South America? You'll probably never see a banana again. That means we will eat what is grown around here, and sold around here. By 'around here', I mean in the very local area. Local dairies. Butchers, farms, growers, markets. And if you don't live near where you work, you're hosed. Assuming that you still have a job when the dust settles."

She was silent for a moment, as were Paul and the boys. "I will need you to talk to the sheriff about this. And the county Commissioners."

"Andrea, I hope they've already figured this out. We're not going back to where we were. Where we were...no longer exists." It was her turn to gas up, then the Jeep.

"I'll have someone in touch with you by the end of the day.....Oh! And I have these for you. Letters."

"Really?" I was floored. A letter from my brother Alex and his wife Amber. They lived in West Seattle..before the quake. I'd feared them both dead after seeing the destruction on TV. The postmark was from Memphis. Five days ago—after the quake. The second was from another of my brothers, in Utah. The third, from my oldest brother in Minneapolis. A fourth from the Paulianos—with a California postmark. "They made it..." I said to myself."

"Who did?" Carl asked.

"Your Uncle Alex and Aunt Amber. This," I said holding up the letter, "was mailed five days ago from Memphis. And this one," holding up Joan's letter, "Is from Joe and Joan. The others are from your uncles in Utah and Minnesota."

"Whoo-hoo! Good for them!" Carl said. "Why was Alex in Memphis?"

"That's where Amber's folks live. They were probably visiting. We Drummonds don't tend to keep track of each other too well," I said.

"So it would appear," Miss Britton said with a smile.

"You should finish gassing us up and get out of here. And go read your letters."

"I will do just that."

After only forty minutes of 'gas duty', I sent the boys back home and Paul and I locked up the store. Paul tossed me a box of 'Snickers' bars, and liberated a box of 'Mr. Goodbar' for himself.

"Be sure to write that down..." I said jokingly.

"Already did," he said in all seriousness.

"How 'bout you stop by the house and pick up a few eggs. My brother-in-law will meet you up there, and you can talk a little trading. It'll take me some time to get up there with the tractor."

"Sounds good. What's his name?"

"Alan. Alan Bauer. Used to live up on Five Mile before it hit the fan. I'll radio him and let him know you're coming."

"I've gotta run back to the community center first, but I'll be by before three."

"Great. See you then."

"Thanks."

After Paul left, and I added some more air to one of the trailer tires with the hand pump, I called both Alan and Karen on the radio and filled them in.

"He's got cattle?"

"And hogs, and goats, and fruit."

"I'm more interested in the beef," Karen said.

"Ditto. Alan, I'd like you to handle negotiations, if you don't mind."

"I'm a little out of my depth here. What is the market rate for beef these days relative to eggs?"

"I have no idea. I doubt Paul does either. So at least it's a relatively level playing field."

"I'll do some thinking. If we can at least compare pre-crash prices one against the other, that'd be a start."

"Yeah, probably a good tactic. I'll see you in a few minutes. I hope the boys kept the gate open."

"I'll make sure they do. John sure has a big smile on his face. What's up with that?" Libby asked.

"I'll fill you in….on a secure channel, if you know what I mean."

"I got it. Out." I could hear her smile.

"Out."

When I finally arrived at the barn, Ron, Karen and Libby were in the middle of the discussion on the net worth of chicken eggs, and what percentage of eggs should be allowed to hatch for breeding stock and for sale.

"Rick, what do you think?" Libby asked.

"I think you're doing fine. We're all trying to make this up as we go you know."

"Lotta help you are," Karen said with a smirk as she handed me a cup of mint tea.

"Thanks. I'll let you play gas-station boy next time."

"Where are the letters?" she asked.

"Right here. I thought we could read them together."

"That's a great idea. We should get everyone over for that."

"We'll do it after Paul leaves then. How many dozen eggs do you have to spare?"

"Honey they're laying a little under five dozen a day. How many do you think we have?"

"More than you need?"

"Yeah. That'd be safe. We don't want them to freeze, and we don't want them to spoil either. We don't really have a conditioned space to put them in right now, we're just hoping we don't lose them."

"So giving Paul five dozen won't hurt."

"No. Not a bit."

"OK. I'll talk to Alan about it. Where's he at?"

"Working on the garage over there. He said the ridge beam's cracked and he's afraid the garage roof will come down. He's putting a brace together for it. He borrowed some wood from the pile next to the Packard, and that two-ton jack from the garage. He said he'd call if he needed help."

"K." I'll go talk to him."

"Radio's quicker," Karen reminded me.

"Right. And honey," I said quietly, "these are for later," I handed her the box of candy bars, and got a big smile and a wink. I popped the ear bud back in and called Alan, and filled him in a bit on my conversation with Paul, and my desire to have him handle the bartering. Of my many skills, that was not one of them. I tended to be a 'buyer', not a 'negotiator.' I let Alan know that I needed to get some sleep before I crashed completely, and let Karen and Libby know that Alan would take a shot at the bartering situation.

As much as I wanted to read the letters, I wanted everyone to be focused on that alone, rather than the daily grind that we were in the midst of. Laundry. The inevitable question of what's for dinner/breakfast. Keeping the fire going. Cleaning out the firebox. Wondering. Mostly, wondering. For me, right that minute, it was enough to know that they were all OK, especially Alex and Amber.

I got cleaned up a little, and turned in for a couple hours of sleep. It was also good to know that I wouldn't be on 'duty' tonight, so I'd be able to catch up on rest a bit more. Even though it was still the middle of the afternoon, I fell right to sleep.

I woke to the sound of rain hitting the skylight outside of my blanket bedroom. I looked at my watch and pushed the light. Three-forty p.m. I got up for a drink of water before heading back for some more sleep.

"How's it going? Did Alan figure out something with Paul?"

"Going OK. Yeah, they decided to for now, trade a dozen eggs for a pound of beef. They both seemed to think that was a good trade. Paul's going to figure out some other stuff too, like maybe trading some chicks for a piglet or two."

"That sounds like something to explore. Any news? I mean on…"

"I know what you mean. Not much new. Endless reports from Texas, Arizona and California. Seems like New Mexico's gone the farthest in ending the invasion. They're saying that we're deep into Mexico in a lot of places."

"I'm thinking they need to mop up here before we go and take on more territory."

"So does ABC."

"What's everyone else up to?"

"Mary and the kids are coming down with the bug that you had, sounds like. Fever, the whole bit."

"Had to happen sooner or later. Your Mom OK?"

"Yeah, she's fine. I might spend the night over there though to keep an eye on things. I don't want Alan or Mom getting worn out."

"Not a bad idea. What's on for dinner tonight?"

"Is that all you men think about?"

"We're but humble peasants ma'am, with simple needs and plain desires."

"Soft shell tacos. I had two packages of tortillas in the freezer."

"Cool. Hope you've got some of that salsa you made last summer."

"You mean that stuff I burned my fingers on?" Karen's first experience with home-grown jalapeño peppers resulted in first-degree burns on both hands, when she wasn't told to wear rubber gloves when 'seeding' them. She spent several unpleasant hours that night with both hands in whole milk. Milk fat helped extract the poison from the skin.

"That's the stuff. That'll kill most any bug."

"Yeah. Or human."

"Only in large doses."

"I've got several quarts in the basement, a pint out here."

"Yum. I'm heading back to sleep for a while. What time's dinner?"

"I think first shift will be at six. With Alan's family down, they'll have soup and sandwiches—light stuff—for those that feel like eating. We'll make sure they get fed, then we'll eat here."

"Rains a nice change. What time did that start?"

"About three. It warmed up too—it's almost thirty five out there."

"Good. About time. A nice melt down would be a very good thing. Wash in some of that ash too."

"Yeah, if you like lots of grey mud. You remember St. Helens."

"I do. It sucked. I'm more concerned about the dust this spring and summer though, if it doesn't get washed in. I don't relish spending the summer wearing a respirator. And that's what we could all face."

"Great. Another inspirational theme."

"I know, I'm a ball of light."

"You are. Now get going."

"OK. I'll snooze some more. Love you."

"You too, sleeping beauty."

"Thanks."

I crawled back into bed and tried to sleep. After a while I succeeded. As I finally drifted back off, I thought of growing seasons and rainfall, and where we'd be in six months. Or three, for that matter.

Seven thirty-five p.m.
Tuesday Evening
January Twenty-fourth

Letters

"January 20ᵗʰ

Collierville, Tennessee.

Dear Rick, Karen, Carl and Kelly—

It's been six days since the quake, and we all pray that this letter finds you all safe and sound and in Christ's care." I stopped for a moment.

"That's my brother's handwriting, but certainly words I've never heard him say before."

"Things change, so do people," Karen said.

"Indeed." I went on.

"Amber and the kids and I were visiting her parents when it hit, her Mom is just out of the hospital for an arthroscopic on her knee. We never knew that we were in that much danger there, nor that the damage in Spokane could ever get that bad. We saw one of the network feeds the first day or so, and then some of the evac buses headed out of town. I assume that with all of your 'just in case' stuff,

that you stayed put. If you did, and you're reading this, we cannot imagine the life you are living right now, nor can we expect things to get better soon, apparently. I will apologize in advance, many times, for all the things I said to you about your preparedness 'thing'. When I was giving you a bad time, I should've been taking lessons. But as the older brother, it was my place to tease you."

"So true," I said aloud.

"Besides that, I thought it was a waste of money, which I'm sure will prove to be dead wrong.

I wanted to let you know (we'll write Jeff and Jack too, and if you run across Joe, I suppose you should tell him too) that we're not coming back. The brokerage firm is toast (literally) and with the pictures of our neighborhood I saw on CNN, there is really no reason (nor probably any physical way) to go back. We're staying here for now, and will be looking for a place near Amber's parents soon.

I also wanted to let you know that I took some liberties with your investment funds—I don't think you'll mind. First, when the market went T.U. on the second day to the point you and I talked about, I sold all of your remaining equities and bond funds and bought a couple of out-of-country AUAG funds, before they really started to take off, and before they then snapped altogether. Played it right for a change. Two days later, I bailed on that and bought physical AUAG. If you reply, I will get you the physical via FEDEX. Amber's Dad still has some pull with the company, and since they're flying relief flights in, he can see to it that a courier-protected shipment can be made. It's here at the house now, just to let you know. Also, if you want out, he can arrange it. Just let me know.

Give Karen and the kids hugs from all of us. Luke and Jaime are being spoiled rotten by the grandparents, which is of course, their due.

All our hopes and prayers,

Alex and Amber"

A few moments of silence after I finished reading passed.

"Good for them. They're damn lucky," Alan said.

"Yeah. They are," I said.

"Dad, what did that mean that he sold your investment funds?"

"I had a pretty good chunk of money invested for my retirement, part of my retirement strategy anyway. Stuff that if it went away, wouldn't kill us. Alex was my broker for those funds, and I told him once that if he ever saw a full scale meltdown get up some steam to sell it and reinvest in something that was going to be around after the smoke cleared. That meant gold, silver, and other metals."

"What did he mean by 'physical?' I don't get it. And what's AU AG?"

"You used to be able to invest in metals 'funds' or physical metal. A fund was like a company that bought and sold the rights to the metal, without actually holding it in their hands. Physical metal is just that. Bullion or coins. Sounds like he cashed in the funds for actual metal. And AU and AG are the periodic table symbols for gold and silver."

"So he saved your money? He changed it to gold and silver?"

"Sounds as if. Of course, it's still a couple thousand miles away. I'm not counting on seeing it ever get here."

"Still, that was astute planning," Ron said.

"What? My doomer mentality? Maybe. I expected the market to melt down. I didn't expect that Alex could move so fast. I wonder how much he saved?"

"No telling, and not something he'd write down, probably. He didn't call it silver or gold."

"Yeah. Prying eyes and Big Brother and all. He also didn't say anything on how things are in Memphis."

"Yeah. That might have to come in a later letter. We'll have to write back tomorrow."

"Next letter. Quick about it Dad!" Kelly begged.

"As you wish. Uncle Jeff's or Uncle Jack's?"

"Uncle Jack."

"He's your favorite. OK. That one next. Here we go."

"January 19th

Dear Rick, Karen, Carl and Kelly—

We have been praying for you all and everyone back home. It is not a pleasant thing to write a letter that may or may not find you alive and well, but we are trusting that God in his Mercy has brought you through this. Emily had a dream of you all, that you were safe and uninjured. We pray that this is so and look forward to the day when we may see you all again, in this world or the next. We feared the worst for Alex and Amber and their precious children, but received an email from him while the internet was still working. They're safe in Memphis with Amber's parents, thank God.

I stopped and said, "This next paragraph's for me." I read it to myself before continuing. I paused, then read it aloud.

Rick I am writing this paragraph to you. You are the head of your family as the Bible has instructed, and instruction and strength you must provide to your wife and your children. You know that I do not say things lightly, and you and I have never talked of the gravity of situations like this. It is my belief that what has happened in the Northwest and what ripples are now reaching the entire country, will strain our Nation as never before. I pray that you when tested, search to Him first for answers, and search the scriptures daily for your strength, your wisdom, and His guidance. Even though I am a number of years older, I believe that of all of the Drummond boys, you and I share this belief with deeper appreciation, fear and wonderment than the others. May God guide your steps and keep you safe.

Karen, you have been blessed with an understanding husband and delightful children. I would urge you too, but I know that you do so already, to ask for His guidance in what I expect will be a much more difficult and different life than what you have expected, and to provide for your husband and children as safe and as loving a home as you can. You are truly a woman blessed of God, as reflected in the faces of your children and the way that they live their lives by yours and Richard's examples. Keep them safe and strong in His word. Equip them as in Ephesians 6:10-13, so that they may be able to withstand in the evil day.

Carl and Kelly, you are both wonderful children and there is nothing we would rather do than hold you both close. Emily and I send our love and our prayers, and ask you to be obedient to your parents and to God, and to learn his word in the future as completely and with the deep understanding that you have in the past. It breaks our hearts to think that you could be hurt in this disaster, but again, we pray that you are safe.

To all of you, things here are OK. We have supplies and places to go should things get bad. Both Jane and Patrick are up north of the Cities, and our dear little Nicole is a joy. And remember not to worry, we don't really live here after all, we're citizens of Heaven, staying here temporarily.

All our love-

Jack and Em"

Karen was crying, as were our kids and Libby. I had a hard time myself making it through that one.

"OK, time for a break. Hon, got any dessert left?"

"No, but I do have something special. I thought we'd need a break. Rocky Road from the garage freezer."

"You, dear, are way too much," I said.

"So Ron tells me too…Oh, did I say that out loud?"

"Yes you did."

"Never mind, then."

We had a good laugh, and two scoops each of Rocky Road. I saved some for Grace, who was home with Mary and the little ones. After finishing up her ice cream, Karen packed an overnight bag and one of the sleeping bags so that she could spend the night at Alan's, to give both Alan and her mom a rest if Mary and the kids took a turn for the worse. It would be one of the very rare nights that we slept apart. Even on business trips or halfway around the world, when we were apart, we both felt that we were missing our best half. I'd never told Karen that until the quake, that I always got choked up when I left town, because I knew that if I did (and I knew she felt the same) that we'd both be blubbering messes on the 'C' concourse at Spokane International.

"OK, two more letters to go. We'll read Jeff's first, then the one from the Pauliano's. Everyone ready?"

"Yeah, if you don't make us all cry," Libby said.

"You mean 'cry again', don't you Libby?" Carl said.

"Not so fast pardner. I saw you tearing up too."

"Never said I didn't."

"OK, here we go."

"January 21st

Ogden

Dear Rick, Karen, Carl and Kelly—

We're all hoping that you're OK and you've made it through or gotten out. The mail's supposed to follow you if you go, but they didn't say how that was supposed to happen. They're not saying much about Spokane, most of the coverage is about the West Side same as always. We did see some video of town, and a helicopter shot of our old elementary school. Looked like part of it went down. We just hope and pray that you are all OK.

The LDS folks down here are working feverishly on both relief efforts and shipments north and other preparations that they're keeping to themselves. It doesn't take a brain surgeon (or an architect in my case) to see the writing on the wall. They're preparing for some serious stuff, and Barb and I are taking heed. Being one of the only non-Mormons in the whole area, we asked a few of our neighbors what to stock up on and they were very helpful. There is no way though, that we're going to have enough time to learn all the stuff that they seem to know, and not enough room to put the stuff, either. Design work all but stopped after the market crashed the first day, with clients calling us up and wanting their retainers back and others up and canceling projects. Our cash-flow plummeted immediately, and if we have a company when this is over, it will be a miracle. Our retirement funds are wiped out too, as is Lynnie's college fund. I hope you took Alex up on his investment strategy, but we haven't heard from him. We hope he made it through, but it looks doubtful. We can't email Jack either, so I don't know if he's heard anything either since the internet went down a couple days ago. The Comcast guy said it's that way all over the country, not just Ogden, so no one knows what's going on. Barb's classes have all been almost deserted, and even though she's teaching college seniors, no one's showing up.

Let us know how you are doing, and if you need to get out of there, we can put you up for a while. Things are getting dicey though, you can tell. The areas with a lot of migrants are starting to have troubles, even here. Better get here quick if you're coming.

Take care and write back soon.

563

Jeff and Barb"

"A little different tone than your brother Jack on that one," Ron said.

"Yeah, that's the way Jeff is though. I hope they're paying attention to what the neighbors are doing and following suit—but I'm afraid it's already too late."

"Let's hear what Joan and Joe have to say," Karen said.

"Will do, my dear. The postmark says Larkspur, California. I think that's between Mill Valley and San Rafael."

"January 20th

Dear Drummond Family—

It's been a helluva thing making this trip, but we finally got here." I stopped for a moment.

"Joe's handwriting. Tough to read."

"We left on Monday no problem. That was the sixteenth. We got here to Don's place this morning the twentieth. It was a bad trip, but we're in one piece anyway. We had enough gas to get almost all the way here, but we gassed up a couple times anyway. I never thought I'd pay fifteen bucks a gallon for gas to damn thieves!

Most of the freeways are OK, but a lot of the overpasses are closed or we had to divert around them. The one bridge over the Columbia at Kennewick was open, but only for two cars on the bridge at a time. Same story on the bridge at Umatilla, and they diverted us away from that big Army base down there, wouldn't say why. After that, we wanted to go over to Highway 97, but they made us go a different way. Ended up in Carson City Nevada!! That's where gas was so expensive. Slow going, and Joan and I are tired of sleeping in the truck. I did sell some of those eggs we took down for nine dollars a dozen! You make some money on those too. Money's going quick, you do that now. Some little bastard tried to rob us once and I damn near ran him over. Couldn't get his money out of the little machine in the wall, and decided I looked like an easy mark. Joan tells me to calm down now and then, but those people are just as good as compost, and if it were up to me, they'd be that now. They didn't get their food stamps either, and they're making all kinds of noise 'bout that too. Well I know and you do too that we're damn tired of paying for them. Gotta end, and now, I say.

Don and Lorene's place is pretty good for now, but we're all thinking of getting out as soon as it warms up a bit, end of February if we can. He's got the acreage for us to do fine, but there's too many people too close and you can already tell that people are thinking of heading for the hills, and that's here. They're starting to go house to house too, those government men from Sacramento, trying to take guns away. Don says that when they get here, they're gonna get one helluva greeting. I've still got my Mauser and I was a good shot too. Can still get a deer if I've a mind to. Men're bigger than deer and not as smart. Didn't like the feeling driving through Sacramento. Felt all wrong, just did. Searched the truck three times, don't know why. So keep an eye on the place for us and guard those hens. They'll get you through this yet, and we'll be back soon enough.

Those illegals are raising hell too. We hear down in Fresno the illegals are getting killed by the legal immigrants when they're trying to stir things up. Not taking any guff, no sir. Different out here though, lotsa money here in this county, and not too many illegals living here. The regular immigrants are just like I was back in '46, fresh off the boat. Work their asses off for next to nothing, and come back for more every day. Never saw people work so hard for nothing, even back in Tolmezzo when I was a kid.

You take care of that wife and kids now, and we'll remember you at Mass.

Joe and Joan P."

"Writes just like he talks."

"I'm so glad they made it all right," Karen said.

"Me too. Not surprised that he took one look 'round and decided that up here was better though."

"You think they can make it back?" Libby asked. "With his son and daughter-in-law?"

"Don't know. We can hope though. He'd be good to have around. Old-world knowledge, and used to making something from nothing. The best kind of people."

"Hon, it's almost time for the news," Karen reminded me. I'd wanted to listen at eight to see if there was anything new going on. The kids shifted seats and got comfortable again, as if they were settling in to watch TV. I turned on the big radio.

"…..ports that the attacks by Mexican terrorists continued after dark in major American cities in the Southwest, but reaching all major Hispanic population centers in the country. Targets are almost universally 'soft' targets, including public buildings, hospitals, shopping centers, theaters and other locations where large populations are gathered. Car and truck-bombs have been used repeatedly, with some set off by remote control. Snipers are also active in targeting police and fire units, with two governors killed in the last six hours by sniper fire."

"From Los Angeles and other cities, reports have come in to ABC that terrorists posing as illegal immigrants have been attacked and killed by legal immigrants and American citizens, and that police and military units have stood by while such actions are being taken, whether the victims are innocent or not. In these neighborhoods, rioting is virtually non-existent, while in more affluent neighborhoods, unrest is being blamed on looters from poor neighborhoods, with more aggressive attacks blamed on terrorists."

"Journalists currently embedded with U.S. military units in Northern Mexico report that all civilians are being disarmed as the military invasion takes place, and that anyone firing on U.S. military units is being literally, wiped off the map. After the U.S. incursion began, large numbers of unidentified combatants began attacking the U.S. units from the rear—from U.S. soil. Arthur Jennick, our embedded reporter, filed a report earlier today that U.S. Army

Airborne units were heavily engaged in Brownsville, Texas, and that the enemy troops were systematically being wiped out within the battle zone. A report of enemy troops trying to surrender, and then detonating suicide bombs was captured by a CBS camera crew. The resulting explosion killed the crew and the reporter, but the tape survived intact and was being broadcast on all major networks all afternoon and into the evening. Because of this tactic, the United States military is no longer accepting the surrender of Mexican troops. For now, it is literally, 'take no prisoners.'"

"Holy crap," Ron said.

"No joke," Carl replied.

"Hate and fear are powerful things," I said as the broadcast went on.

"...ssions are being held at this hour in New York, to discuss postponing the opening of the Stock Market on Wednesday. The President announced that by Executive Order, the Federal Reserve has been disbanded effective immediately, and that the currency of the United States will be backed directly by the Treasury, as was the case until the Fed was created in 1913. Beginning within thirty days, a new currency standard will begin to be put in place, and a transition between the former Federal Reserve Dollar and the un-named currency will begin. Many questions are being raised regarding this transition, especially related to debts, the value of the Federal Reserve Dollar to the new currency, and a rate of exchange. Diana Markham will report further on this developing situation beginning at eight a.m. Wednesday morning, but did tell me earlier that it is interesting to note that since the Fed was created, the dollar has lost more than 95% of its purchasing ability."

"In yet another major story today in a day filled with them, the Vice President has been taken to Bethesda Naval Hospital for unknown reasons. Local contacts at the hospital tell ABC that the Vice President was admitted at four-fifteen p.m. and secured in a respiratory ward in the hospital. The White House has not commented on the Vice President's health."

"Technicians at all major internet service providers are working tirelessly to stop the internet attack set in place just prior to the Chinese military attack on Taiwan and on U.S. forces in the Far East. Internet services world wide have been systematically attacked by a self-propagating and seemingly self-mutating worm that has affected major server farms and all major internet browsers. The attack seems to be multi-faceted, with computer information—especially with regards to financial transactions—corrupted in transit with records of accounts and account owners sent back to mainland China. The new Chinese government is powerless to stop the attack, and in fact has been attacked itself by the computer virus which has been traced back to a Communist Chinese-controlled internet service portal."

"Our final story from the top of the hour, before we go to break, addresses U.S. airlines, already hit by increasing criticism since 9-11. United, Northwest, and American Airlines are expected to declare bankruptcy on Wednesday, citing the dramatic fall-off in international travel since last week, and continued hostility towards the U.S. by foreign nations. U.S. citizens held in these countries boarded what may be the last flights out of those countries by U.S. carriers. Northwest Airlines relationship with KLM airlines was severed today by KLM, in a tersely worded statement. It appears that for several reasons, including escalating fuel prices and declining travel plans, these partnerships are unraveling by the hour. U.S. carriers have noted a ninety-five percent decrease in immediate and long-term travel plans to Europe and non-North American locations."

"Hon, that trip to Paris is off," I said with mocking gravity.

"What shall I do without the latest spring fashions? I simply can't survive without the latest haute couture! Last years fashions? Impossible!" Karen said with an overplayed French accent.

Everyone started laughing at our overacting. "No bon bons, either," I continued.

"Oh! Ze horror!" Karen said as her hands flew up to cover her face in shock.

"OK, enough drama. We better get to bed," Libby said to the kids. Ron was 'up' for fire duty tonight.

"I'll get my things and Alan and I will go be nurses," Karen said.

"OK. Don't wear yourself out, and make sure your Mom gets some rest," I said.

Within a few minutes, the barn had cleared out and quieted down. After we brushed our teeth for the night, I kissed Karen goodnight and watched as she and Alan walked across the field in the rain, silhouetted by the flashlight shining ahead of them. I returned to our 'bedroom', and found both Buck and Ada on the bed, already asleep. 'Well, I guess I'm not sleeping alone.' I thought.

I changed into my sleeping clothes and climbed into bed, a little apprehensive of what tomorrow would bring. 'So fast to change....' I thought.

Wednesday Morning,
January Twenty-Fifth

The late January meltdown was continuing, I thought as I lay alone in bed. There are usually a few minutes each day after I awaken, and before the rest of the bees nest gets stirred up for the day, that I have to myself. I could tell that Libby was already up, and the fire cracked softly in the cook stove as the rain pounded on the skylight. 'Not much outside work today,' I thought.

After a few more minutes, I decided it was time to get up. Buck prodding me with a cold nose in the back of my neck might've had something to do with it. Ron and Libby had taken the 'fire duty' the previous night, and had let me sleep. I pulled on my 'regular' jeans—not the insulated ones for a change—and slipped on some boots and a WSU Rose Bowl sweatshirt. 'Wonder if they'll ever go back?' I thought to myself.

I heard Ada's tail thumping on the floor as I left my blanketed bedroom, waved silently at Libby, and headed outside through the tool room. Ada was keeping Libby's feet warm, while of course waiting for a morsel to drop her way. My well-worn waterproof anorak had its permanent residency in the tool room, and I pulled it on as I tried not to trip over the tools that had been pushed out of the way, and not hung back up on the walls after the quake. In the pocket of the old Cabela's coat, I dug out a pair of forgotten ragg-wool fingerless gloves and a receipt, and realized that the coat had been hanging on the sixteen penny nail for three years, untouched. I was surprised the mice hadn't gotten to it.

I popped the door open and found a different view than that of the day before. What was once pristine white was now mud grey in the half-light of dawn, and the rain was relentless. Our annual precipitation was only around twenty-inches per year, and since the first of the year, we had to be way above average. All of the new snow, fallen after the ash, was gone, and the snow and ice beneath it was going quickly too. The wall thermometer on the barn, normally viewed from the house in the summer, said forty-two degrees. The ash was now a puddling layer of clayey goo, already making my footing difficult, and my boots heavy. I'd only walked thirty feet.

Buck, on the other hand, had no trouble at all, but was now less Golden Retriever and more grey Mud Dog. 'This is going to be a whole big bucket of no-fun,' I thought to myself as I headed toward the outhouse.

After my morning duties, I noted that the TP stock in the outhouse was down to the single roll on the custom-installed sixteen penny nail. 'Better put that on someone's to-do list,' I thought as I walked back towards the barn.

My thoughts of what needed to be unraveled today stopped cold as I heard automatic weapons fire, close by. I ran towards the barn for cover, and Buck of course, went to the fence, barking. I was so shocked by the sound, that I really didn't know where the sound had come from. The hood on the anorak masked some of the sound, and the rain pelting me had obscured even more. Still, it couldn't have been more than a hundred yards off. I was plastered to the south side of the barn, when the door to the Martin's 'bedroom' opened and Ron appeared, Garand in hand and Remington slung over the shoulder. I called Buck back to me. For a change, he obeyed and sat down on the concrete pad.

"You OK?" Ron asked as he passed the shotgun and an ammo pouch.

"Yeah. No idea where it came from though."

"Barn got hit from the north. Rounds went right through the back wall. If we'd've been standing, we'd've been hit."

"Great. Anyone call for help?"

"Libby did, and the cops. Alan's up and reconnoitering up around north. He was up and saw a muzzle flash. He figured two hundred fifty north, beyond that burned up house."

"Why were they shooting?"

"Probably trying to pick you off."

"If they couldn't hit an adult male walking at a constant speed from this range, they're not much of a shot."

"You were lucky."

"So what's our game plan?"

"Good question. If they have full observation of the north side of the barn, we're pinned down and Alan and the cops are going to have to deal with it."

"Or we make a sprint for the house and cut north behind Brad's shop."

That got me a skeptical look.

"Riiiiiight. You first."

"Fine, but you get the shotgun and I get the rifle."

"OK by me," Ron said. We switched weapons and headed toward the east.

"You did tell everyone inside to keep down, I hope."

"I think the splintering of the computer monitor did that well enough. They're trying to hug the floor as we speak."

"Did the cops say they were coming?"

"They said one word: 'Affirmative.' That was it."

"Then I would expect some action, and pronto. If they replied on the radio, they're not going to say much. Too many ears. Ready?" I asked as I was about to sprint across the garden.

"You sure about this?"

"No. But I also don't care to be shot at while taking a leak, either."

"Ready when you are," Ron replied.

"Cover. Now," I said as I ran across the garden, trying to keep my head down. More shots came my way as I headed over the low garden fence and hid behind the small metal shed that held the houses' firewood, the Remington booming three times as I ran. My heart was pounding. 'Bastards,' I thought to myself. Another volley came my way and hit the back of the shed with a 'thwang' sound. I moved to the east some more, knowing that from where the shots were coming from, they could not see me as I left the cover of the eastern edge of the shed, with the view blocked by the neighbor's large shop building. It was up to Ron now, if he wanted to follow. The shotgun wasn't going to do him any good at the likely range we were at, I thought. With the rapid fire of the enemy, it had to be an AK or SKS, just by the sound of the report.

"Ron—Go get one of the Springfields," I called out across the garden. That 870's not going to be much good."

"K," he called back. I climbed over the six-foot fence on the north property line (no small trick even in good weather), and moved up to the back of Brad's shop building. I should next be able to make it to the south side of his house in cover, assuming no one had moved up toward us from that side. I looked back to the barn, saw Ron standing there, and gave him the signal to 'stay put.' He dropped to a knee and took a peek around the side of the barn. More shots headed his way and he dropped like a rock.

"Ron!" I called out as quietly as I could. "You all right?" I got a 'thumbs up' in reply. I was kicking myself for not having a radio. Hopefully, Alan was moving up along the enemy's right flank, and I hoped to either hit his left side, or pop up in front of him. 'Maybe 'pop up' is the wrong term to use,' I thought.

I crouched low, peeked around the east side of the shop, and looked over the side of Brad's house for any activity. Nothing. I sprinted for the south wall, and again, had no fire come my way.

Brad's small house had a covered front porch, with steps entering from the south, a perfect place for me to hide for a moment.

Hugging the house, I went up the stairs and again crouched looking around the corner to see if I could spot the shooter. 'Nothing yet,' I thought. 'Where are the cops?'

Movement....in the brush and limbs piled up in the field behind the burned out house north of Brad's. Two? Three? I couldn't tell. One had a long gun though, and was on his stomach with the bipod equipped gun. 'Easy shot from here,' I thought, 'even without a scope.' My father's Garand however, was a scoped model, with a two-and-a-half power scope and a small flash hider.

I raised the gun and felt the rubber eyepiece touch my face, and carefully took aim. The target moved up to a sitting position and I heard a weapon fire to the west 'Alan,' I thought. I pulled the trigger and the target was down when I looked over the field of vision again. I caught a glimpse of someone running north when I heard more automatic weapons fire from the north. 'Not an AK this time,' I thought.

After about five minutes, I called to the north. A voice called back. 'Marines! Stay where you are!"

I did just that.

A few more minutes came, and two single gunshots were heard, again from the north. Finally, a Marine came into view, and I called out my position. "Advance slowly with weapon safed!" came the booming voice. Sounded like Gunny McGlocklin.

I rounded the house, climbed over the low fence on Brad's north property line, and headed toward the Marine patrol. "Halt," came the voice. "Far enough."

"Gunny McGlocklin, that you?"

"Drummond, right?"

"Yes sir."

"C'mon in. That other fella OK?"

"Far as I know," I turned to call Ron. "RON! You OK?"

"Gotta change my pants, that's all," came the reply.

"C'mon up," I called. He waved back. I could see Alan coming from the west. I deliberately stayed away from the man I'd shot. I really didn't want to see what I'd done to him.

"That'd be my brother-in-law, over there," I said as I shook the Gunny's paw. He'd already collected the weapons from the dead.

"Did a fair flank maneuver. Nice old Garand. May I?"

"You bet," I said as I handed the big rifle over. He handled it like it was part of him.

"Thisn's seen some work. Someone did some nice trigger work on it. And the original M82 scope too. Pacific Theater?"

"Yeah. My father's."

"Marine?"

"No, Army Corps of Engineers," I said.

"What on God's green Earth was he doing with this? This is a specialist's gun."

"No idea. He never talked about it, only that he wanted me to have it, and his other service weapons. Told me to use 'match grade' ammo and it would never let me down."

"Bet this gun could tell some stories," he said, eyeing every detail of the old gun.

"I bet you're right," I said as Alan, and then Ron joined us. Ron had one of the radios, and gave the barn the 'all clear.'

"I'm Alan Bauer. Thanks for coming to our rescue."

"Gunnery Sergeant Scott McGlocklin, USMC. Good to meet you."

"Likewise," Alan said.

"Everyone all right?" the Gunny asked.

"Scared. They managed to perforate the barn pretty well. If they'd've aimed lower, they'd've hit one of us for sure. Kids are scared sh•tless."

"You're lucky. They usually are better shots than this," McGlocklin replied. These were a little doped up. Found a crack pipe on the dash of their car."

"They all dead?" Alan asked.

"You and Drummond here got the first two. I got the ones running away. Looked like one pissed his pants on the way."

"What were the other shots? I heard the rifle, then pistol shots," Ron asked.

"Insurance."

"Huh?" Ron was puzzled.

"That means that there is no chance that they will ever do this again, if I'm correct," I replied for the Gunny.

"Correct," McGlocklin said flatly. "I was passing through north of here when the deputies called. They're otherwise engaged right now up by the river. We're getting ready to go join the real fight down south. I heard the call and found their piece of crap car, and followed the tracks right to you."

"Why…"

"You got food, among other things. They probably saw your fire or smelled it. The scumbags are starting to figure out that five plasma TV's each won't keep them fed. And that all the cash in the world ain't gonna help them much if they're running from the law. Once they knock off the last residents in the neighborhood, they strip it of food, then valuables."

"There are some stores open though, aren't there?" I asked.

"Sure. Just gotta provide I.D. to get in." Ron got a call from the barn, and stepped away to reply.

"Which is then cross-checked against outstanding warrants," Alan said.

"Correct. The local gendarmes have really cleaned up in that one. Let 'em into the store, run the cross-check, when they come out, away they go."

"To where?"

"Main Detention center is set up at the airport, south side, where the old Air Guard base was. Miles of chain-link fence around it, split up into parts, they're living in tents. Can't be a whole lot of things to do other than just keep warm. Which, of course, is the general idea. There are a dozen or so other centers in the city for lesser offenders. If these guys had been caught alive, they'd've been shot regardless for the attack."

"Welcome to the neighborhood," I thought. My brother Joe was likely at that camp.

"It's a tough place these days. They better understand that."

"We sure as Hell do," I said.

"Rick, Libby says coffee's on if we're done out here, and that the Gunny is welcome to join us for breakfast," Ron said.

"Gunny?"

"I'd appreciate that. It's been a long-ass night. I'll be back in a little bit. Gotta check in with the unit and get some baggers out to clean this up."

"Sounds good. We'll see you in a few minutes," I said as we turned back to the barn.

"Ya'll want these guns?" Gunny asked. "We're just gonna scrap 'em. Might be useful soon."

"You sure?"

"Yeah. I'm sure. You want them, take 'em. AK's aren't exactly a precision weapon, but they're OK if you're not serious about your work."

I exchanged a look with Ron and Alan. "Sure, I guess that'd be OK."

"Take 'em then. I'll put it in my report that the weapons were damaged and disposed of," McGlocklin said as he walked off to the north, past one of the dead. "I've already pulled the contraband out of the bags."

Ron, Alan and I picked up the two rifles, two handguns, a sawed-off shotgun and two day-packs of mixed ammunition, and headed back for the barn. Alan had his FRS too, and had checked in with Karen and his family already.

"How're Mary and the kids doing?"

"Still feverish, Mary's probably got it worse than the kids. Karen didn't get a whole lot of rest last night," he said.

"How's your Mom doing?"

"Kansas stock. Eighty five going on fifty."

"I know, getting a little forgetful though," I said as Ron climbed the fence near the barn, back onto our property. Alan and I handed him our guns as we climbed over as well. Buck greeted us as a grey blob.

"How do you propose to clean him off before he goes in?"

"Really good question. I'm thinking a bucket of really cold rainwater or five."

"That'd be a start," Alan said.

"Let me borrow your radio quick. Thought I'd say good morning to my bride," I asked.

"Sure," he said as he handed me the radio.

"Karen, you there?" I few moments passed as I walked around the south side of the barn to look at Alan's house.

"Yeah, are you all OK?"

"Yeah. You?"

"Yeah, scared though."

"Between Alan, me, Ron and the Marines, we took care of it."

"Looters?"

"Worse. Invaders. Gunny said they probably were looking for food."

"Good Lord. What next?" I could hear her exasperation.

"Don't ask. You might not like the answer."

"Great."

"How's Mary?"

"Just a minute," she said. The radio was quiet. "I wanted to be in private. Not good."

"Fever?"

"Yeah. And she can't seem to clear her lungs. Coughing her head off. Whatever she's got, it's worse than a normal flu."

"Keeping after it with meds?"

"As much as we can. Mom said we should go after it with some elderberry tea after she gets something to eat."

"Probably a good idea. Kids the same?"

"They're not as bad, but still not great. Alan's worried sick."

"I would be too. I better let you go. We'll have to figure out a schedule to get you some rest. Can't have you get all sick on us too, or this leaky boat'll go down for sure."

"You'd do fine. But I wouldn't wish this bug on anyone."

"Love you babe, and good morning."

"You too. See you after while."

"Out."

"Out."

I walked over to the garden end of the barn, and Alan was already on at least the second rinse of Buck, who for the world thought this was a really great game. He kept biting at the water as it was poured over him, tail going like mad.

"I'm gonna owe you a single malt for that," I said.

"At the very least. Go on inside. I'll see to the dog and welcome the Gunny in."

"Thanks. There's a pile of old towels and blankets in the tool room, behind the door."

"K. Thanks."

I went back inside and found everyone up and most everyone with a cup of hot tea. I excused myself and went into my bedroom, where I changed out of my ash-caked jeans, boots, and coat, and put on some cleaner, dry clothes. The stack of 'enemy' guns was now located in the corner, emptied of their chambered rounds and magazines. They would all need a thorough cleaning, and assuming that we ever decided to use them, we would need more ammunition. I wasn't sure what calibers they all were, although I knew that the AK's used 7.62 x 39, and I knew that I had five hundred rounds bought for barter because I didn't own that caliber weapon. The handguns could be nine millimeter or .45 Colt. At this point, I really didn't care. The shotgun was all but useless, with a pistol grip and an ultra-short barrel. Hugely illegal since the Nineteen-Thirties. I'm sure it was very effective at injuring or killing a room full of people at very close range.

The boys showed me where the bullets had penetrated the back wall of the barn, and embedded themselves in the front wall. John had already patched the rough holes in the sheetrock with hunks of duct tape. We'd have to patch those up more permanently later. And, maybe think about something more durable on that side....

Libby had assigned the girls to tidy up the barn for our breakfast guest, and help her with breakfast. I was sure that this was only partly because the place needed tidying up, and mostly due to the fact that the girls would freak out if they realized how close we'd come to getting wounded or killed. We exchanged a knowing look as she had the girls mix up a bowl of scrambled eggs, and a big green ceramic bowl of ingredients for pancakes. I remembered my Mom doing the same thing, with the same bowl. 'Forty years ago,' I thought. 'And how things change.'

We had the place pretty well set up for breakfast after about twenty minutes of cleaning, putting away, and cooking. Alan and McGlocklin came in through the tool room, wiping and stomping most of the mud off of their boots, and finally tossing a bucket of rainwater on them before opening the door into the woodshop. The floor drain could handle a little mud, but not on a daily basis, I thought to myself.

"Libby, allow me to introduce Gunnery Sergeant Scott McGlocklin, USMC. Gunny, this is Ron's wife Libby Martin. My wife Karen is over at Alan's house, helping tend a few sick folk."

"Pleased to meet you, ma'am," I could see Gunny's eyes scan the room, quickly settling on the wood stove. "That smells wonderful," he said.

"Coffee, Scott?" Libby asked.

"Yes, ma'am, please."

"Gunny, this is John Martin, Ron and Libby's oldest, this is Marie, their daughter, and my son, Carl, and daughter Kelly." The kids—especially John and Carl—were in awe of the large Marine joining us for breakfast. I could tell that the girls were impressed for different reasons.

"Nice to meet you all. I might get a chance to see my own family in a day or three," Scott said as Libby handed him the biggest mug we had.

"Where you headed? Do you know yet?" I asked.

"Not for sure. Orders are for half the Division to head south pronto. The other half is on standby."

"War might be over by the time you get there," Ron said.

"Not likely. At least, not in California. Mexico will fold up nice and tight, but the Latino neighborhoods are a different story."

"OK you men. Enough of that for now. Scott, we have pancakes, fried potatoes and onions, eggs, and breakfast sausage and orange juice. That sound OK?"

"OK? Ma'am, I've been eating out of MRE's for most of a year. Real food is beyond a luxury."

"Well we will do what we can to make this something to remember then!" Libby said. "Now let's hear about your family and none of this war talk. I'm sure that you'll have time to talk about that later."

Libby and the girls outdid themselves as they prepared 'firsts,' then 'seconds' for our guest. I ate lightly, making sure that Scott ate well and fully. Libby asked Scott if he'd like to try some of our WSU cheese in his eggs, a blend called Crimson Fire. He agreed, and said that his wife Carlita made the hottest eggs on base. I then got out a jar of Karen's jalapeno salsa, and told Scott to have at it. Alan had a single large serving of eggs and a couple pancakes, and excused himself to go back to his house before Scott had finished. The girls passed on the eggs, even without the cheese added, and stuck to pancakes. The boys tried to emulate our guest with just a single bite of the egg/salsa mix, and gave up almost as soon as they started.

"Glad Carlita's out of earshot. This is hotter than hers."

"We'll keep that info code-word only," I joked.

"Affirm."

"So Gunny, what advice can you give us, since you're up and heading out?" Ron asked half-humorously.

Scott considered his question a moment, and again was the military tactician. "Things aren't pacified here to the point where you can go around and be safe like you think you can. Most of the 'normal' people bailed. Those that didn't either have big brass ones or aren't able to string two words together and make a coherent thought. Those are now the ones playing predator. Advice? Don't go anywhere alone, ever. Everyone is armed. I mean the kids too. If they don't know guns they need to, and need to be responsible enough to handle them. Your sheriff has his sh…stuff together way more than I expected him to, to his credit, and so does your local leadership. You need to be low-profile, although that's damn near impossible. You have to stay warm, and that means fire. Fire means smoke, which is seen. An upside to your location is that your neighborhood is relatively far from all of the high-crime areas, but if someone's determined, you will be attacked again."

"Same as it ever was."

"Sure, but now they're armed with AK's and they're using them in the daytime, and you don't have a whole lot of neighbors to call on for help."

"True."

"Listen. You've got a helluva good chance of being just fine. Better than a lot of parts of the city I've seen. Hell, the rich parts of town are burned out holes. The poor parts are pretty well deserted too. I don't know what your population was before, but from where I sit, it's less than half of what it used to be. Probably a lot less."

"That's what the sheriff said on Monday, too," I said. "What's your opinion about the situation nationally?"

"You mean the attacks, the economy in the shi…trash, all that?"

"Sure. Any of the above."

"Bad guys gonna die huge. That's a fact. China screwed up and had a premature eja…shot too soon," he corrected. "That was coming sooner or later regardless. We cleaned up, but that's not over yet. We'll have to see. Mexico, that's another matter. My wife was born in Mexico City, and I'm sure she's more pissed than we are about it. There will be no safe harbor, like the President said. I honestly don't know what the Hell they were thinking. Did they think they could scare us into something? The Japs figured it out right quick. The Mexicans will too. That'll be a bad fight, like Iraq. We don't know who's the bad guy until they're shooting at us. That gets good men killed. They're using car bombs. That kills the innocent. They're attacking hospitals. That's just inhuman. Fine. They're animals, we'll hunt them like animals. The economy's beyond my pay-grade. Not my deal."

"We heard on Monday that the government has a good chance of collapsing."

"The civilian government maybe. Not us," he said as Libby filled his cup again.

"It's gonna be different," I said, looking out the window at the continuing rain.

"That it will, Mr. Drummond. And if we're all really lucky, we'll all make it through this."

We said our goodbyes to Gunny McGlocklin at a little after eight, after exchanging addresses. Both Kelly and Marie gave Scott a big hug, and we were all a little choked up when he had to go. I can still say, that this is one of the finest men I've ever known, even though I hadn't known him long. Wherever you are, Gunny, remember you are always welcome here.

After Scott left, we made up another batch of pancakes and eggs with potatoes tossed in, for Karen, Grace and anyone else at Alan's who felt well enough to eat. After Carl ran it over, we took care of breakfast dishes, assembly-line style.

By nine, Karen was back home and getting ready for some sleep. I dug out my soft foam earplugs that I used to use for sleeping on planes, and she popped them in after we talked about the day's plans. Grace, Kelly and Marie would keep an eye on things at Alan's house while he napped for a while too. Karen told her Mom to call us on the radio if she needed anything. We tasked John and Carl with further patching of the bullet holes in the barn, cleaning out the woodstove after it had cooled, collecting eggs and cleaning up in the chicken shed. With all the mud outside, we all agreed that trying to minimize the outdoor slogging about would be best. We put the dogs' collars on, and when they needed to go out, they'd be leashed.

Around ten, Ron, Libby and I put our rain gear on for a trip over to the community center. The boys had gone through most of their chores by then, and were looking forward to some down-time.

"Dad, can we just veg out today?" Carl asked.

"Once your chores are done, unless something else comes up, sure. I don't want you waking up your Mom though. Let her get up when she's ready. That means, don't go starting up the generator so that you can play video games."

"We figured that already. We can listen to the radio, right? And watch the little TV?"

"Sure. Take notes if you want to—especially if it's something important."

"How 'bout the scanner?"

"That too if you want. We'll run the genny later today to get the batteries charged up. I also want one of you monitoring the radios. Kelly's got one too, so if we need to talk, we can. We'll take one with us to the community center, and if we need you, we'll buzz. OK?"

"Sure!"

"So what have you and John got planned?"

"Cards, maybe read some. Sleep."

"Must be nice to be a teenager," Ron said as he retrieved his glove from Buck's mouth.

I called Alan's house before we left, to let everyone know we were going.

"Kelly, you there?" a few moments of silence passed.

"Yep. What's up?"

"Libby, Ron and I are taking off, over to the community center. You're Mom's sleeping, and the boys are taking it easy. If you need anything, call them first, then us. OK?"

"Sure. We're fine though."

We left the barn through the storeroom, and got in the Jeep for the drive. The Jeep we could hose out, with its thick rubber mats, the Expedition had carpet. Even though I might never put another thousand miles on it, I was still reluctant to goo up the interior. The bullet holes in the Jeep's windows and soft-top had been taped and covered with plastic, but of course it was still a mighty cool drive over to the community center.

The street was nearly clear of snow as we headed south, the greasy grey ash spattering against the fenderwells as we drove. The small store at the corner was closed up, no guards present. The house across the street, though, had an armed soldier camped out on the porch, watching the streets and the store.

Very little traffic had been on the arterial since the melt-down started, and all of the traffic was on the south side of the four-lane road. The county had apparently plowed though, so most of the ash and mud were now piled up on the sidewalk. I could only imagine what several feet of the stuff must've been like in Seattle, with rain on top of it.

A dozen cars were parked in the lot of the community center, more than I'd seen in a while.

"Wonder if they've got the clinic running today?" I said to Ron and Libby.

"They said on Monday that they thought they'd be up and going," Ron said.

"I know what they said, but I'm used to when things 'happen', not when they're promised."

"Born cynic," Libby said as we climbed out of the Jeep. "Oh, almost forgot the letters."

"I have my moods, same as you. Look! Electric lights!"

The lights in the whole building were on—at least those that weren't broken from the quake.

"Generator?" Ron asked.

"No. Line power. The transformer's humming," I said as I passed the squatty green box.

"Cool. Maybe we'll have power soon too," Libby said.

"Not at our place. Not until we do a lot of repair work. The meter and weatherhead were pulled clean off the house."

"Whatever you say. I have no idea what a weatherhead is," she said as we entered the vestibule.

"Where the wires connect to the house."

"Thanks for making it simple," Lib said as we looked around for Andrea.

"I'll check her office. I'll be right back," I said. Libby found the outgoing mail drop for our response letters to my family, and the Martins and Bauer's had written a number of them as well. Several addresses were 'general delivery' only, because they'd forgotten the mailing addresses. Too much dependence on Microsoft to keep track of our lives, I suppose.

I went down the hall to the main office, and found a new secretary, who told me that Andrea was in the building, but under the weather. She directed me to the clinic, which was partly located in the old food bank area in the basement of the building.

"Find her?" Libby said. "I'm interested in meeting the young lady who thinks so highly of my son."

"I'll just bet you are," I said with a wink. "More like, wanting to see if she's worthy."

"I thought I said that," Libby said with a smile.

"The secretary said Andrea's in the clinic, and under the weather. We can see her there if she's up to it." That drew a narrow-eyed look.

"Well, let's go see. If she's sick, though, I'm not sure we want to be around her," Libby said.

"Yeah, probably right. Let's go find out."

We walked down the hall to the stairs to the basement, which was partially lit by windows—intact—and ceiling mounted florescent fixtures. Most of the room was curtained off. It was odd to me to have rooms so bright, and to feel the air-handlers moving air from the hallway into the room. A nurse or nurse's assistant met us at the door, before we entered. Her desk nearly blocked the doorway.

"May I help you?" She asked pleasantly.

"I was looking for Andrea Britton. Is she up to seeing us?"

"I'm afraid not at this time. She's in with the doctor at the moment, and will probably be sent straight to bed when her office call is finished."

"She OK?" I asked.

"Flu bug, that's all," said the nurse.

"OK, thank you. I'll leave her a note if I might," I said.

"That would be fine. You can leave it on the table here for her, I'll see to it."

"Thank you."

I wrote a brief note first, wishing her well, and second, bringing up the idea of getting some teachers together for a restoration of school for the kids. I also wanted to talk to her about the bartering situation, and setting up a formal schedule. It didn't look like the meeting would take place today, though. I finished up my note and turned to go. I looked at Ron and Libby's eyes as they looked into the clinic. I turned and saw what had captured their attention.

The obscuring curtain had opened partially, and the entire room was filled with beds, all occupied. One, farthest from the door, had a bloodstain on the pillow. A young man had coughed up blood.

"Let's go. Now." I ordered.

"Yeah."

We double-timed it up the stairs to the main floor, and out into the vestibule.

"That wasn't 'flu,' Libby said.

"No. Maybe pneumonia. Maybe tuberculosis."

"Holy crap," Ron said.

"Let's get out of here," I repeated. "And we need to stay away from here until we know what's going on."

"Can we go over to the school as long as we're here?"

"I suppose, so long as we don't get into a crowd or near someone who's health may be in question."

She thought about that for a moment. "This is like a quarantine."

"Yeah," I thought. "It might be at that."

"Then never mind. Let's go home."

"I'll second that," Ron said.

I called home on the radio, and let them know that we were coming back. Carl answered and asked why we were done so soon. "Tell you when we get there," I replied.

As we pulled the Jeep out of it's parking stall, I saw sheriff Amberson's cruiser pull in behind us. "Hang on for a sec. That's Mike. Maybe he can shine some light on this," I said as I got out of the Jeep.

"Morning, Mike," I said as I walked over to his car, window already down. The rain spattered on my hood as I talked to the sheriff.

"Gunny said you had a little action this morning."

"Yeah, you could say that. Four raiders. My brother-in-law and I got two, I think Gunny got the others."

"That's what he said. Said to tell you thanks again for breakfast too."

"Seemed the least we could do, since he pretty much saved our lives. Hey, Mike, what's going on here?" I said as I pointed to the center. "This doesn't look like flu to me."

"I know. Me either. But that's what the health district said it is, so that's all we know."

"They're coughing up blood in there," I said. "Andrea's got it too. We were hoping to meet with her about getting a barter store going, and the kids back in school."

"Good goals, but until this bug blows over, I think it's probably a good idea to stay put."

"That's what we're thinking too, I think."

"One thing though, Andrea told me, was about your conversation about moving people around to be closer to their jobs and to places to grow food. I want to talk to you about that in some more detail with the Commissioners. You up for that?"

"Sure, I guess. Presentations and working in meetings is no big deal, but it's a big picture thing that needs to be brought up, thrashed about, and then the real work comes in implementation. It's not going to be easy. Is there any county planning staff left, or did they all punch out?"

"None that anyone can find," Mike replied.

"Oh. OK." My wheels were spinning. "All right then. Let me check my Palm Pilot to make sure my calendar's free."

"Funny. How's two o'clock."

"Today? Sure, I guess."

"I'm heading in at noon. You can follow me in your rig, and if you still have that vendor card, you'll need that on your mirror to make it through the checkpoints."

"Any chance I can stop by my old office?"

"Sure, it's only three blocks from Public Works. Want to see what's left, huh?"

"Sort of. I'd like to salvage some of it if I can...assuming that it is salvageable. There's some books and things I'd like to have."

"Building's still there. A little worse for wear. You should be able to get in, assuming CERT lets you."

"Good. Some of that stuff might be useful."

"Go armed. Our Deputy will check your weapon at Public Works, but you'll get it back when you're done."

"All right. You want me to meet you here at noon?"

"I'll stop out in front of your place. Not sure how long it'll take today to get downtown with this crap on the roads. Monday wasn't bad."

"K, sounds good. You and Ashley doing OK?"

"Yeah, you know as good as we can, all things considered."

"Yeah. See you in a while," I said as I went back to the Jeep.

Ron had listened in from the Jeep. "Field trip, huh?"

"Yeah. I get to go present to the county Commissioners."

"Should've kept your mouth shut," Ron said.

"They're just guys, like us," I said.

"Paid better though," Libby said.

"Right now? Don't bet on it. I think they're earning every dime they're getting. Assuming they're being paid at all."

"So what are you going to talk about?"

"That's the big question, huh? Like I've been saying, assuming that things do not improve much with regards to fuel or repair of the damage, we need to adjust to a new lifestyle. The physical—meaning 'built'—environment that we've created doesn't allow for us to live the lifestyle that our grandparents did. We don't live near where we work. We don't grow food near where we live. We depend on gas and oil for way too much. We don't make anything here anymore. We don't grow what we eat."

"So what do you propose?" Libby asked.

"That we change things. A lot."

Wednesday Afternoon,
January Twenty-fifth

Right on time, Mike showed up out front. Ron and I were already in the Expedition, outside the closed gate. I radioed Karen that we were leaving, and would be back before curfew.

"You better be," she replied.

"Don't worry. We'll be fine."

"Don't forget to give Mike some of those eggs," she said in parting.

"Will do," I said.

"The boys will be back in the observation posts by two," she said. We'd decided to man the positions again while Ron and I were gone. Alan had his hands full already at home, although Mary seemed better, Karen said.

We headed to the main road. Once a two-lane road serving farms and the occasional market center, it was now seven lanes, serving as ugly a strip development as you could imagine. The major shopping mall had been all but abandoned, when a new mall was built near Interstate Ninety. Most of the old mall had collapsed in the quake, including a large call-center built in an old department store. We could see a few locations that had electrical power, almost all located next to main feeder lines. Our first checkpoint was at Dishman Mica, in front of one of Andy Welt's gas stations. It was now marked, 'Out of Gas.' The checkpoints consisted of National

Guardsmen, two vehicles per intersection, manned by four to six soldiers. Regardless of Mike's vehicle, he still had to present I.D., as of course did Ron and I.

The roads appeared to have been plowed here too, with most of the grey ash piled off to the sides of the wide road. Many broken poles were pushed off to the sides, and some of the downed lines had been repaired. We didn't see a single repair crew the rest of the day.

The ash, assisted by the rain and the large snowmelt, had plugged most of the street drains. Three times the water was well over the running boards of the Expedition, in the middle of the street.

The damage from the quake was becoming routine to us. Blown out windows, downed poles, heaved pavement. The Chevy and Ford dealerships had obviously been looted, and a number of empty spaces in the formerly neat rows of cars showed plainly. Dodge, further to the west, seemed to be almost empty of its dozens of Ram trucks, and the new, drum-shaped showroom was now a burned out shell, and partially collapsed. The big metal service building had been torched as well and had imploded. A burned-out minivan was still on a lift, draped in a couple of pieces of melted sheet metal from the roof. We stopped at a second checkpoint at the next signaled intersection, and went through the whole routine again. 'Identification please. State your destination. State your business. Curfew begins at five p.m.'

Continuing toward downtown, our next checkpoint was mid-block, between two home improvement stores and a warehouse store. With the exception of the warehouse store, the large and small stores all appeared to have been looted. A small power tool store, a favorite 'man store' of mine, had a Humvee in its parking lot. The store had been cleaned out. I bought all my spares there for my Troy Bilts and my Honda.

From there on into downtown we had two more checkpoints before we hit Division—the dividing line for addresses in the city. It ran miles to the north, a straight, ugly example of late twentieth century commercial architecture. The last couple miles, which passed through East Central neighborhood, were pretty depressing to me. I used to drive surface streets to work each day (I hate freeways in the city), and enjoyed the small businesses, compact neighborhoods, and old-time feel. Most of East Central now looked more like Sarajevo than part of a fair sized U.S. city.

The downtown core itself was impassible due to debris in the streets from some of the larger buildings shedding their skins and many smaller buildings in complete collapse. The county Courthouse, next to our destination building, the Public Works building was still intact, although part of its slate roof was missing. The Courthouse, built in Eighteen Ninety-something, was modeled after a French castle--complete with turrets. It was by far my favorite piece of local architecture. I was happy to see it had made it this far.

Within a few minutes, we arrived at the Public Works parking lot, and found a place to park, and I gave Mike the couple dozen eggs that Karen had shoved in my hands as we walked out of the barn. He looked a little shocked. "Karen wants to make sure that the Mom-to-Be is eating right," I said. Mike nodded his approval as a couple of uniforms exited. Before we entered the building, we made an effort to get most of the ash off of our boots. A futile task, in the end.

Inside, we signed in on a clipboard, handed a uniformed man our sidearms, and went straight into what used to be the Planning Department's conference area. The Commissioners usually met at the Courthouse, which was probably too damaged to use, I reasoned.

The Commissioner's meeting was already in progress when we arrived, but this didn't seem to be unexpected by the reactions of those present. I'd met all of the Commissioners before in presentations that I gave explaining specifics on projects and various consulting work for the county, but this was different. Mike asked Ron to wait outside if he didn't mind. Ron didn't mind a bit. Meetings weren't his thing.

"Good afternoon, everyone. This is Rick Drummond from out in the Valley. I brought Rick along to present his ideas on recovery. He has some experience in the planning and community development, as you might know. Rick?"

"Thanks, Mike. Commissioners, nice to see you all again, even under these circumstances. Walt, Sammy, you too. General..." I said as I shook his hand, "you've got some good men under your command."

"Yes, sir, I do," the regular-Army general replied, with a distinctly disinterested look.

"For those of you that don't know me or aren't familiar with my firm...or former firm, depending on how things end up, we work in the planning and development sector. Lately, a lot of work on adaptive use, reclamation of industrial sites and wetlands."

"So what does all of that have to do with now?" the most senior commissioner, Earl Williams, said. I was used to his tactics, which varied between Southern-politician condescension and downright hostility.

"Things are different, and will be, from now on. The way that this city grew up and developed, will not be the way it develops in the future. And the future started on January fourteenth."

"What, exactly, do you mean by that?"

"Spokane was founded as a wannabee railroad town, and eventually landed major rail lines to the city. That traffic allowed the city to grow. Streetcars allowed neighborhoods to be built around the core. Those gave way to personal cars, which killed the streetcar, and allowed development to go rampantly wherever it could. And the city encouraged it, and that was 'fine', in that place and time. But all of that, and most of the development—and agriculture, and manufacturing—that's gone on since the early days has been dramatically enhanced by one thing. Gasoline."

"OK, go on," said the lone Democrat, Sam Jackson. Sam was a short, thick, and very black man, not an 'African-American', but simply an 'American.' He bristled at labels applied to race, finding them divisive. I agreed with that sentiment completely.

"Development patterns, pre-gasoline automobile, established small towns within a day's ride on horse or wagon. Cars killed those towns. A day's drive became hundreds of miles, not tens. People shopped farther from home. Bought farther from home. Things stopped being grown nearby. Jobs were now possible far from home, allowing the suburbs and sprawl to happen. That's over."

I had their attention. "We are now in the first days of the Second Great Depression. It appears that almost all oil-producing countries have, or are about to, cut us off. It looks to me like the federal government is about to tank, and the fact that they're pulling our troops back home signals to me that they realize that they're a) not welcome and b) can't afford to be there any longer. So, energy wise, we're pretty well screwed."

"Quite the theory you've got there, Mr. Drummond," Walt Ackerman said. Walt was the county's chief financial officer.

"Yeah, it is, Walt. But you know as well as I that this freight train of debt had to run out of track sooner or later, didn't you? And you know damn well, that the county couldn't run on debt, which is why you have a surplus every year. Right?"

"No other way to run it."

"Well no one in DC knew that. Doesn't matter anymore anyway. The point is this: Without gas, cheap and abundant, most of the developments built since Nineteen Twenty or so are all but dead. Developments built in the sixties through this year are certainly dead. Critical services can only be provided to areas that can survive—meaning a balance of housing, business and agriculture, as well as a connection to efficient transportation and public services. I suspect you already realize that. Historical development patterns allowed, and encouraged, people to live where or near where they worked. Food was grown nearby. Markets were in neighborhoods. People walked to where they needed to go, because they didn't have and didn't need, cars."

"You are implying we write off whole parts of the developed parts of the county?" Commissioner Markweather asked, incredulous. As a former president of the Home Contractors Association, I'm sure he thought I was speaking very evil words. I could see that they were not interested in my 'theory', which would be 'fact' soon enough without their actions.

"I'm not implying anything. I'm telling you that if you live in Northwood, or Liberty Lake, or East Farms—which is now better called East Subdivision—that there are no places to buy food, no jobs nearby, no heart to the neighborhoods. How do you expect people to eat without farming within a reasonable distance of a central transportation link—meaning rail traffic? Rail is a most efficient way of moving goods. The Valley used to have four lines that were spaced across its width, from Downtown all the way into

Idaho. Now there's one. Developments grew up along those rails, then the rails were pushed out by the freeways and roads. I'm telling you that you either encourage people to live where they can work and eat, and foster local food production and manufacturing, or you will see the consequences. Pouring precious resources in the form of neighborhood life support is a cost too dear to pay."

The room was quiet for a moment. I continued on.

"You must realize this, gentlemen. There is a limited amount of time to get ready for the real problem here, and that will be hunger."

"You are out of your flipping mind," Commissioner Williams said. "People in Spokane county will not starve."

"Really. So the two guys that my brother-in-law and I killed this morning, and the two more that Gunny McGlocklin took out were just after my TV? Hell, I feel MUCH better now." That shut him up for a minute...but I was losing this battle.

"I do not know what the population of the county is at present. I do know that large percentages of food were grown here once that stayed here and fed the population. That has changed dramatically since the Sixties. Too much dependence on cheap shipping, so our food is grown elsewhere. Not long ago, there were a half-dozen dairies in the Valley. Meat packers. Bakeries. Farm markets. You could exist without a car. I remember a time when I was a kid, that you flat-out couldn't get a banana out of season. Until two weeks ago, you could get one any time you went to the store. You think that a banana from the Southern Hemisphere is gonna show up some time soon? How about a Florida orange? Hell, how about peaches from Yakima? We have less than two months before winter is supposed to be over, and planting season begins. How are you going to spend those two months?"

The room was still quiet. "I don't know if I'm right or not. I do know that if I'm right, and the county isn't on the leading edge of this, by the time you figure it out it will be waaaay too late."

I went on. "General, you already wrote off some neighborhoods, didn't you? I mean, once they were empty, that is."

"I wouldn't put it that way," he said.

"I realize that. But the point is, that once the people were gone, you did not defend their property. Is that correct?"

"Yes."

"So how can the county defend an un-sustainable and obsolete pattern of development? We aren't going back there, to that lifestyle. My opinion, of course. The resources to live that way are no longer available."

"What are we supposed to do about it?" Commissioner Markweather asked in a sneer.

"You have to reinvent yourselves, and the county while you're at it. If gas and diesel are all but gone, then the remaining fuel has to be used for critical uses only. Communities need to have critical services. Police. Fire. Medical. Utilities. They have to have food, they have to have goods to sell and jobs. And new communities need to be made from what is here, now."

"You realize what you're saying?" Commissioner Jackson said, looking at me over the tops of his glasses.

"Yeah. I do. I've been thinking about this for a week. More importantly, I realized a long time ago that this would come eventually. So have a lot of other folks, and they've been shouted down for years too. Well it's here. Deal with it. We've drawn a bad hand in that we got whacked with an earthquake. Fine. But the rest of the country is in the same shape, other than the physical damage. The financial and social earthquake is just beginning for them."

"That all?" Walt said.

"Isn't that enough?" I said. "I could always tell you how nice it's been living in my barn for the last week an a half." That drew a couple of chuckles. "Or do I bring up the so-called 'influenza' that seems to be all over the place?" That quieted the room.

"We cannot comment on that," Commissioner Markweather said.

"Well I sure as heck can," I said. "It isn't a normal influenza, not like I've ever seen up close, and I'm not exactly a newbie to the virus. My wife's grandmother died in the Nineteen Eighteen flu. I've read all about it. This looks just like it."

"Sammy, shut the door please," Walt said to Samantha Moran, the Boards' long-time administrator. The door clicked quietly.

"This topic will not be discussed," Commissioner Markweather said flatly.

"What, that you have some virulent disease racing through the populace and you think it's a secret? Are you out of your minds? From what I saw this morning, people will die today of it. This is a hemorrhagic influenza or some sort of rapidly advancing tuberculosis. And you know it."

The Commissioners and the General exchanged glances. "We cannot comment," Markweather repeated.

"Because you don't know, or because you can't treat it?"

"Mr. Drummond," the General replied, "the Commissioners cannot comment because they've been asked not to, by me. The CDC is researching it at this time. There is no diagnosis, and therefore there is no treatment regimen. It is not isolated to Spokane county. We may not know what we're dealing with for several days."

"By which time, most of the remaining population may have been exposed to it, or have contracted it?"

"We do not know at this time, the method of infection."

I was getting dangerously close to a regretful outburst. I took a deep breath, and tried to calm down.

"Gentlemen, look around. From what I've seen and the people that I've known that have contracted a fever or worse, including me by the way, and most of my family, there are damn few common threads. No common water. No common food. No weird inoculations, cuts or exposures. That leaves one thing, if you want a blast of the obvious. It's airborne."

"Thank you Mr. Drummond, for your time. We will contact you if we have further need of your services," the General replied.

I decided to quit while I was behind. "Gentlemen, Sammy, good afternoon. Good luck," I said as I left the room. Mike followed. The door closed behind the sheriff. Ron had obviously heard most of the conversation, and stood when we came out of the room.

"Jesus, Rick. Throw some gasoline and nitroglycerin on the fire while you're at it!" Mike hissed at me.

"Mike, there are leaders, and there are fire-fighters. That," I said, pointing to the closed door, "is a room of fire-fighters. They want to react? Fine. But there are things that they need to be pro-active on. What are they going to do, wait 'til it fixes itself? It's not going to happen. The way of yesterday is not the way of tomorrow! Dammit, Mike, people are going to die because of what gets decided in that room. Or what doesn't get decided. If it's an airborne disease, then say so on the damn radio. Tell people to stay inside or away from crowds. Work the solution not the problem. They're working the problem."

"Could be. There's things I can't talk about. You might've made them think though. They're not as dense as they seemed about things out there. They just don't have any answers."

"Politicians shy away from tough decisions. There are no easy ones. Mike, I'm serious. They need to get their excrement in a nice tidy little pile. There is too much work to do in too little time with too much at risk already. Waiting only exacerbates the problem."

"I know."

"I should go before I blow a gasket." I said, looking at the continuing rain coming from the west.

"Remember to use that pass, and keep your lights on and emergency flashers going too. You also need to retrace the same path you came in on."

"Why's that?" Ron asked.

"Patrols have your plate number. You're expected to return on that path. Not doing so would have negative implications, pass or no pass, if you know what I mean."

"Understood. I'll stop by the office and then head home."

"Be home by dark," Mike added.

"Will do. Thanks, Mike."

"You too. You did good, up until the end there," he smiled.

"Yeah, pent-up frustration getting the better of me."

"Understood. See ya."

"Thanks."

We walked toward the main doors, and back through the metal detector. A Department of Corrections deputy signed us out, and handed us back our sidearms and ammunition. The Expedition was across the lot, which was filled with city, county and State Patrol vehicles, and twin Humvees with the odd mounted weapon.

"Nice job in there," Ron said. "Sarcasm was a nice touch."

"Yeah, probably not my wisest moment."

"I got a good laugh out of it."

"Glad I could be so entertaining," I said as we got inside.

"So what do you expect to be able to get from the office?"

"Reference materials, if nothing else. I had maybe fifty or sixty books I'd like to have. Pictures of the kids. If they're intact, I'd like to see if I can get my Mac G5 and the server too. It's got most of the companies' files on it. Between the Mac and the server, the company data is complete. I have the stuff on DVD at home, but the hardware would be nice. And pretty much irreplaceable at this point," I said as we turned the corner.

The office, located in an old brick building that was once a hotel, was located in the daylight basement of the building, with a floor of retail above us, and storage below. A taller wing held more offices and shops. Our space, about two thousand square feet, had fifteen foot ceilings, exposed rafters, and large windows in the granite and brick building. We'd seen a glimpse of it on TV, and I knew that the office wing was a pile, and that the shops above our space had collapsed as well. If we were lucky, our space was still there and not filled with the contents of the upper floor.

I pulled up to the parking lot, and one of the CERT teams was staging in the parking lot. The 'leader' of the team motioned me to stop.

"Good afternoon," I called out through the rain.

"Hello. I hope you aren't hoping to go in there," he replied.

"As a matter of fact, I was. Our office was in the back, in the daylight basement part."

"I'm not sure it's all that stable."

"Understood. Can we look at least?"

"Sure. I'll tag along."

"Hop in," I said.

"Gary, I'll be back in a bit," the leader called to his team.

"I'm Zach Olegson," he said. The young man was perhaps twenty-five, tall, with piercing blue eyes and black hair.

"Rick Drummond. This is Ron Martin. Thanks for letting us look."

"Saw the pass. Figured you weren't just doing this for fun."

"Got that right. Just met with the Commissioners. Probably pissed them off, too."

"How was the General? I've heard he's a real S.O.B."

"Really? Not bad. I think he was playing 'good cop' to the commissioners 'bad cops.'"

"They all think this is some sort of game," Olegson said as we drove around piles of brick.

"Here we are..." I stopped as we saw my former front door. "Well, the ceiling didn't collapse at least," I said as I backed the Ford up to a clear part of the parking lot.

"Yeah. Other than that, it looks like it's just a normal, ordinary pile of debris," Ron said.

"Anyone been inside?" I asked Zach.

"Not since last week. Gamma Team was in there, this is their sector. Body recovery over in the other wing was there last week too."

"Body recovery? This wasn't a residential building. Why was someone there at that time of night?"

"From what I heard, it was a guy and two secretaries. I think they were still 'hooked up' when they pulled them out of the wreckage."

"That paints a picture I'll have a tough time burning out of my brain," Ron said. Zach and I both chuckled at that.

"Mind if we go in?"

"No, but I'll go first. This a recovery operation? Meaning, sensitive materials?"

"Nothing classified, if that's what you mean. Resource materials and equipment, hopefully."

"OK, no problem then. Classified stuff needs to be done with a Defense Department liaison."

"Had much of that?"

"More than I can talk about, yeah."

"Hmmm. OK. Ron, there should be two big flashlights in the glove box, and gloves are in the back."

"Got 'em."

"Zach, lead the way, if you would."

The entire façade of the building had come down in a sheet of brick. The floor—our ceiling—was constructed of three by sixteen joists on twelve-inch centers. Hell for stout, my father would've said. The floor decks were tongue-in-groove three by sixes, fastened to wood columns that were sixteen inches square. The entire frame of the building on our side was intact. The newer portion—housing the office wing--had collapsed completely.

Zach climbed up the pile of bricks and back down into our office. The pile was about three feet deep at the shallow end, where most of the brick wall had fallen outward and not straight down. I followed Zach, and Ron trailed. I played the big flashlight around the room. It wasn't good. Rain was leaking through the ceiling above us, ponding on the ruined oak floor and carpeting.

"Not too bad, Mr. Drummond. You might be able to save some stuff yet," Zach said.

"Yeah, at least it's not pancaked."

"Wrong structure for that. Shear walls took care of most of the shock."

"You sound like an architect. Or structural engineer?"

"Guilty on both counts. Bachelor's in Architecture, Rensselaer Polytechnic, Masters in structural, UCLA," he replied as he looked into what used to be the room that held our server and large format plotter.

"Bi-coastal, huh?"

"Grew up in Troy. Got tired of the cold, and threw a dart at the western U.S. Hit L.A."

"Where do you work in the real world?"

"Used to be Seattle. Big firm, international work, the whole bit. I was on vacation with my wife in Corpus Christi when the quake hit."

"You were lucky."

"Yeah. We were. Looks OK. You should be out of here and home by dark though. It's two forty. Budget your time accordingly."

"Thanks Zach. Take care."

"Will do…" he said as he climbed back out of the office and around to the front of the wrecked building.

"Where do you want to start?" Ron asked.

"My desk. Over there," I pointed to the dark corner. My new flat panel display was still there, same as always, other than the thick layer of dust. "I'll get you started on the library cabinet. Most of the books I have in mind are on that, or were. Get them loaded up first, and I'll see if there's any hardware worth salvaging."

"OK," Ron replied.

We sorted through the wreckage of the library cabinet, an eight-by-eight monster that had had been screwed to the wall. The entire unit had torn loose, smashed one of my employees' desks (obliterating our newest laptop and it's docking station), and shattered on the floor. Within a few minutes, I'd piled up the three stacks of books that were 'first priority', and 'nice to have', for Ron to muck out to the Ford. Next, I went to look over the computer situation.

The leaks in the roof were scattered throughout the office, and ruined at least one of our workstation computers. My G5, display, and most of my hardware was intact though, and I quickly unplugged what I could and put it over near the secretary station near the door, which was completely soaked with water splashing in from the brick pile. Ron grabbed it as soon as I set it down and put it in the Ford. I tossed him my bug-out bag too, which resided under my ancient Steelcase desk.

We managed to salvage quite a bit of the computer network, including a couple of workstations, the large-format plotter and supplies, a printer, and seven of our battery backup devices. There was a lot more 'paper' material that we could've salvaged, but we were running out of time. I handed Ron a roll of plastic garbage bags and had him cover over what we could or load them up in the bags, and then put them in the driest part of the office. Most of what was left were client files....that probably would never be touched again.

"We better go. It's almost four, and curfew's at five," Ron said.

"I know," I said as I loaded the last of my stuff up, looking back at the office. "I spent years in that space," I said almost to myself.

"Yeah. You're free of office-dom," Ron said.

"Yep. And a fearful thing it is," I said as I shut the door and started up the Ford.

"Look at the upside. We scored your little kitchen fridge, three cases of beer, two cases of wine, two cases of Coke, and a fifth of Gentleman Jack."

"Always the upside, leftovers from our last open house. Don't forget the coffee and sugar. I also got the company financial information and checks for the company bank accounts. Which are probably about useless right now."

"How much cash did you have in the company?"

"Checking had about fifty-five grand, which was average. Money market about a hundred eighty grand. Receivables about two twenty."

"Whoa. I had no idea you had that kind of money."

"I didn't. The company did, it wasn't all mine anyway, with partners and all. It's not that much really. You start factoring in what it costs to run a business, you go through a lot of money in a month. Medical insurance alone cost us more than two employees," I said as we headed back across the river on the damaged Division Street bridge.

"Still."

"Doesn't matter. Dollar's not worth much anymore, anyway."

"What kind of debt did you have? I mean the company."

"None. Just paid off our company vehicles, and other than that, it was just day-to-day normal operating expenses."

"Wow."

"Yeah. We were just at the point where we could've made some serious money."

Ron and I were pretty quiet on the way home, traveling east, with only 'official' traffic around us, and not much of that. I tried the radio several times, testing range more than anything. About two miles from home, Karen heard me.

"Everything go OK?"

"Well, they didn't toss me in the clink, if that's what you mean."

"You didn't go off on them, did you?"' Dang. That girl knows me too well,' I thought.

"Not…..right away."

"You'll have to fill us in."

"Ron will probably do that. He's got a better sense of humor about the whole thing," I said as I glanced over towards him. He was grinning.

Once we made it back through the full series of checkpoints, we finally turned toward home. By four forty -five, Carl had opened the gate and we were heading for the barn, with yet another load of stuff that I really didn't have a place for.

"Hey, Dad. Things go OK?"

"Yeah, OK is a good word," I said.

"C'mon, tell him the real story," Ron said as he pulled a case of Henry Weinhard's out of the side door.

"I'll let you, thanks," I said.

"This'll be good," Carl said.

"No big deal, bud. John inside?"

"Yeah. We haven't seen anything all afternoon."

"That is a very good thing."

"Boring."

"Sometimes, boring is good," I said as we went inside the tool room to de-mud.

Ron and I gave Libby, Karen and the kids our report on the trip into town and back. Ron gave the color commentary on my meeting with Mike and the Commissioners, and I only had to restrain his embellishments twice.

"So do you think they'll listen?" Libby said.

"I don't see how they couldn't. Therefore, they won't."

"What happens then?"

"Then they stumble along trying to feed a population with food that isn't all that available, stretching their resources beyond what they are able, until they fail completely."

"Where does that leave us?"

"It leaves me ready for a cold beer while we figure that out," I said. Ron obliged immediately.

While we were gone, Karen had Carl start up the generator, and get our batteries all charged up again. Mary was now out of bed, her fever broken, and both Rachel and Mark were feeling better, but still in bed. Alan had had a low-grade fever earlier in the day, but it was gone when he got up from his nap. Grace, ever strong, hadn't come down with it.

Based on what we'd seen at the center, and what we'd heard downtown, we were especially watchful of our health. We didn't know if we already had the 'bug', or something else entirely, and what symptoms there might be. I'd read a couple of investigative books on the nineteen-eighteen flu pandemic, and asked Karen's aunts, uncles, and parents about their memories of the outbreak. They were mostly children when the outbreak hit in the spring and again in the fall of Eighteen, and Karen's paternal grandmother—her Dad was only a toddler at the time—passed away within a day or two of her first symptoms. Karen's Dad was the youngest of eight.

Exhaustion was starting to be a threat again, too, at least to me. I knew that I needed more rest than I was getting, and that my health would suffer for it if I didn't start taking it easy.

I parked my rear on the folding camp couch we bought a few years back, and took a long draw on the beer, and just sat for a while. Karen and Libby were busy working on 'jackpot noodle casserole' for twelve, as well as a fair amount of cornbread and a pot of elderberry tea. My elderberry plants were only four or five years old, but yielded a fair amount of berries, half of which I'd dried. I remembered finding the web site when I Googled it a year or two before. 'Elderberries.com.' Not real imaginative as far as web site names go, but if it were 'Sambucus.com', I doubt that Google would've found it at all. I archived the site as soon as I found it, as well as all the links. I'd used the tea a couple of times, not religiously, when I felt a bug coming on. Seemed to work, because I never really got sick after I drank a few cups over a day or so.

John and Carl were playing cards, and our girls were over at Alan's helping out where they could, I suppose. I took another drink of the cool beer, and promptly fell asleep in the chair.

Karen roused me from my nap about ten to seven, as the girls were coming back in from the tool room—now appropriately christened the mud room. She was afraid I'd sleep through til morning, without dinner, if she didn't get me up. She was probably right.

"Anyone have the news on lately?" I asked.

"This afternoon. I heard the three o'clock news," Libby said. "They've decided to cancel the playoffs. That seemed to be the big news."

"Well. I hope the world doesn't stop on its' axis," I said.

"Well it will in Green Bay. They were the favorites," Ron said.

"The whole thing seems pretty silly to me right now," I said.

"Lots of things we took for granted do now," Karen said. "Here. Eat up. Between the boys going after thirds and your dogs, you're lucky to get any."

"Thanks." I said.

"Your beer—or half a beer—is in the fridge."

"It's not plugged into anything, is it?"

"No, we made a couple big blocks of ice and wrapped them up in a couple big plastic bags. Works pretty well."

"If it keeps warm like this, we'll have to deal with getting a real refrigerator going again," I said. "Or start freezing a whole lot of ice and build an icehouse."

"You and your projects," Karen said. "You'll wear yourself out yet."

"I know. I'm working on it," I said.

"Work slower on your projects and set realistic goals. You can't save the world single-handedly."

That hit home. "True. But I'd like to save this little corner, OK?"

"Sure, Atlas. It's all on your shoulders," Libby said.

"Obviously you've never read Ayn Rand," I said.

"I have so. Objectivism is self-centered idiocy. And you are no John Galt. The evidence of that is all around you."

"Yeah. That's a fact. No d'Anconia or Hank Rearden either."

"Thank God for that. Those monologues that she wrote for them bored me to distraction."

"On to other news," Karen said. "Alan got the washing machine hooked up this afternoon."

"Good. Just add water and power, and we're good to go."

"What are you going to do for power?" Karen asked.

"Probably the little generator....but we could put the Generac over there, and also run a fridge when it comes time," I said. "Probably have to, on second thought. The startup amperage that the washer motor needs is probably more than the inverter can supply. That's almost a certainty for that big fridge of Tim's."

"Won't that leave us short then?"

"We'll figure out something. Heck, they had line power at the community center today, so it's not that far away. I could probably build another one of those little generators too, if needed. I have all the parts except the engine, and those are all over the place. Tim had two mowers, they're both still there. So that could be the donor for it right there."

"You have another inverter?"

"There's one in a box in the garage. Got it off of the internet for three bucks plus shipping."

"How big?"

"Twenty-three hundred watts normal, forty-six hundred peak."

"Three bucks?" Ron said. "I need you to shop for me."

"Yeah, it was part of a 'grab bag' of other stuff I bought. I planned on putting the inverter on the bucket truck in the spring so I had one-ten power on it for power tools. I just got the package after New Years and tested it, packed it back up and left it in the cab."

"Add it to the to-do list."

"Like I need more to do," I said.

The whole morning was dampened by heavy fog and drizzle. We had unloaded a few of the books and perishables from the Expedition, and done a little more outside work, but other than that, we were all pretty much house-bound. All of the kids, including Alan's over at his place, were restless and eager to get outside or do something other than just sit and be un-entertained.

I was very surprised that they'd lasted this long. Karen and Libby were interested in spending some time talking about getting some schooling going again, now that we had at least the knowledge that 'normal' schooling probably wouldn't be possible for the foreseeable future. That bit of information came from Grace, who's older siblings had been out of school for two solid months in the pandemic of nineteen-eighteen and –nineteen. The entire family, including aunts, uncles, and her siblings, spent those times in complete isolation on the farm. She suggested to Alan, Karen and I that we start adopting that mentality, as much as we could.

"Hon, how 'bout we have a 'movie afternoon' for the kids?" Karen asked me as she warmed up some soup for lunch.

"Works for me. I know that you and Libby want to talk about the school issue, and Ron and Alan are planning on getting that washer set up over at Alan's. I've got some computer work to do, and I'll need to poach a little power for it."

"OK, let's make it a surprise for them then."

"Do you have a movie in mind?"

"Carl retrieved the DVD's from the house, and the TV's got the DVD player built in. I was going to let them choose."

"Works for me. I'll get the generator set up to go, and my computer."

"'K. Keep it quiet."

"Like that will last long...." I said. Alan, Mark and Rachel would join us for lunch (home-canned vegetable soup and fried egg sandwiches), and we'd run lunch back over to Grace and Mary as soon as we could.

After lunch, I helped Ron and Alan get the washing machine water supply set up, from another stored water barrel at Alan's house. The water was set up for filtration, the same as I had at the barn, with more charcoal in the filter. My notes on the computer recommended that we used double the amount that I had in the original filter, which meant that my original filter wouldn't last as long or perhaps be as safe as it might have otherwise.

I heard the small generator start up, so that meant that the surprise was out, and the movie was about to start. Karen was going to make some popcorn on the woodstove, and some of the pop that we retrieved from the office would be served. We had a fair amount of pop, juice and punch in the house, but hadn't felt the need to make a special trip into the basement for it. At least for now, it hadn't frozen and burst. The insulation in the walls of the fruit room, once designed to keep the room cool against the heat from the rest of the house, now served to keep the room warm against the cold of the outside.

For storage volume, I had Alan retrieve two of my storage cans—big galvanized garbage cans actually—that I'd never used for refuse. I had some food-grade plastic bag liners, and these would be the recipients of the stored water.

With some creative use of a battery-powered drill-driver equipped with a hole-saw, we punched a hole in the sidewall of the garage, and into the main filter and the two storage cans. The gutters—which on this house had debris covers—drained to the front corners of the house. We'd restrict the flow on one downspout, forcing more water into the other. The filter was set up on a workbench that was built into the garage, and we stepped the storage cans down a lower level, with an overflow going back out the sidewall at a much lower elevation, onto the ground. The setup took us about two hours to complete, with all the running back to my house and garage for various plumbing parts and fittings. I figured that I had enough additional fittings to build one more of these filter/storage setups for the Martins, and then I'd be scrounging parts. With the addition of a hose bib screwed into the side of one of the cans, there was now the ability to drain relatively clean water into a five gallon bucket, and fill the washing machine. Later, we might be able to plumb it directly, assuming that we didn't get potable water back.....

While I made the last of the plumbing connections, Ron and Alan muscled the Generac generator onto Alan's trailer, along with two ten-gallon cans of gas, and spare motor oil. The house wasn't wired for a backup generator, unlike our place, so connecting power to the washer, the furnace blower, or more importantly, a refrigerator, would for now have to be done with extension cords. The alternative was to build a 'suicide cord', which had male connectors at both ends. Extremely dangerous. Again, depending on how long we were without power, we could also pull the meter out of the meter socket, and wire the generator directly into the supply panel, which would be far safer in the end. I was hoping that we'd have power long before then, of course.

Before I headed back over to the house, I stopped and visited Grace and Mary for a few minutes. Grace was keeping a close eye on Mary, who had eaten lunch and fallen right back to sleep.

"Best thing for her," Grace said. Mary looked very peaceful, and rested. A distinct change from the last time I'd seen her.

"Was it like this in Nineteen Eighteen? I mean, I know you were too young to remember, but...."

"This bad, or worse. I know that when people broke quarantine, the infection spread quick. Two farms on either side were wiped out because the doctor came to the house and spread the flu. My Dad ran him off with his old Sharps rifle before he got the gate open. He never cared too much for us after that."

"Can't imagine why..." I said with some sarcasm.

"He was a nasty old man. Never cared for him. None of us did. Killed himself in twenty-nine. Had all his money in RCA radio stock, bought it in the spring of twenty-nine, after the first time the market went down. Figured it was just a blip. Then BOOM. Lost it all. Shot himself, my Dad said."

"I imagine there is some of that going on now, too."

"Are you and Karen all right financially? Can you get through this?"

"Yes ma'am. We are."

"I know you've got food and supplies put away, which I thought was smart although I've never told you, but what about money?"

"We have some paper money—Federal Reserve Notes—but more importantly we have some silver and a little gold too."

"Good. That'll be the only thing they'll be using, soon enough."

"They didn't have that problem in the first Depression, did they?" I said, not remembering that it was an issue.

"No, the problem then was there was no money to be had. Of any kind."

"Oh. I didn't really know that. I think we're better off than a lot of folks, there then. My parents never really talked about it much. My Dad's family was dirt-poor to start with, so the Depression never really mattered. Mom's family was better off, and didn't notice it much either. Scottish folks, frugal, cheap, a'feared of debt." I paused for a moment. "Grace, I do need your help though,"

"How so? I'm too old and worn out to be worth much," she said.

"Nonsense. You grew up on a working farm. None of us has ever had the kind of experience you've had. Sure, we've collected eggs and run a fair-sized vegetable garden and canned veggies and fruit, but nothing like what you had when you were young."

"Not many have these days."

"We'll need you to teach us, the same as we'll be teaching the kids."

"That's quite an undertaking."

"Can you write down all the livestock that you've had experience with, as well as what was grown on your farm?"

"Sure, but you need more than a farm to make it," she said.

"I know. Linkages."

"Linkages?"

"Community. Support. If you grow cattle, you better have a butcher. If you have horses, you'll need a vet and a farrier and a harnessmaker and a blacksmith...."

"You do get it then," she said.

"Yes, I do."

"Rick, you get me some paper and I'll get to work."

"I'll have someone bring it over. I have some 'inside' work to do this afternoon on the computer."

"What about?"

"A lot of things. How many acres are available on our block for farming, grazing and gardening? How many fruit trees? How much potential firewood? Where are we going to find a dairy cow or a dairyman? The list is huge."

"Get out the phone book. Start there."

"Phones are.... I get it."

"Phones are down. Chances are that the people you're looking for might still be there, along with what you need."

"Right."

"Then you have to figure out how to get hold of them."

"We can do that."

"Then off you go. Send the girls back over with the paper and pencils. They probably need away from my grandchildren, and I could use the company."

"I'll do that. They were planning on talking about schooling for the kids."

"I know of one-room schoolhouses too," Grace said as I got to the door.

"You may be our best resource yet," I said.

"I'm just old, that's all."

"Nonsense. I'll send the girls right over."

"You take good care of that family, Rick."

"It's my job," I said to her as I closed the door to the garage.

Ron and Alan were off again, over to Tim's house, this time to retrieve Tim's big refrigerator-freezer. I'd given them my hand-truck, and didn't feel the least bit guilty in that I was going off to do some less physical labor.
Once I got back to the barn, I told Karen and Libby that their presence was requested at Alan's, and had Karen take a large, three-ring binder and a stack of pencils to Grace. The room smelled of fresh popcorn and mint tea.

"What's all this for?" Karen asked as I handed her the binder.

"Your Mom's been recruited to help educate us on what it takes to farm."

"This oughta be good," Karen said. "I've never been able to get her to write any of her history down."

"She was probably afraid that it would end up being used at a memorial service."

"It is more important to me that her grandchildren and great grandchildren know who she is."

"I know that, and you know that, and I know how your Mom is."

"Well, good for you. Maybe we can get some living history out of her yet."

"You go, girl."

"Got what you need?" Karen asked before she left.

"My biggest problem is that I don't know what I need and what I don't need."

"I mean, do you need popcorn or a Coke."

"Sorry, I'm...."

"........already thinking too hard. One thing at a time."

"K. You're right," I said as I kissed her goodbye.

The kids were already deep into 'Gone with the Wind', with 'Pirates of the Carribean' on-deck, by the time I sat down at the computer. Ada came to join me, I'm sure thinking that I'd share my small bowl of popcorn with her. I did, reluctantly, toss her a few pieces. Pretty tough to resist those brown eyes of hers. In addition to the TV and my computer, I heard the small bar fridge in the shop running off of the small generator. I wondered if that was a smart idea.

"Gone With the Wind?" I asked Carl.

"Kelly's choice. She said that history was repeating itself. We couldn't really argue with that."

"You are still, fourteen years old, right?" I said, dumbstruck. "And she's still twelve?"

"Dad…." He said in a descending tone.

"Just remember that at the end of the movie, life goes on."

"We will, don't take things so seriously, Dad. It's a movie."

"Right," I said as I went back into the woodshop.

I'd listed a lot of things that I needed to do on 'paper' before I used precious power on research. The first thing I did was to get that list into the computer. It never failed to surprise me how much volume my hand-written text took up on paper, and how little space it consumed on the digital page.

One of the big items that I expected to take some real time, was a physical inventory of the neighborhood that we lived in, especially the properties within the streets bordering the neighborhood. We already knew that aside from the Drummond/Martin household, the Bauer's, and Dan and Sandy's place behind us, there was no one left on the block. Dozens of families, now all evacuated, or in some cases, dead.

In my mind, I was focusing the inventory on the available land for grazing and farming, as well as use of available structures for use as barns and sheds. We'd also need to inventory the block and surrounding properties for fruit trees, firewood, and other potential supplies and resources that we could use, should the worst continue to come our way. As I finished up typing my hand-written notes, I looked outside to see the rain pick up from the morning drizzle again into a pounding rain. 'What I'd give to have the NOAA website and its near-real-time Doppler radar image,' I thought.

A few minutes later, Ron came back in through the tool room, soaking wet.

"You OK?" I asked.

"Yeah, done with being outside though. Being a sponge is not what I'm all about."

"Get the fridge over to Alan's OK?"

"Yep. Tested it out, works like a charm. If it gets much warmer out there we'll be needing it."

"No telling what the weather's going to be," I said.

"Anything on the radio?"

"Haven't thought to turn it on," I said.

"Body recovery's pulling that burned out house apart across the street," Ron said, pouring a cup of tea.

"There's a job there's not enough money for,"

"They're using prisoners." He could see the shock on my face. "Guards and shotguns and all. And leg irons."

"How many?"

"Good dozen, three guards with M-16's."

"Wow. Did they find Mrs. Long yet?"

"They're still there, so I don't think so."

"That's gotta be a mess," I imagined, the wreckage of the house collapsing into the basement, walls folding in as the roof fell, then burning for two or three hours.

"Yeah, I don't think they're going to find much," he said. "More dogs out there too. Big pack up north. Saw us and took off."

"They gotta be learning quick. What've you got on for the rest of the afternoon?" I asked.

"Libby sent me over. She wanted to borrow the PowerBook."

"Right over there. I'm using the iMac. I think the batteries are charged up, so she should have a couple hours, at least."

"Sounds good. I'll be right back, then it's nap-time."

"I hear ya. Perfect day for it too," I said as I looked out into the growing gloom. I'd wanted to get down to Pauliano's house and have another look about, but didn't feel the need to get all wet and muddy to satisfy my curiosity. It could wait a day or two, as part of the overall inventory of the neighborhood. I was probably the only one of us who could identify fruit trees without their leaves anyway, I thought.

One good thing, the snow was almost all gone. That would make getting around a little easier, and I could see how much ground we'd have to till, and how much we'd have to clear, before we could plant.

I decided that after Ron hauled the PowerBook in its backpack over to Karen and Libby, and returned for a nap, I'd get back to work. We had about an hour of daylight left, and I decided I better fill the lamps and lanterns before too long. I took the time to feed the slow fire, simmering a stew that Karen and Libby had going for dinner, and collected the lamps. The Coleman lanterns were first, filled with a small metal funnel and one of the gallons of fuel I'd stashed away. The Aladdin's were next, using 'lamp oil', which was really just very expensive kerosene, in my mind. It was a smaller container, and easier to handle. I'd have to fill the smaller container from one of the five-gallon cans soon. Next were the small, old fashioned camp lanterns. I also wiped out the small amount of soot on the glass, which was much less an accumulation than I thought we'd have.

Ron had settled back in, and I rattled about while Johnny Depp swaggered about on screen, trying to convince Orlando Bloom that being a pirate wasn't such a bad career after all. I went back to work. Using my CAD program and an image file from a computer program called Keyhole, I was able to load up a new file that illustrated our block and both blocks on either side of us—the image taken from a satellite. We often used this type of image at work, to map neighborhoods, watersheds, and potential development patterns that might affect wildlife or be built near industrial properties slated for reclamation. I was now using it to map out homes, outbuildings, and available land for farming. Not all that different, unless your life depended on crops grown on that land making it to maturity, so that you'd eat next winter.

The actual area 'take off' didn't take much time. The next step was figuring the types of food to plant, given the exposures to sun, wind, and weather, and what we had available for seed and manpower.

'This was far more of a guess on my part than I ever planned on when I started,' I thought as I fed the fire yet again. This time, I added a couple cups of merlot that was starting to 'go'. Not great for drinking, but sure added some nice flavor to a stew.

While I knew generally how much home-grown food we went through in a year, we could always supplement it with food from other local growers, stores, or frozen goods. When it was gone, it was gone, and we'd go to the store to buy what we needed. Now, I had to start pretty much from scratch--assuming the worst--that what we grew was what we had, and that's all. There were significant elements of our needs that we couldn't grow: Sugar, salt and other basics. I could at least get us a fighting start, present it to everyone else, and have us all tear it apart and put it back together again. We had to start somewhere.

The real mind-blower is how many meals are consumed in a year by a single individual. Assuming three meals per day, plus a midnight snack or two, that is eleven-hundred meals. We now had twelve people here. More than thirteen-thousand meals. And we wanted to grow more than we could use, both for a safety margin, and as barter/sale material.

In order to meet our basic needs, we would literally need to grow tons of food, process it, and store it. Through a series of little spreadsheets I'd built off of some pretty decent information that I'd downloaded from the internet, I was able to predict the fresh and canned food needs we'd likely require for our population. The spreadsheet also provided for frozen foods, but without a prediction on either availability or reliability of power, it was anyone's guess on whether we'd be using freezers as we once did. Pessimistically, I figured that no food would be frozen and stored.

The amounts of 'fresh' food in the spreadsheet showed nearly twenty-seven thousand pounds of fresh food, based on the pounds per meal needed per person, with a guess on how many meals of each type of food might be eaten.

Next, I figured the 'canned' food requirements, which showed me that I needed an additional eight thousand pounds, or nearly twenty-three hundred quarts of stored food, in addition to 'fresh' food such as potatoes, onions, etc. that stored in the root cellar and food we consumed during the season.

I similarly had to figure fruits, which was more of a problem, because I didn't really keep track of how many pounds we canned per year, and there wasn't any digital information that I'd found on it yet.

This all boiled down to acreage required for planting, for vegetables only. Three and a half acres. And this really didn't include enough corn for corn meal, none of the herbs and spices, none of the fruit, no wheat.

The labor required for the production of this food was equally mind numbing. Imagining what it would take, once the ground was broken, it would consume a full time workforce, just to keep up with it all, all of this was assuming of course, that we'd have the domestic water system up and going to provide enough water to produce all of this food.

The total acreage on our block, from street-to-street, was right around fifty acres. Coming up with three that would be farmable, would be no problem. Nearly the whole block had been farmed or pasture at one time, and the family that built our house had owned a large chunk of it.

Convincing everyone else, and me for that matter, would be a little tougher.

The aerial photograph also showed six structures that I thought were barns or livestock sheds in their former lives. I knew that with only one exception—a guy at the north end of the block—no one had any livestock of any kind. His didn't really count—he raised homing pigeons. My neighbors on the block also had two swimming pools, eighteen buildings that looked from the air, and from my memory, like pole-buildings. Most probably RV garages or hobby buildings. I doubted there were any pieces of farm equipment, other than ours, on the block.

I turned on the radio, just before curfew started at five p.m. I heard Karen and Libby coming in through the tool room as I finished up for now.

"How'd it go?" I asked.

"Good. I think we have most of what we need, materials-wise, to home school the kids based on what they brought home or had with them when things blew up," Karen said.

"So who gets to teach what?"

"I'll teach primary, Libby secondary. When Mary gets to feeling better, she can help us both."

"The kids will be thrilled, I'm sure. How's your Mom doing?"

"Good, she's got chili on the stove over there. I brought over some cornbread and some clean water earlier. They're going to turn in early."

"Mary doing better?"

"Yes, much. Still got the cough though, but not as deep in her chest."

"Get much done?"

"Yeah, still a lot to do of course."

"Fill us in over dinner. Smells like it's about done."

"Yeah, my stomach says so too."

"We'll need you to make a run over to the root cellar tomorrow," Karen said. "Potatoes and onions."

"No problem. I needed to go over anyway. I want to count up how many boxes of Mason jars we've got over there."

"You know the rings and lids are in the basement, right?"

"Some of them. The others are over on the shelf."

"How many lids do you have stashed out here? There's three hundred in the house!"

"More than that. Probably a thousand wide mouth, a little less than that for the regulars." I saw the look on her face. "What?"

"I was going to chew you out for having two thousand flats."

"And?"

"And they're not made around here."

"Right. Canada, I think."

"Anything on the radio?" Libby asked.

"Just turned it on. I kinda got into my work. Almost forgot to feed the fire a couple times."

".....fog will continue through the night. Lows on Friday morning are expected to dip into the high teens. Snow expected by Saturday morning, with heavy accumulations in the northeast Washington mountains and the Idaho panhandle. This is KLXY Spokane, it is five p.m."

"Great. More snow," Ron said as he came into the room. Libby asked about his nap as the national news started.

"....markets in New York today, as the Dow Jones dipped to twelve-twenty, the S&P hit one-ninety-one point twenty, and the NASDAQ fell to three twenty-one point ten. Gold, on the other hand, rose to eighteen forty-one, before settling at eighteen thirty-eight. Silver saw similar gains on the speculation that the Treasury would be reestablishing the United States currency based on the silver and gold standard. Silver closed at thirty-one twenty at the close."

"Fighting in the southwest and the former states of northern Mexico continued throughout the day, with consolidation of captured territory being completed as far as three hundred miles south of the former U.S. border. Senator Mardigan of New Mexico called for the immediate annexation of all captured territories, with expulsion of armed combatants south of the new border, which is still in dispute. Comments made on Capitol Hill this afternoon centered on the status

of the border zone, and when—not if—the captured territory would be formally annexed by the U.S. as a protectorate or U.S. Territory. Very few dissenting voices could be heard as the statement was made on the steps of the Capitol."

"Nearby, a massive protest against the federal reorganization planned by the Administration is continuing at this hour on the Mall, with a significant response by the National Guard and regular Army units around the protest. We go now to Curt Wilson on the Mall. Curt?"

"Thank you, David. The Mall is under siege this hour from an unexpected quarter. Well over a hundred thousand people are here, and have been here throughout the day, demanding that the government reconstitute the departments that the Reorganization has eliminated. Employees from hundreds of departments of the government turned out en masse this morning after night curfew ended, and attempted to march on the White House and Capitol buildings. Several Democrat senators spoke at ten this morning, as did several Republicans in the afternoon. Both groups are focused on urging the President and the Cabinet to reconstitute the thousands of well-paying public jobs that until two weeks ago, were often held for life. That is certainly no longer the case, with the abolition of dozens of major departments, hundreds of smaller agencies, and even some Cabinet positions in the largest reorganization—and some say rollback—of the power of the federal government ever imagined. This is plainly a gain for the states and the restoration of the primacy of State's Rights, and a re-focusing of the entire federal Administration on the concept of government as the Founding Fathers originally intended. For many this is a second Revolution. For others, the end of their careers."

"Did I hear that right?" Libby said.

"Yeah. Welcome to Wonderland, Alice," I said. They were now interviewing one of the unfortunate former federal employees.

"....Alice Ankstrom. Alice, you were employed by the IRS, is that correct?"

"Yes, twenty-three years. I just don't know what we're going to do. The government cannot function without us. The President is clearly out of his mind."

"Clearly, the President believes that a new system, and a new, simpler method of generating operating revenue for the vital functions of the federal government means that he can do without the services of the Internal Revenue Service."

"That may well be what his handlers are telling him, but he's wrong. He can't do without us. He can't do without the Department of Education. He can't do without Health and Human Services...."

"But clearly, he feels otherwise."

"He's wrong, dammit. And we're not going to let him get away with it."

"Miss Angstrom..."

"That's 'MS. Angstrom."

"What departments do you think that the people of the United States CAN do without?"

"NONE of course. There was nothing wrong with the government that we couldn't take care of if we were allowed to!"

"This is unbelievable," Karen said.

"Except for one thing. We all know people like her. Just a little more power, and then it'll be all good. Just a little more," Ron said.

"....clearly at odds with the new direction that the Administration is taking the country. I can tell you David that the farther we've ventured into the crowd, the more violent the sentiment is. There are many voices in that crowd calling for the forcible removal of the President and the Cabinet, and their replacement with an interim President—elected by the Congress."

We all looked at each other at the same time. "Like that's gonna happen," I said quietly. The main commentator took over again.

"No comment from the Administration was made following the speeches by the congressmen on the Mall today, other than a printed statement regarding the refocusing of National priorities within a framework that the States could afford. That, in and of itself, drew comment from around the world, including from the European Union, who stated that the United States was systematically being Balkanized in order to avoid the repayment of debts garnered over generations of good faith by the countries of the world. Senator Mitch Andrews, senior senator from Missouri and one of the oldest serving senators in U.S. history, stated that his debt to all countries was paid in full, thanks to his service, and the service of thousands of Americans in Europe and Asia in the early years of World War Two, and his three years spent in prison camps in France, and later Germany. The remainder of his statement could not be printed or broadcast, due to the rather coarse nature of his additional comments."

"Bet he told them to shove it where the sun don't shine," Ron said.

".....in Atlanta, officials of the CDC are at this hour preparing a statement regarding quarantines that have been issued in many U.S. cities. International air traffic has all but ceased due to the economic crisis, which appears to be slowing the spread of the disease. The disease—preliminary identified as an aggressive influenza—has in rare cases killed its victims within twenty-four hours of the onset of symptoms."

"The Vice President remains in Bethesda Naval Hospital, and word has come that his wife as taken ill as well. No comment has been made by the Administration, although rumors are—and have been—rampant throughout the day."

"Fox News is reporting that National Guard, Army and Marine units continue to engage in street fighting with rebels and terrorists in the Los Angeles, Tucson, Phoenix and Southern California regions. While the Department of Defense has not released casualty information, Fox has learned that over seven thousand enemy have

been killed in these urban battles, with losses of U.S. troops topping six hundred. One hundred sixteen of these were killed when a KC-135—a refueling plane transporting troops—was shot down by a surface to air missile during a brazen, daylight attack, while on final approach to Mather Air Force Base east of Sacramento. A small cell of terrorists operating the launcher were beaten to death by civilians before law enforcement officers could respond."

"This is KLXY news. In local news, food shipments coming into the Spokane area are tentatively on hold, after a train containing the food shipment was derailed in northern California, and a caravan of semi trucks was attacked on Interstate Five. The Emergency Management officials in Spokane County urge residents to institute a self-imposed quarantine due to the influenza outbreak. This notice will remain in effect until further notice, and this notice will be repeated hourly. KLXY will now terminate the day's normal broadcast. We will rejoin operations at five minutes before the hour, and will operate for fifteen minutes of news only, terminating at ten minutes after the hour. This limited broadcast is due to the need to perform maintenance on our generator, transmitter, and for fuel consumption. Good evening." Static.

"We really gotta listen to the news more often," I said.

"How fast can things change?" Libby asked.

"Too fast for you to like it, most likely," Karen said.

"Let's have some dinner. I think the big fight scene in 'Pirates' is on. That means it's almost over." I could hear the big battle and that great music coming from the other room, as we went about getting the dinner dishes out."

"So let's hear it," Karen said. "What did you spend your afternoon on?"

I told them. They didn't like it anymore than I did.

After dinner with our niece Rachel and young nephew Mark, Ron and I walked them home through the fog. The rain had finally stopped, and overhead, we could just start to see stars through the hazy cloud that seemed to be trapped near the ground. Other than our footsteps in the wet grass, there was no sound whatsoever. It was very eerie.

On the way back, Ron and I stopped off at the 'facilities' before going back to the barn, then took a few minutes to talk about our needs for food.

"You really think we will have to do all that?" He asked.

"I'd hope not, but I'd hope not to be wrong, too."

"Jeez. What about seeds? You surely don't have enough seeds for that put away, do you?"

"No, I don't. I have enough to plant our garden three or four times over with heritage seeds—those are non-hybrid. We'll need many times that amount."

"Where are you going to get the seeds?"

"I do not know. What I've bought this year—hybrid stuff—won't really make a dent in it."

"Were seeds on any of our shopping lists when we went to the store last week?"

"No, but I bought some anyway. Cleaned them out. Still, thirty packages of seeds isn't going to make much of a dent. We will need pounds of some of it. Many pounds of seed for other stuff."

"Hmm. Better come up with a 'Plan B'."

"Yeah. You let me know how that works out. I haven't been able to."

"Let's get in before the womenfolk send out the dogs."

"Agreed."

Friday
January Twenty-seventh

Karen took the first shift on tending the fire, with Ron and Libby getting a full nights' sleep. I was up from one until five, when Libby woke with her customary need for a cup of coffee and a good book to read before the chaos of the day took over. By the time I went to bed, a little after five, the temperature had dropped again to about fifteen degrees and the wind seemed to be picking up out in the dark.

When Karen and I got up and left our blanketed bedroom, we noticed that Libby was crying quietly. Everyone else was still in bed, and she was listening to the radio on the headphones.

"Lib, what's happened?" Karen asked.

"The Vice President and his wife. They died."

"Oh......." Karen and I looked at each other for a moment and then held each other.

"When?" I asked.

"They just announced it. They swore in....what's his name....McAllen as the new Vice President."

"Who is he?"

"Ex-senator from Michigan. Conservative. Helped the UN figure out that they need to reign in the alleged diplomats living here in the States," I said. "Then told the voters that they needed to take back their government....didn't run for re-election, but they tried to draft him anyway. He told them 'no thanks."

"That one. I remember him. U.S. News skewered him."

"Most of the media did. 'Right Wing Wacko,' I think they said. President speak yet?"

"No. They said he'd speak at noon Eastern time."

"K," I said. 'One more curve tossed our way,' I thought to myself as I poured a cup of too-strong coffee (the way I like it).

"And Rick, I read your notes and your spreadsheets. You made a mistake," Libby said.

"I'm prone to do that, and fairly often, I find."

"Thirteen people, not twelve," Libby said.

"Of course, I figured three families of four. Forgot Grace."

"So it would appear," she said.

"I'll have you review the other stuff too on the computer. This isn't something that I want to make a mistake on."

"With all these teachers around, I'd think you'd want us to check your work," Libby said.

"With all these teachers around, it is the reason that I don't want my work checked!" I said.

Before breakfast, I was shoo-ed out of the kitchen area. I knew that the girls were planning a breakfast soufflé/casserole for breakfast, which would take a little while to prepare and bake. The kids were grazing on some cornbread, more correctly, corn-dodgers (no idea why they're called that. Grace suggested that Karen make some). We'd broken the news to everyone when they got up, and everyone was pretty somber with the news.

While the morning activities were ramping up, I put on my outerwear and took the dogs up to the garage to start inventorying on the seed stocks that I kept in sealed containers in the cabinets there.

The last thing I did as I left the barn was to grab one of the radios and a headset, and put my old .45 in my parka pocket.

The weather hadn't improved over yesterday, just changed in its unpleasantness. The warm rains coming from the southwest yesterday had changed to a bitter cold wind from the north, and would probably bring snow soon. The dogs took off across the garden, Buck trying to bite at Ada's legs—one of his favorite games. She usually responded by soundly thrashing him, usually with him flat on his back completely at her mercy.

The attack came from behind me, no sound other than running feet on the frozen garden soil. I never had time to turn. Buck did, then Ada, and both of their teeth were bared as the first dog hit me in the back, ripping into the back of my old parka.

I was instantly on the ground--the wind knocked out of me--as Buck and Ada both went at the as-yet-unseen first dog. The second and third dogs then attacked Buck as I finally got my .45 out and loosed a round into the ground.

That got Ron moving, but not before I had a chance to drop two of the attackers at point-blank range. Buck and Ada were still working on the first one when Ron ran up and put a slug round from the 870 through its side, then another. It fell dead, jaws still locked on my now-ruined parka, down flying everywhere. Ada jumped back into the fray, grabbing the dead dog's leg and twisting it rapidly, as I shrugged out of my coat and backed away, turning at the carnage.

"You all right?" Ron asked. Karen and Libby and the kids were running over to us.

"I think so. I don't think I'm bit," I said, in shock. "None of this blood is mine, I don't think. Buck! Ada! Come!"

Both dogs came and for a change, sat on command. "Check them over for bites. I couldn't see much, trying not to get my head bit off." Karen and Libby looked the dogs over for damage.

"You sure as Hell dropped those two," Ron pointed. One was a blue heeler mix, the second, a Chow. The first one was the biggest German Shepherd I'd ever seen.

Alan showed up on the run, a revolver on his hip and his stainless Remington marine shotgun under his arm.

"Everyone all right?"

"I think so. Hon? Dogs OK?"

"Looks as if. They were protecting each other, and you."

"Then they better get a damned good breakfast," Alan said.

"How did these three get into the yard?" Libby asked, hands covered with blood from Buck's thick coat, but not Buck.

"Probably under the front gate, or over it. Buck's climbed it before, when he was a pup. These ones were motivated. Probably after the hens. Ron, go take a look to see if they succeeded."

"That was Lucas," Carl said, now joining us. "That was Becky Abrams' dog," he said, pointing to the shepherd. "I don't know the others."

"Wild dogs are probably all over the City by now," Alan said. "Let's get us inside. I'm freezing."

I hadn't noticed, but Alan was dressed in jeans, untied boots, and a single thin, Silicon Graphics t-shirt.

"Thanks for backing us up," I said as we walked back to the barn.

"Exciting way to start off your day, a little dog versus gun," he said.

"Yeah. I thought I was a goner there for a minute."

"If you hadn't had that gun, you might've been," Ron said. "We didn't know anything was wrong until I heard the shots. Chicken shed's fine. You can see where they tried to dig in under the fence and under the wall, though."

"The first one was wild—into the ground. The second and third were into the dogs."

"What about the other four?"

"Four?" I said. I took out the magazine in the .45. It was empty.

"No idea. I thought I only shot three times."

"When in doubt, empty the magazine," Alan said as we went inside.

"Carl, would you wipe down the dogs, please?" Karen asked.

"Sure, Mom. C'mere, Buckster," Carl said to Buck.

My hands were shaking as I picked up my coffee cup and sat down. Karen handed Alan one, and he went and stood over by the stove to warm up, stashing his shotgun next to the two 'captured' AK-47's, the two .45's, and the stupid little sawed off shotgun with the break action. It had been a good gun at one time, a Spartan—made by Remington—single shot, twelve gauge. I'd looked it over the night before. Some jerk had hacked off most of the barrel and most of the stock. Butchered it, was the more appropriate word. It had been a new gun—hardly any wear, and the factory hadn't been making them that long. The previous user had left it filthy, as well as nearly useless.

Kelly brought me a small plate with a couple of the cornbread cakes they'd made, and some honey.

"Dad? You OK?"

"Yeah, Just got scared bad, that's all."

"C'mere," she said as she gave me a big, tight hug.

"Thanks, babe."

Kelly held me for the longest time. "Alan, how're Mary and the kids?"

"Much better. Mary had a good night. Mom's scrambling up some eggs for them."

"Better call and let them know what happened," I said.

"Already did," he said as he took a sip of the black coffee. "This coffee is perfect."

"Your recipe, so it should be."

"What's the game plan today?"

"Well, I was going to inventory the seed stock in the garage, when I was so rudely interrupted. We're way short of the amount of seed we'll need to grow most, if not all, of our own food."

"We gotta get that bartering situation taken care of," he said.

"Agreed. Tough to do though if we're all quarantined. I'm not about to go to the community center after what we saw there," I said.

"Why not try the radio?" Kelly said, still holding on to me. "There's all kinds of talk on the CB. You could ask people on that," she said.

I looked at her again, surprised.

"Very good idea," Alan said.

"Good one, Kel. Have you talked to anyone, or just listened?"

"Listened. There are some weirdoes on there too."

"I'm sure there are. Thanks for using your head. We don't want a whole lot of people knowing where we are and what we've got."

"That's what I thought," she said.

'Dang if this one's not turning out right after all,' I thought.

"Good. Have you heard anyone, or a channel, talking about buying or selling or trades?"

"Yeah. Channel twenty-four. That one seems to have most of it. The two on either side of it too."

"OK, we'll think on that. Keep listening, and write down what you find out that people are trading for, and with what. Money, other stuff, that kind of thing."

"K. Marie and I can do that. We can listen to two channels on the two CB's at the same time."

"Good for you. Get on it after breakfast."

"K."

We gathered in the woodshop for a morning prayer offered by Alan, our hands joined. We had both reason to be thankful, and reason to ask for guidance for our families and our country. More correctly, continued guidance.

After a very filling breakfast, the adults were all banished from the woodshop, and the kids cleaned up and washed the dishes. This gave us time to huddle a bit, and talk a little bit about farming plans, schooling for the kids, and what we needed to do 'today.'

Karen and Libby outlined the general program for school to start on the following Monday. They'd made a list of supplies they'd need for the kids, and we'd need to have a space dedicated to schooling—out of the way of the days' normal activities. We decided that one of the rooms at Alan's, a former bedroom that wasn't used yet, would work for now. Hopefully, after the epidemic passed, a more normal schooling process could take place at the elementary school. That, though, was a long ways off and everyone knew it.

One common goal was to provide a Sunday church service or devotional time. Alan volunteered to prepare a service for Sunday morning. He had served as a lay pastor at his church in the past, and knew both the Scriptures and our needs. Eventually, Ron and I would take a turn as well, I was sure.

Farming plans were discussed only briefly. I wanted to have more information available for everyone with regards to seeds available, the inventory of the neighborhood fruit and nut trees, berries, and other edibles already in the local area.

"Ideally, I'd like to complete a basic inventory—fruit and nut trees, for example—today. Same with looking over my seeds. I wanted to have that done now, except for those dogs."

"No one's going outside without an armed and ready adult with them, period. That's my suggestion," Alan said.

"No argument there," I said. "We should be looking at clearing out the wild dogs too, don't you think?"

"Yeah, and soon. It's only a matter of time before this happens again, or worse."

"OK. What I'd like to do is get the seed stock inventoried. I can tell John or Carl what to do there, and where all the stuff is. That's probably an hour or so job. If they can do that, Ron and I can take a drive around a bit and do a little inventory work up and down the block. We'll have to do a little bit of walking too—which is where the shotguns come in. I figure two hours for that."

"Dad, why don't you just drive the center of the block?" Carl said. "All the stuff you want to see is in the back yards anyway, and there's only a few fences that go partway back on the properties. If you go on to Brad's property, and around the shop, you can drive all the way to the north end. Same thing south of Pauliano's. We used to do that on our bikes."

"Before you got in trouble for same," Karen said.

"Well, yeah. But there aren't any new fences there since then."

"Sounds like a plan to me. I'm all for not slogging around outside in the cold," Ron said.

"In the snow," Kelly added. We looked outside as the small flakes blew over the barn and curled back towards the windows. I could already tell that this would mean 'serious' snow, just by the look of the way it was coming down, and the direction that the snow was coming from.

"We better get going," I said. "If there's berries or other edible stuff on the ground, I'd like to be able to see it without the benefit of a snow cover."

"Brush your teeth and don't forget your gun," Karen said.

I laughed, and not a little. "Sage advice on both counts."

"Stop, you big goof. You think you didn't like going to the dentist before! Try it now, Mr. Leatherman."

"We were all there in December, remember?"

"I remember. I paid what the insurance didn't. Still gotta take care of 'em."

"Always do."

After taking care of my morning face-wash and brushing my teeth, and waiting for Ron to do the same, I reloaded my .45, and Ron topped off the Remington and grabbed another box of shells. We'd have to clean the guns later, along with the AK's and the 'enemy' handguns.

I went over the seed inventory with Carl, directing him to list packages of each seed, ounces if listed, and dates on the clipboard I gave him. I'd bought a fair amount of seed for the current years' garden already, an annual sale at two of the competing seed sellers. I usually bought two years worth of what I didn't collect myself, more because I liked to experiment than anything else....

"Be sure to get the amount of seed corn in pounds, too," I asked Carl.

"How am I going to know that?"

"Bags are in five-pound units. They're in the big red plastic barrel."

"K."

"And take one of the radios. Karen or Libby can listen in," I said.

"Yes sir!"

After Carl (and John, providing protection) went off to the garage, I listened in on Karen's instructions to the girls on getting the research project off and running.

"Look up all of the custom meat companies, butchers, dairies, anything that looks like a farm. Look under 'farming', and be sure to check out 'organic' too.

"Boy, I sure wish we had Google," Marie said.

"But you don't. Have to do it the old fashioned way," I said.

"Which one of you will be listening in on the CB for barter stuff?" Karen asked.

"Both. Marie will be on one channel, I'll scan others," Kelly said.

"Remember, write down what they're looking for, and what someone is willing to trade or pay, OK?"

"Duh, Dad." Kelly said with her mother's smirk.

"Just making sure. Hon, we're off to do our inventory. We'll have the radio with us, and we should be in the Expedition for the most part."

"Make sure your guns are ready. I expect rabies shots are in short supply," Karen said.

"I'm thinking the same thing. We'll need to talk about not taking risks later," I said.

"...said the man who's just been attacked by wild dogs," Libby added.

"Nobody's perfect. Alan? Ready to head home?"

"Yep. I'll listen in on one of my CB's too. Mine are SSB's, so I might pick up something that the girls don't."

"What else is on your schedule?"

"Getting wood in for the furnace, filtering some water."

"Best wait on the wood 'til the boys can help and provide security." I said.

"Yeah, that's what I was thinking too. We better move. Snow's really coming down."

I gave Karen a big kiss before we went out, grabbing both my .45 and my Remington. Ron took the Garand and a 1911 as well.

It seems a little silly now, looking back, that we were scanning for attackers three feet from our front door. Still, we couldn't have known that then, especially in the context of that particular day.

After making sure that Alan made it into his house, we turned the SUV around, and drove out of the property. John provided security with his 10/22, while Carl opened, and then closed the gate behind us. The news guy on the radio was speculating about our new Vice President.

"VP's not even cold yet and they're treating the new guy like some pariah," Ron said.

"Force of habit. It's easier to spew bile than research actual records and facts."

Our first work area was the core area of the block to the north of us. I'd already calculated that the approximate acreage of our block, within the four streets surrounding it, was thirty-five acres. The 'pasture' or 'field' or 'back forty' of all of the homes of on the block comprised about fourteen acres. These calculations were all approximate, based on a three-year old satellite image that I'd downloaded the previous November. I discounted 'lawn' areas in these lots, as they usually had shade trees planted in them as well, which wouldn't do gardens much good. I also had a fair clue as to who had fruit trees, based on the same image—the size of the fruit trees was substantially smaller than big shade trees. It was pretty easy to count them up with a fair degree of accuracy. The next step would be to confirm that they were fruit trees, and what kind. We could then figure out how much fruit we'd be able to produce.

I could tell by driving around if we'd hit any 'nut' trees—I already knew there weren't many. Probably some English Walnut, maybe some Black Walnut, maybe a Hazelnut, not too much else.

"This snow's something," Ron said.

"Winter in the Great Northwest," I replied. "Slow down a scosh," I said as I took some more notes.

"How are you keeping track of all of these?" Ron asked.

"I made a key map of each house, and each probable tree. Makes it quicker than doing it on the fly."

The Presidential address was late. 'Were they ever on time?' I wondered as we finished up the 'north' half. We headed back down to Brad's property, driving through a couple of downed fences along the way.

As we headed back down the street, I saw a Modern Electric truck coming up from the convenience store—Dan, our neighbor, and Alan's next door neighbor. I flagged him down in the street as we pulled in front of our house. I decided to stay on my side of the truck, just in case the flu bug was spreading.

"Morning, Dan, how's it going today?"

"Just a big bucket of crap, same as always," he said, his window half down.

"You and Sandy doing OK? Had the bug yet?"

"No, we're lucky I guess. You hear about Andrea down at the center?" he asked. My heart dropped.

"We saw her...rather, we stopped by the center on Wednesday. She was sick."

"Died this morning. Damn shame," Dan said.

Ron and I were quiet for a moment. "We'll remember her in our prayers."

"We will all need that before this is over."

"You guys ready for some eggs?"

"You bet, if you've got them to spare. I can trade you some sugar and salt. I scored some as a power and water worker when the shipment came in on Tuesday."

"Hadn't heard that food had come in," I said.

"Priority. Relief workers and emergency personnel."

I looked at Ron and he at me. "That doesn't smell exactly right," I said.

"No, it sure as Hell doesn't. We all said so, too."

"Whose idea?" Ron said, through his partially opened window.

"Some moron Commissioner, from what I've heard."

"Sounds about right, 'morons' that is. How much sugar and salt can you spare?"

"Ten pounds sugar, ten pounds salt, per dozen eggs."

'This sounds way too good to be true,' I thought, but I knew Dan pretty well.

"You sure?"

"I'm speaking for seven families." I was quiet for a minute after hearing that.

"Can't do it as proposed." I said. "Two dozen eggs. I know the families you're talking about, and they're all working their asses off trying to get water and power back, along with all those crews from out of town."

"Not anymore. They bailed."

"You're kidding me," Ron said.

"No, wish I were. Can't say I blame them. Most of them left on Wednesday afternoon. Filled up their tanks in their service trucks and took off home. Some of those crews were from Alabama, for Pete's sake."

"Any estimate, now, on getting power back?"

"Well, you know that power's back at the center already. We're working two blocks east, disconnecting all of the houses from both power and water. We'll hook up places that we know are occupied only, and as needed. Water here, will be up by the end of next week, latest. Power, I'm not sure. We're pretty well hosed on parts, and we're scavenging useable gear from unoccupied areas to repair occupied ones."

"When we get power back, we'll still be toast at our place. Alan's is OK, his service connect is still intact. Ours was ripped out when the quake hit."

"We can take care of that. The whole damn crew's had some sort of damage at their homes to fix. Throw half-a-dozen guys at it and things happen quick."

"And we would be mighty grateful."

"Payback for gas and eggs. A lot of that gas you pumped went to run generators at the shop and houses. And I haven't forgotten that propane, either."

"You'd do the same," I said. "I'll have Karen get those eggs ready. Just drop by when you can with the sugar and salt."

"Got it right now. I volunteered for the mission."

"Then your mission is a success."

I called Karen and Libby, and had them box up the eggs for Dan and his fellow co-workers. I had him stay in the truck, and I got the sugar and salt out of the side compartment in his service truck. His window was rolled up. Couldn't blame him, trying not to get the bug.

"Be sure to bring us back the cartons, and any extras you've got laying round. We're running low," Karen said to Dan through his closed window.

"Will do. And thanks again."

"Right back atchya."

Ron and I finished up the southwest corner of the block, as the Presidential Address began. We missed the opening—the radio was cutting out. Not a problem on our end.

"..........the loss of my friend. I express my deepest sympathies to the family on this terrible loss. Vice President McAllen was sworn in early this morning in a private ceremony at a secure location. Since that time, the Vice President has been apprised of all matters of our nation's security and our plans for revitalizing our nation.

The challenges that we face are steep. Decades of government, created and run beyond the means of the people, are being reviewed and downsized significantly. Entire divisions of the federal government are being eliminated. Not downsized, but eliminated and the responsibilities turned back over to the States where they rightfully belong. The entire monetary system will be reconstructed along Constitutional lines, meaning the responsibility of the Treasury and not the Federal Reserve, which according to constitutional interpretation, is illegal and never should have been *allowed. Those types of excesses, and there are many, will be rectified.*

In closing, I have three brief statements to make. First, to those that have invaded our country and killed the innocent, your days are numbered. If you are an illegal alien in this country, consider yourself a viable military target. Second, I ask that you hold in your prayers the sick and injured in this country, and in all countries affected by the pandemic. To those in the Pacific Northwest, your suffering has been long and hard, and we will do whatever we can to alleviate your suffering. We remember you daily in our prayers. Good day."

"Kinda expected to hear from the new V.P.," Ron said.

"Yeah, me too. Although given all we know, I can't say that I blame the President for not putting the guy on the spot in the middle of a war."

"So they think they're going to be able to 're-make' the government. Good luck with that," said Ron as we finished up the south leg and moved to the east. The snow was thick on the hood as we turned back toward the north. A few more minutes, and we'd finished up.

"You can have a revolution peacefully, or you can have one at the point of a gun. So far, this is the former, and coming from the top, rather than the bottom. If they do it right, and don't get shot in the process, there might be a snowball's chance of it actually working."

"And if it doesn't?"

"First, can't go back to the way it was. Can't afford to. Second, the way it was didn't work. Inefficient, wasteful, and deprived the people of their basic rights. The way it was going, they were leveling the playing field by bringing the best and brightest down to the levels that were acceptable to the non-performers. Not a whole lot of incentive to excel when you're being robbed to pay some illegal aliens' medical care and school tab."

"Sure, but the sheer numbers of people that are against them...."

"....Are not insurmountable. But it is dangerous. No doubt."

The news broadcast at noon came on as we pulled into the driveway. John again met us at the gate, with Carl, now armed.

"Hop in," Ron said as the news caught our attention.

"....possible aftershock of the Pacific Northwest's' Domino quake. The preliminary magnitude is a six point three, centered on the Mount Shasta area in California. The quake hit at eleven seventeen A.M. local time, some forty-five minutes ago, with numerous strong aftershocks continuing at this time. No casualties are reported at this time, and seismologists cannot tell if Mount Shasta is exhibiting any visual clues to an eruption due to heavy low clouds."

"This just gets better and better, huh, Dad?" John said to Ron as we pulled up to the barn.

"E-ticket ride."

"Huh?"

"Ron, 'E' tickets were obsolete twenty years before the boys were born....."

The ladies had fresh cornbread and bean soup ready when we got back inside. The girls had made good progress on the phone book, with several butchers, meat shops, and farms within ten miles or so, but only one dairy—in Newman Lake, maybe ten miles away—in the book.

The bartering list was more sparse than I'd hoped, but maybe a couple of days worth of listings would give us a better baseline of the 'prices' of things. One guy had listed his new Corvette roadster, with heads-up-display, for trade. Best reasonable offer.

I spent the rest of the day pouring over the survey information, while Karen, Libby and Ron did some reading on fruit production, and grains. By three o'clock, we'd managed to get a pretty good handle on what we could grow on the land available in both 'dryland' and 'irrigated' lands. Assuming, of course, that Dan was correct in getting our water back on....

Karen and I took a nap (luxury!!) a little after three, sleeping soundly until Libby woke us at five-thirty, per our instructions. Dinner was 're-runs' of more soup and cornbread, with eggs for those who wanted them. Mary and the little kids joined us for dinner, riding over to the barn in Alan's truck. Grace had stayed home, after a busy day of writing. She'd had tea and some tomato soup, and was planning on going to bed early.

After dinner, Alan and the kids headed for home, with the AK's and the captured handguns. Alan would clean them and make sure they were serviceable, should the need arise. The snow was still coming down as we bid them good night, with a half-rack of Seven Up and Mountain Dew under their arms. Kelly and Marie were already in their PJ's, snuggled up under their covers, reading.

Just before seven p.m., I turned on the radio for the late news. KLXY was still broadcasting at five minutes before the hour, until after the news was over, and then shutting down.

"This is KLXY. It is now seven p.m. Pacific Standard Time. We are now joining a live broadcast from the Centers for Disease Control in Atlanta.........The Centers for Disease Control report that the growing respiratory outbreak, originated in Guangdong Province, China, the original location of the SARS outbreak in two thousand-two. This province is also apparently the location of a primary Communist Chinese biowarfare laboratory. The disease, originally noted in European bases of the United States military and the continental United States, now seems to be affecting a sizeable percentage of the population in China and the Asian continent, and is now reported to be spreading unchecked throughout Europe and the Middle East. The curtailing of common air travel between North America and the rest of the world has slowed, but not stopped the spread of the disease, which has an increasing mortality rate as the days pass. At this hour, the Centers for Disease Control estimate that in the Asian theater, the mortality rate could exceed thirty-five percent. No estimates have been released for potential deaths here in the United States, Europe or other regions."

"The CDC has asked the Federal Emergency Management Agency to institute quarantines of all major cities effective immediately, including the cessation of all travel not essential to the war efforts on the southern border and within the contintental United States."

"This outbreak appears to have been deliberately set by the Communist Chinese with a disease that appears to be created in the laboratory. Essentially, this is a weaponized version of the H1N1, or 1918-19 virus, but modified to a more aggressive infectious strain. It is unknown at this time if further mutations are likely and what other long-term effects may be seen. It appears from all indications that either people will be infected, suffer common influenza symptoms and recover within seven days, or they will suffer much more serious effects of the disease and not recover. In the limited number of victims that the CDC has already autopsied, death appears to have come within thirty-six hours of initial infection in hospitalized cases, and twenty-four hours of infection in non-treated cases."

"Given the timing of the outbreaks, it can only be assumed that this was a deliberate attack upon non-Communist Chinese forces as part of an overall war strategy. This does appear to have backfired however, as the virus appears to have mutated already and is aggressively tearing through both the Chinese military forces and the common Chinese people. It is not possible to determine factually, if this is the case, as most former leaders of Communist China have either disappeared, or in some cases have been publicly executed........"

After the broadcast ended at ten after seven, I shut off the radio.

"An early bed time tonight for us, kids."

"I'll tend the fire first shift, Ron said before John interrupted.

"Nope, Carl and I will do the fire tonight. You can all get to sleep all night."

"Give that man a raise...." I said.

"Five eggs for breakfast, instead of the normal four."

"What about me?" Carl asked.

"We'll work something out," John said.

"K. You get mid-shift then. I'll take first."

"Deal."

By eight, we were all ready for bed. Karen and I spoke softly in our blanketed room as John turned down the Aladdin.

"Hon, do you really think we'll be OK?" Karen asked.

"We will if it's God's will. Our lives are in His hands, as they ever have been."

Within a few minutes, I could hear her sleeping.

And so our first two weeks after the Domino quake drew to a close.

6 0

Epilogue

April Seventh

As we approach Easter, April Sixteenth, we look back upon how we've ended up where we are today. This is less an unfamiliar place in an uncertain time than it was a few months ago, but certainly the way we are living in this sunny, busy spring would be unrecognizable by last years' Drummond family. While much has changed, not all is for the better. Not all for the worse, either I must add. This may be simply due to the silently held desire of a forty-five year old to do something different for a while. Well, I'm doing that now in spades. I may not live as long because of our life these days with all of the physical labor, or I may live longer, but at least I know it is a life that I can look back on and have some pride in the impact that I'm having. That alone I suppose, makes it worth it. Still though, there are struggles that are beyond the means of a man to live with.

School started at Alan's house on January Thirtieth, for three hours a day. Chore schedules were established as a 'Til Further Notice', with rotations of egg collection, feeding the hens, doing dishes and laundry, etc. spread amongst the children. The restoration of a working washing machine at Alan's using filtered water meant that laundry was now one of the preferred chores. Cleaning out the chicken shed was universally detested.

A fairly limited bartering network was established based on Kelly's suggestion and her initial research. We were able to discover that our eggs were both in high demand and valuable to those that had goods to trade. One barter partner, Ellen McDonald, who lives a little more than twelve blocks away, traded us twelve dozen eggs for a piglet. We both felt that we got the better end of the deal on that, and have remained friends and trading partners through the spring. Occasionally, we'll team up on a bartering opportunity that usually is beneficial to all. Ellen lost her husband of thirty-six years to the Guangdong Flu, and continues to pray for her daughter and son-in-law. They lived in Tacoma. We provide encouragement to her on those days when memories overwhelm.

Water was partially restored on February Sixth, a couple days after Dan's estimate of the Third, although that didn't benefit us as much as we might've hoped to start with. For Alan, getting water back meant something as simple as checking for broken pipes, and turning a faucet. For our house it was much more of a chore. Our water meter froze up tight, located in the basement and exposed to freezing temperatures in the sheltered, but not weather-tight wreckage of our house. The barn fed off of the meter in the house. On the Sixteenth of February, we had running water in the system after enclosing the laundry room with a door, and allowing the fifty-degree subsoil to heat up the basement again. The rest of the house remained shut off until a couple of days ago, when we tested it for the first time. We still have to boil the water for drinking, but now though, water IS available at the tap....or hose faucet, in the case of the barn. I've cobbled up a real mess of a system for hot water, with a pipe teed off of the faucet, to a water jacket in the woodstove, and out again to another faucet. Voila! Hot water!

The partial restoration of the electrical grid feeding the well pumps and remaining water towers also put power back on the main arterials and some feeder lines. We didn't get power back to our property until four days ago, April Third. With all of the damage to the house, especially where the electrical service came in, we weren't sure we'd have power back at all. The guys (and gals) from four different utility companies helped us put a temporary service in, construction-site style. From the service panel, we ran some temporary overhead lines over to the house, where the wires now run into part of the old service conduit, down into our old panel. Seven of the circuits have some sort of fault in them, and we're tracing them down, piece-by-piece. Fortunately for us though, both the lines to the garage and the barn were undamaged, so now we have line-power four hours a day....but we don't know which four hours!

With luck, by late spring we'll have the destroyed gable on the house rebuilt, and permanent power put back in place. We've got all of the damaged plaster, glass and 'stuff' out of the house, and will be framing the new gable roof this afternoon. The new chimney chase, with the stainless-steel liner from Andy Welt, is already in place and hooked up to the big old Schrader woodstove. The foundation repair work took most of March and part of February to finish, working around all the stuff in the basement that we didn't have room to move.

After the ground thawed out in mid-March, we hand-dug a hole for a new septic tank and drain field at Alan's with plans that I had in my files and some materials provided by the county. The gravity and booster-pump sewer system that we spent millions on will take years of repair before it will operate again, if ever. Alan's was the most difficult of the houses to rebuild. Our tank was left in place, and I'd paid the contractors an extra twenty bucks NOT to fill it with pea gravel years back when the sewers were connected. Other than the pipe connection from the house to the tank, the drain field was still complete. We had our house hooked back up in three days, even though running water inside the house was yet to be restored—I'm still not sure all the pipes are OK, although the test seemed to go OK. The best part, for all parties involved, was the combination of having an electrically heated hot shower at Alan's, in an honest-to-God tub, and being able to use an indoor toilet.

In late February and early March, still under quarantine, we set up part of the hen house for new chicks, and soon had to move a large part of the operation back down to the Pauliano's barns. There simply wasn't room at our place.

Joe and Joan and their son Don and daughter-in-law Lorene, made it back three days ago. Since then, Don and Lorene have started moving out to his cousins' place out near Newman Lake, about ten miles east of here. Don had a fairly good-sized chunk of bottomland out there, and ran cattle and sheep out there in the early Eighties. He sold it to his cousin, who then let it go back into 'native' plants and trees. Evan, his cousin, hasn't been seen since the Domino, so Don's taking it back over. He'll go back to farming and ranching again, having sold his paid-for property down in California for ninety-three ounces of gold. The adjacent property owner bought it, and Don felt it was a good price. We've invited the whole Pauliano clan to our place for Memorial Day—I know that Don and Joe and their wives will be very busy at both houses until then. By then, we'll have a chance to talk and hear how the farm is doing, and how the hay crop is looking. We've got a few head of beef lined up, and Carl and John will be helping buck bales for Don. I'll get to drive the baler. Should be fun.

On the Fifteenth of March, Mike Amberson gave us the OK to pick out a house for the Martin's close by. Given the nature of things these days, Ron and Libby picked a house two doors down from Alan, across the field from our place. The residents of the home were confirmed dead in the quake, although I have no idea how the authorities knew that. We bought it from the county for a hundred dollars silver. The belongings of the former owners were included, although we packed up all of the clothing for barter, and all of the personal effects such as photographs and other keepsakes, for any relatives that might show up someday. Their 'new' house is a little newer than ours, built in Nineteen Fourteen. We're still working on repairing the quake damage, but they'll be sleeping there by the end of next week. In that respect, they'll beat us by a good month, maybe more.

Our garden preparation began as soon as the snow melted off in early March. Over most of last month, we cleared obstacles in the areas we'd chosen for planting, and those that were near available water. We'd managed to secure water rights for the entire block between the families that were present on March first, which meant that we'd have the right to use water from all points-of-connection on the block amongst the families. We clustered most of the tillable land close by the homes, so that we'd be able to keep an eye on it, while reserving larger parcels for grazing, if needed. We're talking about sheep and goats. We'll have to see about that though.

We re-covered two existing greenhouses further up the block and began planting seedlings on St. Patrick's Day. Those two made my small PVC framed greenhouse a poor relation, with fifteen hundred square feet of covered space per house. We heat both of them with box wood stoves that we picked up at barter, although heating season is pretty well done now. Four identical stoves for two thousand rounds of twenty-two long-rifle seemed to be a good deal. Especially since both the buying and selling was anonymous.

We lucked out on the greenhouse timing, too. The early crops went into the ground in mid-March, with the late stuff not going in until May at the earliest—weather's been weird. We'd been trying to get one more roll of the commercial greenhouse skin so we could cover both greenhouses on the same (calm) day. The day we were scheduled to do the work turned out a little windy though so we put it off, and pruned raspberry canes instead. Around one-thirty in the afternoon, I stood up to stretch out a kink in my back. The wall of dirt was just cresting Browne's Mountain as I looked to the south. We'd never seen the like, here anyway. Grace said it looked like her childhood in the dustbowl Thirties. The wall of dirt and ash literally chased us from the fields as it came over the hills south of us at forty and fifty miles per hour. The wind blew like that for three solid hours. If we had skinned the greenhouses that day, we'd have lost them for sure. We now have thirty dozen tomatoes in them, as well as other veggies. I'm sure we'll be dealing with the ash and dust for decades.

On more than one occasion, Carl, John, Ron and myself have had nightmares about shooting the looters that first weekend, and the several 'engagements' since then. The last haunts us deepest, though. Libby was already very concerned about John, who was quiet for days after we learned that Andrea had passed away, and then we had the firefight five days later with a mob of teenagers. He knew that he'd killed at least some of them, as did Alan and I. Seven attacked us, after attempting a raid on the shuttered convenience store in the late afternoon, about an hour before curfew. Four boys, none older than sixteen. Three girls, one obviously pregnant. All armed, working in a coordinated manner. We didn't know that of course, until the last one went down, running toward our barn firing blindly. I see her face with the violet-blue eyes and her long blonde hair, and what I'd left of it after the round from the Garand hit her just above her left eye, every time I go to sleep. I wonder, if knowing what I know now, would I still have killed them, if I'd known they were children only a little older than my own? Could I have not?

And so I pray for forgiveness from a forgiving God. It is difficult to find forgiveness within ones' self, though.

Seven a.m.
April Seventh
Spokane, Washington

CPSIA information can be obtained at www.ICGtesting.com
Printed in the USA
BVOW061806101211

278071BV00004B/4/A